PIGS,
a Trial Lawyer's Story

By Mark Munger

Cloquet River Press
Duluth, Minnesota

ISBN 097200503X
Library of Congress Number 2002115019

Published by: Cloquet River Press
                 5353 Knudsen Road
                 Duluth, Minnesota 55803
                 (218) 7213213
Visit the Publisher at: www.cloquetriverpress.com
Email the Author at: cloquetriverpress@yahoo.com

Edited by J. Bonovetz
Printed in the United States
Cover Art by Rene' Munger

For my father Harry,
a true believer;
And for my mother Barbara,
who taught me to love
books.

AKNOWLDGEMENTS

As a trial lawyer it was my distinct privilege to represent clients throughout the Upper Midwest in state and federal courts. Many of these folks came to me for help in the most difficult and trying of times. There were occasions, at the end of a matter, when I beamed with pride at the result achieved. There were also occasions when the outcome of a case sorely tested my resolve.

Of the memories I carry with me from my days as a trial lawyer, the most compelling are those that recall my legal work for family farmers. This book is dedicated to the men, women, and children of the Midwest who raise our cereal grains, produce our milk, beef, pork, and poultry, and who try to scratch out a living from the reluctant soil.

My deepest thanks to musicians Sarah Harmer and Brenda Weiler, and poet Li-Young Lee, for allowing their words to appear in this work. Please support these talented young folks by buying their art.

Finally, this book is dedicated to the memory of Senator Paul Wellstone. American farmers had no greater friend than the diminutive senator from Minnesota.

Mark Munger
Duluth, Minnesota
November 2002

PIGS,
A Trial Lawyer's
Story
By Mark Munger

Stories from the Lake Superior Basin
www.cloquetriverpress.com

CHAPTER 1

"Ladies and gentlemen of the jury, have you reached a verdict?"

Judge Davidson's genteel voice carried easily across the sparsely decorated confines of the courtroom. The judge's words were projected from high above the gallery in the matter-of-fact style common to those who've grown up in the country. The jurist's inflection carried a hint of authority leaving no question as to who was in charge.

Though the voice was not loud or obviously demonstrative, the judge's confident delivery filled the stark, near silent void between his honor and the others in the room. As Judge Davidson asked the question, a question he had asked countless juries at the conclusion of countless other trials, his eyes squinted behind the bronze frames of his bifocals. Davidson clearly displayed the weariness of someone who'd stayed too long in a profession that devours men and women of lesser stamina.

Davidson's pale face displayed ridges of crinkled skin above faint traces of hair that were once his eyebrows. A suggestion of wisdom was conveyed by the fragile grace of his silhouette.

In the back row of the jury box, a well-dressed woman in a sharply pressed blue business suit rose to speak. Her manner conveyed an impression of means: here was a person of maturity, a person over fifty, trim of body and quick of mind, one of the county's elite, one who wore the exclusivity of her heritage on her sleeve.

"We have, your honor."

The woman's voice was shrill, high pitched, and just a touch annoying. Her words carried with them a tone of obvious self-righteousness that was hard to ignore. The words "we have" were spoken with certainty. She left no room for the listener to attach the slimmest doubt or apprehension to the phrase.

As Judge Davidson watched the foreperson deliver her appointed line, he smiled. The jurist's reaction conveyed an understanding of the trial's likely result long before the verdict was revealed. He knew the lady's heart, her mind, her soul. They both came from privilege. They both spoke the same language. Their speech bore the same patterns, the same inflections. They were not like the others; not like the farmer, the tavern owner, the two ordinary housewives, or the two blue-collar workers comprising the remainder of the seven-person jury. He knew that. She knew that. Soon, the rest of the courtroom would know it.

Davidson nodded towards the Bailiff. Earl Bethard, age sixty-two, a retired Becker County Sheriff's Deputy, filled that role. Bethard had retired from active law enforcement after successive knee injuries forced him first to a desk job and then, ultimately, out of the profession. The deputy's maladies reduced him to the role of a pensioner. Bethard had supplemented his meager disability retirement payments for over twenty years by working in the courthouse as a bailiff. The ex-cop tried hard to bring professionalism and a sense of duty to the position.

The bailiff hobbled across the frayed carpeting covering the stone floor. His predetermined path took him past the bench, directly underneath the watchful gaze of Judge Davidson. Bethard cast a languid smile towards Louise DeSmedt, the court reporter. Louise sat to the left of the judge on a platform between the level of the floor and the exalted elevation of Judge Davidson. The deputy continued on past Maggie O'Brien, the courtroom clerk, who occupied a seat to the right of the bench. Again, the elevation of Ms. O'Brien's station was lower than that of the judge, though somewhat higher than that of the court reporter.

This seating arrangement was repeated throughout most of the courtrooms in the State of Minnesota. By and large, the men occupied the judge's chairs, the seats of power, while the women, the people who controlled the day-to-day operation of the criminal and civil courts, occupied seats of lesser prominence. There were female trial judges located in the larger population centers such as the Twin Cities, Moorhead, St. Cloud, Rochester, and Duluth. But the female lawyers lucky enough to be elected or appointed to judicial posts outside these metropolitan areas generally found themselves mired in the quicksand of family court, imprisoned in the flotsam of broken marriages and child custody disputes.

Though the 1990's brought slow, inexorable change to the bench, it was rare for trial lawyers in Outstate Minnesota to advocate major criminal or complex civil litigation in front of female trial judges, even though, for a time, women held the majority of the seats on the Minnesota Supreme Court. Despite this model of gender-based equality on the state's highest court, from Roseau to Pipestone; from Wadena to Grand Marais; the scene in most county courthouses was identical: the male sat high above his subordinate female employees, occupying the throne of power. Becker County was an exception to this observation. In addition to Judge Davidson, the other jurist holding court in the Detroit Lakes Courthouse was female.

Mrs. Austin, the foreperson, handed the special verdict form to Earl Bethard. The woman adjusted her pleated skirt so that it hung evenly before resuming her seat. Once situated, once assured that everything was in its place, Mrs. Austin did not look up. Her eyes remained fixed upon her hands, hands folded deliberately across her lap. From the determination in her gaze it was clear that she did not want to endure eye contact with the lawyers.

Bethard labored with a noticeable limp and clutched the verdict form in his right hand as he passed before the bench. The retired deputy offered the document to the judge. Davidson nimbly snatched the verdict form out of the old man's hand as Bethard continued on by, the bailiff's progress undeterred by the transfer. The jurist watched the ex-cop return to a seat against the far wall. A slight grin stole across the judge's face as Bethard resumed working on a crossword puzzle.

Behind the cheap Formica tops of the counsel tables, they waited. At one station, the one directly in front of the jury, three defendant medical doctors nervously witnessed the action. Two lawyers represented each defendant; one appointed by the doctor's malpractice insurance carrier; the other retained by the doctor personally to prevent a verdict in excess of his malpractice insurance limits.

At the other table, the plaintiff, Ms. Pelletier, and her lawyer also waited. Unlike the armada of legal and medical talent across the aisle, the individuals at the plaintiff's table seemed vulnerable and somewhat misplaced amongst the dignity and expensive suits of their opponents.

Daniel Aitkins was relatively young but he'd tried many cases before this one. Criminal cases. Automobile accident cases. Land disputes. An odd assortment of product liability lawsuits. This wasn't his first significant case. It wasn't the first time he'd represented a malpractice victim against the medical establishment in town.

Somehow, sitting in the unnaturally silent courtroom, appreciating Judge Davidson's review of the verdict, watching the jurist check each answer to make sure the responses were consistent, the power of the moment made Aitkins uneasy. He felt his heart pound beneath the cotton fabric of his inexpensive white dress shirt complete with button-down collar and red necktie held neatly in place by a tie clasp. The clasp depicted a gold arrow and had been given to Aitkins by his grandfather, the first of three generations of his family to practice law.

"The search for the truth," Grandpa Willard Aitkins had said, "is a trial lawyer's ordeal. Your path must be straight and true, like the aim of a hunter's arrow."

Willard Aitkins had died a month after Danny's graduation from law school, having lived just long enough to see the family legacy assured.

It was March. A blizzard raged outside. Aitkins perspired heavily under the weight of his navy blue wool two-piece suit. The courtroom's atmosphere seemed to thicken, seemed to close around Daniel as an old mechanical clock located high on the wall above the judge's bench counted off the seconds. Davidson's courtroom was large and generous. The ceiling rose twenty feet above the attorneys.

It was not the size of the room making Daniel feel claustrophobic: it was his anxiety.

The attorney's attention was distracted by rapidly swirling snowflakes assaulting the precarious glass of the building's single pane windows. Moist clots of precipitation adhered to the glazed surface and formed intricate patterns against the muted daylight entering the room.

The lawyer's mind wandered back to another occasion, another battle. The LeMaster case. Daniel's first medical malpractice trial. Waiting for Judge Davidson, Aitkins' mind retreated to the LeMaster matter, an occasion in court when everything had gone his way. The young lawyer had been able to turn the night nursing staff of Moorhead Memorial Hospital against the on-call resident. He had convinced the stubborn defense lawyers in the LeMaster matter that they'd heard enough.

That was another case, another time. Once the testimony of Nurse Olson had been completed, the insurers for the hospital and Dr. Stevens settled the claim. Based upon the contingency fee agreement Mrs. LeMaster had signed with Aitkins' office, the firm kept one third of the settlement. It was Daniel Aitkins' first major fee. It was the case that made him a partner.

Movement by Judge Davidson brought the lawyer back to the present, back to the matter at issue. Maggie retrieved the verdict form from the jurist. Unfolding the document, the clerk rose from her chair and cleared her throat. Aitkins felt his client's hand seek his fingers beneath the table. Daniel grasped Ms. Pelletier's moist palm and waited for the inevitable.

Tina Pelletier had been a free-spirited thirteen-year-old girl when the pain struck her down. At first, the tremors of agony came only after meals. It wasn't what Tina ate; it was the fact that she ate. The instant she forced food down, the pain would begin.

Betty Pelletier, Aitkins' client, was a single mother. Though Betty quit school at fifteen when she found out she was pregnant with Tina, though she suffered through a brief, violent marriage to the child's father, though the beginning of her life with her daughter had been tough, Ms. Pelletier managed to find work as a waitress at the local Ojibwe gambling casino run by White Earth, her home reservation. The meager wages and tips she earned provided them with food, shelter, and a few amenities. She could not afford private health insurance.

For routine check-ups and exams, Tina went to the local tribal clinic near Round Lake. Patients at the clinic paid for their medical care on a sliding scale based upon what they could afford. A doctor with the Indian Health Service, a family practitioner, Dr. Lisa Envold, saw Tina for the stomach aches. X-rays, upper and lower GI studies, and blood chemistries were done. Dr. Envold opined that an obstruction of the small bowel, caused by adhesions left from post-natal surgery to repair an abdominal fissure, were the cause of Tina's pain.

The child was born with a gap in the skin covering her stomach. The fissure had been surgically corrected at birth. Dr. Lisa wasn't certain, but as an educated guess, felt that the surgery left significant scar tissue, which caused the small bowel to hang up on the adhesions. It was the doctor's theory that each time the bowel got stuck on the scars, the organ would twist, cutting off the blood supply, causing pain. She recommended that Tina see a specialist, a gastroenterologist. Dr. Envold said Tina wasn't in any immediate danger. There wasn't an urgent need for the suggested consultation. Betty Pelletier had thanked Dr. Envold and taken her daughter home.

It was only a matter of days before Tina's symptoms returned. This time, the pain did not abate. It robbed the girl of her cheer, her whimsy. She was unable to concentrate in school. Her grades plummeted. She became quiet, reclusive, and spent two days curled up in a fetal position on the couch, clutching her belly in agony. Betty Pelletier knew that her daughter was gravely ill. She had no choice but to call Dr. Envold.

Three days later, after much red-tape and delay, Tina was seen at Detroit Lakes Specialized Medicine, Ltd., a practice group of three internal medicine specialists housed in a single story brick clinic adjoining Detroit Lakes Lutheran Hospital. Dr. Rudolph Bongaard, Jr. saw Tina. He was a general surgeon, Detroit Lakes being too small to support a gastroenterologist on a full-time basis. Bongaard was also the proud owner of a championship quarter horse mare, Mary's Sheba of Becker. The day the doctor saw the Pelletier girl he was due to be at a horse show by 5:00pm. Tina was scheduled to see the doctor at 4:30pm. The girl arrived early.

"So, Tina, your mom tells me that you have a tummy ache. Let me have a look, will you?"

The young Indian girl, dressed only in a hospital smock, reclined on the examining table. She turned her head to avert her eyes, concentrating upon her mother's face as the doctor roughly manipulated her abdominal wall. Betty Pelletier noted a wave of pain descend over her daughter. There was no outcry from the child. And when the surgeon attempted to examine Tina's lower abdomen, the girl's cheeks turned rubicund. The doctor's gesture, though strictly professional, clearly embarrassed her.

Privately, Bongaard hated to see another patient from the reservation on referral from Indian Health. The agency paid too little and took too long to pay the pittance authorized. Every test, every x-ray or procedure not done in the outmoded IHS clinic had to be pre-approved. The whole system turned him off. Try as he might, he could not disguise a similar disdain for Indian patients themselves.

Though Ms. Pelletier and her daughter seemed nice enough, Bongaard regarded Native people in general as ill kept, poorly nourished, and alcoholic. It was difficult for him to examine the child in a vacuum when he believed this, when in his heart he was convinced that this was her heritage.

His physical exam of the girl took only a few minutes. Its rapidity and the doctor's curt manner led Ms. Pelletier to believe that her daughter's condition was not serious. It was a perception that the physician reinforced with words.

"Ms. Pelletier, could I see you outside the exam room? Tracey, you can get dressed and wait for your mother in the lobby."

His use of another's name made Tina cringe. Her reaction was internalized but obvious to her mother. Betty Pelletier knew how hard her daughter struggled in school, in her life, to be someone, to be Tina Pelletier. The white skinned doctor had taken the child's self, her pride away in one moment of insensitivity. Betty and the surgeon exited the room to discuss the child's condition in private. After dressing, Tina passed them in the hallway. The little girl's cold stare, her black eyes fierce and hateful, locked on the physician as she passed him. If the doctor noted Tina's expression, he ignored it.

"I'm puzzled why Dr. Envold sent your daughter here. I don't find anything wrong on exam. Her pain is not reproducible. There's no fever, no obvious sign of infection or distress. Her tests are within normal limits. May I ask, how is her mental health?"

"Mental health? Why, it's been fine. She's a little high strung but a wonderful kid. Hard working, loving. Good grades in school. Lots of friends. Why do you ask?" Betty Pelletier replied.

"Frankly, we see similar problems in a lot of young women entering puberty. Often times they get upset, uptight about the changes they're going through. This unrest can manifest itself physically, not uncommonly as stomach pain," the doctor opined.

Bongaard handed the woman a packet of medicine wrapped in silver foil.

"Here."

Betty Pelletier recognized the pills to be Valium.

"Have her take two of these if the pain returns. If the pills don't help, have her see Dr. Envold again."

"But what about Dr. Envold's view that the pain is related to her fissure surgery?"

"Ms. Plaintier, that couldn't be. The symptoms would be reproducible. Don't worry yourself about this, ma'am. She'll be fine once she passes through this rough spot."

Her surname misspoken, the Indian woman was shown the door. Two days later, after the abdominal discomfort became severe, after a gastroenterologist and psychiatrist concurred with Dr. Bongaard's diagnosis of emotionally induced angst, Tina withered in distress in the Mental Health Unit of Detroit Lakes Lutheran, her small bowl completely obstructed. She remained there, trying not to complain, trying to listen to her mother's admonitions that she should "knock it off" and "be a good girl", until the tissue strangled itself. Once that occurred, there was no saving the child. She lapsed into a septic coma and died.

When George Simonson, a local probate attorney and a member of the White Earth Tribal Council approached Dan Aitkins and asked Aitkins to take the Pelletier case, the white man hesitated. It was one thing to sue an inexperienced resident physician as in the LeMaster case. It was quite another to bring a wrongful death case against a small town's most prominent doctor claiming that the physician neglected his professional duty towards a helpless Indian child. But when the details of Tina Pelletier's death became obvious to Daniel after a cursory review of the girl's medical records, Aitkins agreed to take on the case.

Danny Aitkins knew that it wasn't enough that Dr. Envold held a professional opinion that Tina Pelletier's death was caused by an obvious small bowel obstruction. To prove a case against the defendants, Aitkins had to show that the obstruction caused Tina's death and that it was the negligence of the physicians that killed her. Negligence without causation would not suffice. He had to prove both.

To do so, the attorney assembled a team of board certified specialists to review the conduct of the defendant physicians. Aitkins hired a pathologist to link any negligence found by the other experts to the cause of death. On paper, in the form of written reports, each of the experts appeared confident and strong in their views; strong enough to sway a jury of seven hometown jurors that Tina Pelletier's death was not an act of God but an act of malpractice caused by the collective failure of three reputable doctors to adhere to the standards of care.

Then there was Dr. Envold. The Native American community, the community from which she derived her personal satisfaction as a healer, began a subtle campaign of pressuring her to stand behind her opinions. Reluctantly, at the risk of being ostracized by her own profession, the doctor agreed to testify on behalf of the plaintiff. But when the time to point to the truth came, when she sought to defend her opinions before the jury, Dr. Envold collapsed under the collective onslaught of the defense lawyers.

Her views as to the cause of Tina's death became mere guesses; the unsubstantiated theories of a family practitioner; mere speculations when compared to the learned positions of the three defendant doctors and the platoon of distinguished expert witnesses called at trial by the insurers; expert witnesses who had written text books and prestigious journal articles regarding the causes of and appropriate treatments for bowel obstruction.

At the conclusion of the cross exam of Dr. Envold, her words became so confused, so illogical, that Aitkins did not interpose a single inquiry on re-direct.

The questioning of plaintiff's hired experts, those out-of-town, out-of-state professional witnesses that Aitkins relied upon, fared little better. Despite hours and hours of meetings and discussions with each of them to hone their positions, so that their collective story formed a seamless, brilliant edge of knowledge, Aitkins had not been prepared for, and did not anticipate, his adversaries' theory of the case.

Dr. Emil Scholts, the Becker County Medical Examiner, the man who completed Tina Pelletier's autopsy, was not the subject of a discovery deposition prior to the trial. Aitkins did not question the man because Scholts' opinions were succinct and clear. The ME's conclusions as to the cause of death were set forth in great detail in his autopsy report. The bottom line, the end result of his examination of the dead child's body, was that her death was occasioned by "an obstruction of the small bowel with septic consequences resulting in coma and death."

When the defense called Scholts to the witness stand pursuant to subpoena, Danny Aitkins felt he was ready for anything the man would say. Except for what the man did say.

"Dr. Scholts, thank you for your review of the protocol you observed in conducting the autopsy in this tragic case."

Attorney F.W. Barnes, lead counsel for the defense and personal friend of Dr. Bongaard, spent nearly an hour going over the precise details of the dissection of the corpse of Tina Pelletier. In stoic Germanic fashion, Scholts described each intrusion he made into the little girl's cold body with negligible emotion. Aitkins took sporadic notes, confident that Barnes was wasting valuable time on a boring preliminary inquiry.

"Dr. Scholts, is it customary for you to dictate your findings as you perform an examination? In other words, is a tape made which is later transcribed into the official autopsy report?"

The question caught Aitkins off guard. His eyes left the idle doodling he'd been engaged in during the introductory questions of the Medical Examiner. He focused his gaze on the face of F.W. Barnes as the veteran attorney stood up and stepped out from behind the counsel table. A meager grin formed across the old advocate's face. Aitkins recognized the gesture as the same disingenuous, less-than-honorable "I've got your balls in my hand" snigger the younger man had encountered in the past.

F.W. Barnes, tall, distinguished, every inch an aristocrat, his sixty-something-year-old head covered with wave upon wave of glorious silver hair, made sure Aitkins saw the grin. Barnes' gesture was for no one else in the courtroom, on the planet.

Aitkins had first encountered that smile as a young lawyer fresh out of law school. He was representing a woman who claimed injury to her shoulder in a slip and fall accident. At trial, Aitkins' client provided an oral medical history devoid of any reference to prior shoulder injuries. When Barnes inquired, the experienced barrister approached the woman with a stack of medical records. In full view of the jury, Barnes used an overhead projector to display innumerable medical records referencing previous shoulder injuries incurred by the woman, many of which had involved litigation and the recovery of damages for pain and suffering.

Confronted with his client's dishonesty, Aitkins sought to withdraw from the case. The judge had refused his request. The case went down in flames. Daniel remembered his adversary's smile from that first bitter encounter.

Scholts' response to Barnes' question brought Aitkins back to the present.

"That's standard procedure."

"In this instance, we've looked at Exhibit 19, the death certificate, and Exhibit 20, which is your report. You've indicated that you completed both of these documents and signed them?"

"I signed them. The report and the certificate were typed by my secretary, Joan."

"Do you find any significance in the fact that you did not personally prepare the documents?"

"Yes."

"How so?"

"I've listened to the tape, the actual tape made while I was performing the autopsy. There's a difference between what was dictated into the tape and what appears on the report as transcribed by my secretary. A material difference."

Sensing that he was about to be surprised, Aitkins scrambled to his feet.

"Objection, your honor. Failure to disclose. May we approach the bench?"

"You may."

Seven lawyers left their tables in mass exodus and circled around Judge Davidson.

"Your honor, interrogatories were served upon the defendants asking for all records, tapes, statements, writings, photos, or the like relevant to this case."

Aitkins argued in a whisper, out of the hearing of the jury, as he continued.

"This tape was never disclosed. Until today, until this very moment, I didn't know that a tape existed. I ask that the tape be excluded and no further reference be made to it during the remainder of the trial."

"Preposterous, your honor," F.W. Barnes said.

The defense lawyer leaned in and cast a depreciating glance in Aitkins' direction.

"Mr. Aitkins requested those items, that's true. But his demands sought only those things held by the defendants. Dr. Scholts has always maintained possession of the one and only copy of the tape. He is a witness, not a party to this action. Any request for production served upon the defendants is inapplicable to him. Had Mr. Aitkins subpoenaed Dr. Scholts and taken the man's deposition, plaintiff would have discovered the error in the report as I myself did. Mr. Aitkins made no such inquiry. He has no grounds upon which to complain."

Barnes was right. Aitkins knew it. The court knew it.

"The objection is overruled. You had your chance, Mr. Aitkins. You chose not to depose the man. Let's get on with it. The tape is admissible," Judge Davidson said through tightly clenched teeth.

The attorneys returned to their seats.

"Now Dr. Scholts, you have the tape, the actual tape of your dictation of the autopsy of Tina Pelletier?"

"Yes sir, I do."

"And this tape, the contents of this tape, are they in any way different from the typed transcription of the report? The report prepared by your secretary?"

"Yes they are."

"Could you tell the ladies and gentlemen of the jury just how the tape and the report differ?"

"The report, the one typed by Joan Wilson, states that my conclusion as to cause of death was: 'obstruction of the small bowel with septic consequences resulting in coma and death.' What I actually found, and what I actually said on tape is quite different. Because of the age of the infarct, the degree of damage to the bowel tissue, and because of other scientific evidence I found on microscopic examination, what I actually said was: 'sudden, recent

16

obstruction of the small bowel with septic consequences resulting in coma and death'''.

"What is the significance of this clarification?"

"The word 'sudden' means an unforeseen, unpredictable event. And the term 'recent', well, that means I found physical characteristics in the tissue samples I took from the site of the infarct that indicated to me, as a trained pathologist, the event causing the complete obstruction of the bowel took place only hours before death. From what I found, and from looking at the tests done by Dr. Envold in the week preceding death, the opinions of plaintiff's experts are grossly incorrect. This little girl did not have a complete obstruction of the small bowel when she was placed on the Mental Health Unit."

The ME paused, took a breath, and began his testimony anew.

"She had adhesions, that much is true, and had them since her corrective surgery at birth. But the combination of adhesions and the small bowel obstruction took place only in the last four or five hours of Tina Pelletier's life. The condition came on suddenly, without warning, and caused her to lapse into a coma due to the immediate, unfortunate suffocation of the blood supply to her intestinal tissue."

"Doctor, in your opinion, was this bowel infarct, the one that killed the child, present when Tina Pelletier was examined and treated by the defendant doctors so that they should have diagnosed and treated the condition, thereby preventing the unfortunate loss of this child?"

"Absolutely not. Because of the age of the infarct, based upon what I saw on autopsy, there was nothing to diagnose or treat at the time these gentlemen saw the child," the ME testified.

Daniel's mind was dragged back to the moment.

Maggie the clerk unfolded the pages of the verdict. Three years of Daniel Aitkins' professional life were lost amongst the questions, amongst the "yes" and "no" answers the jury was charged with placing upon the special verdict form.

"Question One. Was Dr. Bongaard negligent with respect to the care and treatment of Tina Pelletier?"

Aitkins felt his client's hand close tightly on his wrist. Betty Pelletier's fingernails dug into his flesh, cutting off the circulation. The lawyer stared at his client, taking in the tawny brown of her complexion and her large almond shaped eyes, eyes moist and near tears. He couldn't concentrate on the courtroom clerk as was his custom. The attorney didn't turn his head to watch the clerk announce their fate. There was no need to. He saw the result of the trial reflected in his client's face. She knew, from a lifetime of prejudice and hate, from a lifetime of struggles. She knew.

"Answer: 'No'."

Daniel felt his heart drop to the floor. Tears dripped onto the yellow legal pad placed on the table before him. The moisture blurred the black marker ink set down upon the page, smudging the finely scripted words of his final argument, an argument, an effort that had accomplished nothing.

He tried to think of something conciliatory to say to his client. He wanted desperately to comfort her. The lawyer maintained a pained silence. The client observed his upset. She smiled at him with a slim purse of her lips.

"Thank you for believing in Tina, Mr. Aitkins. I know she's grateful that at least one person other than me stood up for her. We did the best we could. We told the truth. There's nothing more we could do."

Daniel watched the Indian woman rise from her chair, gather her ragged overcoat and stocking cap, and begin her long walk. Aitkins noted that his client's gait was heavy and that her steps were labored as she moved across the carpeted floor. The woman exited the courtroom, leaving the attorney to contemplate, to argue with God, as to whether truth and the law can ever be reconciled.

CHAPTER 2

It wasn't a night that one would normally spend on the beach. In fact, there was no beach. An insignificant strip of exposed earth rose above the lake's ice. Hummocks of rigid sand formed a hedgerow between the snow-covered lawn of a city park and the frozen lake. Alone, amidst the briskness of the spring wind and the stinging snow, its texture sharp and jagged, the despondent attorney sat. Huddled before a heap of burning driftwood, propped against the smooth trunk of a discarded oak timber, the lawyer studied the evening.

The tree trunk that Aitkins used as a backrest had been lost years before. It had broken free from a raft of thousands of identical logs towed across Big Detroit Lake sometime in the distant past. The timbers had been bound for a sawmill located across the lake. Whether the logs were released by natural disaster or human error was a long forgotten piece of local trivia.

He rested against the cold solidity of wood. Reflected fire danced across the chilled skin of his face. His contact lenses were dirty, causing him to constantly rub his eyes. He gripped a frigid glass bottle of Miller Genuine Draft in a bare hand despite the cold. Two smaller logs formed the sides of a windbreak around the fire. The wall buttressed the attorney from the surging wind. Danny Aitkins hunkered down, regaling in the warmth and primitive light of the fire. He was well on his way to being drunk. He was unrepentant, though he was violating city ordinances by drinking on a public beach and by having an open fire without a permit.

"Danny," the lawyer mumbled to himself through the thickness the beer brought to his tongue, "you're one stupid son-of-a-bitch."

His arms became animated as he chastised himself. He flung his appendages upward to greet the coldness of the April night and to mock God. Beyond the meager comfort zone of the fire the air was brutally cold. Aitkins shook his head with vigor as he protested. Short yellow fibers rested neatly against the base of his neck. Before he'd conformed, he wore his hair longer, putting it up in a ponytail. Now he was out to make money. He needed to look the part. His hair was still his pride and joy but it was no longer a topic of conversation. The attorney laughed as his shadow danced across the frozen ground but behind the strained lunacy, Daniel's heart was hollow.

"You should have seen Barnes' cross exam coming from a mile away," he chided. "Should have remembered about the tape. Knew that medical examiners always keep a tape. But you didn't, you stupid, pompous jerk. You didn't."

His faux gaiety disappeared. His back ached where he'd had the fusion, a subtle reminder that he knew better than to test a surgeon's work by sitting on frosted soil. He stood up, experiencing a familiar prickling sensation in his spine.

"Don't be so damned hard on yourself. Shit even the old man said he would have never guessed that Barnes had such a card to play. If a trial lawyer of forty years experience like dad couldn't see it coming, how could you? You're only thirteen years out of law school, thirteen years into the war. Don't fault yourself. Besides, even you couldn't change the truth."

Aitkins tossed his empty bottle through the air. The container landed next to a Coleman cooler full of beer and redundant ice.

"You're better than that. At least you thought you were. Told everyone so, those that would listen. You told them about the girl's case. They agreed with you. But it's you who lost her case, Danny. Suck it up. You made your bed so lie in it. Admit you screwed up. Get on with your damn pitiful life."

The phrase "get on with your life" echoed in the young advocate's head as he opened another Miller and staggered over difficult ground. He reclined before the fire. Embraced by a circle of heat, he wrapped himself in the thick down of a sleeping bag.

"Get on with your life."

The words gnawed at him, ate away at him like a slow acting toxin.

"What life?" he asked softly, "what life?"

He studied his shadow and waited for the lake to reply. Across the ice, the lights of Detroit Lakes suggested the limits of the city. Considering the pale white glow emitted by the village, Danny realized that he could identify the owner of nearly every structure in town. He knew these people. They were his people. Why hadn't they been able to see the truth?

He'd lived here all of his life. At times, the little city was a warm, loving place. In some respects, the city's familiarity seemed like the embrace of a mother. Then again, like an over-protective parent, the place could be suffocating, smothering in its day-to-day sameness and predictability.

He'd been so young, so full of idealism when he walked onto the campus of the University of Wisconsin in Madison to study law. He'd spent his years in college at North Dakota State in Fargo gleaning all he could from the works of Ursula LeGuin, Rachel Carson, and Henry Thoreau.

Aitkins chose learning the law as a means to help save the planet, to save mankind from itself. Three years of studying under the Socratic Method beat such nonsense right out of him. Three

20

years of fending off the demeaning ridicule of law school professors, pseudo-intellectuals who'd never picked a jury, never tried a case before the bar, never billed an hour of work as an advocate for someone's cause, stifled the bright light of his imagination and creativity. His law professors had, in every sense of the word, beaten his idealism into a dull conforming light of practicality.

Raised in a family that traced its roots back to the halcyon days of the Farmer Laborites, rural Minnesota Progressives who claimed the governor's seat in the 1930's as their brief interlude of success, Aitkins thirsted for political and legal truth from the time he was able to form a thought.

He graduated from NDSU with a degree in political science and left Western Minnesota for three years of law school in Madison, a city renowned as a bastion of liberal thought. He soon found that the reality of the grind, the inescapable conformity of law school crushed him. He bore few fond memories of Madison save for those of Virginia Hostler.

It hadn't been planned. He hadn't left Julie Marie Norton in Detroit Lakes with an engagement ring on her finger just so he could chase around. He and Julie had been high school sweethearts. Friends first, lovers after their friendship matured. She was a writer, a poet, a creative force, and a woman of great promise. She was brown-eyed with a pleasant face and dirty blond hair accented by a full, quick smile. Her hair hung down to her waist when they first met, its wispy ends touching the seductive curve of her bottom. As time passed, as their lives became more ordered and serious, her hair became shorter.

Julie's cheeks were dimpled, set off by little creases that cast attractive shadows over an engaging mouth when she smiled. She was argumentative and temperamental, as quick to anger as she was to laugh. He liked her mercurial nature right from the very start of their relationship.

"Danny, I don't know if I can wait three years."

Sitting near the fire on the beach years after Julie spoke those words, Dan Aitkins could still hear her voice, could still see the look of uncertainty on her face as if it was yesterday. Alone on the frozen beach of Big Detroit Lake, he smiled as he recalled the gentle pull of the Ottertail River passing beneath them, a full moon standing watch over their naked bodies.

Idle thoughts wandered through the lawyer's mind between sips of beer. After their swim, they had made slow, passionate love on a faded blanket beneath the protective shadows of box alder trees. He'd promised that three years would fly by, that he could stay true to her until he finished law school. Though skeptical, she had agreed to wait.

Aitkins was nearly as good as his word. He kept his nose clean, studied hard, and came back to visit Detroit Lakes every chance he got. Sure, he saw other women and desired them, wanted to discover them, as he had discovered Julie. But each time such feelings intruded, each time he felt ready to lose control, he thought of her and he fought the urge to stray.

On a whim, Aitkins went out with Dave Johnson, a classmate. They clerked at the same upscale, politically liberal downtown Madison law firm. Johnson was from Chicago, a big city boy with money. He was silky smooth and suave around women: a professional with the ladies. Dan Aitkins was a hick from the Corn Belt, a kid from a small town in love with his high school sweetheart. From the first time Aitkins watched Johnson talk to a woman, flatter her, tease her, make her blush, the Minnesotan was in awe of Johnson's power over the feminine gender. Aitkins had never been able to attempt the same sort of deception: he found the small talk, the lies, the false leads, and unattainable expectations shallow and crass.

Danny's brain told him to stay clear of Johnson, to avoid going out with him at all costs. But in a moment of weakness, Aitkins gave in to the enticing danger of a night out on the town with David Johnson.

"Mary, Virginia, this is my good friend Danny. His father's a plastic surgeon in Melbourne, Australia. His mom's a romance novelist. Perhaps you've heard of her? Katrina Aitkins?"

Johnson squeezed himself between two long-legged young ladies that evening without so much as a bat of an eye as he spun his usual web of deceit.

"Is that true, Mr. Aitkins? Your dad's really a doctor?" Virginia asked politely.

"Danny. Please call me Danny. At's what all me friends call me."

Virginia was model thin and tall, taller than Aitkins. She wore her blond hair cropped short to accent her classically featured face. Her eyes were an opaque gray. Her bright red lipstick was in stark contrast to her milky skin. She watched him through an intense, unnerving gaze, as if she could see right through the lies. But she seemed genuinely interested in him. Or at least interested in the person she thought he was.

"At's right. Me mom's a writer, me dad's a doctor. Does boob jobs, tush lifts, you know, the cosmetic stuff."

He fell into the role easily. Why? Why did he do it? With Julie waiting and their wedding day only three months away. Why, with the minister and the guests all ready, with the presents bought and wrapped? Why?

Later, after the bar closed, the four of them walked to Johnson's house together. It was a tepid March night, nearly seventy degrees. Daniel strolled alongside the blond, his hands shoved deep into the front pockets of his well-worn trousers. He followed along, not really knowing or understanding what he was doing with her, where they were headed. All the while, he felt Ginny studying him. He was unsure whether they were connecting or simply drifting along, accompanying their friends to a destination.

Johnson's house was located at the edge of the University of Wisconsin campus. It was a ramshackle duplex. Most of the building's exterior displayed peeling white paint. Nearly all of the spars of the covered front porch were cracked and broken.

Inside, Johnson's half of the structure continued to emphasize the building's general state of decadence. Broken plaster, soiled shag carpeting, and disintegrating walls confirmed that the place's ultimate demise was only a few years away. The sole items of value in the dimly lighted living room were a huge Marantz stereo and Johnson's album collection.

Their host placed an LP on the turntable. The opening strains of *Suite: Judy Blue Eyes* disguised an awkward silence between Dan and the girl. Thankful for familiar music, Aitkins left the room, returning momentarily from the kitchen with four bottles of beer.

"I love this song," Virginia offered in a voice as soft and gentle as spring rain.

Her words were said with reverence, as if she didn't want to intrude upon the music. She swayed gently to the beat of the song as she walked through the living room towards him. She grasped the cold neck of her beer bottle with grace. A faint echo of a smile crossed her lips, vanishing before Aitkins could determine its sincerity.

She retrieved the album cover from an end table next to Aitkins and stared intently at the photograph of Crosby, Stills, and Nash on the jacket.

"You look something like Graham Nash," she observed. "Sound something like him too."

"Eee's English, love, not Aussie. He used to be with the Hollies. But thanks for the compliment."

She laughed. Her expression of delight was limited to fragile air escaping her lips. Her laugh wasn't forced or contrived. It matched the subtle nature of her other gestures. Her manner was so different from Julie's directness, Julie's assertiveness. Ashamedly, Aitkins began to consider what his date would be like in the thralls of orgasm.

Ginny's curiosity satisfied, she placed the album cover down on the black plastic dust cover of the turntable and joined him on the couch.

"Where do you suppose Dave and Mary are?" Virginia asked in a slightly provocative voice.

The law student shifted uncomfortably on the davenport but didn't answer the woman's question.

"I think they went into the bedroom," she whispered.

Ginny smiled. The edges of her mouth tensed. It was clear she was interested in Dan as she nodded her head in the direction of Johnson's bedroom. Aitkins looked down the unlit hallway but kept his thoughts to himself. He was thankful that the music of Stephen Still's guitar drowned out whatever sounds being released from his friend's bedroom.

"It's Mary's twenty-second birthday. I think she feels like celebrating," the woman advised.

"I see."

Aitkins became aware of the girl's hand resting on his inner thigh. Her intent was demonstrable through the denim of his jeans. Shamefully, he became aroused.

"I've got something to confess."

He abandoned the accent. The motion against his leg stopped. Ginny lowered her mouth to the beer bottle. Her lips surrounded the opening provocatively as she took a long draw of liquid.

After fourteen years, Aitkins still remembered the tiny droplets of moisture clinging to the cool glass; how sensuous the curve of her neck looked as she swallowed the liquor. How beautiful she seemed.

Whether his recollection was accurate or merely the result of the alcohol he'd consumed on that evening so long ago, he was unable to reconcile. In memory, when Ginny's image came to him, she was always the same. She was flawless. Perfect.

"You're married, aren't you?" she had asked defensively. There was certainty in her voice that, if he answered in the affirmative, she would vanish.

Danny remembered the indecision he felt as he considered the question. Aitkins squirmed on the couch as he fought with himself, seeking honesty in the depths of need, want, and guilt. The truth would have been: "yes, all except for the ceremony." But those were not the words he uttered on that evening in Madison. Instead, he lied. Maybe not legally, maybe not in terms of perjury on the witness stand. But morally, spiritually, as a Christian, he lied.

"No. It's just that, well, I'm obviously not Australian. I'm from Western Minnesota. A little town called Detroit Lakes."

24

"No shit. Did you really think I fell for that accent?" she asked through a smirk.

He looked into her eyes. They were not judgmental. They appeared to be searching for a sign from him that he was ready to commit some part of his real self to the evening.

"I guess that was pretty lame. I'm not very good at small talk."

"You're doing fine right now."

"That's because you're easy to talk to. I've never met someone so ready to listen, so unwilling to condemn. That's a rare trait."

"Thanks."

Her hand brushed his cheek. The movement lacked pretense.

Sitting on the beach more than a decade removed from the event, he recalled how her mouth found his. It seemed, in memory, to have taken hours. He felt it was an eternity that she kissed him, at first with curiosity, and then, as their blood began to rise, with intensity. In reality, her intimate gesture had lasted but a moment, though each tick of the clock on that evening drew him further and further from morality, honesty, and fidelity. Even still, he had wanted more from that first encounter.

She made it plain it was not going to happen. Aitkins had studied the woman's face. She wore a slight, puzzled smile. Her reaction seemed to recognize the delicacy of the situation.

"I don't think you're that shy. Just remember, they'll come a time when I'll expect you to reciprocate."

Ginny's eyes had carried with them a sense of understanding. Her face remained, from that moment on, a portrait of guilt that he would carry with him forever.

They retreated from the battered sofa, exited the house, and walked down the hillside. The couple followed a well-worn path to Lake Mendota. Next to the water, under a clouded sky, they sat on a concrete bench and held hands. Daniel allowed Virginia's head to rest upon his shoulder as she breathed deeply of the fresh spring air.

Daniel had silently vowed, after kissing Virginia goodbye, after exchanging telephone numbers, after she drove off just ahead of dawn in her rusted Opal GT coupe, that he would never see her again.

It hadn't worked out that way. He continued to see Ginny Hostler. And they continued to advance their intimacy until he took her to bed. After each of their couplings, in the repose of resolution, he would lie next to Ginny, fighting pangs of remorse that stole across his naked body.

"I love you, Danny."

She'd spoken the dreaded words after one such tryst, after a night of passionate lovemaking in her apartment. It was painful to hear words that he himself felt but dared not utter. Or had he felt love at all for her? Perhaps it was only lust, a momentary infatuation spawned by distance and time. Whether he loved the woman was beside the point. He'd made a promise, a vow, to Julie. And he knew, whatever his transitory feelings for the young woman next to him, he still cared for the writer back in Detroit Lakes.

Daniel had feigned sleep that evening. Virginia did not press her intentions. Her words carried hot and potent poison that he dared not acknowledge.

"Can a man love two women?" he'd asked himself against the lonely pain of decision. He knew the answer was "yes". Would either woman understand? He knew the answer to that question, then and now, was "no". Smarter men then he: men of wealth, power, and politics, had tried to divide their love equally between two women. They all invariably failed. He knew from that first night at David Johnson's apartment that what he desired, what he was attempting, was impossible.

Dear Ginny:

I write this to you because I am a coward. You've given me so much. You've awakened something in me, made me feel alive and loved. But I can't keep seeing you. I've been less than truthful with you, and I hate myself for it.

I should have told you this when we first met. I'm ashamed that I didn't. So much has happened between us. I might as well just say it. I'm engaged to someone else.

Under the circumstance, I think it's best that we don't see each other again. You deserve more than half of my attention, even if I was free to give it to you.

Take care. You're beautiful, kind, and decent. I'm a bastard for manipulating you this way. If it makes a difference, I'll always remember you and I'll always bear the hurt of having to leave you

Love,
Danny.

He never gathered up the courage to talk to her, to explain his deception in person. He mailed the letter, moved to another apartment, stopped hanging around with Dave Johnson, and vanished from Virginia Hostler's life forever. But try as he could, her memory, her touch, the bits and pieces of their fevered moments together, clung to his subconscious, lingering like bits of forbidden conversation within the dialogue of life. Years later, Ginny was still there, watching, always watching.

Staring at the deteriorating ice of Big Detroit Lake, the lawyer tried to force the tired image of the Wisconsin woman from his mind. The beer weakened the defenses of his psyche and allowed melancholy to linger. As he sought sleep within the marginal comfort of his sleeping bag, Danny Aitkins sensed that Virginia was beside him. He was certain he felt her blond hair tickling the wind-hardened skin of his face. Her legs sought him, wrapped around him. Her accusing eyes stung him, peering scornfully into his soul, seeking a response to an old recrimination. A remembrance of her perfume engaged his olfactory nerves.

Virginia had not been brilliant or smart like Julie Norton. But she had been so considerate, so kind, so at peace with herself. She was satisfied to be a clerk in a dress shop, to drive fast in her beat up old sports car, and to have someone love her. What happened to her after she read his letter? Did Dan's selfishness, his lies, hurt her? Or had he overestimated his impact upon her life?

"Just like Tina Pelletier's case. I should have thought it through before I got involved. Another bonehead move from Becker County's supreme bonehead."

Seeking relief from the wind, Daniel pulled the sleeping bag tighter around his torso. As Aitkins fought personal demons, he tried to avoid reliving Julie's reaction to his confession. His attempt to forestall recalling that painful moment proved unsuccessful.

"You bastard. How dare you go out with someone else only months before our wedding? How dare you?" Julie had cried out.

He'd admitted the affair one night when he was home from Madison on break. They were having a drink in Zoro's Bar in downtown Fargo.

"I didn't mean for it to happen. It just did. It's over. I swear. I'll never see her again," he confessed.

Julie studied his face through angry disbelief.

"You slept with her, didn't you?"

There was an unkind hesitation before he replied.

"I don't know what I was thinking. Maybe it was the beer. Or being so far away from you. I don't know why it happened."

Julie's eyes welled with tears. Her voice quaked.

"Damn you, that's no excuse. Haven't I been away from you? Haven't I been just as lonely? You don't see me fucking the first college boy who compliments my tits, do you? Well, do you?" she gasped, her breath short and desperate. "How can I ever trust you, believe you? I loved you. And you slept with some woman you barely knew."

"It wasn't like that," he'd whispered.

He knew the words were wrong before they were released. It was too late. They escaped. They were out there for Julie to hear. He could not take them back. He could not sugar coat them or replace them with more intelligent, less injurious phrasing.

"Christ, Dan, what the hell do you mean? Do you love this girl? Is that it? Christ, if you love her, I won't stop you from fucking her."

Julie had bit her lip. The skin burst apart. She began to bleed. Serious bright red liquid dripped onto her angora sweater. After that night, she never washed the garment. After that terrible moment, when their love hung suspended on a cliff of revelation, she placed the stained sweater in her closet as a reminder of what he'd done.

Swallowing hard, Aitkins reflected on the moment when she sat in Zoro's crying, bleeding, ready to break apart. What was he to say? If he told her that he loved Virginia Hostler, that he was still in love with her, he would lose them both. There would be no wedding. But if he lied, if he told Julie that he had no emotional debt to pay regarding the woman from Madison, there was a chance, a glimmer of hope. The choice had not been difficult.

"I don't love her," he whispered. "She filled a physical need, a longing. That's all. I love you. From the first time we walked around Alden Lake after Elmer Stevens' wedding to this very day, I love you."

Julie became quiet and left the bar. He found her hours later, sitting on a park bench overlooking the Red River. They endured several weeks of slow, cautious rapprochement. Eventually, the emotional storm clouds passed. She proclaimed a truce and announced a wary forgiveness. Against all odds, the wedding went on as planned.

"Lord, I'm only thirty-seven but this damn world seems to want to knock me down."

Aitkins' half-hearted prayer was spoken through a tarry wall of self-pity drawn from the most secret levels of his soul. He shoved another piece of driftwood towards the center of the fire, so lost within his private gloom, so caught up in the personal aspects of his courtroom defeat, that he forgot the ultimate reason he was sitting next to the icy expanse of Big Detroit Lake. The lawyer forgot that he was there to mourn the passing of a thirteen-year-old Indian girl killed by neglect.

CHAPTER 3

A feeble April sun was just clearing a line of maple trees when the farmer made his first trip through the nursery. The smell of pigs settled over the man as he opened the door to the barn. It was an odor that would render most city dwellers unconscious. The stench had no effect on Dean Anderson.

Certainly, the farmer smelled the hogs. But after living in close proximity to animals for all of his life, the odor had simply become a part of him. It was a constant. No matter how many times he tried to leave it, wash it away, or out run it, the smell was always present.

Dean Anderson stood in semi-darkness on the imperfect floor of the nursery building and instinctively activated a double pole light switch. One hundred and fifty stations rested on each side of an isle running down the middle of the building. Three hundred bred sows and gilts, together with their litters, occupied the space: eight piglets on average per female, twenty-seven hundred pigs in all. The sounds of infant animals nursing, suckling on their momma's teats, drowned out the discontented grunts of the hungry sows and gilts. It was another routine day in a routine life for both Dean Anderson and his hogs.

The farmer pushed an empty metal feed cart down the aisle. He stopped in front of a feed station, reached up, and grabbed a frayed loop of rope. With a steady pull, Anderson drew the steel funnel of the feed chute towards the waiting conveyance. The other end of the chute was anchored to a stainless steel grain bin, its fastening bolts rusted by the caustic atmosphere of the barn. As the flume descended, the farmer opened a sliding door, which allowed feed to fall noisily into the hopper of the cart. Watching the grain tumble, Dean Anderson contemplated how it was that he'd become a pig farmer.

Anderson's father had given him ten sows for a 4H project when he was nine years old. Dean's older brother Ervin helped him build a lean-to off the old dairy barn to house the swine, helped him pound cedar fence posts into the hard soil, and string wire for an electric fence to contain their modest herd. They won first prize at the Swift County Fair in Benson, Minnesota the third year they raised pigs. Betsy the champion sow, all four hundred and eighty- five pounds of her, took home "best of show".

Erv and Dean bred their sows with Duroc and Hampshire boars, genetically engineering the pigs to thrive in the sweltering humidity of summer and the sub-zero cold of winter. They were partners. They made big plans for the future; plans that ended when Erv joined the Marines in 1971. Ervin Anderson came back from

29

Vietnam, one of the last soldiers drafted to serve in that confusing conflict, nine months later in a flag-draped casket.

Most days, Dean Anderson thought about Erv and what life would've been like if they were still partners, if Erv had survived the war. The farmer often contemplated how much easier life would be with his brother's big-boned face, framed with waves of thick blond hair, accented by a perpetually goofy grin and large, floppy ears sitting on top of a lanky six foot five frame, around to help Dean Anderson through life. How much better the sun once felt; how much brighter the stars once burned when Erv was alive. But Ervin wasn't alive and he hadn't been for over thirty years.

When Dean married Nancy Groth, a local girl from town who'd never known farm life, there had been only his father, mother, his younger sister Sherry, and some of Nancy's family to help move Dean and Nancy onto the old dairy farm they bought in Becker County. The distressed farmhouse might have seemed crowded to most as folks hauled box after box of clothing and personal belongings into the dwelling. To Dean, Ervin's absence on that day made the home seem vacant.

Catching himself in mid-thought, the farmer noted that feed pellets were spilling onto the concrete floor of the nursery. Anderson grasped the spout and swung it back into position against the metal skin of the feed bin. Shutting the access panel, the farmer twisted a rusted piece of bailing wire to secure the funnel.

It was seven in the morning. Dean's boys were already awake and working. Chad, the youngest, had been the first one up. Chad started each day by mucking out the old dairy barn where the family's two milk cows were stabled. Though only ten years old, Chad contributed his fair share of labor. In fact, by a city kid's standards, standards that his mother had grown up with, Chad Anderson was employed full-time. The boy put in more than forty hours a week on the farm: milking the cows twice daily, feeding and raising his own laying hens, marketing eggs for extra spending money; helping his mom till, plant, and weed a two-acre vegetable garden that supplied the Andersons with fresh berries and produce for the better part of each year. Then there were the seasonal chores, like driving the old narrow-front Allis Chalmers tractor during haying season or guiding the Allis' seven-foot wide snow blower through the accumulated drifts of winter.

Matthew Anderson, Dean and Nancy's oldest son, was starkly different in physique from Chad. Whereas Chad favored his mother in that he was thin like a rail with honey-colored hair and blue eyes; Matt was short, powerful, and stocky, built like his father and his paternal grandfather. Matthew's eyes and hair were dark brown, close to the color of the Becker County soil when it was freshly turned.

The oldest Anderson boy had seen fit to quit high school in tenth grade. He told his parents he'd had enough of teachers, rules, and education. It was a decision allowed by Minnesota law but one never really sanctioned by his parents. Once Matt dropped out of Detroit Lakes High School, the conversations between father and son became strictly cordial. No pleasantries were exchanged. No personal concerns were shared between them. Theirs became a simple economic bond based upon the day-to-day reality of farm work. Dean Anderson needed his son as a skilled, conscientious employee. Matt needed the room, board, and the two hundred dollars per week pay he drew as a wage. Though the father and son reached an arrangement of convenience, their unspoken conflict continued to tear Nancy Anderson up inside.

"Why can't you let Matt live his own life, make his own choices? He'll come to realize he needs to finish school on his own terms. You're being too hard on him," Dean's wife had urged that morning.

"Me? What about him? The only thing...the one thing I ask of our kids is to stay in school, to graduate and give themselves a chance to become someone, to be something other than a filthy pig farmer stuck on a Godforsaken plot of land for the rest of their lives. There's no hope, no future in that, not these days, Nancy. Not with corporate farms destroying our way of life."

"We're doing all right, Dean. We've made a pretty good go of it."

"That's past, Nance. The time of the two-hundred-acre family farm, whether it's grain, turkeys, hogs, cattle, or milk cows, has passed. The damned corporations, the foreigners, the big-city processors, they've got the power now. They're stealing everything in sight. Instead of buying raw product from us, the family farmer, they buy our land, buy us out, and replace us with a factory farm."

"Is it really that bad? Martha Hemshaw's boy, Andrew, he's doing well over by Perham milking cows. He's not much older than Matt and only half as smart. Isn't there a chance Matthew can do the same?"

"The Hemshaw's have a thousand acres of the best land in the Ottertail River Valley and only one kid. Giving their boy four hundred acres of prime land, subsidizing his costs with interest-free loans for operating capital, those are things a rich man like Earl Hemshaw can do that I can't. If Matt wants to go out on his own, he'll start off deep in debt to the FHA, provided they take him on. I can't afford to keep him working here much longer as it is. And we can't split up this rinky-dink operation. How would we? Split it between three boys? And what about Millie? The four of them would each get enough land to raise a few apple trees and a chicken or two and that'd be about it."

They routinely held such discussions, though not as long or agitated as they had that morning. Nancy was upset, near tears, when they were done. Dean had stomped out of the kitchen in silent frustration, forgetting his coffee in the process, and nearly knocking his daughter off the back stairs as he stormed away.

At twenty years old and the oldest offspring, Millicent Anderson was bright, articulate, and good-looking in athletic, healthy fashion. She had graduated from high school with honors, valedictorian of her class, and was awarded a full scholarship to Concordia College in Moorhead, a private Lutheran school located fifty miles west of home. She chose to stay on the farm and work at the Detroit Lakes Perkin's Restaurant as a night manager.

"School can wait," she told her parents.

She wanted to earn enough money for at least one year at Notre Dame, where she'd also been accepted as well but awarded only a partial academic scholarship. Turning down a good Lutheran school, where all four years of her education were guaranteed, on the off chance that she might eventually mingle with unsympathetic Roman Catholics was an unpopular decision with her Missouri Synod Lutheran parents.

"There's a good possibility you'll run out of money and never finish school," her father initially admonished. But Dean's stern warning dissipated over time. Millicent was his only daughter and by virtue of that status, eligible for special paternal dispensation.

"Hi dad".

Millie kissed her father dryly on the forehead, brushing by him in her haste to get inside. Though she had just worked a full twelve-hour shift at the restaurant, she was expected to help her mother with household chores. The farmer determined, from the lines of exhaustion accenting his daughter's features, that she was bone tired. It was obvious she wanted to finish her duties and crawl into bed.

"Hold on, darlin'."

Dean grasped his daughter's arm and pulled her back towards him enveloping her in a hug.

"Sorry I almost knocked you down," he said.

"That's OK. You look frazzled," she replied.

"It's nothin'. Parent stuff. Go on in and give your mom a hand. She could use it."

He watched the girl open the storm door. As his daughter departed, the porch light cast a luminescent glow over Millie's feminine form.

My little girl, the farmer thought, *has become a woman. Where the hell was I when that happened? Where did the years go?*

Later that morning, Dean Anderson had come across Matthew in the finishing barn where the boy was feeding fifty to sixty pound feeder pigs their grain. Feeder pigs are not breeding animals but meat stock; pigs confined indoors to be fattened into two hundred pound plus butcher hogs for slaughter, satisfying America's demand for pork roast, ham, bacon, and pork chops.

"Matthew, where's Joey?"

"He's with Chad. They're in the nursery. You done with the farrowing barn yet?" the boy responded.

Matt's message slid across his tongue. His tone was flat. His words were a reflection of facts punctuated with an inquiry about work. As cool as the boy's countenance appeared, Dean Anderson detected regret on his oldest son's face. Being who he was, what he was, Dean Anderson didn't press his impression.

"Nope. Heading that way now. See to it that you look at that lame hog over there will ya?" Dean Anderson had said.

The farmer gestured towards an animal in obvious pain.

"No need to get docked for him. Mend him if you can, cull him if you can't. It's no big loss: the freezer can stand a few more roasts in it anyway."

Matt nodded before tossing the remaining feed into galvanized troughs in front of each hog pen. His eyes remained fixed on the work. He never looked directly at his father. Matt's breath became scarce. The door closed and the young man's attention returned to the labor he'd chosen.

Dean Anderson next ventured into the farm's nursery, where newborn pigs are moved after being weaned from their mothers. Fed another special grain mixture, the piglets are raised in the nursery to feeder pig weight. After achieving their target size, some of the animals are sold as feeder pigs, some are held as breeding stock, and some are sent to the finishing barn to be fattened into market hogs. It all depends upon health and genetics. It's a simple progression; farrowing house to nursery; nursery to finishing barn; finishing barn to market.

The farmer had walked into the nursery to sounds of pigs in ecstasy. Joey and Chad were feeding pelleted corn to the nursery animals. The concentrate being used in the nursery was nearly identical to the feed being given the sows and gilts in the farrowing house.

"How's it going boys?"

It was clear from the man's demeanor that he'd freed himself of the irritation that resulted from dealing with oldest son. Dean

Anderson smiled. Chad and Joey looked up from a feed cart, an ancient wooden contraption constructed from discarded plywood, old bicycle tires, and baling wire.

"Great. These pellets are a whole lot cleaner than the ground stuff we were using. Seems like it takes awhile for them to get used to the texture though," Joey said.

"That's typical. Pigs are particular about changes in diet. Sometimes it takes a day or two. But if they're healthy, they're hungry. They'll be at it soon enough," the farmer advised.

"Millie home yet?" Chad asked.

The boy discarded his feed scoop and raced towards his father as he spoke. Vaulting through the air, the youngest Anderson child landed in his father's arms before wrapping himself around Dean Anderson like a leech.

"She's home, Chaddy boy, she's home. She's in the kitchen with mom. You boys better hurry. The school bus'll be here in twenty minutes. You need to get showered and changed. Can't have the two of you going off to school smelling like hogs, now can we?"

"I'd go smelling like cow crap if it'd keep Betty Mae Clemson away from me. She's always making faces, sending notes around about me. If I smell, maybe she'll leave me alone."

"Sounds like Betty Mae's sweet on you. Little girls often show their love in very peculiar ways. Be nice to her. That'll confuse her for sure. She won't expect it. Understand? Come on now, off you go. Help Joey finish this up so you're not late for the bus."

The boy jumped away and scurried back to work.

"Dad, are you coming to see my track meet today? It's against Fergus. Should be a great meet," Joey inquired.

"Can't. I'd dearly love to see you lap those guys from the 'Falls. Maybe next time. Matt and I have to deliver some hogs to West Fargo."

"OK," the middle Anderson son replied, disappointment clear in his juvenile voice, the boy's lament poorly concealed.

Dean Anderson was rarely able to attend his children's functions. He'd missed Millie's graduation night, her valedictory speech and all. A calf had come breech. He'd missed Matthew's first and last game as a starting quarterback for the Detroit Lakes Junior Varsity football team two years ago. A sow had gone wild, "hog wild" as it were, and destroyed the wooden enclosure around her, trampling her own litter and seven other litters before the hog farmer and Jake Benson, a neighbor, could put her down. Matthew Anderson never played another football game, not after he looked up into the stands searching for the familiar face of his father only to find that the reassuring features of Dean Anderson were not there.

34

The farm. It was always the farm and the accursed pigs. They took up every waking breath, every ounce of energy, every moment he could muster. The farm was his life. There was nothing beyond the boundaries of the place for Dean Anderson. When he was younger, it hadn't bothered him. Now, as he contemplated midlife, the claustrophobia of his trade seemed ready to suffocate his dreams. The stranglehold he endured at the hands of his profession made him vow that none of his children would become farmers, that all of them would finish high school and go on to places of higher learning.

Dean had smiled as he stood in the nursery and placed a world-weary hand on Joey's back. Looking at his middle son, the farmer witnessed tears form in the corners of the boy's eyes. Anderson's gaze took in the big blond head of hair, the shape of the mouth, the dangling earlobes. Joe was tall and raw-boned at fourteen. He was different from the others.

Whereas Matt favored Dean, and therein probably resided the problems between them, and Millie was clearly a mixture of her mother and father, and Chad was a carbon copy of his mother; Joey was the spitting image of Dean's older brother Ervin. He was going to be a big, powerful man, an athlete. Dean wanted his middle son to realize this potential. The father pushed the boy in that direction in hopes of insuring that Joey would never become a hog farmer. But the farm demanded so much; there was so little time for the father to play with his children.

After visiting the nursery, Dean Anderson entered the farrowing house. Despite the fact that his boys were good workers, Dean retained the job of caring for the breeding females and their nursing young for himself. The litters were the farm's cash crop, its future, the operation's source of income. Until the young pigs were completely weaned and separated from their mothers, they were fragile and susceptible to disease. It was the farmer's job to insure that the piglets survived weaning by carefully monitoring their feed and by medicating the mothers against insidious swine diseases such as Lepto, Parvo, and Pseudo-Rabies so that the immunity of the sows and bred gilts was passed on to their young through their mother's milk. There was an unrelenting and ever-expanding list of diseases that could wipe out a gestating swineherd. It was Dean Anderson's job to insure that such a catastrophe never occurred on his watch.

The hog farmer pushed the feed cart down the center isle of the farrowing house. At intervals, he carefully placed a three to four pound ration of feed in each animal's trough. Moving from crate to crate, Anderson visually inspected the health of the sows, gilts, and their litters. It was rare for him to find distressed or dead pigs. A few piglets expired during birth, but if they survived delivery, the piglets rarely perished in the Anderson farrowing barn.

The ration that Anderson poured out for each sow and gilt was a high protein pelleted feed with a corn and soybean base. It was finely ground, pelleted feed: "FGP" for short. According to Stevenson's Sci-Swine, the product's manufacturer, the complete feed contained sixty-nine percent corn and twenty-three percent soybean meal, the remainder of the formula being medications added by the mill depending upon the age and type of pig being fed. Dean Anderson was trying FGP feed for the first time.

The farmer had always mixed, ground, and medicated his own livestock feed. A month earlier, Stevenson's Sci-Swine Mill in Detroit Lakes had commenced advertising FGP feed. Using manufactured pellets eliminated the need for Dean Anderson to rely upon his own corn crop. It also eliminated the time consuming tasks of mixing, grinding, and medicating the rations. Anderson knew the guys at the mill and trusted them. Though the complete feed stacked up as more expensive per ton, the projected savings in labor and the decreased amount of waste the farmer expected to find around the troughs after feeding seemed to outweigh the additional expense.

Stevenson's had delivered the grain, a week's supply, from its local mill. Anderson used up the remaining grind and mix sow and nursery rations in his feed bins before the truck arrived. The farmer was careful to remove any residue from the bins before the new feed was unloaded. This was the first day that Dean Anderson was feeding his animals Stevenson's pellets.

As the farmer struggled to move the fully loaded cart along the uneven surface of the floor, he sensed something different about the feed. He couldn't put a finger on it. It was a feeling, an uneven impression. He grabbed a handful of pellets and held the mixture to his nostrils, searching for the telltale odor of spoilage. There was no scent to the feed save for that of the molasses used to bind and fortify the pellets. Satisfied with his impromptu inspection, the farmer tossed the pellets back into the hopper of the wagon and continued to work. The adult animals moved right for the feed as it filled the troughs. They didn't seem as concerned about the pellets as the boys at the mill had predicted. Anderson shrugged off his premonition and made his way through the farrowing house, weighing in his mind the possibility of slipping away to do some late-season ice fishing in hopes of making Joey feel better about his father's inability to attend the track meet.

"Maybe", he mused, "Matt will go with. Fishing might help us mend some fences."

But the farmer knew that the chances of his oldest son going fishing were slim. Dean pushed that glimmer of reconciliatory hope back to where it belonged, back to the realm of impossibility.

The first chores of the morning behind him, Anderson left the farrowing house at a leisurely, done-with-the-job-pace. He utilized a well-established path through melting snow to make his way back to the house. Winter's cold was being supplanted. Water pooled along the edges of declining snowdrifts. An oblong sun rose to the east. A breeze swept across the farm, stealing in from somewhere over the horizon. Anderson stopped at the back porch and rested a muddy work boot on a wooden stair tread.

The man watched two white tail deer, a doe and her fawn, nibble sprouts of new grass along the edge of the forest. The mother sniffed the morning air nervously, her head high and alert, her tail raised in warning. The fawn, its tawny hide covered by white spots, stood beside its mother on ungainly legs and continued to graze.

"Sometimes, I guess it's worth it."

The hog farmer spoke with reverence as he watched the deer.

"Sometimes no other job compares."

Dean Anderson opened the storm door and reached for the crystal knob of the entry panel leading into the kitchen. The oak door swung heavily. The aroma of recently brewed coffee and freshly baked caramel rolls greeted the farmer. The hinges of the portal creaked. The deer bolted, disappearing into the woods surrounding the farm, leaving only a memory of elegant beauty behind.

CHAPTER 4

"**Aitkins**, Murphy, Ordell, and Aitkins. How may I direct your call?"

Beth Monson, the law firm's receptionist, answered the telephone with a cheerful voice. It was her job to screen calls, to funnel clients and potential clients to the appropriate attorneys.

Each of the four partners in the firm handled certain aspects of the law. No one attorney handled every type of case that came through the firm's doors. Their practices were specialized, reflecting the personal aptitudes of the individual lawyers. There was a sophisticated written methodology used to account for production and rainmaking, the bringing in of new business. But the written policy wasn't always followed, resulting in a compensation system that was more informal than intended.

Ms. Monson was short, barely over five feet tall and pleasant to look at. She favored slacks, rarely exposing her legs, her greatest physical attribute. Danny was puzzled by Beth's lack of understanding that her plain rounded face, nondescript eyes, distressed hair, and nearly concave chest were in need of some assistance if she intended to find a second husband. Beth was newly divorced, having tossed her husband Barry, an uncontrollable pot smoker, out the door. The divorce wasn't final but Danny could tell that the receptionist was anxious to move on. She was over thirty and it was obvious by the way she studied the firm's male clients that Beth Monson was in the hunt for husband Number Two.

If she'd wear shorter skirts, Danny thought, *Beth would do OK. She's got the nicest legs in Detroit Lakes.*

"Mr. Aitkins, there's a gentleman calling from out near Island Lake, a Mr. Anderson. Do you want me to take a message?"

"What's he want?"

"He says it's about some bad feed. Something to do with pigs. Sounds upset. I can take his number if you'd like."

Beth's voice sounded like a tin whistle. It wasn't her fault. It was the hangover. Her voice startled him just as he placed his head down on his desk. Aitkins was physically ill and thoroughly depressed. He wasn't in the mood to talk to some hayseed about a lost pig or two.

Christ, he thought, *just what I need. Some poor bastard barely hanging onto his shit-ass forty whining to me about a couple of dead hogs.*

Somewhere deep inside his head Daniel heard the voice of his father, Emery Aitkins, the first "Aitkins" in the firm name, talking to him. Emery was the founder of the firm, having actively practiced law in excess of forty years. Danny's father had instilled in the younger man a belief that the rejection of a meritorious claim would lead to the usurping of good local cases by the "fat cats" from the Twin Cities. This fear was so ingrained in Danny's litigating soul that it overpowered his physical condition. He was compelled by his father's admonition to talk to the man.

"Put him through," Daniel muttered.

It was Aitkins' first day back after the Pelletier verdict. He'd spent a long, cold, and lonely evening drinking near-frozen beer. He'd been so deep in reflection that he forgot to call his wife. Julie had been clueless as to where he was. He avoided a scene with his wife by calling her from the office after a shower and a change of clothes at the YMCA. He kept clean underwear, socks, neckties, dress shirts, and an old sport coat in his locker at the "Y". The call to Julie had been anything but easy.

"I lost the case," he had advised.

"Where have you been? It's six o'clock in the morning. I've been worried sick."

"Julie, I lost the case."

"I know. Emery called. He's worried about you. Where the hell have you been all night?"

"On the beach."

"In April? Are you nuts?"

Silence. He had trouble concentrating over the din in his head.

"What beach?"

"Detroit Lake. By the Park. I bought some beer, built a fire. Spent the night in an old sleeping bag I had rolled up in the back of the truck. I needed some time to sort out what those bastards did to that little girl, how they got away with killing her. I'm sorry I didn't call."

"You can't keep doing this to me. I have to know where you are. We've got three kids. How the hell did I know you weren't in some accident, lying in some ditch?"

The attorney's head had pounded in a merciless tempo, keeping time to the syllables of his wife's discourse. His stomach had churned relentlessly. He'd intentionally emptied its contents, vomiting up beer and half-digested food to stop his vertigo. Two Pepcid hadn't helped. In his languor, memories of the innumerable times that he'd screwed up in his life swirled around him.

"I'm sorry. It won't happen again."

"I've heard that before."

"I mean it. I just needed to be alone, to work things out. Three years, Julie. Three fuckin' years of my life I spent on that case. Those sons-of-bitches in their white coats and fancy shoes killed a little girl and they walked away. Those egomaniacal bastards in their three-piece suits defended their clients without regard to the truth. Where's the justice in that?"

There had been a long pause as his anger dissipated.

"How are you feeling?" she'd inquired in a more compassionate voice.

He hadn't responded immediately to her question.

"After the beer, I mean. You know you're not supposed to drink," she added.

Julie's reminding him of his frailty stung him. Her question forced the attorney to confront the fact that, at thirty-seven years old, he'd endured two back surgeries and invasive probing of his mouth and digestive tract to determine the cause of intermittent stomach pain. He kept his theories about his stomach ailment to himself. He alone knew that the pain commenced shortly after he was sworn in as a lawyer. Danny Aitkins had long ago come to grips with the reality that the stress of his profession was killing him, piece by piece; or, as in the case of the Pelletier verdict, occasionally in large chunks.

His wife's words revealed a future for Daniel that seemed more depressing than the post-binge landscape of his hangover.

"I'm OK. The beer didn't seem to affect me too much," he lied. "I know I shouldn't have done it. But I did."

"I'll only ask this once. Were you alone last night?"

The inflection in her voice had acquired an injured tone. The pain she'd felt years ago, a hurt caused by his betrayal of her trust, festered just beneath the veneer of their relationship.

"What the hell do you mean by that?" he asked, the volume of his voice rising in upset.

He knew what she meant. She meant Ginny. She meant sex, intimacy, deception, and the loss of trust that clouded her love for him. Aitkins knew it was a damn good thing she didn't know about Melanie.

Melanie Ingersol Barnes had been his second mistake. Six years ago, after Julie had given birth to their youngest child. It happened at a time when Julie was buried beneath a thick cloud of post-partum depression. Daniel thought that he was up to the task, that he could sacrifice his need to be the center of attention for the greater good of their marriage. He'd been wrong.

Melanie had been in Julie's crowd back when they all went to Detroit Lakes High School. She was someone that Daniel dated. Theirs was a limited courtship; they had so little in common, the liaison hadn't lasted. In the dim light of history, Aitkins recalled that his perception of Melanie was that she was aloof. They'd shared no prolonged period of intimacy, no intensity of contact, no real

40

passion. Once their fling was over, Dan began courting Julie and his romantic connection to Melanie slipped away.

After Daniel and Julie were married, Melanie Ingersol drifted back into their lives when she married Michael Barnes, F.W.'s youngest son, a fellow lawyer, a defense lawyer, another high school classmate, and a friend of Dan's.

The couples became inseparable, vacationing together, attending legal seminars and conferences financed by their respective employers. Despite the closeness between them, there was a hidden aspect to Michael Barnes that, when it was fully disclosed confounded even Danny.

Lawyers, by ethical caveat, keep settlement funds for their clients in trust accounts. Pending distribution of the money, the accounts serve as escrows. Attorneys are precluded from commingling their operating funds with client money by the canons of ethics. The Barnes Firm, the largest firm in Western Minnesota at twenty-two lawyers, eight of whom were partners, with offices in Moorhead, Fergus Falls, and East Grand Forks, maintained several such trust accounts. The funds held in those accounts belong to the clients, not the lawyers. It's a simple differentiation, a line that sometimes becomes blurred by an attorney's personal failings or greed. In the case of Michael Barnes, the line vanished very much like the lines of cocaine Michael snorted up his nose.

"Danny, I don't know what to do. Mike's disappeared. The Lawyer's Board, the police, his firm, everyone is looking for him. Do you know where he is?" Melanie had asked during a tense telephone exchange.

She still called him "Danny". He preferred it to "Dan" or "Daniel". The juvenile form of his name reminded him of an innocent, less-stressful time. It sent a flood of memories cascading over him to hear the woman use the moniker. There had been a moment of silence as the import of her distress sunk in.

"I thought you might know where he is," she added.

The woman had called him at his office, her voice frail and panicked. He drove immediately to her home. The missing man's father hadn't asked for his help. The wife of his best friend had. Daniel did what he was asked.

"No Mel, I haven't heard from Mike in days. What's up?" he inquired when he arrived at the house.

Daniel had heard the rumors. Detroit Lakes is a small town. News of unseemly behavior doesn't stay private or buried beneath prestige for long. He'd heard the whispers of Mike's downfall long before he arrived to comfort Melanie in the home she shared with her husband, long before Danny entered the old rambling monster of a brick mansion sitting high above the west shore of Big Detroit

Lake. He had stood at the ornate stonework of the front entry, gently knocking on a door crafted of black walnut, an expanse of water fanning out below the house like the carefully tilled fields of an English manor, until Melanie greeted him at the door with bloodshot eyes. They embraced fleetingly before she led him into the living room where they sat heavily on a black leather sofa. Their discussion was solemn; their words confined to low murmuring even though the Barnes children weren't around. He didn't volunteer any of the gossip he'd heard and she didn't ask to hear it.

"Mike's been doing coke," she blurted out. "Been into it for years. Didn't you know?"

"No Mel, I didn't. Hell, I never would have guessed it."

He lied to her. In an effort to protect her from the viciousness of the rumor mill of their small town, he told a minor untruth.

"This is such a Peyton Place. How'd he hide it? How'd you find out?" the lawyer asked.

"A month ago, I caught him going through my purse. He was tearing it apart, his eyes desperate. He said he needed cash. Before that, his mother had loaned him money a few times. Then she cut him off. F.W. wouldn't confront him about the problem, though I think Mike's parent's got wind of it before I did. They couldn't have the Barnes name defiled-no, not them. When they refused to advance him any more cash, he resorted to digging through my purse. I'd suspected what was happening for a few months. Then I found a bag of white powder in the pocket of one of his jackets. I watched him closely after that. I could tell he was getting strung out."

She stopped, took a short sip of warm coffee, and continued.

"Anyway, I finally confronted him. He denied it but I persisted until he broke down and cried. His moods were so unpredictable, so volatile; it really didn't take much to push him over the edge. He swore he'd get help. He went to Fergus Falls Mental Health Associates for a few outpatient sessions. That was a mistake. I should have put him in the hospital. But things seemed like they were getting better. And then, yesterday, he just up and left."

Thinking back, Aitkins recalled how odd it all seemed, before he knew, before he sat with Melanie Ingersol Barnes in her living room talking on that forlorn morning.

Clark Stuart, Michael's supervising partner at the Barnes Firm had been making Michael's court appearances for months. In hindsight, Aitkins should have realized something was amiss when the managing partner steps in to handle routine pretrial motions, discovery conferences, and scheduling appearances. Stuart's presence on behalf of the young defense lawyer commenced long before Mike's disappearance. Apparently, the partners knew one of

42

their own was sick but, given the law firm's desire to preserve its reputation, the principals did nothing meaningful to arrest their young partner's downward plunge.

"I should've known. Clark was obviously covering for him, taking care of minor things in court. I never put two and two together," Dan revealed through a pained expression.

Melanie had placed her hand on his. He recalled her skin as cool, just as it had been back in high school. But there was something about her gesture that was different from the "ice queen" persona he remembered from their youth. Her touch stirred him in ways that he had no right to be stirred and caused a rebirth of feelings.

"It's been difficult for all of us. Julie being out of sorts after the baby, Michael reduced to stealing change from my purse. Life certainly doesn't get any easier as we age, does it Star Baby?"

She'd used the nickname that she'd given him in their teens, in reference to the Guess Who song of the same name. Physically, he'd been a poor excuse for a varsity football player. Blond hair stuck out of the top of his head like the end of a mop. Five foot nine; mostly bone, little muscle, weighing one-forty-five soaking wet his junior year when he occasionally played on special teams.

As a senior, bulked up to one-sixty-five, he worked his way into the starting lineup as a free safety and became something of a local legend because of his small stature and vicious hits. He became a baby-faced football star. A Star Baby.

The telephone rang. The incoming call interrupted Danny's mental wanderings.

"Hello, Mr. Barnes," Melanie answered.

Aitkins found it odd that, after years in the family, Melanie resorted to formality with her father-in-law.

"Found Michael? Where? Oh my God...no...You must be kidding. There must be some mistake. Oh please Mr. Barnes, not Michael..."

She dropped the receiver. A chill apprehended her shoulders. Sobs convulsed Melanie's body while F.W's voice, distinguished and plaintive, continued to ramble on as the telephone receiver bounced at the limit of its elastic cord.

"Melanie..." the voice repeated.

Aitkins retrieved the phone as the woman clutched her body.

"It's me, F.W., Dan Aitkins. What's up?"

"It's a good thing you're there. I may not like your politics or your clients but you've at least got brains enough to talk to the girl."

"About what?"

The father took a breath.

"Michael's dead. My secretary found him this morning when she came into work. He shot himself in the stomach, the stupid fool.

43

In the stomach, Aitkins. Bled to death. Left a terrible mess all over the office. Dragged himself from his desk down the hall to the front door. He left blood everywhere."

There was a mechanical quality to the father's voice as he related the death of his son. Danny was astounded that a parent could describe the death of a child in such an orderly fashion.

"What the hell happened? Why would Mike kill himself?" Aitkins paused, realizing that he'd called his friend by the shortened version of his first name. F.W. Barnes never called his son anything but "Michael" and insisted that those referencing his son follow his lead.

"Melanie says he had the drugs under control, that he was trying to get sober," Danny inserted.

"I don't know anything about drugs. But I do know about money. Client money. He left a note. Told Clark he'd taken in excess of one hundred and fifty thousand dollars from our trust accounts. Described a scam where he'd call the involved insurer and tell it that the case had settled for say, fifty thousand, when it actually settled for twenty-five. He'd get the fifty thousand, sign the check over to himself, cash it, deposit twenty-five to distribute to the plaintiff, and pocket the rest. He stole, Aitkins, from some of our oldest and best clients. The damage he's done to the firm's reputation may well be irreversible."

There it was. The father's first and foremost concern was not for his troubled son but for the law firm.

Aitkins didn't respond. He placed the receiver back on the hook, eliminating the old man's insensitivity.

Nothing happened between them that day. Danny called Julie and told her about their friend's death. He and Mel embraced gently, shrouded in silence. There was nothing sexual or passionate about their actions. He was simply a strong shoulder for her to cry on in a time of extreme need.

A week after Michael Barnes was laid to rest in the damp Western Minnesota earth, after the two Barnes children went to stay with Melanie's parents, giving their mother a period of respite before having to face the world as a widow, before she figured out how to climb out from underneath the emotional and financial ruin her husband's death had caused, she asked Dan to visit her at what had been their home, a home that had been sold and was about to be occupied by strangers. The new owners were due to move in within the week. Melanie asked Aitkins to drop by and help her sort through her husband's things.

"Look at this picture. This was taken on the day that you, Michael, and I went to Emily's cabin. Remember? The sky was dark, the lightening flashed, but you two still went water skiing. What were we? Sixteen?"

44

She passed him a color Polaroid; the hues faded and mute. Four teenagers posed in their swimsuits in front of a Larson speedboat. The kids smiled broadly, holding cans of soda against a dark, threatening sky.

"Sixteen," Aitkins agreed.

"That was a long time ago. Seems like a lifetime ago."

"Or more."

"Look at this one. You and I at the homecoming dance."

In the picture, his hair was much longer, his face leaner, his mouth far more relaxed and youthful.

"Michael took Michelle...," the woman hesitated, seemingly unable to recall the girl's surname.

"Prate. Michelle Prate. She had great legs," Danny answered.

"Only you'd remember that. You were the most impossible flirt. But for a skinny guy, you sure were handsome."

He studied the photograph. A feeling of primitive sensuality, adolescent and terrible, surfaced from some place deep within.

"I didn't feel so handsome. I felt like a dork."

"Why?"

"Zits, skinny arms, no muscles. That stupid lock of hair on the back of my head standing straight up like a rooster's comb. I just remember feeling like a total dork."

"I didn't think of you that way."

It was a revelation that he never expected.

"You didn't say anything different."

"I should have. But I felt the same way. Awkward, unsure."

"You?" he asked incredulously.

His disbelief was genuine. She had been the most popular and sought after date in his class. That he went out with her at all, even for the briefest period, had, in Danny's view, been purely an accident, a lapse in her social calendar.

He stared intently at the photograph. The four of them. Children dressed up like adults. Mel wearing an expensive gown; lavender he thought, though the colors of the picture were too faded to confirm his memory. Despite the photo's decay, he was able to resurrect impressions of the evening from what remained.

Daniel recalled Melanie Ingersol's flaming red hair, tied up off her neck, here and there an irrepressible curl escaping to dangle provocatively above her freckled shoulders. His mind fashioned details from the grainy photograph with little effort, allowing him to envision the low-cut front of her gown, two spaghetti straps holding the fabric above her bosom, her flat chest looking grand and exquisite in a push-up brassiere.

He knew from a single encounter in the back seat of Eddy Sorenson's '67 Dodge Dart that the bosom created by the bra was an illusion. He knew because she had allowed his timid and inexperienced hands to excitedly explore beneath her Moorhead State T-shirt as they parked behind Lester Scherman's Mink Ranch one night on Torchlight Lake Road. Over the intervening years, the acrid smell of mink held a special place in Dan Aitkins' heart. The thought of those more innocent times stirred Daniel as he sat next to the woman on her couch. The emotions he felt were wholly inappropriate for the setting. And yet, he could not vanquish them.

"You were so beautiful. I was a smuck. Look at that goofy mane of yellow hair. I looked like am emaciated John Denver."

"I had no bust before the kids were born," she observed. "And look at that awful mess of hair. I never could keep it under control. I hated that I had red hair, that I stood out. What did you ever see in me, Danny?"

He hadn't thought of her like that, as she was in the picture, youthful and desirable, for a while. The question caught him off guard. He searched his mind for an answer, a response that wouldn't make the two of them uncomfortable. But none came to the mind. He simply shook his head and placed the photo back in the pile.

Melanie Barnes did not retract her gaze. Even though he tried to avoid her eyes, purposefully sorting through the memorabilia of his dead friend arranged in front of them on the coffee table, he sensed that she was staring at him. The intensity of her inspection made him nervous.

"Why didn't we stay together?" Her question drifted towards him in a soft, velvety lilt. "I really liked you. Always have. Your smile, your sense of adventure. What happened to us?"

In truth, he knew that there had never been an "us". *That's what I should say*, he thought. Instead, his remarks took an entirely different approach.

"I don't know, Mel. That was a long time ago. I guess I was never really sure where I stood with you. I never got the impression that you cared. You seemed so distant, so removed. Like you were waiting for someone, or something, better to come along; like I was only a momentary distraction to kill some time."

"That's not true. I fell for you. Big time. Maybe I didn't show it, didn't know how to let you know. Maybe I wasn't mature enough to handle what it was I felt. But I loved you Danny Aitkins, I surely did."

Her use of the "L" word caused him to shift uncomfortably on the couch. Their talk brought back memories of Ginny. He tried to switch topics, to escape the glaring reality of the impending encounter, a liaison that would only cause them agony. She didn't let him retreat easily.

"I'm frightened. I'm so alone. I don't know where to go, what to do, where to turn. It's like I need someone beside me to defend me against the unknown, to prevent me from fading away into nothingness," she whispered.

Before he could respond, before he could tell her why he couldn't stay, why such a thing was impossible, how it would tarnish them forever, how it would weigh unpleasantly in their minds each time they met, each time they spoke, she eased him off the couch. She pulled him firmly and directly behind her, towards the bedroom, the bedroom that she had shared with his best friend, a friend who rested dead and silent in the hard clay of the grave.

He half-heartedly tried to resist her lead. His efforts were more cerebral than physical; his mind told him to stop, that it was forbidden, impossible. But no words came out. His body yearned for her, yearned to explore the intimacy of her soul. Still, as they crossed the threshold into her bedroom, he managed to speak.

"We can't do this. It'll never be the same. I love Julie. I always have. I always will."

"Sssh, Danny. I know. I don't ask that you love me in return. Just hold me. Don't think. Don't explain. I know. I know."

Reflexively, he reached around the woman, encircling her in his strength. His embrace was tentative. He thought his feigned lack of interest would forestall the inevitable swelling of his passion. His mind continued to command his arms to push her away, to retreat. His heart and his loins told him to draw her ever closer, to ease her pain.

Her body pressed tightly against his chest, compressing her breasts as they kissed. Daniel noted that Melanie had put on weight. It was good weight, weight that softened the edges of her features. The weight made her more a woman, differentiated her from the young girl he petted with and kissed to a breathless frenzy in the back seat of the Dodge. Decades ago, she had allowed him those small pleasures until his hands found her nipples, whereupon she had abruptly, and probably, wisely, ended his juvenile exploration of her body.

Carrying two children had created curves that hadn't been there in the Dodge. She surprised him by flashing her tongue, cherry red against the clean brightness of her teeth. The scarlet contrasted sharply with her complexion. He recalled that she had not been particularly adept or interested in open mouth kissing. The fleeting touch of her lips, her tongue tickling the soft skin of his cheek, caught him off guard. His mouth opened to receive her. He drew her in.

His eyes met hers. Her eyelids remained tightly clenched, like she was trying to forget whom she was with, where they were, what they were doing. Or perhaps this was how she made love; in the dark, with her eyes closed. Because he had never been with her, he couldn't say which was the truth.

Aitkins looked at her face. The slightly freckled skin was smooth. Laugh lines accented her eyes and the corners of her mouth. These hints of maturity made her more interesting, more attractive. Hers was a kind face. Not stunning, not chiseled in its perfection, but caring and gentle, wholly unlike the face that he remembered from their youth.

Concentrating upon the movement of their bodies, his hands slid down her bottom and settled on the coarse fabric of her blue jeans. His fingers felt the details of the cloth. His hands surveyed the curves of her buttocks. Slowly, his fingers caressed her from behind. As his fingers stroked denim, her breathing became more rapid.

Melanie's hands grasped the skin of Daniel's neck. His right hand found the tail of her flannel shirt, Michael's shirt, and pulled it free of the waist of her jeans. The tips of his fingers found her bare abdomen. He stroked the rippled skin, exploring flesh made uneven by stretch marks caused by her pregnancies.

She began to pant. He unfastened the top button of her Wranglers. His thumb found the beginning of her intimacy and followed it through the soft fuzz of her pubic hair. His movements were without urgency. Melanie let out a haunted moan as his thumbnail moved closer to her essence.

Her arms locked around his neck. She arched her back. Her tongue explored the enamel of his teeth. Her left hand followed his right thigh to where his erection strained. Her fingers sought him through his slacks. His mind raced, seeking a reason to release himself, his soul, to her. His fingers fumbled with the buttons on the front of Melanie's shirt before exposing the soft fabric of a seamless white bra. She shed the shirt effortlessly. He released the hooks of the bra.

As the undergarment drifted downward, he stared at her breasts. Creamy skin heaved towards him with each stroke of his absent hand, a hand lost, enraptured, in a far-off, distant rhythm. His head leaned towards the pink nipple of her left teat. She urged the pliant flesh towards his lips. His mouth closed on her skin. She tasted of erotic tension. It was so wondrous, so breathtakingly beautiful. He knew in an instant that it was wrong. He stopped. Standing there, lost in the ecstasy of her, his blood boiling to the tempo of man's most ancient song, he stopped.

"I can't."

"God no, Danny, not now."

Her despair reflected an animal lust. Her inflection bore no understanding beyond an expression of raw passion.

"Don't leave me like this. No one will ever know. I swear. No one," she said.

"I will."

Aitkins had kissed the woman on her cheek, gathered his clothes and left, fleeing the unfulfilled promise of his youth. After that day, Melanie Barnes never mentioned their encounter. She never remonstrated about what might have been. And Danny Aitkins made certain that he did not repeat the folly he'd made after Madison. He never confessed his sin, or near sin, to his wife.

"You know what I mean. Were you with anyone?" Julie repeated, her words calling his attention back to her voice.

"No, Julie, I wasn't. I sat on my sorry ass on cold sand getting pig-eye drunk watching driftwood burn."

Danny Aitkins slammed the phone down. He knew that he would apologize later. He always did.

"Hello?" a quizzical voice said over the intercom.

"Yes?" the attorney answered.

"Mr. Aitkins, my name is Dean Anderson. Anderson Hog Farm. I got your name from Dr. Thomas at NDSU. He says you two have worked together."

"I know Ivan. Good guy. What's the problem?"

Aitkins inhaled hot coffee. The stuff was poisonous to his stomach but it was the only cure for his self-induced condition. He winced. The liquid stung. He popped another Pepcid and gritted his teeth.

"I bought some feed from a local elevator. Somethin's wrong with it. Don't know what. Thomas is doing some checking. Three hundred sows and bred gilts aborted their litters. The little ones in the nursery threw up after eating a similar ration. It's a disaster, Mr. Aitkins. A total disaster."

"Sounds like it. Sounds like Thomas has the bases covered. Has your own vet been out?" the lawyer asked.

"Dr. Guttormson was here last night. He's the one that put me in touch with Thomas. I fed the new feed yesterday morning. By nightfall, excuse the French, all hell broke loose. I called my vet immediately. He saw the aftermath, saw the mess. He thinks the feed is the culprit since only the animals on the pellets had problems. It looks like I'm gonna need a lawyer."

Aitkins tried to clear his head.

"Tell you what, Mr. Anderson. I'll drive out and see you folks next week. I'm sorry to have to make you wait but I'm just swamped. Is that OK?"

"I'd rather have you come sooner but if you're booked up, you're booked up. Nothin' you can do about the dead pigs at this point anyway. How much will this all cost me?"

"Won't cost you a thing. We work these on a contingency. If I get you a settlement or a favorable jury verdict, we take a third after expenses. If you get nothing, you owe us nothing, including the expenses we advance. Some lawyer's bill for expenses if they lose. We don't."

"No offense, but you sound kind of young. I mean, these feed outfits; they'll hire some Twin Cities or Fargo lawyer. I need to feel comfortable with you before you drive all the way out here. How old are you, anyway?"

Aitkins sighed. He'd offered his services to the man, explained it wouldn't cost a dime, and still Anderson wasn't satisfied. Other attorneys would have pulled the plug right then, said their good-byes, and let the potential client find someone else. Good trial lawyers don't need to beg for clients. Aitkins was a good trial attorney. But he also knew that the farmer had reasons enough to error on the side of caution. Anderson's livelihood, his future, had been aborted onto the floor of the family barn. Dan refrained from sounding hurt or upset.

"I'm thirty-seven. Been in practice thirteen years. I'm Board Certified as a Civil Trial Specialist, which means I spend my time in court, not on the telephone attempting to avoid trial. Lot's of folks these days on television and in the phone book say they're 'contingency fee' attorneys. Some even claim that they're 'trial lawyers'. Most of 'em haven't tried a jury case, but if they have, it's a once-in-a-decade occasion. That's not the way I practice law. Dr. Thomas can vouch for that."

It was the truth. Danny Aitkins and experts from NDSU had worked together on a number of stray voltage cases, situations where rural electric cooperatives found themselves in court because of allegations that uncontrolled electric current had infiltrated milking systems, causing the affected cows to produce less milk.

Cows, yes. Aitkins knew something about cows. But the lawyer had to admit, if asked, that he knew virtually nothing about pigs. He had a couple of feeder pigs at home, on his hobby farm. But he was no expert. Fortunately, his potential client didn't inquire about Dan's expertise in cases involving swine.

"No question, Dr. Thomas is one of your biggest fans," Dean Anderson admitted.

"How about it, Mr. Anderson. I'll come out to visit. If you like what you see and I like the way the case comes together, we can partner up. If you're not sold on me after our visit, well, there are 20,000 other lawyers in the State of Minnesota to choose from. Agreed?"

"Sounds fair. Thank you. I really appreciate you taking the time to talk to me."

Dean Anderson stayed on the line long enough to provide the attorney with directions to the Anderson Farm. After the farmer hung up, Aitkins buzzed his secretary, Eunice Marshall.

"Eunie, pull together a new client packet for a product liability case will ya? You know, copy of the firm brochure, my business card, a retainer agreement, authorizations, client history form-the works. Put it in my briefcase. Make the appointment for next Thursday, at 9:00am. Dean Anderson's Farm. I have the directions."

Eunice Marshall was a forty-something professional. Graying brown hair, broad hips, and thick shoulders. Bright eyes of negligible color set deep in perpetually tan skin. She was a large, brilliant woman with two kids, a ten-year-old boy and a twelve-year-old girl, who had lost her husband to colon cancer when he was only thirty-eight. That was eight years ago. Aitkins doubted that Eunice had been on a date since.

"You're supposed to meet with Alison Buckvold, you remember her don't you?" the secretary asked sarcastically. "She's wrapping up the investigation on that ATV roll-over case. She found a witness you're gonna love. You two are meeting him at 9:30am on Thursday. Should I cancel?"

"No. See if Dee Dee can handle it."

"OK."

Dee Dee Hernesman was the firm's only associate. Short, stocky, with thinning black hair, faint hazel eyes, and a stark face, Dee Dee was nothing to look at in Aitkins' view. But Daniel didn't select employees, male or female, based upon looks or academic achievement alone. He looked for a combination of brains and street smarts. Hernesman had graduated first in her class at the University of North Dakota at Grand Forks but that wasn't why she got the job. After interviewing her and finding out she'd finished her undergraduate degree in three years, while playing varsity softball, Danny Aitkins found the intangibles he valued in an employee. Dedication; strong work ethic; determination: these were the reasons the newest attorney in the Aitkins firm was being paid twice the going rate for associates in rural Minnesota.

She'd been with them four years and was on the verge of becoming the first female partner in firm history, a probability that had Emery Aitkins, the patriarch of the firm, considering retirement.

The intercom buzzed again.

"It's Eunice. Dee Dee can take it. She says she's up to speed on the file."

"Great. Thanks, Eunie. Hold my calls. I've got a splitting headache."

"I wonder why."

"Save the moral critique for National Boss' Day. Just keep the damn phone from ringing."

"Grouch."

The trial lawyer slipped off his boots. He peeled soft leather away from his sweat-soaked stockings, observing, as he deposited the boots on the floor of his office, that the footwear needed polish. The silver toe plates of the boots displayed similar evidence of neglect. He made a mental note, such as he could in his condition, to clean up his boots before meeting with Dean Anderson.

Aitkins shut off his notebook computer with a jab of his index finger. Resting his stocking feet on the desk, the lawyer closed his eyes, leaned his head back against the neck support of his leather chair, and tried to ignore the pounding in his temples.

As his mind floated along the edge of sleep, a place dominated by serene pools filled with small-mouthed bass, the intercom interrupted his day-dream and caused a lovely vision of leaping fish to burst into a thousand fragments.

The call was from Julie.

"I'm sorry for doubting you. I know you love me. I know you wouldn't do anything to hurt me. I'm sorry."

He pondered what to say. How would she respond if she knew he had once nearly slept with Melanie Barnes? What would she do if that awful truth were ever known? She'd leave him for sure. That much he could count on. He'd been granted one reprieve. There would not be another.

"It's not your fault. It's mine," he said softly. "I once gave you cause to doubt me. It's only natural that what I did comes back to haunt us. Don't blame yourself for my stupidity. I should have called."

"I love you, Danny."

"I love you too."

"I've got a roast on for supper."

"Sounds good. I'll leave here in a minute or two. I'm almost done."

"Don't forget Adam has a playoff game tonight in Bemidji. You in any shape to drive?"

"I'm fine. I'm on my way."

Despite a mammoth hangover, the attorney had put in a full day. Danny's stomach had settled. Rising from behind the desk, Aitkins pulled on his boots, turned off the lights, and left his office. On his way to the exit, the lawyer stopped at his secretary's workstation. Eunice's chair was empty. It was after five. All of the offices were dark except his father's. Emery's space was the most spacious room in the place. The senior partner occupied an office larger than the firm's conference room. Light escaped from a crack at the bottom of the patriarch's closed door. Danny heard his father's voice, distant and tired, dictating interrogatories into a tape recorder. The son hesitated.

I should say goodnight to the old man, he thought.

Daniel considered his suggestion.

No. He'll grill me about the Pelletier case. How I lost it. What went wrong. I'm not up for that bullshit tonight. In a few days, we can have that talk. Not tonight.

"Good night Emery," the son mumbled as he walked down the hallway towards the lobby.

Outside, the litigator dodged puddles left by melting snow. The sun had departed. Aitkins' boots splashed through depressions in the paved surface of the parking lot. As Danny loped towards his truck, he considered his new client.

That's premature, Aitkins corrected himself in mid-thought. *Potential new client.*

The lawyer smiled as he produced a key and unlocked the driver's door of his hard-driven Ford Ranger pickup truck.

"Tomorrow," Danny observed as he slid into the driver's seat, "tomorrow I'll have to try and learn something about pigs."

CHAPTER 5

Bemidji State University's hockey rink was cold. Despite the mild spring weather outside, the metal and concrete interior of the arena was bone chilling. The temperature didn't seem to matter to the Pee-Wee hockey players from Detroit Lakes or their opponents from Bemidji.

"Starting in goal for the Detroit Lakes Lakers, Number Thirty-three, Adam Aitkins," the announcer declared.

"Keep 'em out Adam. Stay up," the goalie's father yelled.

Daniel and Julie Aitkins stood with a small knot of fans on top of the bleachers located in the visitor's section.

"How's the head?"

"It'll be all right," Danny replied to his wife's question. "I hope Adam stays away from that flopping shit he seems prone to."

"Daniel, it's a youth hockey game. Relax, would you?" his wife urged. "Where are Amanda and Michael?" she asked, referencing their two youngest children.

"I gave 'em each a buck. They're checking out the concession stand. They'll be back once the money runs out. Not much you can buy at a hockey rink for a dollar. Give 'em about a minute."

Fred McVean stood on the bench behind the other Detroit Lakes fans. He leaned forward to make his presence known.

"Hey, Aitkins, your kid has had a pretty good year."

McVean was, to Danny's way of thinking, the biggest jerk of all of the parents with kids on the team. Physically imposing at six two, two hundred and fifty pounds or more, McVean made sure everyone within earshot knew he'd played hockey in Europe after a stint in Junior A's in Canada. It was rumored he had a tryout with the North Stars before they fled the state for Texas. He didn't make the cut, mostly because he was a goon, a cheap shot, and his audition for the bright lights came on the heels of the USA Hockey Team's gold medal effort in the 1980 Winter Olympics. His style wasn't what the "bigs" were looking for at the time. McVean was pushing forty. His best days on the ice were behind him.

McVean's son Erik was a chip off the old block. He was a brawler. Pee-Wee hockey doesn't tolerate brawlers. But that didn't deter Erik McVean. He was the most talented, and the most penalized, member of the team. It seemed utterly lost on the father that his son could have been a premier player in the league, likely a star on a traveling team, a level above his current station in the sport, if Fred McVean saw fit to encourage his son's more positive attributes; skating, stick handling, and teamwork. It struck Aitkins as funny that a man who professed to be an expert about hockey couldn't detect his own son's shortcomings.

To make matters worse, the Canadian, dull-witted, and low on personality, was Adam Aitkins' sixth grade math teacher. Despite all this history, Aitkins tried to forget to whom he was talking, tried to remain sociable and polite.

"Thanks Fred. We'll need Adam to stand up tonight. We haven't come within two goals of Bemidji all season. They're rated fourth in the State in B-1, you know."

The attorney didn't turn to face the other parent. His eyes remained fixed on his son's warm-up exercises. He knew that McVean's next comment would likely contain some small criticism of Adam's abilities. The big man didn't disappoint.

"Your kid needs to concentrate on hockey. Erik eats, lives, and breathes hockey. That's what gives him the edge he has. If Adam works a little extra in the off-season, next year, who knows? He might just find himself a spot on the A-team backing up the Olson kid."

McVean's reference to Dallas Olson, the starting goalie on the Pee-Wee A traveling team, dredged up angry recollections of the tryouts Adam had endured that past autumn. Most of the impartial observers, if such humans exist within the realm of Minnesota Youth Hockey, had pegged the two goalies as dead even, with Matt Masterson as number three. When the rosters were posted in late October, Masterson, to everyone's shock, was listed as the second goaltender on the traveling team. Adam was the sole goalie on the B-1 squad. The kid cried for a week. Aitkins came within seconds of calling the hockey association to ball out the whole damn lot of them. At his wife's patient urging, the lawyer let it pass.

In Danny's view of the world, the lawyer was certain that Masterson, a kid with no skating skills and limited reflexes, made the traveling team on the strength of his father's financial contributions to the program. It was no coincidence, or so Aitkins' believed, that Arnie Masterson's son made a squad with the phrase "Masterson's Bar and Grill" embroidered on the team jerseys, the result of the elder Masterson's generous donation to the team.

"I'm sure Adam will give it his all next year, Fred. Whatever happens, happens."

"I just hope he knows that a win here puts us in the regional playoffs in Duluth. That's as far as we can go in B-1, that's our State Tourney."

"He knows, Fred. Believe me, he knows."

Adam Aitkins, a thin-boned, smallish child, had vomited most of the night before the big game. The stress of the upcoming District Championship was nearly too much for the child and his parents to bear.

"What an asshole."

Julie's comment slid surreptitiously between her lips. Her husband heard the words plainly. Dan figured that Fred McVean also heard the insult. If the math teacher caught the criticism, he ignored it. The game began.

Bemidji came out flying. In the first five minutes, the home team put ten shots on net. They were quality chances, all of which Adam saved. He stood his ground, not dropping to the ice unless he was left with no other option. He had brought his best game with him.

With three minutes to go in the first period, Shawn Johnson, Bemidji's star forward, found himself free with the puck on his stick in the Lakers' end. Cutting to the crease, one hand steering the puck on the end of his stick blade as he held Erik McVean off with his other arm, Johnson flicked the puck on net. It was not a hard shot. It was the type of assault that any Pee-Wee goalie could stop.

Anticipating that Johnson would swoop in for the rebound, Adam slid across the net and went down, stacking his pads, reaching with the curved blade of his goalie stick to guide the puck into his body. Believing Aitkins had the shot covered, Erik McVean lessened his pursuit. Johnson beat the slowing defender to the rebound and poked at the rubber disk with the heel of his stick blade. The puck bounced high over the sprawling goalie and landed in the net. Johnson's momentum carried him into the crease, knocking the net off its mooring pegs.

"Man in the crease. Man in the crease," the elder McVean screamed. "Goddammit ref, that can't count. He can't interfere with our goalie like that."

Fred McVean was incensed, likely embarrassed that his son's lack of sustained play caused the goal. His face turned the color of flame. His arms gyrated. He left his perch in the stands and tried to climb the Plexiglas along the top of the boards. Both referees, former Bemidji State University stars, skated away from the angry fan, ignoring his admonitions. The officials stopped in front of the Detroit Lakes net, placed the goal back in position, and signaled for a center face-off. Adam Aitkins looked into the crowd. Despite the distance between them, the son detected bitter disappointment on Danny Aitkins' face. The child turned and slammed his stick against the goalpost.

"Calm down, Adam. There's lots of game left, son. You'll get it back," his mother encouraged.

Julie Aitkins knew the depth of the sports connection between her husband and their oldest son. In her view, it was an illogical, almost sinister bond in her view. Adam was a gifted student, a wonderfully bright and energetic person on the verge of adolescence. And yet, the only thing that seemed to be of importance to her oldest child was athletic competition.

She wanted to stop the two of them, right there, in the middle of the game, and tell them how God-awful stupid they both were. She wanted to shout out to her wounded son how proud she was that he was out there at all. But a philosophical approach to the sport of hockey would be lost on most of the parents and other players. She refrained from embarrassing Adam and confined her comments to traditional fan banter.

"I wish to hell he wouldn't look at me like that during a game."

Dan Aitkins turned away from his son and looked steadily into the eyes of his wife as he spoke.

"He makes me feel like he's doing this only for me," Dan added.

"Well isn't he?"

There was truth behind Julie's words. Dan had been the one to push the kid. He had been totally swept away by the USA's victory over the USSR in the '80 Olympic Games. He vowed, listening to the final seconds of the jubilant conquest of the communists, that if he ever had a son, the kid would play Minnesota's sport, a sport that Dan Aitkins had never mastered.

He tried to control his expectations, tried to instill in the boy that hockey was an amateur sport played for fun. But he grossly underestimated the subliminal messages he'd sent the boy over the years. Daniel also underestimated the importance placed upon the sport by the athletic establishment in the North Star State. Just as football in Texas is not merely a game but a lifestyle, hockey in Minnesota, no matter the level, no matter the quality of competition, is never just a game. Try as he and Julie might, they could not overcome the emphasis placed upon the sport even in the seeming backwaters of Detroit Lakes amateur hockey. It was either accept that hockey was not a sport, it was a lifestyle, not just for the player but for his entire family, or quit. And Adam Aitkins, despite his small size and average athletic skills, possessed one trait in common with his father. He would never voluntarily yield; he would never leave something unless it was on his own terms.

"I wish to hell I never got him involved in this stupid sport," the lawyer reflected.

"Too late now. He loves it. Behind all the stomach aches, crying fits at cut time, and late night or early morning practices, he lives, eats, and sleeps hockey," Julie observed.

Aitkins avoided looking at his wife, thereby avoiding the truth of the matter. He focused his eyes on the players floating across the ice.

"Let's just hope he hangs together tonight," the attorney suggested.

57

The Lakers mounted an offensive threat. Erik McVean, known throughout the league as a talented but selfish player, took off on an end-to-end rush and blasted a wicked slap shot off the Bemidji goalie's chest protector. With the goaltender scrambling to retrieve the puck and force a face-off, McVean poked the puck free, sending it on end across the crease to Lisa Ricari, the only girl on the Lakers team. Detroit Lakes' leading scorer pulled the puck free of the tender's out-stretched catching glove and tucked it neatly into the upper right corner of the opposing net. Lakers 1, Bemidji 1.

A horn sounded the end of the first stanza. Ricari knelt to one knee and pumped a gloved fist into the air, Gretzky style.

"Damn, that girl has some moves, eh McVean?" Daniel observed.

"She's OK. But she'll have one hell of a time next year moving up to Bantams. She's too small. They'll take her head off."

"I doubt it. Adam says she can take any boy in the seventh grade. She's a tough little lady."

"There you go again, talking out of your ass. Stick to what you know best: suing people. Or football. At least that's a sport you played, or so I hear. Leave the hockey analysis to those of us who played the game," the Canadian muttered.

Julie pulled harshly on the poplin fabric of her husband's jacket, jerking him away from a confrontation.

"Forget him. He's an asshole. Let's get some coffee," she whispered.

Aitkins followed his wife's lead and stepped down from the bleachers.

"But he's such a pain-in-the-ass. I'd like to pop him one right in the middle of those false teeth of his. He'd kill me, that's for sure. But it'd be worth it just to try to knock that smirk off his fucking face."

"Watch your language. There are kids around."

"Oops. Sorry, Jules. He just gets me all wound up."

"He's an idiot. Forget him."

The announcer's voice broke through their dialogue.

"Saves for the period, for Detroit Lakes, Aitkins-fifteen. For Bemidji, Troyson-seven.

Another Detroit Lakes parent placed a hand on Dan's shoulder.

"Well, we're making a game of it, anyway. Adam's sharp tonight."

"Let's hope he stays that way," Aitkins responded without meeting the other man's gaze.

As they stepped onto the cement floor, Julie resumed their discussion.

"That's great Dan. I can see the headlines: 'Local lawyer jailed for assault on teacher. Teacher sues for millions.'"

"It'd be worth it. It'd make me forget about the Pelletier disaster."

"You're like Michael. You'll brood a long time over that case, Mr. Do-Gooder Attorney."

His wife's reference to their empathetic youngest offspring made him smile. She was right. Michael and he were alike in that respect, the child being reduced to tears whenever they passed a dead raccoon or skunk on the highway.

It was a case that would leave its mark upon him forever. Aitkins knew that. It was a case that, for the first time in his legal career, had the attorney questioning the integrity of the jury process.

Losing was one thing. There were always good and substantial reasons for a jury to rule against your client or your position. Fifty percent of all civil trials end up in the loss column. Seventy-five to eighty percent of all medical malpractice cases end up as failures for the plaintiff. He knew the statistics, could recite them from heart. He'd come to accept them as part of doing the dirty business of trial work. He could accept and had accepted losses in the past. But not this one: not this case. The jury's decision, even with the mistake that he'd made on discovery regarding the Medical Examiner, made absolutely no sense. The failure of the jury's collective logic ate away at him.

Couldn't they see that the pathologist was simply covering for his buddies, the local doctors? Couldn't the jurors ferret out myth from reality?

He tried to suppress the face of Tina Pelletier, to erase her from his thoughts as he walked through the crowd beside his wife. Another child, his own son, needed his thoughts and prayers tonight. But the dead Indian girl would not yield center stage so easily.

They stopped in front of the concession stand. His wife, her hair neatly arranged, her figure attractive and alluring even when concealed by a winter parka, pulled out a five-dollar bill and handed it to a woman behind the counter. Harsh artificial light cast a halo across the cashier as she made small talk.

"Aren't you the mother of the DL goalie?" the woman queried, nodding slightly towards a button bearing Adam's likeness pinned to the front of Julie's coat.

"Yep."

"Your son is playing a great game. There were two or three shots in that first period that I swore were certain goals. This is the best game anyone has played against us all year. We've only lost a couple of games and all of them were to A-teams. Make sure you tell him he played a great game, however it turns out."

"Thanks. I will."

Neither team scored in the second period. Both squads put ten shots on net. Adam remained strong as his team began to push the larger, faster Bemidji kids around the rink. His concentration was solid, his catching glove, flawless and exceptionally quick. The home team seemed stunned and lifeless, confused by the intensity of the smaller Lakers, a team they had mastered easily during the regular season. The Bemidji unit was disorganized and unable to capitalize on their home ice advantage as the horn sounded, ending the second stanza.

The home team came out skating with abandon at the opening face-off of the concluding session.

"What the hell did their coach give 'em in the locker room?" Aitkins mused aloud, wondering what device, what artifice, the Bemidji mentor used to pump up his team during the second intermission.

"It's called coaching," McVean asserted. "Bemidji actually has someone coaching its team who played hockey. Stan Laaksonen. Stan played for the U of M. His boys know how to play the game. Our guy is nice and everything, a good fellow. But he's a basketball man. He can't even skate. That's the difference."

Both goalies stopped the first opposing shot on net. The Lakers turned it up a notch, pulling themselves to a plateau they'd never reached during any regular season contest against the Beavers. Their defense consistently crashed the net and sent the puck along the boards. As Aitkins studied the play of his son's team, he began to resent the audacity of McVean's comments. Bob Hustead, the Detroit Lakes coach, was a wonderful, caring man, a good father, and a hell of role model for the kids. Aitkins' blood boiled at the contentions made by the Canadian. His anger surged towards an obvious point of escape. Julie intercepted his reaction before it was verbalized. A swift, sidelong glance of disapproval from his wife tightened the attorney's lips, silencing venomous words before they escaped.

"Bob has done a hell of a job. He knows the kids. To me, that's the most important thing a coach can bring to the table: the ability to understand each of the young people playing for him or her. As long as a coach can do that, teach the fundamentals, and be fair, that's all we can ask for," Dan replied.

"That's fine for Squirt hockey. This is Pee-Wees. These kids are out there to win games, not learn skills. If they don't have the skills by this age, they shouldn't be on the ice."

It was Julie's turn to feel anger rise within her. The bile cut like a sharp piece of glass digging into the lining of her gut. Danny noted her upset and, repressing a smile, touched her cheek, a gesture meant to dispel her urge to launch into McVean.

Dennis Lampson, one of the Laker defenders, skated skillfully with the puck. He controlled the rubber disk with the blade of his stick. His eyes found Lisa Ricari racing towards center ice with no one between her and the Bemidji goalie. Certain she'd sprung free of the opposition, Lampson launched a lazy cross-ice pass towards his teammate. Black hit black as a Bemidji player intercepted the puck with the friction-taped cradle of his stick. There was nothing to stop Shawn Johnson from scoring at the other end of the ice but the scrawny profile of Adam Aitkins.

Lord, let him stand his ground. Don't let him go for the fake, Danny silently prayed. The plea was not said for the benefit of the lawyer's ego but for the benefit of his child. Aitkins hoped this subtle distinction would convince God to grant his petition. He'd be proud of his child no matter how the game turned out. He honestly believed he had no personal stake in the outcome of the contest. Aitkins glanced at the clock. There were thirty seconds left in the game.

Johnson's legs churned. His skates dug into the ice. He was a good skater and shot right handed with power. Adam guessed that the winger would tend towards his forehand, going with his strength. The younger Aitkins had already stopped three of Johnson's slap shots from the point on power plays. He'd robbed the kid on two rebounds at the doorstep. All those shots had come from the forehand. Adam believed the Bemidji player had something to prove, that he wanted to bury a shot from his dominant side to end any question as to who was who on Bemidji's home ice. The tender set up for the forehand.

At the top of the left face-off circle, Johnson veered right and increased his speed. The forward's eyes were riveted on the upper right hand corner of the goal over the tender's left shoulder. Adam sensed the shot would be aimed there. He tensed, waiting for Johnson's stick to be drawn back, waiting for the shot to come. He could see the puck sliding towards his right. The goalie watched in nervous appreciation as the blade of the forward's stick protected hard rubber.

Anticipating the shot, Aitkins moved his catching glove to cover the spot Johnson aimed at. Simultaneously, the goalie went into the splits to protect the corners, keeping his stick in a neutral position to block the "five hole" between his legs. He'd committed himself. There was no turning back.

With deceptive quickness, Johnson pulled the puck back into his body and carved away from the waiting glove and stick of the goaltender. With Adam's weight and momentum forcing the goalie to the left, the Bemidji star stretched his arms away from his opponent and directed the projectile. Too late, Aitkins realized his error and fought to counter gravity. With the tender down and helpless, Johnson launched a soft backhand shot over Adams's outstretched leg. The puck fluttered through the air like a wounded hummingbird before striking mesh.

A siren erupted signaling the goal. Before the teams could gather at center ice for the face-off, another horn announced the end of the game. From the Bemidji bench, a mass of players vaulted the boards and mobbed their goalie. At the far end of the arena, the Lakers quietly consoled Adam Aitkins, patting him on the back or touching his stick with theirs in appreciation of his effort. After his team left the rink, the goaltender fell to the ice, his face awash with tears, his bare midriff exposed and chilled by the cold ice beneath him.

"It's hell being the wife of a trial lawyer and the mother of a hockey goalie," Julie Aitkins mumbled.

The woman didn't look at her son as she spoke. She averted her eyes out of sympathy and not embarrassment.

"I guess some of my choices in life haven't been the best," her husband observed.

The attorney's wife glared at her husband. She was near releasing a diatribe about her mate's selfish pride, about his inability to understand that not everything in the world revolved around him. But something in Danny's eyes told the woman that he knew this was not about him: it was about their son.

"I swear. If that son-of-a-bitch McVean says one word about Adam and I find out about it, I'll kill the jerk myself," Julie Aitkins promised.

Danny pulled his wife towards him and, despite being surrounded by others, kissed her full on the lips. Though normally uneasy with public displays of affection, she didn't protest. As they descended the gray metal stairs of the bleachers, their boots pounding audibly against stamped aluminum, a smile formed across Daniel's mouth.

"What?" Julie queried.

"I can see it now," Dan responded.

"What?"

"'Disgruntled PTA mom turns homicidal at a youth hockey game and slays obnoxious Canadian living in Minnesota on a work visa. Ottawa government asks for extradition of the mother for possible execution.'"

"One problem with your headline."

"What's that, dear?"

"They don't have the death penalty in Canada."

"Thinking about it then, are you?"

"Nope. Wouldn't be worth my time."

Julie Aitkins pivoted on the balls of her feet. Her perfume smelled florid and feminine. The scent mixed easily with the odor of her cleanly scrubbed skin. The smells distracted Dan Aitkins from his son's pain. The attorney's grip tightened as he relayed a gentle squeeze that told his wife something sensuous and seductive was destined to take place between them later that evening.

Thirty minutes after the ending buzzer Adam emerged from the visitor's locker room. He carried his hockey pads loosely over one shoulder. A sweat-stained equipment bag hung from his other arm. Moisture dripped from the child's black hair, the tendrils cut to the bare scalp on one side of his head yet remaining nearly shoulder length on the other. The goalie stopped in front of his parents and leaned heavily on his stick.

"Can I carry somethin'?"

Michael reached up and latched onto the heavily taped handle of the goalie stick. Wordlessly, Adam let the battle-scarred prize fall into his younger sibling's arms. Michael scooted off across the smooth concrete floor of the lobby dragging the heavy object behind him.

"You played a great game. Twenty-six saves. That's a good piece of work," Dan offered.

The elder Aitkins touched his son gently on the arm. The boy retreated, not so quickly as to convey upset, but slowly, deliberately, as if to remind his father that he still needed his privacy.

"Thanks. It doesn't feel so great. We could have won it in overtime and gone to Regions if I'd stopped that last shot. Now the season is over. It's all my fault."

"Goalies don't win games by themselves. It takes a whole team. You did the best you could. Some things are just not meant to be. You can't dwell on it. Pick up your feet, one foot at a time. You start tomorrow with a clean slate."

The family walked out into the cool night. Adam lagged behind, decidedly unconvinced that the sun would rise in the morning, weighed down by a heavy belief that he was a failure to himself, his team, and to his father. Against the shadow of the arena's great mass, Michael danced along the edge of pavement, dueling imaginary dragons with the tender's stick. Amanda Jane walked beside her parents, quiet and introspective, striding unnaturally to keep pace with the adults.

Ground fog crept across the surface of the parking lot as cold night air met asphalt that had been warmed by the day. Moisture hung over the Aitkins family like a wet towel. Julie leaned against Dan as the parents waited next to their van for their oldest child. Discretely, the woman reached up and tugged playfully on her husband's earlobe.

"What's that for?"

"For being you. You know, you could stand to follow some of your own advice."

"Whatdoya mean?"

"'Don't dwell on it. Pick up your feet one at a time. Get on with your life.' Sound familiar?"

Daniel looked up. The night was overcast, preventing him from viewing the light of distant worlds. He knew he'd given his son perfunctory advice, advice dispensed out of a can of pseudo-psychology retrieved from some bargain-priced parental advisory store.

Even if there was value in the admonition he'd given Adam, the trial lawyer knew, in the darkest reaches of his soul, that no dime-store logic could protect him from Tina Pelletier's ghost and the specter of his defeat at the hands of F.W. Barnes.

CHAPTER 6

The advocate had not discussed the Pelletier verdict with his father. Daniel managed to limit his encounters with Emery Aitkins to brief greetings and partings, appearing to be too busy for an in-depth parlay with his father. It was likely that, in addition to losing the case on the merits, Ms. Pelletier would be hit for the costs of defense; the expenses incurred by F.W. Barnes and his cohorts in defeating the malpractice claim. Expert witness fees, mileage, filing fees, and the like would very probably result in thousands of dollars of costs being taxed against Ms. Pelletier. Such a judgment would likely force the woman into personal bankruptcy.

In addition, the financial impact of the loss on the Aitkins Firm went far beyond negating the firm's one-third contingency fee. There was also the loss of hundreds of hours of uncompensated attorney time to be considered. And, though the rules of ethics allowed, and indeed required, that Betty Pelletier be held financially responsible for the costs incurred by the Aitkins Firm on her behalf, in reality, the firm had never, in the forty-plus years existence of the partnership, charged such costs back to a losing client.

Dan knew he couldn't escape such a discussion forever. At best, he was only delaying the inevitable.

An alarm screeched. 5:30am. Dan's eyes opened but his wife didn't stir. Julie was not an early riser. She seldom woke before 6:30am unless there was an urgent need to do so. It was an in-service training day for teachers. There was no need for her to rise since both Julie and the children had the day off.

Dan stretched and felt the back of his hand touch his wife's bosom. He inadvertently brushed the smooth fabric of her teddy with his hand as he reached to shut off the alarm. His gesture did not wake her. The attorney rubbed his eyes and pushed the snooze button on the alarm. Through the dimness of half-opened eyes, he stared at her torso. Julie's breasts were flat and loose. The white skin of her chest contrasted with the residual tan of her shoulders and with the suggestion of nipples concealed beneath cloth. After fourteen years of marriage, the sight of his wife's half-revealed body still held the same exhilaration, the same thrill, as it had in the meager light of his father's 1977 Oldsmobile.

"That must count for something in this horseshit world," he mused.

He reached over to stroke the fabric of her nightgown, thinking that he might arouse her. He hesitated. Neither of them were much good at early morning romance. A smile crossed his lips as the odor of his own morning breath signaled the end of his intentions.

"Christ, today's the day of the Johnson Deposition. Damn, I forgot to bring the file home to study last night," the attorney muttered impatiently, raising a corner of the wrinkled blanket.

Aitkins stood up in the darkness of the bedroom. Only the distant glow of an insignificant wall fixture distributed illumination. Pale yellow light pulled shadows out of angles in the ceiling, casting elongated shapes across the space. The third floor had been a walkup attic until it was remodeled. The renovated space contained their master bedroom, a huge walk-in closet for Julie's clothes, and a modest bathroom.

Unfinished seams in the sheetrock were visible despite the poor light. Danny had vowed to tape and mud the joints himself as his personal contribution to the renovation project. The lawyer never seemed to find the time to complete the job.

An oversized oval window, its surface black as ink, interrupted a wall. The window was nothing more than an odd geometric disturbance in an unornamented plane. Shapes of unpainted gypsum sloped gently from the peak of the roof to the floor. The window had not been trimmed out. A pile of unstained oak gathered dust in a corner, the wood intended to be stained and nailed in place as trim. All in all the room appeared decidedly unfinished.

By daylight, one could look out the window and study the gentle flow of the land, take in a small stream that interrupted the uniformity of a pasture, the still waters of a livestock pond, and the undulating hills filled with oak forest that marked the limits of the Aitkins hobby farm. None of these details were available for scrutiny at the hour of Danny's awakening.

Grabbing a sports jacket, a freshly pressed pair of Lee jeans, and a Tasmanian Devil necktie, the lawyer removed a clean pair of flannel briefs and a pair of white socks from a battered chest of drawers. Fully dressed, Aitkins searched beneath the frame of their brass bed until he located his cowboy boots. Danny pecked his wife on the cheek as he left the room carrying the boots in one hand. Julie did not stir.

"What the hell," he thought. "I don't need to know much about the Johnson file. They've been friends of my family forever. I'm not taking the deposition; just sitting in to protect old Ben's interests. Piece of cake."

He tried to justify his failure to read his calendar, tried to use self-deception to fool his subconscious into believing that being unprepared wouldn't create stress. His stomach and bowels told him otherwise. An urge to go rushed over his body like a great wave crashing upon a Gulf Coast beach. He scurried into the bathroom. Aitkins was barely seated when his body emptied itself in a mad, nervous explosion. He sat on the toilet, alone in the dark, thinking about why Ben Johnson needed his help.

Ben's son, Emil, had sued his father over the death of Elizabeth Johnson, Ben's wife and Emil's mother. The family had been in town last 4th of July for the annual parade. Ben spent too much time that day in Burley's Bar. He wasn't normally a drinker but for some reason, that was his course on July 4th. After polishing off his tenth tap beer, Ben insisted on driving the eight miles home from Detroit Lakes to Pelican Rapids. Liz reluctantly climbed into the front seat of their Delta 88 after voicing a mild protest.

Sharon Johnson, Emil's wife and Ben and Elizabeth's daughter-in-law, occupied the back seat. Emil wasn't along. He'd left town with the kids to go fishing, taking his leave right after the parade concluded its serpentine journey through downtown Detroit Lakes. It was well after dark when Ben coaxed the old sedan out onto the highway.

Somewhere west of Cormorant, Minnesota, the beer finally hit Ben Johnson. With his female passengers engaged in animated conversation about how much weight Emma Jorgeson had gained after her second child, the man dozed off. Sleep came on suddenly. Ben's chin came to rest on the plastic of the steering wheel. In an instant, the vehicle crossed the centerline of the two lane highway, careened into oncoming holiday traffic, and was struck broadside, just to the rear of the front passenger's door, by a Ford F250 pickup pulling a trailer full of turkeys.

The violence of the collision shoved the Olds across the pavement like a slingshot, spinning the heavy car in a complete circle before the front tires caught the edge of the gravel shoulder. The sudden change in driving surfaces, in conjunction with the steep slope of an adjacent drainage channel, launched the vehicle into the air, catapulting the car into a grove of maples standing near the right-of-way. The car smashed into the trees just as Ben Johnson came to. Instant deceleration was Ben's first memory of the accident. It was also his wife's last.

Impact with the unyielding trees caused Elizabeth's body to confront violent forces within the passenger compartment of the automobile. The right side of the car, the side occupied by Mrs. Johnson, slammed sideways into a tree just ahead of the center post, collapsing the passenger side door, causing the tree to intrude deep into the vehicle. Though Liz Johnson was seat-belted in, her body was thrown sideways into the hard plastic of the center console, splitting her forehead open from her hairline to the bridge of her nose. The awful violence of the crash snapped the second cervical vertebrae in her neck, severing her spinal cord as her head rebounded to the right.

67

Elizabeth's disfigured face came to rest. Her eyes stared blankly at the ceiling. An additional impact occurred when the car struck another tree. This final collision threw Sharon Johnson, who had not been wearing her seat belt, forward between the front bucket seats. Sharon's head collided with the dashboard, crushing the cassette deck. Her right arm became trapped under the body of her mother-in-law. Elizabeth's rare breath rustled the muslin of her daughter-in-law's peasant blouse as the older woman declined, as her chest became still.

Ben Johnson's right hip bore the force of the impact. Bone exploded through the skin of his thigh, through the thick fiber of his slacks, showering the interior of the car in blood. Before the old man's body reacted to the pain of the fracture, the front end of the Delta slammed into a final maple, forcing Ben Johnson's head into the steering wheel, rendering him unconscious.

Sharon Johnson sustained a concussion, a lacerated forehead requiring sixty-eight sutures, a broken nose, and a compression fracture of her third thoracic vertebrae in the mid-back. She spent a week in Detroit Lakes Lutheran Hospital. Six months after the accident, by the time of Ben Johnson's deposition, she was still unable to recall the event. She'd returned to her elementary school teaching position in Bismarck, North Dakota but she could no longer lift books or use her arms in a repetitive fashion due to the residual affects of her spinal injury. Sharon was also plagued by nightmares. She rarely slept without seeing the lifeless, bloodied face of Liz Johnson staring at her. She was traumatized and remained in fear of driving. She was twenty-seven years old.

They buried Elizabeth Johnson. There was no autopsy. The cause of her death was self-evident. Ben Johnson, her loving husband of forty-one years, had killed her. Ben didn't attend the funeral. He was fighting for his own life.

The force of the steering wheel striking Ben's face caused his neck to fracture. Pieces of vertebrae splintered off from his spinal column and floated freely around the third and fourth joints in Ben's cervical spine. His neck injury was similar to that experienced by his dead wife, though because the fracture was lower in the spine and incomplete, the old man did not perish.

During eight hours of neurological and orthopedic repair, the stricken man's spinal canal was cleared of bone. Nerves were decompressed. A disc, crushed and mal-aligned gristle meant to serve as a cushion between the bony vertebrae, was removed to allow the remaining portions of healthy bone to be fused together, creating a solid union at the level of injury. A piece of Johnson's hip bone was sliced into small wedges, inserted in his neck, and held in place by wire to secure the fracture site. In time, the grafted segments would connect the vertebrae above and below the injury, creating stability.

Four days after Ben Johnson's cervical surgery, another surgical team repaired Ben's shattered right leg. The force of the side impact, the impact that killed his wife, had disrupted the contours of Johnson's femur, the largest bone in his body. The final head-on collision with the tree, the crash that ultimately stopped the forward progress of the car, caused the already disrupted femur to tear into the upper thigh muscle providing stability to the hip. Both the femur and the leg muscles needed to be rebuilt. A stainless steel plate was screwed into the two disconnected ends of the femur, drawing the bones into alignment. A small section of cadaver bone was wedged between the ends of the fracture and held in place with more wire. The gap that had been created by the shattering of the femur was thus bridged. The cadaver bone would, if the operation were successful, adhere to the natural bone of the leg, filling in the space.

Even before the accident, Emil Johnson and his father didn't have the best of relationships. As the only son, there being two daughters, Margery and Lucy, Emil had been expected to take over the family business in Pelican Rapids, Johnson's Variety Store. Emil started working in the store, a collection of small, outdated departments that had a difficult time competing with the mall in Fergus Falls and the plethora of shopping alternatives available only an hour away in Fargo-Moorhead While still in high school, it became apparent to the boy that he and his father could not work together. They saw things too differently. The son was also too proud, too sure of himself, to listen to his dad's advice.

By his senior year in high school, Emil came to dread the twenty hours a week that he was required to put in at the store. Two weeks after graduation, he left Pelican Rapids for the Air Force. He never moved back home. His desertion of the family business was an open wound, a hurt that festered for years, a scar that Elizabeth Johnson tried to close through tireless efforts at reconciliation between her husband and her son.

Negotiating the bare maple stairs descending from the attic, Dan Aitkins pondered the chasm between father and son in the Johnson family. He found it impossible not to relate to the valley of sorrows between the generations.

It started when Danny was a kid, a little boy, nine years old, trying to play baseball. From the start, he was terrible at the game. He wouldn't know it for another two years but he was as blind as a bat. No one postulated that the reason he swung wildly at the ball was because he couldn't see. That discovery occurred when Daniel turned twelve. By then it was too late. He'd lost the years that he could have played in the major leagues with his friends, years that he could have traveled with them to away games in Fergus Falls, Fargo, Warroad, and beyond. He stayed in the minors until he was twelve and no longer eligible to play. Then he quit the sport. Baseball was his first love and his first glimpse at the hard-edged reality of the world.

Emery Aitkins had tried, in his own way, to help his son. He spent time, what little he could spare away from the office, throwing pitch after patient pitch to the kid in the backyard every spring before tryouts. But patience and practice alone couldn't overcome Dan's near-sightedness. Even when Emil tossed slow, easy meatballs towards his son, the kid's futile efforts to connect failed.

In the end, the father did not yell. He did not chastise. He simply walked away. No words were ever exchanged between them about Daniel's athletic failure. A distance grew between them out of subtle neglect fed by the son's belief that his father had, for whatever reason, given up on him.

The September he started seventh grade, Jennifer Aitkins, Danny's mom, took Dan to see old Doc Hyndes, the local ophthalmologist. Hyndes knew in an instant, after watching the boy squint heavily to read the largest of the letters on the eye chart, that the child couldn't see anything more than a few inches from his face.

"Mrs. Aitkins, how's the boy been doing in school? Any complaints about seeing his work, the blackboard, that sort of thing?"

"Funny you should ask that. His performance in the first two weeks of school this year has been dismal. He complains that he can't see the board from the first row of seats."

"Little wonder. Danny's near-sighted in both eyes. I'm surprised he can even walk, much less read a blackboard, without eyeglasses."

"How could the school nurse have missed that? She tests kids every year."

Old Doc Hyndes looked up and smiled at Mrs. Aitkins as he replied softly.

"She's no eye doctor. She sees hundreds of kids. Daniel's not the first child to get passed over. The good thing is, we caught the problem early this school year. You get his prescription filled and you'll notice a big change in this young man."

"Will glasses help me play sports?"

The boy's eyes grimaced tightly as he tried to focus on the old man's face.

"They sure will, tiger. You'll be surprised at what you're able to do once you can see what game you're supposed to be playing."

"Will I be able to hit a curve ball?"

"I'm a doctor, son, not a magician. I'll give you sight; you'll have to put in the effort to take it from there."

And he had. Once Dan Aitkins got his new glasses, and later, his first pair of contact lenses, the improvement in his athleticism was miraculous. Though he never again played baseball, he became the starting point guard on every basketball team he played on until he graduated and he became a force on the Laker's varsity football team.

Maybe the distance between them didn't really begin with baseball. Maybe it started earlier, when they both realized that they had disparate personalities that were difficult to reconcile. The boy had been born with his mother's incurable romanticism while Emery Aitkins was a pragmatic cynic. His parent's respective outlooks on life were as different as their expressions of spirituality, their views on the hereafter, and the necessity of worship and prayer. Simply put, Jennifer Aitkins, though a chronic alcoholic and a terrible mother to Daniel and his sister, Audrey, was a believer, a God-fearing Evangelical Lutheran trusting in the ultimate satisfaction of Christ's saving grace. Emery was, as in all other things, at best an occasional adherent of the Gospel. Daniel never really knew what path his father was walking when it came to issues of the soul. It was one of life's topics that remained unexplored between them.

Whatever the true cause of their schism, the gaping hole in their relationship was omnipresent from Dan's earliest memory of his father. Emery wanted his love. The son knew and understood that fully. But it wasn't clear that his father was capable of asking for that love, or returning that emotion to his son in equal measure. It felt, at times, to Danny, as if he was supposed to love his father as a sort of tribute that a parent expects to be paid as a matter of course for conceiving and raising a child.

The attorney's face was flush from exertion. Danny stopped in front of a coffeepot in the kitchen of the quiet farmhouse. He caught his breath and sought to release the tension lodged in his breast. Whether the anxiety came from the unpleasant prospect of being present at Ben Johnson's deposition, or was a reaction to his fleeting reflection upon his life-long struggle to honor his father, was unclear.

Aitkins grabbed the metal handle of the glass coffeepot and poured steaming liquid into a plastic travel mug. Light began to ascend. He looked out a window. The lawyer's eyes searched the new morning for signs of life.

Two horses and a steer stood motionless in hoof deep snow, the shaggy remnants of their winter coats sloughing slowly onto the hard-packed ground. Heavy vapor curled upward from their nostrils as the livestock contentedly chewed the residue of a hay bale. A truck appeared across the meadow. The animals watched the progress of the vehicle as it passed by. A bulk tanker was headed down the gravel township road to Jensen's Dairy Farm to pick up milk. Aitkins studied the silver surface of the tank, the rising sun reflected in the polished metal, as the truck disappeared around a bend. The animals dropped their heads and nuzzled the remaining hay, pawing expectantly at frozen ground.

The young lawyer took a draw of coffee, secured the travel mug's lid, and picked up his overcoat. Placing the garment over an arm, Danny retrieved an Australian bush hat from a wooden peg in the back hallway before venturing outside.

Standing in the easy atmosphere of morning, Aitkins tried to forget the past, tried to set aside his differences with his old man. But somehow the day, despite the freshness of oncoming spring, seemed bleak. The sun appeared hesitant. A sense of bitterness remained with the lawyer as he climbed into his pickup and headed towards town.

CHAPTER 7

"Mr. Anderson, Jason Billington, Stevenson's customer service. I heard from the Detroit Lakes Mill that you might have a problem. What's going on?"

The call came unsolicited. Beyond making an initial complaint following the abortions, which prompted the mill to retrieve unused pellets from his farm, Dean Anderson had not spoken to the boys at the mill. He'd only talked to his veterinarians and the lawyer about his problem. And yet, someone had told Stevenson's corporate honchos enough about the situation to prompt the regional head of customer service to call.

Dean Anderson was sitting down to Sunday dinner. He didn't like interruptions during the Sabbath meal. It was the one time during the week when all of his children, including Millie, were usually home. Sunday was the only fragment of normalcy left in their routine in terms of quality time together.

"Dad it's long distance. Someone from Stevenson's," Millie had said, trying to hand her father the remote telephone.

"Take the number," Dean replied gruffly.

Nancy, agitated by the abortion calamity that had hit their swineherd like a tornado, insisted that he take the call.

"Mr. Billington, I can't explain what happened other than to tell you that I fed our sows and gilts your feed and shortly after, they began to abort. It continued until every last one of the animals was barren," Dean Anderson advised after accepting the phone from his oldest child.

"Very unusual, Mr. Anderson. Never heard of such a thing outside of a disease situation. How are you vaccinating the sows and gilts?" Billington asked.

"We medicate for all the usual swine ailments. I can't see this being an illness; our other animals appear to be fine, except the weaned piglets in the nursery. They threw up the pelleted food. Some of them died, though the majority just got sick and wouldn't eat."

"Difficult to assess the possibilities without being there. I understand that the folks at NDSU haven't found anything of significance in the feed."

"That's true. But they suspect the pellets. Something about Microtoxins."

"Mycotoxins. They'd be looking for poisons caused by fungal growth, mold, and whatnot. Doubt you'll find anything in our feed. We have strict quality control; use only dry corn and soybean meal for our pellets. You need wet, substandard product to cause a Mycotoxin problem. And even then, it's usually an isolated situation

73

limited to a few sows, maybe a litter or two aborted over a whole herd. Never heard of mold causing anything like what you claim."

Anderson had become upset with the man. The farmer stood up, pushed his pine ladder-back chair away from the long narrow harvest table occupying the better part of the kitchen, and retreated to his study. Dean Anderson's study had been a pantry at one time. The Andersons had opened the space up, adding a Franklin stove and a large arched window overlooking the family vegetable garden. It was Dean Anderson's only retreat in the house, the one place none of his children dared bother him. The room also held Dean's computer. It was where he sweated over their monthly bills.

The farmer clutched the remote phone against the sweatshirt covering his shoulder. A low flame licked the bottom log of a pyre left smoldering in the cast iron firebox of the stove. He opened the glass door and tossed a dry piece of aspen onto the embers.

"Look Mr. Billington, all I know is that my litters are dead. Thousands of pigs that I counted on to make it through the year are gone. They never made it to being born, much less weaned. The only thing that anyone can point to is your company's damn feed."

He felt an inkling of regret that he'd cursed over the telephone. His religious convictions, deep and abiding in the Missouri Synod tradition, generally curbed his desire to cuss.

"That's the long and the short of it, I reckon," he continued.

"I know you're frustrated..." Billington interrupted.

"Frustrated isn't the word. Angry is a better term for what I'm feeling right now. Two years ago, I bought salt supplement from your mill. It turned out to contain three times the sodium it was supposed to. I lost three of my milk cows. Without question, your adjuster paid for the loss. I sang the praises of Stevenson's up and down the Ottertail Valley. Now when I'm in real trouble, the kind of trouble that can do in my farm, you tell me you can feel my pain but I don't hear you offerin' to take care of the damage your product caused. You tell me it's got to be somethin' other than the feed, that it can't be your fault. That's why I talked to a lawyer, Mr. Billington. I was expecting this."

The mention of the attorney had caused a palpable change in the company man's tone.

"Don't be hasty, Mr. Anderson. Like before, maybe there's a reasonable way to resolve this. I'll tell you what. It's only a few hours by plane from Fargo to Des Moines. I'll reserve two round trip tickets for you and the missus. You drive to Fargo and I'll take care of the rest. We'll have a cab waiting for you at the Des Moines airport and a hotel room reserved for you downtown, right up the street from our building. You come down, without a lawyer, without any obligation. We'll talk it over and see if something can't be done on a nonadversarial basis. OK?"

74

"I'll have to run it by my wife."

Anderson placed the phone down on the warm surface of the oak desk and left the room. Nancy was starting to wash the dinner dishes. Dean's plate of food remained on the table. His portion of roast beef and mashed potatoes, covered with cold, congealed gravy, remained half-eaten. Millie's eyes followed her father as he entered the kitchen, her hands submerged in rinse water.

"This customer service guy in Des Moines wants us to fly down there and meet with him. He wants us to come without a lawyer to see if we can settle the matter," the farmer advised.

"Dean, you know we can't afford to be flying off to Iowa. We don't have the time and we surely don't have the money." Nancy replied.

"They'll pay for it. It'll only take a day or two."

"Where we gonna stay in Des Moines? Who's gonna pay our expenses? We'll have to eat out."

"They'll cover it all."

His wife stared at him, seeming smaller and more vulnerable than Dean remembered. Her gaze wore a frightened uncertainty. Dark rings, a detail he hadn't noticed before, circled her eyes, bearing witness to her hard life.

This isn't what she needs or what she deserves after all she's put up with on this place, he thought. *It's not fair. She's too young to look so worn out, so tired.*

He considered their infant son Jeremy, a child born between Millicent and Matthew. In those ugly circles of flesh around his wife's once vibrant eyes, he saw a mother's anguish at finding her baby son motionless and dead in his crib, the victim of SIDS. Within those dark creases of skin, he also witnessed his wife's pain of watching her twin sister Emma die from cancer.

All Dean Anderson wanted, all he had tried to do, was farm his little piece of earth until the mortgage was paid off, until the land was his. Then he would stop. He'd take Nancy away to Maine, Oregon, Utah, or Montana. Somewhere where either an ocean or the mountains dominated the horizon. But the farmer saw, in the eyes of his wife, the impossibility of escaping their fate, a fate made clear by the destruction of their animals by forces beyond their control.

"They'll pay for all of it. But they want both of us to come. I think we should," Dean urged.

Even as he said the words, he was reasoning with himself. If they approached the situation as a gentleman and a lady, perhaps they could avoid the turmoil of a lawsuit. A trial was something that would weigh heavily upon Nancy. He was not looking forward to a long, protracted legal entanglement. Dean Anderson and his family had better ways to spend their time.

"If you think it's worth it, I'll go," she had agreed.

He nodded, leaving the women to the dishes. Passing the boys as they played cribbage at the far end of table, Dean Anderson noted that Chad was winning.

"Why don't you give your mom and sister a hand and put the clean dishes away?" he asked.

The tone of the father's rebuke was harsh. He realized that he was taking out his financial distress on his children. The call from Iowa had upset him more than he was willing to admit.

"After this hand, dad," Joey said meekly, recognizing the edge to his father's words.

The farmer nodded again, a slight acknowledgement of his son's response, and retired to the study where bright flames cavorted across the face of the stove. Anderson picked up the phone.

"When do you want us? I can get away the next few days. After that, with our problems and all, we'll need to be back here to determine our next course of action."

"I'll have tickets ready for you at the Fargo airport tomorrow. Window or aisle?"

"What?"

"Do you want to sit in the aisle or by a window?"

"Window will be fine."

"Call the Northwest desk first thing in the morning. If the tickets aren't there, call me immediately."

The man continued to rattle off more details of the trip.

"Looking forward to meeting you, Mr. Anderson. Mrs. Anderson too," Billington concluded.

"We'll be there."

Nancy flew poorly. Despite strong religious beliefs, she had an innate fear of the unknown and a healthy respect for the potentiality of accidents. Anxiety gripped her the moment they boarded the DC9 in Fargo. Her upset multiplied when they boarded a small commuter plane to fly from the Twin Cities to Des Moines. Her terror reached its zenith with the plane's unorthodox approach into Iowa's capital city.

The turbo prop had banked sharply above Des Moines to avoid a small thunderhead. A wind shear caught the aircraft as it made its final approach. The gust caused the airplane to dance excitedly over the flat expanse of Iowa beneath them. Nancy gripped her husband's sleeve with a power, with a physical strength that the farmer had only seen displayed by his wife during the final push of childbirth.

A few hundred feet above the flooded banks of the Des Moines River, the aircraft leveled out. Muddy fields roared past them, seemingly within reach, as they watched the ground loom large. And then, with a gentle bounce, they landed. Nancy Anderson remained rigid, unable to relax, until the wheels of the plane ceased to revolve. It was a short, quiet cab ride to their hotel. The couple registered. Their room was paid for in advance. The farmer and his wife freshened up before their afternoon meeting with Stevenson's.

The wind had quieted; the rain had subsided. The Andersons felt out of place as they walked arm in arm to the Stevenson's Building. Nancy wore a long black skirt and a navy silk blouse beneath a charcoal colored wool coat, a garment that Millie had given her. Dean was protected from the elements by a heavy brown greatcoat, a substantial article of clothing that was at least twenty years old. Underneath, he wore his one and only suit. The outfit had cost him two hundred dollars off the rack in Fargo six years ago. He'd worn it twice. Both times he felt constrained by the garment's finery.

Their destination was a gray granite building standing eighteen stories above a main avenue in downtown Des Moines. Stevenson's Sci-Swine's regional office was located on the top floor of the structure. The farmer and his wife entered a cage-style elevator in the lobby. A panorama of the cityscape greeted them as the antiquated car deposited them in the corporate reception area on the eighteenth level. The view was dominated by the state capitol located across the Des Moines River. The watercourse was swollen and in danger of overflowing its banks as it snaked through the trees defining its borders. Brown floodwater threatened a system of artificial dikes erected to protect the city.

"May I help you?"

A heavy-set middle-aged black woman in an expensive red business suit addressed them. The woman's desk was oval, carved out of the same expensive gray and pink granite used to finish the floor and walls of the suite.

"Mr. and Mrs. Dean Anderson to see Mr. Billington. We have an appointment."

"He's expecting you. Go right through the double doors," the woman advised.

Dean Anderson pondered the woman. There was an essential element of humanity buried in the contours of her features. The Minnesotan tried not to stare. He'd seen few black folks in his lifetime. There were only a handful living at any one time in all of Becker County. Those that called the farming community "home" were mostly adopted kids of white parents. It was an unusual event for Dean Anderson to converse with a black person.

The farmer noted, in the instant he spoke with the receptionist, that her eyes were piercing and that her lips were smooth and covered with red lipstick, the color in striking contrast to the tone of her skin. From the pattern of her speech, she was obviously well educated. As he walked away from the desk, he wondered what the woman's family was like, whether she had children; what her husband did for a living; whether she had ever lived outside the confines of Des Moines, Iowa.

Dean Anderson kept his thoughts to himself as he followed his wife through the suggested doors. At the end of a broad passage, they saw another set of identical doors constructed of the same significant oak. The doors opened by themselves as the couple approached.

"Good of you to see us on such short notice, Mr. and Mrs. Anderson."

Dean Anderson recognized the voice to be Billington's. The executive proved to be a petite man with an uncertain smile. Billington held one of the doors open for the Andersons. Plush carpeting cushioned their shoes as the husband and wife entered the space. Billington himself wore delicate, pointed shoes that squeaked when he walked. His blue suit was smartly cut, perfectly tailored to his slender form. He wore a blue and yellow silk tie fastened to his starched white shirt with a glimmering clasp. Whether the medallion boasted membership in Rotary, the Masons, or the Knights of Columbus, was uncertain.

The executive took their coats and extended his right hand to Dean Anderson in the process. The farmer shook Billington's appendage. The flesh of the small man was damp and cold to the touch.

"Please, have a seat at the table next to me folks," the man offered.

Billington's head boasted a small face. His skin was ruddy and devoid of hair. The customer service man's lips were minikin and pale as he surveyed the farmer and his wife during the interval it took for them to become seated.

Four additional men joined them. Each of the other executives was also dressed to perfection. Dean Anderson did not focus on them. He felt nervous and out of his element. The Minnesotan faced his wife. Nancy's eyes were fixed upon her lap; staring at her folded hands, at her task-hardened hands and unadorned fingernails. It was obvious to the farmer that his wife's nerves were no better than his were.

Billington introduced the other men. Two lawyers. A feed nutrition expert. The vice-president of the swine division. The farmer did not catch their names. Dean Anderson concentrated his attention inward, attempting to harness his anxiety. He barely heard the words the claims man uttered.

"Well now, Mr. and Mrs. Anderson. No sense beating around the bush. Covington here, our best swine nutritionist, has had a few conversations with your vet and the folks at NDSU. Tell them what you know, Ralph."

Another slender man, obviously a runner, under thirty, boasting thin black hair and an insignificant mustache, replied in a monotone.

"The testing done up your way wasn't conclusive as to the cause of your problems. Dr. Guttormson, your vet, confirmed that he saw a few fetuses on the floor of your barn. But he didn't say how many, nor did he verify the full extent of your situation."

Dean Anderson looked up from the polished surface of the conference table. The gray and pink stone of the furniture reflected dull light from outside. There was no sun. Low rolling clouds, cumbersome and threatening, blanketed the city. The farmer struggled to make his words pointed and strong. They came out sounding angry.

"Guttormson knows what happened. The whole breeding herd was wiped out. It hit the sows, the gilts, and some of the young in the nursery. Those were the only animals that had a problem. They were the only pigs that got your feed. It has to be the feed."

"Not necessarily so. I can cite you eight or nine swine diseases, haemophilus pleural pneumonia being one possibility, which cause massive abortion storms," Covington stressed. "Our quality testing is done at the pelleting plant in Grand Forks. We use only top-notch corn. We sold thousands of bushels of the same mix that you claim is defective to other farmers across the Midwest, Manitoba, and Ontario. Yours is the only complaint we've received."

The farmer's dander rose. He'd come to Des Moines to discuss a fair resolution of their problem, a problem that, in his own mind, had only one cause. It was the feed: the pelleted feed that Stevenson's sold him. There was no other possibility.

Dean Anderson pushed himself away from the furniture while trying to maintain some semblance of calm, trying to control the storm of anger rising within.

"Then why in God's name did you drag us all the way down here? To play with our minds? To give us false hope that Stevenson's actually would stand behind its product when the chips are down? Come on, Nancy, I think we'd better head out before I say something to these gentlemen that I'll regret."

Dean Anderson assisted his wife out of her chair.

"Please sit down. Covington here is merely trying to explain that there may be other reasonable explanations for the loss you experienced," Billington argued. "Nothing in this world is certain, Mr. Anderson. Agreed? I mean, you must admit, there could be other causes of your problem, causes other than our product."

Billington's tone wasn't pleading despite his obvious desire to keep the Andersons in the room in hopes of an early resolution of the claim.

"I don't see it that way," the farmer retorted.

The couple resumed their seats. Dean Anderson's dislike for all things corporate boiled to the surface. His unease was palpable to his wife, revealed to her by the tautness of her husband's facial muscles.

"I know you don't. However, I must point out the reality of an extended legal battle," Billington observed.

One of the lawyers, a fat, well-groomed man, spoke up in a gravel edged voice.

"What are your actual out-of-pocket losses to date, Mr. Anderson? If Stevenson's could offer you a sum of money today, realizing that you don't have to pay a lawyer, what would make your operation whole? This would be without consideration of who's at fault, mind you. There would be no admission of responsibility by the company."

"You mean Stevenson's would pay but not admit that their product did this? That doesn't seem right," Mr. Anderson said.

"Right has nothing to do with a lawsuit. Every civil claim, whether for the death of a loved one or the loss of livestock, is about money," the attorney opined. "Even if an apology was possible, and I assure you that it is not, an apology would not remedy your claimed economic situation. Money is the only therapy that can cure that ill."

There was a haunting pause in the conversation. Dean Anderson did not consult his wife as he delivered a response.

"One hundred thousand dollars. That's what it will cost us to cull the sows and gilts and raise new breeding females and start over. That amount represents only a portion of what we'll lose because we'll miss two farrowing cycles. We'll lose all the animals from those litters."

"But you can buy sows on the open market at auction for far less," Covington asserted.

"Won't work. We run a closed herd. We only import boars for insemination. All the other animals are bred, born, and raised on our farm. That's why we don't have a disease problem. You start bringing in outside animals and all hell will break loose, if you'll pardon the expression."

Nancy glanced at her husband. She was a church going woman and didn't approve of such language. Though disappointed in her husband's choice of words, she held her tongue in deference to his authority in business matters.

"That's admirable. But Stevenson's is looking for a mutual resolution of this situation. Perhaps I could characterize our position as being willing to fund a Chevrolet to replace one wrecked in an accident. We're not prepared to buy you folks a new Cadillac," Malachi Stone advised.

Billington reached into a brown expansion folder and retrieved a white envelope with dainty fingers.

"This is the best and final offer of settlement we will make. Lawyer or no lawyer, I can assure you that if you do not accept it, Stevenson's will defend this case all the way to the Minnesota Supreme Court," the customer service executive said.

The businessman slid the envelope across the stone tabletop towards the farmer.

"There will be no last minute settlement of this case on the courthouse steps. That's not the way we operate," Billington added.

Dean Anderson looked at the envelope. He listened to Billington's admonition. The farmer's distrust increased with every vowel and consonant uttered by the Stevenson's employee. Dean Anderson ripped open the envelope with unsteady hands and withdrew a green bank draft and a stipulation of settlement.

"Twenty-five thousand dollars. No lawyer's fees, no expenses, no long court battle, no jury trial to upset the members of your family. Today and today only, this amount is yours. Tomorrow, you go see your lawyer and the offer is retracted. There will be, as Mr. Billington indicated, no subsequent negotiations," Stone reiterated slowly, for effect.

The farmer scrutinized the legal papers. Nancy Anderson leaned to whisper in her husband's ear. He believed he knew what she would want him to do without hearing the words. He anticipated the depth of her fear of a prolonged court battle. He anticipated that she would urge the hasty acceptance of the offer.

"Tell the son-of-a-bitch to shove his Chevrolet up his ass," she advised.

Dean Anderson pivoted on his buttocks in disbelief.

"What did you say?" he whispered.

"You heard me. Tell that pompous jerk we'll see him in court," the woman responded.

"Are you sure? It's a lot of money."

"It's a lot of money if we hadn't lost our sows. It's one quarter of what we lost at a bare minimum. Tell the man."

Shaking his head in disbelief, Dean Anderson replaced the documents in the envelope before sliding the papers across the table.

"I'm sorry, gentlemen. You seem to have upset my wife. We can't accept your offer."

"Surely you can see that there is little likelihood that you'll do better at trial. The risks of court, the risks of failure are great for you and your family. Please, reconsider," Stone said quickly.

"Quite frankly, my wife has never been known to cuss. You must have really riled her up. She says you can stick your offer up your collective asses. That's about as plain as I can make it," the farmer related.

The couple stood up, retrieved their coats, and left the room. Behind them, five corporate executives sat in stunned silence, rendered speechless by the poker-playing prowess of a farmer's wife.

CHAPTER 8
The Autumn Before

It had rained on the plains of North Dakota for as many weeks as he could remember. The crops needed moisture in August, when the sun was still high and the ground was a sea of hardpan. Every afternoon, the winds had come busting in from the northwest, stirring up the precious topsoil, tearing it free of the ground, carrying it away. The crops had taken off like lightening during the spring on the strength of early rains and heavy heat. That growth hit a standstill by late July.

Dave Mueller had prayed then, prayed for rain to boost the cereal grains and corn growing on his land back to growth. Either he prayed too vigorously, prayed too often, or God was determined to toy with the North Dakota man. In any case, too much September and October rain had come.

Mueller was a grain farmer. He raised wheat, barley, and a little corn. No livestock. Four thousand acres of prairie went under the plow every spring on the Mueller place. He was forty-seven years old and a bachelor. He didn't need to farm. He had no dependents, no debts to speak of. He could have taken the path of leisure like others of his generation. There was a ready market for good farmland. There was nothing stopping Dave Mueller from selling his place and moving on except history.

The white frame house he lived in was the same house he'd been born in. He was the fourth generation German Catholic to inhabit the dwelling and farm the land. In his short tenure, Dave Mueller hadn't done much to improve the home itself. The only major alteration he made to the house was the purchase and installation of a satellite dish. Not one of the new mini-dishes but a huge, commercial-sized unit that he'd bought ten years earlier so he could watch the Bison play football. He was an alumnus of North Dakota State University. He never missed a game.

Mueller stood, a short, stocky man with two day's ragged beard covering his round face, beneath the covered front porch of his house. The roof of the veranda sagged towards the south end of the building, where a post was beginning to disintegrate from wood rot. Pale emerald shingles contrasted with vivid forest green moss growing between the squares of asphalt. Rainwater poured freely over the edge of the awning, cascading into gutters already filled to capacity. David clutched a hot cup of coffee in his thick right hand and watched low, broiling storm clouds parade across the open landscape on the heels of a quickening wind.

Every low spot in the farmyard, in the fields, in the riverbed that cut through his property, was full up with the rain. The driveway and the narrow gravel service road leading from his land to the paved county two-lane highway were reduced to soggy, rutted paths. Only the rocky crowns of the driving surfaces remained above the temporary pools. There was a serious question as to whether the driving surfaces would remain dry much longer.

"Damn the rain. When's it gonna stop?"

There was no one around to hear the farmer's question. Given his recent experience with prayer, he wasn't expecting an answer from God.

"Pray for rain, get the Great Flood. My corn is going to be nothing but shit by the time I get it in," Mueller muttered between thoughtful draws of coffee.

It was mid-October. The corn, a small but important portion of the Mueller Farm's total annual production, was the last crop on the place waiting to be harvested. No matter how careful Mueller was, no matter how long he waited; the kernels would not dry. There was little hope that the sun would provide much warmth. Nights were fast becoming cold. Frost had already hit the lowlands of the Mueller place. When the ice melted, it simply added more water to the soggy corn. When Mueller went to sell his corn at the local elevator in Larimore, west of Grand Forks, the stuff would already be beginning to mold. He'd be docked for moisture content. He'd be lucky to come out of the year dead even given the loss he'd already taken on his wheat crop for a similar deficiency.

The farmer extended a mud-covered work boot and kicked at a half-eaten apple lying on the wooden deck of the porch. The fruit spun crazily out into the storm and caromed off a 1000 gallon LP gas tank sitting in the side yard.

Bonnnng...

"Gonna have to bring the corn in as soon as the rain stops and we get a day or two of good weather. Can't afford to let it stand too long or the snow will be flying. Get what I can off it and hope for the best," the farmer intoned.

Mueller's voice was flat. He wasn't a person prone to emotion. This was not the first corn crop he'd raised that would come out a loss. It surely wouldn't be the last. He tossed the remaining coffee out into the weather. Carefully wiping his boots, he opened the storm door to the house and went inside to escape the howling wind.

A week passed. A dull October sun briefly warmed the plains. The interlude allowed Dave Mueller and his neighbors to fire up their harvesters and gather the remnants of one of the worst corn crops in years. Hour after hour the big machines hacked away at waterlogged stalks, peeling cobs away from plants, depositing the precious cargo in hoppers. One could hear the moisture in the vegetation as the stalks were squeezed in the harvesting mechanism. One could detect the sound of water dripping from the plants as the tractors passed by.

Jed and Tom Quegley helped Mueller out. They were local boys. The brothers boasted sandy hair and gangly limbs. They worked like the devil during the day and drank like fish at night. No matter how severe their hangovers, they made it to work by 4:00am every morning. At ten dollars an hour, the boys were a bargain. But each hour they spent struggling to bring in the wet crop cost Mueller. Delays in the field due to rigs getting mired in the low spots for hours on end, additional maintenance, extra fuel; all the expenses of a poor crop began to add up. Mueller had no alternative. Letting the corn stand was not an option. Given its moisture content, it would sprout mold and be rendered useless. It was either pay the Quegley's, and get the corn in now, or throw in the towel and let it rot in the field.

Marge Martin drove Mueller's corn to the Larimore elevator. She was an owner-operator of tractor-trailer units. Big hipped, flat chested, and consistently ornery, Margaret had thighs as thick as Dave Mueller's waist. She was a tough businesswoman and a tougher critic.

"What the hell is this shit?" the trucker bemoaned.

"What do you mean?" Mueller responded.

"This corn-it's wetter than a beaver's tail. How in God's name do you expect to sell this garbage?"

"Hey, do I tell you how to drive? Last I looked, you weren't much into farming, Marge. The whole county has corn like this. It'll be all right if they cut it with some drier stuff," Mueller replied.

"Seems like you'd be better off firing up your corn dryers and drying it yourself."

"No can do. They're LP gas fired. With the cost of propane, I'd go broke. The stuff's so wet it'd take a week just to bring the moisture down from twenty percent to fifteen percent. I'd still be docked for wet corn anyway. Better to just take my lumps now and cut my losses."

"You're the boss. I'll send Earl and Bennie over for the other two loads. See you at the elevator," Martin advised.

All of North Dakota had experienced an inordinate amount of autumn rain. The entire grain crop of the state; barley, wheat, oats, and corn was adversely affected. Still, the Dakota's fared better than the Western Provinces of Canada where heavy snow destroyed two-thirds of the grain crop in Manitoba and Saskatchewan. Because of the failure of the Canadian harvest, Mueller hoped that his corn, even in its less than desirable state, would command a better price than could be expected. Demand, he reasoned, would drive up the price and cover most of the added expense of the wet harvest.

"She measures right at nineteen percent, Dave. Afraid all I can use this for is mixing. Really not much good even for that. Best I can go is salvage price."

"Christ, Ed. At that rate, I should have burned the crap and filed a crop insurance claim. Can't you do any better than that?" Mueller asked.

"Sorry. Price is the best I can give. I've already got more of this junk corn than I'll ever be able to use locally. Plus I'm already full up with all that crap wheat I bought off you. We've only got a small operation here. You know that. I've got a bin of Number One corn from last year that I can cut this wet stuff with and that's it. I'm gonna have a hell of a time breaking even if I unload this shit on another elevator," Ed LeFaive, the manager of the Cooperative said.

"Yeah, right. With Canada down to next to nothing for production, this corn's gotta be worth more than you're offering. It's just gotta," Mueller asserted.

LeFaive stood next to the moisture gauge. Darkly complected, in his early seventies with thin flowing white hair that fell to his shoulders, and an elegant beard to match, time had clearly taken its toll on the French-Canadian. A trace of a Quebecois accent colored his softly spoken words. LeFaive was known as a fair man, a man who valued the Cooperative's customers and relied upon them to sell to him at a slightly lower price during times of plenty. In return, he normally bought grain from those same customers at a slightly higher price during times of scarcity. But the situation presented by the influx of poor corn precluded him from offering a premium. LeFaive's price was, Dave Mueller knew, the best that could be expected.

The farmer kicked a plank wall, the pine boards long devoid of whitewash, and tossed his cowboy hat to the ground as he stomped off the loading platform in anger. The little Canadian watched his customer in careful silence.

Mueller stood next to the idling tractor-trailers and contemplated three loads of rotting corn. His neck ached. His hands were numb. Hard work in the fields had yielded hard luck at the elevator. Three truckers sat in the cabs of their rigs in silence. Marge Martin held her tongue as the farmer anguished over his circumstances.

The man turned and began to slog back through the parking lot. Approaching his hat, the farmer grabbed the Stetson and rudely shoved it back on his head without breaking stride. Mueller climbed the wooden stairs of the loading platform, pulling his hat down until the webbing pinched his ears, before nodding his acquiescence.

"I'm sorry, David. It's the best I can do. I'll be lucky to sell your corn for what I'm paying you. Here, take a look under this black light," LeFaive advised.

The manager stepped away from a small fluorescent bulb and a microscope mounted to a table. Mueller removed his hat and bent at the waist to peer into the equipment's eyepiece.

"See that coloration? That's fusarium," the Co-Op man said. "The stuff is loaded with it. So is every other load of corn I've taken in. Unless I get rid of this garbage right away, or spend several weeks drying it, and I don't have the money or manpower to do that, this corn'll get hotter than a furnace and burn itself up."

"I know you're doing the best you can here, Ed. Let's get on with it."

"Just want you to understand. If this stuff stays together in one bin, or it's used as feed for gestational animals, all hell will break loose."

"Mycotoxins, right?"

Mueller was standing upright, looking into the dark eyes of the elevator man as they spoke. The legal implications for both were obvious.

"You got it. The poisons this mold puts out can completely destroy the breeding cycle of a dairy or swineherd. That's the problem with corn as wet as this. You've gotta be careful where it goes, what it's used for."

The men stepped into the elevator office to draw up a check. Marge Martin shifted her diesel into gear and pulled her trailer forward. Bill Wilson, a skinny teenager working for the elevator as a laborer, climbed down from the loading platform and helped the trucker remove the canvas tarp covering the corn. Pungent air boiled off the fetid grain. The smell of rotting corn burned the youth's nostrils as he reached into the trailer to remove the loosened tarp. The woman jumped down, landing sharply on the dirt.

"What the hell are they gonna use this for?" she mumbled to herself in disgust as she observed the festering corn.

No one at the Larimore elevator responded to the trucker's question.

CHAPTER 9

Signs of spring greeted Daniel Aitkins. Against the backdrop of a blue sky over Island Lake, the lawyer witnessed a pair of bald eagles soaring high above the trees intent upon courtship. As the lawyer's pickup truck turned from a paved highway onto the dirt drive to the Anderson Farm, a flock of Giant Canada Geese flew noisily above the roadway. Deer nervously browsed along the edge of the right-of-way. But it wasn't until Aitkins exited his truck that he realized the totality of the seasonal changes at hand. The odor of several thousand hogs crammed together in one small space assaulted Daniel as the attorney left his Ranger to follow a bare cement walk to the front door of Dean and Nancy Anderson's home.

A thickly built man appearing to be in his mid-forties stepped out of the shadows.

"You must be the lawyer."

The farmer extended his right hand.

"You must be Mr. Anderson," Aitkins responded, noting that his potential client's grip was firm.

"Dean Anderson. Call me Dean. No one but Pastor Eckman calls me Mr. Anderson."

"Likewise. Call me Danny. Or Dan."

"Let's go into the house. My office is all set up for us. After that, we can take a walk around the place if you like."

"Sounds fine, Dean. Sounds real fine."

The men climbed the steps to the front porch. Aitkins noted that the home appeared to be well cared for. The white paint on the clapboard siding was only a year or two old. A thick coat of gray enamel protected the planks of the porch deck. The windows of the house were wooden double-hungs. The glass appeared to be sparking clean; the frames, without rot. The home's front door was varnished wood of a three-panel design. There was no storm door. Anderson held the door open as the lawyer entered the house.

Wide boards of native pine covered the floor of the vestibule. The wood was freshly shellacked. Aitkins noted that the interior walls of the home appeared to be original lathe and plaster. Small cracks in the plaster were evident. The defects were concentrated where the walls met the ceiling. The flat surfaces of the home were clean and painted a uniform eggshell white. Historic fixtures hung from the ceiling and bathed the space in old light.

Aitkins instinctively stopped in the foyer to remove his cowboy boots.

"No need to do that, Mr. Aitkins. You're company," Dean Anderson advised.

"Trained that way. And it's Dan, remember?"

"Sure thing, Dan."

The lawyer pulled off his footwear and followed the farmer down a narrow corridor. The warmth of a low fire in a woodstove greeted them as they entered Anderson's study. The smell of burning wood reminded Aitkins of pleasant occasions spent before the fireplace in his own home.

"Nice office. Better than mine by a long stretch."

"Thanks. Have a seat. I think Nancy is free. She's got some coffee and blueberry muffins in the works. Plus I want her to get to know you and help me make a decision on how we handle this thing."

Anderson's comment conveyed a subtle reminder that Aitkins had not yet been hired. Dan tried not to let concern show. He wanted this case. Wanted it bad. By all indications, these were quality folks. Unlike some of the injury victims that came to his office for help, he doubted whether the Andersons had any skeletons in their closets ready to pop up and make things dicey during the discovery process. Daniel's years of experience told him, at first blush, that these were people he wanted to represent.

The farmer entered the room with his wife. Nancy Anderson was thin, though not to the point of being frail, with long blond hair pulled in a bun. She wore a pair of faded Lee jeans, a loose fitting sweatshirt, and tennis shoes. She was tall for a woman, as tall as her husband, with well-defined features. Mrs. Anderson wore no makeup but was, at least to Dan's eye, pretty in simple fashion, though her bright blue eyes seemed, at first glance, to express a fatigue that her posture failed to disclose.

"Honey, this is Mr. Aitkins. Oops, I mean Dan."

The farmer's wife extended her hand. Aitkins grasped it. The attorney found that the woman's grip was nearly as strong as her husband's was. Blue veins stood out from the pale Nordic skin of her forearm where the sleeves of her sweatshirt were rolled up. The bulk of the sweatshirt hid the woman's figure. The palm of her hand was moist.

"Pleased to meet you. I'll be right back with muffins and coffee. Do you take cream or sugar?" the woman asked.

"Just black."

"I like him already. A man who drinks his coffee black has got to be OK," the farmer quipped.

Mrs. Anderson quietly closed the door behind her as she left the room.

"So tell me about this abortion storm," Aitkins said.

"It was bad. Hit every bred sow and gilt. We had our neighbor Clyde Armstrong come over and do ultrasounds on our entire female breeding stock. Nearly a hundred percent of the ones that should have been bred were no longer pregnant. Damn near all of our litters were wiped out," Dean Anderson related.

Nancy Anderson opened the door and carried a tray full of cups and muffins and a pot of coffee into the room. The woman placed the tray on top of her husband's desk and poured coffee for her guest. As she bent towards Aitkins to hand him a cup, a strand of her hair fell loose and hung suspended in the air near her left ear. The lawyer's attention was immediately drawn to the tuft of yellow and, for the first time, he noticed how striking the woman was.

"Thanks, Mrs. Anderson," he said, using formality in an attempt to conceal his awkwardness.

"Nancy. Call me Nancy. "

Her words conveyed sincere politeness.

"Have a muffin. Our daughter, Millie and I picked the berries last summer. They're a sight better than the ones you get in the store," Mrs. Anderson said.

The woman handed the attorney a pastry. Blue blotches stained the exterior of the muffin. Aitkins took a bite of the offering.

"Great muffins. Just like my wife Julie makes. Always uses wild berries. The tame ones just don't have any flavor. They're full of too much water, I think," Danny said.

The woman nodded and passed her husband the plate of muffins and a cup of coffee. She sat easily in an oak side chair next to the desk cradling a mug in her hands. Nancy Anderson stared at the embers of the reluctant fire, seeming content to eavesdrop on the conversation.

"Like I said over the phone, Guttormson and the folks from NDSU are behind us one hundred percent," the farmer advised. "The only thing anyone can come up with as a cause for the abortions is the pelleted feed. Dr. Thomas at NDSU thinks it's linked to mold in the feed. Can't really say for sure yet because the stuff was in pellets. He's suggesting that we get the feed analyzed. I'm waiting to find out how much to send, how to package it, and the like," Anderson continued.

"Sounds like the elevator is liable for breach of warranty and strict liability, not to mention negligence. If that's the case, they're liable for all of your damages, including lost profits," Daniel Aitkins observed.

The farmer looked intently at the lawyer. His eyes bored straight into the soul of the other man.

"What do you figure our chances are?"

Aitkins leaned forward and put his cup on the edge of the desk before he replied.

"If we can get scientific support for your theory that the pellets were tainted and the mold caused the problem, good. Better than fifty-fifty. But it all depends on who our experts are and what they're willing to say."

Dan felt the woman's eyes leave the mystery of the fire and fix upon him. He sensed she was anxious about the prospect of going to trial.

"Of course, there's always the possibility of settlement. Out of court, you understand. Happens all the time," Aitkins interjected.

The farmer released an audible sigh. His wife pushed herself back against the hard oak of the chair. Dean Anderson's voice was quiet.

"I don't think so, Dan. At least, not in this case."

The farmer took a long swig of hot coffee. The liquid surged down his throat as he looked away from the lawyer.

"We already tried that. Stevenson's flew us down to Des Moines, to their regional headquarters, to discuss the case after I told them we were gonna see a lawyer," Dean Anderson revealed.

Aitkins rose to his feet and walked a short distance before standing in front of a window. The lawyer stared absently at trees surrounding the yard.

"Did they make you an offer?"

"Yes."

There was a long pause in the dialogue.

"How much?"

"Twenty five thousand, about a quarter of what I figure they owe."

"What did you tell them?"

Aitkins turned towards the farmer as he asked the question. The tension in the air seemed to pass. Dean Anderson's face broke into a wide grin.

"Nancy told them to shove it up their ass."

The woman's eyes darted. She didn't speak. Aitkins felt the corners of his mouth draw into an involuntary smile.

"I can't picture Mrs. Anderson using that sort of language."

"Trust me. She can use it where it's appropriate. And it was," Dean assured the attorney.

Danny studied the farmer's wife. Her cheeks were red. She coughed nervously and whispered.

"They deserved it, the sanctimonious bastards. I meant every word I said."

Aitkins chuckled.

"I'm sure you did."

"They told us that it was their only offer. That if we got a lawyer, there'd be no more negotiating," she whispered.

"Might be the case, Mrs. Anderson, might not. No way to tell until we get the case served and filed and we have their undivided attention," Danny said.

The farmer's eyes narrowed. His tone became serious.

91

"Can you stand toe to toe with big city lawyers? I mean, Stevenson's is a multi-national company. I'm sure they'll hire the best money can buy."

The man was to the point. The lawyer respected clients who were courteous but succinct.

"We've got the experience in our office to handle this case. We have all the computer technology and personnel we need to represent you at the same level as any other firm in the state," Dan answered.

"I don't really care about all that. I'm asking about you. Are you up to it? I'm not hiring your firm. I'm hiring you. If the firm comes along with you, fine. But I don't want us to come to an understanding with you only to have some snot-nosed associate handling this thing. I want you to do the work, to be there in court for us."

Aitkins walked over to his briefcase, opened it, and withdrew a three-page document.

"Agreed. You hire me and that's who you get. I may have my staff work on certain aspects of the file but I'll be there each and every time anything critical needs doing," the lawyer advised as he handed a document to the farmer.

"This is our standard retainer agreement," Aitkins continued. "What it says is that if you hire us, it's on a contingency basis. We recover anything over and above the twenty-five thousand offered you; we get paid back our expenses and one-third of the recovery after that as a fee. If we don't prevail, if you get nothing, we get nothing. We eat our fee and our expenses."

Nancy Anderson rose and poured herself another cup of coffee. For the first time, Anderson noticed the inscription on her coffee mug. It read:

If you don't like the coffee, make it yourself.

The lawyer grinned. There was more to the woman than was obvious at first glance.

"You don't have to let me know right now. Take a few days to think it over and get back to me," Danny added.

The farmer's wife reached across the papers, found a flare marker in a plastic organizer on her husband's desktop, turned the document to the last page, signed her name in neat cursive script, and handed the pen to her husband.

"I don't have to think about it. You seem genuinely interested in us as people. You're a little young for this big a case, but then, so are we. Sign the form, Dean," the woman commanded.

The farmer studied his wife with amazement. She was usually the cautious, contemplative one. Dean Anderson scrawled his signature across the document.

"Thanks for the confidence, Mrs. Anderson. You won't regret it," Aitkins said.

The attorney added his signature to the agreement.

"Just so you know. We can't afford to lose this case, Mr. Aitkins. Our farm is on the line here," the woman revealed.

Before the lawyer could reply, Nancy Anderson picked up the tray and left the room.

"She's a pistol," Dean Anderson said through a suppressed chortle. "Can't say as I've ever seen her as riled up about anything. She's right, you know. We can't afford to lose this thing. Our bank says they'll hold off foreclosing until the case is over. I talked to Chase House at the bank. He's on board. But we're gonna end up a year or two behind schedule even if we can settle outside of trial," the farmer noted.

Aitkins studied the wide face of his client. The lawyer detected a hint of desperation behind the man's words.

"Let's take that stroll around the place. It seems like as good a time as any for you to teach me something about pigs," the lawyer said.

Anderson placed his cup on his desk and escorted the attorney to the back door. Outside, the men walked the path leading to the farrowing barn. As he accompanied the farmer on a tour of the farm, Dan Aitkins experienced a sudden weakness in his knees. Whether the instability was from drinking too much coffee, the after-affects of his football career, or the consequence of a sudden increase in responsibility, the litigator couldn't say.

CHAPTER 10

Danny contemplated the venue of the Anderson case. His recent bad luck in state court was likely to reassert itself if Judge Clermont Davidson was assigned the Anderson matter. The Andersons' claim would be best served by bringing suit in United States District Court. That way, Aitkins would be assured that Davidson wouldn't have a shot at getting the lawsuit on his docket.

Lawyers are entitled to remove a judge once per case in Minnesota State Court without cause. Dan Aitkins had never invoked that provision of law. Practicing his craft in a small town, in a small district, he avoided making enemies on the bench. Clermont Davidson, despite his routine disdain for plaintiffs in personal injury cases, wasn't the worst judge in the district. But the old man was thin skinned. If Dan filed, the judge would remember. And in subtle ways, ways not subject to formal inquiry or discipline by the Judicial Standards folks, the veteran judge would make Aitkins suffer.

It wasn't that the young trial attorney was a fan of the federal civil litigation system. He despised the rigid application of rules and procedures that were the hallmark of the United States District Courts. But he was willing to bow to rigidity to preserve a fighting chance at a just result for his client.

"How's the Anderson Complaint coming, Dee Dee?"

"It's already done and on its way."

Aitkins stepped into the cramped quarters occupied by his associate as they spoke. Ms. Hernesman had her back to her boss, she busily typed away on a computer keyboard. Thin black hair hung short and even against the neckline of Hernesman's flowered blouse. When Dee Dee looked at Aitkins, her mottled hazel eyes caught the morning sun and sparkled in uncharacteristic fashion.

"You weren't around. I knew how anxious you were to get it filed. I ran it by Marcus before it went out," the associate explained.

Her reference was to Marcus Ordell, one of the other partners in the firm. Ordell was a veteran litigator with twenty-five years of trial experience. He was a careful, cautious man, though somewhat lacking in style.

"Marc made a few minor changes. I sent it out by Federal Express."

"Where's it venued?" Aitkins asked.

"Fergus Falls. I figured we'd want a rural jury rather than a bunch of suburbanites from the Twin Cities passing judgment on our clients."

"Dee, there hasn't been a jury trial held in the Federal Courthouse in Fergus Falls in decades," Aitkins mused. "I hope whichever federal judge we draw can find Ottertail County on a map."

"If we get lucky and have trial set for next summer, there won't be any problem getting a federal judge up here during fishing season."

"Unless we draw one of the women."

"That's sooo sexist," the associate moaned, drawing out the word for effect. "Girls like to fish too."

The boss changed the tenor of the conversation. He wasn't about to be drawn into an equal rights debate. He avoided such topics with Hernesman because she nearly always bested him.

"What theories did you plead?" Danny asked.

"Strict liability, negligence, negligence per se under the Minnesota Adulterated Feed Act, and breach of implied warranty under the Uniform Commercial Code."

"What about express warranty?"

"There weren't any made so far as I could tell," Hernesman advised.

"What in God's name is the 'Adulterated Feed Act'?"

"It's a state statute. If a feed manufacturer supplies a product containing anything deleterious, the fact that the feed contains something unintended means the maker of the stuff is per se negligent. It places the burden on the other side, on the defendant, to rebut presumed negligence."

"Where on earth did you come up with that?" Aitkins asked.

"Research, boss, plain old research. Once you get Online, finding what you want is a snap. Far faster than that old 'by the book' method you keep fumbling around with."

"That's why you're here, Dees. You're here to do the heavy lifting and make me look good. Maybe you're right. Maybe you can give me a lesson on the computer when things are slow."

"Slow? If things slow down, I'll find myself unemployed and out on the street with the kids Minnesota's three law schools keep dumping into the practice."

"Four."

"How's that?" she asked.

"Now it's four schools. St. Thomas in St. Paul just added a law school. But don't worry, Ms. Hernesman. I have a feeling you're in the driver's seat right where you are."

"I've heard that before."

"Not from me."

It was a done deal. Dee Dee was going to make partner before year's end. Aitkins had already insured that his existing partners, including his old man, were on line. The only questions remaining were: when would she be anointed and what ownership share would she assume?

Several days later the Anderson Complaint returned from Minneapolis with a form Summons to be served on Stevenson's Sci-

Swine. Dee Dee routed the documents to a process server in Winnipeg for personal service on the North American headquarters of the company. The fact that Andersons were claiming damages in excess of $50,000.00 against a foreign corporation gave concurrent jurisdiction over their case to the United States District and Minnesota State courts.

Shortly after the affidavit of service came back, Daniel received the telephone call he'd been expecting.

"Mr. Aitkins? Jim Thompson. I'm in town for a Bar Association meeting. I'd like to stop in and chat about the Anderson matter. Stevenson's has hired me to defend the case."

Danny knew his opponent by reputation. James Thompson was a local boy; an African American born and raised in Fargo, North Dakota. "Big Jim" ended up working as a defense lawyer in the Twin Cities where he built an impressive career defending the likes of Ford, GM, Pillsbury, and assorted other multinationals. He was a millionaire many times over, commanding a law firm of seventy-five partners and twice as many associates from the top floor of the Henderson Building in downtown Minneapolis. The sixty floor monolith was named after the founding partner of the firm, Gene Henderson, who had long since passed away leaving Thompson and others to carry on the work of Henderson, Bradley, and Smythe. The founding litigator left no children to foster his legacy of devotion to the elimination of plaintiff's claims in the courtroom. Big Jim Thompson stepped willingly into the void left by the old man's demise. Thompson became a partner at the tender age of twenty-seven, managing partner at thirty-eight, and CEO before his fiftieth birthday.

Sounds about right, Aitkins thought, *hiring a dedicated gunslinger to fend off my pesky little lawsuit.* The lawyer knew better than to denigrate Thompson's client so early in the game. He kept his opinions to himself.

"Never had the pleasure of working with you before, Jim."

Aitkins' use of the term "working with" was deliberate, meant to convey a sense of mutual respect and a tacit acknowledgement that they were both, within the bounds of advocacy, seeking justice.

"From the looks of the Complaint, seems like you really know your hogs," Thompson offered.

The younger man felt a subtle swelling of pride. He took pleasure being known around Western Minnesota as a trial lawyer who outworked his adversaries. A feeling of superiority began to shroud Aitkins' judgment as he reflected on the countless hours he'd spent with Dean and Nancy Anderson learning the ins and outs of their closed herd farrow to finish swine operation.

"I'd like to stop in while I'm in town and talk about the case before things get too heated. Do you have a few minutes you can spare sometime later today?" Thompson asked.

"Sure. Looks like I'm open from two until three or so. You know how to get here?" Aitkins asked.

"DL isn't that big. I'll find you. I'll be there around 2:30pm."

When the defense lawyer walked into Aitkins' office, Dan realized why everyone called the man "Big Jim". Thompson had played football, defensive end, for the University of Minnesota Gophers back when the team was still "Golden". Even at the peak of his professional life as a lawyer, decades removed from his last gridiron contest, Thompson remained an imposing figure. Burdened by a London Fog overcoat and a heavy briefcase, the former football star extended his hand, the palm pink and bright in contrast to the darkness of the rest of his skin. They shook hands. In Big Jim's embrace, Daniel felt the residual power of extreme physical strength.

"Nice to meet you, Dan."

The defense lawyer's eyes, brown and small, nearly Oriental in aspect, remained steadfast. Aitkins was aware that he was being scrutinized from behind a veil of false pleasantry.

"Same here. How can I help you?"

"Well, I'll be candid," Thompson began. "I thought you could outline for me, being that I'm not familiar with your clients' operation, what their claims are and why they think Stevenson's is at fault for the loss. Just the bare bones will do."

Dan studied Thompson as the man settled into a soft chair in front of the lawyer's desk. Thompson scanned the walls of the office, feigning interest in the diplomas, photographs, and awards arranged against the drywall.

"I see you were a football player. All Conference D-Back, eh? Must have been one hell of a hitter at your size," Thompson noted.

"I'm not sure why I keep that thing there. That was a long time ago," Aitkins replied.

"I hear you. It's been a lifetime since I put on a pair of cleats."

There was gentleness about the man that unexpectedly caused Aitkins to ease up his guard. In a matter of minutes, the young advocate was laying out his case, detailing his clients' financial losses, their theories of recovery, to his adversary. There was no hesitancy in Aitkins' delivery; no sign of caution as Daniel poured out every last facet of the Andersons' claim, as he knew it. When the plaintiff's lawyer was finished, he had no inkling of what Thompson had gained from the exchange until the older man extended his hand, intent upon leaving.

"Expect our answer in a day or so. It'll be fairly straightforward. Nothing fancy. I'm not into gamesmanship. May have to raise a few unique defenses to preserve them but it sounds like this case may end up settling before trial."

"My client received an offer from Stevenson's a while back," Aitkins disclosed.

"Really? That's news to me."

Dan focused his gaze. He wasn't convinced that this was the first time James Thompson had heard about the settlement offer.

"I think they offered twenty thousand. Sort of a 'take it or leave it deal'."

Dan misrepresented the amount of the offer to see if the ex-Gopher would reveal anything.

"I don't know about 'take it or leave it,'" Thompson replied. "Some underling in the claims office usually generates that stuff. Stevenson's is self-insured. I'll be dealing directly with their General Counsel in Winnipeg. I'll keep you posted as to what I find out. Being that we're in federal court, there'll be enough pressure brought on both of us to settle. The case will go through pretrial with a magistrate. Magistrates like to resolve cases to keep their judges happy. They don't like being told that corporate parameters have been invoked. Executive policy doesn't get very far in the federal judicial system."

The big man left. As Aitkins watched one of the wealthiest lawyers in Minnesota depart, the Detroit Lakes native realized that he'd been played and played by a master. Though it felt like his pockets had been picked, like his wallet had been lifted, Danny Aitkins found it hard to harbor ill will against the man.

I'll have to be more careful when I'm left alone in a room with Big Jim, the lawyer thought as he began to work on client files.

CHAPTER 11

The case was assigned to the Honorable Morton Triton McNab, a curmudgeon of a jurist and Chief Judge of the United States District Court for the District of Minnesota. From the outset, Aitkins knew it was a bad sign.

McNab was a Reagan appointee: a man prone to demagoguery and demeaning depreciation of trial counsel. Nearing retirement, McNab didn't much like civil cases. He tolerated claims based upon federal statutory authority; he despised cases filed in his bailiwick based upon diversity of citizenship.

Dan Aitkins had been before the unhappy, embittered judge only once before. Danny's client, a hockey player from the University of Minnesota, suffered the end of his college career when a steel rod implanted to secure a fractured arm failed due to metal fatigue. The surgeons and the hospital lined up behind Aitkins and pointed their collective fingers at the manufacturer of the hardware, a medical supply company based in Kentucky. A metallurgical engineer from the Institute of Technology on the Minneapolis campus of the "U" supported the case. Despite McNab's views regarding civil cases, the federal judge came down hard on the manufacturer's attorney.

McNab's ego precluded allowing a Magistrate Judge, an appointed subordinate of the District Court Judges, from handling settlement sessions. Aitkins had been fully prepared, based upon the old man's reputation, to be assaulted for clogging up the magnificence of the federal justice system with frivolity. But someone got to McNab and turned him, turned him defiantly against the out-of-state defendant who had denied the University its star right wing from Thief River Falls, Minnesota.

It was sometime after Dickie Mills, the injured player, pocketed his check for $200,000.00, braced by an annuity paying an additional five hundred dollars per month for life, and after Aitkins' firm socked away its fee, that Dan learned where the pressure had come from. He'd guessed that it had something to do with McNab's wife being the sister of Justin Nealy, one of the Regents appointed by the Governor to oversee the running of the University system. He'd been right. The rumor mill confirmed that McNab, himself a Golden Gopher Alum, had been taken aside by his brother-in-law, another conservative Republican. McNab was unceremoniously berated for nearly granting summary judgment to the defense. Nealy's tongue-lashing, backed by subtle entreaties by other alums, turned the tide.

Though Aitkins emerged from the Mills case victorious, the ease at which a federal judge changed heart resonated within the advocate. It made Daniel wary and untrusting. There was little he could do but accept the fact that McNab now held the fate of the

Anderson Farm in his hands. Unlike Minnesota State Court, where a lawyer is entitled to remove a judge at the outset of the case without divulging any reason for the removal, Federal Court does not allow the removal of a judge except for bias established after a full-blown hearing. Such removals, Aitkins knew, were few and far between.

Big Jim Thompson's team of associates filed their Answer promptly. As promised, it was a straightforward denial that Stevenson's product was in any way a cause of the abortion storm. Buried within the text were assertions that the claim was barred by the expiration of the statute of limitations, that the cause of the incident was rampant disease and animal husbandry problems in the Anderson operation, as well as implications that the Andersons' neglect and carelessness caused their pigs to die. The final paragraph raised the defense that, even if something had happened, it was "de minimis" (of minimal consequence) and that the damages incurred by the plaintiffs were less than the $50,000.00 threshold required to maintain federal diversity jurisdiction.

"What the hell is this?" Daniel Aitkins exclaimed.

The attorney sat at his desk examining an Order from the United States District Court of Minnesota. His eyes darted across the single page document. A hot glow blossomed across his face.

Emery Aitkins heard his son's lament and stopped in the open doorway to Daniel's office. The father was short, thick of thigh, noticeably overweight, but dressed impeccably in a navy blue blazer, tan slacks, and a silk tie. His hair was buzzed into a 1950's crew cut; the gray fibers flecked with the sandy coloration of his youth. His eyes, small and murky gray, were set immediately next to an imperial nose. Emery's white dress shirt was impeccably tailored and pressed. The man's impressive belly protruded over his belt, concealing the waistline of his trousers.

"What's up?" the older attorney asked.

The younger lawyer looked up. Several pieces of correspondence sat on the desk in front of him. He wasn't interested in the other mail. Danny Aitkins was only interested in the Order.

"That asshole McNab. He dismissed the Anderson claim, suis sponte, without Thompson even filing a motion."

"What the hell are you talking about?" Emery queried.

"Here," Daniel said, handing his father the legal document.

There were few occasions when father and son actually worked together. Their egos were so charged; they had determined early on that the office would be better served if they kept a working distance from each other. It was unusual for Danny to take Emery into his confidence.

"Of all the pompous arrogance. What the hell does that little primrose asshole know about hogs, the value of litters, or any Goddamnthing, for that matter?"

Emery's eyes, clear and without the need of artificial assistance at seventy years old, studied his young partner.

"Well, what the hell do you do now?" the older man asked.

"The dismissal is for failure to state a federal diversity claim. It's without prejudice. The only thing I can do is re-draft the Complaint and bring the case in State Court," Danny stated.

"What about Davidson?"

Father and son had not said much to each other about the Pelletier case. Emery had tried to make casual conversation about the case's outcome several days after the verdict. His efforts had been rebuffed. Still, without delving into the specifics of the trial court's rulings in the Pelletier matter, the elder Aitkins knew Davidson. He'd tried dozens of cases against the judge when Davidson was a defense lawyer. He'd had enough matters in front of the senior judge of Becker County to know Davidson's demeanor on the bench. There wasn't a bone of compassion or empathy in the judge's makeup when it came to plaintiffs, regardless of the merits of a case.

"I'll have to file against Davidson if it gets assigned to him. I've got a fifty-fifty shot that he won't be assigned and that Judge Enwright will. I'll take Enwright in a minute. She's new but she's fair. I worked with her on the Civil Rules Task Force. Her heart is in the right place."

"Filing against the old man won't endear you to him."

"Dad, give me some fucking credit. After the looks and body language he exhibited in the Pelletier case, I'm convinced he poisoned the jury. There's no way that case should have been a defense verdict. I won't let him hear this case."

Danny's voice grew loud. Anger built in his father's face.

"Fine. Do whatever it is you feel you need to do. Just don't toss another hundred grand into a pisshole," the elder Aitkins curtly warned.

Emery handed the document to his son and retreated. His abrupt departure was a matter of course. There had been many angry exchanges between father and son in the past. His father's reference to unreimbursed costs lost as a result of the Pelletier debacle reminded the younger attorney that the defeat had inflicted significant financial pain on their firm.

"Beth, get Dee Dee in here, will you?" Aitkins commanded over the intercom.

"What's gotten into you? You don't have to shout," the receptionist retorted, her words slightly slurred by a peppermint in her mouth.

101

The lawyer hadn't realized that the tone of his voice was still elevated from the exchange with his old man.

"Sorry. I'm just P.O.'d. Get Dee Dee for me, will you?"

"She's at lunch. I'll make sure she sees you as soon as she gets back."

Two weeks later, a revised Summons and Complaint, bearing the heading of the Minnesota District Court, County of Becker, was served upon Stevenson's. Within days, an Answer, nearly identical to the one filed in federal court, was provided by the defense. Aitkins filed his client's case with the clerk of court a day after the Answer came in.

Judge Davidson was assigned the file. Aitkins quickly served a Notice to Remove. Judge Harriet Enwright became the trial judge. There was talk on the street that Davidson was furious, that he had salivated at the prospect of presiding over the Anderson matter, a matter that had been profiled in the *Becker County Agricultural Gazette*, the local newspaper. *The Gazette* was a prime source of local information. August Johnson, the old Swede who owned the tabloid, came to the area from New York City after a stint as a reporter for the *New York Times* back in the late fifties.

An ardent Democrat in a predominantly Republican area of the State, Johnson regularly latched onto obscure causes and bits of news in an attempt to advance his personal political beliefs. He'd written a short piece on the Anderson lawsuit being filed in the context of foreign multi-nationals taking over all aspects of American agriculture. He'd pointed his toxic pen directly at the defendant.

Davidson wanted the case, wanted to rise to Johnson's challenge and try the lawsuit under the harsh light of journalistic scrutiny. He never got the chance because an upstart attorney took the old judge out of the game before it started.

Big Jim also filed a motion. He demanded the right to inspect the Anderson Farm, to bring in a team of scientists and veterinarians to secure water samples from the farm's wells, blood and tissue samples from the Andersons' hogs, and generally scour the place in search of alternative causes for the abortion storm.

Dan Aitkins knew better than to oppose the motion. He had already funded similar excursions by Dr. Elias Guttormson, the Andersons' local vet, and Dr. Thomas, the toxicologist from NDSU. The results of those inspections were pending. Dean Anderson assured Daniel that the tests would be negative for swine diseases.

"We had a little bout of pneumonia sometime back," his client had disclosed, "but we vaccinated the herd and we haven't had a problem in over three years."

"What about your management practices? The wells you use? Any other possibilities as a cause for the abortions?" Danny had asked.

"We're clean."

Judge Enwright wouldn't hesitate to grant Thompson's motion. Aitkins advised Big Jim that there'd be no opposition to an inspection. Aitkins knew there would be many occasions to draw his battle sword as the case progressed towards trial. Contesting the obvious would not endear his clients' cause to the trial judge. Thirteen years of litigation had taught him to pick his battles, to choose his positions carefully.

The morning was an inferno. Heat waves rose off the tarred roadway as Danny Aitkins drove east through hills. Oaks, maples, aspen, and birch were in full leaf. Early June rains made the landscape blossom. White sunlight, abstract and pure, cloaked the rolling landscape. Waterfowl; mallards and wood ducks for the most part, sat contentedly upon the green water of small potholes along the roadside carefully shepherding newly hatched offspring. Aitkins glanced at his watch. His pickup truck didn't have a built-in clock. The defense inspection was set to begin at 9:00am. It was 8:30. He was still ten miles away. Danny pushed the accelerator towards the floor.

Three immaculate white vans, all stenciled with the same logo and corporate identity, *Swine Scientific and Agricultural Resources*, were parked along the edge of the Andersons' gravel drive. As Aitkins arrived, dozens of men and women outfitted in white rubber suits, reminiscent of alien invaders from a "B" movie, milled around the vans. One man towered above the others. Aitkins recognized Jim Thompson instantly.

"What in the world is going on?" Danny asked as he approached the defense lawyer.

"The suits aren't as daunting as they seem," Thompson explained. "They're for the protection of the Andersons' herd. Just in case anyone from our team was at another swine farm and forgot to wash off any debris or fecal matter from their clothing or boots, Dr. Bronski, our swine expert, insisted that we all wear these suits to preclude any possibility of outside contaminants affecting the animals or skewing the test results."

"Looks like you went a little overboard, Jim."

"That may be. But Stevenson's is taking this case very seriously. They're willing to spend what it takes to win."

"I can see that," Danny replied.

Aitkins watched the crowd of experts and technicians extracting testing equipment, notebook computers, and sampling devices from the vans. An insipid feeling of dread crept over him.

This is serious shit, Aitkins thought.

"Mind if I talk to my clients before you get started?" Danny asked.

"Not at all. We'll need a good half hour before we're ready," Thompson replied.

Dean and Nancy Anderson stood in the shade of their home's covered front porch. The farmer raised a glass tumbler to his lips as Aitkins approached. Whole milk; warm, thick, and freshly squeezed from the udder of one of the farm's milk cows, flowed down Dean Anderson's throat in a single, audible swallow.

"What in the world is going on?" Dean Anderson asked.

There was an edge of concern to the man's voice.

"They're here to inspect the place like we talked about," Aitkins explained.

"I know that. But a dozen people? Maybe we should have fought them on this."

"We went over that," Dan emphasized. "Judge Enwright would've granted the motion no matter how we argued it. Like I explained, I'd rather not waste time fighting things we can't win. Let's save our fight for the real war in front of the jury."

Aitkins felt the focus of Nancy Anderson's eyes. Her gaze was, in many ways, predictable. There was a sense of inevitability about her. It was something that Danny had come to appreciate from the many conversations he'd had with the Andersons. Throughout their talks, he'd noted a continuous fatalism, the recognition of being unable to control the outcome of events, lurking behind Nancy Anderson's pretty eyes.

"They should be done and out of here by noon," the lawyer advised.

"I hope so," the woman murmured.

"We've got a lot of work to do. Our replacement gilts are close to breeding. If we can get a good result from the new females, things might look a little better," Dean related, taking a deep breath of the close air. "It all depends on the boars and the weather. This heat isn't helping."

The farmer wiped his forehead with the sleeve of a blue flannel shirt. Aitkins noted that the needle of the thermometer on the house stood at eighty-seven degrees. It was a little past nine in the morning.

Thompson approached the porch accompanied by another tall man in an identical white uniform. Both men wore facemasks suspended around their necks. Hoods cloaked their heads. White latex gloves covered their hands. Thick rubber boots, white and spotless, concealed their feet. The big lawyer's companion displayed a meager face accented by a sparse beard and a thinly distributed mustache.

"Mr. Aitkins, I'd like you to meet Dr. Chuck Bronski, head of Swine Scientific. He's the fellow that will be coordinating our inspection."

"Pleased to meet you, Mr. Aitkins," Bronski said in a falsely gregarious voice.

Aitkins shook the man's gloved hand.

"Same here, Chuck."

Danny deliberately used the expert's first name, declining to legitimize the man by calling him "doctor". He knew Bronski was a veterinarian by trade, a world-renowned consultant on swine diseases and nutrition, a man who operated a multi-million dollar firm from the relative obscurity of Wadena, Minnesota, a little wayside rest of a town in Central Minnesota. Aitkins didn't see the need to emphasize the man's expertise in front of the Andersons.

"We're ready to start. Dr. Bronski thought taking the tissue and blood samples from the boars, gilts, and sows should be the first order of business. That way your clients can get back to farming. We'll do the feed, soil, water, and air samples after that."

"Dean and I'll walk with you, if you don't mind," Aitkins said.

Thompson conferred with the expert before replying.

"Dr. Bronski sees no problem with that but you'll have to wear a suit. Never know what you might have brought with you on your clothes. Mr. Anderson is fine as he is, given that this is his place and whatever he's got on him came from his own herd," the defense attorney stated.

"You gotta be kidding. I'm not wearing one of those outfits," Aitkins objected.

"Has to be that way if you're coming along to observe," Thompson insisted.

Aitkins began to sweat a few minutes into the ordeal. Restricted by the impervious membrane of the white suit, beads of moisture formed in recesses of his body. After a half-hour, his clothes were drenched as the farmer and his attorney accompanied the team of scientists from structure to structure. Dean explained the day-to-day operation of his swineherd as the inspection progressed. In each building, including those inhabited by unaffected animals, technicians drew blood and acquired tissue samples from the animals. Under the dim artificial lighting of the shelters, Dr. Bronski and two other vets carefully examined selected animals, taking temperatures, listening to heart sounds, inspecting the overall health of the herd.

Several hours later, Danny Aitkins removed his suit and deposited it in a canvas sack marked "decontamination" next to the last of the white vans. His blue jeans and red "We Fest" golf shirt

105

were soaked through and his hair; short, blond, and matted, hung limp, as if someone had dumped a bucket of water over his head.

"That should do it," Thompson remarked as he helped Dr. Bronski place a tray of plastic bottles filled with well water into a small refrigerator in the cargo area of a van.

Despite the heat and the constriction of the suit, Big Jim's hair, the fibers coiled neat and tight against his sable scalp, appeared dry; his blue short-sleeved dress shirt and vibrant red tie appeared crisp and untouched by sweat.

He's one cool customer, Aitkins thought. *He'll be trouble in the courtroom.*

"Thanks for your hospitality, Mr. and Mrs. Anderson. Dan, I'll be in touch," the big man said as he entered the lead van.

Twelve rubber wheels bit into the hard-packed gravel of the driveway as the vehicles drove away. Dust rose in the hot air, drifted across the brittle dry grass of the lawn, and settled on the broad wooden steps of the front porch.

"I hope you're up to dealing with this sort of thing," Nancy Anderson offered as she watched the caravan turn onto the asphalt highway. "That colored fellow seems to know what he's doing."

Aitkins didn't respond to his client's comment. His immediate attention was focused on the sudden onset of a headache.

CHAPTER 12

Big Jim Thompson was as smart a lawyer as the State of Minnesota had ever seen. Despite the fact that he'd been born and raised in the Fargo-Moorhead area, not far from the venue of the Anderson trial, Detroit Lakes being less than an hour's drive east on US Highway 10 from Moorhead; despite the self-proclaimed egalitarian nature of the people of the Great Plains when it came to issues of race and culture, Thompson knew that the appearance of a black attorney defending a multi-national corporation against the allegations of a local white farmer, would sorely test the notions of racial neutrality aspired to by the good citizens of Becker County.

Ignoring skin color and religious differences come easy when a black man isn't in your backyard accusing your Lutheran neighbor and his saintly wife of trying to pull the wool over the eyes of a local jury. Thompson needed help; someone respected by the community who would act as a buffer for the ingrained bias against an urban African American asking tough questions. There was only one man that fit the bill; a stellar defense lawyer and someone intimately connected to the pulse of the people of Western Minnesota.

"Mr. Barnes. Jim Thompson. We've met a few times at the Minnesota Defense Lawyer conventions in Duluth."

The call had been an easy one for Thompson to make. His only worry was that Barnes' ego would intervene and derail the notion of hiring F.W. Barnes as local counsel on the case. Barnes likely wasn't happy that Stevenson's, a company he ordinarily represented, chose a Minneapolitan to defend the Anderson claim. Thompson sensed his hunch on this point was accurate from the slow, acidic tone present in the older attorney's response.

"I recall meeting you, Mr. Thompson. Impressive man, as I recall. Big fellow."

"Bigger than some, smaller than the present governor," Thompson admitted. "At any rate, I don't suppose you've heard about the case that Dan Aitkins has going against Stevenson's Sci-Swine?"

There was a pause. Thompson guessed that Barnes was struggling with a response. *However he answers*, Thompson thought, *Barnes' words will be well thought out.*

"Sure, I've heard of the claim. Done quite a bit of work for Stevenson's in the past," the older man disclosed.

The unstated premise behind the comment was Barnes' burning question: *why would Stevenson's hire some yahoo from the Twin Cities to defend a case in my backyard?*

"Well, and this is between us as attorneys who are representing and have represented Stevenson's, there's a lot more at stake here than a six figure damage claim," Big Jim related.

The telephone line remained silent. Thompson imagined the steady beat of the older man's heart as Barnes considered the matter.

"How so?"

"I can't go into all of the details but suffice it to say that it's unlikely that Anderson is the only farmer who received pelleted feed with a potential for causing problems. I'm not saying Stevenson's knows anything for certain but there are financial considerations present in this case that are infinitely more serious than one farm being affected," James Thompson advised.

"You mean that this thing has the possibility of erupting into a class action?"

Business owners of every stripe deplore similarily-situated plaintiffs joining together in class action lawsuits; whether advanced in cases alleging the concealment of the harmful effects of asbestos, fraudulent inducement claims aimed at Big Tobacco, or in discriminatory employment lawsuits targeting large employers. Barnes' intuition was astute. Thompson moved on.

"It's a possibility. We're still trying to track down the potential cause of the Anderson abortion storm. It may well have been precipitated by disease insidious to the plaintiffs' farm and totally unrelated to the pelleted feed. Test results are pending. But for damage control purposes, the folks in Winnipeg have made it clear. And the orders from world headquarters in Paris, where no one gives a good Goddamn that the legal system we're working under has nothing to do with the Civil Code of France, are to fight this thing to the death. Scorched earth. No prisoners."

Barnes remained quiet as the big man took a breath.

"I want you to be local counsel. I've heard good things. This case needs the touch of regional adeptness that I can't bring to the table. What do you say?"

There was hesitancy in Barnes' response. Thompson believed it was for effect; that the old man was jumping to get on board, to begin ringing up the hundreds of billable hours the case would require.

"When you say 'local counsel' just what does that mean? There are lots of ways to be 'local counsel'-from merely appearing as a figurehead at hearings to rolling up one's sleeves and getting down and dirty," Barnes said.

"The later. You'd be right there with me, in the thick of it. I answer to Winnipeg. I'll be directing the ebb and flow of the case in terms of strategy. But you'll be in on the day-to-day decisions."

"Sounds like one hell of a fight. Young Aitkins is a smart kid. But I don't think his firm has much left in its coffers for a war chest. I just beat the pants off him in a medical mal case that I should have lost," Barnes revealed.

Thompson sensed the old man was reluctant to finish his thought.

"Why do you say that?"

"How's that?" Barnes asked, his attention elsewhere.

"Why were you able to win a case you shouldn't have?"

Silence hung between the men. Barnes' voice was soft and deliberate as he replied.

"The dead girl was Indian. That might not make much of a difference in the Twin Cities but it meant everything up here."

Thompson felt apprehension settle over his mind. Concern came to rest in the place he retreated to whenever he recalled incidents of racial prejudice and hatred he'd experienced during his life. Despite his internal discomfort, Thompson didn't hold the admission against Barnes.

"That's why I'm calling. Stevenson's wants me on the case," Thompson continued. "I've done a lot of multi-national litigation for them on cases far larger than this one. They didn't suggest local counsel. I did. I'm a realist. As a black man, even though I grew up in Fargo, I know these people. They're as nice as pie on the outside. But on the inside, they're no different than Crackers from Mississippi. I can't let my pride get in the way of the realities of life. We need you, Frank. What do you say?"

No one called F.W. Barnes by his first name. Not his wife Lillian, not his surviving son, Samuel, and certainly not someone he'd only met under the most casual of circumstances. Barnes let the error pass.

"What's my billable rate?" F.W. asked.

"That's up to me. I have carte blanche to spend whatever I need to stuff a sock in this case. I'm billing out at my normal hourly rate for complex litigation."

"And what might that be?"

"Be realistic, Frank. The legal market in Fergus Falls is a little cheaper than in the Twin Cities. I'm billing at three hundred and fifty dollars an hour."

"Two hundred and fifty per hour is what I charge for similar work," the old man announced.

"That'll be fine. Do you folks have a good local investigator we can use to run down a few things?"

"Bobby Morgan. Ex-Chief of Police in Detroit Lakes. He's a bulldog with a soft bite. Why?"

"Dr. Bronski, the chief veterinarian we've got working on the case..."

"I know Bronski," Barnes interrupted. "He's a consultant to most of the big swine operators in the Midwest. Farrow to finish hog expert, as I recall."

"That's the guy. He's from Wadena. Anyway, he's fairly certain there's disease in the Anderson herd. Even if it isn't the actual cause of the abortions, if there's a bug present, we can use it to our advantage. I'd like to send an investigator to talk to Anderson's customers to see if any of them experienced health problems in their herds after buying pigs from the plaintiffs," Thompson advised.

"Morgan's your man. He's out of town right now on another job. I'll have him call you when he gets back," Barnes agreed.

"That'd be fine. I'll be up in your area again next week. We can sit down and go over the case in more detail. Until then, keep our little discussion just between us, OK?"

Barnes noted a hint of uncertainty in Big Jim Thompson's voice. By reputation, Big Jim was calm, cool, and collected even in the most heated courtroom struggle. Barnes wanted to ask the man a little more about the lawsuit. The old man wanted to dig a little deeper into whatever secrets Thompson held in confidence but F.W. Barnes' inquiry was left for another day.

CHAPTER 13

Pitiless rain assaulted the cab of Dean Anderson's Ford F250 King Cab as the vehicle ran a two-lane highway deep into Eastern North Dakota. Dan Aitkins sat in silence in the front passenger seat as the truck's oversized radials hummed along the wet pavement. Their first stop was Lisbon, a tiny crossroads situated on the Sheyenne River southwest of Fargo. The rain was as unrelenting as it was false, a momentary squall rolling in across the flatness of the land. There was not enough substance behind the weather to undo weeks of heat or to spell the arid atmosphere.

"Tell me again what Hansmeyer said," the lawyer urged after a considerable lapse in conversation.

The farmer stared straight ahead. Though Aitkins didn't know his client all that well, it was clear that the man's mind, in fact the entirety of his being, was full of rancor. Only after a lengthy pause did Dean Anderson finally reply.

"He said that a private investigator showed up at his place and started asking all kinds of questions. About how many feeders he buys from me in a year, about whether he'd ever had any problems with my hogs."

The truck lurched across a significant pothole in the blacktop. Overhead, the clouds began to part. Hesitant drops of water spattered the windshield as they drove out into sunshine.

"But that wasn't the half of it. The guy started saying how my pigs are infected with haemophilus: that pneumonia likely erupted on my farm and wiped out my breeding stock. That's the part that frosts me. Spreading lies, the sonofabitch."

Anderson's grip on the neoprene steering wheel became excruciatingly tight. Aitkins studied his client's face, contemplating what to say.

"There's the turn onto Number 32. It's only a few miles to Everett's place from here," the farmer muttered between clenched teeth.

The Ford passed the hamlets of Englevale and Elliot before turning onto a dry gravel road leading into the Hansmeyer Farm. The landscape was parched and vacant except for a grove of wilted cottonwood trees lining the river. The Sheyenne River itself was thirsty. A desperate sun hung above the cultivated fields. The Ford passed farm after farm of planted cropland. Nothing looked healthy; not the corn, shriveled and dry; not the soybeans, short and brittle; not the cereal grains, small and withered.

Just after Englevale, Anderson made a sharp left onto a path leading through a tumbled down two-plank fence. There had once been white paint on the boards. Now the fence was mostly bare wood weathered by the prairie sun.

"Everett's a pretty shrewd guy," Aitkins' client revealed. "He always makes a good deal on my feeders. Simple operation he has here. All he does is raise other people's hogs from forty pounds to butcher weight. He's strictly a finisher. Dabbles in some fancy Indian cattle, supposed to be able to live without much water, eat the worst weeds and grass, and out-produce other stock. Another one of those 'newest and best things' waiting to take off."

"From what you've told me, he's pretty wary of buying anymore hogs from your farm at this point," the lawyer observed.

"Wary? He's heading for the hills. He usually buys three or four times a year. Good orders. He's not buying squat now, all on account of that investigator from Stevenson's."

Aitkins let his client's words sink in. The truck pulled up to the Hansmeyer spread. The home was a traditional two-story farmhouse. The structure's presentation was defined by an enclosed screen porch. Fresh yellow paint and white trim accented the neat and tidy atmosphere of the dwelling. Pansies and marigolds framed both sides of the concrete walk leading to the home's front door. A rusted International pickup and a pristine Cadillac Eldorado occupied an area immediately in front of an old garage. The siding of the utility building matched the weathered entry fence. The garage's white paint was significantly absent. It had been the better part of a decade since its pine clapboards saw paint. Carefully trimmed lilac bushes delineated the perimeters of the buildings. The poured concrete foundation of the farmhouse was painted white, matching the home's trim.

"Hansmeyer keeps a neat place, don't he? Not a twig or blade of grass out of place," Anderson murmured as the two men exited the truck. "Said he'd be in the first finishing barn when I talked to him. It's right out back."

Both visitors were dressed in cowboy boots, denim jeans, and short-sleeved shirts. The farmer wore a white T-shirt. Daniel wore a polo shirt with the brand name of a horse dewormer embroidered across the base of a pocket located just above the lawyer's heart. The two men walked briskly despite somber heat.

"How you fellas doing?" a voice called out as they approached the low profile of the first of the pole buildings. The steel sides of four identical barns gleamed white in the summer air. Yellow roofs reflected waves of hot air into the atmosphere. A strapping man of more than six and a half feet stepped out of the doorway of the barn and extended his right hand in greeting.

"Sorry about the situation, Dean. Hope you understand."

"Everett, we've been doing business for over ten years. If I had a disease problem in my herd, you'dve heard about it from me."

"I'd like to think that's the case. But the fellow from the law firm, he really got to me. I'm afraid until the dust clears, I'll have to buy elsewhere. Once your pigs have a clean bill of health, that'll change things."

Hansmeyer offered a calloused hand to Aitkins.

"You must be the lawyer fella Dean is so high on. Sorry I'm such a mess but your client didn't give me much notice. I'm short handed: the wife's in Fargo at some craft doings at the Mall. My boy is at the elevator getting supplements for the cattle. You caught me a little off-guard."

Aitkins studied the man. Hansmeyer's grip was firm but not exhaustively so. There was a look of skepticism, of wariness in the farmer's eyes that told Aitkins it would be a long time before Dean Anderson sold any more pigs to Everett Hansmeyer.

"Here's the thing, Mr. Hansmeyer..." Daniel Aitkins began.

"Ev," the man interrupted. "Call me Ev."

"OK, Ev. The thing is, I'd like to know exactly what this investigator said. I think I know the man. The Barnes Firm uses him all the time. Guy by the name of Bobby Morgan. Used to be the Chief of the Detroit Lakes Police until he got caught with his pants down at a stag party for his nephew. He and one of the strippers got a little too cozy for Mrs. Morgan and the upstanding citizens of DL. He took his retirement and moved to Fergus. Got divorced. Don't think he married the stripper, though I heard they were living together. Anyway, that's the kind of man you're dealing with."

"Come on inside," the farmer motioned, ignoring the attorney's revelation. "I've got some fresh lemonade in the fridge. It'll do us all some good to get in out of the sun. It's too damn hot for June."

The men followed their host into the house. Aitkins surveyed the interior of the home as he sat down uneasily at the kitchen table. Nothing in the eating area had changed since the house was built in the 1940's. The gas range, the sink, the refrigerator were all vintage post-war manufacture. Painted wooden cupboards, the shelves open to the room save for drapes hanging from miniature curtain rods, lined three of the four walls. The fourth wall consisted of double-hung windows overlooking a vegetable garden. The garden wasn't much to look at. The summer had scorched the plants and seedlings past repair. Oak wainscoting covered the bottom third of the kitchen walls, the wood painted white with canary yellow trim: the exact reverse of the exterior color scheme of the home. Hansmeyer retrieved a glass pitcher, its surface clouded by pearls of moisture, and three glasses. A strong odor of hog permeated the room as the man poured lemonade into tumblers.

"I don't much care what this Morgan was or is except that he claimed he had information that Dean's hogs were infected with HPP at one time, hadn't followed protocol, and were likely carriers. Now, since I only deal in feeders and don't breed, HPP isn't going to wipe me out. But if my pigs come in contact with it, or I buy infected hogs and sell HPP positive stock, you know who's gonna get sued. It ain't gonna be just Dean. It'll be me."

"Ev, that's so much bull. We had HPP a few years back. But we vaccinated and have never had another problem once the disease ran its course. They're just trying to scare off my customers so I'll cave in and settle cheap. They've got to you; they got to the Amish folks down the road at Cogswell. Hell, they've talked to every last customer on the list I gave them as part of my Answers to Interrogatories. My sales are drying up as fast as the Sheyenne River because of these guys," Anderson advanced in a pleading voice.

The North Dakotan looked away. His message was firm.

"Dean, I just can't risk it. You get a Vet to sign off on your herd. Then we'll talk. Not before. This Morgan, he says they got proof that a farmer over in Wheaton just off the Mustinka River, some guy named Tynjala, bought some of your hogs at auction. He was going to use them as breeders, replacement gilts, I guess, and two weeks later, he had a massive HPP breakout. Nearly wiped him out. If that had been me who sold your pigs at auction, I'd be up to my rear end in lawyers just like you. No offense, Mr. Aitkins, but that's not a place I want to visit."

Their discussions with the Amish followed a similar pattern. The members of the religious community located near Cogswell, North Dakota, just north of the South Dakota line, were not open to purchasing Anderson hogs. Dean's major sources of feeder pig sales had evaporated.

Dusk settled to the west as they drove towards I-29 on Highway 11. Both men were tired: tired of driving, tired of the incessant sun, tired of the dryness. They were nearly to the freeway before Aitkins finally asked a question he'd been mulling over in his mind since they left the Hansmeyer Farm.

"Is there anyway this guy from Wheaton can support Morgan's claim that your hogs infected his animals with HPP?"

"That'd be Pavo Tynjala, the Finn," Anderson replied. "Lot's of flash, not much substance in terms of farming know-how. I didn't know he was desperate enough to resort to going to an auction for breeding stock."

"Whatdoyou mean?"

"Any hog man knows you don't go to an auction to buy breeding stock. If you're running a closed herd farrow to finish operation, you might occasionally buy feeders to fill up your grower-finisher barn. You'd quarantine 'em first, a minimum of thirty days, before you introduce them to your other finishing hogs. But you'd never be so stupid as to inject auction animals into a breeding operation. That's asking for trouble. The chance of a disease outbreak ruining your farrowings is too great. A bug kills off your little ones, well, you're in the same boat I am."

Aitkins looked out the passenger window and fingered the vinyl covered door panel of the Ford. The lawyer's eyes remained concealed from his client as he continued his questioning.

"Could some of the pigs you sold at auction have been HPP-positive? Is it possible that those pigs infected Tynjala's herd to the point where he had abortions in his sows and bred gilts?"

Aitkins felt a small component of pride well up inside. He'd quickly learned that a sow was a female breeding animal that had already raised a litter. Bred gilts were female pigs going through their first pregnancy.

Dean Anderson kept his eyes on the road as he responded to the question.

"HPP doesn't cause massive abortion storms. That's a red herring. It can cause the odd abortion; it can certainly make pigs ill and listless, even kill adults if they're not treated. But large scale abortions? That's not HPP."

The farmer frowned as he finished his statement. A touch of uncertainty appeared behind Dean Anderson's coal black eyes, an uncertainty that was unsettling to Danny Aitkins.

CHAPTER 14

Bobby Morgan hit them all. He didn't miss a trick in meeting with Dean Anderson's customers and spreading it on thick. He used all the techniques he'd learned as a cop to leave small shadows of doubt in the minds of Anderson's connections, shadows strong and certain enough to cut off the farmer's economic lifeblood.

Danny Aitkins suspected that the ex-policeman hadn't crossed the line into the unethical or committed actionable libel. Morgan's words had been carefully chosen: his assertions were repeated as mere rumors, not stated as fact. Aitkins knew his client's farm was on the line. The bank would only hold off foreclosure for so long. It had been four months since the abortion storm. Feeder pig sales from the Anderson place had dried up. Butcher hog prices were in the tank. His clients were desperate. Civil litigation moved slowly, Aitkins had warned them, sometimes too slowly.

"He can't get away with talking to my customers and leaving the wrong impression, can he?" Dean Anderson had asked.

"It's not nice, but then, commercial lawsuits rarely are," the attorney had counseled. "Your herd had HPP, in fact, from the blood test reports that came back from NDSU, there are still remnants of the infection in your animals. Your herd may be asymptomatic. That doesn't mean that what Morgan told your customers wasn't true."

"It's a pile of crap. We haven't lost a hog to pneumonia in three years."

"Doesn't matter. You had or have HPP. That's what Morgan is telling folks. And since it's the truth, it's not defamatory."

"Can't you do something?"

Aitkins had paused and watched the blood drain from his client's face. They had been sitting in Anderson's study. The room was hot and close. The house was not air-conditioned. Even with all the windows open, the atmosphere was stifling. Dean Anderson sat in front of his PC, the screen blank, as he thumbed reams of bills and receipts for expenses that he couldn't meet.

"I can take a stab at threatening a libel suit. But I don't think it'll have much impact. We're playing with the big boys here and they don't scare easily," the lawyer had advised.

"Bobby Morgan is one horse's ass," Daniel Aitkins observed a few days later while seated in the conference room of the Barnes Law Firm in downtown Fergus Falls.

"Aitkins, watch your language," F.W. Barnes retorted, casting a reproachful gaze in Dan's direction.

"He's been running all over making untrue assertions to the Andersons' customers."

"How so?"

Aitkins was dressed in a short-sleeved shirt and khaki slacks as he studied the defense lawyer's demeanor. A cheap Daffy Duck necktie, one his wife bought him for a long-departed birthday, hung loose around Dan's throat. The top button of his shirt was open in a futile attempt to forestall perspiration.

Barnes was dressed in a light blue custom-tailored summer-weight suit. Pinstripes accented the light cotton fabric of his outfit. A blue tie broke up the starched white of the defense attorney's shirt. The cuffs of his garment broke at the wrists, exactly where they were supposed to. Silver cufflinks secured the sleeves. The old man's hair was meticulously groomed. Waves of silver cascaded across his head in neat rows. There was no hint of sweat anywhere about Barnes, something that Aitkins found utterly remarkable.

"He's been telling Andersons' customers that their herd is infected with HPP and, by inference, that the abortions on the Anderson place were caused by disease."

"Well?"

"It's not true."

Barnes folded his hands and placed them confidently upon the walnut surface of the conference table.

"Oh, please. You've seen the results of the blood tests from NDSU and Dr. Bronski. There's no doubt that your client has HPP in his herd. We've got scientific documentation that HPP causes abortions in sows and bred gilts. That's a part of our defense, that and the fact that your client used oil and lindane to fight mange in the dead of winter which accelerated the effects of the HPP."

Barnes' position was nothing new. There had been disclosures of the factual defenses claimed by Stevenson's in the Interrogatory Answers served upon Aitkins by Big Jim Thompson. Aitkins knew that Barnes was right: that while Morgan's intent in revealing information to Dean Anderson's customers was anything but honorable, no rules had been violated, no untruths had been told. Still, Aitkins wasn't about to concede.

"Bullshit, Barnes. Morgan went over the line when he told other customers that Tynjala's herd suffered losses due to HPP. There's no proof of that and Tynjala has never made a complaint to Dean Anderson on that score."

Barnes' eyebrows rose. A smirk crept slowly across his thin lips. Aitkins' flashed back to the times in his career when F.W. Barnes had caught him napping and stung him.

"But he will, Daniel, he will," Barnes promised. "He's going to bring a lawsuit against your clients for losses in the hundreds of thousands of dollars. Alan Ignatius of St. Cloud will be representing Mr. and Mrs. Tynjala. If I'm not mistaken, the Summons and Complaint is just about ready for service."

Aitkins' face, despite a significant tan, flushed crimson.

"You bastard. You know that Ignatius is an unscrupulous slime who'd sue his own mother for wrongful birth. The guy lost his judgeship in Stearns County for falsifying affidavits in his own lawsuit. As a lawyer, he's been disciplined by the Board of Professional Responsibility. You of all people should know the measure of Alan Ignatius."

It was clear that Aitkins' assault on Ignatius upset the defense lawyer. Barnes rose from his chair and leaned close to Aitkins as he spoke.

"Get out. Get out of my office, my building, my town. I don't want to see you again unless and until there's a court reporter or a judge present. Alan is a dear friend and a classmate. He had a rough go of it because of the bottle. He's straight and sober. He's a church going man who has redeemed himself. How dare you cast aspersions on him. How dare you."

"You're so full of shit," Aitkins' muttered angrily as he rose, intent upon leaving the room, "that your eyes should be brown instead of that crap-ass blue. I know what you're doing here, Barnes. You're fabricating a lawsuit to distract us, to draw our attention away from your slight of hand tactics."

Aitkins was nearly out the door when he turned and issued a parting shot.

"It won't happen again, old man. What happened in the Pelletier case will not happen again."

The defense lawyer chuckled to himself as Daniel Aitkins exited the building.

CHAPTER 15

The feeding trials at NDSU went well. The university staff fed pregnant rats the tainted grain. Besides noting significant feed refusal, culminating in an actual loss of weight in the gestating animals, the lab technicians discovered that all of the rodents in the study suffered massive and complete abortions of their litters. A control group fed pellets from another manufacturer gained appreciable weight and delivered their offspring without incident.

Mass gas spectrometer analysis of the feed taken from the bins at the Anderson Farm revealed that the pellets were contaminated with Mycotoxins, the poisonous residuals of fusarium mold.

"Give me the short course on Mycotoxins, Dr. Thomas," Dan Aitkins asked as he sat in the professor's office on the campus of North Dakota State University in Fargo. The office was really no more than a cubicle. Concrete blocks, painted manila white, formed the walls of the room. An imitation walnut door, its vinyl surface disturbed by a narrow window of thick glass, the glass reinforced with imbedded wire, occupied the better part of one wall. Metal brackets supported sagging bookshelves along the other three walls. Particleboard shelving held innumerable books. The shelves were demonstrably taxed by the plethora of research volumes and manuscripts.

A metal desk, institutional and inexpensive, tan in color and complimented by a swivel chair and two metal side chairs, was crammed beneath a break in the informal library. A couple of diplomas, a smattering of pictures of the professor's family boasting two grown daughters and a diminutive wife, and an assortment of framed quotations from Einstein and other scientists, defined the space above Thomas' desk. Two brand new Gateway computers, linked to the Veterinary Science Department's network, occupied the entirety of the work surface.

A CD in the DVD drive of one of the CPU's played *Something More Beside You*, a tune by the Cowboy Junkies, a Canadian alternative band with a distinctly smooth sound. Aitkins' feet tapped the floor in time to the music as the lawyer waited for Dr. Thomas to respond.

"Fusarium has been around as long as there have been plants," Thomas said. "Back in the 1920's, experts began to study the effects of wet conditions on cereal grains, including corn. Used to call it 'scab'. There've been a lot of horrific outbreaks of fungus over the years. Recently, it's hit our area hard, harder than in the past. There's no question that moisture is the operative environmental factor causing these outbreaks. Fusarium, in all its sub-forms, is always around. But it becomes epidemic during wet years."

Ivan Thomas looked like a scientist. The professor hadn't converted from the thick plastic eyeglass frames of his youth. Small tufts of white hair stood up behind Thomas' ears. His scalp was flecked with brown age spots. The spots had once been freckles. Somehow the blemishes had merged together to form deformities in the man's sunburned scalp. The professor's short, compact form was covered in large part by a white lab coat. The North Dakota sun had scarred his small ears. Bright pink skin revealed itself where the weather had stripped away old layers of tissue.

"Dr. Stack of our faculty prepared this report," Thomas said, handing Aitkins a manuscript of several pages. "It's a little technical but it gives you a good understanding of where fusarium comes from and how long it's been studied. You can keep this."

"Thanks," Aitkins responded, accepting the document. "I've wondered how a farmer who grows grain, or a company that mills feed is supposed to be able to tell when fusarium is present. Is there an easy way to detect the presence of Mycotoxins, some method that elevators use?"

"Mycotoxins themselves require sophisticated analysis under a mass spectrometer. That's expensive equipment requiring someone with years of specialized training to operate. But noting the presence of fusarium itself, the mold if you will, isn't tricky. Odor, the smell of must in a handful of grain, is the best way to detect fusarium. Some elevators also use black light to show the presence of mold. That's not uncommon. It's relatively fool-proof and cheap technology."

Aitkins slid his chair across the linoleum to better hear the professor.

"Here's some information I pulled off the Internet from the Canadian Grain Commission," Thomas advised. "Stevenson's home office in Winnipeg works with the Commission. They're the governing body in Canada regarding the inspection and grading of Canadian Grain. There are similar regulatory bodies in the States that companies, like Stevenson's, must answer to."

Additional papers passed between the men.

"But what about this particular case? Your report was a little hard for me to understand, what with the abbreviations and all," Aitkins asserted.

"There's a good study from North Carolina included in the paperwork I just gave you. It really lays out the Mycotoxin/fusarium situation quite nicely. The bottom line is that, even though the government, American or otherwise, may set out certain 'safe' limits for various Mycotoxins in livestock feed, there's a lot more to it than artificial limits."

"How so?"

"Observation can tell a farmer far more than scientific analysis. How an animal, be it pig, horse, or cow, reacts to feed can be a real tip-off. Where there's initial feed refusal, as was demonstrated in the rats we used, that's a good indicator something's amiss. Once an animal gets hungry enough, initial refusal can be overcome. But noting it in the first instance tells us all is not right with the feed. And the number one cause of feed refusal in swine is the presence of mold in the feed."

"Fusarium?"

"Now you're tracking. Identifying the genus of fusarium is the next step. In the samples we received, the mold itself wasn't preserved to a degree where we could make that determination. What's left are the Mycotoxins, the poisonous offspring, so to speak, of the mold. DON-deoxynivalenol, was found in the Anderson sample. The Canadian studies talk about DON levels of one part per million, 1ppm, or greater, as being toxic to swine. At lower levels, there can be partial feed refusal. At higher levels, there can be a total abhorrence to eating the tainted grain. The levels found in the Anderson sample were 2ppm or so. That's enough to account for temporary feed refusal in both swine and rats. But that doesn't address the issue of the abortions."

Aitkins had reviewed the feed analysis done by NDSU. He knew that other Mycotoxins, poisons with impossible to pronounce names, had been detected. He was uncertain of the importance of the findings.

"DON, unless it's found in huge amounts, doesn't cause reproductive problems," Thomas continued. "What we look for is zearalenone. That's a Mycotoxin that, even in miniscule quantities, and we're talking parts per billion, or ppb, can wipe out the reproductive abilities of a gestating sow or gilt."

"That's listed in the report you sent me," Aitkins observed. "I remember trying to pronounce that word."

"We found it all right, in concentrations of between 35 and 100 ppb, depending upon the sample. There's no question, in my opinion, that zearalenone was the likely cause of the abortion storm. Look at this reference."

Thomas retrieved a report from the stack of documents he'd presented to the lawyer. Using his index finger, the scientist directed the attorney's attention to report.

"Read this. It confirms that zearalenone adversely affects the reproductive abilities of pregnant swine. It notes that the symptoms of zearalenone poisoning include reddening of the vulva, increased size of the vulva, and increased size of the mammary glands in early pregnancy, before the milk comes in. What's being described is the hyper-hormonal impact of the toxin: it unnaturally speeds up gestation to the point of causing 'embryonic mortality'-spontaneous abortion of incompletely formed piglets."

"But the study talks about levels of 100-200ppb," the lawyer corrected.

"There are other studies which indicate that if you have feed refusal and observation of physical symptoms regarding the reproductive tract, together with any significant level of the toxin, the feed is the culprit. There's no doubt in my mind that Dean Anderson's hogs were fed tainted pellets. And judging by the levels of DON found, the stuff used to form the pellets was terrible grain. Must have come in wet, hot, and full of fusarium mold."

Danny pushed himself away from the scientist's space and stood up, his outlook on the case appreciably brighter.

"Dean tells me that the pellets he bought from Stevenson's are some sort of new fangled mixture, 'FGP' I think he called them," Aitkins said. "Part corn, part soybean. Any idea which of the two components is responsible?"

"Can't tell for sure because we were unable to isolate the mold itself. But if I were a betting man, I'd bet on the corn. We've had more fusarium problems with corn. Plus the formula uses nearly three times as much corn as soy meal. Can't put a percentage on the probability other than to say that it's likely the corn is what caused Mr. Anderson's problems."

"Are you willing to stand behind these opinions at trial?"

"No question."

"What about HPP as a possible cause of the abortions?"

"Swine diseases are a little outside my area of expertise. But from what the Andersons' Vet tells me," the doctor paused, "what's his name?"

"Guttormson."

"Yes, I knew that. Guttormson says HPP isn't capable of causing widespread, immediate abortions. He'll state that, I believe, for the record."

"Yes, he's told me that."

"Then there shouldn't be a problem."

Aitkins thought for a moment as he studied the volumes of biology and plant pathology texts on the shelves.

"Is there anyone else you'd recommend me talking to? I don't mean to sound ungrateful. We want you to testify for the Andersons. But is there someone else in your field that you'd recommend as an additional source?"

Thomas strained hard at the lawyer. Aitkins winced, fearing that he'd upset the professor. The man's reply was absent any negative inflection.

"Robert Ojala at the University of Minnesota. He's the world's foremost expert on Mycotoxicology. I can run this by him, if you like."

"You know him?"

"Went to college with him. Bob's a great guy. He'll be happy to do me a favor. If he's agreeable, I'll hook you two up."

Aitkins' reached out with his right hand.

"I don't want you take this the wrong way. The Andersons appreciate everything you and NDSU have done. But one of the lawyers on the other side of this thing has burned me more than once. I want to make sure it doesn't happen again," the lawyer confided.

The men shook hands.

"No problem. You and I've worked together before. I'm old enough and wise enough to let you do your job," the professor advised.

The lawyer retreated. Dr. Thomas' voice called the attorney's attention back into the cubicle.

"Aren't you forgetting something?"

Dan Aitkins turned around. The professor approached the attorney with a letter sized-envelope.

"What's this?" the lawyer responded as he accepted the folio, adding it to the materials he was carrying.

"My bill," Dr. Thomas said through a significant smile.

CHAPTER 16

"The plaintiffs pass the jury for cause."

Becky Connor, the attorney representing Emil Johnson in the action against his father, left the podium and returned to her place behind a counsel table in the Becker County Courthouse.

Ms. Connor was a corpulent woman with short blond hair, cracked lips, and less than beautiful eyes. Her neck was full: her chins, multiple. In her early thirties and married to a local undertaker, Becky Connor was a chain smoker, a mother of three young girls, and an avowed work-a-holic. She was a stickler for detail in the courtroom, a person able to work long hours on minimal sleep.

"We'll take our morning break while the lawyers make their selections. Ladies and gentlemen of the jury, don't talk to anyone, including your fellow jurors, about this matter. You can shoot the breeze, make small talk, but don't discuss this lawsuit. Stay close by. You can smoke outside but be ready to come in when the bailiff calls you back."

Judge Harriet Enwright stood up. Her black robe flowed off her narrow shoulders towards the floor. She was young for a trial judge. She'd been appointed to the post a year earlier, a judicial selection of Governor Ventura, who, despite a litany of other faults, drew accolades from Becker County voters when he named Harriet Enwright to the bench.

The judge removed her robe in her chambers. Beneath the wool garment she wore a pair of casual slacks, a tan silk blouse, and well-used brown pumps. Her auburn hair was shoulder length. There was no sign of tan, or an attempt to tan, over any portion of her exposed flesh. Being young and new to the job, she worked long hours. She was unmarried, though seeing a fellow from Alexandria when their schedules allowed. She was thoroughly devoted to her job. She wanted to make her mark in the judiciary and to eventually ascend to the Minnesota Supreme Court. She knew that she didn't have the political connections to get there without working herself to the bone.

"Angie, could you come here a minute?" the judge called out softly to her court reporter, her right hand assistant.

Angie Devlin had been the court reporter for Judge Andrew Slattingren, Harriet's predecessor. Though the new judge had the option to hire whomever she chose to serve as stenographer, Judge Enwright felt duty bound to keep Angie on. Devlin was good at her job, which was a major consideration. And the new judge, while in private practice as a family lawyer, had represented Angie in her second divorce. She felt obliged, having been the woman's lawyer, to now become her boss.

"What's up?" Angie asked.

Devlin walked into the room wearing a brilliant red outfit: a carefully arranged skirt, matching jacket, and delicate pink blouse. Expensive pearls adorned her perfectly formed neck. Whereas the judge's clothing concealed her bust and her form, the court reporter's suit left the observer with little doubt as to her gender. Angie Devlin was all woman. From her bleach blond hair to her razor sharp artificial nails, painted a brazen red, Ms. Devlin was a looker.

"I need a couple of Tylenol," the judge moaned. "And a glass of water."

"Coming right up. Pretty tough case, eh?"

Angie was originally from Regina in the heart of the Canadian prairie. Her voice contained a subtle inflection of Canadian culture despite the fact she'd lived in the States for thirteen years.

"I just don't get it," Judge Enwright replied. "How can a son sue his own father. How can the man sleep nights?"

"He probably doesn't."

"You may be right. I wish to hell they'd settle this thing before the family is torn apart."

"That's the old family law attorney in you talking."

The judge walked to her desk and sat heavily on the soft vinyl of her chair.

"You're probably right."

"I'll get you that Tylenol."

"Thanks."

Bright sunlight flooded the judge's office, her chambers, in the basement of the courthouse. Around her, diplomas, awards, and judicial appointment documents adorned the walls. There was a single photograph, a picture of her now-deceased parents, hanging behind her. She rarely looked at the portrait. Harriet's father had murdered her mother in a rage over her mom's inability to cook a decent meal. Then he stuck the handgun in his own mouth and left Harriet, an only child, without immediate family. That was back when she was getting her law degree at the University of Vermont. The picture was taken a month before the incident. It was one of the few photographs remaining from her earlier life. There was a knock on the heavy wooden door.

"Come in."

Becky Connor, representing the plaintiff; Dan Aitkins, representing Ben Johnson personally; and Tenley Adams, the attorney representing Ben Johnson's insurer, entered the judge's chambers.

"You got a minute judge?" Ms. Adams, an experienced insurance defense litigator in her mid-fifties asked.

"Sure. How can I help you?" the judge asked.

Tenley Adams, her platinum hair cut shoulder length, her waist and hips concealed by an oversized pantsuit, began.

"We've reached a settlement in this case, your honor."

"How so?"

Aitkins stood in front of the judge's desk and spoke up.

"Emil's waiving his claim for excess damages against his father."

"Waiving them, as in giving them up completely?" the judge inquired, a note of incredulity behind her words.

"That's right. The family finally sat down and talked. Emil's sisters persuaded him to accept the liability settlement previously offered by Ms. Adams," Becky Connor related.

"Sort of a sudden way to see the light, isn't it counselor?" the judge mused.

Aitkins spoke up again.

"In Becky's defense, she's been trying to get her client to listen to reason for months. He was told countless times that there was no more money short of collecting against his father's assets. His sisters finally got him to see the folly in that."

Empty space hung between the attorneys and the judge. White light filtered into the room through dirty panes of window glass. Specks of dust, fighting gravity, floated in the air.

"I'll draft the dismissal," Tenley murmured.

"That'll be fine. Tell your client, Ms. Connor, that he did the right thing."

"I'll tell him, judge."

The attorneys began to leave.

"Mr. Aitkins, a word with you if I might?" Judge Enwright asked as the female lawyers departed.

The trial lawyer rotated on his heels.

"Have a seat."

Aitkins claimed an uneasy perch on a vinyl-covered chair next to the jurist's desk.

"Dan, you know I'm assigned to the Anderson matter. I'm not going to say anything that could be construed as violating the Rules of Judicial Conduct."

There was a delay in the judge's delivery.

"But tell me, what's the status of the case?"

"We've got a scheduling conference coming up next month in front of you. Discovery is cooking along. No major problems," the attorney replied.

Dan wanted to tell her, to scream out at her, that the bastard Barnes was at it again, that Aitkins' client was on the verge of bankruptcy and that the defense was pulling out all stops to defeat him. But that would have been improper.

"I look forward to trying the case. Sounds interesting. Good lawyers on both sides. You got any help?"

A paternalistic tone infected Harriet Enwright's question. They were friends. She knew him, knew his moods, and his liabilities, including his affection for the bottle.

"I've got it covered."

Concern became obvious in the woman's eyes as she watched the lawyer's mouth trap the phrase.

"Take care of yourself, Daniel. And say hello to Julie for me."

"Will do," Danny mumbled as he departed.

After a moment of reflection, the judge donned her robe, opened the door, and walked back into her courtroom to explain to the jury that the case they were impaneled to hear had just been settled.

CHAPTER 17

Bruce Tollerude strolled down a sidewalk in downtown Fargo under the constant impression of an August sun. He passed the building housing Prairie Public Broadcasting, a studio he'd visited during fund-raising telethons for the local PBS and NPR affiliates. His course brought him beyond the opulence of the Radisson Hotel. At the Fitzsimmons Building, an old sandstone structure rising four stories above the banks of the Red River, the attorney turned, pushed the hard glass of a revolving door, and entered.

Tollerude wasn't much past forty but he was a force throughout the Red River Valley in terms of deal making. He had connections to every local economic development authority, through his own network or that of his wife Ingrid, a woman of independent means and a distant relation to the Cargill Family, purveyors of grain and commodities; the largest family-owned business in the State of Minnesota. Bruce Tollerude held positions on many boards of directors for local manufacturing, agricultural, and software companies. As a lawyer, Tollerude often skirted the Rules of Professional Responsibility by acquiring equity positions in commercial concerns, trading billable hours for economic ties to companies that looked to be on the rise.

Together, he and Ingrid made a formidable financial duo. There was no love, no shred of decent marital existence between them beyond the money. Neither of them particularly cared. It was a union they had both contemplated knowingly, trading emotion for stability. There were no children. There would never be any children.

"Bruce Tollerude to see Alan Upton."

The lawyer announced his presence to a male receptionist in the lobby of the Fitzsimmons Building. An irradiant white and blue sign loomed behind the desk, proclaiming that Tollerude was standing in the lobby of the Fargo branch of The First Farmer's Bank of Montreal.

"Go right in. First door on the right, Mr. Tollerude. Mr. Upton is expecting you."

Tollerude moved with surprising agility. His brown hair remained perfectly in place as he paced towards the Vice-President's office. Though he was a large man, the lawyer's ambulation defied his size: a residual benefit of the many hours of tennis and handball the counselor had played over his lifetime. His dark pinstriped suit was perfectly matched to his physique. His black wingtips were polished to luminosity.

"So good to see you, Bruce," the banker gushed.

Upton extended his right hand and ushered the lawyer into the Vice Presidential office.

The banker was very young. Twenty-seven. He'd been hired as Head Teller right out of college, becoming Assistant Personnel Director a year later. His deft handling of several sexual harassment claims, cases he worked on with Tollerude's associate, the now deceased Michael Barnes, elevated Upton, first to Special Assistant to the President in Montreal, and then, upon his return to his hometown of Fargo, North Dakota to Vice President of the Bank's regional flagship location.

"Please, have a seat."

"I always enjoy talking to the Midwest's smartest young executive," the lawyer said with false sincerity. If the banker detected the barrister's condescension, he didn't let it show.

There were no windows in the office. The building had been remodeled to accommodate the regional bookkeeping and computer functions of the bank. With the changes, the old President's office (the building had once housed an independent family-owned bank) was wiped away, and with it, a wondrous view of the River from the top floor of the structure had disappeared.

Upton was relegated to a small and decidedly mundane space on the ground floor where he kept tabs on his immediate charges when not overseeing the banking chain's national and international interests. The upper three floors of the building were reserved for Regional Operations. The Vice-President spent most of his time there, unless there were men and women of importance on the property. Those folks he greeted in his office, such as it was.

"This just a social call? Another pitch for more donations to Ducks Unlimited or the Nature Conservancy?"

"Hardly. I've got a serious problem," Tollerude disclosed.

"You don't normally bank with us, Bruce. Tied into Wells Fargo pretty heavily, as I recall."

"It's not a personal situation. Client related."

Upton's eyes, little pods of distorted color, scrutinized the big man seated in front of him.

"How so?"

"Stevenson's Sci-Swine, the Canadian feed manufacturer and elevator owner is one of our biggest clients."

"One of our largest depositors as well. They have sizeable payroll and loan accounts with just about every Minnesota, North Dakota, and Iowa branch of Farmer's."

Another pause. Recognition crept into Tollerude's eyes. The gesture didn't make it to his lips.

"But somehow, I get the sense that you knew that," the banker said.

"Of course. You can't represent a business client like Stevenson's and not know where the assets and liabilities are. And it's the liability portion of the equation that brings me here."

Upton knew the history of Stevenson's. Beginning as a family-owned elevator and granary in Winnipeg, the company had blossomed at the end of the Great Depression, displacing many rural cooperatives across both the Canadian and the American Midwest. The company was just a tick behind Cargill with respect to the bottom line. In the deregulation and consolidation craze of the 1980's, a French concern, Justere' Decroix, made a bid for every outstanding share of Stevenson's stock. In one swift move, Justere' acquired the grain giant and began to make an assault on the American feed and commodities industry with aggressive marketing and cutthroat pricing. The company was healthy, as healthy as it had ever been. Tollerude's disclosure puzzled Upton. He was unaware of any recent liabilities incurred by the French grain concern.

"I haven't heard of any significant problems within Justere's. Given my principal's connections, I would have heard about anything of importance on the radar screen."

Tollerude moved uneasily against the smoothness of the leather chair. A look of conflict cascaded across his face.

"What I'm about to tell you is confidential and cannot be revealed to anyone outside this room. Understood?"

Upton nodded.

"We're, my firm that is, is involved in a little lawsuit with a farmer from Detroit Lakes by the name of Dean Anderson. A small farrow to finish hog operator. Anderson claims he bought some pelleted feed from Stevenson's Detroit Lakes' elevator, fed it to his gestating sows and bred gilts, and suffered abortions in his herd. Claims all of his litters were wiped out."

"Any chance of settlement?"

"Tried that. Des Moines office of Stevenson's made a very reasonable offer, which was immediately rejected. Our firm is working with Jim Thompson of Minneapolis. There's a local guy on the other side, a guy who's questionable in terms of ethics and ability. We've handled cases against his firm for years. Any way, our marching orders from Winnipeg, and of course, from Paris, are to dig in and defeat the claim. No holds barred, no further offers."

The banker raised a plastic container of Red River Wash, a local brand of bottled water that had no connection to the neighboring river other than the fact it was bottled in Moorhead, to his lips. Upton drew heavily from the container before asking his next question.

"Was there something wrong with the feed?"

It was an imprudent inquiry. Upton meant it as such. He was uncertain of the lawyer's intentions and wanted to flush them out and get down to the essence of the meeting.

"Anderson says the feed was contaminated with mold. Mycotoxins."

"Microtoxins?"

"Common mistake. No, Mycotoxins. Poisons created by mold."

"Any proof of it?"

"Not much. And it looks like Andersons' pigs were infected with disease at the time they were fed our client's pellets."

"So why are you here? Seems to me that Stevenson's is on top of things," the banker observed.

The words were tinged with a level of impoliteness meant to prompt the attorney to move the dialogue along.

"Things should go fine in front of a jury. But you never know. We've drawn an inexperienced judge, Harriet Enwright, a woman with very little history in terms of complex litigation. Can't tell where she'll come down on important issues like summary judgment and damages. Winnipeg wants us to put pressure on Anderson and his lawyer."

"Pressure? Like interrogatories, depositions, motions, that sort of litigation stuff?"

"Pressure from outside sources."

"Such as?"

"We've already cut off Andersons' feeder pig sales. Our investigator made some inquiries of the plaintiffs' chief customers. They're all off the grid for now. But we need to push Anderson to the wall. We've told him we won't offer another settlement. But that's posturing. We will. But we want him soft and compliant before we get to that point."

Upton drained the last of the bottled water. His voice grew insistent.

"What does Farmer's Bank have to do with any of this?"

The attorney stroked his chin. His facial skin was smooth and tan from hours of playing doubles tennis under the prairie sun at the Fargo Tennis Club. Tollerude reached across the space between his chair and the edge of Upton's desk and delicately but firmly placed his right hand on the thick plate glass protecting the desktop.

"Chase House."

"The manager of our Detroit Lakes branch?"

"The same."

"And?"

"We want you to talk to him."

"About what?"

"About calling in Anderson's line of credit and foreclosing their mortgage," the lawyer revealed.

Upton's eyes drifted to the ceiling. His hands clasped the arms of his chair in a grip of defiance.

"That's not a call I'm about to make. Chase knows his customers, knows whether Anderson is good for the money or not."

Tollerude moved to the edge of his seat. He was all over the banker like a hungry mosquito on the naked ass of a camper. His eyes spread wide, his teeth became visible as he spoke.

"So you'd risk Stevenson's pulling their accounts from every Farmer's Bank in the Midwest and going over to Wells Fargo just for the sake of preserving appearances?"

The threat hung between the two men like a boulder momentarily impeded by a tree during an avalanche.

"Are you trying to intimidate me? Because if you are, you can march your sanctimonious ass out of my office," the banker replied.

Upton's insult had no visible impact upon the lawyer.

"No one is trying to intimidate a multi-national banking corporation. I'm simply stating fact. Anderson is behind on his line of credit, which can be called by your bank anytime after sixty days of delinquency. He's also four payments behind on his mortgage. His sales figures for the last three months are dismal. On paper, by the numbers, he cannot survive another three months unless your bank continues to carry his obligations. I'm asking you to do what you're empowered to do by law. Call the loans."

"You want to take his farm away? That's a pretty drastic penalty for simply bringing a lawsuit. What's the downside for Stevenson's here anyway, a few hundred thousand? That's pocket change," Upton said.

"There are reasons behind my request that I can't divulge," Tollerude added cryptically. "Like I said, we're only asking that you call the loans. Once Anderson's feet feel the fire, you can do whatever you want with them. Give them more time or foreclose. We could care less."

Upton stood up. His voice was flat and empty.

"I'll have to run this by Montreal."

"You'll find that the skids there have already been greased. Stevenson's General Counsel in Winnipeg recently called your boss. You'll find no resistance from your superiors to doing what the law allows you to do."

Tollerude eased his bulk out of the leather chair, stretched his thick legs, and smoothed his trousers.

"Stevenson's appreciates your understanding in this matter. You'll see a noted increase in their financial reliance upon your institution in the very near future," the lawyer promised.

Before the young banker could protest, Bruce Tollerude was out the door, walking down Broadway with a renewed feeling of superiority.

CHAPTER 18

"**Come** on, McVean, put the ball across the plate," Danny Aitkins shouted.

The attorney-turned left fielder slouched over home plate; bat in hand, crowding the bag, hoping to send the softball over the outfield fence.

Fred McVean wound up and threw an underhand pitch past the lawyer.

"Strike two," the umpire barked.

Aitkins raised his right hand for time, backed away from the plate, and stood up. He was guessing that, with the count full, McVean would come with another fastball. It was the bottom of the seventh. There were men on first and third. Two out. Masterson's Bar and Grill, McVean's team, had a tenuous one run lead over Mitch's Auto Care. One swing from Aitkins, a player known more for his defense than for his batting average, could end it either way.

Aitkins was right. The Canadian threw a fastball over the outside edge of the rubber. Dan's eyes watched the low trajectory of the big ball. He took an easy cut, not the home run swing everyone was expecting, but a compact, abbreviated slash with the titanium bat. Metal collided with leather. The ball sliced towards where the shortstop would normally play. Because Aitkins batted left, the entire infield, including short, had shifted towards first base. The ball skipped into the outfield. The left fielder stood in line with second base, his shoes touching the warning track. There was no one within a hundred feet of the ball as it skirted off the hard, rain-deprived turf, and rolled on.

Jake Lambert bolted from third and crossed home plate with the tying run. Stanley Oldfeather, the Mitch's player on first, got a good jump. His legs churning, his long black hair whipping behind his head, the wiry Ojibwe took a wide turn at second, looked at the third base coach, and saw the sign to stop at third. Aitkins could tell, from the powerful strides of the Indian, that the man wasn't about to heed the base coach. There would be a play at home plate.

Wade Pekkila, Masterson's center fielder, retrieved the ball on the run. He scooped the softball up with a bare hand, planted his rear foot, and launched the sphere towards the cutoff man. The ball sped through thick August air without arc, thrown directly on line, with no wasted energy. It landed smartly in the receiver's glove. The shortstop, Bill Pearson, spun and launched an identical throw towards home.

Oldfeather knew the ball would beat him in. His only choice was to go hard into the catcher, Ted Hughes, the weakest player on the Masterson Team. The ump moved into position to make the call. The ball slammed into the catcher's mitt just as the Indian dove headfirst towards the plate. Oldfeather was looking to slide around the tag and touch home with his right hand. The Ojibwe's hand sought rubber. Hughes placed his meager weight forward to absorb the impact of the certain collision. The catcher attempted to protect the ball with his right hand. Oldfeather's shoulder struck the catcher's arm before the ball was secure. The force of the Indian's assault knocked the little catcher on his ass. The ball popped loose and rolled across the dusty ground.

"Safe," the umpire intoned.

Downtown Detroit Lakes was crowded when the team finally made its way to Masterson's Bar for their victory celebration. Mitch's had won the tenth annual "We Fest Softball Bash", a fast pitch tournament occurring during the "We Fest" country music festival held outside of town at the Sioux Pass Ranch. Aitkins' intention was to stop at Masterson's, have a tap beer and head out. Julie and the kids were at her parent's cabin on Lake Bemidji and wouldn't be home until Sunday night. He was alone on a Saturday because his wife no longer enjoyed watching him play softball. She'd seen too many pulled ligaments, too many sprained ankles, too many raspberries on his thighs when he tried to slide in shorts. Julie made it clear that his playing days were near an end. He was looking at this as his last hurrah, his last year of competition.

"Hell of a hit," one of his teammates said, slapping Aitkins across the upper back as they walked into the bar.

"Thanks."

"I'll buy the first one. After that, they're on the hero," Oldfeather said, his face fixed in a full smile.

"A pitcher of St. Pauli Girl," the Indian said, reaching deep into the rear pocket of his baseball shorts for his wallet. The bartender nodded his head, pulled a tap, and filled a plastic pitcher with beer. Glass pitchers had been the norm at Masterson's until plastic came into vogue. Plastic didn't shatter when thrown in anger against a malfunctioning jukebox.

Rich Devens, Mitch's pitcher, conversed with a female friend from Perham standing next to him. Aitkins didn't catch her name. Devens grew tired of the dialogue and returned his attention to his teammates.

"Hell of a hit, Danny. I'll bet McVean doesn't show up. He'll never get over losing the title game in his own tournament. This little baby's going to look mighty nice down at the garage."

Devens stroked the cheap metal and plastic first-place trophy as he spoke. A statute of a male batter in mid-swing adorned the top of the prize. Tucked beneath the trophy was an envelope containing a check for two hundred and fifty dollars; first prize money. The amount equaled the team's entrance fee for the tournament. They'd come out dead even, discounting the trophy and the free beer.

"You're probably right. That big Canadian is one sore loser," Oldfeather added. "And a horseshit math teacher."

"Got that right," Aitkins agreed.

Other players arrived. The team claimed a table. The trophy was placed in the center of the table, in a place of reverence. Masterson's filled as other players, their wives and girlfriends, wandered in. It was dinnertime. Aitkins was hungry. He hadn't eaten since he gulped down a Coney Island hotdog at noon. The Budweiser clock on the wall claimed it was six in the evening. That was bar time. It was really five forty-five.

Countless women passed by. Aitkins' teammates, their voices growing louder and more obnoxious with each pitcher of beer, threw out assorted catcalls and comments. The lawyer remained quiet. He had a good buzz on. His face was warm, his humor high. He'd just won a championship, one of only two his rag-tag team had ever managed to claim, and he had the night to himself.

Then he saw her. There was no mistaking the red hair, the stark skin, the elegant pattern of freckles on her forearms. Melanie Ingersol Barnes was in the bar. Danny's heart began to race. She didn't see him. She was wearing white Capri slacks. The cuffs of the pants ended at her shins. Her toes were bare, exposed by sandals; the nails clipped short and polished a brilliant orange. It was the most bizarre, yet intriguing, color of nail polish Danny had ever seen.

Melanie appeared slender and toned. Her chest had returned to the minimal attraction he recalled from their early dates. Her iridescent green eyes, their color forming marked exceptions to her complexion, were distinguishable. She wasn't alone. Her companion kept a loose hand on her right buttock. The hand belonged to Bobby Morgan. Seeing the investigator with Melanie Barnes brought Aitkins' temper to an unreasonable boil. He had no claim on his best friend's widow. In fact, if he'd ever had any claim on her, he'd yielded it long ago. Still, the reality of Robert Morgan escorting Melanie Barnes drove a spear of hate through the attorney's heart.

She saw him. She moved towards the lawyer with Morgan in tow. Aitkins set his beer down on the plastic surface of the table and watched her advance. The neatly clipped edges of her hair bobbed with each stride. There was mystery, angst, and passion in her every step. He felt like he was going crazy. Thoughts that he'd suppressed for the better part of five years boiled to the surface.

"Hi Danny."

Her voice was soft, pleasant, and had not changed one iota.

"You know Bob," the woman added.

135

Aitkins stared hard at the ex-cop. Morgan was a full head taller than his date, nearly a full head taller than the lawyer. A thick paunch had settled in over the retired chief's mid-section but his forearms, left exposed by his T-shirt, were well muscled.

"Only by reputation. How's it going?" the lawyer asked.

Aitkins didn't make a move to shake the man's hand. He wanted to see how Morgan played it.

The cop's lipless mouth broke into a weak grin. Morgan removed his right hand from his date's bottom and extended it to the attorney. A moment of decision loomed for Aitkins. He considered ignoring the gesture.

"Nice to meet you," the ex-chief said as Aitkins grasped the man's hand and shook it.

"Same here," the attorney replied without enthusiasm.

"Melanie tells me you were Michael's best friend."

"That was a long time ago."

The woman studied the attorney. She knew, from their friendship and her romantic encounters with Danny, as brief as they had been, his moods, his temper, and his sudden changes in attitude. Dan Aitkins was doing a good job of keeping his feelings concealed.

"It was a long time ago. How are Julie and the kids?" the woman asked.

"Great. And your two? How's life in the Cities?"

"The kids are fine. I can't complain. I'm thinking about moving back, probably to Fergus. I've had enough of big city life."

Melanie's eyes darted. She watched Bob Morgan's response to her disclosure. The ex-cop seemed pleased.

"Would you excuse me? I need to hit the john. Haven't gone since our first game this morning," Morgan admitted. "Be right back. You want anything from the bar Mel?"

"Just a Coke."

"Got it."

The investigator waded through the crowd. There were more and more people in the bar.

"So how's life, Star Baby?"

Melanie's eyes danced. If she bore any animosity against him due to his sudden discovery of morality during their encounter in the Barnes bedroom, it didn't show. Her hand settled gently on his forearm. Her touch was warm and careful, as if he was a piece of expensive china.

"Doing fine, except I'm in the middle of a big-ass pissing contest with F.W. and a guy by the name of Thompson from Minneapolis," Aitkins said. "That's got me stressed. But what's new? I've never handled my job with particular ease."

"You guys win that?"

136

She changed the subject, gesturing towards the trophy. The table was crammed with empty glasses and pitchers. Most of the softball players were lit up to the gills. The beer was flowing freely. Not a single member of the outfit was sober enough to drive.

"Yep," Dan responded.

"He won it, Miss Barnes," Devens interjected through a slight slur. "Danny knocked in the winning run."

"That true?" the woman asked, eyeing the prize in the center of the table.

"It was just a single. No big deal."

"Same Dan as always. Never ready to admit when you've done something spectacular," Melanie observed.

Aitkins glanced towards the bar. Morgan was trapped in a line of patrons waiting for service. The ex-cop was the last person in line. They would have time to talk before the cop came back with Melanie's soft drink.

"Where's Julie?" the woman asked.

Dan hesitated before responding.

"She's at the cabin with the kids. Won't be back until tomorrow night."

"She trusts you that much?" Melanie said with a provocative wink.

"You should know better than anyone else just how safe I am," the lawyer whispered, the beer making him brazen.

"I guess that's true."

He wasn't sure why he did it. As Melanie Barnes stood next to him, Danny grabbed the woman's wrist and pulled her into his lap.

"What's gotten into you?" the woman asked, her words edged with concern.

"Isn't this why you came over to see me, sweetheart? So we could get reacquainted, so we can finish the rest of our sorry little opera?"

His voice took on an unreasonable tone. She struggled to break free. He would not let her escape.

"What the hell is going on?" Morgan yelled as he arrived at the table.

"We're just two old friends having a reunion," Aitkins offered.

"Let the lady go."

"Fuck you."

"What did you say?"

"I said, on behalf of this wonderful woman, whose company you don't deserve, and on behalf of the Anderson family, whose lives you've screwed up, I said clearly and plainly, fuck you!" the lawyer declared.

It was an embarrassment. Morgan was sober, much larger, and far quicker than the drunken advocate. The investigator broke Aitkins' hold on Melanie Barnes, tossing Melanie's Coke into the lawyer's face for good measure.

"You fuckin' cunt, I'm gonna kick your ass," Aitkins screamed, rising from the table.

The crowd dispersed. Danny dove at the midsection of the bigger man. Morgan sidestepped the assault and leveled Aitkins with a right cross to the chin. The attorney was down. He was out. There would be no fight.

CHAPTER 19

Danny's eyes resisted sunlight for as long as they could.
A shaft of illumination danced across his face in cadence to slowly shifting drapes. The bedroom was awash in light. The air was cool, the result of night breezes that had migrated through the house during the lawyer's slumber.

The fingers of Dan's left hand, his dominant hand, touched the edges of his nose, where the orifice merged with the smooth skin of his cheeks. Taut flesh, swollen, and tender to the touch, reminded him of his stupidity.

"Fuckin' jerk," the lawyer mumbled to himself as he sat up in bed.

Aitkins realized he'd caused his own demise. He was at a loss to explain why he'd selected that moment in time to play the fool. That he still held feelings for Melanie didn't answer his inquiry. He'd held those feelings close to his heart during the intervening years and never acted upon them. He knew where she lived, that she'd taken a job as a bookkeeper in Burnsville, to the south of Minneapolis. Julie, one of Melanie's close friends before Michael's death, maintained sporadic contact with the woman. Through Julie, the lawyer remained aware of the details of Melanie Barnes' new life.

"What the hell was I thinking?" the attorney asked, stroking swollen tissue. He rose from bed. He'd slept beneath the coverlet, never making it beneath the sheets. Aitkins was still dressed in his softball jersey, the synthetic fabric odiferous and grass stained. His baseball shorts lay in a crumpled ball on the hardwood floor. The attorney had worn his briefs and stockings to bed. As a result of fitful sleep, Aitkins' baseball socks had migrated significantly, clumping around his ankles.

The attorney moved gingerly towards the bathroom. Outside, a crow cawed. Daniel inventoried the damage to his face in front of an antique mirror in the lavatory.

"Shit," he muttered, noting that the bruising from Morgan's single blow had spread. Purple and red occupied the prominence of his cheek, surrounding a bloodshot, half-opened eye. Aitkins' throat was parched. There was a deafening hum behind his eyelids, a constant and steady pressure of pain caused by a mounting hangover. The tap took several seconds to dispense cold water. He lowered his mouth and gulped.

Danny considered calling Julie. He'd forgotten to touch base with her last night. After the punch, there wasn't much about the evening that he remembered. The team had loaded him into Devens' Taurus. The pitcher brought him home. Beyond that, how he got in the house, how he got undressed and into bed was a complete mystery.

He walked into the bedroom. The telephone's LCD screen blinked at him. There were three messages. He sat on the edge of the bed and raised the receiver to his ear to listen to the recordings.

"Dan, this is Julie. I just wanted to find out how your team did. Give me a call in the morning. Hope you had a fun and safe day."

His wife's voice bore no upset. It sounded as if she was genuinely allowing him the night, giving him time off from husbandhood and fatherhood to enjoy himself.

A second call had come in a little before five in the afternoon on Saturday.

"Mr. Aitkins, Dean Anderson. I need to talk to you right away. A deputy came by with some papers. The bank is calling our line of credit and beginning foreclosure. I know it's the weekend but Nancy is about to have a nervous breakdown. Call me as soon as you can."

Message number three was a repeat of Anderson's earlier call. The client's voice revealed mounting anxiety. Aitkins knew he needed to call the man. He also needed a shower.

It was difficult exiting the comforting pulse of the water. After toweling off, the attorney dressed and headed downstairs. Hot coffee scalded the lawyer's mouth. Danny sat at the kitchen table and scanned the Sunday edition of the Fargo Forum. A slice of freshly buttered whole-wheat toast remained half-eaten on a ceramic plate. His call to Bemidji had gone reasonably well. His wife was happy that Mitch's had won its first tournament in three years. She would have been far less supportive if she knew what her husband's face looked like at that moment. Aitkins decided she'd learn about the fight when she came home. There was no reason to upset her before then.

The attorney's balance remained suspect as he walked to his pickup truck. He'd decided to drive to the Anderson Farm rather than call his clients. A phone conversation wouldn't accomplish much. He needed to be present to assuage the Andersons fears.

Aitkins didn't know what words he'd offer to accomplish that result. He also didn't understand Chase House. He'd met with House a week earlier, on another matter. The banker hadn't brought up the Anderson lawsuit. Dan had. There was no doubt when the two men got done talking that Farmer's Bank had agreed to delay any action regarding the line of credit or the mortgage until the case with Stevenson's was tried or settled. House hadn't placed any conditions or limits on his promise. Chase House had always been a man of his word. He was Aitkins' personal banker. There was no accounting for House's sudden change in position.

Warm air flooded the cab of the Ford as the lawyer drove unsteadily towards his client's place. Aitkins couldn't think straight.

Residual beer upset the natural channels in his brain. Remnant alcohol made the understanding of complex ideas illusive and transitory. It took considerable concentration for the attorney to keep the truck in its lane. Though he wasn't drunk, the impact of the liquor was omnipresent.

"What happened to you?" Dean Anderson gasped as the farmer opened the front door.

"Met up with a friend of yours. Mr. Robert Morgan."

Anderson studied the bruise covering the middle third of his attorney's face. The farmer's eyes focused on the swelling that distorted Dan's features. The lawyer entered the farmhouse.

"You look terrible," Nancy Anderson murmured. "What happened?"

"Says he met up with that private investigator, Mr. Morgan."

Nancy Anderson's voice was edged with curiosity.

"How'd you get like that?"

"I was acting stupid. I'd like to say we had a knock down, drag out brawl as to how he's been spreading rumors about the Anderson Hog Farm. I'm afraid I wasn't that gallant. I got myself in a situation I shouldn't have. Let's leave it at that."

"Well, it must have been one hell of a fight," the hog man insisted.

"One punch. He threw it. I caught it."

The farmer whistled.

"A little old for brawling, aren't we?" the woman asked, her words steeped in scorn.

"I'd have to agree," Aitkins replied. "Now, let's sit down and talk about your situation."

Dean Anderson handed the lawyer the legal documents as they moved from the hallway into the kitchen. Fresh orange rolls sat steaming on a plate. Coffee percolated contentedly on the stove. Golden fingers of sunlight danced over the polished surface of the table as the farmer and the lawyer sat down.

Mrs. Anderson moved effortlessly across the maple floor. Her hand gripped the coffeepot as she poured hot liquid into three cups. No children were evident.

"Where are the kids?" Aitkins asked.

"Church. Millie, our oldest, has the day off. She took them. She also made the rolls, says they're your favorite, says you order them whenever you're in Perkin's," Nancy responded, pushing the warm pastry and a cup of coffee towards the lawyer.

"We thought it best if the kids weren't here for this," Dean Anderson interjected.

The farmer's wife sat in a chair at the opposite end of the table a considerable distance from her husband. Her eyes were set hard in concentric rings. Her fingers nervously tapped the sides of her coffee mug.

Aitkins studied the documents. The Andersons were four month's past due on their payments to the bank. Their excuse, that a third party had put them in that position, wasn't a legal defense against the bank's claim. The lawyer's head pounded despite the four aspirin he'd consumed. He realized that his clients were about to lose their farm and there wasn't a damn thing he could do about it.

CHAPTER 20

Matt Anderson, the oldest son of Dean and Nancy Anderson, waited in the meeting hall of the Grafton All American Club. The drive from Detroit Lakes to Grafton, North Dakota, a little town along US Highway 81 an hour or so northwest of Grand Forks, had been uneventful. It was Matt Anderson's first militia meeting.

Two men dressed in faded army fatigues stepped onto a meager stage, a small platform positioned in the front of the room. A podium and an antiquated microphone stood on the stage. One of the men, a short balding figure not yet mired in middle age, carried a roll of fabric under his left arm. The man and his assistant unveiled a large banner of white felt with twelve-inch lettering and secured the pennant with hooks implanted in the dirty wall. The pennon boldly proclaimed:

GREAT PLAINS MILITIA
FIRST PATRIOT DIVISION
Grafton, North Dakota.

An official looking emblem in red felt was displayed beneath the words. Anderson could not identify the details of the emblem from his seat in the second row of folding chairs. The individual who'd carried the banner and seemed to be in charge stood behind the microphone. The other individual on stage, a seedy looking white male, his face scarred from long-departed acne, a day's growth of beard on his chin, assumed an "at ease" position off to one side of the podium.

Anderson's right hand held a pamphlet he'd downloaded from the militia's website. The language in the tome was strong, proclaiming the need to fight back against the unholy invasion of America's farmlands by multinational corporations backed by non-Christian foreign governments. The young farmer was intrigued; interested in learning how the entrenchment of alien companies and the resultant cheap immigrant labor injected into Midwestern farming communities from Mexico, Cambodia, and Somalia, could be challenged.

There was also a personal issue requiring Matt Anderson's attendance. The pending foreclosure of his parent's farm, the pre-destined extinguishment of his family's ability to make a living demanded his attention because Tom Murphy, Aitkins' partner in charge of handling foreclosure cases, hadn't done much to mollify the Andersons' concerns.

"All rise," the short man commanded, "and recite the Pledge of Allegiance with me."

The audience rose to its feet. Those in uniform raised their hands in military salute. Those, like Matt Anderson, wearing the clothes of farmers, shopkeepers, and laborers, placed their right hands over the left side of their chests. A forceful rendition of the Pledge ensued. Matt Anderson had forgotten the words. He mumbled along as best he could.

"Be seated. Welcome. You all responded to our invitation to come and see what we're all about here at the Great Plains Militia," the apparent leader began, speaking in a fatherly tone of voice.

There was none of the bombast, the twisted vile that Matt Anderson had seen in television renditions of various militia factions, infecting the man's delivery.

"I'm Commander Eli Bremer. Most of the time, I'm a cattle farmer out near Edinburg. But on the first and third Mondays of every month, and for our one week retreat in the summer, I'm the leader of the First Division of the Great Plains Militia."

Bremer's eyes sparkled as he continued.

"Sergeant Vincent will pass out a copy of our Code of Conduct to each of the visitors. After he does that, I'll talk briefly about who we are, what we do, what we stand for. Then, we'll break so you can ask members of the Militia any questions you might have. There'll be refreshments and snacks. Feel free to ask anything you want, anything at all. And please, stay and get acquainted with the other men that have come here tonight."

Vincent provided a leaflet to the new people. Matt Anderson accepted a copy and began to page through the document as Bremer explained the concept of becoming a Patriot.

"We're indebted to George Mason, a Framer of our American Constitution, who forever preserved our place in the scheme of government by declaring that the Second Amendment, the founding precept of the militia, applies to all male citizens except elected public officials. Each one of you, as lawful voters and residents of this country, already belongs to the militia."

Bremer paused. He was subdued and restrained in his diatribe. His words sounded logical and coherent. Matt Anderson was captivated by the tone and tenor of the speech.

"Recognition that the people, the militia, because of the Second Amendment, have the absolute duty, and note I say duty, not right, to carry arms, is essential to the preservation of our nation. Why duty? Is it not the duty of each man to preserve the safety and the sanctity of his marriage, his home, his family? Isn't that the duty each man is born into?"

The commander raised the volume of his voice slightly.

"Article I, Section 8 of the Constitution gives this great nation the tools to raise and organize a militia of the people to serve this duty. 'Is this being done?' I ask again, "Is this being done by the powers in Bismarck, by the powers in St. Paul, Pierre, or Washington?'"

There was a break in the address as the speaker's words sunk in.

"Is it?"

"No," mumbled the crowd. Matt Anderson did not answer.

"That was a pitiful response. I ask again, is our government, whether state or federal, organizing the citizens of this land, and I mean here friends, all white, male, Christian Americans who were given their citizenship status by our forefathers as opposed to those who have illegally acquired such rights since the Constitutional Convention; I ask you, 'Is our government organizing the Militia as required by Article I, Section 8?' Answer me like you mean it, brothers."

"No!" the crowd shouted.

"It isn't that complex, it shouldn't be that hard. Every able-bodied male between the ages of seventeen and forty-five must be called, is called, to service, to carry a legal firearm and serve in the militia of the people. But why haven't you been called up, why haven't you been required to serve? Simple. The military industrial complex, with support from foreign multi-nationals, including the corporate gluttons that are destroying the American family farm, won't allow those in power to follow the law."

Bremer gulped ice water from a clear glass mug he retrieved from the podium before continuing.

"This conspiracy involves money, the transfer of assets from good hard working American families to folks that have no business owning American soil. A flood of Godless immigration of heathen humans and foreign influence has swept across this nation in defiance of the protections of life, liberty, and the pursuit of happiness guaranteed us in the Declaration of Independence and codified in the Constitution. We are, gentlemen, looking at the overthrow of our way of life, of our history, and our Constitutional Democracy, because the militia has, for too long, remained impotent and silent. It is time for action. It is time for good Christian men like ourselves to follow the law, to take up arms in lawful but forceful accommodation and see to it that America is preserved for Americans!"

There was a sustained cheer from the gathering as the commander's voice rose in a contrived crescendo. Blood boiled hot in the young farmer's veins as he found himself standing and applauding the speaker with vigor.

"Won't you join me, brothers? Won't you take the vow and answer the call as a member of the Great Plains Militia? Your country needs you. Your family needs you. Your God needs you," the commander exhorted.

145

Afterwards, the gathering broke into small knots of men talking eagerly about Bremer's message. Though the Commander had never mentioned a specific race, ethnic group, or religion as a potential adversary, amongst the newcomers, there were significant and common references to "Jews, Africans, and Asians", all uttered in disparaging tones.

Matt Anderson found his way to the bar. He was not old enough to drink in North Dakota, or Minnesota, for that matter.

"What'll you have, son?" the bartender asked.

"A Bud Lite."

"You twenty-one?"

"Sure."

The man scrutinized the farmer.

"I'll take your word on it," the bartender said, passing a cold bottle of beer to Anderson.

The boy handed the barkeep a five.

"No, no, it's on the house. Commander Bremer's compliments. And there's no tipping. He's got you covered."

Anderson felt a firm grip on his left shoulder. He turned to confront the person responsible while holding the Miller tightly in his right hand. To his surprise, he came face to face with Bremer.

"I'm Eli Bremer. You can call me Eli."

The man didn't attempt to shake Anderson's hand.

"Pleased to meet you, commander. Matt Anderson."

"Ah yes, from Minnesota. Detroit Lakes, as I recall. You sent me an email. And it's Eli. We don't use rank unless we're in session or training. This is the militia, not the army."

Bremer's teeth gleamed in the artificial light. His smile was large and genuine. There was an aura emanating from the man, which established that he valued those interested in his cause.

"So, what did you think of the speech? Any questions or points you want more detail on?"

"No, you laid it out pretty clearly. I do have a personal matter I'd like to discuss with you, if I could."

The commander studied the boy. Bremer was suspicious of newcomers. The FBI and the ATF had hounded him in the past when he'd been sloppy, when his recruiting and training methods had become careless. Anderson was too naive to be a spy. The boy was so wet behind the ears, so obviously born and raised on a farm, Bremer knew in an instant that the youth wasn't a plant.

"What's it concern?"

"I'd rather not talk about it out here in the open. Is there some place we can go?"

"Sure. Come on back to the office. The All American Club won't object. We're the only ones using the building tonight."

Bremer flicked on a light. An incandescent bulb hung loose from the ceiling, providing irritating illumination.

"Have a seat," the man said, gesturing towards an abused chair. Anderson sat down. Bremer eased his way into a battered imitation leather chair behind a photographic wood desk. There was hesitancy about the older man as he sought to sit down.

"Anything wrong?" Anderson asked.

"Gulf Storm. One of the unlucky ones. Took a bullet to the low back from one of our own. Guy discharged his M16 automatic right into our platoon when we were passing his position. He was bringing the weapon down from port, thought the safety was on. It wasn't. I was lucky. He killed the two guys next to me. Sort of disputes the notion of 'friendly fire' when you watch two guys die for no good reason."

"Must have been terrible."

"Not as terrible as sending American troops overseas to save the investments of rich American Jews."

Bremer let down his guard. An angry hatred overcame his speech. There was an inflection in the man's words that had been wholly absent from his public discourse. Anderson felt the man's pain and determined that, given what the commander had seen, where he'd been, Bremer was entitled to his opinion.

"How can I help you?"

"Well, I want to join. I think what you said about family farm's is right on. But my reasons for joining are more personal."

"How so?"

Matt Anderson looked away from the man to escape the Patriot's blue eyes.

"My dad's place is being foreclosed. He could use some help."

Bremer followed the boy's eyes as they avoided his.

"That's a little out of my ballpark. Doesn't he have a lawyer?"

"We've got a couple of them. But they can't stop what's happening. There's supposed to be a Sheriff's Sale in October. Something about an expedited process. The bank claims my old man isn't using his best efforts to provide cash flow. There's nothing the lawyers can do."

Anderson turned his head and looked directly at the militiaman.

"I read on your website that you've been able to call upon the militia to stop foreclosures in Montana and North Dakota."

"True. In specific, isolated instances. But tell me, what's the basis for the foreclosure? You said hogs. Hasn't your dad been able to sell enough animals to keep afloat?"

"Always. He and I don't see eye to eye on lots of stuff. But one thing I know is that he's a good farmer. He plans things out, doesn't overextend. He's careful but willing to try new approaches."

147

"So why's he in trouble with the bank? By the way, which bank is involved?"

"First Farmer's Bank of Montreal."

"Those bastards? They've been slowly buying up family-owned banks all over the place. Those asshole Frogs, eating up our little banks like dead flies."

It was clear that Bremer wasn't fond of foreign financial institutions.

"We're in trouble because my dad bought some feed from Stevenson's Sci-Swine. Stuff was loaded with mold but hidden because it was in pellets. The mold wiped out our litters, wiped out our operating money."

"There a lawsuit?"

"It's due for trial in December. It's on a fast track, according to our attorney, Mr. Aitkins. But the trial will come too late to save the farm."

Bremer pondered the information. He stroked his short black hair from the tip of his widow's peak to the base of his neck.

"There's more," the boy added.

"Go on."

"The attorney's for Stevenson's got all of our customer's riled up against us. Claimed we've been selling diseased pigs. We can't sell a hog to nobody we've done business with in the past."

"Lawyers are assholes. Any truth to the allegations?"

"None. Take this one guy, Tynjala. He bought our pigs second hand, at an auction. He has a farrow to finish farm. Shouldn't be buying anything at auction on account of the potential to infect his breeding animals. Well, he says our hogs infected his animals with disease. Could have been any of the animals he bought. But he says it was us."

"Sounds like your family has a real full plate. I'd like to help but..."

The Patriot's eyes fixed on the boy. A nerve twitched on the young farmer's cheek. Disappointment invaded the boy's face. Bremer reconsidered the youth's appeal.

"I suppose I could place a few calls, get some members of the Administrative Counsel to consider a response. You'd have to take the oath, become a member, before I call a meeting."

"No problem. I'm ready to join."

"It's not that easy. We'll need to do a background check and make sure everything is on the up and up..."

Matt Anderson's eyes betrayed concern.

"Not that I think you're anyone other than who you claim to be," the commander advised. "When you've been around the movement as long as I have, you know the snakes from the saints.

148

But it's standard operating procedure. You fill out this application form, I'll take it from there."

"Thanks. I really appreciate your considering this," the young man said, a note of calm reasserting itself in his voice.

"I'm not one to make speeches and then rest on rhetoric. I'll need to know some of the details about your parent's case: the names of the lawyers, the judge, and such. Just jot it down on this note pad and leave it with the form," the older man advised, pushing a single page document across the desk.

"I will."

The militia commander extended his hand to the boy.

"Welcome aboard, Anderson. I'm sure there's something we can do to help out."

"That's why I came, commander. That's why I came."

CHAPTER 21

Dan Aitkins wasn't able to give the Andersons much hope. He rued the fact that he'd walked into their home with a busted up head clouded by alcohol. In Danny Aitkins' view, Dean and Nancy Anderson deserved better than that. Still, he had come out to their place on a Sunday. Most lawyers would have made their clients wait until business hours. Like doctors, fewer and fewer attorneys made house calls.

During the meeting, Dan had admitted that they faced an uphill battle against the bank. Time would run out on the foreclosure matter before the jury heard their claim against the feed manufacturer. Then there was the fact that even if the Andersons prevailed against Stevenson's Sci-Swine in court, the award might not be enough to save the farm. And Stevenson's could appeal: first, as a matter of right to the Minnesota Court of Appeals, then to the Minnesota Supreme Court. The later appeal would be discretionary; if the Supreme Court wanted to hear it, they'd hear it. Even if the second level appeal was denied, Aitkins' clients were looking at a minimum of six additional months before the case was resolved. All of this, of course, presumed that the jury saw fit to find for the Andersons.

Back at his place, Aitkins saddled up his quarter horse mare. The buckskin stood patiently in front of a pole barn, reins looped loosely around a tamarack fence rail, as the lawyer slid a wool saddle blanket, the fabric woven by Native hands, the cloth boasting interspersing blues and blacks against an off-white background, across the thick flanks of the animal. With considerable effort, the lawyer removed a cattleman's saddle from a wrought iron saddletree and gently placed the leather seat on the horse's muscular back.

It was early evening. A slight chill cloaked the river bottom. Late summer frogs chirped and peeped as the last visages of sunshine warmed the shallow ponds and ditches. There were no flies or mosquitoes to speak of.

Aitkins had checked the answering machine before he saddled up. Julie had called a second time. She and the kids were staying at the lake another day.

"Maybe you can come up and join us for the evening. We can have breakfast together if you don't have a heavy morning at the office," her message suggested.

As a creative writing teacher at Detroit Lakes High School, Julie had summers off. It was the time of year when she became selfish. She coveted every moment she was free to write. Summer was her window of opportunity; a lapse in her hectic world where she could simply stare at the walls of her writing space and create. She'd won two grants for her creative prose. The first, from the Minnesota Department of Children and Learning, enabled her to take a one-month leave of absence from her teaching job and attend a writer's conference in Burlington, Vermont. Her second award, a honorarium from the Loft, a private literary foundation located in the Twin Cities, placed her in the inner city of Minneapolis for two weeks during Christmas break one year where she taught bright but impoverished children the love of the written word.

Dan had returned his wife's message through her cell phone's answering service.

"Sorry, Jules, I won't be able to make it. I've got a big day. The Anderson case has taken a turn for the worse. I'll be up to my elbows in pig shit, if you'll excuse the term, come first light. Call me when you get in. Love you."

Fog touched grass as the evening air embraced the warm ground. The horse, Pumpkin, moved out casually, following a well-defined trail. The steady gait of the horse betrayed its experience: Aitkins trotted Pumpkin often; loped the animal occasionally; galloped the horse rarely; and only once or twice let her go full out. The attorney's horsemanship skills were rudimentary. He'd never taken riding lessons. He'd learned to manage a horse on his own. He was blessed to own a forgiving mount.

Thick foliage concealed the trail from an adjacent highway. Noise from passing traffic didn't concern the quarter horse. The Ottertail River flowed next to the path. The stream was silent in its course. Aitkins said nothing to the animal. They followed the water's channel for the better part of an hour. A mild headache began to assert itself. Aitkins reached into the front pocket of his jeans, adjusting his weight as he rode, and removed four Advil. He ate the medicine dry and on the move. Despite the onset of the headache, Danny relished the solitude of the maple and willow lowlands. There was something primitive and innately curative about the ride.

It was dark when the lawyer arrived back at the farm. Pumpkin stood patiently as the attorney undid the leathers, removed the heavy saddle and equipment from the animal's back, and turned the horse out into the pasture. Peepers and bullfrogs achieved a crescendo as Danny entered his home.

There was a hang-up on the answering machine. Aitkins didn't recognize the number. While Aitkins studied the caller ID, another call from the same number came in.

"Hello," the lawyer answered.

For a considerable space of time, there was no response.

"Hello," Aitkins repeated.

"Danny, it's me."

The attorney sat down on a kitchen chair.

"Hello," he whispered sheepishly.

"I just wanted to make sure you're OK," Melanie Barnes said. "I didn't leave a message because I thought Julie might be home. I didn't know if you told her about the thing with Bob or not."

Thing with Bob, Aitkins thought. *How diplomatic.*

"She's not coming home until tomorrow. I haven't talked to her. She doesn't know about her husband's paltry attempt at pugilism," he said.

"Are you hurt?"

"Just my pride. A nasty shiner and a bruised ego. The pain is gone. The hangover was far worse," he disclosed.

There was a break in the discussion.

"Mel, about what I did..."

"Forget it. You took me by surprise is all. I over-reacted. We go way back. I should've told Bob to cool his jets. It would've passed," she said.

"I was an asshole. I'm no fan of Bob Morgan's but I got what I had coming to me. I apologize."

"Apology accepted."

The texture of the woman's speech changed.

"There's something more you should know."

"Oh, Christ, you're not going to marry that jerk, are you?"

Laughter exploded from the other end of the telephone.

"Get serious. That was our first date, if you can call watching Bob play softball and going out for a beer a date. He's been married twice. I'm fairly certain he's no longer the marrying kind. Bob's paid child support and alimony through the nose. He's lost two houses in the bargain. I don't think he's interested in anything that lasts over a weekend. Besides, he's too old for me."

Aitkins ventured to the refrigerator, removed a bottle from the shelf, and filled a tumbler with milk. The liquid coated his throat. The lawyer thought long and hard about Melanie Barnes and Bob Morgan together. The daydream seemed more like a nightmare.

"I just wanted to make sure you're doing OK," the woman offered.

"I'm fine. Where are you living anyway?"

"The Cities for another few weeks. But I'm moving to Fergus. I'll be living right off downtown. In a cute little two-story. The kids love the place; love the town and the school. I can walk to work in about three minutes."

"You find a job as a bookkeeper?"

"Heavens no. I went back to school and got a two year certificate as a paralegal."

"You're gonna work for a law firm?"

152

"That's how I met Bob. I knew him by reputation. But now, I'll be working with him. That's how come you saw us together at the bar. "

Aitkins dropped the glass. Whether the tumbler slipped out of the lawyer's grasp, or whether the lawyer purposefully released the container was unclear. In any event, the glass fractured into innumerable shards of crystal when it hit the floor.

"Is something wrong?" the woman asked.

Danny Aitkins mumbled something about being tired before hanging up the telephone.

CHAPTER 22

Fireflies danced across the verdant green of a freshly cropped pasture. Night fell. Insolent snipe flew erratically above a gravel driveway, twittering off as Dean and Nancy Anderson walked by the birds' nesting place.

The meeting with their attorney had left them shaken. Aitkins had tried to console the couple but his words offered little comfort. There was something amiss; something wasn't quite right with the counselor. There was an odd essence, an uncommon strain about Dan Aitkins when he sat down in their kitchen and tried to mollify their fears. After their meeting with the lawyer, the Andersons determined that they were going to tell the children; tell them that the farm was in jeopardy; that the place was probably as good as gone.

Across the Great Plains, August's heat waned. Pleasant, pre-autumnal air arrived over Western Minnesota. Changing seasons brought clear skies and the slow declination of the sun. Dean and Nancy Anderson struggled to bear up under the intolerable weight of knowing that their home could be lost. It was time to share that burden with their children.

"Millie home yet?"

Dean's voice appeared calm, though inside, the farmer's nerves were near the breaking point. His wife had cried brief tears when the foreclosure papers were served upon them. But now, as Nancy Anderson moved across the gravel drive next to her husband, wearing khaki shorts and a clean white cotton blouse, her muscular arms and legs caramelized by the summer sun, her blond hair cut short and bleached nearly white by natural radiation, the woman's blue eyes remained dry. She was steeled against the ultimate unfairness of the situation. She had vowed to remain strong, to portray a calm exterior for the sake of her children.

"She just took a shower. She'll be joining the boys in the kitchen," Nancy responded.

They matched strides despite the woman's height advantage. They did not hold hands. The intimacy of their life was a secreted reality that rarely bore fruit in public. It wasn't that they weren't capable of passion. Their reluctance was a product of ingrained modesty. Their demurrer concealed their emotive bond from the world at large.

"This thing with the bank, we can't let it hurt Millie's chances of going to Notre Dame," Dean said, a strong current of guilt coloring his words.

"I agree. But she may end up better off in terms of aid if the farm is sold," his wife said.

The man grasped the woman's wrist.

"Don't say that, Nance," Dean Anderson whispered. "Don't ever say that. No matter what happens, losing the farm, no matter how much I belly ache about this place, can't be construed to be a good thing. Not for us, not for the children."

"Dean, be realistic," she replied carefully. "If we don't have the farm, can't rely on its income, Millie will likely qualify for a full ride."

"She already has one at Concordia. It's her choice to traipse off to Indiana in search of opportunity. Whatever happens, our being taken off the land, off the place we've worked so hard to create, isn't going to help us or our kids."

The wife stared blankly at her husband.

"I thought we were going to talk to them and prepare them for the worst."

Dean Anderson nodded.

"We are. But we don't need to leave Millicent with the impression that the demise of this place is written in stone. Things might change between now and the sheriff's sale. That's a full month away."

Nancy nodded reluctantly. She accepted her husband's desperate optimism as they resumed their slow walk towards the farmhouse. A slight moon rose in the east. Bullfrogs croaked in low tones, augmented occasionally by the higher pitched voices of insects.

The Anderson family assembled in the kitchen. Millie and Matt sat on one side of the table. The two younger boys sat along the opposite wall. Dean stopped at the range and poured coffee from a simmering pot on top of the stove into a porcelain mug. Nancy sat on a chair at the far end of the table, her hands settled into the denim folds of her jeans.

"We need to talk," Nancy Anderson said in a firm voice. "Your father has something to say," she added.

A look of anguish stole across the farmer's face as he placed his coffee mug on the table and steadied himself by placing his left hand on the back of a chair.

"Seems that the bank won't let us slide on our mortgage any longer. They say they're worried that our lawsuit won't pan out, that we'll over-extend ourselves before the matter is resolved."

Matt's dark eyes flared.

"That's so much bullshit."

"Watch your language," Nancy admonished.

"It's not like you haven't heard it before, mom. I'm so pissed off at that bank, I'd like to take my twelve-gauge out and give Mr. House a piece of my mind," Matt replied.

Anger flashed in the boy's eyes. The clarity of the threat unnerved Dean Anderson.

"Stop such foolish talk. Chase House isn't pulling the strings. The boys in Fargo, maybe even Montreal, are behind this thing. Someone got to him. Chase is just following orders to keep his job. Can't rightly blame him."

Millie shifted uneasily.

"I have the money I've saved for my first semester at Notre Dame. You can have that if it'll help. I've got over ten thousand dollars."

The farmer cast a wistful glance at his only daughter.

"Thanks Millie. But that's only a fraction of what we owe. The bank's made it clear that we've got to bring the mortgage note and the line of credit current. Not a penny shy. Otherwise, they'll hold a Sheriff's Sale come October fifteenth."

"What about settling our case against the elevator, dad?" Joey asked, his eyes near tears.

"Isn't going to happen before the deadline," Dean Anderson explained. "The defense lawyers have motions for judgment and other tricks up their sleeves pending. Until the judge decides those, there won't be any more offers. Maybe not even after that."

Chad, the youngest Anderson child, began to sob. The youth's head fell to the table, coming to rest in a smooth nest of skin created by his bare forearms. The boy's mother left her seat and knelt beside him, stroking the base of his neck, massaging kinks that had formed deep in the muscle in response to his father's disclosure.

"We're not going to let them take away our farm," Nancy Anderson promised, her words cloaked in infinitesimal deception.

"Your mom's right. We'll figure out some way to refinance the place before then," Dean offered.

Matthew ignored the falsehood manifested by his father. In his mind, the boy was far away from the table, far away from the pretended solutions swirling about the Anderson kitchen. His mind was fixed on the Patriots. They would be the key. There would be no need to resort to paying homage to another bank, another institution controlled by similar interests. Commander Bremer would have the answer to their predicament. Of that, Matthew Anderson was certain.

CHAPTER 23

Julie Aitkins' large brown eyes bore down on her husband as he stood in their bedroom. Danny Aitkins knew that it would not be easy to explain the bruises and the great prominence of disrupted cartilage defining the center of his expressive face. He didn't realize how truly difficult the moment of confrontation would be until that instant.

"Something you want to tell me?" his wife intoned, staring unwaveringly at her husband's wounds.

"I sortof got into a fight."

"Sortof?"

"OK, a guy took a couple of swings at me before I could put him down," the lawyer fibbed. Once the words were out of his mouth, there was no turning back. The deception was set in the concrete.

"Who was it? And why would you, a thirty-seven year old father of three, get into a bar room brawl?"

"Did I say it was a bar room brawl?"

"Where else does someone end up a face like that? At the grocery store?"

Dan Aitkins was partially concealed by the darkness cast by the irregular angles of the attic ceiling. His wife stood motionless in the middle of the doorway to their bedroom clutching her suitcase in one hand. Without warning, Adam, the oldest Aitkins child, crowded into the vestibule beside his mother.

"Wow, what happened to you?" the boy asked, staring quizzically at his father.

"Your dad got in a fight when he was drinking at the bar after his softball game."

Dan grimaced as his wife related her best hunch as to how the injuries occurred. The attorney had no basis to object to her supposition because it was true. A sheepish cloud descended over the lawyer and forced him to retreat deeper into the unlit room.

"That really what happened, dad?"

"Go put away your stuff. We'll talk about it later," Danny admonished.

"Maybe your father will give you some self defense pointers," Julie related sarcastically. "He must have some pretty good tips to share, coming out of the fight on top like he did."

The woman's venomous assault did not let up once the child was out of earshot.

"That's how it happened, isn't it? You got in a fight, sitting in a bar. Which one?"

"Masterson's"

"Really bright, Dan, really bright."

The woman edged her way past the man and dropped the luggage.

"You can unpack my suitcase. I'm taking a shower. Then we'll talk about how a lawyer, father, and husband ends up in a fight in a downtown bar."

Aitkins was about to interject a defensive dialogue. The bathroom door slammed shut, ending his ability to communicate with his spouse. Dejectedly, Danny opened the soft-sided luggage and began sorting soiled clothes from clean garments.

Despite the emotional distance between the lawyer and his wife, as Danny's fingers touched the satin of his wife's unworn bra, primeval urges rose from the depths of his being. The lawyer's index finger traced the delicate lace of the undergarment. He carried Julie's clothing, opened a dresser drawer, and placed the garments inside.

His arms laden with dirty blouses, shorts, and assorted attire, the attorney made the descent to the basement laundry. When he re-entered the bedroom, Julie was sitting on the edge of their bed in a flimsy nightgown. Light entered the space indirectly. Pale green gauze outlined the contours of Julie's body. The woman's right hand clutched a hairbrush. She pulled the appliance through her soggy hair, avoiding her husband's eyes as he picked up the empty suitcase and placed it in their closet.

"Are you going to tell me why you got into a fight?" she asked, her words coated with upset.

"There's not much to tell," the lawyer said in an apologetic tone.

Aitkins debated with himself as to whether he should reveal the truth to his wife and admit that he pulled Melanie Barnes onto his lap in front of a bunch of drunks in a weak moment of carnal lust. He'd already lied about the fight itself. He had nothing to lose.

"Some drunk thought I was someone else. He came at me without so much as a hello. He got in a couple of good ones before I could react."

"So you didn't do anything to provoke him?" Julie asked. Her lips were absent lipstick. The skin of her mouth was parched from the sun. There was a strong hint of skepticism in her voice.

"No. I was just in the wrong place at the wrong time."

Julie Aitkins' studied her husband's eyes. She sensed that he was not being candid. But she was tired, tired from the kids, tired from the drive. She didn't have Daniel's stamina for inquiry.

"See if the urchins are in bed," she mumbled as she resumed brushing her blond hair.

"OK."

On the second floor of the house, Amanda Jane, ten years old and on the verge of blossoming into adolescence, was tucked into a corner of her bed. A lamp burned brightly on a nightstand. A Harry Potter book was casually placed upside down on the table's scratched surface. Danny kissed his sleeping daughter's cheek and extinguished the light.

Down the hall, Michael fidgeted on the bottom mattress of his bunk bed set.

"Mike, it's time to turn in," the father intoned.

"Aw, come on dad, I want to hear about your big fight."

"Who told you I was in a fight?"

"Adam."

"Well, he's not supposed to be blabbing it about. You get to bed. We'll talk about it tomorrow."

"Did you whoop him good, dad?"

"We'll talk about it tomorrow. Good night," Daniel said sternly as he turned out the light.

Adam sat at his desk writing in a journal. At thirteen, he'd discovered his mother's love for the written word. The youth was so engrossed in his work that he didn't notice his father enter his bedroom.

"What you working on?"

The boy looked up.

"Dad, knock next time, will ya? You scared me half to death."

"What ya writin'?"

"Short story about an out-of-shape bar owner who ends up knocking out the middle weight champion of the world when the boxer is drunk and obnoxious in the guy's bar."

"Fiction?" the lawyer asked through half a grin.

"Mostly," the boy responded with a chuckle.

"Don't burn the midnight oil too long. You've got a barn to clean tomorrow."

Adam pivoted on the smooth pine of his desk chair.

"Do I have to? I don't even ride the stupid horses. Only you and Amanda care about 'em. Why don't you clean the barn with her?"

"That's enough lip. You get twenty bucks a week for chores. Amanda is going to Fargo with mom to help her get supplies for a writer's workshop in the Twin Cities. I'm tied up and the horseshit is nearly to the ceiling. Tomorrow's the day and you're the man. Got it?"

The boy grunted. Danny let the response pass. The father knew the boy and knew that the job would be done before the lawyer came home.

Their bedroom remained warm. Heat collected along the seams of the sheetrock and hung above the bed. The room was dark and quiet save for the patterned breathing of his wife. Aitkins stripped to his boxers and crawled beneath a cotton sheet. It was too hot in the attic to use anything more substantial. The windows were open. There was no breeze.

As he lay next to his wife, Aitkins' nostrils detected the aroma of his wife's newly washed skin. He cast furtive glances at her sleeping form, studying the round profile of her jaw, the loose fibers of her hair, the quivering of her closed eyelids. He wanted to touch her skin. In his mind, he could picture her becoming aroused, her eyes open and hungry.

And then, just as the vision of his wife neared perfection, another portrait entered his mind. Melanie Barnes, her eyes defuse emerald, overpowered his thoughts and exorcised Julie's form. He felt himself growing down there, down where all things human are created, where all wars begin, and all fortunes are ruined.

There was no escaping the image of his former high school sweetheart as Daniel Aitkins fought for sleep. The red headed woman would not disappear.

CHAPTER 24

The week following Julie's return from Bemidji taxed Danny Aitkins' patience. He and Dee Dee Hernesman spent the better part of five days reviewing thousands of pages of feed invoices and receipts sent to the Barnes Law Firm in Fergus Falls by Stevenson's headquarters in Winnipeg, Manitoba. The lawyer was looking, searching for something that would confirm the opinions of his two primary experts; Dr. Ivan Thomas, the veterinary toxicologist from NDSU and Dr. Robert Ojala, a plant pathologist from the University of Minnesota's St. Paul campus. The opinions of the plaintiffs' experts dovetailed perfectly.

Dr. Thomas' feed trials with pregnant rats showed that feeding the suspect pellets to rodents resulted in initial feed refusal, and, subsequently, abortions. Bob Ojala, one of the top forensic plant pathologists in the world, a man who spent the better part of each year in the field researching the growth of fungi under natural conditions in the remote corners of the planet, was similarly confident of a connection. He was ready to testify that, given the experiences reported by Dean Anderson, given the laboratory findings of NDSU, and given the presence of DON and zearalenone, as measured by both NDSU and the U of M, there was no question that fusarium mold had been allowed to infiltrate the product sold by Stevenson's long before the feed found its way onto the Anderson Farm.

The University of Minnesota researcher's opinions were not reduced to a written report. Danny Aitkins had a week remaining before he was required to disclose the views of his experts. His intent was to find some shred of evidence, some written link, between the pellets sold to Dean Anderson and the corn used to make Stevenson's product during those remaining seven days. If the attorney could determine the origin of the corn and prove that Stevenson's purchased it with the knowledge that it was riddled with fusarium, the liability battle would be one step closer to being won. Such a link was not in the documents provided to him. Aitkins assigned Dee Dee Hernesman the task of tracking the relevant invoice down while he pursued other aspects of pre-trial preparation.

One component of the Andersons' damage claim was establishing the pregnancy rates of the sows and bred gilts prior to the abortion storm. The plaintiff's records reported a ninety-three percent conception rate. The issue wasn't whether that conception rate was in effect at the time of the abortion storm; the breeding records of the herd made it clear that this figure was an accurate assumption. The issue was: Could Dean and Nancy Anderson prove that the abortion storm wiped out nearly all of the bred litters?

Clyde Armstrong raised silver fox, turkeys, and hogs on a forty-acre parcel south of the Andersons, near the Redeye River outside the hamlet of Evergreen, Minnesota. An odious bouquet greeted Dean Anderson and Dan Aitkins as the men arrived at Armstrong's ramshackle home. Pigs wandered about the place as if they owned it. There was no delineation between swine yard and front yard. Around the home, the soil had been turned into a quagmire by the ever-ambitious snouts of Armstrong's hogs. Piglets scurried off, frightened by the sudden deceleration of Aitkins' Ranger pickup. Adult animals lifted their nostrils high in the air, sniffing for scent. Though it was September and long after the usual period of heavy fly infestation, the filth around the place allowed the continuous breeding of vermin. Swarms of black flies, their wings beating feverishly, dodged in and out of the few decaying trees in the yard that had not been claimed for firewood.

"This is where our expert lives?" Aitkins asked.

Dean Anderson, his forearm resting against the warm metal of the truck outside the passenger's window, studied the dwelling, the outbuildings, and the ebb and flow of the unfettered pigs.

"Yep. This be the place."

"You've got to be kidding."

"Nope. Clyde's been doing ultrasounds since his daddy passed ten years ago. He's the best there is around here, believe it or not."

"He better be good at something. It sure as hell doesn't look like he's a cracker jack at farmin'," the lawyer muttered.

The men stepped out of the truck and onto hard dirt. A heavy-set man, his breath labored and difficult far beyond his apparent age, appeared from behind the house.

"Dean, how's it going?" the fox rancher said, wiping his right hand across an already mud-stained white T-shirt before offering Anderson the appendage.

"Could be better, Clyde. How about you?"

"Doing fine. I read the article in the paper. The one about the lawsuit. I hear Judge Davidson is real burned up that he's not on the case. He goes to our church, St. Benedict's out by Butler. Don't have much use for the man, as pompous as he is. But that's another story."

"That's why we're here. You did the ultrasound on my gilts and sows when I had the abortions."

"I surely did. That's something I'll never forget. Never seen a mess like that in all my twenty-nine years."

Aitkins narrowed his eyes under the brim of a "Fighting Sioux" baseball cap. He scrutinized the young farmer from head to toe. It would take considerable work to clean up Armstrong and put him in front of a jury. Jurors would respect a hard working farmer, so long as his smell didn't knock them off their chairs. Aitkins felt a smile creep across his lips.

"Come on up to the house. We can sit a spell and talk in peace and quiet away from these flies," the farmer offered.

They entered a three-season porch that occupied the entire front of the house. Aluminum storm windows and screens defined the enclosure. The screens were torn. The white vinyl flooring of the entry was stained with mud. Armstrong motioned for his guests to sit on an old sofa, the fabric oily and malodorous from use.

"How can I help you out?" Armstrong asked.

Dean Anderson sat next to his lawyer, carefully avoiding contact with the more significant smudges on the davenport.

"We're gonna need you to testify at trial about the ultrasound results..." Dean explained.

"As well as tell the jury what else you observed when you were out at Dean's place," the attorney added.

"I surely can do that. I keep a record of each test I run in this here book."

Armstrong pulled a beleaguered spiral notebook out of the top drawer of his desk. The desk matched the rest of the room; battered and clearly salvaged from some other life.

"What day did you say it happened?"

Anderson related the date of the abortion storm.

"Got it. Shows I tested all three hundred sows and replacement gilts in the farrowing barn five days after the incident. Two hundred and sixty-eight of them tested open. And remember, I was also there the morning after the abortions. Dean called me to bring up some medicine. I saw a whale of a lot of dead piglets, fetuses only a few weeks along, mashed into the concrete. The sows were trying to clean them up."

"Clean them up?" Aitkins asked.

"Eat 'em. The moms do that when they abort. Fancy lingo is 'reabsorbtion' but all that means is that the mommas eat their own."

The lawyer tried not to let the younger man see the wave of disgust wash over his face. He was unsuccessful.

"Ya, it's pretty gross. Anyway, I saw an awful lot of hogs in the making being cleaned up by the females. Pretty close to every sow or gilt, as I recall."

Armstrong stretched his limbs inside the confines of his blue and white striped overalls. His boots were caked with various kinds of manure. His shirt was too small and failed to cover the pink skin of his flanks, where his belly conflicted with the snaps of the overalls. Thick folds of flesh flowed along the farmer's waist where the T-shirt proved inadequate to cover his girth.

"You boys want some coffee? Just made a pot," Armstrong asked.

Outside, the sun climbed above the limited trees shading the front of the house. Late summer light sifted through the leaves and branches. Aitkins and Anderson followed the path of their host with their eyes. The man lumbered across the room to a Mr. Coffee unit sitting on top of a metal file cabinet. There was a distinct hesitancy as both men waited for the other to answer. Danny Aitkins pushed the lump in his throat down into his gullet and spoke.

"Sure. I take it black."

Dean Anderson smiled hesitantly.

"I'll take the same."

A loud commotion erupted from inside the house. Squeals, followed by the sound of hooves pounding against hardwood flooring, erupted from behind the door leading into the home's kitchen.

"Junior, you quit stealing Ellie's food in there, ya hear?"

An unrepentant grunt was the only response. The bachelor poured two cups of coffee and handed each guest a filthy cup filled to the brim with scalding liquid.

"Damn hogs. Let 'em inside and they think they own the place."

The lawyer and client looked at each other. Their eyes considered the steaming coffee as the pet pigs of Clyde Armstrong, a massive boar and an undersized sow, nudged open the kitchen door and ambled through the porch to join their kin out in the yard.

CHAPTER 25

Daniel sat heavily on the seat of a toilet surrounded by the gray metal walls of a restroom partition. Thoughts of the past few weeks screamed across his mind against a backdrop of anxiety.

Julie's reaction to his battle scars from the encounter with Bobby Morgan had been predictable. What would have been unpredictable was how long it took her to pack up his stuff and toss it onto the front lawn of the farm had she known the wounds were the result of Melanie Barnes sitting on his lap.

"What the hell really happened?" she had repeated as she stared at the swollen tissues of his face that morning.

"I told you last night. I had a little problem at Masterson's."

"You started it, didn't you?"

"I told you how it started. Some guy cold cocked me, thought I was someone else."

"Tell me you weren't drinking."

There had been a lengthy interval of silence. Julie shifted on the balls of her feet as she waited for his response. The lawyer's eyes focused on his wife's hips, thickened over time by childbirth. Her suntanned legs had called out to him from beneath the crepe sundress that hung free of her skin. He avoided a close inspection of her eyes. The attorney knew that the burnt ginger lurking there was inflamed with animosity set hard against the normal kindness of her face.

"I had a couple beers. No big deal."

She had turned and walked away.

The lawyer shuddered. He transferred his weight across the plastic toilet seat as he remembered the sound of the back door to the farmhouse slamming, as he recalled the puzzled expressions on the faces of the three children left standing before him in their kitchen earlier that day.

Jim Thompson began the depositions of the Andersons with polite efficiency. The questioning was conducted in one of the three conference rooms of the Barnes Law Firm. F.W. Barnes, James Thompson, and Malachi Stone, Stevenson's in-house counsel, occupied one side of a cherry table. Bobby Morgan leaned his chair against a wall and scrutinized the proceedings from a distance. The ex-cop's presence intimidated Aitkins. Ralph Covington, Stevenson's nutritionist, sat at the other end of the room. Covington's hand never left his pen as the veterinarian scribbled notes during the testimony.

165

The depositions began at nine o'clock in the morning. The thermometer on an adjacent bank building announced that the temperature was already eighty degrees outside.

The Bugle Building, Barnes' headquarters, had once housed the radical press of the Fergus Falls Republican Bugle, a long-departed daily newspaper belonging to another age, an age when the populace of Western Minnesota derived all of its news and information from gossip or local newspapers, the gossip being somewhat more reliable. It should have been cool and pleasant behind the protection of the solid yellow bricks of the structure, especially with the assistance of central air conditioning, but it was clammy in the room.

"I must apologize, Aitkins. The air conditioner seems to be on the fritz."

Dan watched his opponent as F.W. Barnes related his explanation. The young litigator watched the defense lawyer's eyes. Aitkins scrutinized the clothing of the men seated across the table from him. All of the men except Thompson had removed their suit jackets and placed them on the backs of their chairs before Aitkins and his clients entered the room. Big Jim wore a crisply pressed khaki summer suit. The other members of the defense team wore short-sleeved white dress shirts and loosened ties.

The plaintiff's lawyer was sweating. He sat heavily on the thin fabric covering his chair. Daniel's suit was appropriate for a deposition conducted in air-conditioned comfort. It was not designed for the conditions in the room. Upon closer scrutiny of F.W.'s demeanor, Aitkins was convinced that the atmosphere of the space, the slowly rising thickness of it, was contrived. He was certain that Barnes had shut off the air conditioning as a ploy.

Thompson's pattern of speech was elegant and practiced. His questioning was masterful. The inquiry conducted by the black attorney drew information out of Aitkins' clients, first from Dean Anderson, and then from Nancy, cleanly, like a skilled surgeon's blade excising a tumor. It was Dan's pattern to interrupt examinations of his clients by tossing out inane objections as a method of disrupting the opposing attorney's train of thought. Thompson's mastery caused Aitkins to remain strangely mute. There was no glaringly obvious point in the interrogation for him to interject himself and delay the proceedings. Thompson's exam was calm and efficient.

"I believe that's all the questions I have," James Thompson advised.

Danny glanced at his watch. Though not much time seemed to have been taken up by the defense lawyer's inquiry, it was slightly past noon.

"We've got Dr. Covington this afternoon, at one o'clock?" Barnes asked.

The men began to organize the papers in front of them.

"That's right. Shouldn't take more than an hour or so," Aitkins responded as his clients rose from their seats. He watched as the court reporter, a woman Dan had never seen before, a stenographer Thompson brought with from the Twin Cities, organized narrow sheets of shorthand paper neatly into the crib of her steno machine.

"Maybe the air conditioner will be working by then," Aitkins quipped, noting that every crevasse of his suit was stained with perspiration.

"I'll see what I can do," Barnes clucked, his remark revealing a hint of animosity.

"I'm sure you will."

They sat quietly at a table in a small downtown cafe eating sandwiches and sipping unsweetened ice tea.

"How did we do, Mr. Aitkins?"

Dean Anderson's mouth was full of liverwurst, white bread, and mustard as he spoke. His wife chewed quietly on a BLT, bits of tomato hanging expectantly over the edge of the whole wheat bread suspended in the air above her plate.

"Remember, it's Dan," the lawyer chided. "Real fine. Thompson is slick, I'll grant him that. Smooth. He got what he needed on the pneumonia issue, the use of lindane and oil to spray mange, and some other points of contention. He'll use what he got to paint you and Nancy as poor operators, folks who don't follow their Vet's recommendations, folks who live on the margin."

"I thought it went pretty well," Dean responded, an injured aspect to his words.

Danny realized that his client felt betrayed by the lawyer's candor.

"That's not to say Thompson got anything from you or Nancy that we hadn't already put out there. You both did fine," Daniel added quietly.

The farmer's wife raised a glass of tea to her lips. Thin red tissue parted, revealing slightly crooked teeth. Aitkins averted his gaze, relishing her raw, uncluttered beauty without being obvious.

"Has anything happened with Tynjala?" the woman inquired, referencing the farmer who had threatened to sue the Andersons.

"Nothing. I suspect that old Pavo talked to someone, perhaps his lawyer, and came to the realization that his claim against you was a lot of smoke. I wouldn't worry about him," the lawyer counseled.

167

Nancy Anderson's blue irises stared significantly. They finished lunch in silence.

"Dr. Covington, you say that you're a veterinarian by training. What sort of practice were you engaged in before coming to Stevenson's?"

Aitkins was back at work. Adrenaline cascaded through his veins. Cross-examination was his forte'. Covington was young, only twenty-eight years old, and likely inexperienced in the ways of litigation. Aitkins sought to take the man out as an expert, to render him a testimonial eunuch prior to trial.

"After graduation from the University of Wisconsin Veterinary School, I worked as a veterinarian in the United States Air Force for six years."

"That doesn't leave much time for you to have worked for your present employer."

"I've been with Stevenson's a little over a year. I was honorably discharged fourteen months ago. Came to Stevenson's immediately after discharge."

"Now you've offered opinions, as set forth in Exhibit 2 to this deposition, Defendant's Answers to Interrogatories, Second Set, regarding the impact of HPP and the use of lindane and oil for mange control."

"Is that a question?" Barnes interjected.

"It is."

"Then ask it in the form of a question."

Aitkins felt the short blond hairs on the back of his neck rise. His clients sat quietly beside him. A cloud of seething hatred broiled up inside the litigator's gut. He wanted to reach out and physically choke the old man, to strangle him where he sat. The attorney struggled to maintain his composure.

"Point noted. Do you understand the question, sir or should I have the reporter read it to you?"

"That's not a question, Aitkins. Ask a question," Barnes repeated.

Dan held his temper.

"I can answer it," the witness offered. "Yes, I gave certain opinions in this case to Mr. Thompson and Mr. Barnes regarding HPP and the use of lindane and fuel oil to treat mange."

"Thank you. Now, I'd like to explore that a bit with you. I note from your resume' that you're originally from New Jersey. Were you raised on a farm?"

"No, I grew up in Newark. I've always loved animals, always had a dog, a golden retriever. But I wasn't raised on a farm."

"Any of your immediate family have a farm that you visited or worked on growing up?"

"Nope."

"When did you first work with livestock, and by that term, I mean, hogs, cattle, milk cows, and the like?"

"When I was at Wisconsin in Vet school."

"No exposure to livestock before then?"

"Not on any consistent basis. I went to a couple of State Fairs growing up, maybe a field trip or two during high school. But nothing formal."

Aitkins paused and took a deep sip from a water glass sitting on the table. The container felt cool and pleasant against his heated skin.

"So your first exposure to working with pigs, hogs, swine of any sort, was during your veterinarian training?"

"That's right."

"Describe that for me."

"Well, we had some involvement with hogs on a farm located off-campus. We worked fairly intensively with all the livestock. I sort of gravitated towards working with hogs, sort of specialized in them early on during my studies."

There it was. A slight insertion of pride, of willfulness, into the proceedings by the young professional. He was beginning the process of building his credentials as an expert regarding swine diseases. It rankled Aitkins to think that the smug young punk in front of him wanted to sit in judgment of his clients, folks who had lived their whole lives with animals, who knew more about the day-to-day health and care of pigs than some smart-assed New Jersey brat with a professional degree could ever hope to learn.

"How many hours, in total, do you believe you spent working exclusively with pigs while undertaking your studies?"

"I couldn't begin to say."

"Thousands?"

"I don't know."

"Hundreds?"

"Objection, asked and answered," Big Jim interrupted. "He said he doesn't know."

Thompson's brief remark was colored with annoyance. Aitkins felt the sting of the disruption. He knew he shouldn't take the inflection personally, that the attorney was simply making a minor point. For some reason, maybe due to the stifling heat of the room, maybe due to the rising discomfort in his stomach caused by the all-too-quick ingestion of the sandwich at lunch, maybe due to old wounds and hurts sustained at the hands of big men on the football field, Aitkins overreacted.

"Goddamn it, Jim. I'm simply trying to find out how this silly little joke of a witness can claim to hold professional expertise regarding the care and raising of farm animals. I mean, let's be real

169

here, kids. Dr. Covington likely wouldn't know if the pig in front of him was a sow or a boar, given his background."

Aitkins' words erupted from some place deep within and were blurted out without thought. By the time Danny realized that his remarks had crossed the line, that his diatribe was an unprofessional outburst, it was too late.

"That's it. We're finished here. I will not, and I repeat, I will not, tolerate the abuse of a witness by counsel. There is no call for your remarks, Mr. Aitkins, no call at all. Come on gentlemen, this deposition is over," Big Jim announced.

Thompson's clean-shaven face appeared dry and free of sweat. He rose from behind the table and gestured to Barnes and the others that the event was concluded.

Aitkins did not want to come back to face Covington at some later point. He wanted to complete his interrogation and move on. Each day that the discovery process dragged on brought his client's farm closer and closer to auction. There was less than a month remaining before the foreclosure hearing was to be held. He didn't have time for pride. Daniel didn't have the luxury of allowing his ego to be mollified. A knot formed in his throat. The lawyer threw out a desperate entreaty.

"Jim, I apologize to Dr. Covington and to everyone in this room. You are absolutely right. That was uncalled for. It won't happen again. Can we finish this?"

"It's up to Dr. Covington," Thompson said. "Doctor?"

"Let's get this over with," the young nutritionist hissed.

The Vet sat his rail thin frame, his body angular and quick from miles of long distance running, hard against Danny as the expert awaited the next question.

During the following hour, Dr. Covington adroitly testified that, despite the fact that he had only worked with dogs, cats, parrots, and fish as a veterinarian during his years in the Air Force, he'd managed to become an expert regarding hogs and hog farming during his fourteen months at Stevenson's. His conviction in that regard was deeply held and unshakable. Aitkins eventually came to realize that he was beaten. He ceased his assault upon the young man's confidence and threw in the towel.

"What was all that about?" Dean Anderson asked as they left the Bugle Building, the three of them walking hesitantly against the lingering humidity of late afternoon.

Aitkins remained silent.

"Dan, what the hell just happened in there?" the farmer repeated.

The lawyer, his disheveled suit coat draped loosely over the moisture-stained sleeve of his dress shirt, walked mutely towards his truck. Sunlight formed a bright halo above the advocate's head as Danny Aitkins fought hard to place one heavy step in front of the other. The litigator waved the farmer's question off with a tired flip of his hand before entering his pick-up and heading for home.

CHAPTER 26

Tom Murphy, the partner in Aitkins, Ordell, Murphy, and Aitkins working with the Andersons to halt the foreclosure of their farm, failed.

On the day of the auction, a cold mist blew over the hog farm propelled by a heavy breeze. Dean Anderson watched a parade of pickup trucks, punctuated by a smattering of passenger cars and vans, pull onto the lawn of his place. His soul was gripped by an unrelenting desire to walk into his study, open his gun cabinet, remove his lever action Winchester 30-30, load the magazine with bullets, and confront the mob. Instead, he sat quietly on a pine bench under the eaves of his front porch holding a metal camp cup full of hot cocoa. His wife had left for town, taking all of the children with her except Matthew. The oldest Anderson boy was lurking somewhere inside the house, sullen and ashamed by the events unfolding before them.

Four Sheriff's Deputies scrutinized the prospective buyers. Occasionally a friend or an acquaintance would wander past the farm implements and equipment parked unnaturally on the front lawn of the place and approach Dean on the porch. These were his friends, his neighbors, people that he'd known for years, folks he'd broken bread with at church or talked shop with at any number of small businesses around the area. Despite the connection, they were on his place looking for bargains, steeped in the knowledge that Dean Anderson's misfortune was creating an economic opportunity for them.

The auctioneer had arrived earlier that morning with his wife. Dean Anderson didn't respond to the auctioneer's attempts to engage the despondent farmer in conversation. The Anderson family had followed the requirements of the court's order and moved all of their farm equipment; the tractors, the hay balers, the plows; in short, anything of value related to their operation not affixed to a building or to the land, out into the open, where the auctioneer placed a price tag on each item. But compliance with the court's mandate did not require the farmer to make small talk with the auction man. Anderson remained mute as the auctioneer attempted an apology before tripping ungracefully backwards down the steps of the front porch in retreat.

"I can't believe some of these people," Matt said as he slid out the front door and sat wearily on the far corner of the bench occupied by his father. An "International Harvester" ball cap, a hat that Dean had worn as a young man and saved for his oldest son, rested on Matt's dark hair, the strands still wet from a shower.

"Some of these folks are supposed to be our friends."

"That's the hurt of it, son."

172

Matthew waited for further comment, for some sort of embellishment, from his dad. There was only elongated silence as the wind picked up and sent newly fallen leaves skittering across the fading lawn.

The crowd was significant. Perhaps three hundred people were gathered across the early autumn grass scrutinizing the machinery. Their conversation created a deep, low hum of words, sounding something akin to an enormous swarm of honeybees reflecting on a field. Most of the spectators clutched white Styrofoam cups of complimentary hot coffee provided by First Farmer's Bank. Here and there, clusters of onlookers stopped to catch up on gossip, to discuss the weather, the fate of the Fargo Red Hawks minor league baseball team, or the latest agricultural and educational proposals by the State's enormous bald-headed governor.

"Sorry to have to go through with this Dean," Chase House mumbled as he climbed the stairs towards the farmer.

The young banker had always been a shining light in Dean Anderson's estimation; one of the few in the banking industry who said what he meant and meant what he said. Until he caved in to whatever pressures were being exerted upon him regarding Dean and Nancy Anderson's loans, Chase had been not only their banker, he'd been their biggest supporter and booster. Now, all that had changed. He was, in Dean Anderson's view, a man who could be bought for a price like all the rest. The farmer didn't have time to waste on such men.

Anderson grunted and refused to engage the financial officer in conversation.

"I think you better get off our porch steps," Matt remarked, disgust and loathing clear beneath his words. "Dad's just liable to knock you on your ass if you don't keep your distance."

"I just wanted...."

"Like I said, Mr. House, get off our porch. Until the house gets foreclosed on, we own it. You get offa it."

The boy's father gazed steadfastly into the crowd, ignoring the young banker as his oldest son dealt with the situation. Dean tightened his lips, to avoid saying anything foolish, to refrain from jeopardizing his position with the bank any further. House shook his head with sadness and left the man and the boy alone under the cover of the porch.

As the throng began to converge on the hay wagon being used as a stage for the auctioneer, Dean Anderson shifted on his rump. Tom Murphy mounted the stairs and sat down wearily next to his client.

"Danny would have been here personally but I think it's too painful for him."

173

Anderson pursed his lips and sent a large deluge of spit out into the cool air.

"Painful for him?"

An opening occurred in the conversation. "I'm the one losing my Goddamn farm."

Murphy, a heavy set man in his late forties with a balding palate and bright pink skin, folded his hands across the thick denim of his blue jeans and stared hard at the crowd.

"I know that Dean. So does Dan. And he feels awful about it. He wanted to have something put together with Stevenson's in terms of a settlement but they're playing hardball. They won't even entertain an offer until Judge Enwright hears their motion for summary judgment next month. Once she rules, presumably in your favor, they'll be singing a different tune."

"Some good that'll do," Matthew interjected. The boy stood at the very edge of the porch scanning the assembly, watching with anxiety as his neighbors milled purposefully in front of the little auctioneer.

"Matt, we've pulled out all stops. Dee Dee is working fulltime on your case with Danny. The firm is into this thing for a lot of scratch with all the experts we've fronted. Dan's doing the best he can under the circumstances."

"I know that. Just don't compare what he's feeling from a distance to what my family and I are going through. See that? My friends and neighbors have turned into sharks, ready to feed on my dying carcass," the farmer whispered.

The words rolled off Dean's tongue without rancor. There was a pattern of reluctant acceptance in his voice.

"I think I'll head down there to make sure House follows protocol. I'll see you after the sale."

The lawyer trudged slowly across the painted wood of the porch and walked carefully down the front stoop.

Just before the auctioneer began his opening speech regarding the terms and conditions of payment, as each audience member gingerly thumbed the plastic bid numbers they'd received from the auctioneer's wife, numbers they'd soon be raising into the air to depict their offers, a yellow school bus, old and surging desperately under the weight of a full load, rounded the corner of the Anderson driveway, drove around a pair of sawhorse barricades erected by deputies to restrict traffic, and came to an abrupt halt in the middle of the startled gathering.

An efficient looking man in his thirties, dressed casually in brown summer weight slacks, a tan rain-resistant windbreaker, and brown lace-up work boots, exited the bus with a bullhorn in his hand. Behind him, forty other men, all dressed for the weather, filed out of the big yellow bus onto the trampled grass.

174

"See here now..." the auctioneer objected as the new arrivals took up positions in the crowd. His remarks were cut off by the man with the bullhorn.

"I'm Eli Bremer from Grafton, North Dakota, a friend of young Matthew Anderson, one of Dean Anderson's sons. Dean's the owner of this here farm. He's your friend, your neighbor. I've come to ask you to consider what you're doing, consider the evil that you're participating in, by taking part in this auction, the selling off a family's life."

Hoots and jeers began to assail the stranger as he waded into the crowd. Bremer's companions formed a corridor of support as the commander walked towards the hay wagon. The press of the audience prevented the deputies from moving against Bremer as the militiaman strolled quickly across the lawn.

"Hear me out, friends. This thing you're about to do is wrong. The Andersons are victims of corporate greed and corruption. Their farm is being sold from beneath them because they dared to challenge the big internationals that are ruining our way of life by merger, consolidation, buy outs and, when that doesn't work, intimidation and litigation as is being done here."

"Stop this disturbance at once," a deputy shouted as Bremer arrived at the stage. The militiaman ignored the order and climbed the steps to the wagon.

The frightened auctioneer vanished from the wooden platform, leaving the stage to Bremer. Militia members took up positions around the perimeter of the hay wagon.

"Go back to where you came from," a husky voice shouted from the assembly.

"We don't need your kind here," another yelled.

"On the contrary, you do. We were asked to come here by young Matt Anderson. I represent the Great Plains Militia, Grafton Chapter. These other men are from all over the region. Most of them, myself included, are farmers just like you. George Winchip down there in the orange and camo rain gear drove all the way from Terre Haute, Indiana to answer our call. He's here; we're here, to help our friend Matthew and his family fend off this insidious, treacherous theft of their home by Stevenson's Sci-Swine and the Farmer's Bank."

"Go back to North Dakota," someone yelled against the weight of the wind and mist. Other voices began to join in, calling for an assault on the platform to silence the intruder.

"Give him a chance to speak," a spectator, someone not obviously linked to the militia, shouted. "Let's hear what the man has to say."

A cascade of catcalls erupted. Individuals in the midst of the customers began to nod their heads in agreement with the lone voice of support. Soon, the mood of the majority of those standing in front of the wagon was altered. They were now in favor of giving Bremer a chance to talk. The deputies, seeing there was little hope that they would make it through the mob unscathed, realizing that the auction crowd itself had been strategically sprinkled with militia plants and sympathizers, migrated to their squad cars to call for backup.

"Friends, thank you. The action that Farmer's Bank has taken, with the full support and blessing of Stevenson's, is not just about Dean and Nancy Anderson. It's about all of us, living here, on the edge of the prairie, farming the land, raising livestock, feeding the world. Do you realize that the multi-national conglomerates control nearly every facet and every component of food production in this country? That's a fact, a fact that we as farmers must recognize and come to grips with. Slowly, agonizingly, our way of life, like the Andersons here, is being ripped away from us by these international hoodlums."

There was a din of acknowledgement from the crowd. The folks milling around Dean Anderson's farm knew the score, knew that their days as family farmers, unless something drastic took place in the agricultural economy, were numbered.

"How can this be? How can the fat cats eat up farm after farm after farm? Replacing folks like the Andersons here with large corporately run facilities? With huge polluting, inefficient, unhealthy concentrated feedlots? Simple. They have the support of the banks, institutions like Farmer's, another foreign company spreading its poisonous web across this great land of ours, wiping out our family banks, savings and loans, and credit unions in the name of corporate greed."

"He's right," a woman shouted from the crowd, her hand raised in a militant fist towards the gray sky.

"That's it sister, that's the spirit. So you ask, 'We hear you, brother Bremer, but what can we do about it?'. Every political action starts as a small bit of snow rolling down a slope. With each turn, the snowball gathers speed and weight. It grows in significance. Today, let this auction be the beginning of a political avalanche. Turn away, return to your farms and your homes untouched by corruption. Refuse to buy up the Anderson Farm bit by sordid bit from these cowards and vagabonds. That's what you can do today, tomorrow, and so long as you breath the sweet air of the prairie."

A thunderous applause cascaded across the lawn. Dean Anderson leaned heavily against a wooden post. His son stood next to him on the front porch of their home, the boy's hands firmly entrenched in the back pockets of his faded green work pants.

"How in God's name did you ever come up with this?" the farmer asked, his words choked with emotion.

"It's called the Internet, Dad. You should try it some time."

A smile crossed Dean Anderson's face. He watched with clear eyes and a soaring heart as the prospective buyers headed towards their vehicles, leaving the farmer to marvel at the depths of his son's creativity.

Matt Anderson's plea to the militia resulted in the cancellation of the auction. Though neither Dean Anderson nor his eldest son knew it, Eli Bremer's sudden appearance was an act of civil disobedience that had its roots back in the Populist Farmer-Labor movement of the early twentieth century in Minnesota. The militia had repeated the stalemate tactics used by Populist farmers back in the Great Depression when hordes of disgruntled men would converge upon farm auctions and disrupt the sales, preventing the displacement of their friends and neighbors.

"I want to thank you and your men," Dean Anderson said, approaching the school bus, extending a worn hand to Bremer as the Dakotan was about to board the vehicle.

"No thanks necessary. Glad we could be of assistance," Bremer replied.

"I don't know how you managed, but you sure turned the crowd."

Bremer smiled, his teeth small and crooked, an odor of sweat emanating from his body.

"It was nothing. Put a few folks in the midst of them, tell them what they all know, what they all want to hear. I didn't do so much."

Anderson studied the man's features as they stood beneath the clouded canopy of the Western Minnesota sky. There was something slightly odd, something marginally troubling about Eli Bremer. Dean Anderson couldn't put a finger on it. But it was there.

CHAPTER 27

It wasn't only his drinking. There was something insidious and far more threatening, in Julie Aitkins' estimation, behind her husband's pervasive dolor. She wasn't sure what it was. Calling it a "mid-life crisis" didn't explain it; the term merely affixed a convenient label on Daniel's advancing melancholy.

She knew that she'd become progressively less lithe and supple after the birth of each child. There was a thickness about her waist. Danny gently suggested the two of them needed to get in shape shortly after Michael, their youngest, came along. She knew that what Dan really meant was that she needed to hit the gym and hit it hard.

"Why in the hell did he marry me?" she often wondered over the course of their union, reeling from some small slight or insult cast in her direction by her husband, recoiling from remarks directed at minor flaws in her imperfect nature.

She believed, despite compliments from others to the contrary, that her face was ordinary. She thought her profile was clean and honest. Her looks, to her way of thinking, benefited from her eyes; an aspect about them made her more physically appealing than she really was. Her hair was dirty blond, turning truly dishwater when deprived of the sun by the long Minnesota winters. Her figure was, in her estimation, unexceptional.

She was standing in their bedroom. Danny was late for dinner. Julie realized that the Anderson case was a difficult cross to bear, that the litigation challenged her husband's considerable intellect and stamina. Still, she missed having him home, moody attitude and all. The school year was well underway and the kids rarely saw their father before they left for town on their respective school buses. Dan was always up by five, feeding their two horses, their steer, and their three feeder pigs, before showering. He downed his first cup of coffee between the barn and the bathroom, living as always, on the run, at peak rpm's. Evenings were supposed to be dedicated to family time. The past few weeks, Julie ate with the kids while Danny worked at the office long into the night. In some ways, the woman felt like a widow.

Julie undressed. Her eyes avoided the full-length mirror attached to the lavatory door. Years ago, she relished seeing her nude body. She loved every curve. She was not like some women, abhorrent of her own flesh. But that had changed. She no longer relished looking at herself. There was nothing in particular that caused this alteration of habit. It just was.

Over the years of their marriage, they had made love in every room of the old farmhouse. On the kitchen table. In the drafty living room beneath the cracked plaster of the ceiling, before the roaring flames of a mid-winter fire in the tired brick fireplace, its security suspect, its draft, temperamental. On the floor of the basement as they unpacked boxes after they moved in, Julie eight months pregnant and barely able to walk. On top of the hard maple surface of their dining room table, candles burning fiercely at each end of the platform as Danny bucked and bucked and bucked against her, nearly breaking the middle leaf of the table before she came. And hundreds, maybe thousands of times, within the sweet softness of their antique bed.

Lately their couplings had become perfunctory and rare. Sometimes, as Dan entered, she felt the old tension, the sudden raw unsheathing of every nerve in her body, and it was wonderful. But such occurrences now constituted the exceptional evening. And their intercourse, both physical and verbal, had become limited almost exclusively to the night. Sometimes it happened. Sometimes, Danny came the way she was used to. Violent. Shuddering. Like Thor rendering open the side of a stubborn cliff with his hammer; a sudden silence, followed by a rush of exhaled air, a breath that had been held for minutes, as her husband climbed, climbed, climbed an imaginary mountain, winning some wondrous altitude.

Most often now, all she felt was a small shrug, a slight hint of release. Only the cessation of his motion told her that he was finished, that his urge had been satisfied. But was he satisfied? Did she still satisfy him?

Julie Aitkins did not step across this mental threshold as she slipped on a flannel nightgown. She did not ask herself if there was someone else. Prospects of betrayal could not be entertained. She would not go there. She'd been there before.

Her breasts, hanging slightly lower than in her youth, shifted as she walked across the cold wooden slats of the floor to the bathroom. The kids were in their rooms. She doubted that Adam was sleeping. It was only nine-thirty. Michael had zonked out on the couch watching *X-Men* for the zillionth time. Amanda had excused herself to do homework in her bedroom right after supper, right after Dan called.

"Hi, Jules."

"Where are you?"

"Still at the office. Working on the Summary Judgment Motion in the Anderson case."

"Dinner's cold."

"I should've called earlier. I'm so into this thing. Time just slipped away."

Julie hadn't argued. She knew the seriousness of the matter he was working on, how his insides were churning, how his bowels were

179

moving. The pressure. He was always fighting it. The problem was, as Julie Aitkins saw it, Danny wasn't a player. He litigated from the heart. He rarely took soft tissue automobile cases because he couldn't hitch himself, couldn't connect his inner self, to such a speculative star. Once in a while he was forced to take a whiplash case because Emery insisted. But Dan generally only took matters that contained an element of sympathy. He left the ordinary and the mundane for his old man and his other partners.

Worse yet, Julie knew early on that Danny was a horrid poker player. His face, his speech, his demeanor gave away every little deceit. In contrast, Emery was a master at negotiating with opposing attorneys and insurance companies. The senior Aitkins could bluff with the best of them. Sadly, at least in terms of professional attributes, Emery failed to pass along whatever genetic material allowed him to succeed at deception.

Her writing languished. That was the thought that manifested itself in Julie Aitkins' mind as she crawled underneath the goose down comforter on their bed. The brass legs of the pallet were coated with a thin veil of dust. Larger pods of fluffy debris; feathers and assorted leavings, were hidden beneath the box spring on the hardwood floor. Housework was not a priority for either of them. Daniel demanded little of her in that respect, which is exactly what Julie provided.

Her novel wouldn't move. She'd worked on the book over the summer in the writing studio that Danny built for her in the loft of the barn. The room was airy and boasted a wonderful view of the hobby farm's meadow and of Rocky Run, the little tributary of the Ottertail River that meandered through the farm's hayfield. There was good natural light; a couple of well-placed electric fans to keep the room cool; a small refrigerator stocked with flavored water, ice tea, and several bottles of expensive wine; a microwave and a coffee maker; within her private space above the animals.

More days than not over the summer, she found herself looking at a computer screen, unfinished thoughts and useless sentences staring back at her. She had never experienced writer's block before. Always, when she turned on her computer, or, in the days before computers, when she wrote her stories, essays, and poems in long hand, the words had flowed with grace and ease.

Sure, there were occasions where she needed to re-work things. There was always editing to be done. She'd never been afraid of trashing an entire concept, even a completed work, if, in the end, it didn't sit right on the page or sound right in her head. This summer had been different.

Now, here it was, the middle of October. The book had a beginning, a middle, but, definitively, no end. The protagonist, a Catholic nun named Sister Mary Kathleen O'Shea, was defined. The plot concerned the Sister's Irish upbringing and the passage of time, the slow parade of the nun's life, as the woman slid helplessly into maturity, longing to know a different path, a different sort of love.

This was the sum and substance of what Julie Aitkins, Loft Laureate, decorated essayist, and teacher, had been able to fathom from her muse. She was nearly finished with a first draft but couldn't bring the book to a place where Sister Mary's story rang true. The writer longed to feel her fingers sing across the keyboard as words erupted from her brain without prodding. Julie's inability to complete her first novel dogged her as she cracked open someone else's bestseller and tried to pass the time until her husband came home from the office.

CHAPTER 28

Emery Aitkins pulled into the front yard of his son's hobby farm in a shiny blue Chevrolet Suburban. The air was crisp with the onset of fall. Around the perimeter of the neatly trimmed lawn, between the old farmhouse and the pole building, maple, oak, and assorted other deciduous trees stood in resplendent color.

"Hey old man," the younger Aitkins called out from behind an open screen door leading to the home's back porch.

"What a morning," the father replied, exiting the warmth of his vehicle to confront the chill of the day.

High clouds provided a thick ceiling above the landscape, preventing the tendrils of the sun's ascent from becoming visible above the rolling hills surrounding the hobby farm. Leaves rattled restlessly as meager wind touched their fragile surfaces. The family's two horses and steer contentedly nuzzled the last of the summer's grass in the pasture adjoining the barn, the building's white steel walls and roof wet with early morning dew.

There had been something of a truce between the two men following the disastrous results of the Pelletier verdict. Nothing had been said. The son had not come to the father and bared his soul as the result of some great epiphany. Their unspoken accord was more the result of steady, progressive recognition by the elder Aitkins that his son was a terrific trial lawyer. Though Emery said nothing, the accommodation in their relationship was palpable.

With his mother dead, after years of silent struggle with the bottle, having failed to beat her chronic alcoholism after enduring treatment after treatment in the finest recovery centers in the Midwest, and his sister having also passed away, the young lawyer felt desolation. Danny had come to realize that Emery, the last surviving son of Herbert and Linda Aitkins, was all that he had left besides his immediate family and an odd assortment of distant cousins. Had Emery not softened towards his son, Daniel contemplated attempting his own version of reconciliation with the old man. Now, as the young attorney walked across the wet grass of the front lawn to greet his father, Dan realized that his personal acquiescence was unnecessary.

The young lawyer visited his mother's grave in Brainerd, Minnesota, near the last treatment facility she had attempted, once a year, on her birthday. He had not visited his sister's grave in a long while. Audrey's face, her haunting eyes, dry and withered from self-starvation, remained too vivid, too full of anguish, for him to contemplate. Awful memories forced Daniel to avoid Audrey's burial plot in the Grace Lutheran Church graveyard located on a little knoll outside of Detroit Lakes. He knew that his only sibling rested in a grove of willows, the long, weeping limbs of the great trees shading her rest during the height of the summer sun, protecting her from the fiercest winter winds. That was enough. Someday he would visit. But for now, the image of her tomb was more than enough.

The elder attorney was dressed in new Carhart trousers, a thick polar fleece pullover, and finely polished leather hunting boots. He'd offered to help Danny, Adam, and Julie put up three hundred bales of freshly cut alfalfa Dan had purchased from a neighbor. Despite his father's wide girth and ruddy complexion, the old man was in excellent shape. Emery thought the exercise would be good for him and that time spent away from the office with his only child would be beneficial to them both.

"That's the hay?" Emery remarked, pointing to three wagons piled high with square bales of alfalfa.

"Yep. Three hundred of 'em. You bring gloves?" Danny asked.

"Nope."

"That's all right. I've got an extra pair. Bought 'em at Menard's in Fargo. Canvas and leather. Should last a while. You'll need gloves to pick up the bales by the twine."

The men walked towards the house.

"Got any coffee?" the father asked.

"Pot's on. Julie whipped up some scrambled eggs and bacon. Last year's butcher hog. He's real tender and flavorful."

Emery, a head shorter than his son, looked away from his boy and studied the advancing light of the new day across the scarlet, yellow, and orange finery of the forest.

"Ducks'll be flying soon. We should take a run out to Postal Lake and see if we can't pass shoot a few teal."

"Maybe tomorrow. I can ditch church one Sunday, I'd guess," Danny said through a mischievous smile.

They entered the kitchen and sat at the table while Julie bustled between the stove and their plates with breakfast. Adam sat in his seat; half asleep; picking at his eggs, a slice of toast coated with homemade apple jelly half eaten to one side.

"What's the problem?" grandpa asked, tousling the youth's hair as he spoke.

"Nothin'."

"He doesn't think he should have to put up hay since he never rides the horses," Julie advised.

The teacher stood in front of the sink scraping burned edges of egg into the garbage disposal as she talked. Her hair was pulled tight against her face. She wore a battered terry cloth robe and well-used slippers of matching material. Her facial skin was dry and without makeup; her eyes seemed tired, as if an aspect of weariness had burrowed deep inside her physical self. To her father-in-law,

Julie Aitkins remained pretty. Not beautiful. But pleasant to look at, sensual in an old fashioned sort of way.

"How's the novel coming?" the older man asked, knowing that the woman was working steadily towards completing her first book.

"Tough," she admitted, wiping her hands on a dishtowel draped over the corner of the porcelain coated sink. "I'm having a heck of a time with the ending."

"Writer's block?"

"Somethin' like that," she admitted, sitting heavily beside her son. Her hands, the fingers short, thick yet feminine, reached across the surface of the table and removed two slices of toast from a plate.

"I don't envy Julie," Daniel interjected. "Teaching all day and then trying to find time to write at night, during odd hours on the weekends, along with all the demands of being a mom to our three brats."

Adam looked up from his food, his mouth full of eggs. His eyes contained mock anger.

"Yes, you-a brat," the father repeated, reaching across the table to squeeze the adolescent's cheek.

"Knock it off," the boy chirped, annoyed to be part of the day's events, longing to spend his Saturday morning deep inside the cozy confines of a quilt.

Dan climbed the hay elevator into the loft, a space adjacent to Julie's second floor writing room, to await the arrival of bales. Julie and Adam worked the hay wagon, sliding and tossing bales to the cement floor of the barn where Emery loaded the squares, two at a time, onto the slowly churning links of a John Deere conveyor.

Every now and then, the electric motor handling the load proved insufficient to carry an overly wet bale. Hay full of late autumn moisture temporarily caused the equipment to seize up; leaving bales stuck half way up the measure of the conveyor.

"Unplug the motor," Dan shouted whenever the equipment locked up. His father would disconnect the extension chord. The young attorney would scramble down the elevator, one foot on either side of the conveyer chain, until he reached the offending bale, dragged the square up the apparatus, and deposited it on the plywood deck of the loft.

"All clear. Start her up," he'd proclaim. The bales would resume their steady parade.

Dust filled the dimly lighted confines of the barn. Three incandescent bulbs provided paltry light. Four of the five stalls of the structure were empty. The larger animals remained outside,

184

content to graze. One stall held the family's pigs. Three butcher hogs squealed and pranced back and forth, annoyed at their confinement.

Though the temperature outside never rose above fifty degrees, the interior of the barn became warm. Sweat rolled across Julie's face and arms as she struggled to slide the last of the bales across the wooden deck of the trailer towards her oldest son. The two younger Aitkins children remained sound asleep as the crew finished their work, as Daniel stacked a last row of alfalfa against the building's eaves.

"That was quite a load," the young litigator admitted as he slid down the metal frame of the elevator.

"Got quite a workout up there, did you?" his father asked, pounding Dan on the back. "You had to do a lot of quick thinking to stack all that hay in that little space."

"Beats the old barn. Remember hauling the stuff bale by bloody bale, Adam? Up that old ladder? Never knew whether the floor of the old barn would hold the load. Never knew when a rung on the ladder was gonna break under your weight."

The child spoke.

"Am I done?"

"Yep," the father replied.

"I gotta get ready for practice."

The boy jumped from the hay wagon and ran out a big sliding door towards the house.

"Practice?" the grandfather asked.

"Hockey. Tryouts start in a couple of weeks. They've got some free ice time before then. Jules, you taking him in?"

The lawyer's wife pulled a piece of hay out of her hair and lowered herself cautiously from the wagon.

"I was going to work on the book, maybe get Michael and Amanda to pick some apples for a batch of jelly. We're almost out. The jar we used this morning is all we have left from last year."

The adults left the dark interior of the barn, emerging into the subdued light of the overcast day.

"I can bring him to town," Emery offered. The old man's skin was red from effort. His breathing was labored. The work had been more than he'd expected.

"You sure dad?"

"No problem. I'm going in to the office to work on some files anyway."

There remained one point of contention between father and son. Danny avoided the office on his days off. He rarely drove into Detroit Lakes to work on the weekends unless he had a trial or a hearing the following Monday. It was a small difference between the men that, over the years had sometimes festered into angry

185

confrontations. Daniel looked at his father's face. There was no animosity present. Something had truly changed in the old man.

"OK," was all Dan replied.

"Tell Adam to get his stuff together and bring it out to the truck," the older attorney told his daughter-in-law as she made her way towards the back door of the farmhouse. "I need to talk to Daniel."

"He'll be right out. Thanks for all your help," the woman responded in a voice coated with fatigue.

They ambled towards the fenced pasture restricting the grazing livestock.

"Horses are looking fit," Emery remarked, the tone of his words clearly indicating the comment was idle small talk. "That steer ready to be butchered yet?"

"Next spring. Needs a little more finishing," Dan replied. "What was it you wanted to talk about?"

A note of minor unrest infected the young litigator's voice. He stared at the horses. He removed his work gloves and held them in one hand.

"This Anderson thing. You need any help?"

There was no challenge in the father's address; only an expression of concern colored his words.

"I've got some time," Emery added softly.

"Dee Dee has been a blessing," Dan remarked quietly. "We've got it under control. Thanks for the offer. I'll take you up on it if things get hairy."

The veteran lawyer placed his right hand, the skin smooth and unmarred, evidence of years of paper work, on his son's shoulder. He was about to tell his only child how proud he was of him; how many compliments he'd heard from folks that had been represented by Daniel or had seen him at work before the bar. But it was not in the father's nature to pass on such accolades. Emery's discrete gesture would have to be enough.

CHAPTER 29

Dee Dee Hernesman became a partner in the firm. There wasn't time for a party or an extended celebration. She was knee-deep in documents, additional responses to the discovery demands she had drafted and served by mail on Stevenson's a month earlier. Twelve boxes of paper had been shipped from Winnipeg to The Bugle Building in Fergus Falls. In the basement conference room of the Barnes Firm, the air cool and moist, Dee Dee waded through a mountain of reports, memoranda, and correspondence; searching, searching for anything that would provide documentary evidence that Stevenson's knew that the raw corn used in the feed sold to Dean Anderson contained fusarium mold. There was nothing, nothing in the boxes that linked cause and effect. She was unable to discover a "smoking gun".

"Zilch, Danny. A big fat zero."

Hernesman sat, her body limp from a straight week of manually inspecting thousands of pages of material provided by Big Jim Thompson, her spine pressed against the vinyl back of a chair in Aitkins' office. Her short hair was in disarray. Her eyes were glazed.

"I told you so."

"You don't have to be so smug. I thought for sure they'd cough up something we could use," the female attorney retorted defensively.

"You're not playing with some insurance company here, Dees. You're in the big leagues now. Stevenson's isn't about to keep incriminating evidence where it can be found, if they keep it at all. Likely we'll just have to go with what we've got."

"How you doing with Dr. Ojala?" Hernesman asked, referring to the University of Minnesota Mycotoxicologist they'd retained to bolster the feeding trial results and analysis of North Dakota State University.

"I haven't heard back from him since I sent the samples he requested last month. I should touch base with the guy. Maybe he's got something we can use next week in the summary judgment hearing. I need to give him a call," Aitkins added, jotting a reminder to himself on a Post-It note.

"I was thinking. Maybe we should go up to Winnipeg and inspect the entirety of Stevenson's documents regarding their feed mill operation. Serve them with a Subpoena through Hague protocol, catch them off-guard," Dee Dee suggested.

A glimmer of intrigue crept into the woman's voice as she spoke. Aitkins liked how Dee Dee Hernesman thought. She had that "never say die" dedication, together with brains and superior negotiating skills, that make up a complete trial attorney. In many ways, Dee Dee Hernesman's considerable abilities were already outshining those of her mentor. Dan didn't mind. The more she could do, the less was left to him. He had no axe to grind with Dee Dee. He accepted her capabilities. In fact, he relished them. Her entry into the ruling class of the firm was welcome. She had earned her place.

"Give it a whirl, Dees. Book us at the Fort Garry, right by the railroad station. Two rooms."

"Duh. You think I'd let you sleep anywhere near me in some foreign city?"

"Canada hardly constitutes exotic turf, Ms. Hernesman."

He wanted to add.

"Besides, Dee Dee, I thought you swung the bat from the other side of the plate," but he didn't.

Even though they were now partners and therefore equals, he knew better than to speculate as to Hernesman's sexual preference. If there were anything he needed to know about her personal life, she'd eventually tell him. If not, then it was none of his business.

"Exotic enough for me. I'll book the rooms. How's your schedule?"

Aitkins scrutinized a calendar resting on a far corner of his desk.

"Adam begins Bantam hockey tryouts next week. But it's better that I'm not around for that. Julie can handle it. She's less likely to punch someone out than I am."

Hernesman rose from the chair. Her dirty hazel eyes glimmered.

"I would've thought the shiner Bobby Morgan gave you taught you a lesson about starting altercations at your age."

Danny smiled but said nothing as the female attorney left his office. The door swung shut.

"Mr. Aitkins? Dr. Ojala on line 1," Beth Monson, the firm's receptionist intoned over the intercom.

"That's amazing," the lawyer murmured to himself, reaching for the receiver. "I mention the guy's name and he's on the line."

"Hello, Dr. Ojala. Dan Aitkins here."

The professor spoke in a reserved voice, a voice wholly unlike the enthusiastic tone Aitkins recalled from their earlier meeting on the St. Paul campus of the University.

"Mr. Aitkins, I'm afraid I have some bad news," the plant expert said.

Daniel let the message glide through the air. He envisioned the samples he'd sent to the doctor spilled across the floor of the lab or, worse yet, spoiled in the process of delivery.

188

"What's up? Something wrong with the samples?"

"That's not the problem."

"Then what is the problem, Dr. Ojala?"

"It seems that I spoke too soon about undertaking this project. All outside consultations go through the Department Head, Dr. Fujimatsu. Usually routine. Not this time."

Acid crept into the attorney's mouth.

"Whatdoyou mean?"

"Seems that Stevenson's is in the process of funding an endowed chair for our School of Veterinary Science, something to the tune of $300,000.00. Before I agreed to assist you, I looked into any potential conflicts in terms of research or development we might have done for Stevenson's. Nothing surfaced. I'm afraid this endowment thing was below the radar, as they say."

An ache formed across Danny Aitkins' forehead. Blood began to pool, pushing urgently against the skin of his scalp.

"When did you find this out?"

"An attorney from the University called me yesterday. In-house fellow. Don't recall his name. Stevenson's inked the deal earlier this week. Fairly quick decision for a major gift. But it happens that way sometimes."

The lawyer sat in stunned silence. He gazed at two brown expansion folders before him on his desk, folders that contained the life and essence of the Anderson Hog Farm and its case against the feed manufacturer.

"Sorry I can't help out. I'd love to work on the case. I don't get involved much with the legal system. I was sort of looking forward to spending some time in a courtroom."

Aitkins didn't respond.

"One more thing," the professor added.

"Yes?" the attorney replied.

"Where should I return the feed samples? Under the circumstances, I don't feel comfortable keeping them around for any length of time."

"I'll have to get back to you on that."

"Don't wait too long. I'm uneasy holding evidence in the case. I hope you understand."

"I understand perfectly," the lawyer muttered before hanging up the phone.

CHAPTER 30

Summary Judgment. A defense lawyer's blade; a finely honed edge of pre-trial procedure meant to cleave the meat of a plaintiff's case from the bone. A process often used to dispatch a claim altogether, before a sympathetic jury can use emotion to render a big damage award against a defendant.

Judge Enwright's domain. The basement of the Becker County Courthouse had been remodeled into a jury-ready courtroom. As the least senior judge, Harriet Enwright drew the short straw, the subterranean space. She didn't mind. She knew that eventually she'd either outlast Clement Davidson and claim the prestige and historic decor of the upper-level courtroom or she'd make it to the State Supreme Court, in which case, her chambers would be in St. Paul; all marble and smoothly oiled wood; high ceilings and muted conversations with important people about the state of the judiciary.

Harriet sat rigidly behind the bench. Below her station, her court clerk Mark Olson and Angie Devlin her court reporter occupied their seats. Their collective attentions were captured by the voice of a large man standing behind a counsel table where three other well-dressed individuals occupied chairs.

"Your honor, opposing counsel. I'm James Thompson representing Stevenson's Sci-Swine. We've brought a Motion for Summary Judgment under Rule 56 of the Minnesota Rules of Civil Procedure. Our brief is fairly exhaustive so I won't repeat much of what is in there. I know this court's reputation for thoroughness. I'll just highlight a few of our key positions and then entertain any questions the court might have."

Thompson's dark skin shone under the bright lights of the room. His great height seemed to bump up against the suspended ceiling as he began his remarks. The stark white of his dress shirt contrasted with the deep tones of his African heritage. A yellow necktie formed a focal point, drawing the judge's attention directly to the center of the lawyer as he spoke.

"Our contentions are two-fold. First, that there is insufficient scientific evidence in the plaintiff's submissions to the court, in the form of expert affidavits and discovery responses, to sustain any claim. Specifically, the court must note that the levels of the purported Mycotoxins found in the feed purchased by Mr. Anderson from my client do not, by any stretch of the imagination, violate any laws or regulations of this State or the USDA."

Thompson paused and stared directly at the judge. His confidence was palpable as he let the import of his message settle in.

"The court will note that all of the authorities we have cited require findings of Mycotoxin contaminants, such as those alleged here, to be present in significant parts per million. The DON and zearalenone detected by NDSU, and, I might add, not detected by the University of Illinois Poison Control folks upon submission by our expert, Dr. Bronski, were reportedly found in concentrations thousands of times less than levels required by the cited authorities."

Judge Enwright cleared her throat. It was her usual course, unlike some of her colleagues, to inject herself into the lawyer's arguments and ask questions. In a fashion, she was preparing herself for the appellate bench where jurists routinely dive into dialogue with the advocates and rarely allow attorneys to build up a head of steam during oral argument.

"But isn't that why we have jury trials, counsel? Your expert says one thing; Mr. Aitkins' expert says another. The sifting of facts, the battle of positions...isn't that better played out in front of a jury?"

The defense lawyer smiled. He'd anticipated the court raising the issue, calling his attention to the time-honored precept that any issue of material fact in dispute was for jury, not judge, not summary judgment, determination.

"That was true before *Celeotex*. And *Daubert*."

Thompson affected a French pronunciation of the federal case, extending and softening the word. "Dow bare" was the way he phrased the case name.

"This court is well aware that elements of *Daubert* have been embraced by our appellate courts."Junk science' and 'mere guesswork' cannot be allowed to defeat a motion for dismissal. We assert, with all due respect to NDSU and the folks named as experts by plaintiffs, that the court in this case is being lead down the primrose path of junk science and speculation. Plaintiff's experts are applying standards regarding Mycotoxins that have no scientific basis."

F.W. Barnes sat quietly at the table. Judge Enwright looked fleetingly at the old man. It was obvious that Barnes was piqued, that he relished the chance to undress Danny Aitkins. Enwright knew that Barnes' delivery, his oratory, would have carried an entirely different inflection, more personal, more focused on the audacity of young Aitkins perpetrating a fraud on the court by pursuing a nuisance claim. Her attention swung back to the argument at hand.

"We've cited, in our submission, an utter lack of scientific testing and authentication behind plaintiff's premise that the almost non-existent levels of Mycotoxins involved in this case could cause any disruption of the breeding cycle of healthy pigs. Couple that with the fact that HPP was, at one time, obviously rampant within the Anderson herd, and that residual traces of the illness remain yet today, together with the ill-advised and dangerous process of spraying the hogs with lindane and fuel oil to rid them of mange, and it is abundantly clear that this case cannot be left to a jury to decide. It is squarely within the province of this court, as the gatekeeper, to prevent plaintiff's fanciful speculation from being pursued any further."

Thompson raised a paper cup of room temperature water to his lips and drained the contents in one swallow. Barnes and Malachi Stone, Stevenson's in-house counsel, leaned towards each other and conferred as the big lawyer scanned his notes.

"Our second point is that even if there is a plausible claim here regarding Mycotoxin contamination, and somehow, Stevenson's bears some responsibility for that..."

The attorney paused before redirecting his thoughts.

"I might add at this juncture that there has been absolutely no showing that Stevenson's had any knowledge of the presence of fusarium mold in the grain used to manufacture the batch of pellets in question. There has been no deposition taken, no discovery made, linking the grain used to make the feed sold to the Andersons back to its source to show the condition of the corn when Stevenson's received it. Another crucial failure in the link, the chain of evidence, in our view."

A deep breath by the big man.

"But in any event, the more important point is, that, under *Superwood* and the line of cases after it, this court must scrutinize the plaintiffs' claims for damages with a clear and dedicated vision."

"How so?" the judge asked.

There was no sign that the interruption flustered the veteran litigator.

"Very simply put, this was, the sale of the feed was, a transaction between two commercial entities. Stevenson's, through its Detroit Lakes facility, and the Anderson Hog Farm. *Superwood* limits damages between commercial entities. The caselaw simply does not allow a non-consumer transaction, in other words, a business deal as we have here, to open up a seller to damages above and beyond losses caused by defects in the property sold. All damages sought must be recoverable under the Uniform Commercial Code."

"In English, Mr. Thompson."

A brief smile stole across the judge's face. All of the attorneys in the room, including Daniel Aitkins, grinned at the jurist's subtle jab.

"Surely. Sorry about that. What I mean to say, and what *Superwood* requires, is that the plaintiffs be limited in their damage claim to the difference in value between tainted and untainted feed. Even if you buy the Andersons' view of things, and we certainly don't concede that it's reasonable, the most that the Andersons could claim as damage in this case is the entirety of their feed bill for the pelleted feed. Less than $5,000.00".

"Seems fairly harsh to the court, Mr. Thompson."

"Harsh or not, Judge Enwright, that's what we believe to be the status of Minnesota law in this regard."

"And what if the court determines that, for whatever reason, *Superwood* doesn't apply? Say, as an example, and by advancing this argument, I don't mean to infer that I am anywhere close to adopting it, I were to find that the Andersons, as a family owned farm, do not meet the *Superwood* criteria for an arms length transaction given the bargaining disparity between the parties. What then?"

"Of course, we don't believe such a distinction exists in Minnesota law. But if you made such a determination and the matter was tried, having not adopted our thinking on *Daubert*, then several other questions must be addressed.

'What portion of plaintiffs' losses were caused by HPP and the use of oil and lindane to treat mange?'; and: 'How long a period of time is reasonable to allow plaintiff's to rebuild their herd and mitigate their loss?'

It's our position that these issues shouldn't confront the court. The case should never reach that point. But if for some reason, our motion is denied and the case proceeds to jury, our brief does discuss the fact that plaintiffs should have been able to purchase replacement breeding stock at auction, with all necessary safeguards to prevent the invasion of outside disease, and been back to a 'pre-abortion storm' level of production within six months."

"And the significance of your distinction?"

"Plaintiffs are advancing a claim that it would take two years to get back on their feet. The damages set forth in their discovery responses are in the six figures. That's simply nonsense."

Thompson's use of the derogatory term "nonsense" was the first crack in the defense attorney's performance. Judge Enwright let the remark pass. She left it to Aitkins to attack the defendant's position, allowing her neutrality to remain unquestioned.

"Anything further?"

"Just this. Plaintiffs have been unable to prove any knowledge on Stevenson's part that the corn used to manufacture the pelleted feed was contaminated with fusarium. This point is vital because, as I have already stated, even plaintiffs' own experts concede that the levels of Mycotoxin found in the samples they studied in this case were well below FDA, USDA, and Canadian Grain Commission Guidelines. Couple that lack of factual connection with the affidavit of Dr. Bronski, a world-renowned expert in swine, wherein he makes it clear that low levels of the Mycotoxins found by NDSU would not, under any circumstances, cause gestating swine to abort their litters, and there simply is no scientific or factual basis upon which this matter can be allowed to be tried before a jury," Thompson argued, the texture of his voice clearly indicating he'd completed his remarks.

"If you have any other questions, I'd be happy to answer them at this point."

"I think you covered them, Mr. Thompson. I'll hear from Mr. Aitkins after a five minute recess."

The jurist rose from her seat. Her law clerk, a recent graduate of Drake Law School in Des Moines, Brad Peters, studied the defense lawyers as he rested his pen on a yellow legal pad covered with notes, notes that would eventually form a recommendation to Judge Enwright as to how the case should be decided. The lawyers stood up in respect as the judge left the room.

Danny approached his client. Dean Anderson sat patiently in the front row of an array of old church pews used for public seating. Aitkins leaned over to speak privately with the farmer.

"How do you think it's going?" Anderson whispered.

"Between you and me, I think we're weak on negligence and strict liability. I'll try to keep those theories alive but the law isn't on our side. Breach of Warranty for sure. The most interesting claim we have for the judge to chew on is negligence per se."

"How's that?"

"The sale of tainted feed violates Minnesota statutory law."

"Statutory law?"

"Laws passed by the legislature as opposed to common law; common law being created by precedent, past decisions of the court."

"What's the difference?"

Aitkins smiled at Angie Devlin as the stenographer floated lazily past the men. Exotic perfume followed the court reporter as she moved. Aitkins struggled to keep his mind on his work as the woman left the suggestion of a smile behind her.

"If I can get the judge to buy that negligence per se applies, even in the face of *Superwood* and its progeny, we have a little easier burden. Show the feed was contaminated with mold, a violation of the statute, and we've proven negligence. The more arrows in our quiver, the more likely one will hit the target."

"All rise".

The bailiff called the hearing back into session. Danny took his seat behind the counsel table.

"Mr. Aitkins?"

194

"Your honor, I don't want to belabor the arguments already raised in our brief. I'll try to address the areas of Mr. Thompson's dialogue that came to mind as he argued."

The lawyer stopped. Aitkins carefully scrutinized the defense team. Thompson smiled lightly. Barnes didn't acknowledge his adversary. Daniel resumed his argument.

"First, let's start with the obvious. *Superwood* requires two things for a recovery in tort:

One. There must be damage, to person or property, caused by the defective product, other than the product itself. That point of the *Superwood* test, as later enunciated in *Hapka v. Paquin Farms*, a 1990 Minnesota Supreme Court decision, is met here. The property claimed to have been damaged is the Anderson herd. Clearly 'other property'.

Two. The buyer must not be a merchant of the kind of goods purchased from the seller. That point of the test is also met. Dean Anderson, who is here today in the courtroom, is not and has never been a commercial feed miller or seller of livestock feed. In that sense, he is not a 'merchant' under the caselaw or under Minnesota Statute 604.10, the law clarifying *Superwood* and *Hapka*."

Aitkins looked up from his outline. There was an obvious frown on Harriet Enwright's face. She scanned the courtroom over her reading glasses.

"But Mr. Aitkins. Isn't the sort of thin distinction you're drawing here, claiming Mr. Anderson is not a 'merchant', disingenuous? I mean, it's absolutely clear that he's a commercial entity of some sort. He's a farmer seeking profit, and thus it seems, he's involved in commerce."

"Agreed. But the commerce he's involved in, and has been involved in, is the raising and sale of hogs, not the sale of feed. With all due respect to the court, there must be a distinction made here, as there was in *Zumberge v. NSP*, where the Court of Appeals held that a farmer's claim against an electrical supplier for stray voltage damage to his milk cows could proceed both under the Uniform Commercial Code for Breach of Warranty and under common law theories of tort."

"I know the case. There's a world of difference, isn't there, between a farmer purchasing electricity from a large power company and the situation here. I just don't know that your distinction passes muster."

Aitkins grimaced but did not engage the court in further debate. He knew the tort claims were weak given the legal precedent stacked against him. He knew Harriet Enwright, knew she rarely changed her mind once she dug in her heels. He moved on.

"Mr. Thompson seeks summary judgment of all claims in this matter, not just those relating to negligence and strict liability. He's

195

cited the Court to the United States Supreme Court holding in *Daubert* for the proposition that our expert witness testimony cannot sustain our claims. *Daubert* would be binding precedent if Mr. Thompson and Mr. Barnes were arguing this case in United States District Court, where it began. But the federal court refused to hear this matter and it's now here, in this jurisdiction. Minnesota procedural and evidentiary law apply. And, unfortunately for the defense, our Supreme Court recently rejected the stern language of *Daubert*."

Aitkins made a point to pronounce the case name "dow burt", avoiding the pretentious accent affected by the defense.

"How so?"

"A case just came out, *Goeb V. Tharaldson,* a decision from the Sixth District, Judge Hallenbeck in Duluth, I believe."

"I know Judge Hallenbeck. A stickler for evidentiary matters."

"Well, the Supreme Court affirmed Judge Hallenbeck's decision that *Daubert* does not apply in Minnesota. The effect of the ruling is that our time-honored system of gauging expert testimony remains in place. Under Minnesota law, the affidavits submitted by the plaintiff more than sustain a cause of action before the jury on all theories advanced."

"I follow your argument as to liability. But what about the defendant's position as to damages?"

"One last point as to the theories of liability, if I might?"

"Make it brief."

"No one has discussed Stevenson's violation of the Minnesota Commercial Feed Act, Minnesota Statute 25.37. We raised the contention in our original Complaint that the feed, by containing fusarium mold and Mycotoxins deleterious to swine, was adulterated and in violation of the statute. If the point is proven before a jury, the doctrine of negligence per se applies."

"How does that square with *Superwood's* preclusion of tort claims in commercial settings?"

"That's my point, judge. Even if you accept defendant's argument that, because the Andersons are merchants unable to sue for tort losses, there is nothing in *Superwood* or *Hapka* that deals with a commercial seller violating a statute. Negligence per se would still apply."

"Interesting. Go on."

Big Jim shifted uneasily in his chair. Barnes looked at the judge. Daniel intercepted the old man's glance and winked ever so slightly at the veteran litigator. Barnes' face flushed crimson. The defense lawyer quickly averted his eyes.

"There's an exhaustive review of the law of negligence per se in *Alderman's v. Shanks*, a case involving a violation of the Uniform Fire Code. In that case, our Supreme Court determined that a

196

party's failure to adhere to the Fire Code was grounds to find that party negligent per se. The only issue for the jury in that case, as it would be here, was: 'did the defendant violate the law?' If the answer is 'yes', then the defendant is negligent. I believe that the doctrine applies even if you buy into Mr. Thompson's position that this is a commercial transaction."

"What brings you to that conclusion?"

"If negligence per se is not imposed in such situations, then the court is creating an exception for businesses to break the law without suffering civil liability. There's something fundamentally unfair and inequitable in allowing a business that right when a consumer who violates the same law would be subject to tort liability."

Daniel detected movement. The lawyer noted that Malachi Stone's prodigious left leg was shaking violently as the corporate lawyer listened to Aitkins' argument.

"Lastly, I'd like to dispel the notion advanced by Mr. Thompson that, even if plaintiffs' claims are limited to Uniform Commercial Code Breach of Warranty remedies, that somehow the UCC precludes a recovery of lost profits. Under many Minnesota cases, including *Frame v. Hohrman*, a 1949 decision involving lost profits in milk cows caused by a disease brought into the herd by a newly purchased heifer, there's no question that the Andersons are entitled to sue for lost profits. So long as speculation isn't an element of the award, lost profits can be recovered. I thank the Court for its indulgence and I'll answer any questions that you might have."

"Does the defense have any brief rebuttal?" Judge Enwright asked.

Jim Thompson rose and advanced an uninspired response. He knew that Aitkins had all but conceded the issue of negligence and strict liability. The younger man's arguments had been calculated to allow the judge to discard those theories but retain Breach of Warranty, and perhaps, negligence per se, for trial. Thompson limited his remarks. He was done in fifteen minutes.

"What'll happen now?"

Dean Anderson stood on the sidewalk outside the Becker County Courthouse. The farmer studied the face of his attorney. Danny Aitkins had appeared nervous at the beginning of his argument but had warmed to the task. There had been a deep, desperate burning welling up in Dean Anderson's gut while he listened to Thompson's masterful oration. He was amazed that the young lawyer responded so well given the defense lawyer's reputation, the details of which Aitkins had shared with the farmer.

By the end of Danny's address, Dean Anderson was confident he would get his day in court.

"The law clerk will review all the cases and statutes," Aitkins replied. "Then he'll draft a written order for the judge to review. Judge Enwright will accept some and reject some of what the clerk recommends. Eventually, a written decision will be released. That'll take a couple of weeks. With the trial pushed back until after the first of the year, we still have time to put the rest of our case together. The parties have agreed to cut off discovery on December First."

"There's something more we need to find out?" the client queried.

A brisk west wind howled over the low rooflines of a building across the street. Aitkins shaded his eyes against the sun.

"I'd like to find some link between the pellets and the farm of origin. I'd love to be able to pin down whether or not Stevenson's knew the stuff was crap when they got it. That's one thing left on the burner. But it's a long shot. Then I need to touch base with that Vet you told me about. What's his name again?"

"Horace Brewster. He's a consultant to the Amish and Hutterites. Lives over by Leonard, North Dakota."

"We need someone else to swing the bat for you now that those dirty bastards knocked Doc Ojala out of the picture."

A wary smile crossed the farmer's face.

"Dan, don't you ever get so pissed off you just want to kick the crap out of those assholes on the other side?"

Aitkins' mouth broke into a broad grin.

"You saw what Bobby Morgan did to me. I'm afraid my brawling days are over. I'll stick to the courtroom. I'll be in touch after I meet with our economist from Moorhead State, Andy Nelson. I went to high school with him. He's totally behind us."

"Take care, Smokin' Joe," Dean Anderson quipped, referencing another retired pugilist as the farmer watched Danny Aitkins saunter away from the first good day they'd spent together in the courtroom.

CHAPTER 31

Jim Thompson crowded into the rear seat of a battered red and white Chevrolet Caprice with F.W. Barnes, Malachi Stone, and Dr. Ralph Covington. A young woman, resplendent in a tailored business suit, low heels, nylons, and flowing red hair occupied the passenger side of the bench seat in front of the men. A sour faced Metis, his thick black hair oiled to the scalp, a perpetual scowl carved on his suntanned face, maneuvered the car through the stop and go traffic of the western neighborhoods of the city.

"Ms. Barnes, have you been to Winnipeg before?" Mr. Stone asked, his voice barely audible over the roar of the car's engine.

"Many times. My parents came up here a lot on vacation. Friends of theirs had a little cabin; the Canadians call them 'cottages', on the east shore of Lake Winnipeg."

"They say it's an impressive body of water," the Iowan offered.

"More than impressive," F.W. Barnes advised. "Over three hundred miles long. You're in igloo country by the time you get to the north end of the lake."

Big Jim Thompson didn't join the conversation. His narrow eyes studied the passing neighborhoods.

"Not much fishing, though. Too shallow and warm. Big catfish by the dam, where the Red River comes in. Upwards of forty pounds," F.W. continued.

Barnes didn't look at the corporate man as he added additional detail. F.W.'s eyes studied the profile of his daughter-in-law. He had never told his son, never told the woman, how lucky Michael had been to find her. A glimmer of regret crept into his consciousness as he watched Melanie's delicate eyelashes beat reflexively. There might have been a time to offer his opinions while his son was alive. Now, all he could do was provide Melanie a job and insure that his grandchildren had a roof over their heads and a hot meal on their plates. Sentiment didn't have a place in their lives now that Michael was buried beneath the Ottertail County dirt.

"Can you eat 'em?" Stone asked.

"Only if you like stinking pesticides," the Metis blurted out, spitting a wad of chew into a paper cup on the floor between himself and the woman. "Damn farmers. Always dumping crap on the land, screwing up the works."

The Canadian's words descended into an inaudible diatribe rendered in an indecipherable language.

Ms. Barnes ignored the expectoration and turned to watch the passing streets of the provincial capital. The leaves had long since fled. There was no snow; only fragile grass, its resilience lost in death, covered the ground. No birds landed in the branches of the naked trees. There were no butterflies or insects buzzing the empty air. Her eyes, their hue, the color of Lake Michigan greenstone, teared up as she compared the barren landscape to the wilderness of her own heart.

"Anything wrong, Ms. Barnes?"

Jim Thompson's enormous palm rested on her right shoulder with insignificant weight. The delicacy was something she did not expect from so large and powerful a man.

"She gets this way around the holidays," F.W. said softly. The older man's voice skirted compassion. The attorney's restrained concern was as close to tenderness as Melanie Barnes had ever witnessed from her father-in-law. "Michael's absence seems to upset her most around the holidays."

"I'm sorry," the black man murmured, his voice soothing and considerate as his fingers gently grasped her shoulder in a subtle embrace before retreating.

"I'll be fine," the woman said.

They checked into the Fort Garry, an old palace of a hotel constructed of stone and steel by the railroad back near the turn of the Twentieth Century. Melanie's heels clicked briskly against the polished floor of the lobby as they walked towards the elevators.

"Mel," a familiar voice cried out.

Danny Aitkins identified the unmistakable figure of his best friend's widow from his seat in the hotel bar. As the lawyer approached the paralegal, he quickly realized that she wasn't alone.

"F.W., Jim, Mr. Stone. Fancy meeting you folks here," the trial attorney quickly inserted, hoping to mask his enthusiasm for the woman. Aitkins extended a hand, perfunctorily greeting each of the men. He refrained from hugging Melanie. He simply patted her forearm and chanced a glance into her eyes. There was no indication that she shared his exuberance. The advocate struggled mightily to bury his disappointment.

"Ms. Barnes and Mr. Stone will be covering the examination you're conducting at the Stevenson's Document Center," Thompson advised. "F.W. and I have other business to attend to."

"I'm sure," Aitkins responded.

He knew that the two trial attorneys would be meeting with the powers that be at Stevenson's to discuss the case. Judge Enwright had ruled exactly as Daniel had predicted. Negligence and strict liability were out. Negligence per se and all the UCC claims were in. The judge imposed no restrictions upon the plaintiffs' ability to claim damages and invoked no limits regarding the testimony of Dr. Guttormson and Dr. Thomas. The jury would hear it and hear it all.

"What's that supposed to mean?"

F.W.'s face turned ominous.

"Easy, big fella," Danny said, placing his palms up in front of his face as if to deflect an anticipated assault. "I guess I'll see Mr. Stone and Ms. Barnes tomorrow morning. Eight sharp, right?"

"Right," Malachi Stone responded, his thick face devoid of detectable emotion.

"See you then."

"Bye," Melanie whispered as her companions advanced towards the lift. She watched Danny's eyes light up as the word floated in the air. She sensed there was something new between them, something terrible and beautiful that she'd nearly held, nearly captured before. An image of Julie Aitkins sought to interrupt her rapture, sought to insert itself into the depths of Melanie's longing. She fought the specter, battled the essence of her friend, a woman that she admired.

"What?" Daniel murmured. "What is it?"

"I'm going running at six tomorrow morning if you want to join me."

Bing.

The elevator car arrived.

Dee Dee Hernesman entered the lobby from outside the hotel. Her attention was fixed on her partner. She watched Aitkins touch Melanie Barnes lightly on the cheek with the tip of his index finger, their faces illuminated by the glow of a chandelier. The red head turned sharply on her heels, escaping an awkward moment with grace, and entered the waiting elevator.

"And what, pray tell, was that all about?" the female attorney asked as she approached her partner.

Danny didn't immediately acknowledge his partner's presence. Dee Dee grabbed the man by the front of his flannel shirt, the fabric worn smooth; its red and white squares muted with age, and repeated her question.

"What the hell was that all about?"

His face flashed.

"Nothing, Dees. It's nothing. We're just going running in the morning. She's working for F.W."

"On this case?"

"Yep."

"Isn't that going to present a problem?"

It was Aitkins' turn to ask the question.

"What do you mean?"

"I'm not blind, Danny. I saw the way you looked at her. A person can learn more from one look than you can learn from reading a thousand books."

Aitkins felt himself draw inward.

"You're letting your imagination interfere with your common sense. We're going running, that's all," Daniel offered weakly.

201

Aitkins turned and headed towards the pub, intent on finishing his Molson. Ms. Hernesman shook her head in disbelief and followed her partner to his table.

CHAPTER 32

The litigator crawled beneath the thick comforter of the king-sized bed. The sleeping platform occupied one wall of Aitkins' room at the Fort Garry. Delicate flowers, feminine and subdued, embracing yellows and browns, adorned the wallpaper; paper freshly hung as part of a refurbishing project. High above the reclining lawyer, plaster walls met a freshly painted ceiling. The only light in Aitkins' room came from the screen of a color television. The set was tuned to Winnipeg's local station, the A-Channel. Aitkins watched the news, pretending, for the benefit of himself, to be interested in the provincial politics of Manitoba.

In reality, all he could think about was the soft luminescence of Melanie Barnes' alabaster skin; the way her thick red hair rested on her shoulders; the suggestive movement of her thighs against her skirt as she left him in the hotel lobby and entered the elevator car; her virescent eyes, turning from murky green to stark emerald as she studied his face, as she tried to discern his intentions.

Julie was far away, taking care of their children, unselfish in her devotion to their family, to their unity. She was a striking woman in her own right, a woman who made love with the passion of a teenager, a woman who had seen him through the turmoil of his apprentice as a trial lawyer. Loyalty. He owed Julie his. There were a hundred reasons he should have been thinking about his wife and children as he lay in the warm sheets of the hotel bed. And yet, his mind was on someone else, a woman who was his friend, his wife's friend, the widow of his best friend.

Aitkins hadn't run in months. His stomach seemed to be losing its tone with the approach of winter. He tried to keep the weight off by intermittent exercise and doing physical labor around the hobby farm, by doing chores; like putting up the three hundred bales of freshly mown alfalfa cut, raked, and baled by his neighbor, Jimmy Titus. In the close humidity of the barn, Dan's father had tossed bale after bale onto the cranky old John Deere hay elevator, its metal frame rusted and nearly devoid of factory paint, the electric motor taxed to its limit by the heavy cargo. Danny picked up and stacked every one of the three hundred thirty-five pound bales. It was hard, hot work. As a result of such chores, Aitkins felt that he was in good shape. Somehow, it didn't take long for the edge of his summer chores to wear off and for the thickness of oncoming winter to reclaim his middle.

His running pants, black nylon with a thin linen lining, occupied the seat of a chair across the room. Well-worn Nike cross trainers, the soles nearly absent tread, the uppers faded and beaten by countless miles of jogging on gravel roads in years past, hung across the back of the chair by the laces. He feared the morning.

Melanie was a serious runner. She was capable of putting together six-minute miles without breaking a sweat.

"I'll be lucky to put in one eight minute mile," Danny muttered, watching a demonstrator on television being arrested at an Animal Rights Rally at the Forks, the reconditioned tourist area near the confluence of Winnipeg's largest rivers. Aitkins' attention was captured by the fanatical screams of the protester as the mesh fence she'd padlocked herself to was cut by a police officer using a gigantic bolt cutter. The attorney hit the off button on the remote, plunging the hotel room into darkness.

Lights outside the hotel windows cast shadows across the room's furniture. Dan rested heavily on his back, the fusion site well cushioned by the bed's ample mattress. He tried to push lusty images of Melanie Ingersol Barnes out of his mind. She kept fighting her way back, overriding his attempts at mental fidelity. It was well after two o'clock when his eyes finally closed due to the great weight of his fatigue.

"Ready to go?"

She was dressed in running tights, a nylon shell, and flashy New Balance running shoes. Her thighs, the exquisite shape of her calves, were accented by the tight fit of the running gear. Her hair was pulled into a sparse ponytail. Feathery strands of red mane were woven through the adjustable strap of a "Winnipeg Moose" baseball cap.

"I'm as ready as I'll ever be. Where'd you get the cap?" Daniel asked.

"Bought it at the Portage Mall. Clearance. We'll go at your pace if you like."

"Hey, I haven't been running in like three months. I went two miles with Adam last week and thought I was gonna die. Let's keep the potential for a heart attack to a minimum, shall we?"

His maroon and gold "Minnesota Gophers" pullover was stained with an odd assortment of oil and paint. He'd last worn the coverlet working in his garage. He didn't have a hat. As they walked against a fierce wind, a hint of snow in the air, the temperature below freezing, Aitkins silently lamented the fact that his head was bare.

They maintained a slow, easy pace. Melanie barely exhaled as they trotted lazily towards Holy Trinity Anglican Church. Bare tree limbs framed the exquisite architecture of the cathedral. A bell tower cast a shadow. Heavy clouds boiled as the joggers passed the sanctuary. Aitkins looked at the woman. Her eyes stared straight ahead.

The attorney pondered their run. Aitkins' contemplated his inability to maintain a platonic distance from Melanie Barnes, a woman who had rejected him, and then desired him during a time of turmoil and upset in her life. As he ran away from the religion embodied in the stones of the Anglican church, no great moral awakening presented itself.

"You doing OK?" she asked, her breathing easy, her legs and feet marking time against the concrete.

"OK," Danny managed to exhale, his side beginning to clench, his lungs beginning to burn. "How far do you want to go?"

"I'd like to get at least three in."

"I think I can make three at this pace," the lawyer offered with little conviction in his voice.

"You sure?"

"Yep."

They turned east and headed towards the Forks, seeking the river bottom and the natural pull of water. Below the crest of the banks, there was no wind. Dan felt a revitalization of his physical abilities, a rebirth of the runner's high he'd been away from for so long, as they negotiated a trail along the Red River.

"That's a little over two out. If we turn back now, we'll put in four," she advised.

"About all I can handle," Danny admitted, a new stitch across his low back presenting itself as they climbed a hill.

He failed to note the merger of nature and city that enveloped them. His eyes were riveted to the gentle sway of his companion's form as she led the way back to the hotel. His attention was fixed on the poetry of her strides, on the strength of her hamstrings as she stretched out and increased her speed.

"Slow it down, Mel. I'm about done in."

"Come on, Star Baby, I know you've got it in you," she teased, throttling back a bit as they turned onto Main. The Romanesque facade of the Fort Garry loomed obvious against the horizon. Her feet pounded the asphalt. Her pace increased.

Daniel tried to find fourth gear. It wasn't there. Melanie Barnes pulled away from the lawyer and ran the last four blocks alone, sprinting briskly until she came to rest in front of their hotel.

"Nice run," she said, looking at the watch on her left wrist as Danny jogged up to the woman. "Seven and a half minute miles. Not bad for an old out-of-shape football player."

She removed her ball cap and smiled. Danny tried to respond. He couldn't. His breathing was labored; his pulse pounded in his temple. The lawyer bent at the waist, his hands on his hips.

"Maybe I pushed you a little too hard," she added quietly, concern evident in her voice.

"I'll be fine. It was a great run," he replied, chancing a glance at his companion.

Her smile hung between them. Danny Aitkins sensed there was a world of potential heartache for them both in that beautiful grin.

CHAPTER 33

The basement of Stevenson's warehouse, tucked beneath a towering feed manufacturing complex, was bathed in penetrating cold. Box upon box of receipts, memos, and correspondence surrounded a small table in the center of the room. Massive sandstone blocks, carved years before from some long-forgotten quarry, formed the foundation of the building and defined the limits of the space where the attorneys worked. Light bulbs hung randomly from ancient fir beams; timbers supporting the great weight of the three stories of additional storage and offices above the basement level of the structure. The fixtures threw half-hearted light across a poured concrete floor. Much of the perimeter of the room remained dark and inaccessible without a flashlight.

Daniel Aitkins and Dee Dee Hernesman began their inspection with boxes closest to the table. Hour after hour they scanned the disorganized, unindexed mass of documents. Searching. Looking for any connection between the paperwork and the pelleted feed manufactured in Grand Forks and sold to Dean Anderson through the Detroit Lakes elevator.

The stunt pulled by the Grafton Militia had delayed the auction and foreclosure of Dean and Nancy Anderson's farm. Jury selection was set to begin January Fifteenth before Judge Enwright. The foreclosure had been postponed by the bank, much to the chagrin of Stevenson's, until after the verdict. Chase House had finally, after the debacle at the auction, stood up to his superiors and convinced them that, whatever corporate shenanigans were in the works between Stevenson's and the First Farmer's Bank of Montreal, the auction sale of the Andersons' assets could wait.

"Not finding much in the way of organization to these files," Dee Dee observed, talking in low tones as she bent over a carton, working through a collection of manila folders and documents. "They all seem to be pretty much randomly tossed into boxes."

Melanie Barnes sat off to one side of the table. Malachi Stone, dressed casually in wool slacks and a long sleeved navy blue sweater, sat across the table, studying a file folder. Ms. Barnes scrutinized the work of the opposing attorneys, making note of each box opened, ready to make copies of any documents retrieved by Hernesman or Aitkins so that she could retain the originals and pass them along to Big Jim Thompson and F.W. Barnes. An ancient copier purred next to the paralegal, waiting to laboriously churn out copies, though none had been requested.

Danny stood next to his partner, a file folder in his hand, scanning invoices from the Grand Forks feed manufacturing plant.

"I get the feeling that we're not going to find what we're looking for," Aitkins whispered. "Look here."

He handed the file to the female attorney. They were both dressed in corduroy slacks and loose fitting sweaters. The room's musty atmosphere embraced more than a century of trapped odors and hung over them as they labored. Dee Dee studied the materials handed to her.

"The trucking invoice for the load sold to the Andersons isn't in there," Aitkins murmured. "It's like it never happened."

"Deliberate?"

"No question in my mind. Stevenson's has either removed it and destroyed it or secreted it somewhere in this mess," the senior attorney observed, glancing across several hundred assembled uninspected cartons of material. "If it's here, it'll take a long time to find it."

"I'm a little confused," Hernesman said, handing the folder back to Aitkins. "Why are you so interested in finding a tie between the farm of origin and the load that went to the Andersons? The judge tossed out our tort claims. We don't need to prove fault."

Aitkins studied the faces of their adversaries. Stone was deeply engaged in his project. Melanie Barnes appeared to be preoccupied with paperwork. Danny fixed on the faint gray of his partner's eyes.

"You're probably right, at least in terms of the law. But think of the impact on the jury if we can find out where this crap came from and prove that it was rotten on the day Stevenson's took it in. All the niceties of warranty and negligence per se won't mean a damn thing if the jury thinks that Stevenson' tried to pass shit off as sirloin."

"We don't have a lot of time left to put our case together," Hernesman noted. "Trial's in less than two months and discovery closes the First of December. That doesn't give us much time to find a link."

"This is our only shot. If we don't find it here, we'll go with what we've got."

Aitkins quietly crossed the distance between himself and Melanie Barnes.

"Ms. Barnes," he interrupted.

"Yes, Mr. Aitkins?"

Dee Dee Hernesman suppressed a giggle. She was standing in the shadows, pretending to be engaged in her work, as Danny addressed the paralegal. Hernesman recalled that her partner's eyes had danced when he discovered Melanie Barnes was working on the document retrieval project. Dee Dee had seen them interact in the hotel lobby.

She'd also been in the Fort Garry breakfast room, watching the artistry of the hotel chefs when Danny and Ms. Barnes strolled into the room after their early morning jog. Hernesman made it a point to scrutinize the nuances of Melanie's performance as the other woman sheepishly joined her father-in-law at a table across the largeness of the dining room, her entrance with the enemy concealed from the old man by a crowd of customers.

It was indisputable that Ms. Barnes felt something for Daniel Aitkins. It was there in the woman's gait, in her brief hesitation as she separated from Danny.

She's a friend of Julie's, Hernesman thought as the paralegal had taken a seat to begin a false, animated conversation with F.W. Barnes that morning. *What in the world are they doing?* Dee Dee had asked herself.

Dee Dee had wanted to say something, to verbally assail her friend and bring him to his senses about the reality of his life, his responsibilities to Julie and to his three kids. She had stifled the urge and made small talk as they waited for breakfast.

Watching the couple in the basement of the warehouse, emotion and angst written so obviously in their respective eyes, she felt twinges of both regret and anger that she had not said something to Daniel. She liked Julie, thought highly of her as a mother, as a teacher, and as a writer. Dee Dee had read early portions of Julie's novel. The female attorney was an English major herself, an avid reader, and a poet, albeit a poor one. There was an indisputable quality to Julie's writing, literary turns that few authors from the prairie could sustain over the scope and breadth of a lengthy work of fiction.

Sadness replaced anger as Hernesman watched the couple's charade unfold.

"Seems that the delivery invoice involved in our case has been misplaced," Aitkins reported to Melanie Barnes. "You know anything about that?" the lawyer added with skepticism.

Dan handed the yellow folder to the woman. She scanned the contents of the packet. Her eyes viewed the material over the thick black plastic frames of her eyeglasses; cheap "cheaters" purchased from a Fergus Falls five-and-dime.

"Should be right with the others. Malachi, you know anything about this?"

Stone raised the great weight of his large head and stared at Aitkins.

"Everything that we have, you have, Aitkins. If it's not there, it doesn't exist."

"Seems sort of odd to me, counselor, that the only invoice missing in over fifty invoices in a row would be the one pertaining to this case," Aitkins quipped.

"Odd or not, if it exists, it's in the boxes. I resent your insinuation," Stone replied.

Dan smiled. His discourse with the corporate lawyer made Stone uncomfortable. There was a tremor to the man's voice. Aitkins knew he'd hit a nerve. What it was, exactly, Danny couldn't say, but there was something about his inquiry that put the Iowan in distress.

"I'll take you at your word, Stone," Aitkins responded, gently retrieving the folder from the legal assistant.

"And I'll take you at yours," Stone added solicitously.

Noon arrived. Aitkins and his partner took a break. They walked across the street to an ancient lunch counter. The cafe was full of Stevenson's employees, predominantly tired men wearing green Carharts boasting corporate logos embroidered over the left front pockets of their shirts. The conversation in the restaurant was loud and animated, ranging from discussions about American-based teams dominating the NHL, to diatribes about the dismal exchange rate between American and Canadian currency. Dan and Dee Dee found a small table in a remote section of the café and sat down.

They'd finished inspecting thirty boxes. Aitkins was certain that their search was futile. He watched a young woman approach their table, mindful that their time in Winnipeg was short.

"Hi. My name's Kathleen. Here're a couple of menus. Specials are on the back. Can I get you anything to drink?"

The waitress was in her late teens, fighting acne, and smelling of French fries and grease. But her manner was pleasant, her accent, obvious. Behind retreating puberty, an adult face was emerging. In a couple of years, when her face cleared and her body matured, she would become an attractive woman.

"I'll have a Coke," Dee Dee said.

"Coffee's fine," Aitkins added.

"Take anything with it?"

"Black."

"I'll be right back."

He retracted his gaze.

"You're so obvious," Dee Dee remarked.

"What?"

"Staring at that little girl. You should be ashamed of yourself."

"I wasn't staring."

"Sure, Danny. You just reminded me of something my big brother Alex told me just before I turned eleven."

Aitkins appreciated his partner's broad face. There was no question in his mind that she was a lesbian. Not that it mattered. She was a friend, a confidant, and a great lawyer. He was interested in any wisdom she had to impart.

"What's that?"

"'All men are pigs'."

There was little Danny Aitkins could say. The evidence was indisputable. He kept quiet and waited for his coffee.

CHAPTER 34

They planned to have dinner at Tommy's Americana, a trendy, out of the way hole-in-the-wall on a poorly lit back street off Portage Avenue. Before he left his room, a wave of guilt, thick and oppressive like the firmament stalled above the Canadian prairie, descended over him. A stifling wave of nervous anticipation sought him out and tried to force his will as he dressed in the brightly illumined lavatory of his hotel room. The television was on. An old Sherlock Holmes movie provided dissonance to the moment. The telephone rang.

"Hello?"

"Danny, it's me."

"Jules," he answered weakly, urging unruly strands of short blond hair into compliance with the bristles of a brush as he spoke. He stared at his reflection in a mirror over the bathroom sink. Danny Aitkins didn't like what he saw.

"I miss you," his wife said dryly. "What's up with the case?"

"We'll be through tomorrow. Dee Dee and I haven't found a smoking gun. I doubt that we will."

The report of a rifle rang out. Basil Rathbone's companion collapsed onto the moist earth of a London graveyard as the detective crouched low in anticipation of another round being fired. Gray fog drifted across the dead man. Danny was distracted by the movie.

"I've got some good news."

"What?"

"Adam made the Bantam A's."

"You're kidding me."

"Nope. They brought in some coaches from Thief River Falls to make the selections. The committee didn't know the names of the kids until after they made their picks."

"I can't believe it. Last year he was number three. It sure didn't look good."

His wife released a small, gentle laugh.

"He's an Aitkins, remember? He doesn't give up easily."

"I'm sorry I missed it."

The lawyer paused to reflect on his words.

"No, really I'm not. I always get so wound up. Better you were there. Tell him we'll celebrate big time when I get home," Daniel said.

"I will. Drive safe and come home in one piece, OK? We all miss you."

"How are Michael and Amanda?"

"Great. They're over at the Olson's watching videos. They'll be back before ten."

Danny tucked in his long sleeved sport shirt, the color of the fabric a vibrant green, and zipped the barn door of his blue jeans. He watched the age in his face dissipate as he talked to the woman he'd loved for over sixteen years.

"Give them a kiss for me, will you?" he added.

"How about one for me?"

"You know that I'd kiss you senseless if you were here," the lawyer whispered. "Along with doing other things."

"You're bad, Daniel Emery Aitkins. Very bad."

"I'll see you tomorrow."

"I'll be waiting," she replied, inserting a flirtatious inference.

The lawyer hung up the phone. His conversation with his wife had reiterated everything that was right with their lives. Every good and decent thing that connected him to Julie had made its presence known during the short, fleeting minutes of their long distance connection. And yet, the magic of their union could not dislodge the image of Melanie Barnes from his mind. Despite his best intentions, he could not prevent his departure from the Fort Garry Hotel.

They walked to Tommy's together. He did not embrace her or touch her in any way during the interlude in the lobby or on their journey through Winnipeg. She matched him stride for silent stride as they followed familiar lanes towards their destination behind the Portage Place Shopping Centre. His pace was brisk and determined, leading her to believe that something was amiss.

The attorney stopped in front of the restaurant and took in the entirety of the woman. Her flaming red hair was held in place by a hairpin. Her cheeks were pink from the cold, making the natural color of her lips less obvious. Light displayed by an ornate street fixture in front of Tommy's revealed that she was dressed casually in slacks, a thick winter wool coat cut narrowly at the waist, and brown cowboy boots. It was cold. Her exhalations drifted from her mouth. A look of apprehension rested in her eyes.

"What's wrong?" she asked.

"Nothing."

"Don't lie to me, Dan. We're both grown-ups. We've been down this road before. Something is eating you."

He hesitated.

"Julie called."

"Oh."

"Adam made the Bantam A's."

"That's wonderful. I know how hard he's been working. You must be very proud."

"I am."

213

Her bare hand, chilled by the winter air, touched his exposed wrist.

"What is it that you want from me, Daniel? What is it that makes us keep doing this to ourselves?"

She studied the faint blue of his eyes, seeking an aspect of truth.

"I'm not sure."

"We're friends, you know. We can remain friends; have a nice meal, talk about life and old times. There's certainly nothing wrong with that. Julie's my friend. You may not believe me; hell, she probably wouldn't believe me if she saw us right now. But that's the honest to God's truth. Whatever this is, understand I know that it's fleeting, and that I'm OK with that."

Aitkins tried to avert his eyes.

"Don't turn away. Look at me. I'm not a fool. I know you love Julie. Hell, I love her. She's been there for me, in more ways than you can ever know."

He steadied himself, fighting off a wave of nervous shivers.

"What do you mean?"

It was her turn to look away.

"She knows about what happened when Michael died. Between us, I mean."

The revelation startled him.

"How?"

"I broke down once, afterwards, when she and I were packing Michael's clothes for The Goodwill. She asked why I was so upset. I blurted it out."

"She never said a word. All these years, she never said a word," Danny whispered.

"She loves you. She didn't want to confront you. It was something that happened against a tremendous hurricane of grief. I think she understood that. She didn't like it. Obviously not. She didn't talk to me for months afterwards. But, eventually she called. We talked it through."

A Dodge minivan, loaded with teenagers, roared past them.

"Smootchy, smootchy," immature voices called out derisively as the vehicle zoomed away, rounding the corner on two tires.

Melanie smiled.

"What'll we do now, Star Baby?" she asked.

"How about getting something to eat?"

"Only if that's what you want."

"It's what I want."

He held the door for her. Snowflakes descended. Danny's eyes lingered on the woman as she passed by. He felt numb. He was oblivious to the delicate touch of alighting snow. Sounds of congregated humanity emerged from the building. A surge of warmth embraced Danny Aitkins' troubled face as he followed Melanie Barnes into the restaurant.

CHAPTER 35

They found a table. Tommy's was famous for two things; thick Black Angus steaks and live folk music. It was happenstance that the couple chose Tommy's that night. Sarah Harmer, one of Danny's favorite singer-songwriters, a Canadian artist he'd first heard perform at the Winnipeg Folk Music Festival, was the entertainment. They would have an hour and a half to eat their dinner, down a little wine, and contemplate where they were headed, what boundaries they were willing to cross, before the singer took the stage.

Greenery obscured the couple from the other patrons. A mass of ferns, palms, and other plants, vibrant despite the chill of the season, concealed their location from all but the most vigilant eyes. Around them, out in the main concourse of the restaurant, under a universe of artificial stars, galaxies, and planets, servers darted between booths and tables carrying heavy trays of beef, pork, and assorted seafood. The Pub's owner, Tom Jacobs, a wealthy software designer, had come to Winnipeg with a hefty fortune of American coin in his purse seeking to fashion a new reality in the form of an upscale eatery featuring live music. Jacobs insisted on providing the highest quality presentation for his customers. Live seafood was flown in once a week from whichever coast had the better selection. Frozen fish did not touch the plates of Tom Jacob's customers.

Tin signs, salvaged from gasoline stations, warehouses, and antiquated retail establishments from across North America adorned the brick walls of the building's interior. Remnants of plaster; white and distinct, clung to the mortar spaces between the bricks, evidence of the past life of the structure. A weathered Mobil Oil sign, its winged steed faded from its signature red to a subdued pink, covered the wall behind Danny. Melanie Barnes sat across the table from the attorney sipping a glass of rose'.

The air was thick with cigarette smoke. Aitkins noted that the people of Canada seemed to enjoy their tobacco and beer at levels in excess of those attained by their American cousins. Neither he nor Melanie smoked. He'd tried it as a thirteen-year-old kid, sneaking Kent's out of the vending machine at the Lakes Bowling Alley back home. He lasted a month as a serious smoker. The habit never held an appeal.

Liquor was another story. When he took his first swig of Boone's Farm Apple Wine at Maggie Swanson's fifteenth birthday party, he knew that alcohol was special. The soft, easy glow that came over him as he loaded his brain up with fermented liquid; the natural, lazy disappearance of his inhibitions around girls, the mellow, hazy

216

bliss of knowing more about life and where he was headed all came to him as near sacred revelations each time he befriended the bottle.

For a long time, Daniel didn't consider himself to be an abuser of alcohol. He didn't believe that he needed to curb his appetite for booze; at least until the night he ended up in an unfamiliar house in downtown Fargo after a touch football tournament. His team won the tournament and went on a tour of nightspots in Fargo. There had been a linking up with some young women, a ride back to their place with two or three other players in tow. Everyone but Danny had disappeared into separate bedrooms, leaving him alone with one very stoned girl. She turned out to be fifteen. He was married, with one kid at home, and another on the way. Finally, in the wee hours of the morning, the realization that he didn't know where he was, or who he was with, gave him fleeting insight.

"Maybe I have a problem."

His teammates had been preoccupied. He called an old friend. Mitch Colliard didn't ask why Danny needed a ride. The situation was obvious when his friend walked into the apartment and found the teenaged girl passed out on the couch.

"Shit, Danny."

"I know. I gotta get the fuck out of here."

"What were you thinking?" Mitch asked as they headed out the door, out into the blazing heat of the Indian summer night.

"I wasn't."

There had been other times, other places where alcohol placed him in jeopardy. Each time, on each occasion, he managed to dodge true difficulty. He swore to himself as he approached forty that it was over, that he could stay off the sauce on his own, without intervention, without some fancy-pants shrink or group of reprobates guiding his hand. And he did it mostly. Until Bobby Morgan cold-cocked him in Masterson's Bar, he hadn't been drunk since the night on the beach, lamenting the death of the Ojibwe girl. After his confrontation with the PI, he returned to relative sobriety, touching only a glass or two of wine with his wife, a beer or two with the old man after putting up hay.

"The wine's good," Melanie observed, avoiding any conversation of substance, feeling out her companion's mood as they waited for their server.

A carafe of rose' stood in the center of the table. The clean lines of the container merged with the freshly laundered white of the tablecloth, lending an atmosphere of class to the place. Danny sipped readily, holding the thin stem of the wineglass in his left hand as he considered his female companion.

217

"Something wrong?" she asked, tilting her head, resting her delicate chin on pale hands.

"I was just thinking about the Andersons. How this whole thing has fucked up their lives. Before this case, they were like any other hard working Midwestern farm family struggling to make ends meet. It's all changed for them now, regardless of how this turns out."

"What do you mean?"

"They've lost faith. Not in the religious sense but in the system. They'd always been able to work out disputes with their neighbors. Never needed courts to sort it out. I can see it in Dean's eyes when I talk to him. Even if we win this thing, he's been beaten. The corporations have won."

Melanie pursed her lips. The allusion to Stevenson's role in the demise of the farmer's trust unnerved her.

"Can we pick a different topic? I'm tired of talking shop. Besides, my client has a different view of things. I don't know that it's productive to air our differences here. It doesn't accomplish anything or change what's happened."

"Agreed. How are the kids?" Danny asked.

"They're doing well. I thought the move to a small town, after five years in the Cities, would be traumatic. They both took to it. I guess it's where they belong."

Danny raised his glass and drained the wine. He reached for the carafe and refilled his goblet.

"And yours? I know Adam must be elated to make the A-Team. How's Amanda Jane? She's such a sweetie."

"Still pulling my chain. I'm not sure I'm cut out to be the father of a girl. She's so different, so wily when it comes to knowing how to get to me. The boys, even little Michael, come straight out and say what they mean. Amanda is so good at taking an alternative route, persuading me to accept her position. It drives Julie nuts."

The mention of Julie's name disrupted their rapport. Whether there was something untoward in the air, whether the night would end in romance or mere friendship, the denotation of Danny's marital status brought reality into the equation. Uneasiness colored Melanie's face. Her hand shook slightly as she lifted the crystal glass to her lips and swallowed the remaining liquor.

"Ready to order?" a young waiter asked, his words effeminate, his demeanor helpful and polite.

The man was in his early twenties. He sported no earrings. A single yellow rose adorned the left side of his neck, a vulnerable position for such an emblem.

"How are the broiled scallops?" the woman responded.

"Fresh. Flown in yesterday. That would be my first choice if I was ordering seafood."

218

"I'll take the scallops, tossed salad with vinaigrette. I'll skip the potato."

"Lovely. And for you sir?"

Aitkins held a leatherette menu in his hands.

"The Porterhouse any good?"

Melanie smiled.

"I thought you were trying to lose weight."

"I am. Just not tonight," Daniel responded, his trademark grin returning.

"Again, an excellent choice. How would you like that prepared?" the waiter asked.

"Medium rare. Thousand Island on the salad."

"Potato?"

Aitkins handed the menu to the waiter.

"I'll skip the potato," he said, winking to Melanie Barnes. "Watching my weight, you know."

The gay man did not leave the table immediately. His eyes surveyed the respective ring fingers of his customers. He noted that the man and the woman both wore wedding bands, though the woman did not have a diamond on her finger.

"Special occasion?" the waiter asked politely.

Melanie looked at the attorney. She reached across the linen tablecloth and grasped Daniel's hands in hers.

"You could say that," she replied, the wine settling over them like a forgiving blanket.

CHAPTER 36

Sarah Harmer walked across the stage, guitar in hand, and took her place on a stool.

"I love her. Loved her the moment I heard her at the Folk Fest," Dan whispered.

They had moved into the lounge, their bellies full of good food, their heads full of rose' and indiscrete thoughts. Melanie sat next to him, emboldened by alcohol. The details of his companion's face, measured through the equalizing gauge of inebriation, swept Danny away, caused the shackles of obligation to disintegrate. His eyes followed the curves of her body concealed by a fawn-colored sweater. His vision rested on the defined edges of her hair, where the red fibers touched her shoulders.

Melanie focused on the performer. Sarah Harmer sat lightly on the four-legged stool and began to sing. The words to the song were poignant:

> *Was it something I said, somewhere in her head*
> *I just asked for the answers given.*
> *20 minutes up the road just off the great highway.*
> *I won't be around here for long,*
> *I did not come to stay.*
>
> *You'll know in a little while if this was meant to be*
> *Are you afraid of you?*
> *Are you afraid of me?*

Melanie didn't call the words of the song to Daniel's attention. She knew that the man was conflicted enough about who they were, where they were headed. He didn't need another reason to analyze, to contemplate.

"What a beautiful song," was all she said.

"It's called 'Westray'. It's one she used to do with her band," he replied.

Their eyes met. A second carafe of rose' was empty. A tide of anticipation crested between them. He pulled her face close to his and kissed her lips. Her breath was hot and tasted of garlic and scallops and butter.

"What's that for?" she asked.

He studied her.

"I'm not sure. It just seemed like the thing to do."

She patted his thigh.

"It's appreciated. It's been a long time since I was kissed by someone I cared about."

The emotion caught him unawares. He hadn't mapped out where they were going. Though the wine didn't prevent him from understanding the consequence of his actions, the steady warmth of the liquor, the languid embrace of its influence, destroyed any remnants of moral resistance. Being drunk made the path seem clear and abundantly less encumbered.

They listened to the set, holding hands, making small talk, ordering more wine. Her fingers were light and dry, not at all like his. Sweat leaked off his palms as he anticipated the culmination of the night. A steady song of sorrow pulsed through his veins, trying to overcome the powerful biology he and Melanie had loosened upon themselves. But the cautionary tune was drowned by rose'; reason was eclipsed by reflex.

The man and woman passed Holy Trinity Anglican Church, the chapel they'd encountered earlier. Yellow light, strained through old glass, fell upon a thin layer of new snow covering the ground.

Daniel felt a sudden urge to burst through the doors of the place. Though he was an Evangelical Lutheran, he knew there was a close theological umbilicus running between his denomination and that of the great stone church looming before him. His mind fought hard against the booze. He sought an acknowledgement from within himself that confession was the right course and that infidelity was not.

"What are you doing?" Melanie asked as he halted in front of the structure.

The lawyer took in the enormity of the building. The complex lines of the roof and bell tower gathered his attention and drew him closer; closer to doing the right thing, the holy thing. The thick stones of the church's exterior walls reminded him of the moral teachings of The Carpenter. He released his companion's hand and began to climb the front stairs of the church, disturbing the snow as he ascended.

"Danny," she said.

Her voice trembled. He'd done it to her before. Not so long ago, he had brought her to a place of vulnerability and supplication only to desert her, only to leave her desperately full of desire. The lawyer turned and looked at the woman, his expression distorted by shadow.

CHAPTER 37

Her room was on the seventh floor of the Fort Garry. He held her hand in a needy grip as the elevator climbed through the interior of the hotel. His fingers lost feeling. He prayed that, his decision having been made beneath the cross of Holy Trinity, a decision made in disregard for the purity symbolized by the crucifix, he would not encounter Dee Dee Hernesman.

"We don't have to do this."

Melanie stood hesitantly in her room. The woman's fingers pressed the fabric of her slacks against her thighs in a display of nervous anticipation. Her hair curled from moisture. Her nose displayed a salmon hue, the effects of night air. She was barefoot. Her toes dug into the thick fibers of the carpeting.

"I know."

"Once we do this, we can't undo it," she whispered.

"I know," he replied.

Her room was open to the hallway. The attorney's body was centered in the doorway. Dan leaned against the wooden trim of the doorframe; the color of the door, the color of the room, a muted yellow.

"I know you love Julie. Don't think that I expect something more out of this."

He didn't know how to respond. His feelings were a mass of fits and starts; a short-fused disarray of emotion and lust. Did he love her, this woman who was once married to his best friend? In what way? Would the night turn him into something, someone that he could not live with?

Images of his parents. The adults fighting. He and his sister Audrey, a girl killed by anorexia, in the grave some twenty-three years already, cowering in a corner of Audrey's bedroom on the second floor of their house, raced through his mind. His mother and father had loved each other once. But his father's life became devoted to work. His mother's life became devoted to gin, a non-prescription remedy for a husband's neglect. Pint and half-pint bottles of Gordon's were secreted throughout their rambling house on the shores of Big Detroit Lake. A nip here, a nip there to help mom ease through long boring days as a housewife: an intelligent woman held captive by her upbringing and society. A woman who stood placidly by while her daughter vomited up meal after meal until she perished. It meant the end of Audrey. It meant the end of a marriage. It meant the end of love.

Ghosts. Would they reappear to assail his own children if he pursued the inevitable consequences of the evening? The balance

222

was broken. His life could not be brought to center. There was no turning back.

Danny closed the door and advanced towards her, his gait unsteady, his head light from wine. There was no hiding behind the alcohol. It could not serve as a convenient excuse for what was to take place. This was their doing, he and Melanie's. He'd have to live with that.

She didn't move. He touched her cheek. His fingers stroked her crimson hair. The flesh of her face flamed slightly. Her breathing was rapid. His hands rested on her hips. He pulled her closer. He felt himself rise: not a gentle stirring but a rapid acceleration of flesh. Daniel's finger explored the edge of Melanie's sweater. He found skin. He found the stretch marks he'd encountered years before. His fingers traced the scars. He massaged the rim of her navel.

"Are you sure this is what you want?" she asked.

His mind was distracted by her words. There was a kindness; an understanding to her voice that was comforting and alarming at the same time. He knew in that instant that Melanie Barnes was someone he could love. There was honey and there was poison in that realization.

"Yes. Is it what you want?"

She didn't respond. Instead, her mouth covered his. Her tongue, its surface moist and erotic, forced its way between his teeth. Her eyes closed.

His right index finger followed her stomach to the waistband of her slacks. His left hand supported the small of her back as he undid the snap, as he slid the zipper down. Fingers traced the fabric of her panties. He felt her warmth and touched her there. She shifted on her feet. Her eyes opened. There was a longing, a desperation, displayed in her pupils. The scent of human femininity rose and mixed with the fragrance of Este Lauder clinging to her skin.

He slid her slacks to the ground. She attempted to undo his belt.

"Wait," he whispered.

He knew that he was out of control. He was slightly drunk, fighting a rush of guilt. If the night was to have any meaning, patience would have to flow and flow like a river.

A hand moved beneath the sweater. Another hand held her upright. His fingers found the rim of her bra. His hand embraced the entirety of the breast restrained by the undergarment. He slid the sweater up to her chin. He explored delicate skin with his teeth. Her left hand found his zipper and unzipped it. Her fingers searched his flannel boxers. He was hard. Her nails dug into him. She stroked the base of him.

Then, they were naked in her rented bed. Danny tried to suppress the image of his wife, of Julie's nakedness; the tones of her skin, the color of her nipples, the coloration of her most intimate hair; attributes in stark contrast to the details of the woman he was with. Excitement swept Julie's portrait from his mind. The woman turned and, in an instant, he was beneath her.

Daniel's hands grasped Melanie's hipbones. She rose from the bed. He massaged the space between her breasts. He refrained from touching her nipples, though she begged him to, as his tongue tasted her intimacy.

"Oh," the woman murmured, a small shiver enveloping her body. "Oh."

She came hesitantly. He was not used to that. He was used to fireworks; the largeness of orgasm totally encompassing his partner. Apparently, Melanie was not built that way.

He rolled out from beneath her, rose from the bed, walked across the room, and sat silently in an easy chair. Outside, snow continued to drift towards the ground. A slight wind began to stir. As guilt ascended Danny's soul, she came towards him. Her weight depressed his body into the chair as she climbed onto his lap. Melanie eased him inside of her. Danny Aitkins felt her warmth, felt the grip of her as her hips began to rise and fall. Her breasts trembled. His mouth found a bosom. Faint musk colored the taste of her vague nipple, reminding Danny of whom he was with, of where he was headed. He knew now that there was no turning back, that it was what he wanted; that it was what he'd always wanted.

CHAPTER 38

Sunlight streamed through a window. The allure and attraction of the rose' was gone. The woman remained. He was in her room, in her bed. The enormity of that circumstance dawned harshly. Peach fuzz covered Melanie's spine like soft down. The lawyer contemplated the junction of vertebral bodies beneath the woman's skin and considered what he'd done. She had been right to say it as she had: once such a thing is done, there's no undoing it.

The thing was done, all right. Maybe he was too. Aitkins left that sad thought for another day, another reality. For the moment, he knew that he needed to return to his room and get dressed for another day of reviewing files. After that, he faced a long drive back to Detroit Lakes with Dee Dee Hernesman. A thick layer of silence would likely wedge itself between the attorney and his partner when and if she figured out the truth.

There was that word again. Truth. Truth hadn't served Daniel Atkins very well. Trouble was, lies didn't work out so well either. The times he'd tried to lie, to his parents as a little kid; to his teachers at school; to his wife, he'd always failed. Lying wasn't going to save his marriage or his sanity. Silence might. There was a razor thin line between remaining silent about a thing that needed telling and lying about it outright. It was a line Danny realized that he would have to negotiate.

"How do you feel?" the red head asked, her face hidden from him, the skin of her back brightened by the day's first light.

"My head feels fine. I think I'm over the wine."

Her voice trembled as she continued.

"It's not the wine I'm concerned about."

"Oh."

She turned beneath the blanket, her nakedness covered by a sheet. She held the linen fast to her chest as she spoke.

"And?"

A wave of significant uncertainty crossed the attorney's mind.

"I'm not sure what to make of this," was all he could think to say.

"This?"

"You and me."

Melanie's eyes grew wide. An inappropriate grin touched the smooth edges of her lips, lips rendered pale and lifeless by an exhaustion of spirit.

"Danny, sweet Danny. There is no you and me. There is you and Julie. I know that. You know that. Don't pretend last night can somehow unbind those ties."

He eased himself out of bed. He stood naked in the center of the room and thought back to the prior evening. There was a notion stuck in the back of his mind that the world would never be as it had been before.

"Before," he whispered to himself as he bent to retrieve his clothes.

"What?" Melanie asked, a hint of anxiety encroaching on her speech.

"Nothing. I was just muttering. I better get dressed and get ready for another thrilling day at the warehouse," he replied.

It was not that they had made love. It wasn't even that they had made love again, the second time more natural, less frenzied, in the Missionary way, with his body writhing on top of hers, with Daniel's arms holding himself off her as he came, and the both of them waiting, waiting for her orgasm, which eventually arrived as a slight shiver that seemed inconsequential.

It was that his life, his marriage, no matter how closely he guarded the truth, could never, would never, be the same. History had seemed so certain before he and Melanie spent the night together. History should have included a long, loving, and vital marriage to Julie, three kids, wonderful memories; an ability to simply compute what they shared, from the date he said, "I do" until their respective deaths. That history could not be made; it could not be remembered because it would be a lie, a myth. It was this loss of history that swelled beneath Dan Aitkins' skin like an irritating boil. Problem was, and would always be, that the cure for the illness, lancing the boil with the sharp needle of truth, would be worse than the malady.

"Don't feel obligated to treat me differently," she offered as he pulled his pants on over his bare feet. "I knew what I was getting into when I asked you to go running."

He stared hard at her in disbelief, focusing the blue of his irises on the suggestion of her form hidden by the folds of the sheet.

"I can't help but feel obligated, among other things," he whispered, touching the bare skin of her shoulder for balance as he bent over, lightly brushing her forehead with lips parched by alcohol.

A crowd had already formed in front of the cooks by the time the lawyer made his entrance into the dining room of the hotel. Dee Dee was nearly done eating, her mouth full of the last bits of a spinach and mushroom omelet by the time he selected an entrée and made his way to her table.

"Where were you last night?" the female attorney asked.

Aitkins shrugged and changed the subject.

"Great food they have here, eh?" he noted.

Hernesman grunted, dismissing his comment.

"Don't tell me. I don't want to know. I hope you know what you're doing."

"Doing? Why Ms. Hernesman, I'm doing fine. Very fine, thank you."

He tucked a cloth napkin into his jeans and sat down across from the woman. His fork was poised to assault a stack of flapjacks and sausage when Melanie Barnes walked into the room. Her eyes met his. She smiled, a faint gesture to the hopelessness of their connection, and continued on towards Malachi Stone and F.W. Barnes. The defense lawyers were seated in a remote alcove of the restaurant, pouring over a red file folder, engaged in heated conversation.

"I'm telling you, F.W., it was right here, in this folder. I haven't let it out of my sight since we arrived here in Winnipeg," Stone said, his voice irritated and difficult.

"Then where is it now, Malachi?" Barnes interposed.

"I don't know."

"Incompetence, that's what this is," Barnes asserted, looking directly into the Iowan's eyes. "I knew it was a mistake to allow you to maintain security over the documents."

Stone's face flushed.

"Frank, that's uncalled for. It'll turn up. I'll retrace my steps. I'll find it."

"Gentleman," Melanie offered in a whimsical tone, seeking to mollify her superiors as she approached.

"Ms. Barnes, how lovely to see you. You're looking well this morning. Care to join us?" Stone asked.

The plump lawyer rose from the table and retrieved an extra chair.

"Are you ordering?" F.W. asked, a look of concern on his face. It was unusual for her father-in-law to make such an inquiry. The remark caused her to take inventory of herself.

Why is he looking at me that way? she thought. *It's almost as if...*

She dropped the conjecture, confused by an apparition of her dead husband. In the blaze of an instant, there he was, alive and strong, before the drugs, before he snorted his life away. He was making love to her, doing things that Danny Aitkins didn't know she needed, in ways that only Michael knew. Her eyes went vacant as she tried to bind him, as she sought to put Michael's ghost to rest.

"Is anything wrong?" Stone asked, placing a hand on the paralegal's wrist.

"No, I'm fine. I'll just have some coffee."

Danny found it impossible to stop staring. She was radiant. She was striking and vibrant. His adoration was painfully obvious.

"Stop eyeballing her. Do you want everyone in here to see you gawking at that woman?"

Dee Dee's admonition brought Aitkins' attention back to their table. He shut his eyes and concentrated on eating the mountain of food in front of him.

"Dan, it's really none of my business but I've never been one to keep quiet when I see something that needs addressing."

Aitkins swallowed a lump of pancake, the batter thick and coated with maple syrup. He tried to voice an objection to the anticipated lecture but found that the food rendered him unable to speak.

"What in God's name do you think you're doing? I know you. You're not some player who can screw yourself purple and then forget about it. You've got ethics. You've got morals, though lately, those seem to be in some doubt. Don't you realize how much you have? How much you've got to lose?"

The attorney drained a glass of apple juice. He fought the urge to weep.

"Nothing happened."

"Bullshit, Dan."

He repeated the lie.

"Nothing happened."

"I don't get you. A beautiful wife. Great kids. A nice house. The respect of your colleagues. Good friends. What the hell gives? Don't you know that what you're doing puts everything at risk? Not just a tiny, insignificant part of it, Daniel, but the whole of it. Where the hell are your brains?"

Aitkins stabbed at a link of sausage with his fork. The lawyer raised the meat to his mouth only to find that he had lost his appetite.

CHAPTER 39

"Sorry I forgot to call," the lawyer apologized.

What he could have said, if he wanted to lay the truth at his wife's doorstep during the long distance call, was:

Sorry I forgot our marriage vows as I fucked your friend repeatedly last night while you were at home, taking care of our kids.

But of course, Danny Aitkins didn't say these things.

"That's all right. The kids didn't get home until late," Julie replied.

"I was in bed before midnight," he said, which, in the strictest of terms, was true. That he happened to be in bed with another woman wasn't a revelation he was prepared to make.

"When you coming home?"

"Dees and I are at the border right now. Should be back in about three and a half hours or so. She's picking up perfume and some other stuff at the duty free shop."

"Dee Dee uses perfume?"

There was an air of disbelief in his wife's expression.

"Sure. Why does that surprise you?"

"Well, I thought...oh, never mind."

"Ah, the old preference thing rears its ugly head again, eh Jules?"

Talking the old talk with Julie, sharing the same sense of humor he'd shared with her for the entirety of their adult lives, the shame of his unspoken infidelity momentarily retreated.

"Well, it sure seems to me that she's not walking on the same side of the sidewalk as I am," Julie said.

"I don't ask and I don't care," Danny observed, watching his partner apply fragrance samples.

"I love you," he offered, meaning every word of it despite the circumstances.

"I love you too."

The drive home was complicated by the onset of a blizzard that nearly closed the interstate between Grand Forks and the Canadian Border. Brittle flakes of snow pelted the sheet metal of the Ranger as their pace slowed to a near crawl. It was five hours before the truck finally turned into the Aitkins' driveway. The house was dark as the lawyer carried his leather overnight bag and briefcase through the back door and into the kitchen. Dan deposited his luggage in the entry and flipped on a light. A roast beef sandwich, mashed potatoes, gravy, and steamed carrots occupied a paper plate on the table's wooden surface. Amanda had positioned a handwritten note next to the cold food:

Dad: I love you!

He put the paper plate in the microwave and filled a coffee cup with unsweetened orange juice from a cardboard carton retrieved from the refrigerator. The house remained ominously silent as he sat down to eat.

"It can't happen," he whispered to himself, digging into the warm beef. "It won't happen again," he vowed to himself as he drank the sour juice.

That night they made love. He took great pains to attend to his wife's every need. He was slow and methodical, rendered obedient and compliant by guilt. They came together, beneath the eaves of the old attic, their bodies understanding each other, their desires merging with each other. When he kissed Julie goodnight and rolled over on his side in search of sleep, Danny's eyes focused on the outline of their barn, its shadow long and desolate outside the window as he tried to fathom the enormity of what he had done.

CHAPTER 40

The settlement conference was scheduled for Judge Enwright's chambers in the basement of the Becker County Courthouse in Detroit Lakes. Daniel Aitkins and James Thompson had discussed hiring a private mediator, an attorney with experience in achieving settlements through Alternative Dispute Resolution, or ADR, to resolve the case. But the parties couldn't agree on a neutral facilitator; Thompson wanted someone from the Twin Cities; Aitkins wanted someone from the western part of the state, someone familiar with agricultural issues. In the end, the attorneys agreed that Harriet Enwright could conduct a non-binding settlement conference before the end of discovery. The court selected the Monday after Thanksgiving as the date for the conference.

Hernesman and Aitkins returned from Winnipeg empty-handed. They had been unable, after two days of searching, to uncover any documents showing the place of origin for the suspect corn. Previously, Dean Anderson had provided them with his receipt from Stevenson's indicating the date of delivery, the date of the feed's manufacture in Grand Forks, the amount delivered to the Andersons, and the like. But they had no information about where the moldy corn had come from. It was a missing link that weighed heavily on Dan's mind as his trial preparations began to take shape.

Big Jim Thompson brought his wife Rita, and their ten-year-old daughter, Ajudica, to Fargo to spend time with his folks over the Thanksgiving holiday. His parents were elderly and stubborn. Though he made it routine to point out to his folks the lack of African American culture abiding in the Red River Valley, they didn't seem to care. They'd made the Valley their home since Jerome Thompson. Jim's father, came to the area with the Air Force in the late fifties. They had raised six kids in the lily-white neighborhoods of Grand Forks and later, Fargo, and they were satisfied with what they'd found there. Despite an untoward word now and then, overall, it had been a good life, a proud life. Jim had no choice but to bring his family back home to Eastern North Dakota for the holidays. His parents weren't about to travel. They wanted to end their stay on this Earth planted in the rich soil of the Red River Valley and no amount of haranguing from their son would change their resolve.

Jim brought his wife and daughter to Detroit Lakes once their holiday visiting was done. They were slated to leave from DL for Minneapolis after the settlement conference concluded. Ajudica was due back at the Breck School, an Episcopal Preparatory Institution in Minneapolis, Tuesday morning. The lawyer booked a hotel room for Sunday night so that his daughter could take advantage of the

231

pool and so that he and Rita could take advantage of the soothing heat of the hotel's Jacuzzi.

Thompson was protective of his only child. Rita was forty-four. The chances of them having another child were negligible. The attorney lamented that he had found his wife, a woman clearly his mental and spiritual equal, so late in life. He was past forty when they married, worn out from a lifetime of pitiful affairs of the heart that never went anywhere. When they met at a recognition dinner held for the Hennepin County Public Defender's office, where James donated significant amounts of billable time to help out the underprivileged, the ex-football star had been immediately smitten by the tall Negro woman with radiant brown eyes and keen cheekbones.

But it was as they sat next to each other during that dinner and talked about life as black professionals in the Midwest, where Rita Evers revealed that she was a dentist, working in the poorest neighborhood of Minneapolis, that he fell in love. She was the woman. No if, ands or buts about it. Rita Evers had to be his wife.

James pursued Rita with vigor. She was flattered; at least until her connections downtown let her in on Jim's reported flare for brief, messy trysts. Inexplicably, Rita stopped returning telephone calls and ceased responding to his entreaties to get together.

Later on, during walks along the shores of Lake Calhoun in the midst of the trendy Uptown neighborhood of Minneapolis where Big Jim owned a condo, and on innumerable visits to museums and art galleries, Rita came to understand that the Nay-Sayers were wrong: that James' avowed womanizing was a sad pretense perfected by an introspective giant of a man whose pursuit of excellence, on the football field and in the courtroom, left him with only the vaguest of inclinations as to how to enjoy an intelligent woman's company.

He watched his daughter, her tiny arms and legs flailing as she jumped into the deep end of the Holiday Inn pool. Rita was in the hotel room putting on her swimsuit. There was a chill outside. Drifts of fresh snow collected against the exterior walls of the hotel. More snowfall was predicted over night.

The lawyer eased his massive frame into the spa. He'd endured two complete reconstructions of his knees. Now, in his mid-fifties, Thompson's knees affected his daily life. It was the price he'd agreed to pay when he put on a football jersey and accepted a scholarship. There wasn't any regret. There wasn't any anger. It was what he needed to do to get through school, to become what he was. A father. A husband. A lawyer.

232

Three other adults sat around the pool. A nondescript white couple sat under an umbrella enjoying cocktails. A skinny white man in blue jeans, wearing a tattered "Indiana Hoosiers" sweatshirt, sat across the way, his eyes downcast and riveted upon the latest edition of *People Magazine*. Two other kids, white and older than his daughter, played with Ajudica in the cold waters of the big pool.

"Careful AJ," the lawyer cautioned, watching his daughter run pall mall across ceramic tile surrounding the pool.

"OK daddy," the child answered, her words distorted by laughter.

Thompson rested his head against the rim of the hot tub. Steam rose around him. Big Jim closed his tiny eyes.

The Anderson case was not one he wanted to try. He wasn't afraid of losing. He was convinced that the facts would be seen by the jury in a defense light. That wasn't why he hesitated to bring the matter to trial. He'd taken the Andersons' depositions; he'd walked their farm; studied their records; seen their struggles and travail reduced to mere numbers on balance sheets. They were fine people; the sort of folks his parents would befriend. He was tired of doing corporate bidding. His heart had swung, after years of defense practice, to side with the underdog. He wanted to settle this case and move on. Stevenson's was vehement that no offer above twenty- five thousand would be authorized unless the matter could be settled under a confidentiality agreement. Thompson could pay up to fifty thousand if the Andersons agreed to keep the settlement quiet. He knew fifty grand wasn't enough.

Big Jim emitted a sigh.

"Where's AJ?" Rita asked, approaching the spa in a bright orange one-piece suit, the cut of the fabric revealing the curves of her body.

Jim opened his eyes and smiled. His wife's hair was held in place by a yellow kerchief. Her bronze skin shone magnificently under the phosphorous lights of the Holidome. He knew he was a lucky man, a blessed man.

"She's right over there, with the other kids," he said, nodding towards the big pool.

"Where?" the woman asked.

The lawyer's eyes focused. The two white kids, a little boy and a little girl wearing arm floats, splashed urgently in the shallow end of the pool. Ajudica was nowhere to be seen.

"Excuse me. Have you seen my little girl? She was just in the pool," Thompson asked as he approached the couple under the umbrella. The strangers looked up, their faces reflected in the attorney's concerned eyes.

"Last I saw her, she was going to use the restroom. You looked to be dozing off so I pointed it out to her," the woman answered, gesturing with her right hand towards a door. "That was about five minutes ago."

"Thanks,"

"Where is she?" Rita Thompson asked as she walked over to the group, the volume of her voice rising with each word.

"They said she went to the bathroom," James responded, his feet slapping against the wet pool deck as he moved out in search of the missing child,

"That other fellow, he followed her out," the woman added loudly as the lawyer's hand grasped the handle of the stainless steel exit door.

Thompson turned his head, his eyes full of knowing.

"What?"

"That strange looking dude," the male added. "My wife says he left here right after your little girl did. Looked to be in a bit of a hurry."

Ajudica wasn't in the woman's restroom. She wasn't in the lobby. She wasn't in their hotel room. She was gone and so was the skinny white man in the "Hoosier" shirt.

CHAPTER 41

Becker County Sheriff Isak Iverson scrutinized the face of the man in his office. Snow was piling up outside, carried across the landscape on the back of a fresh wind out of Saskatchewan. The African giant seated before the lawman was deeply troubled. His wife was overwrought and was being comforted by Liz Taburn, the department's only female deputy, across the way, in an intake room. Though the walls of the Law Enforcement Center were supposed to be sound proof, Iverson could distinguish the mother's mournful wail as he studied the attorney.

"I don't know what to think," Iverson began.

James Thompson hung his head between his massive thighs; his leg muscles constrained by the nylon fabric of his warm ups. The sheriff took in the enormity of the lawyer. There was little question in Iverson's mind that Thompson could have played professional football in his prime.

"There's nothing, nothing at all that I can think of that would lead me to suspect anyone would want to harm Ajudica," the black man mumbled.

"Could this be about you? Or your wife?" the officer asked gently.

"I don't see how. I'm a civil trial lawyer. My wife's a dentist. It doesn't make any sense."

Iverson had dispatched a squad to the Holiday Inn as soon as the missing child report came in. His deputies were able to determine that Ajudica had left the lobby of the hotel with the white male. She didn't appear to be struggling with the man so the desk clerk paid the child's departure little attention. Only after the little girl was reported missing did it dawn on the hotel employee that the child had not arrive with the white man, but had, instead, arrived with her black parents.

A maintenance worker in the parking lot shoveling snow provided a description of the stranger's vehicle. A late 1980's vintage GMC Safari Van. The custodian didn't get the license number. But he remembered the color of the vehicle; blue-where the vehicle hadn't decayed to rust. The Safari also boasted a "Jesus Saves" decal on the rear bumper, the lettering red and sharp, the sticker nearly new.

"We've got every squad in the area, municipal, county, and state, looking for the van," the sheriff offered. "But you're sure you can't think of anything that will help us zero in on why this happened?"

Thompson's eyes watered as the big man struggled to think, to uncover some bit of information, some piece of data he could share with the police that would lead them to his daughter and her abductor. There was nothing, nothing at all that stood out; that raised itself to his consciousness. James Thompson shook his head despondently and covered his face with his beefy hands.

"Let's take a stab at shaking something loose, shall we?" the sheriff said, leaving his desk to stand next to the attorney.

The peace officer placed his withered left arm, the result of a farming accident that had severed the major tendons of the wrist when Iverson was seven years old, against the wall to support his weight. The lawman looked intently at Thompson through cloudy hazel eyes, the eyes of someone a few months away from pension. A thick gray mustache, long and trimmed in the fashion of Wyatt Earp, drooped below the sheriff's hawk-like nose. Iverson was tall, nearly as tall as the ex-football player, but delicately thin, teetering precariously over the black man on spindly legs that seemed to end at the officer's armpits.

"What you in town for?" the sheriff asked.

Vagrant wind rushed through diminished caulking surrounding the building's windows.

"I've got a hearing in front of Judge Enwright tomorrow."

"What kind of case?"

"Civil lawsuit. Involving Stevenson's Sci-Swine."

"The Anderson thing?"

Thompson's eyes opened and focused on the sheriff.

"That's right. How did you know?"

"Anything more than a stubbed toe is news in this town. It's been in the paper a couple of times. Surprised you didn't know that."

The lawyer shrugged his shoulders.

"I guess I did. Barnes told me, I think. I must have let it slip my mind."

"I also had some deputies out at the Anderson place when those militia boys showed up and got the auction sale postponed," the sheriff deadpanned. "Any chance your daughter being taken has anything to do with the case?"

Incredulity boiled to the surface and was released.

"What in God's name would taking my little girl have to do with a lawsuit?"

Iverson's imperfect hand touched the top of Thompson's solid shoulder.

"You never know, Jim. Stranger things have happened."

"I just don't understand how they could be related."

"May not be. But, until something else turns up, we have two possibilities. One, this is a random act by someone with a bad propensity. Or two, it's somehow linked to you or your wife."

Thompson's spine shook with upset. Images of his daughter in the clutches of a stranger; terrified, uncertain of what the man

236

was after, why he had taken her, riding in the back of a filthy van against the anger of the oncoming snowstorm, flicked off and on in his mind like a terrible movie. There were other, more sordid thoughts lingering beneath the images. He fought them, battled to keep them from manifesting. They were unthinkable.

"You go see your wife," the sheriff urged. "You two need to be together. Don't worry Mr. Thompson, we'll find her. We'll get her back. I know this country. I don't believe the man in the van does. That's an advantage he didn't reckon with when he took your daughter."

The attorney rose in increments and walked out of the room, hesitant in his movements as he crossed the hallway to console his wife.

CHAPTER 42

"You've got mail," an electronic voice declared.

"Matt, you've got an email," Dean Anderson observed aloud.

The farmer was seated at the family computer in the living room of the Anderson farmhouse. The CPU boasted an outmoded 486 processor that was too slow and a hard drive that was too small. Dean's office held a Pentium unit that, in contrast to the 486, was lightening quick. The Pentium was for work, for the family farming operation. The kids were relegated to using the old electronic dinosaur in the front room.

Anderson happened to be sitting at the 486 because it had his favorite game, a discontinued version of "Phantom of the Opera", on it. All of the Anderson kids had solved the mystery and were no longer interested in chasing the Phantom around the Paris Opera House. Dean had been hard at it for three months but was only half way to mastering the game.

He'd logged on under his oldest son's screen name through AOL to locate hints regarding the game from the manufacturer's website. The farmer couldn't remember his own password for AOL. Matt's entry code was saved, making the service provider easy to access on the old computer. The email message intrigued Dean Anderson. Who was the email from? Should he violate his son's privacy by reading it? He could always read it and save it as "new", preventing Matt from knowing that the message had been read. The hog man contemplated the screen. His fingers thought for him:

Matt:

A word of caution about George Winchip, our compatriot from Terre Haute. He's not someone to keep an acquaintance with. He's been talking about using drastic measures, ala Oklahoma City, against Stevenson's, the bank, or Stevenson's lawyers. I don't think there's anything behind it but one never knows. I'd keep my distance. He moved over here, was working in Grafton at the hardware store but just took off. He didn't give any notice. Chances are; he's headed back home.

Just a word to the wise. I hope things are coming together for the trial. Talk to you soon.

Eli Bremer
Bremer1776@ndpatriots.com

The revelation shocked the farmer. That someone who knew his child, someone who'd been on his farm, would contemplate domestic terrorism premised on some twisted misunderstanding of the Bill of Rights, was beyond Dean Anderson's comprehension. He printed a copy of the message, depositing the hardcopy of the email in the rear pocket of his work pants before restoring the message to its original state, saving it as new, precluding Matt from discovering that his privacy had been compromised.

"I'm sorely troubled," the farmer revealed as he walked into the kitchen. His wife was standing over the sink peeling fresh peaches for pie.

"How's that?"

"Matt."

"What about Matt?"

"Where is he?"

Nancy Anderson dried her hands on her apron as she looked at her husband.

"He went to town to see Suzie Ashcroft. Millie went with him. What's wrong?"

Dean sat on a kitchen chair. His callused fingers withdrew the printed email from his pocket. The farmer handed the paper to his wife.

"This is terrible," she muttered, returning the message to her husband. "Did you know that he was mixed up in this sort of thing?"

Dean raised his eyes. Age had set hard against his wife's pretty features, accelerated by the uncertainty of the looming trial. Her disposition, her naturally soft persona, had turned stern in the face of anxiety. She didn't need this. He didn't need this. There was too much at stake as it was.

"I suspected he was going to some meetings and such. He's slipped away a few times, probably to head up to Grafton to see this Bremer character. I thought it was harmless, a lot of show and not much else. I was wrong."

"What you going to do?"

Anderson stood up, walked into the back hallway, stopped, pulled a winter jacket over his arms, and slid leather choppers on his hands.

"I'm gonna bring the note to the sheriff," he replied.

"In the middle of this storm? Can't it wait until morning?"

Lightening ignited the night sky. Thunder rolled ominously over the house.

"This can't wait. It may be a hoax. It may be for real. I can't take the chance. Folks close to Timothy McVeigh had the opportunity to stop him and didn't. I couldn't live with something like that."

She sighed. There was exhaustion and fear in her gesture.

"If Matt comes back, don't tell him about this," the farmer advised.

Nancy Anderson nodded. The woman's pale blue eyes followed her husband's thick form as the man opened the door and walked out into the teeth of a November blizzard.

CHAPTER 43

George Winchip didn't like people. Not just selected individuals; he despised the whole unwashed, irreligious, spiritually impoverished human horde. That said, the fact that the Indianan was capable of kidnapping a ten-year-old girl from a hotel right under the nose of her adoring father wasn't due to exceptional planning, cunning, or criminality. His success in gaining temporary physical custody of Ajudica Thompson was based upon blind luck.

He had originally planned to go out big, like McVeigh. But his act of terrorism wasn't aimed at the United States Government. That act in the sorry play of the militia movement had already been staged and could be recounted in the distressed faces of the folks left behind in Oklahoma after ammonium nitrate lit up the skyline of their beloved city. Winchip's prey, a quarry that he selected out of personal animosity, was to be a multinational corporation involved in the agricultural business, a company dedicated to vertically integrating the nation's food supply.

The militia man spent many hours casing supermarkets until he realized that the collateral damage he would cause by blowing up a grocery store located in the center of a shopping mall would likely surpass even McVeigh's insurgency. A terrorist, a Patriot, and a loner though he was, Winchip didn't want to be branded a lunatic who killed children, pregnant women, and old folks.

"Besides," the white supremacist had mused, "that concerto has already been scored."

Winchip was fifty-five years old and other than a younger brother who had a differing philosophy, the Hoosier was without any family to speak of. Twice-divorced and on the lam for failing to pay alimony to his most recent ex-wife, a thirty-year-old woman with an appetite for soap operas and credit cards, he left his home state at the earliest opportunity, loading all of his worldly possessions into his van.

At one point during his meager existence, George Winchip thought he'd make a damn fine farmer. He'd have succeeded, he surmised, if the big boys, the multi-national agricultural syndicates, hadn't eased small family operators like himself out of the dairy markets in the '80's, when he was just getting his herd started, when he was juggling his wife Nora's demands for cash with his natural tendency to doze off when he was supposed to be working.

Foreclosure came swiftly once his futile attempt to farm hit the skids. He blamed his demise on faltering milk prices. He blamed it on a lack of available credit. He blamed it on feed, medication, and heating expenses; on anything but his own lack of motivation.

When Eli Bremer's email seeking militia assistance out on the Great Plains hit the Indiana Patriot Web Ring, the message sent a shudder down Winchip's spine. There it was, clear as crystal; his road to Beulah Land, to Glory. All he had to do was get on up to North Dakota and ingratiate himself to the local Patriot commander. There appeared to be plenty of opportunities for George Winchip to shine out on the prairie, plenty of chances to right the wrong that had been done to him back home.

The Safari plunged through darkness. Snow ricocheted off the van as it headed west, away from Fargo on I-94. Winchip was bound for Bismarck, the capital city of North Dakota, where he'd rented a small efficiency apartment in an old tourist motel out on the western edge of town. He figured on making a call to the black lawyer using a calling card he'd purchased with cash. There'd be no way to trace the call. By the time the authorities figured out where he was calling from, he'd be gone and so would the girl.

There was a .357 under the front seat of the vehicle. He didn't figure that there'd be any occasion to use it. The storm had closed off the freeway behind him. The concentration of snow was diminishing as they headed west. Soon, they'd drive out from under the blizzard into a fierce winter night on the plains. No one was tailing them. No one would find them, at least, not until he did what needed to be done.

The girl hadn't put up much of a fuss until he tried to force her into the van. He had all he could do to push her flailing body through the sliding rear passenger door of the Safari. There had been one other person, a maintenance worker, out in the parking lot when the girl began to fight back. It didn't appear to Winchip that the janitor paid much attention to the fracas.

As the wheels of the van slapped against the wet pavement of the Interstate, Winchip's captive intermittently tried to work herself free. The driver had no sympathy for her plight. George Winchip didn't care for people, reserving a special hatred for blacks and anyone other than white Anglo-Saxon Protestants. Catholics and Jews were also down there, at the bottom of humanity, with the colored masses, in his opinion.

To Winchip's notion, America was a country founded upon Conservative Protestant ideals and values; faith, honor, fidelity, precepts that fornicating races, the Africans, the Chinese, the Mexicans, and the others could never adhere to; fundamentals absent from the creeds and morals of the Papists and the Zealots.

His hate was something handed down to him by his father, Adrian, a man who had once been the Grand Dragon of the Indiana Ku Klux Klan. His father's legacy was a heritage of intolerance

241

formed during the economic distress of the Great Depression when Adrian Winchip watched his white neighbors lose their jobs to illiterate immigrants and migrant blacks willing to work for starvation wages.

"You best quit fussin' around back there, you hear?"

There was no sound from the terrified girl.

"I know you're listening. You do as I say, missy, an things just might work out fer ya."

A sudden shift in the wind caught the van. The vehicle bounced across two lanes of blacktop. The tires of the Safari caught the edge of the pavement. The van bucked like an overeager bronco. Winchip battled the steering wheel. He was no match for gravity.

Just outside of Bismarck, the van careened off the pavement and plowed headlong into a freshly deposited drift of pristine snow. Winchip was unharmed. He remained belted in the driver's seat. Ajudica fell onto the floor and rolled across filthy carpeting, becoming lodged between the front and rear seats of the Safari as the vehicle came to an abrupt stop.

"You OK?"

There was no response from the child.

"I said, is you all right?"

Silence.

Red lights caromed off the ceiling of the van's cockpit. A North Dakota State trooper's squad pulled in behind the stricken vehicle.

"Shit," Winchip muttered, his eyes dancing around the interior of the van. "If he sees the girl, it's all over but the shooting. I'm not ready to make a stand, not here, not in the middle of this crapper of a state," the Hoosier lamented.

He pushed the girl's body under the rear seat and draped a tattered sleeping bag over the unconscious child. Winchip's right hand searched desperately for the comforting wooden grip of his pistol. The weapon wasn't within reach. The abrupt stop had dislodged the .357 from its hiding place. George Winchip would have to rely upon his wits as his only defense.

"Good evening, sir," a trooper said as he approached the van. The officer's body was shielded by the Safari's chassis. "Looks like you need some help."

The cop turned on a flashlight and threw a beam of light across the van's cabin.

"Might be able to rock her out. I haven't tried that yet."

"You from out of state?"

Winchip paused. He'd replaced the Indiana registration with North Dakota license plates liberated from an identical Safari in downtown Fargo. The license numbers wouldn't match the van's

242

VIN. Winchip hoped that the cop's inclination for thoroughness was moderated by the tenacity of the storm.

"What makes you say that?"

"The accent," the trooper related. The law enforcement officer's hazel eyes stared at the driver. His gaze carried a heavy dose of scrutiny.

"Oh, that. I'm originally from Kansas City. I'm living up in Grand Forks."

Disbelief crested across the officer's face.

"Doesn't sound like Kansas to me."

"Kansas City, Missouri."

The trooper grunted.

"May I see your driver's license?"

Winchip dug into the rear seat of his trousers and produced his wallet. He lifted a plastic North Dakota license, the identification indicating Grafton as his place of residence, and handed the plastic card to the cop.

"Everything seems in order," the officer said after a review of the card, handing the ID back to the Indianan.

"Mind if I give rocking it a try?" Winchip asked.

The officer nodded and stepped back. Light snow continued to fall. The militiaman gunned the engine. The Safari strained against the grip of the snow. Winchip slid the gearshift into drive. The van sputtered forward. He slammed the shift into reverse. The vehicle surged backward, its tires spinning against frozen earth.

"Ease up on the gas," the officer yelled over the roar of the engine.

"Sure thing."

With a steady pull, the van's all-wheel-drive inched the vehicle back onto pavement.

"Thanks."

"You slow down, now, you hear? Once you get to Bismarck, stay put. This freeway is closed to traffic. You must have just missed the gates closing." The cop paused and reflected on the stranger's face. "Where'd you come from, anyway?" he asked.

"Fargo," Winchip offered, realizing as soon as he revealed the truth, he'd made a mistake.

"I figured as much. Stay put once you get to town. Next time, you might not be so lucky."

The trooper touched the brim of his campaign hat and started to walk back to his cruiser.

The Patriot took several deep breaths to calm his nerves. He glanced at the lump of little girl hidden by the sleeping bag. The child had not stirred. Winchip reached for the automatic shift and planned a cautious exit, an exit designed to maintain his anonymity. Winchip put the van in gear. His eyes scanned the rearview mirror for traffic. The State trooper was headed back towards the Safari with his weapon drawn. There was a look of determination on the officer's face. Winchip had no choice. He slammed the vehicle into reverse.

CHAPTER 44

Danny Aitkins engaged the Ranger's four-wheel drive as the truck sped towards town. The call from Nancy Anderson had found him in the midst of cleaning a stall in the barn. He'd left the job unfinished. He didn't bother changing his clothes. That he stunk like horseshit didn't matter. Getting to the Becker County Law Enforcement Center to intercept Dean Anderson, before his client blurted out the contents of the email to Sheriff Iverson, was crucial. Danny had been called

by a deputy, a former client, regarding the taking of Ajudica Thompson. He was aware of the sheriff's suspicion that the kidnapping was somehow related to the Anderson lawsuit.

With the information provided to Danny by Nancy Anderson over the phone, Iverson's hunch took on an aspect of plausibility. If there was a link between the Grafton outfit and the disappearance of the girl, Aitkins wanted to get Iverson's assurances that Matt Anderson wasn't a suspect before Dean handed over the email. The lawyer downshifted the four by four. The truck slowed for a stop sign and made a left turn onto wet pavement without coming to a complete stop.

"Dean," Aitkins called out, recognizing his client from a distance.

"Dan. What are you doing here?" the farmer queried as he walked across the Becker County Law Enforcement Center parking lot.

The lawyer jumped out of his pickup and closed the driver's door without slowing.

"Nancy told me what you're up to."

The farmer stopped.

"Didn't figure on that. Why would she call you?"

Aitkins caught up with his client.

"She thought that you could use the benefit of my counsel before you gave up the email. She's right, you know. Before you hand the goods over to Sheriff Iverson, we need assurances that the State won't go after Matt."

Anderson's eyes widened.

"For what? He hasn't done anything."

"I know that but we don't want to take chances. As I understand it, Matt hasn't even seen the message yet. And, so far as you and Nancy know, he's only been an occasional visitor to Grafton."

The farmer nodded his head.

"You're the lawyer," Dean said, handing the copy of the email to Aitkins.

Dan read the document under the streetlights surrounding the jail.

"Who knows whether this Winchip character is for real or not? But, it seems to make sense. If he wanted to get back at Stevenson's, or a company like that, hitting their lawyer isn't all that far fetched a strategy."

Aitkins pushed an intercom button on the exterior of the Law Enforcement Center.

"Dan Aitkins to see Sheriff Iverson."

"Nice to see you, counselor. Come on in," a familiar voice responded.

There was a loud click. The lawyer and his client entered the facility.

After outlining the information contained in the email, and after considerable discussion between the sheriff and the on-call Assistant County Attorney, Sheriff Iverson assured Aitkins that the boy would not be charged. Dan handed the message to the lawman.

"Shit, who knows whether this is related or not," Iverson muttered.

Jim Thompson stood up, walked over to where the sheriff and Aitkins were conferring, and scrutinized the email.

"Seems to me, Sheriff Iverson, we don't have much else to go on. May well be something worth looking into," the black attorney urged in a voice betraying exhaustion. His wife was resting in an adjacent room after taking two sleeping pills. Their daughter had been gone for eight hours.

"All right, Jim. I'll get a man on it, track down this Winchip's mug shot, if he has one in Indiana, and get it out to all the departments in the Dakotas, Minnesota, Manitoba, and Western Ontario. I'll have the County Attorney get a search warrant signed by Judge Davidson and coordinate the search through the North Dakota prosecutor. It's pretty thin but Davidson will sign just about anything."

Within the hour, Winchip's criminal record, mug shot, and fingerprints had been retrieved via computer from the State of Indiana. There was nothing in George A. Winchip's criminal history to suggest violence. Contempt of Court for failure to pay child support. Kiting bad checks. Burglary. Welfare fraud. But no sexual assaults, no terroristic threats; nothing to denote that George Winchip had a vicious propensity.

Eli Bremer was rousted from bed by the North Dakota authorities. The commander proved to be fully cooperative. A search of Winchip's room at Edna Pease's Board and Lodge in nearby Oakwood, North Dakota revealed precious little information about the Indiana man or where he was headed. His clothing, his computer and peripherals, the majority of his personal items, and an odd assortment of furniture remained behind in Winchip's rented room. A piece of useful information, an article from the *Minneapolis Tribune* entitled "Ten Minority Couples of Power in the Twin Cities", featuring a photograph of Rita and Jim Thompson in formal attire at a performance of the Minnesota Orchestra, was found in Winchip's garbage. A passage in the article had been circled in red:

Nationally renowned trial attorney James Thompson and his dentist-activist wife Rita, manage, despite their hectic professional lives, to make their ten-year-old daughter Ajudica's activities a priority.

Ajudica's name was underlined.

"Seems we may be on to something," Sheriff Iverson related after receiving a faxed copy of the news article from the Grafton Police. "It looks like this guy targeted the little girl, most likely because Mr. Thompson represents Stevenson's. According to this Bremer fellow, Winchip's got a bee in his bonnet about big corporations taking over family farms. Can't say as I've ever run across anything like this in all my years of policing."

Big Jim Thompson buried his head in his hands and let out a guttural wail. Aitkins crossed the floor of the conference room.

"Jim, they'll find her. Now that they know who they're looking for, they'll find her."

"He's right. We had the van I.D. and a half-assed physical description of Winchip. Now we have a lot more. We'll nail the sonofabitch, I'm sure of that. We'll catch him before anything happens to your daughter," the sheriff asserted.

Thompson's Anguish rose.

"How in the hell do you know he hasn't done something already?" the black man cried out in a voice loud enough to wake his wife in the room next door, in a voice loud enough to wake the dead.

CHAPTER 45

The Indianan hadn't spent time planning what to do with the girl once he arrived in Bismarck. Though George Winchip had aspirations of a McVeigh-like exit, he lacked McVeigh's dedication to detail. In his mind, the Patriot had worked it through to the point where he had the girl, they were safely hidden away in the motel, and he'd made a triumphant telephone call back to the black attorney.

The dialogue he was to have with Jim Thompson was unwritten. Whether the girl would be released, terrorized, or sacrificed hadn't been determined in advance of the taking. Beyond the taking, nothing that occurred was scripted, including Winchip's decision to run over a North Dakota State trooper with a van.

Winchip's Safari hurtled towards the trooper. Officer Dwight Rogers, twenty-seven years old with four years on the job, understood the import of the vehicle's sudden change of course. The driver of the van, the man Rogers finally recognized as the fugitive described in a bulletin from Minnesota, meant to run the trooper over.

Rogers held his 9mm tightly in one hand as he scurried out of the path of the marauding vehicle. Diving to his left, the lawman cleared an embankment and rolled through ankle deep snow before coming to rest in a ditch. There was one clear opportunity. Rogers drew a bead on the driver's profile through the tinted glass of a window.

Crack.

A round left the barrel of the automatic.

Thipppp.

The bullet penetrated glass.

Rogers steadied the muzzle of his weapon. A brutal spasm embraced the suspect as the projectile tore into the man's temple. The kidnapper did not cry out. Winchip's forehead struck the Safari's plastic steering wheel. The van spun out of control before becoming mired in the snow. The Safari spewed oily exhaust into the night air as all four wheels of the vehicle continued to rotate.

The trooper maintained his weapon at the ready as he approached the passenger side of the van. The side window was shattered. Glass shards littered the front seats of the van. There was no sign of life from the driver. Rogers cautiously opened the door and reached in with his free hand. The trooper searched for a pulse. There was no movement of blood within the Patriot's carotid artery

"Call for you sheriff," a dispatcher advised over the intercom.

Sheriff Iverson manipulated his lanky form and rose from his chair. Jim Thompson and his wife were propped against each other on a water-stained davenport. Aitkins and his client had left, their obligations having been fulfilled.

Iverson loped out of the room with the stiff-legged gait of age. Within seconds, he returned, a significant smile embedded upon his craggy face.

"Jim, Rita, that was the Bismarck Police. State Patrol found your little girl."

Both parents erupted off the couch.

"Is she all right, sheriff?" Rita Thompson asked, tears forming. "Is she all right?"

"Is my baby OK?" the attorney added, holding his wife tightly with one hand while brushing away his own tears with the other.

Iverson's smile broadened.

"She's got a little bump on her head. Seems Winchip tried to run over a state trooper and ended up with a bullet in his brain for his trouble. But Ajudica's fine. Other than taping her up and tossing her in the van, he never laid a hand on her."

"Thank God," the woman murmured.

"Amen," James Thompson added.

"She's coming back with Trooper Rogers, the officer who saved her, as soon as she's done at the hospital. They're just patching up a little cut on her forehead. Then she'll be on her way back."

The defense lawyer looked up at the wall. He'd lost track of time. It was 2:00am. Jim Thompson was due in front of Judge Enwright at 10:00am for the Anderson settlement conference. There was no way he was going to argue the value of dead pigs tomorrow. He and his wife were going to devote their time to their only child. Barnes could handle the conference. Barnes was fully capable of stonewalling the plaintiffs and advising the court that Stevenson's was not about to offer anything more than fifty thousand dollars to settle the case.

Dan Aitkins made his way up to bed. Julie was already fast asleep. The trip to the Law Enforcement Center had taken longer than expected. Aitkins hadn't anticipated hanging around, trying to console Thompson and his wife about the loss of their little girl. He hoped she was all right. He said a prayer, a genuine request for divine intercession as he climbed into bed. Maybe there was someone listening. Maybe.

Danny Aitkins needed somebody to pray for him. That was a thought that he had repeated over and over to himself each day since he'd returned from Winnipeg. Residual lust for another woman had become fixed between the lawyer and his wife, though Julie Aitkins hadn't said anything to her husband about his lack of passion.

Other than one brief intersection the night he returned from Winnipeg their paths had not crossed in bed. Aitkins hoped that Julie was giving him space because she knew a trial was looming; perhaps the trial of his career. He theorized that she couldn't know about the other. He wanted to believe that there was no trace, no evidence of his infidelity to be uncovered. He hadn't been forced to lie, which would have immediately revealed the truth. The attorney was convinced his wife was cognizant of the pre-trial dissonance that accompanied his trade. Danny assumed that Julie was simply allowing him distance to prepare for the case.

His feet inadvertently touched the smooth skin of his wife's ankles as he slid beneath the bedcovers. Julie did not stir. Somewhere in the house, a faucet dripped. The pattern of the water's descent matched the attorney's labored breathing. Danny Aitkins sought sleep. The trial lawyer closed his eyes and attempted to disassociate himself from the sounds of the house; from the uneven respirations of his slumbering wife; from the imprinted memory of Melanie Barnes' audible acceptance of his desire. The lawyer found that he couldn't still the noise.

CHAPTER 46

F.W. Barnes held tight to the money. He offered $40,000.00 to settle the Anderson claim with the requirement that the terms and conditions of the settlement remain confidential. Judge Enwright cajoled and pushed the defense lawyer to increase his offer into six figures. There was no budging the old man. Aitkins made a final settlement demand of $225,000.00, a sum large enough to cover the firm's expenses, a reduced lawyer's fee, and adequate redress for the Andersons.

"You folks are so far apart, it'll take a jury to decide who's playing the better poker," Harriet said after a short but frustrating attempt to mediate the case.

"How are the Thompson's doing?" the judge inquired of F.W. as the participants in the settlement conference, including Malachi Stone, Jason Billington, Dan Aitkins, Dee Dee Hernesman, and Dean and Nancy Anderson, rose from their respective seats in the courtroom and headed towards the exit.

"Thankfully, the little girl wasn't harmed. She's still scared out of her wits but at least she's alive. To think of what could have happened," Barnes related as he gathered up his file and deposited the papers in his briefcase.

Judge Enwright stood up from behind the bench, lifted a glass of ice water to her mouth, and emptied the tumbler.

"I heard that the trooper who saved her used some quick thinking," the jurist added.

"One shot to the head. The crazy militia guy tried to run over the cop with a van," Aitkins offered. "It was a good thing the child was out cold for the worst part of it."

"She'll have nightmares all the same, I suspect," Judge Enwright observed. "I hope Mr. and Mrs. Thompson are doing as well as could be expected."

"They'll be fine. Jim will be here for the pretrial. He's a tough bird. He'll get past this," Malachi Stone observed.

"See you the first week in January for that pretrial," the judge added, exiting through the private door to her chambers.

The courtroom emptied. Aitkins sat in a chair close to the jury box. His mind imagined the faces, clothing, and attitudes of the Anderson jury. He began to create voir dire questions in his head. Who would he want as jurors? Some folks with farm backgrounds. A liberal or two. He'd stay away from employees of grain elevators and small business owners. They'd be personally interested in the outcome of the case or too used to being sued.

Aitkins pressed his palms into the wool fabric of his dress slacks. He straightened his Snoopy tie and adjusted the collar of his sport coat. There were twelve seats in the jury box. There was a need for twelve jurors only in felony criminal trials. The Anderson case would require seven jurors. They'd start with eleven candidates. If none of the eleven were stricken for cause, for medical disability, or outright prejudice or bias, then each side would strike two, leaving seven to serve.

A sharp pain announced itself. It was a month from trial but Aitkins' anxiety was already starting to build. Soon, he'd be on the toilet four or five times a day. Once the jury was picked, the symptoms would ease up. Then he'd resume eating. But up until those seven people were selected, his body would make him pay dearly for the privilege of representing Dean and Nancy Anderson.

"You coming?" Dee Dee called out from behind the half-opened door to the basement courtroom.

"Be right there."

It wasn't all bad. Those times when the jurors saw it his way, when they did justice according to Danny Aitkins, he soared, climbing to heights normally only occupied by birds of prey. The trouble was, those days were few and far between. With the advent of the insurance industry's campaign announcing a "litigation crisis", juries became stingy: unwilling to listen to claims of personal injury or personal loss. He'd had his fill of citizens turning deaf ears to their neighbors. But it was impossible to knock everyone who thought like a John Birch poster boy or girl off a jury. There was only so much you could do with two lousy strikes.

The advocate's eyes studied the rich grain of the hickory and oak woodwork adorning the room. Aitkins' attention came to rest on the flags of the United States and the State of Minnesota standing behind the bench. The flags represented the ideals of two separate constitutions, written documents preserving the rights of citizens to have their civil causes of action heard by juries of their peers. That was the essence of democracy. That was the essence of justice.

"Somehow," Aitkins mused as he left the counsel table, "I've got to convince these folks to do their duty, to ignore the ads and the hype. It ain't gonna be easy."

"Are you coming or not?" his partner called out through the partially opened door.

Dan didn't respond. Instead, he jerked the door open, pulling the doorknob from Hernesman's unsuspecting grasp. As their faces met, he smiled.

"What the hell were you doing in there, meditating?" Dee Dee asked her partner as Danny joined her in the hallway.

"Sort of. Contemplating justice."

The woman scrutinized the man.

"You feeling OK?"

"As well as can be expected. Where are the Andersons?"

Hernesman shrugged.

"They got tired of waiting for their philosopher king. They went to get a table."

Danny Aitkins stopped as they approached the exit.

"What?" Hernesman asked, her eyes quizzically studying her partner.

"Nothing."

"Come on, what's up?"

The litigator smiled.

"A little philosophy isn't a bad thing, you know," Aitkins quipped.

"If you say so, Mr. Lawyer man," the woman responded, skepticism apparent in her voice.

CHAPTER 47

Matt Anderson considered his decision as he tossed fresh hay into a corral confining beef cattle. A weakening sun shone behind the youth, creating exaggerated shadows as the boy worked. Matt's breath curled upwards in the icy air. He was dressed for the weather in an insulated denim jacket, work boots, and worn-out army fatigues. A ball cap covered his short black hair.

He hadn't meant to hurt anyone. In retrospect, his decision to join the Grafton Patriots had been a mistake. A little girl, someone the age of his youngest brother, nearly suffered unspeakable atrocities at the hands of a lunatic. It was on him, whatever had happened to the black child. It was his fault.

Matt mounted the torn seat of a Polaris four-wheel ATV, the frame distressed and battered, the chrome and plastic covered with frozen mud. He started the vehicle and pulled a trailer away from the fence line. The cattle contentedly munched their feed. Matt knew that he'd made the right choice. Telling his parents, especially his father, about his decision, wasn't going to be easy.

Dean Anderson didn't know that the oldest Anderson boy had passed his Graduate Equivalency Exam, obtaining a GED diploma. Nancy Anderson knew this but was sworn to secrecy. She had attempted to uncover the reasons behind her son's reluctance to share the news with his father. Matt simply clamed up and explained that he'd tell his father when the time was right.

Matthew never knew his Uncle Ervin Anderson. The man was long dead and buried, relegated to legend, by the time Matt came into the world. Dean referenced his departed brother only on disparate, removed occasions, never really providing much in the way of detail, absently casting off-the-cuff references to something Erv had said or done and little more. What the young man did know was that the passing of his uncle set his father against the military as a career. The rigor of that opinion was going to make it tough for the oldest son of Dean and Nancy Anderson to tell his parents that he'd enlisted in the Marines.

Pulling the trailer with the Polaris, the black sides of the sheet metal conveyance dented from hard use, Matt debated how and when he should tell his folks. He was over eighteen. His enlistment was irrevocable. The die had been cast. All that was left for him to do was the telling of it. As he drove the vehicle, he spent time thinking about how and when the revelation should be accomplished.

Unexpectedly, Millicent walked into the machine shed, her form willowy, her hair, limp and damp. She carried a cup of hot chocolate in her hands.

"Hey," Matthew said as he straightened up from unhitching the trailer.

"Beautiful day," Millie asserted, handing the cocoa to her brother.

"Thanks. I could use somethin' to warm me up."

She was dressed in a hand-me-down sweater that had been knitted by her mother years before.

"What's up?" the young man asked.

"Nothing. Just came to bring you the hot chocolate."

Matt studied his sister. She was a woman in the fullest sense of the word. There was a time when he'd tried to ignore that she was female because acknowledgement of that fact disturbed him in ways that were unnatural. But now that he'd weathered the storms of adolescence, the young man had come to a place where he was comfortable with his sister, comfortable that they shared a common heritage and home. They were closer than they had ever been.

"There's something I need to tell you," Matt Anderson said.

What's that?"

"You've got to promise not to say anything to mom or dad. Leave that up to me."

Millie's bright face turned sorrowful.

"This isn't about a girl, is it?"

The possibility of an unplanned pregnancy involving any number of girls from town crossed the woman's mind.

"You know I'm smarter than that."

She revealed her teeth through a weak smile. A shiver descended across her upper back.

"I hope so," she responded.

There was no way to soften the information, no way to sugar coat it. He simply tossed out the news at her, letting it hang in the November air between them.

"I joined the Marines."

Her eyes immediately clenched.

"Holy shit," she muttered.

Matt reached for his sister's hand and drew her in.

"It'll be fine," he whispered.

"Are you crazy?"

"No. It's something I've been thinking about for awhile."

"Matt, it's the fucking Marines."

The woman's use of that particular four-letter word astounded her brother. He'd never heard her utter so much as a "hell" or a "damn" over the course of their life together.

"Couldn't you have joined the Navy or the Air Force? At least you wouldn't get shot at and end up like Uncle Erv," she postulated.

"The Marines have the best package and the most openings in electronics right now. Mill, I want to go to college when my four years are up but I don't have the grades. I don't have your smarts. Hell, I was too stupid to even finish high school. With the money and some training, I figure that'll get me started so I can make something of myself and get me off this shit hole of a farm."

His sister's eyes lifted.

"This place is not a shit hole. It's our parent's lives reduced to sweat, toil, and work. I won't stand you denigrating everything they've worked for. I just won't", she announced.

"You know I don't mean it like that. I just mean farming's not for me. Never has been. I think you're the only one in this family who understands that."

The young woman looked into her brother's dark eyes. There was something captured there that was mature and confident. It was a look that she'd never encountered in him before. Reflexively, she kissed his cheek. The texture of his face was smooth, like that of a child.

"I know," she admitted. "I just hope this isn't some spur of the moment thing because of what happened."

Millicent wanted to add that a severe reaction to the abduction of the little girl would be easily understandable. She wanted to tell her brother that he shouldn't beat himself up over the incident. He couldn't have known what his contacts with the militia would manifest. There was no predicting what course a bigot's hate would run. But she didn't say those things to Matthew. It was obvious that he knew them.

Matt released his sister.

"I've thought about this for quite a while. I decided to enlist long before the kidnapping. That's not why I'm doing this," he expressed, as if he able to read her mind.

His eyes took in the confines of the shed. The ceiling rose above them to a great height. There was no light in the building save what infiltrated through an open service door. Dean Anderson's three tractors, assorted trailers, and equipment, items that had once been on display for auction, were neatly stored against the walls of the structure. Shadows of machinery accented the corrugated steel interior of the place as the young farmer tried to envision himself in the dress blues of the Marine Corps.

"When are you going to tell the folks?" Millie asked.

"Tonight."

"Wait until tomorrow. I gotta go to work. I'm on until midnight."

"OK."

Matthew watched his only sister walk out the door. As she moved away, the man remembered that he had something more to say.

"Mill," he called out softly.

She turned.

"Yes?"

"When are you going to leave for Notre Dame?"

She shrugged.

"Maybe next fall. I still need to save some more money."

He smiled.

"You should just take the Concordia scholarship. You'd be sitting pretty."

She laughed. A tiny flutter of air vibrated her lips.

"That's not what I want."

Matt nodded.

"We Anderson kids can be stubborn, can't we?"

The young woman didn't respond. She left her brother to his work, his point having been made.

CHAPTER 48

The Perkin's Restaurant on Highway 10 was full of luncheon customers. Dean and Nancy Anderson slipped into a booth ahead of Aitkins and Hernesman by taking full advantage of patronage. Millicent Anderson was on duty when her parents arrived. She ushered them to a booth. Despite the milling crowd of customers, no one complained.

"How'd it go this morning?" the daughter asked as she handed her parents menus. The young woman smiled, concealing her brother's recent revelation from the adults.

Dean looked at the offerings and responded without making eye contact.

"We didn't settle."

"That's too bad. Did you make any progress?"

Nancy smiled. Her face appeared to be fighting a sense of desperation.

"Not really. They're not in the ballpark," the mother replied.

"Dan and his associate, Ms. Hernesman, will be joining us," Dean advised, still reflecting on the menu.

"I'll set two more places."

Millicent left her parents to retrieve additional silverware, napkins, water glasses, and menus.

The farmer and his wife ignored the background noise. Dean glanced above the edge of the bill of fare; the pages laminated in plastic, and cast a surreptitious eye at his wife. There was no question in the farmer's mind that the looming trial was taxing his spouse. She was ready to break under the pressure. In recent weeks, she'd seen her doctor for an irregular heartbeat that needed correcting with a pacemaker. The procedure was to take place after the trial. Dean was convinced that stress was the root cause of his wife's cardiac symptoms.

"It'll be all right," he urged in a calm voice, his hand coming to rest on his wife's forearm. "We'll get through this."

She didn't respond. After a moment of contemplation, the woman forced a weak grin.

"Maybe I shouldn't have told them to go to hell in Des Moines."

Dean grinned.

"I don't think that would have made any difference," the farmer said.

A deputy walked across the dining room towards their booth. At first, Dean thought the man was looking beyond them. The determined path of the deputy made it clear he was coming to speak to the Andersons.

"Mr. and Mrs. Anderson?"

"Yes," the farmer replied.

"Deputy Johnson. I've got some legal papers for you."

The officer produced a small packet of documents and handed them to Dean.

"We have an attorney. Shouldn't these go to him?"

"This is a Summons and a Complaint. I have to personally serve the papers on you. Have a nice day."

Deputy Johnson avoided a prolonged discussion, quickly leaving the Andersons' booth to reduce the attention his presence directed towards the couple.

"What is it?" Nancy asked.

"Shit."

The woman's eyes narrowed. Her voice dropped.

"Dean, watch your language. You're in a restaurant."

"Sorry. That damn asshole Barnes is at it again. Danny warned this might happen."

Anderson spoke in low tones and ignored his wife's admonition. His blood pressure was up. It was clear that he was angry.

"Dean, please tell me what you're talking about."

"We've been sued by Pavo Tynjala."

"The hog farmer from Wheaton?"

The farmer looked up from the pleadings.

"The same."

"What for?"

"I don't get all this legal mumbo jumbo but I know that he talked to Bob Morgan, Barnes' investigator, and made allegations that his herd got HPP from animals we sold him."

The woman became alarmed.

"Why are they doing this to us?"

"Because they can," the hog farmer replied.

Daniel Aitkins and Dee Dee Hernesman entered the restaurant.

"Hi, Mr. Aitkins," Millicent said through an exuberant grin. "My folks are in the back. They're expecting you."

Aitkins returned the smile. His eyes carefully took in the young woman, noting her poise and striking features without staring or lingering.

"What's wrong?" Hernesman asked as the lawyers approached. Mrs. Anderson was wiping tears from her eyes with a cloth table napkin.

"Those bastards," Dean Anderson said.

"What are you talking about?" Aitkins prodded, standing over the booth as his partner sought to console Nancy Anderson.

"Read this," the farmer demanded, thrusting the Summons and Complaint at Aitkins.

259

"Shit," the lawyer noted.

"What's it about?" Dee Dee whispered, trying to maintain confidentiality in a room full of eavesdropping ears.

"That son-of-a-bitch Barnes and his buddy Thompson."

"What?"

"He got that shark from St. Cloud, that rotten scum bag Alan Ignatius to take on Tynjala's HPP claim against the Andersons."

Dee Dee rose from her crouched position to study the papers.

"That asshole," she murmured.

"My thoughts exactly. They planned this, timed it so as to hit us just as we're getting ready to present the case against Stevenson's. They're trying to break us, pulling out all stops to make us spin our wheels and expend all our resources so we'll take their offer."

Dean Anderson watched crimson ascend across his attorney's face.

"Can you handle this?" the farmer asked with more than a slight influence of skepticism.

Aitkins crumpled the legal documents and shoved them into the depths of the rear pocket of his dress slacks.

"We can."

"You've already got two partners working full time on this. How can you afford to devote any more people to representing us?" Nancy Anderson asked, a tear sliding down her cheek.

Dee Dee waited for Danny's response. She was doubtful that the firm could dedicate another attorney to defend the Andersons, no matter how serious the situation. They were stretched thin in terms of personnel. Other cases, cases of significant worth and merit, needed attention. Now their client had been hit with a lawsuit, a claim that would divert precious manpower and money away from the looming trial. Hernesman searched the eyes of her partner for recognition that there was no hope; no way could their operation stand up against the latest onslaught from the defense. She was surprised by Danny's reply.

"My old man is itching to get into this fight," Aitkins observed. "He's been salivating to take a chunk out of Alan Ignatius for years. If you ask my dad, he thinks the cheating slime should have been disbarred, that the Lawyer's Board was spineless when the time came to deal with F.W. Barnes' crony. He'll relish this chance. He'll grab it and run like a little kid with an ice cream cone on a hot day," the lawyer said with a flourish.

"You sure about this?" Hernesman asked out of the hearing of their clients.

"Abso-fucking-lutely," Dan Aitkins replied.

CHAPTER 49

The drive to Horace Brewster's ranch, a two hundred acre spread set in the narrow valley of the Maple River just outside of Hope, North Dakota, was uneventful. Hernesman and Aitkins made the trip through a prairie landscape embraced by winter. White, black, and gray were the only colors on nature's pallet save for the occasional conifer, though even the green pines seemed to take on an ebony aspect under the limited light of the season.

There was no snow in the air. Outside, the wind was still, the mercury hung close to zero. Hernesman's Volkswagen Beetle, one of the new type, hugged Highway 32 as the roadway curved and sliced through the fertile soil of the Great Plains. Farm fields, their crops harvested, lay dormant beneath modest snow. Here and there, splotches of brown earth were visible where late November sun had melted the precipitation. It was the Friday after Thanksgiving and they were working.

"This Bug has a nice ride for a little car."

"You can't beat the Germans for engineering. You could spend a lot more on a Porche or an Audi but why? This car has all their attributes at half the price," Hernesman mused, turning up the music on the car's CD player as they drove.

"Who's this?" Aitkins asked, listening to an unfamiliar folk singer urging the strains of a sorrowful lament from his guitar.

"John Gorka."

"Can't say as I've ever listened to him."

"He's one of my favorites. This is some of his early stuff."

Danny reclined his head against a headrest and closed his eyes.

"There's something I've been meaning to ask you," Dee Dee remarked, her tone tender and gentle.

Aitkins opened his eyelids. He wasn't interested in receiving a lecture from his partner about marriage, truth, and honesty. He knew that's what she was warming up to. He knew he had it coming.

"How's that?" he answered weakly.

"That night in Winnipeg, was she good?"

There was no subtlety in Hernesman's approach. The rebuke behind her inquiry was obvious.

"What the hell are you talking about?"

"Dan, don't be so stupid. I'm not the only one that knows what went down at the Fort Garry Hotel."

The lawyer's eyes opened.

"What do you mean?"

"Jim Thompson saw the two of you arrive after your dinner together. You weren't being very discrete, you know. The way he tells it, you had your tongue half way down Melanie Barnes' throat waiting for an elevator."

"Fuck," Aitkins muttered.

"That's what I thought," Hernesman interjected. "Does Julie know?"

Dan looked out the passenger's window. Obtuse light greeted his eyes. The fingers of his right hand stroked the skin of his forehead.

"Of course not."

"You're going to tell her, aren't you?"

"Are you out of your mind?"

Dee Dee downshifted and made a left hand turn. The wheels of the Beetle bit into frozen gravel.

"Danny, I know you. You keep this thing bottled up inside of you, you're gonna have a freakin' heart attack. You did the crime; you gotta fess up and do the time."

Aitkins turned and faced the female lawyer. Her hazel eyes betrayed sincere concern. His face was chalky, as if someone had drained his blood.

"She'll kick my ass out of the house. It will be the end of us, her, me, the kids."

Hernesman shifted the car into fifth and accelerated down a straight stretch of country road. Trees whipped by the Volkswagen. Clouds seemed to stand still as they sped through the desolate countryside. An abandoned barn, its sides painted a deep royal blue, boasting matching blue shingles, stood solitary and alone against the pewter sky. No birds or other animals were apparent. There was an absence of life in the world they passed.

"Because of one mistake? I don't see Julie doing that. Maybe a little cooling off period, some counseling, promises from you that it won't happen again."

Dan looked away in shame.

"This isn't the first time," he admitted.

Dee Dee Hernesman considered her response carefully.

"I'm not an expert on this kind of stuff. At least, not with respect to your lifestyle. But it happened to me. I had a partner, a girlfriend..."

A pause.

"Yes, Dan, you're idle wonderings are correct. I'm gay. Anyway, she stepped out on me, actually fell in love with someone else for a brief time. We were undergrads together. We worked through it."

Aitkins returned his gaze to the woman.

"What happened?"

"She died of leukemia during our senior year. But we were back together when she passed away. I forgave her. Julie can forgive you too, if you're willing to let her."

Aitkins pointed a finger out the windshield.

"Here we are. Doc Brewster's place."

The Bug drove under an arch of Ponderosa pine timbers bearing a large wooden sign with painted letters that proclaimed:

MAPLE PASS RANCH.

Road divided pasture. Cattle and stock horses grazed on slices of hay carved from large round bales of alfalfa deposited across the meager snow. The Volkswagen crossed a narrow bridge, a span constructed of railroad ties and timbers suspended above the gurgling course of the Maple River. The water was shallow and clear, flowing easily across smooth stones.

"How you folks doin'?" a smiling man, his face suntanned and weathered from years of riding herd, greeted them as they exited the automobile. "Cute little car," he added.

"Thanks," Hernesman responded, offering her bare hand. She stood eye-to-eye with their host, noting that his hair was snow white, that his brown eyes reflected signs of developing cataracts. "Doctor Brewster?"

"That'd be me. You must be Dee Dee."

The veterinarian pumped the woman's hand with enthusiasm before turning to greet her companion. The gesture was clearly from the heart and not perfunctory.

"You must be Aitkins," the man said turning to greet Danny.

"That's me. Good of you to see us on such short notice, Doctor."

"Call me Horace. 'Ace' for short. When I was a pup, my brothers tried calling me 'Hore' as a nickname but my ma, God rest her soul, put a stop to that early on. It became 'Ace' pretty soon thereafter. Come on up to the house. Helen, the wife, she made fresh coffee and Saskatoon muffins before she left for town."

Aitkins walked next to the man. Brewster was a shade shorter than the attorney. It was a rare occasion for the trial lawyer to have a height advantage over a companion.

"Saskatoons?" Hernesman inquired.

"You gotta pardon her, Ace. She's from the city. She's probably never even seen a June Berry before," Aitkins observed.

"June Berry?" Hernesman queried.

Brewster opened the front door. The dwelling was a recently completed log home. The walls of the place were impressively solid;

263

constructed from the same Ponderosa pine that formed the fencing along the drive and the entrance arch to the ranch.

"They're deep blue. Taste somewhere between an apple and a plum. A little tarter than a blueberry but similar in size and color. So blue they're nearly black when they're ripe," the veterinarian added.

"A prairie delicacy," Aitkins said, taking off his trademark cowboy boots and depositing them neatly on a throw rug inside the front door. "The city of Saskatoon was named for all the June Berry, or Service Berry trees, that grew where the city developed. They're raised commercially up in Canada."

"Like a 'pick your own' strawberry farm," Brewster rejoined.

A massive stone fireplace dominated the home's Great Room. A log stairway climbed to a loft overlooking the main living area. The floors were constructed from wide boards of yellow pine, done in crude pioneer style and shellacked to a glare. A fire raged in the firebox. Smells of fresh pastry and coffee permeated the air.

"Have a seat," the doctor advised, pointing to a snack bar delineating the Great Room from the kitchen. The cabinets of the cooking area were constructed of carefully selected pine, lightly varnished so that the natural color and grain of the wood remained pronounced. Hernesman and Aitkins climbed onto two wrought iron stools and rested their elbows on the ceramic tile surface of the counter. Aitkins placed the expert report section of the Anderson file on the tiles beside him.

"Muffin?" Brewster asked, removing steaming Saskatoon-laden baked goods from the oven.

"I'll try one," Hernesman said, reaching for a pastry with her bare fingers. "Ouch."

"Careful, they're hot," the Vet added.

Aitkins used a paper napkin to retrieve two muffins from the muffin tin. Brewster pushed two empty plates towards the attorneys. Aitkins studied the oatmeal embedded crust of the muffins, here and there the caramelized coating of the food disrupted by indigo. Dan slid a plate to his partner.

"Coffee? Either of you take cream or sugar?" Brewster inquired.

"We both take it black," Hernesman advised, her mouth half full of butter and berries. "These are wonderful."

"I got the recipe for Helen off the Internet. Even an old dog like me can learn new tricks."

"You don't look that old," Aitkins quipped.

"Sixty-seven come next May," the rancher said, beaming proudly. His teeth were a vibrant white; their perfection defying his reported age. His hands and forearms burst with sinew and strength. Horace Brewster was a man who'd live another two or three decades unless something untoward like cancer or ALS struck him down.

"No way," Dee Dee added. "I'd guess you were in your late forties."

"Good clean Christian living," the veterinarian winked. "A little wine, a little bread, a little love, but none of them in too large a quantity."

The lawyers laughed and sipped coffee. The muffin plate was nearly empty by the time they retired to the Great Room to talk.

"I've gone over the materials you sent me from Dr. Guttormson and Ivan Thomas at NDSU. I've also taken a look at the stuff Stevenson's is relying on from Chuck Bronski and his buddy, Kelly Long at the University of Illinois Animal Poison Control Lab."

The doctor gathered his thoughts.

"It's too bad you couldn't get Ojala on board. He's the best there is. But it doesn't surprise me Stevenson's got to him. They throw a lot of money around to keep experts quiet. He's not the first one they've bought off. He won't be the last."

"I'm interested in using you as an adjunct expert," Aitkins advised. "Andy Nelson, our economist at Moorhead State put Dean Anderson on to you. Said you're not only a top-notch Vet, working with the Amish and Hutterites, but you're a rancher and hog farmer yourself. That intrigued me. I think you're the kind of man a jury will really respect; one who doesn't mind getting his hands dirty."

Brewster sat deeply in a leather recliner. The rancher drew a mouthful of coffee from his mug. A sheepish grin replaced the Vet's smile.

"That's some praise. You've got high expectations. I don't have Bronski's international reputation. Do you realize that, right now, he's over in Poland as a consultant? He's been to India, China, and God knows where else, all at the behest of foreign governments. He's a consultant to every multi-national feed and seed supplier, not to mention all of the major pork and beef producers. Chuck's credentials would fill this room."

Hernesman studied the rancher as the man caught his breath.

"Me, on the other hand. I've got my DVM. I do nice work for some of the bigger locals; consult with the Amish and the Hutterites. I'm respected in a radius of a hundred miles from Fargo and that's about it."

Aitkins grinned.

"Well, Detroit Lakes is within a hundred miles of Fargo."

The doctor laughed. His face stretched, displaying a hint of age around the corners of his mouth.

"So it is. I like your clients. They've got some things to work on but, overall, they're quality people working hard, trying to make

265

it a go. These big companies, I get a little work from some of Stevenson's competition but I don't like doing it. They have too much control, too much power."

Aitkins nodded.

"Vertical integration?"

"That's only the half of it. Sure, the big feed and livestock companies are taking over the food chain on the meat, poultry, and diary side. But you know what? It's even scarier on the crop side."

"How so?" Hernesman queried.

"Ever hear of the 'killer gene'?"

"Nope," the female litigator admitted.

"Me neither," Dan added.

"Well, here's how it works. A seed company sells corn seed to a farmer. Use Anderson as an example. Anderson plants Brand X corn to grow livestock feed or maybe to sell sweet corn to Green Giant or Libby or someone else. They're all part of some larger corporate structure now anyway. Anderson harvests his crop and, like farmers' have done for thousands of years, he saves kernels for next year's planting. That's if he got a good yield and liked the disease resistance of Brand X. Guess what?"

"What?" both lawyers blurted out at once.

"The crap won't grow. Brand X has installed a 'killer gene' in the corn that precludes germination. The kernels can't be used the next year to start another crop. Anderson is captive to Brand X, or has to switch to another brand, which of course, will also have a 'killer gene' spliced into its product."

"That sucks," Danny Aitkins muttered.

"That's an understatement," Brewster corrected, his smile having disappeared.

There was a deep and significant silence in the Great Room as the occupants watched flames engulf scrub oak logs in the fireplace.

"So you'll work with us?" Daniel finally asked.

"Not an issue. I'd love to be able to take the stand against Chuck Bronski. Deep down, he's a decent guy. But he's so far into this expert witness thing, he'll say whatever he's paid to say. This case is simple. Your clients bought FGP pelleted feed. They fed it to their pigs. The corn base was contaminated, adulterated to use Ms. Hernesman's term, with mold. The mold was concealed because the corn had been re-formed into pellets. There were Mycotoxins in the feed that caused feed refusal and the massive, complete abortion of all of the litters being carried by the Andersons' breeding herd. It's a very simple case. Stick with simplicity, Mr. Aitkins and Ms. Hernesman. You can't lose."

"Is that a guarantee?" Aitkins asked, rising from his seat and picking up the file.

"Ain't nothin' guaranteed in life but death and taxes," the veterinarian retorted. "And there's an awful lot of folks who get away without paying their taxes."

The lawyers donned their winter coats and walked out onto the porch of the log home.

"We'll do fine. Leave the answers to me, folks. All you need do is come up with the right questions," Horace Brewster said with a subtle wave of a well-muscled hand to the departing attorneys.

Dee Dee Hernesman had more questions. They were for her partner. She asked her questions inside the Volkswagen as they headed back to Minnesota through the fading light of day. Her inquiry concerned a certain red haired woman and events that had taken place in the capital city of Manitoba. They were questions that Danny Aitkins did not want to answer.

CHAPTER 50

Obsession begins as a small seed of attraction. Sometimes the seed sprouts quickly, grows to its full height, and then dies a rapid death. In other circumstances, desire matures slowly, over the long course of time; sometimes over months, sometimes over years, sometimes over a lifetime.

Danny Aitkins' compulsion for Melanie Barnes ignited like a slow burning fuse following the death of Melanie's husband and Dan's best friend. She was a widow. The moral restrictions that applied while Michael was alive were stripped away by the young lawyer's untimely suicide. Daniel's obsession was fueled by an unnatural combination of envy, grief, and passion. He was able to harness his demons for a time. He thought he was strong enough, that his love for Julie was resilient enough, to best the desire he felt, that he repressed, for Melanie Ingersol Barnes. He had been wrong.

"Can we meet for lunch?"

In other circumstances, under other conditions, his telephone call would have been innocent, the call of one friend to another to schedule a casual meeting. Given the events that had transpired in Winnipeg, the call was anything but chaste.

"Danny, are you out of your mind?"

Her answer had taken him aback. He had envisioned her ready acceptance of a sultry, heated affair; surreptitious liaisons propelled by mutual longing. He considered a response. There was no reason to mince words. The attorney blurted out what was on his mind.

"I need to see you."

"I don't think that's such a good idea. We're on opposite sides of a lawsuit. If F.W. gets wind of what happened in Winnipeg, I'm likely out of a job, father-in-law or not. I can't afford to lose this position," she said, talking in low tones, the door to her office in the heart of the Bugle Building closed to prying ears.

"It's too late. Dee Dee tells me that Thompson already knows, or at least suspects something between us."

Silence.

"Shit," Melanie whispered.

"Let's get away from here, maybe have lunch in Grand Forks. I know a nice little place by the river, Italian. It doesn't have to be any more than lunch."

There was a lapse in the conversation.

"Danny, do you really know what you're getting into? One night is something that can be forgiven. Starting something more long term is a whole 'nother matter. You realize what that means? Is that something you really want to risk?"

The lawyer's blood was racing. Considerations of morality slipped away. Distant walls of resistance were being assailed by his physical needs.

"Mel, I know what I'm asking. I'm asking an old friend to go to lunch."

"Then why not have lunch here, in Fergus?"

A valid point. If nothing was going to happen between them, if the meeting was indeed innocent, why not see Melanie in public, out in the open?

Because I want more than lunch, the attorney thought. *I want you.*

"There's a nice little lunch counter right next door. If F.W. already knows about us, or has some suspicions, then why not put those inklings to rest by walking into our office and asking me to go to lunch?" she requested.

Food was not what he wanted. He wanted the taste of her skin, the smell of her hair, the wonder of her body. Given the way the conversation was directed, he acquiesced.

"I'll be there at noon."

"I'll be waiting. Want F.W. to join us?"

A nervous laugh erupted from Aitkins.

"Not particularly."

"Well, I'm gonna ask him any way. He'll say 'no' but it'll knock him off track."

"If he says yes, it'll be a lot tougher to digest the food," Daniel mumbled.

F.W. didn't accept. The ruse worked; it confused the old man. He was beginning to suspect something was brewing between his daughter-in-law and the ambulance chaser. Melanie's invitation to join them for lunch caught the defense lawyer unawares and cast doubt upon his supposition. Melanie saw this in the old man's eyes when he declined to accompany her to the cafe.

They ordered sandwiches and cups of soup. Aitkins had a cheeseburger; she had a turkey and Swiss on rye. Melanie sipped hot tea; the lawyer drank chocolate milk. The couple sat across from each other in a booth removed from the other customers, near the restrooms and the rear exit to Caroline's Corner Counter.

"So, what's up?" the woman asked.

Melanie was dressed in a smart blue blazer, matching wool slacks, and a white silk blouse. Her hair was cut short, shorter than it had been during their brief encounter. Her eyes seemed tired; her smile, less than exuberant.

"Not much. Adam's hockey schedule is a real killer. The other two are playing basketball which is a lot less intense."

"Michael's already playing?"

"They start young."

"Amanda's playing too?"

"Well, she's on a team. I wouldn't exactly call what she does on the court 'playing'. More like 'social interaction.' She tends to gab a lot and forget why she's out there."

The paralegal laughed. There was little joy behind her expression. They resumed eating their sandwiches in silence.

"Danny."

"Yes?"

The woman's eyes peered over her teacup.

"Why are you here?"

He took the last bite of his sandwich.

"I needed to see you."

Her face flushed. There was a growing sense within the woman that their informal get together had been a bad idea. She felt the return of a steady flame, an unquenchable attraction.

Aitkins' eyes sparkled. Desire became obvious on Danny's face as the ghost of their past clamored to have its chains stricken, its appetite satisfied.

"You're seeing me now," she whispered.

"You know what I mean."

"How long can this go on?" she asked.

The attorney looked away. The woman's question burrowed into his brain.

"I don't know."

"What is it that you want from me, Danny, other than my bed?"

"Isn't that enough?"

His face was flushed. Her hands reached across the table and found his.

"You can't blame this on wine," she advised.

"I know."

Her house was a modest bungalow two blocks off the main drag. The yellow two-story was surrounded by massive oaks. The leaves of the trees were stiff and frozen. Her bedroom was small, containing a modest twin mattress, a maple headboard, a matching dresser, and an end table with a brass lamp. The light was off as they undressed.

He found her just as he had before. This time, the guilt was more easily defeated. This time, her response was more animated. They were learning from each other. His hands found ways to reach her. Her soul found ways to receive him. A tide of passion lapped, then crested, at the shore of orgasm in the shadowy confines of her room, the air smelling of sweet oils and humanity, the atmosphere still save for their panicked breathing.

Afterwards, his arm rested across the gentle curve of her chest. She was lying on her back, studying the plaster ceiling, her breasts bare, the reddish nipples smaller, once they had finished. He watched the restrained rise and fall of her chest, as he thought of something appropriate to say. There was nothing he could come up with to relate his feelings. Within his heart, his soul, there was more for her than mere sexual attraction. There was something else. Maybe it was love. Love like he felt for Julie? That couldn't be. He knew he was incapable of sharing the mature, rarefied love he had constructed in his marriage with another woman. Love like he once felt for Ginny? That was closer, though his tryst with the young blond had been an indiscretion of youth; and this, this liaison with Melanie, was an entirely planned and calculated event of maturity.

The woman beside him rolled off the mattress and walked into the bathroom. Instinctively, he knew it was time to leave. He rose from her bed, the sheets damp with his seed, and began to pull on his underwear. Daniel dressed in silence, leaving the house without saying goodbye.

CHAPTER 51

Bruce Tollerude, F.W. Barnes, Malachi Stone, and Jim Thompson flew from Minneapolis to Montreal. They were joined, in the magnificent city built at the confluence of the Ottawa and St. Lawrence Rivers by Ellen McNally, Stevenson Sci-Swine's General Counsel; Albert Boise, President and CFO of Justere Decroix, Stevenson's parent company based in Paris, France; Pierre Montrose, President of the First Farmer's Bank of Montreal; and Renee LaCrotte, Assistant General Solicitor of the Bank.

Beneath the towering shadow of Mount Royal, the bluff dominating the City of Montreal, the participants gathered at the Marriott Chateau Champlain. There was much work to be done. The clock was ticking. Investors were getting anxious.

"Let's start with a discussion of this pesky lawsuit you're handling in Minnesota," Ellen McNally began.

The barrister was a sparsely defined woman of great height. Her eyes were colorless; her hair, a universal brown. There was no definition to her hips and bust; nothing save the fact that she wore a skirt gave any indication that McNally was, in fact, female. Her cheeks were devoid of powder. Her ears were absent finery. She was, in a word, plain.

"We're on top of the Anderson matter," Malachi Stone observed. "Mr. Thompson and Mr. Barnes have taken steps to limit Stevenson's exposure."

"How so?" Albert Boise, who, despite being French, spoke English better than most of the individuals in the room.

"We've eliminated as many possible claimants as we can, preventing this thing from getting out of hand and snowballing into a class action lawsuit," Thompson inserted.

The black man's eyes appeared tired. He was thinking about his daughter and the fact that the law was once again taking him away from his little girl. The separation was made more painful by uncontrollable recollections of the afternoon at the Holiday Inn pool in Detroit Lakes. He was using pills, non-prescription stuff, to help him sleep. The medicine left Thompson drowsy, unable to make quick decisions, though the lag time in his thought process appeared to be noticeable only to the lawyer.

"In American football parlance, we'd call it an end around," F.W. Barnes interjected. "We tracked down all of the other folks who received pellets from the same lot as the plaintiffs and made significant offers, more than we'd originally planned to spend, to get the other potential cases resolved."

"Why not settle the Anderson claim as well?" Pierre Montrose, head of First Farmers Bank, rejoined. "With what's at stake here, wouldn't that be the prudent thing to do?"

Montrose's' English was infected with the influences of his native French-Canadian tongue. There was an odd discrepancy between the Canadian's inability to speak English without an accent and that of Boise, a native Frenchman, whose English bore no such inflection.

"I'll handle this," Ellen McNally said. "It's not as simple as all that. We'd love to settle the Anderson claim for something in the low six figures. But the plaintiffs' attorney refuses to give us a confidentiality agreement. We can't afford to have word of a significant settlement leak out at this point. We're in hush-hush negotiations with two mid-level American commodities firms. The margins are thin right now. There's a lot of skittishness on both the Canadian and American trading boards. A six figure case may seem insignificant in the scope of a ten billion dollar deal but any adverse publicity, and I want to emphasize 'any', could knock us out of the running and bring another player into the game."

"I might add that, though we're relatively certain we've taken care of the majority of the possible claims from other buyers of the same lot involved in the Anderson case," Bruce Tollerude revealed, "the margin of error is such that we may have missed a dozen or so customers."

The American continued.

"Couple that with the distinct possibility that other lots from the Grand Forks mill were likely contaminated and you can see that keeping a lid on this, to include the seemingly inconsequential claim of the Andersons, is a must for this merger to move forward," Tollerude concluded.

"The Bank is wary of getting involved in financing any mergers or acquisitions if even a hint of a class action suit looms on the horizon," Ms. LaCrotte observed. "Any such filing would preempt our participation in the financial arrangements."

There was no tension in the room. Each of the professionals spoke in a restrained manner, a manner suited for the business of high finance and corporate acquisition.

"When will the Anderson case be completed?" Montrose asked.

"Trial is set for January Fifteenth in Detroit Lakes and should last two weeks. After that, presuming there's a defense verdict, the matter should be concluded. There's a chance the plaintiffs might take an appeal but the odds of that being successful are less than ten percent if the jury determines the facts in our favor."

"The bank can accept those odds," LaCrotte said.

The female solicitor from Quebec was a tiny woman with short gray hair, gray eyes and equally gray skin. Thick eyeglass frames of blue plastic dominated her face, making it difficult to discern her nose. She wore pale blue eyeliner and cobalt lipstick, the tones complimenting her silver business suit.

"And if the plaintiffs prevail?" Boise inquired.

"Then we negotiate to pay off the judgment, or we appeal, depending upon the amount owed and the willingness of Mr. Aitkins, the plaintiffs' attorney, to be reasonable," Tollerude added. "In any case, we'll delay post-verdict matters long enough so that any payment takes place after Justere Decroix has completed the transaction and acquired the target company. Once the merger is agreed to, the new entity will be in a much better position to compete in North America and Europe."

"People, we need this merger," Albert Boise stated with an emphatic nod. "Without it, the company cannot continue to expand its operations as set forth in the five year plan adopted by our Board of Directors. With First Farmer's backing, we can do this thing. But we've got to be careful. We've got to hold our cards until the player across the table has been drawn into our game."

"And that, folks, means that we must keep the Anderson matter out of the national media. Occasional articles in the local paper have had no impact on the viability of the pending deal. But widespread speculation as to a class action lawsuit would be another matter. That would be ruinous," McNally said, leaning forward to retrieve a tissue to wipe her nose.

"It's been taken care of," Tollerude advised. "The local press hasn't printed any more diatribes since I paid the editor a visit and showed him a proposed libel complaint asserting Stevenson's claim for punitive damages. The paper will report on the trial and the verdict but there won't be any big hoopla over the fate of the Anderson Farm coming out of the press."

Boise stood up, a short, medium-built man with a shiny head and no excess body fat. He was dressed casually, unusual dress for the corporate head of a multi-billion dollar business. As he walked to a window and scrutinized the snow-covered hillside of the city, his eyes, thin slits of murky brown and green, focused on the beauty of the season. It was near Christmas. He would be home, back in the suburbs of Paris, tomorrow. He'd be able to see Jean, his male paramour, and celebrate the birth of the Christ Child at home. The thought of an intimate holiday dinner and midnight mass at the stone Roman Catholic church in the center of his village made the tycoon smile.

"Good. We're all in agreement," Boise said as he turned to face the other participants of the conclave. "We'll push forward and make this thing happen regardless of what occurs in Minnesota."

The heads of the lawyers and bankers nodded in unison as waiters broke through the massive paneled doors of the conference room to serve lunch.

CHAPTER 52

He found himself fighting the runs after every meal. There was a quiet desperation about Daniel that Julie had seen before. She thought it was "the case". It was that. It was also more than that.

Danny tried to continue jogging as a means of coping with the stress. The stress of the looming courtroom conflagration. The stress of the burgeoning relationship with his wife's friend, the widow of a departed colleague. His mind told him that it would be easy to call Melanie Barnes on the telephone and end it. End the dissimulation. End the looming catastrophic destruction of his marriage. Time and time again, as he worked late into the night on the Anderson file, his hand would reach for the receiver to call her, only to retract, constrained by his heart.

They met once more before Christmas. The taste of her skin, the essence of her, lingered. He could not rid his senses of her. Within the engagement of making love later that same day to Julie, the remnants of Melanie Ingersol Barnes drifted across his mind like a morning breeze across a Midwestern pasture. The images were worse than they had ever been with Virginia. They were far more intense, more distracting. During the weeks that followed, it became obvious that Julie was troubled by his ineptitude, his lack of patience, as she sought him within the warm confines of their marital bed. He wanted Julie, wanted to please her but it was beyond Daniel's meager abilities as a lover to overcome his sin.

"What's wrong?" his wife asked. Julie snuggled against her husband, her naked body entwined with his. She stroked his hair, noting that the blond tendrils were beginning to display significant flecks of gray.

"I'm not sure."

"Is it something I'm doing?" she inquired, injury apparent in her voice. There was pain, the pain of a wife's failure to please her husband, trapped within the words.

"It's not that."

She touched his flank. Her fingers followed the definition of his ribs to his waist with elegant delicacy.

"Then what?"

"The Anderson case."

"Are you sure that's all?"

"That's all."

Once again, he'd climaxed too early. The dysfunction happened with increasing regularity. An out-of-step ritual had displaced their wondrous unity, the blissful cadence of their shared history.

"Are you sure?"

She softened the query. She didn't want to pry too deeply. There was a danger that he would withdraw, that he would clam up and abandoned their conversation without resolution.

"I'm sure. It's late. I have to get up early."

"Tomorrow's Saturday."

"I know. I promised Amanda I'd take her to an auction over in Park Rapids. A bunch of quarter horse mares are up for sale."

Julie Aitkins rolled over, reached for the switch on the table lamp next to the bed, and turned off the light. She remained unsatisfied, both with her husband's answer and with the results of their lovemaking.

"I like that one, daddy," Amanda Jane yelled with glee as they watched a dozen or so grade mares parade around the livestock arena at the Hubbard County Fairgrounds on the outskirts of Park Rapids, Minnesota.

The girl's gloved hand pointed to a high-boned, spirited gray mare with a black mane and three black stockings. The horse pranced with assurance. There was nothing about the animal that was reserved. She carried her head high and regal, as if she felt superior to all the other equine flesh on display.

"She's a beauty, all right," Danny acknowledged. The attorney's eyes followed the animal as it cantered smartly across the frozen earth of the corral. Clouds of vapor drifted from the herd as the horses went through their paces at the direction of two wranglers mounted on matching palomino geldings. The men wore thick sheepskin coats, black cowboy hats, black cowboy boots, and leather gloves against the marginal air.

"Can we see her up close?" Amanda asked.

Aitkins nodded to his daughter.

"Stanley," the lawyer shouted over a din of hooves. "She wants to see the gray."

They were at the arena ahead of other buyers. Danny had defended the owner of the auction house on a drunken driving case, got him acquitted after a two-day trial, despite a breath test showing that Stanley Kubiak was driving with twice the legal limit of alcohol in his blood. The cop forgot to turn off his portable radio when he administered the Intoxilyzer test. The printed test report contained the abbreviation "RFI" alongside the blood-alcohol rating, .25. The green prosecutor didn't know what the letters stood for.

Danny had waited until the jury was impaneled, until jeopardy had attached, before educating the Assistant County Attorney. "RFI" meant Radio Frequency Interference. The Intoxilyzer handbook advised that a test with the designation "RFI" was not a valid test. Danny had studied the text cover to cover. He knew what the letters stood for. By the end of his argument, so did the trial judge. The case was dismissed.

Stanley Kubiak edged the mare across the surface of the corral towards Danny and his daughter. The cowboy swung out of his saddle and stood next to the horse. He looped his hand through a bridle on the gray and held the animal so that the lawyer and the little girl could enter the enclosure. Kubiak's partner moved the other horses into the sales barn.

"She's a real goer," Kubiak said. "She's had two hundred hours of training. You gonna ride English or Western?"

Amanda gently stroked the shimmering flanks of the animal. Her face broke into a wide smile.

"Western."

"All her training's been Western," the man advised. "She's out of the snaffle and into a curb bit. Just a light touch and she's off. Turns and cuts on a dime. She'll make one heck of a barrel racer or roper."

Aitkins walked around the animal. The mare stood still against a winter sky accented by the brilliant blue of unencumbered altitude. The creature's eyes followed the attorney as he studied the quarter horse's profile.

"Any bad habits?" Danny asked.

"None. I bought her from a lady over by New York Mills. She had Barry Evans over there train her. Ever hear of him?"

"Can't say as I have."

"He's one of the best."

Aitkins stood eye to eye with the horse. The animal wasn't nervous. She didn't prance or exhibit any trace of uneasiness.

"Why'd she sell her?"

"Lupus. She's dying of lupus."

"That's tough."

"She had three nice horses. The other two are already spoken for. Personally, I think this one's the best of the lot."

"The auction sheet says thirty five hundred. That your bottom dollar?"

Stanley smiled. The man was missing significant numbers of teeth. Those that remained were stained deep brown from chew.

"Shit, Dan..." the horse trader stopped after he realized a ten-year-old girl was standing next to them. "Sorry about that Miss. What I meant to say was, for you Dan; I can let her go for twenty-five. That's exactly two hundred over what I paid. It'll cover my expenses and the cost of dufus over there helping me for the day," the man related, pointing to Stuffy Pembroke, the other rider.

"Can we take her on approval, say for a month?" Aitkins queried.

Kubiak squinted and let fly with a huge wad of spit. The mixture spattered against the frozen earth with force.

"Don't see why not. If you're not happy with her, I'll take her back. Full refund. OK?"

The auctioneer reached across the underside of the horse's neck and shook Amanda Jane's hand.

"You wanna take a spin on her right now?"

The girl's eyes grew wide.

"Sure. What's her name?"

"Penelope's Hope. Hope for short."

Stanley tied the horse's bridle to the top rung of the corral and pulled the saddle and blanket off his cutting horse. In a matter of minutes, the cowboy had adjusted the stirrups and reins to fit the girl.

Amanda mounted the gray with ease and put the horse through a walk, canter, trot, and a run. She had the horse stop, turn, and work smartly through a variety of elementary Western movements.

"Wow, she's great," Amanda observed, bending over the animal's mane to stroke the horse between its ears. "I like her already."

"Can you drop her off at my place?" Aitkins asked.

"As part of the deal? Man, Aitkins, you are a tough negotiator," the cowboy moaned. "Seeing as how I owe you, consider it done. I'll have her there before dark," Kubiak added with a sincere smile.

The lawyer pulled out his checkbook and filled out a draft for the purchase price, carefully writing "Thirty day approval" in the memo section of the instrument, before handing the document to Kubiak.

"I'll put through the paperwork to register her once you've decided she's a keeper."

The lawyer and his daughter said their goodbyes. All the way back to their old farmhouse, Amanda beamed with pride and talked endlessly of Hope.

CHAPTER 53

White powder blanketed the field. The teams, seven players to a side, lined up on the visitors' twenty-yard line. Danny Aitkins wore an old football jersey, the sleeves ending at the elbows, over a blaze orange deer hunting sweatshirt. The hood of the sweatshirt bounced on the attorney's neck as he pranced in place, waiting for the opposing center to snap the ball. The attorney wore black sweat pants, the knees torn and open, exposing the white cotton fabric of his long underwear, and old football cleats, spikes that hadn't been changed in two decades. His shortly cropped hair, a contrast to the flowing locks that he'd displayed during games past, was tucked neatly beneath a purple and white stocking hat. In games gone by, Danny had shoved his blond mane under a hat only to have the hair free itself during rigorous play. Aitkins' hair, reduced to a comfortable length appropriate for a father of three, remained secure beneath his cap. It was Christmas Eve morning. The Lakers Class of 1981 was having its annual touch football skirmish on the snow-covered turf of Detroit Lakes High School's home field.

"Hut, hut, hut," Able Jenson, the starting varsity quarterback in '82, recruited to supplement declining participation in the annual contest, received the ball. By the curious rules of old men, everyone was eligible as a receiver. Six bodies feigned to block and then sought openings in the defense in which to catch the football. Jenson took a three-step drop, evaded a rusher and looked downfield. Tim Andrews, the wide out from Aitkins' class who caught eight balls their senior year for touchdowns, setting a record with eight hundred and seventy-nine yards receiving, a mark that stood for ten years, still lean and lanky as he approached forty, sprinted towards Aitkins.

Danny was playing safety. He was the only defensive back set off the line of scrimmage. His eyes followed the progress of Andrews as the accountant pushed along. Andrews' movements required significant exertion. The end came straight at the D-back. Aitkins back-pedaled, anticipating a move from the wide-out. The accountant threw a head fake towards the sidelines. The attorney bit, realizing too late that the end was doing a buttonhook. Jensen delivered a wobbly pass into the midsection of his target twenty yards down field. The receiver clutched the ball, completing the reception.

Aitkins was intent upon preventing Andrews from gaining additional yardage. Danny was oblivious to the warnings of his teammates.

"X pass," Dwight Simpson, a nose tackle turned over-the-road-trucker, bellowed from a distance. "He's got a trailer."

Aitkins realized that he'd been had. Snowflakes fell as the lawyer tried to stop his forward momentum. Blake Eagleclaw, a back-up running back from Aitkins' class, stepped high as he raced towards Andrews. Before Aitkins could block the tailback's path, allowing another defender to take care of the end who was now standing still, Andrews delivered a pitch to Eagleclaw. The Native man fielded the underhand toss cleanly, dodged Aitkins' diving attempt to tag him, and raced down the sidelines. Visitors- 6, home- 0.

"Christ, am I out of shape," Danny moaned as Dwight Simpson waddled over to where the lawyer was standing.

"And you haven't gotten any smarter over the years, either," the nose tackle remarked, spitting a wad of phlegm on the clean white snow. "Park Rapids pulled that one on you with just about the same result, as I recall," the trucker added through a wide grin.

"Let's see you chase after that crazy-legged aborigine," the lawyer responded.

"Not my job," Simpson observed. " I covered my man."

"I had two men to cover," the attorney said defensively. "Who the hell was supposed to handle Eagleclaw?"

"That'd be me," Larry Nevis, a lanky probation officer with a bulging gut, admitted as he sauntered up. "He blew right by me."

"Good thing none of us does this for a living," Aitkins observed, smacking Nevis across the buttocks with a chopper-covered-hand. "Our kids would all starve."

The breeze lifted the loose snow, mixing the flakes in delightful confusion. As the players took their positions, Eddie Anstett, a former place-kicker and linebacker, now a university professor, lined up for the kick-off. Anstett's arm dropped. The ball was launched. The contest and the snowfall continued.

Across the field, a solitary figure walked into the stadium, climbed concrete stairs into the bleachers, swept loose snow off the cold metal bench, and sat down to watch the game. Patterns of lacey flakes danced around the woman's flaming red hair. She huddled inside a Hudson Bay blanket she'd bought in Winnipeg, the fabric thick and warm, as her eyes followed the antics of the men: men long passed their best years on the gridiron. She didn't want to call attention to him, to make tongues wag and rumors fly. But it was too late for that. They needed to talk. There was nothing she could do. She took a chance, driving up from Fergus Falls on Christmas Eve, leaving her kids, Megan and Josh, with her mother-in-law and father-in-law overnight, a chance that Danny Aitkins was still participating in the annual game.

Her instincts were correct. He was there, all five-foot-nine of him, dashing across frozen ground, slower, less graceful than he had been in high school, trying to recapture the thrill of games long past. She imagined him, as he had once been, a wisp of a thing, a man in the making, intercepting passes, delivering punishing tackles. Given the circumstances that brought her to the field, she tried not to smile. She couldn't help it. Daniel made her smile. It's why things were the way they were between them.

Dan noticed the woman after he picked off one of Jensen's wounded ducks and ran in unmolested for a touchdown, bringing the home team even with the visitors. At first, he wasn't able to make out Melanie's face. It puzzled him why anyone would venture out on Christmas Eve morning to witness the poor play of gridiron has-beens. As Aitkins tried to fathom the identity of the lone fan sunlight fought through the clouds and the diminishing snowfall to illuminate her face.

"You guys keep playing, I gotta go see someone," he said quietly.

"How can we play with only six guys?" someone asked.

"They can only send five men out for passes. I'll be right back."

"Lawyers," Jensen mused. "Always changing the rules. Nathan, play center this set of downs. You're ineligible."

"I'm always the guy who doesn't get the ball," Nathan Berg, former third-string-linebacker-turned-music-teacher, moaned.

"Next series, four tosses your way, I promise. Line 'em up."

Aitkins' mind was full of concern: *Why is she here? Doesn't she realize that it's dangerous, that everyone out on the field knows who she is?*

Behind him, Danny heard Simpson ask one of the other players.

"Who's the chick?"

Someone said her name.

"Melanie Ingersol. Barnes now, I guess."

"What's she want?" another voice added.

"She's a good friend of Julie and Dan's," Jensen related.

The attorney didn't climb into the stands. He stood at the bottom of the bleachers, the steel railing pressed against his chest, and leaned towards the woman to talk.

"Hi, Ms. Barnes."

Her reply was elongated.

"A little formal aren't we, Mr. Aitkins."

"What brings you out so early on Christmas Eve morning?"

She stood up, holding the blanket around her body like a shawl. She wore a red beret on her head, the felt pulled down on her ears, the bare ends of her hair protruding from beneath the cap. Her hands were covered in black leather gloves. She wore Mukluks laced above her shins and a down ski jacket. The boots and coat matched the color of her cap, complimenting the color of her hair.

"We need to talk," she said, carefully negotiating the slippery stairs.

"OK," he replied, puzzled anticipation clear in his voice.

"Can we walk a little? I don't want to be make a scene in front of that crowd," she requested.

"Scene? What's there to make a scene about?"

They strolled down the sidewalk.

"I just don't think the 'boys' need to be in on our conversation," she advised.

"Fair enough."

His mind began to race. Speculations tumbled into each other. Did she want to call it off? Had Julie somehow found out and confronted her? Had F.W.? Had Dee Dee? Was there someone else?

Maybe it's that fucking Bobbie Morgan, he conjectured.

There was no traffic. The wind was at a lull. The storm had stopped. Their boots crunched against fallen snow as they put distance between themselves and the game. She began to talk. There was a frightened, upsetting tremor to her words.

"I don't know how to tell you this," she began.

Water slid down her face. Her lips appeared vulnerable. Her eyes were nearly closed, as if she was in utter, unrelenting pain.

"What?" he asked, his hands shoved inside the pouch of his sweatshirt.

He was cooling off. The sweat he'd accumulated playing football was dissipating. Cold infiltrated his joints. Her voice cracked. She emitted a brutal sob. A convulsion of upset shook her body. He stopped to allow her to regain her breath.

"What is it Mel?"

"I didn't think it could happen. I was so careful. I tried to make sure I wouldn't do this to you, to Julie."

Aitkins placed a hand on each of the woman's shoulders and forced her to look into his face.

"What are you talking about?" he asked, a seed of recognition beginning to grow inside of him.

She stared blankly, recalling how long it had been since her cycle, how long it had been since she experienced the cramping, the disorientation, the monthly fatigue. Recounting her self-deception, the weeks of refusing to buy a test and pee on a stick, she broke down.

"I'm pregnant," she blurted out.

There came after those words the saddest, most morbid loneliness that Daniel Aitkins had ever experienced. A thought crossed his mind. It was an evil, unfair, and despicable notion that loomed so large and so gross between the man and the woman that Melanie was able to see the idea form, determine its ghastly intent, and intercept it before it was expressed.

282

"It's yours, Danny. The baby is yours. I haven't been with anyone else."

CHAPTER 54

Julie's parents, her two sisters, their husbands and kids, showed up early for Christmas Eve dinner at the Aitkins' farmhouse. A sculpted Norway pine stood in the archway between the dining room and the kitchen of the home, its lights twinkling in a resplendently archaic glow. Antique ornaments and bubble bulbs, the liquid quietly percolating beneath opaque glass, adorned the tree. Strings of fresh popcorn wound through the tree's graceful limbs in Currier and Ives fashion.

Neatly wrapped packages rested under the lowest branches. The presents were adorned with gaily-printed paper and shiny ribbons. An odor of cooked goose hung over the rooms of the dwelling as the adults sat on thickly cushioned living room furniture drinking eggnog, studying flames in the fireplace. Above the yellow and orange tongues of fire, a porcelain Jesus reclined in a manger, his parents, a few angels, and the odd shepherd standing watch. Three Magi seemed to be in suspended animation a short distance away; trying to reach the Christ Child but never making any progress. The rambunctious laughter of children at play, cousins tearing wildly through the place, echoed distantly from the upper reaches of the house.

"Where's Danny?" Ethel Norton, Julie's mother asked as she nursed a hot drink.

"He had to go to work for a while. A big case that's coming up for trial," Julie observed, her hands shaking slightly, the inflection of her voice quaking.

In truth, Julie didn't know where her husband was. He had called just after noon, indicating something had gone wrong with the Anderson case that needed immediate attention.

"On Christmas Eve? My entire family is coming for dinner. I hope to hell you're gonna be back to eat," she had asserted.

"I can't make any promises. It's a mess; that's all I can tell you. Things are falling apart. If I don't get over to the office, we could lose the trial before it starts."

There was something unsettling behind the man's words. Something intangible crept into Daniel's speech and convinced Julie that what he was saying was true, that a crisis was looming. Against her better judgment, knowing the toll litigation had already taken upon her husband's health, she relented.

"Get back as fast as you can," she said.

Masterson's Tavern was deserted. Other than Danny Aitkins, there was no one in the bar besides the bartender.

"Shouldn't you be somewhere else, Dan?" Sharon Sylvester, the barkeep, asked as she poured the lawyer another shot of Jack Daniels.

He considered the woman's question. The answer was 'yes'. It was four o'clock in the afternoon. It was Christmas Eve. He should be home. He kept his own counsel and didn't respond.

An old Western played on the television set anchored above the bar. A band of Indians had some poor white family cornered in their crude house, arrows raining down from the sky, flames lapping at the log walls of the structure. A weird, unnatural smile formed on Aitkins' lips.

"Hey Sharon, ever notice that not a single savage in these old movies is actually played by an Indian?"

"Can't say as I ever thought about it, Dan. But now that you mention it," she said, pausing to study the screen, "I see an awful lot of white guys wearing makeup whooping it up."

A weak laugh escaped the attorney.

"It wasn't that funny," the bartender observed.

Aitkins was half way to oblivion. The booze went down easily after the first couple drinks. He hadn't tasted whiskey in years. It tore up his insides, cut the soft flesh of his stomach like glass. But beer was too slow for what he was seeking; the utter, significant destruction of memory. When the first shot had been poured, Daniel sat for a good long while staring at the amber liquid, contemplating what he'd done. There was enough shame, enough grief, to destroy a man lodged within his personal recrimination. In the end, he knew the whiskey wouldn't make it all go away. The best he could hope for was that, for a few hours, the booze would delay reality.

The first shot was harsh. The alcohol had stormed through his system, disrupting everything in its path. The second was less vicious. By the third shot, things were as they had once been; his body seeking the steady hum of pastoral dimness that sour mash provided. Time ticked off the clock above the bottles neatly lining the back bar. It was well into late afternoon. His house was full of obligations, obligations that he wanted to avoid.

Danny's fingers clenched the whiskey glass as he recalled her face, her eyes. His hand gripped the elevated base of the container as he struggled to hold back the wave of upset welling inside him. He hoped the booze would form a temporary dam against emotion, a dam that would hold long enough for the lawyer to determine a course of conduct, a plan of action. He found the storm to be too great; the rising of the tide was too swift for mere chemicals to defend against. And yet, he drank on, pouring booze into his body in a futile attempt to insulate himself from the truth.

He'd placed the telephone call to his wife from his cell phone. She thought he was still at the office.

285

"How the hell did this happen?" he had asked Melanie as they stared blankly at each other under a brightening sky outside the high school football stadium.

"I missed a pill," had been her deliberate response.

"How in the fuck could you do something so stupid?"

Daniel's voice had contained acrimony. His basic human decency retreated. He could not face his own moral shortcomings so he lashed out at the messenger, trying to destroy the message.

Melanie Barnes had sobbed uncontrollably in the wake of his verbal assault. Her arms dropped away from the Hudson Bay blanket, allowing the covering to fall onto the snowy ground. Her body shook with unnatural anguish. He knew he had gone too far, that his response was wrong. There was no blame, no accusation to be made beyond looking in the mirror.

"What are you going to do?" he asked, picking up the blanket and draping it around her shoulders.

There was a quixotic despondency about her that Dan had never witnessed in the woman. A shiver assaulted the attorney's bones, the chill of the unknown, not the weather. Aitkins altered his question slightly.

"What are we going to do?"

There was a spark of recognition from Melanie Barnes.

"I'm Catholic."

The words escaped into the cold air from the woman's tightly clenched mouth.

"I know," he replied.

"What do you expect me to do?" she asked in a wounded tone.

"I can't father a child with you," he asserted.

"You already have," she answered, a note of defiance evident.

"How far along are you?" he asked, ignoring her response.

The game was breaking up on the field. The players looked in the couple's direction.

"Eight weeks. It must have happened in Winnipeg."

"There's still time to deal with it."

"Not for me."

"Mel, do you have any idea what this will do to Julie?"

She looked down in shame. Tears began anew.

"I think I have a pretty good idea."

He wasn't about to attempt to persuade her to have an abortion while standing on a public sidewalk. Though the entire scenario was unseemly, pushing that particular issue out into plain view seemed unjustly morbid.

"Are you all right, physically I mean?" he asked, nudging the discourse in a different direction.

286

"Not so bad. I've tossed my cookies a few times. It seems like things have settled down."

A pair of wayward bluebills, ducks caught too far north for the time of year, sliced across the gradually opening sky. White clouds piled carelessly on top of one another across the taconite heaven as Danny Aitkins struggled with his thoughts.

"Mel, can we talk about this after Christmas?"

She had winced: He couldn't tell if the reaction was pain or a depreciating smirk.

"I guess we'll have to."

The lawyer had embraced the woman's slender frame, determined to ignore the beating of the fetal heart within her as he held Melanie tightly to his chest.

"Another shot?" the bartender asked.

"Just the bill," the lawyer said.

Danny Aitkins paid his tab, pulled the frayed hood of his orange sweatshirt over his head, jammed his hands into his mittens, and headed home to celebrate a very different sort of Christmas.

CHAPTER 55

He never saw the cop car until it was too late. The Ranger slowed briefly for a stop sign before rolling through the intersection intent on making a turn.

"Know what you did back there?" the Detroit Lakes cop, his face clean shaven, his skin smelling of cheap after-shave; his uniform crisply pressed as if it was the kid's first day on the job, said through the open driver's side window of Aitkins' truck.

The lawyer gripped the steering wheel of the Ranger tightly as the beam of the policeman's flashlight swept through the interior of the Ford. Danny downed two peppermints as soon as he saw the red lights come on. The candy wasn't powerful enough to divert the cop's scrutiny.

"I kinda rolled through the stop sign," the lawyer said, carefully forming his words.

"You also didn't signal your turn. Could I see your driver's license and insurance information?"

Danny reached into the pouch of his sweatshirt for his wallet. It wasn't there. He opened the glove box. Still no wallet, though he did find the insurance card. He handed the document to the officer.

"I can't find my wallet," Aitkins admitted, a nervous smile touching the edges of his face.

"What's your name and date of birth?"

The lawyer recited the information.

"I'll be right back. Please remain in the truck."

He was almost out of town when the cop pulled him over on a darkened stretch of Highway 34. He hadn't called home despite the fact it was well after five, the appointed time for Christmas Eve dinner. The cop sauntered back.

"Seems to be in order, Mr. Aitkins. You been drinking tonight?"

The officer looked at the driver through thick eyeglass lenses as he returned Aitkins' insurance card.

"I've had a few."

"I'd like you to do a few field sobriety tests."

The attorney studied the ceiling of his truck's interior as he mulled over the cop's request. Aitkins tried to recall how many shots he'd had. The last one he could remember was number five. Five in a little over three hours. He did the math in his head. Given his weight, he should be fine.

"Sure. What's your name? I don't think we've met."

"Wayne Markum. I just started last week," the officer obliged.

Illuminated by the headlights of the squad car the lawyer walked an imaginary line on the uneven gravel shoulder of the roadway. Daniel stood on one leg and counted. He followed the point of Officer Markum's pen as the cop sought to determine whether the muscles of Aitkins' eyes had the characteristic bounce of intoxication. The lawyer breezed through the alphabet.

"I'm gonna have to take you down to the Law Enforcement Center," Markum said after the tests were completed.

"Arrest me?"

"That's right."

"Why?"

"Because I believe you've been driving while under the influence."

"Come on, Officer. Have a fucking heart," the litigator pleaded, his words beginning to slur more significantly the more emotional he became. "It's Goddamn Christmas Eve."

"Please step out of the truck with your hands above your head," the cop commanded.

"Why are you doing this to me?" Danny moaned as he opened the door and complied.

The cop placed the suspect in handcuffs. A stern look flashed across the officer's brow.

"Because you're under the influence of alcohol."

"I thought I did fine on your tests."

"You missed "h" and reversed "u" and "v" in the alphabet. The horizontal gaze test was positive for intoxication," the policeman related before reading Aitkins the Miranda warning off a printed card.

"I think I'll remain silent until I can talk to an attorney," Daniel responded.

Sitting in the back seat of the squad behind a mesh barrier, Aitkins felt weak.

"We better get to the jail quick. I gotta go."

"Don't be pissing in my car," the young cop scolded.

"It's the other," Daniel related.

"You're a lawyer right?"

Aitkins looked at the officer.

"Yep."

"Well then, counselor, I'd appreciate it if you didn't shit in my squad car."

Under the intense fluorescent lights of the Law Enforcement Center, Aitkins was read the Implied Consent Advisory, giving him the option to decline an Intoxilyzer test of his blood alcohol level as measured by breath. He agreed to take the test. The results came back at .10, right at the legal limit for DUI.

"Dees, it's me," Danny whispered, out of handcuffs, sitting at a brown metal desk in the intake room of the facility.

"Danny, where the hell are you? Julie called looking for you. She thought you were at the office."

"I'm in jail."

"What?" the female attorney shrieked across the receiver.

"Not so loud," the lawyer admonished, the clouds of intoxication beginning to disperse, a pitiless headache beginning to form behind his eyeballs.

"Why are you in jail?" the woman asked in a more restrained fashion.

"DUI."

There was a short silence.

"You take a test?"

".10"

"Shit."

"That's what I said."

"I'll call Harriet and see what I can do. You shouldn't have to post bail."

"Thanks. Can you come down and pick me up? They won't let me drive home."

A slight chuckle, an expression that was out of place for the somber moment.

"What was that for?"

"Danny, are you nuts? Of course they aren't going to let you drive home after arresting you for DUI. I'll be over as soon as I talk to Judge Enwright."

"Thanks."

"Oh, you'll owe me a lot more than a mere 'thanks' when we're through, Danny Aitkins."

Dee Dee came into the Law Enforcement Center to get him. Aitkins didn't know that there was another person in Dee Dee's vehicle until he opened the front passenger's door to the Volkswagen and saw a woman sitting in the front passenger's seat.

"That's Carol," the female litigator said as Daniel closed the door, opened another, and entered the vehicle.

"Nice to meet you, Carol," Aitkins said, trying to be polite. He didn't extend his hand to the woman and she didn't extend hers.

Carol was nondescript, as ordinary as toast. Her face was round and cheerless. Her eyes were without distinction. There was nothing exceptional about her physical self that struck the man as the Bug pulled away from the curb.

"Pleased to meet you, Mr. Aitkins," the stranger responded without emotion.

"So Daniel, tell me just what the hell you were thinking? It's after seven. It's Christmas Eve. Julie said you were supposed to be home for dinner by five. Where were you all day?"

290

"Not now, Dees. Just get me home."

He watched his partner's face boil, her grimace visible in the rearview mirror.

"Look Dan. I really don't care what the hell you do to yourself. It's none of my business. But you took us away from a quiet Christmas Eve together. I had to connect with Harriet at home. She wasn't the 'on call' judge but I sure as hell wasn't gonna give Davidson a jingle to see if he'd let you walk without bail. So maybe you should be a little more considerate of others, especially me, before you tell me to kiss off."

He knew she was pissed. There was no mistaking the tenor of her voice.

"I'm sorry. It's been a lousy day."

"You think it's gonna get any better when you get home?"

Silence. He hadn't even thought about Julie, her family, the spoiled dinner, the unopened packages, the disappointed kids.

"Fuck."

"For a trial lawyer, you sure don't have much of a vocabulary," his partner responded.

It was the last comment he heard from Dee Dee as they sped towards his home over deserted rural roads west of Detroit Lakes.

The house was unnaturally quiet. Adult voices emanated from the living room. His eyes were bloodshot. His body was sore from the football contest. Daniel's soul was tired and defeated as he leaned heavily against a wall in the home's rear entry and pulled off his wet spikes, the white athletic tape holding the soles of the decaying leather soiled by the effort of his play.

"Where the hell have you been?"

Julie stood in the shadows, her arms crossed beneath her chest, her posture demanding.

"Let's not do this tonight," he mumbled.

"Why did Dee Dee give you a ride home?"

"It's a long story. Can't we do this in the morning?"

Her eyes flashed so brilliantly that, even in the depths of darkness, he could see her anger. There was venom, a broken vial of poison, running through her at that moment.

"Great. We'll have a blow out argument on Christmas Morning, right before we traipse off to church. That'll be just fucking super," she cursed before pivoting on the balls of her feet and exiting the room.

A plate of food, the goose flesh, potatoes, carrots, and dinner biscuits stone cold and unappetizing, sat on the wooden surface of the kitchen table. A warm glass of milk stood next to the meal. He poured the room temperature liquid down his throat. Instantly, the thickness of the milk coated his digestive tract, bucking him up for the long walk into the living room.

CHAPTER 56

Christmas morning. He tossed and turned all night. Partly because of the booze, mostly because of Melanie. The brittle, suffocating notion that another woman was carrying his child set hard against the base of his skull. Children. Laughter. He rolled over on the couch in the basement television room, the air cold and smelling of dirty laundry. There was no light; no window to the outside world. Santa had come. It was time to get up and face the day. Reluctantly, he climbed the basement stairs.

Adam ripped through packages. Michael sat in a cardboard box. An unassembled plastic spaceship, the size of a small dog, and assorted action figures were strewn about the living room carpeting. The child held a figure in each hand as the imaginary men battled for control of the universe.

Amanda sat quietly on a chair, fingering a collection of new clothes and assorted books. A shiny black western-style saddle, a red bow taped to the horn, leather stirrups gleaming against the colored lights of the Christmas tree, rested at the girl's feet.

"Hi Dad," Amanda said, dropping a yellow and green sweater as she dashed to his side.

The girl's cheeks reddened from the effort of her sprint. She pecked her father on his neck with small, tender lips.

"Get what you wanted from Santa?" Danny croaked gamely, his head pounding, his ears ringing.

"Thanks for the saddle," his daughter whispered, concealing her words from her youngest sibling.

"Sssshhh!" the lawyer warned through an exhausted smile.

Dan was dressed in flannel pajama bottoms. His chest was bare. His eyes took in the enormity of his circumstance, his life. Julie was not in the room.

"Mom's in the bathroom," Adam offered.

"She make coffee?"

"Yep. She seems upset," the oldest Aitkins child observed.

The litigator pondered the statement. He shuffled across the frayed carpeting towards the kitchen without comment. His hands trembled slightly as he filled a mug. He sat, his bones tired, his mind clouded, on a hard chair and stared out into the darkness. Day had not yet broken. It was only six thirty-five.

"Shit," he muttered, burning the inside of his mouth with coffee.

Outside, a tow truck exited the driveway and lumbered away. Despite her rancor, Dee Dee had made arrangements to have Danny's Ford Ranger towed from town.

A toilet flushed. Daniel listened. He detected sounds of his wife's feet padding down the upstairs hallway. The lawyer rose, poured a cup of coffee for his wife, and followed the sound of her footsteps.

"Dad, see the neat rocket ship Santa brought me?" Michael intoned as Aitkins waded through the debris-strewn living room.

The lawyer stepped cautiously over torn wrapping paper as he made his way towards the stairs. He stopped and hesitated, his mind elsewhere, before responding.

"Wow, that's sure something. I'll be back down in a bit to see the rest of what you got."

The atmosphere in the attic was stifling. All the heat of the house had accumulated near the rafters. He found the door to their bedroom closed but unlocked. He balanced the coffee cups in one hand, careful to avoid spilling the contents, and opened the portal.

"Julie?" he whispered as he stepped over the threshold.

There were no lights on in the room. The shades were drawn. He moved cautiously across the hardwood floor, nudging discarded garments with his bare toes as he walked.

"I brought you some coffee."

Utter quiet.

He sat down on the edge of their bed and set the cups on a nightstand. His fingers reached out through the dimness and found his wife's bare shoulder.

"Julie, we need to talk."

She stirred but did not face him.

"About what?" she muttered.

"About yesterday."

"Oh, you want to tell me how sorry you are for ruining Christmas?"

He had expected her to be wounded. Daniel knew that he needed to tread lightly.

"That and why I was late."

"Dee Dee already told me. She called before she went to get you."

Aitkins shifted his gaze from the reclining form of his wife, the outline of her uncovered torso and legs coming into focus as his eyes grew accustomed to the light.

"Oh."

The woman suddenly turned over in bed, rose to her knees and struck her husband in the face with an open hand.

"Christ, Julie, knock it off," the lawyer yelled, grabbing his wife's wrist, turning flesh against bone as he tightened his grip.

"You're hurting me, you sonofabitch. Get your fucking hands off me," she screamed as she struck at him again with her free hand.

He responded by grabbing her wrists and holding them tight against his chest. He contemplated hitting his wife. Anger compelled him to retaliate. Honor bade him to refrain.

The attorney bent over his wife and tried to console her.

"I'm sorry, Jules."

"Get the fuck out of my house," she retorted between tears. "Take your shit and get the fuck out of my house."

He released her.

She cowered against the wall.

"It's Christmas. Can't this wait until tomorrow?"

"If you don't leave now, I'll call the cops. I'll tell them that you assaulted me. You don't want to spend a night in jail, do you, Mr. Big Shot Lawyer?"

Tears poured off her face. He clenched his fist. He wanted to lash out, to strike her. A blow against his wife would be a blow against himself. That's what he needed, what he wanted to feel; the complete and final destruction of his own existence. He looked deeply into his wife's frightened eyes and lowered his hand.

"Alright," the lawyer said painfully. "What'll we tell the kids?"

"Just get dressed and get the hell out of my house," the woman repeated.

"I need a shower."

"Take one somewhere else," she sobbed.

Aitkins retrieved a suitcase from the closet and began to toss underwear, socks, and casual clothes into the valise. He determined that he'd come back later for the remainder of his clothing. All he could think of was retreating, getting as far away from his wife's steady, pulsating hatred as he could.

He slipped into a pair of jeans retrieved from the back of a chair next to his wife's makeup table. His hands fumbled with the zipper and the snap of the trousers. The lawyer slid the rough wool of a sweater over his bare skin. His eyes darted around the room. His boots were nowhere to be found. He pushed his bare feet into his Nike running shoes, the toes of the footwear shiny from use, the laces tenuous.

"I'll call you later," he said. The words were distorted by a lump in his throat.

"Don't bother."

"Jules..."

"Don't fuckin' bother."

Danny Aitkins knew better than to press the issue as he walked out of the bedroom.

CHAPTER 57

"Dad," the lawyer revealed in sibilated tones over his cell phone.

"Hello, Daniel. Merry Christmas," Emery Aitkins replied.

"Yeah. Merry Christmas."

"I've got the ham all ready."

"I won't be coming over."

A shocked silence.

"What the hell are you talking about? Someone sick? Not little Mike again. I told you, he needs those tonsils out. That'll perk him right up."

"It's nothing like that. Julie and I had a fight."

"On Christmas. What the hell could you be arguing about on Christmas?"

The Ranger's tires pounded against the pavement as the truck pulled north, towards the Canadian Border.

"I got a DUI."

Danny listened to the old man's breathing and envisioned Emery's face as the elder Aitkins tried to contain his wrath.

"What the hell are you talking about?"

"After the football game. I stopped in and had a few. A DL cop pulled me over for not signaling a turn."

"You take a test?"

"Yep."

"And?"

".10"

"Ah, Daniel. I've told you before you need to tone it down. Son, I think you have a drinking problem."

That's the least of my worries," the young litigator thought, giving consideration to the enormity of the things his father did not yet know.

But Daniel didn't have the stomach to lay it all out for Emery during a cell phone call. He kept his mouth shut while he waited for the rest of the lecture, a speech he'd heard nearly every year since his mother died of acute alcohol poisoning.

"Your mother killed herself with booze. Is that what you want? To leave Julie a thirty-seven-year-old widow with three little kids? I think it's time you took a long look at yourself. You need to get into a program."

Danny wanted to shout "up yours, you old hypocrite." He wanted to point out that his mom wouldn't have resorted to alcohol as her confidant and friend if her husband had paid her even minimal attention. He didn't disgorge the old arguments, the old hurts, mostly because they weren't entirely true, and because his father's observation about his son's boozing hit too close to the mark.

"Why don't you come over so we can talk?" the old man suggested, his tone modified, his heart beginning to soften.

"I can't. I need to take some time to sort through some stuff. When I figure out a few things, I'll come over. It'll be a couple of days."

"Danny, it's Christmas. Do you want your kids to remember this kind of Christmas? Because I'll guaranty, despite all the wonderful, sweet memories of every other Christmas morning they may experience, this one, where mommy and daddy fought and daddy stormed out of the house, is the one they'll remember."

"It's more complicated than that," the younger attorney asserted. "And I didn't storm out of the house."

Danny realized his father was crying.

"Son, I love you. I don't want to lose you. You're all I've got left."

Tears clouded Dan's vision.

"Promise me you won't do anything stupid."

A veiled reference to Michael.

"I promise. I gotta go. I'll call you in a day or two."

"I still don't think you should do this to your kids."

"I gotta go," Danny insisted, sobs choking out his words.

Danny hung up the cell phone. He turned off the power so that his father couldn't call back.

The tears flowed like rain as Aitkins pushed the little six-cylinder. The odometer displayed 120,000 miles. There wasn't much more juice under the hood. Light ascended. The sun rose from behind the banks of the Red River off to the east. He passed the Grafton exit. The sobbing subsided. The thinking began.

His plan was simple: he had no plan. Danny's mind was torn into segmented, unrelated partitions. One sector attempted to rationalize and deal with the events of the morning, to understand why he had fought with his wife. Another isolated vector tried to fathom the import of Melanie Barnes, her love for him, his love for her, the fetus growing inside her that they had conceived.

"More like ill-conceived," he said beneath his breath, no humor in the pun.

The yellow disk of the rising sun appeared over trees demarcating the riverbed. Above the ribbonous highway, there were no clouds. A faint memory of turquoise accented the ceiling above the broad prairie.

His mind tried to sort through his alcohol use, his insistence upon medicating his way through life with booze, as the truck bounced north.

"The old man's right," he said above the hum of the tires. "I need help. It'll have to wait until after I figure out this mess with Mel."

The radio was silent. No CD's played in the changer. The peace didn't provide an answer; not for the complex and dangerous reality that had arisen from his desire for the red headed woman.

And yet, deep within, he wanted to see her again. To hold her again. To taste the salt of her breast; to feel the pulse of her heart beating against his naked chest. He was shamed by his thoughts.

He stopped at the Canadian Customs building to use the bathroom. Great torrents of piss erupted from inside, the result of too much whiskey and an equal measure of coffee. He bought a pre-packaged ham and cheese sandwich, a bag of peanuts, and a plastic jug of orange juice. Breakfast. Christmas Breakfast. Breakfast with Santa.

The wind fashioned the freshly fallen snow into a smoothly flowing quilt. There were no drifts to speak of. A vast expanse of ivory covered the dormant land. Here and there, ravens cawed from power poles, waiting for a vehicle to hit an animal, thereby assuring the winged scavengers of their next meal.

He bypassed downtown Winnipeg, making a brief stop in the suburbs, before heading north towards Winnipeg Beach. There was a little motel there with inexpensive winterized cottages. He'd formed the beginnings of a plan, of an approach, as the Ranger bounced across the Border. There was nothing in his hasty arrangements that answered the Melanie question. Theirs was a situation so large and so frightening that the attorney carefully avoided bringing it to the forefront of his thoughts.

"Fifty-five dollars a night Canadian," a clerk said as Daniel stood impatiently behind the registration desk at the Crying Loon Cottages.

An expanse of ice, as smooth as mother of pearl, commanded the American's attention as he stood in the lobby looking out a picture window frosted by escaping heat. Lake Winnipeg was frozen from shore to shore. The lawyer would hear no waves crashing; experience no cries of seagulls, as he pondered life from the warmth of a rented cabin.

Aitkins handed the clerk his credit card. The man listed heavily to the left. He stood precariously on a badly twisted right leg. The clerk's eyes were bloodshot. His "Go Blue" sweatshirt, the message referencing a Winnipeg football team, was spattered with tomato sauce. A modem dialed and admitted a beep of acceptance. A receipt was printed.

"There you go. Just one night, right?"

"That's my plan. We'll see what happens."

"You're in Cabin Seven. The last one on the right. It's got a great view of the Lake."

"Thanks."

Aitkins removed his suitcase and a cardboard box from a storage area behind the driver's seat of the truck. The jump seats were folded up, out of the way, and secured to the walls of the cab. Bottles in the cardboard box clanked as the lawyer walked from the Ranger to the cottage.

Danny flicked on a light switch, illuminating the living room of the cottage, and set the box and his luggage on a couch. He took a brief tour of the place. Two bedrooms. A kitchenette. A bathroom with a standard 1960's porcelain tub, plastic shower curtain, oak vanity, sink, and toilet. Aitkins stopped at the thermostat and turned the LP gas furnace up.

It wasn't particularly clear in his mind why he had chosen Canada as the place to die. He knew that few human beings had his luxury, the luxury of choosing the time, date, and location to conclude their personal story. Michael had done it. He'd been wise, in retrospect, the attorney mused, to see the light so clearly, so early. Before more mistakes were made. Before more people were hurt.

Danny selected a glass from the kitchen cupboard and filled it with ice from the freezer, twisting the plastic ice cube tray to force cubes into the sink where he retrieved them and placed them in the glass. He withdrew a bottle of his wife's medication, sleeping pills prescribed by their family doctor, from the front pocket of the winter jacket he'd tossed over an arm of an easy chair. After opening the drapes covering the front window, he switched on the television, found an old movie on a cable channel, pulled out a liter of Windsor from the cardboard box, and returned to the kitchen.

The attorney broke the seal on the whiskey bottle, one of four in the box. He poured amber liquid over the ice cubes, watching intently as the booze filled the tumbler. He listened to the noise of ice cracking in the glass and to the groans of lake ice shifting beyond the frozen beach. An otherworldly premonition swept over the lawyer. His shook. He fumbled with the cap on the medicine bottle. He aligned the arrows, opened the container, and dumped a cluster of sleeping pills onto the smooth vinyl surface of the kitchen table.

Danny's eyes welled. There was no mistaking the finality of what he was about to do. He could have done it like Michael, with one of his hunting weapons. But removing a shotgun or rifle from the Aitkins family gun cabinet on Christmas morning, in the presence of his children, would have caused more questions than he had time to answer.

Visions of Michael Barnes dragging himself gut-shot across the soft fibers of his office carpeting, the effort staining the entirety of the main floor of the Bugle Building in blood, was an image Daniel did not wish to leave for his wife, his children, or for Melanie. His way was cleaner and the end result would certainly be the same.

The fingers of his left hand cupped the medicine. His right hand lifted the tumbler full of booze. A fragrance of bourbon permeated the air. The lawyer closed his eyes and tried to bring an image of heaven to mind as cool glass touched his lips.

CHAPTER 58

Melanie Barnes prepared to drive to Willmar, Minnesota where her parents lived. Her kids were already there. Melanie's in-laws, F.W. Barnes and his wife had driven the children to Willmar the evening before. She normally would have been with her parents for Christmas Eve Mass, would have spent the evening hours following the service drinking white wine, laying out the kid's presents, and talking with her mother. But Melanie had begged off Christmas Eve with the promise that she would arrive early on Christmas morning.

"Work", she had lied. "I have to work. We're getting ready to go to trial."

It was a small falsehood but one, as the only daughter, she felt she had the right to assert. Melanie was an only child; the result of her parent's marrying late. She didn't mind being their only progeny. It suited her.

She teased the short ends of her hair with the plastic bristles of a hairbrush as she sat on a stool in front of a mirror. Her arms and legs were thin, far thinner than they had been in years, the result of running three miles a day to lose the residual weight gain from her last pregnancy. The green highlights of her eyes danced in the glass. Her complexion was enhanced by her condition. Hormones surged and raced within her like wild comets across the night sky.

Melanie placed a white hand, the pale skin augmented by dark freckles, over her stomach. The child hadn't revealed itself as yet through hesitant wriggles; the beginnings of movement that she knew would soon become apparent. Her other hand slowly drew a tube of muted color across her lips, the lipstick complimenting her ivory skin. She fought an urge to weep as she studied her face in the mirror.

"What are we going to do?" she asked.

A vision of Daniel and her, walking hand in hand through tall prairie grass along the edge of a corn field, the stalks crisp and ready for harvest, her stomach round, their hands entwined in an overt embrace, soared through her mind. It was possible.

Anything is possible, she told herself.

Julie wouldn't understand. Julie wouldn't forgive. But an accommodation could be made. She and Danny could make something of a life together. Her children loved him. His own kids would not suffer. He'd be there for them, at all their events, cheering them on. She'd stay in the background when it came to his kids. That way, time would heal Julie's heart to a degree, to where they could once again be in the same room, at the same time. The baby had changed everything. It had to change everything. She could not let go of the premise of a new life that the reality of conception made possible. Julie was a friend. That would be affected. It had to be. There was no other way, no other path that made sense.

The woman slipped out of her robe and stood naked in the yellow light of a table lamp. The stretch marks were beginning to tighten; the little scars were knitting together. She pulled her cotton briefs on one leg at a time, carefully tucking wayward wisps of reddish hair into the waistband of the panties. Her hands fumbled briefly as she sought to secure the clasp of her bra, to force her breasts into confinement within the wire cups of the garment. The normally pink areolas were beginning to darken. Her nipples were tender and sore. She pulled a pair of panty hose over her legs and underwear, taking care not to run the nylons with the freshly painted nails of her toes.

Melanie dropped a slip over her head, concealing her thickening body, and draped a cotton shift, the style smart and mature, over the sheen of the undergarment. Her fingers, accented by her polished nails, drew conservative pumps onto her feet, completing the process.

Outside, her decrepit Audi remained stubborn. Though the temperature hadn't fallen below zero, the car's reluctance to start was patent. Sitting on the stiff leather of the driver's seat, her forest green wool dress coat and matching mittens insulting her from the cold, Melanie Barnes methodically turned the ignition key. She was hesitant to give the automobile fuel. She knew that pumping the gas would flood the fuel-injected power plant. After a few false starts, the motor roared to life. She shifted the transmission from neutral into first, released the clutch, and pulled out onto the street.

She took a right and passed the Bugle Building, the place where she worked, the place where her husband had worked before her. As she drove by the old structure, its bricks neatly tuck-pointed, the glass of its windows shining clean, she encountered fleeting sorrow, a lingering recollection of Michael's death. Melanie's right hand found the radio dial. She tuned in a local public radio station. Someone, perhaps the departed poet himself, was reading *A Child's Christmas in Wales,* a short story by Dylan Thomas, on the air. She smiled. Michael, being a quarter Welsh, had always revered Dylan Thomas. She'd contemplated having Danny Aitkins read *Do Not Go Gentle into that Good Night* at her husband's funeral. F.W. Barnes had vetoed the idea. There was a lack of concentration, a distance, in her attitude, as she drove out of town, as she listened to the lyrical voice on the radio. She never saw the oncoming semi-tractor and trailer swerve into her lane.

CHAPTER 59

An expansive void opened above him. The vault extended infinitely. There was a searing anxiousness in his soul as his body moved towards light. It wasn't that he was afraid of what he would be called upon to reveal. The attorney anticipated his confession beneath the cross would be difficult. For grace to attach itself, for the power of the resurrection to nurture and cleanse Danny Aitkins, there would need to be a concise acknowledgement of his multitudinous sins: lust; desire; adultery; deception.

His legs were weary beyond his thirty-seven years; thirty-eight come the twentieth of January. Sadness settled over the attorney. A mantle of despair weighed the man down, precluding a swift journey towards the crucifix. His feet lagged behind his legs. He forced his body forward; every movement, every inch of progress, an exercise in agony.

"May I help you?" a voice asked from behind the veil of ebony.

The question reverberated.

"Are you looking for someone?" the voice gently insisted.

The voice was that of a woman. A feminine form approached. The figure entered light from darkness. The woman appeared to be in her late fifties. Artificial illumination, broken into a spectrum of color by the stained glass windows of the cathedral, touched the short gray hair of the female priest. A black skirt touched her shins just below her knees. Her red blouse parted at the neck, revealing a white clerical collar. He could not determine the color of the woman's eyes.

"Is there something I can do for you?" the woman repeated. A trace of uncertainty, perhaps fear, fear that she was vulnerable and alone in the darkness of the church with a recalcitrant stranger, disturbed her speech.

Daniel stood up. He wanted to explain, in rational terms, what he was doing in a foreign city, away from his family, early in the evening on Christmas Day. There was no controlling his emotions. The attorney began to sob.

"Why don't you have a seat?" the reverend suggested, pointing to the finely polished wooden pew with her delicate hand, distant lamps of the city casting a kaleidoscope of reflected light across the bench.

Aitkins resumed his seat.

"I'm Ingrid Hubbard," the cleric offered reassuringly. "What brings you to Holy Trinity Episcopal Church?"

The lawyer's mind raced down a plethora of unrelated avenues of thought before eliminating a multitude of possible responses.

"I came here to die," Aitkins whispered.

A draft circled inside the old church. Beginning near the hard surface of the stone floor, the zephyr soared upwards until it lingered adjacent to the timbered beams and rafters of the ceiling. The lawyer's quiet words were snared by the errant air and carried to the limits of the space.

"To Holy Trinity?"

A brief respite ensued in their conversation.

"No, to Winnipeg."

"May I?" the woman asked, seeking permission to sit down.

He nodded affirmatively.

The priest sat down next to Daniel and studied his face. Her fingers touched the back of the attorney's left hand.

"Are you ill?"

"You might say that," he reflected, trying to harness his tears.

"If you don't mind my boldness, what is the nature of your malady?" she asked.

He raised his head. His eyes locked on the woman's.

"Life," he replied.

"Something concerning a personal situation?" she asked perceptively.

"That's an understatement," the lawyer lamented, additional tears streaming down his face.

Indirect lighting accented the finely crafted altar of the sanctuary. The cleric's eyes left the man and fixed upon the cross adorning the Eucharistic table.

"Do you want to talk about it?" she inquired, maintaining a professional demeanor.

The attorney stared blankly at the woman. There was something about her that, despite his anguish and circumstance, hinted at salvation.

"OK."

"Why don't you start with why you think you want to die."

"I'm not so sure that I want to."

"That's a positive step. Why did you think that suicide might be the answer?"

Danny's eyes averted.

"I can't see a way out of the hole I'm in."

"How so?"

Time seemed to stand still as the attorney pondered a painless way to reveal his secrets. His mind circled around the terms he would have to use. He sought a clever means of saying what needed to be said without infecting the words with self-condemnation and loathing. There was no path available to Daniel Aitkins that would accomplish such a neat trick.

"I had an affair with one of my wife's friends. She's been a friend of mine as well for years, since high school."

The woman's grip tightened. Her fingernails dug into the back of the litigator's hand.

"I see. Does your wife know?"

"No. At least, not about the most recent situation. She knows that we nearly had an affair some years back, when the woman's husband, my best friend, killed himself."

Rev. Hubbard let the import of the disclosure sink in.

"So this wasn't the first time."

"Well, sort of. Gees, this is awkward, talking to a female priest like this."

"Don't think of me as female. My gender isn't the issue," the woman advised. "Go on."

"That other time, we came close but I stopped it before it went too far."

"And this time?"

"I couldn't."

"You mean, you wouldn't?"

Her judgmental inflection stung.

"I guess that's true. I wouldn't," he murmured.

"Is your wife a Christian?"

"Yes. We're both Lutheran, ELCA."

"Ah. I thought you were an American," the priest intoned, nodding significantly as she listened. "Don't you think you ought to put it out there for her? I mean, I assume since you're here, in a strange church, in a foreign city, contemplating ending your life, that the thought of telling her the truth has crossed your mind."

Someone opened a door to the church.

"Hello," another female voice called out from a distance.

"Mrs. Wharton," the priest replied, the rector rising to her feet as she spoke. "I'll be tied up for a few minutes. Would you mind starting the coffee and tea for after the service?"

"Surely," the elderly parishioner, her head covered with a vibrant orange scarf against the cold, said. "I'll get to it right away."

"Thank you. I shouldn't be but a moment or two," Ingrid Hubbard advised.

"Sorry about that. You know, you haven't told me your name," the cleric observed as she returned her focus to the man. "You don't have to if you'd rather not."

"Daniel."

"A strong Biblical name. I'm sorry, Daniel. Where were we?"

"You wanted to know if I was going to tell my wife about the affair."

"When you use the term affair, I expect you mean that this was more than one occasion?"

"Yes."

The woman winced.

"Do you love her, this other woman I mean?"

"I think so."

"Do you love your wife?"

"Definitely."

"Are there children?"

Right to the rub. There were not only children from his marriage; there was the unborn, unspoken prospect of another child from his relationship with Melanie.

"We have three," he related, concealing Melanie's pregnancy from the priest.

"Christ teaches all of us to forgive. Do you think that your wife...what's her name?"

"Julie."

"Do you think Julie can begin the long and difficult process of forgiving you if she knows?"

Sounds of coffee cups rattling from the social hall echoed across the sanctuary.

"Mrs. Wharton's way of letting me know she'd appreciate my assistance," the woman said through a meek smile. "And?"

"I don't think so. She's a wonderful wife and mother. But I've hurt her before. I don't think there's enough love in the world to make her forgive me for this."

"Christ's love isn't confined to this world, Daniel. You may be surprised at Julie's capacity to forgive if she's the Christian woman you say she is."

The attorney's throat constricted. His eyes burned.

"It's more complicated than that."

"You want to leave your wife for this other person?"

Tears.

"It's not that."

"Then what?"

He felt as if the mortar sustaining the integrity of the church was about to let loose and bury him in a deluge of stone.

"The other woman, Melanie's her name," he leaked through quivering lips.

The priest's hand moved to the attorney's upper back and stroked the fabric of the man's winter jacket. The gesture was meant to calm the lawyer but had no visible effect on the man.

"Yes?"

"She's going to have a child."

Rev. Hubbard's chin tilted. The movement allowed her eyes to focus upon the significant beams of the building's rafters. She inhaled sharply.

"The child is yours?"

Aitkins' cascade of sorrows increased.

"It seems so," he admitted in a whisper.

"There's no doubt?"

"None."

The cleric nodded demurely as she stoked his shoulder.

"I want you to wait for me in my office. There's a davenport there you can lie down on. I need to deal with Mrs. Wharton. But I'll be back, I promise. I want to explore some things with you, maybe offer you some possibilities you haven't thought of."

"There's no way out of this," Aitkins' moaned.

"In a sense, you're right. Nothing I say will change what you've done. But grace is a strange and wonderful gift from God. I can't promise everything will be the same if we can find the path to God's grace in this, but perhaps there's some aid and comfort I can give to you that will allow you to see that all is not lost, that your wife may still be able to forgive and love you despite what you've done."

The minister rose and extended a hand to the lawyer. Her grasp was deceptively strong, as if she had prepared the entirety of her life to wrestle with sin. Danny accepted the gesture, stood up, and followed Ingrid Hubbard down a dark hall passageway; thankful that shadows concealed his face.

CHAPTER 60

Strains of *What Child Is This?,* the notes mellow and golden, floated through the cathedral. The melody was propelled by subtle Celtic fiddle, mandolin, acoustic guitar, and squeezebox. The music woke the attorney from a deep slumber.

Danny Aitkins' eyes fluttered. He strained to lift his tired body off the couch in the rector's study. The Christmas hymn disturbed the desolation of his predicament, massaging his despondency with familiar melody. He forced his torso into a seated position as images of the past claimed his attention.

The whiskey glass had touched his mouth, chilling the tissue, bringing the implausibility of suicide into focus. A young girl had ridden a Morgan, he couldn't tell the horse's gender from the picture on the television, across a field of native grass. The character was about Amanda's age. He watched the horse and rider gallop across far hills, the glass of booze poised in one motionless hand, a fistful of pills in the other.

The day after visiting Park Rapids, they'd taken Amanda's new horse, Hope, and his mare, Pumpkin, for a long trail ride. A recollection of his daughter's eyes haunted him. The wideness of her smile, the unburdened joy on her face as she rode Pumpkin, and he rode Hope, captured the attorney's heart and forced the booze away from his mouth. His life had been spared by the intervention of an old movie and not a very good one at that.

Danny had called Julie from the cottage. She refused to talk to him. Adam picked up the phone. It had been a painful conversation with his son. Before the lawyer dialed home, he flushed the whiskey and the pills down the toilet.

"I love you; you know that, don't you? And your brother and your sister," he had told his oldest child.

"Mom too?" Adam whispered. Uncertainty became wedged between them during the intervening silence.

"Mom too," Danny had agreed.

The return path through Winnipeg had led him directly to the old church. He could have avoided Holy Trinity by following the highway east of town. But Daniel was unable to ignore the building's attraction. There was magnetism about the place. He felt a need for religion. The temple's power had touched him earlier when he stood on the cathedral's steps with Melanie, contemplating all that was right, and just, and true.

The door to the pastor's study opened.

"How are you doing?" the female priest asked.

"Better."

"You slept through the entire service."

"Maybe it's for the best. I don't feel much like confronting God right now," the attorney whispered.

"Maybe not. But at some point, you'll have to make your peace, at least some version of it, with both God and your wife."

Aitkins stood up from the couch.

"I think I better get going."

"You're not thinking of driving back to the States tonight, are you?" the woman asked, her voice knitted with concern.

"Tomorrow. I've already taken up too much of your time."

Her hand touched the fabric of his long-sleeved shirt.

"Please sit down. The parishioners can fend for themselves. They know where the cups are," she said with a fatalistic smile.

"All right. I am pretty light headed," Aitkins admitted, taking a seat on the sofa.

"While you were sleeping, in between thinking about the birth of Christ and a hundred other things that crossed my mind, a pearl of wisdom from another time, another culture, made its presence known to me," she confided.

"What's that?" the lawyer inquired in an exhausted tone.

"Well, it's a Buddhist precept but I think it fits where you find yourself. The saying goes something like this: *Give infinite gratitude to the past; infinite service to the present, and infinite responsibility to the future.*"

Dan's eyes stared blankly.

"What's it mean?"

"I think, for you, it means that you need to consider the years of marriage you and Julie have given each other, the children you have brought into this world, the blessings that God has showered upon you during your time together, and look upon these gifts with gratitude. The service to the present: that's where you're going to have to own up to your actions: with God, with Julie, with your situation. You must serve the present as Jesus would demand."

"How do I do that?"

"That's a journey only you can make. But I'd suggest that it includes coming to grips with your infidelity, seeking counseling, and accepting whatever other help you might need to insure this never happens again."

"And the future?"

Ingrid Hubbard looked away from the man before she responded.

"Therein lays the darkest, most difficult passage of your walk. You've created a life with another woman. You're morally responsible to be a father to that child, regardless of the relationship you have with the child's mother, which, if you honor the past and give service to the present, will only be marginal contact, enough to function as the child's parent, and nothing beyond that."

They sat quietly, bathed in the amber light of a decorative stained glass lamp perched on top of the preacher's desk. Muffled footsteps and casual conversation intruded from the hallway.

"Where are you from?" she finally inquired.

"Minnesota."

"I figured that. Where in Minnesota?"

"Detroit Lakes."

"I'm not familiar with that city. Are there counseling resources available near your home?"

He nodded his head. Random tears fell, staining the flannel pattern of his shirt with moisture.

"Lutheran Social Services has a branch office. I know a few folks who work there, people I trust."

"Good. That's a start. Here," she said, removing a business card from a plastic container on top of the desk. "Call me anytime. I'd like to be of help, if that's something you'd accept."

"Thanks," the attorney mumbled, depositing the card in his wallet.

"You sure you're going to be OK?"

"I dumped the pills and whiskey. I'm going to get a good night's sleep at the Fort Garry and head home at first light," Danny advised, unwittingly providing the minister with the first reference to his chosen method of suicide.

They stood up. Reverend Hubbard hugged the man. Her embrace was pastoral and strong.

"Don't wait too long to tell Julie," she urged. "This isn't something that will become easier to deal with over time."

"I know."

The Anglican priest escorted the lawyer down the corridor and into the sanctuary of the Gothic church. Suspended lights, their bulbs ineffective across the vast distance of the interior of the cathedral, cast shadows against plaster. The priest and the attorney advanced across the carpeted floor. They arrived at a door. No words were exchanged as Daniel Aitkins stepped out into the cheerless evening.

CHAPTER 61

F.W. Barnes made it to the hospital just as the surgical team was preparing to enter the operating room.

"I'm her father-in-law", he said, with uncharacteristic concern.

The lawyer passed his fingers reflexively through his silver gray hair as he stood at the nursing station on the surgery floor of Fergus Falls Catholic Hospital.

"I see," said a short blond LPN manning the desk. The woman's eyes held an appearance of genuine kindness. "Dr. Norstan, the neurosurgeon on call, just came in. He's going into the OR with her right now."

"Can you tell me what happened?"

"Police called it in. A semi-driver swerved to avoid a couple of kids sledding next to the road. The truck hit her head on."

Barnes' eyes clouded.

"How is she?"

"Can't really say. She's unconscious and she's had significant chest and head trauma. The shoulder harness failed. She apparently struck the steering wheel with her forehead and chest. We'll know more when the CT and X-rays come back."

Barnes waved at the woman, a slight gesture of appreciation. He found a hard plastic chair in the waiting area from which to begin his vigil. His wife was home, telephoning the Norton's. Julie's parents and her children still did not know that she'd been in an accident.

Technicians floated in and out of the OR suite, carrying samples to the lab; returning with test results and radiological films. A physician exited the operating room and conferred with the desk nurse.

"Mr. Barnes," the blond LPN called out as the doctor retreated.

The defense lawyer left his chair and approached the nursing desk.

"Yes?" he asked.

"The lab results, x-rays, and CT scan just came back," she said through transparent hesitancy.

"Do they show anything?"

"Well, you're daughter-in-law's a lucky young woman," the nurse offered, using the adjective "young" though Melanie was approximately the same age as the LPN.

"How so?"

"There's a subdural hematoma but it's small. Dr. Norstan thinks it will resolve without surgery. She's got a nasty fracture of the orbit of her right eye, which may or may not involve the right optic nerve. He's waiting for the orthopedic surgeon to get here, Dr. Teri Tonsina, before repairing that. Chest films show a lot of bruising and a collapsed lung. They'll reinflate the lung momentarily. A broken left wrist, where she must have tried to brace herself. Nothing appears to be a major problem."

"Thank God for that," the lawyer intoned, his hands folded as if in prayer.

"Amen," the woman responded out of respect.

Barnes returned to his seat to await further news. His attention drifted off. The old litigator recalled the smiling faces of Michael and Melanie on their wedding day, at St. Bonifice's Catholic Church in Detroit Lakes, the city the Barnes family called home until Michael completed law school. Shortly before Michael's graduation from the University of Iowa, F.W. shocked his wife by announcing that he had merged his four person practice with a firm of similar size, bought a building in the heart of downtown Fergus Falls, and made an offer on a stately mansion along one of the tree-studded avenues up the hill from the Ottertail River, only a few blocks from the new office. Michael's nuptials were the last significant connection between the Barnes family and the city of Detroit Lakes. There was something fitting that his son's wedding day was the closing scene in that act of the old man's life.

A feminine hand touched the right sleeve of his dress shirt.

"Mr. Barnes," a voice said.

His eyes focused on the woman standing in front of him.

"Ms. Aitkins?" F.W. suggested, the man's hesitancy the result of a distracted mind.

"That's right. Sorry I startled you. Please, call me Julie."

"Not a problem," the old man responded.

"Dee Dee heard about the accident from one of her pals in the sheriff's office and called me. How's Mel doing?"

"From what they tell me, it could have been much worse. Some bruising around the brain and in the chest. A broken eye socket and wrist. But overall, not nearly as bad as it could have been."

"I'm glad. She's been a good friend over the years."

The attorney's eyes narrowed. Barnes struggled to withhold his opinion regarding the woman's husband.

"Where is Mr. Aitkins? I expected he'd be here with you," the defense lawyer inquired, maintaining an element of formality to the conversation.

Julie drew a large breath.

"He's out of town."

"On Christmas Day?"

"It was sudden. Something he had to take care of."

312

The woman's tone of voice made it clear that she was uncomfortable with the subject. Barnes let the matter drop.

They sipped tepid coffee and watched CNN on a color television mounted to a white wall on a black metal armature. Strangers, their family members having surgery or just arriving by ambulance, came and went. The traffic on the unit was light, as if sensible folks avoided being hurt or succumbing to illness on Christmas Day.

Sometime later, just after Julie Aitkins placed a call to Emery Aitkins at her house where he was minding the kids, a lean and lanky male dressed in hospital clothing, slipped off his facemask and walked into the waiting area.

"Mr. Barnes?" the man inquired.

"That's me," F.W. advised.

"Dr. Norstan. Stanley. Please call me Stan."

The doctor's eyes darted around the room.

"Can we talk somewhere?"

"This is one of Melanie's friends. You can speak in front of her in confidence."

The surgeon glanced at the woman.

"'Fraid not, Mr. Barnes. We need to talk privately."

The elevator doors opened.

"June, Alfred," Barnes shouted, recognizing Melanie's parents as they exited the car.

"F.W.," Melanie's father responded weakly.

"This is Dr. Norstan. He wants to pass along some information about Melanie."

"Stanley, Stan Norstan," the doctor offered, reaching out with a slender hand to welcome the stricken woman's parents.

June Ingersol wept. Her husband, a small, bookish man with remnants of scarlet hair interrupting short gray stubble covering his scalp, shielded his eyes with his hands against the harsh waiting room light.

"Let's find some privacy," the surgeon suggested, sliding his arm behind the weeping woman, urging the couple towards a quiet corner of the room. F.W. Barnes resumed his seat.

Anesthetic smell wafted over the operating suite as they stood apart from the other visitors.

"How is she?" Alfred asked the doctor.

"She's doing fine. She had a fractured orbit of the right eye that Dr. Tonsina repaired, a bump on the head that'll likely resolve on its own, some other bruises, a collapsed lung that we've re-inflated, and a broken wrist that we've set."

"Thank God," June moaned, nearly passing out at the revelation.

Melanie's father scrutinized the physician. There was something lingering between them that needed to be said.

"What is it Doc? You look like you're not quite finished."

"This is a little delicate. I normally wouldn't tell you but, in your daughter's condition, there are decisions that need to be made that she isn't capable of making."

"I thought her condition was stable."

"It is. But she's still not coherent. Given the level of her head injury, I don't expect she will be competent, in the fullest sense of that term, for another forty-eight hours or so. That delay might cause significant complications."

"What sort of complications?" the father asked.

Stanley Norstan drew a deep breath.

"As I said, I'd normally leave this to her to tell you. But given that a decision needs to be made soon, you'll need to be the ones to make the call."

"As to what?"

The doctor drew another breath.

"Your daughter is approximately ten weeks pregnant."

June's insignificant sobs suddenly stopped.

"Are you sure?" Alfred Ingersol inquired.

"Blood test says that's the case. We confirmed it with an ultrasound just to be sure."

"But how...? She isn't even seeing anyone that I know of," Mrs. Ingersol interjected.

"I can't tell you who the father is. But there is one, that's for sure," the surgeon said, stating the obvious.

"What's the decision that needs to be made?" the father asked.

"The trauma to your daughter's chest has compromised the fetus. The baby's heart tones aren't quite right. There's a chance that the infant may have suffered injury due to reduced or interrupted blood flow."

"What kind of injury?" the father asked.

"Perhaps to the brain itself."

More subdued weeping from the mother. Alfred grasped his wife around the shoulders.

"What's the decision that needs to be made?" the man repeated.

"There's a possibility that what we're seeing is only a temporary situation and that the blood flow was never reduced to the point where it will have a lasting effect. The decision that you must make on behalf of your daughter is whether you want her to stay here, in a Catholic institution and simply have the fetus monitored, or have your daughter brought to another facility for a D and C. There's some uterine bleeding that may or may not resolve. Doing a D and C would insure that she won't lose any more blood."

"Absolutely not," June replied, her eyes staring intently at the physician. "We're Catholic. So is our daughter. She'll stay here, in God's hands. She would not, under any circumstances, allow an abortion of a child to save herself."

"Because of the fetal inconsistencies and the intrauterine bleeding, not doing a D and C might compromise your daughter's recovery. There's a chance, and I can't break it into a percentage that the OB-GYN might not be able to arrest the bleeding without doing a D and C. If the bleeding continues, your daughter's life is at risk."

"The answer, as my wife so aptly pointed out, is 'no,'" Alfred Ingersol repeated.

"I respect your decision. I'll tell the on-call OB-GYN when she gets here. I'm sure both Melanie and the baby will be fine."

The Ingersol's watched the surgeon glide towards the operating room. They looked at each other with uncertainty, cognizant that they could not share what they had learned with the other people in the waiting room.

CHAPTER 62

"Where's your mother?" Danny Aitkins asked his youngest child as the attorney walked into the kitchen the next morning.

"Hi daddy," Michael squealed. The boy left the table, abandoning a peanut butter and jelly sandwich, a plastic spill-proof cup, and a sliced apple.

"Where's mom?" Aitkins asked again, hugging the child. The son returned the embrace and retreated to his seat.

"She's in Fergus Falls, at the Catholic Hospital," Emery Aitkins responded from the living room.

Daniel deposited his suitcase on the floor and kicked off his tennis shoes.

"Where in God's name have you been?" the older man asked in an incriminating voice as he entered the kitchen.

"Not now dad. Why's Julie at the hospital?"

"Melanie Barnes was in an accident."

The message struck the young litigator like a hammer.

"What?"

"She got hit head-on by a semi. Hasn't come too yet but it's expected she'll make a complete recovery. Julie went back to the hospital this morning to be with Melanie's parents."

Danny didn't offer any further observations. His mind wrapped itself around the distinct possibility that his wife and a host of others now knew that Melanie Barnes was pregnant. All the twists and turns of that supposed reality began to unwind, suffocating him in their enormity.

"I better drive down there to be with her," Daniel said.

"Julie's expecting you. She's none too happy about Christmas. I'd walk real softly around her if I were you," Emery counseled, his tone softening.

Daniel studied his father's face. There were lines crossing the man's rugged forehead that the son hadn't noticed before. It was likely a vein or two would pop right out of the old man's skin if he knew that Dan's allusion to "being with her" could also refer to being with Melanie Barnes.

"Yeah, I'm sure she is. Hopefully she won't start in on me in front of a bunch of other people."

"Julie's smarter than that. She'll keep her mouth shut until she gets you home, on her own turf," Emery observed, his lips curled into a genteel smile. "Then I'd suggest you take cover."

"I'll just take a quick shower and head out, if that's all right with you."

The father took in his son's profile through hazel eyes. Emery rubbed the base of his thick neck.

"Go ahead. I've got nowhere else to be. Give Melanie my regards if she's awake."

Danny forced a smile.

"Where are the other two kids?"

"Adam's at practice. One of the other parents took him. Amanda's out in the barn. She was pretty torn up about Christmas. You'll want to step lightly around her for a few days," Emery advised.

"She's a lot like her mom," Danny responded.

"She's just like mom," Michael chimed in.

Daniel gave the boy a pat on the head.

"Wanna see what I got from Grandpa?" the child asked.

"When I come back, we'll play with all your new toys," the lawyer promised.

Under the intermittent pulse of the shower, the force of the stream unpredictable due to the aging pressure tank supplying the water system, Dan scrubbed his skin. His hands slid a bar of soap across his thighs, across the wet mop of his pubic hair, and up his stomach. He picked up a washrag and scrubbed his shoulders, neck, and back. As his fingers moved across the base of his spine, they lingered on the fusion site, touching the edges of the disrupted skin, feeling the unnatural thickness of the scar.

The lawyer kept his eyes closed. He struggled to prevent snapshots of himself and Melanie, alone and in bliss, from intruding. He fought urges that demanded to be addressed. His fingers worked shampoo into his scalp as he struggled to avoid attending to desire.

Danny altered his thinking. He began to pray for Melanie. An evil notion passed through his mind. The thought lingered and attempted to take root. There was a possibility that the woman would fully recover but that the fetus, their mutual problem, would not. He banished the rumination. The lawyer sought to recall some semblance of piety from his soul. As he rinsed suds from his short blond hair, the attorney battled demons of his own creation under the inconsistent flow of the shower.

Toweling himself off in front of the mirror, he studied his body, his face. Gray intruded into the hair of his chest and at his temples. The alterations were minimal. He noted the passage of the years more in his joints and in the stiffness of his bones than in his overall appearance. Mornings were the worst. Driving from Winnipeg, his legs had cramped, his hands had tingled after only an hour behind the wheel. The lawyer massaged his calves and closed his eyes.

Julie sat next to June Ingersol in the waiting room. Alfred paced the floor, casting sidelong glances at an action thriller playing on the television. Dee Dee Hernesman stood in front of a male nurse, an RN, manning the reception desk.

"Hi," Danny said as he stepped out of the elevator and approached his wife.

"Hey," Julie responded without enthusiasm, barely lifting her eyes in acknowledgment.

"How's Mel doing?" he asked, avoiding a confrontation with Julie by directing the question to the injured woman's mother.

"She's starting to come to," June Ingersol responded.

Daniel cast a nervous eye towards his wife as he contemplated the possibility that Melanie had already said something about the pregnancy to one of the people seated in the waiting room.

"That's great. How'd it happen?"

"Truck swerved into her lane as she was leaving Fergus. The driver was trying to avoid some kids who came sliding down a hill and out into the road on their sleds," Mrs. Ingersol reported.

"She's gonna be OK?"

"That's what the doctors say. She has a couple of fractures, a hematoma. But everything else seems in order," the mother related.

Something about the way she related the phrase "everything else seems in order" sparked alarm in the lawyer.

I'm just being paranoid, Danny thought.

"Can she have visitors?" he asked.

Dan realized that his question carried an intimate edge. He watched his wife's eyes flare. Julie remained quiet, turning her attention towards a magazine in her lap.

"Just go over to the desk where Ms. Hernesman is standing. They let two in at a time, but only for five minutes," Alfred Ingersol offered.

Daniel walked unsteadily across the polished linoleum.

"Hey there, Aitkins," Dee Dee observed. She hugged her partner and whispered into his ear.

"This can't be anything but awkward for you."

He nodded slightly.

You don't know just how awkward it is, he thought.

The attorneys entered the ICU. Ten beds were lined up, five against each wall of the long room. Drapes hanging from stainless steel rails secured to the ceiling provided privacy for the patients. Melanie was in the first bed on the left.

Daniel's eyes took in the tubes, the glowing screen of the monitors, and the forest of IV bags hanging from the metal post alongside the patient. He placed a warm hand on the woman's cool skin. Dee Dee kept her distance.

"I'm so sorry," he murmured through trembling lips. "I am so damn sorry."

318

The woman's eyelids flickered. Her eyes opened. Melanie struggled to focus on his face.

"That you, Danny?"

The morphine affected her motor skills. Her speech was slurred.

"Yes," he answered.

"Is everything OK?" she asked.

He glanced over his shoulder at his partner. A puzzled look formed on Dee Dee Hernesman's face.

"Yes," he replied.

"Is that what you want? For everything to be OK?"

He thought a moment. He marveled that, even under significant medication, Melanie was discrete in her questioning.

"Yes."

"Are you sure?"

"Yes," he lied. Of course he wasn't sure. Of course he had thought about the accident destroying the life growing inside of her, of ending the most intrusive, life-altering by-product of their affair. For a brief moment in the shower, he had even prayed that it was so. But now that it wasn't, now that there would be a child, he had to lie.

"I feel so tired," she whispered.

Her eyes closed under the weight of the narcotic.

"Dee Dee's here," he said.

The woman smiled.

"Dees?"

"Yes," the female attorney replied, approaching the patient.

"Thanks for coming."

"No problem. You'll be out of here in a flash," Hernesman offered.

"You're not here to give me your card or anything, are you?" Melanie quipped.

"The lawsuit against the trucker can wait," Dee Dee answered through a smile.

Melanie grinned but said nothing more as her guests quietly exited the room.

CHAPTER 63

Ghastly cold lurked inside the Aitkins farmhouse. Daniel had been unable to bring himself to confess. It wasn't that he was unwilling to disclose his sins to his wife. The matter was complicated by the fact that the Anderson trial was set to begin. The pretrial was only a week away. For his clients' sake, the litigator could not risk coming clean on the eve of trial. Danny's confessional would have to wait until after the jury decided the case.

They wandered past each other in the big house, making idle chitchat but never connecting. His wife's mood was disturbing. She was itching for an argument. He kept his distance. He took to sleeping in the basement. The children, even little Michael, perceived the strain. The adults in the home had come to an unhappy ceasefire akin to the numerous truces in the Middle East or Northern Ireland. Soon, as in those wretched places, their truce would break apart. All hell would let loose.

When he was around, Julie retreated to her studio to write. Daniel didn't know how far she'd progressed on her novel. The last they had spoken of the book, Julie had nearly completed a rough draft of the manuscript. He'd asked to read it. She said it wasn't ready, that he could read it when it was finished. Though he was anxious at the thought of having to reveal his terrible secret, he was counting on success with the book to soften the blow. He knew that such an accommodation was unrealistic, that the circumstance he was about to relate could not be lessened or reduced by anything positive that took place in their lives.

In the evenings, while Julie wrote, he ferried the kids to their activities. Adam's hockey took up an enormous amount of time. Emery helped out, taking the younger children to their basketball games, making the occasional road trip with his oldest grandson for out-of-town hockey tournaments. Despite an appearance of normalcy to their day-to-day lives, there was an uneasy, distasteful balance in the home that needed to be addressed.

After, Danny thought as he drove to the hospital to see Melanie again. *After the verdict.*

The lawyer had dumped out all of the booze in the house except four bottles of Julie's wine, which he moved to her studio and locked in her supply cabinet. His wife had the only key. She never said a word to him about his flurry of sobriety. Doubtlessly, she thought it was the result of his DUI. He didn't tell her any different.

Emery put him in touch with Lawyers Concerned for Lawyers, a group of attorneys and judges who intervene to save the lives of others in their profession plagued by chemical dependency. He went to lunch with a lawyer from Perham who was in the program, a guy he knew from intermittent dealings. He joined AA and started attending meetings in Park Rapids to avoid seeing folks he knew. Danny Aitkins missed more meetings than he made.

But, he thought, *it's a start.*

Counseling was more difficult to swallow. He kept Rev. Hubbard's telephone number in his wallet. From time to time, when he was alone, Aitkins would draw the business card out of its hiding place and study it. He never called the priest. He never called Lutheran Social Services.

That can wait until after the shit hits the fan, he told himself on those occasions, sitting alone, feeling the weight of guilt pressing down on his body in the solitude of his office. *I'll need more than just a little counseling once Julie knows.*

She was sitting upright in a chair. Megan, Melanie's nine-year-old daughter, and Josh, her seven-year-old son, were seated on the edge of the bed with their legs dangling in the air. The children were watching cartoons on television, giggling with delight at the antics of imaginary dinosaurs.

"Hi rug rats," Daniel said. He liked Melanie's kids but he didn't know exactly how close to get to them. The fact that their half brother or sister was alive and growing inside their mother caused the attorney no end of confusion when he was in the company of Melanie Barnes' children.

"Hi, Mr. Aitkins," the children responded through exuberant smiles.

"Why don't you kids go find grandpa and get him to buy you some breakfast? I need to talk to Mr. Aitkins alone," Melanie suggested.

The children scooted out the door.

"Grandpa," they shouted, running helter-skelter down the hallway.

"Cute kids," Danny noted in a disingenuous tone.

"We need to talk," the woman said, scrutinizing the man's profile.

"I know."

"When are you going to tell Julie?"

The room was still for a moment.

"I was thinking that it could wait until after the trial."

Her eyes studied him.

"That makes sense. But no later. I'm starting to show," she added, shifting uncomfortably in the chair.

"Does it hurt much?" he asked, pointing to an ominous bruise covering the right side of her face where the fracture had been repaired.

She gestured with her left arm, the wrist encased in plaster.

"Not much. The headaches are gone. My memory is pretty much back. The bleeding's stopped."

"That's good," he said softly, standing over her, nervously shifting from foot to foot.

"Danny, I don't expect anything from you."

He stopped swaying.

"What do you mean?"

"I know you still love your wife. What happened between us was a terrific, stupid error in judgment by two people who've never grown up. When you tell her, tell her you love her and that you want to remain her husband," she directed.

"I don't think it was a mistake," the lawyer observed. "I think it was foolhardy. I think it was juvenile. But I won't call what happened between us a mistake."

Her eyes closed.

"Having a child with someone other than your wife is about number one on the big mistake board, Daniel."

"That part, I'd agree with."

"I've made it clear why I can't change that portion of this sorry scene," she murmured.

"I wish you'd reconsider," he urged.

"I can't."

"Then I'll have to live with your decision."

"We'll have to live with it. You, me, our kids, your wife, our families. There's a lot to consider here, Star Baby, beyond the you and the me in this equation."

"Agreed."

He knelt next to her and smoothed strands of her matted hair with his hand. His fingers found her mouth and followed the curve of her left cheek. The tip of Danny's index finger caught a bead of salty moisture from her eye as it descended.

"I don't know what'll happen, Mel. You know I never meant to hurt you."

"I know. But it does hurt, Danny. It does."

"I'm sorry."

"I think you better leave," she whispered.

"OK."

The lawyer kissed the woman on the forehead. His lips grazed taut skin. Memories; illicit, wondrous, and full of agony, flooded over Daniel Aitkins as he turned to leave the mother of his unborn child.

CHAPTER 64

Domesticity demanded the couple's attention despite their unprecedented silence towards each other. Upon Dan's return from Winnipeg, after the complete and utter destruction of Christmas, the lawyer fell deeply into the preparation of the Anderson case. In the back of his mind, the knowledge that he was going to be a father for the fourth time loomed large, universally threatening to push the lawyer back towards the bottle and, ultimately, to that dark place where whiskey and pills remained suspended before him like the Holy Grail. He resisted the urge to cash it all in. The vision of his daughter riding her horse across the verdant grass of a new spring, the vision that had appeared within the acidic reality of the rental cabin along the shores of Lake Winnipeg, sustained his spirit. Whenever his mind wandered close to the edge of self-destruction, Amanda's face appeared and defeated his suicidal ideations.

Julie moved through their life with uncertainty. She was puzzled by her husband's disappearance on Christmas after a seemingly minor altercation. She sensed that greater troubles fermented beneath the surface of their relationship.

The Anderson trial? He was always testy and inconsolable just before trial. This felt different. Financial woes? They were always present. Throughout the duration of their marriage, the couple had always spent more than they made. This year was nothing out of the ordinary in that regard. They were no more or less in debt than before. Another woman? Given Daniel's track record, it was possible. She knew about the girl in Madison and about Melanie Barnes. That he had, by Mel's own admission, cut the affair off at the pass, so to speak, before consummation, did not make that history more palatable to Julie Aitkins. It merely confirmed that Danny operated on a higher moral plane than some folks but on a lower moral plane than others.

Distance had formed between them. At the dinner table. In the bedroom. Around the children. Polite pleasantries, perfunctory pecks on the cheek, had become the fruition of their bond. It distressed Julie that their relationship had deteriorated to such depths in such a short period of time. She had not signed on for a cardboard marriage. There would come a day of reckoning. Just when she would approach Dan about their situation was an open question. But she knew that it would have to be done before the glue of their present accommodation became too firmly set.

Beyond their problems as a couple, Julie found herself preoccupied with her craft. She remained mired in an inner turmoil regarding her first novel. There were women that she knew from her writer's group at Concordia College in Moorhead, The Prairie Writers and Poets Workshop, who had already published collections of their poetry and short stories. A friend, Isobel Jameson, had publishers offer hundreds of thousands of dollars in advance money for her debut novel, the feverish competition occurring as the result of a bidding war engineered by Isobel's literary agent. Julie recognized that she was rapidly approaching forty. For whatever reason, being a loving wife, a wonderful mother, and a well-respected teacher were not enough. Those considerable accomplishments did not feed her ego. She needed more. More than Danny was providing, more than her job and her children were capable of yielding. More.

On the plus side of the ledger, she was comforted to know that her husband was no longer drinking. She hadn't seen Danny sip so much as a beer since he returned from Canada. While Julie Aitkins had never considered her husband an alcoholic, there was always the suspicion in the back of her mind that his vulnerable ethos, more succinctly, his need to feel loved by everyone he met, did not need the added burden of sorting through artificial emotions prompted by alcohol. It was a good thing, she surmised, that Danny had ceased to drink. It was also a good thing that the City Attorney had agreed to give Daniel Aitkins a break. Her husband had been granted a deferral of prosecution on the DUI charge. If he stayed clean for a year, with no alcohol offenses of any sort, and maintained his sobriety, the criminal matter would disappear. Julie knew Dee Dee Hernesman had gone to bat for Danny and brokered the deal. She was hopeful it was the end of an embarrassing footnote to their Yuletide debacle.

The attorney's eyes studied the face of the judge. Daniel Aitkins was hunkered down behind a table in the courtroom, listening to James Thompson explain to Judge Harriet Enwright why the case couldn't, at this late date, the day of the final pretrial, be resolved.

"We've tried your honor. I've gone to my people in Winnipeg on a number of occasions since the completion of the mediation session before this Court. The company is worried about a succession of unprincipled claims, perhaps a class action suit, if word of a settlement in the Anderson matter hits the streets. Mr. Aitkins has indicated that his clients are not willing to sign a confidentiality agreement. It would seem that all hope of an amicable resolution has been exhausted," the defense attorney advised.

"Mr. Aitkins, is confidentiality really an issue?" the judge inquired.

Daniel rose.

"That and the small matter of the amount offered. Stevenson's has never come close to six figures. This case cannot be settled, with or without a confidentiality clause, for anything less than something in six figures. What that something is doesn't lend itself to debate unless and until the company is at least in the same ballpark as the plaintiffs."

"Mr. Aitkins has a point, Mr. Thompson. Seems that it's pretty tough to ask the plaintiffs to sign an agreement to keep the settlement amount sealed if you're client isn't willing to negotiate the amount."

Thompson narrowed his eyes and confronted the judge. It was clear to Aitkins that the defense lawyer felt he was being pressured to increase his offer.

"With all due respect to the court, we believe we've given plaintiffs top dollar for their claim in terms of our outstanding settlement proposal. I take issue with the court being involved in judicial arm twisting at this late stage of the proceedings."

Harriet Enwright remained unmoved. If she was upset by Thompson's candor, she didn't let her emotions show.

"I'm sorry you feel that this judge is resorting to 'arm twisting' Mr. Thompson. I'd prefer to call it a 'friendly suggestion' that the parties move closer to each other in hopes of resolving their differences," she advised through a loose smile.

Thompson's large face broke into a grin, the edges of which nearly concealed the man's miniscule eyes.

"Sorry about that, your honor. Got carried away by the heat of the moment. We'll keep talking. I can't promise anything. But we'll keep the avenues of settlement open."

"That's fine, Mr. Thompson. And, Mr. Aitkins...."

"Yes," Danny responded, rising once more to address the judge.

"Perhaps you should think about taking something off your last demand so as to promote a response."

"I'll talk to my clients about that, your honor."

"You do that. And talk to them about signing a confidentiality agreement as well. We'll see you folks back here on January Fifteenth at eight in the morning to mark any trial exhibits and go over any motions that need to be addressed. Trial will begin at nine o'clock sharp. If the matter settles, please make sure you call my clerk, Mr. Olson. Your case is the only one slated for trial that week. I'd hate to call in jurors if the matter is resolved."

The two attorneys gathered their files and moved towards the rear of the basement courtroom.

"How is it that F.W. and Stone aren't here today?" Aitkins observed as the men began to leave the room.

"F.W.'s under the weather. And Stone, well, as much as I hate to admit it, he's up in Winnipeg trying to shake loose a few more dollars to settle this case," Big Jim replied, chuckling lightly beneath the words.

"Gonna take a lot more than just a few dollars," the plaintiffs' lawyer responded lightly.

"American or Canadian?" Thompson quipped.

"We'll take either. But don't forget about the exchange rate." The defense lawyer smiled.

"I won't. Can you come off the two-twenty-five?" he asked.

"I don't generally negotiate against myself," Danny responded as the attorneys walked up the stairs to the lobby of the Becker County Courthouse.

Thompson stopped as they reached the top of the staircase. The man's massive right hand found Aitkins' wrist.

"Cut the first year law school bullshit, Aitkins. Your clients don't need two hundred and twenty-five thousand dollars to replace their lost pigs and rebuild their herd. Give me a number that they can live with, something in the low six figures, and I'll sell it to Stevenson's."

Aitkins' eyes fixed on the pupils of his adversary. Unlike Barnes, a man he would never trust, Daniel sensed there was an honesty, an integrity, to James Thompson, perhaps a trait ingrained in the man by the experience of being one of a handful of black students in his graduating class at Fargo North High School. Or, perhaps, an attribute passed along by his parents.

"I'll see what I can do."

"Better get to me before the end of business today," the defense attorney added. "Stone should have something for me by lunch. Give me a call after you talk to the Andersons. But do it before four this afternoon. I know the clock is ticking and that my people aren't interested in settlement of this case on the courthouse steps."

Aitkins smiled.

"That's what they told my clients back in Des Moines."

"Trust me when I tell you today's the day. After four, we're at war," Thompson said.

The huge lawyer burst into laughter.

"What?" Aitkins asked. "What's so damn funny?"

"I can't stand that pompous ass Johnny Cochran. Here I am using verse, like his dim-witted 'if they don't fit, you must acquit.' Lord, I am losing it," the man moaned. "Aitkins, please settle this damn thing so I can go home to my wife and daughter," the man said, combating a resurgence of laughter.

Daniel winced. He wasn't concerned by the possibility of doing battle with Thompson. The plaintiffs' attorney was so deep in trial preparation that it no longer mattered to him personally, in terms of his health or well-being, whether they played it all out before a jury or not.

326

His reaction was to the fleeting notion that he was going to be a father again, an idle thought that passed from his subconscious into the foreground of his mind. He stood under a wall clock. The hands of the instrument indicated that it was ten-thirty in the morning. His eyes went blank. His heart began to pound.

"Did you hear me?" the defense lawyer asked.

Aitkins nodded.

"Are you all right?" Thompson inquired solicitously.

"I'm fine."

"Before four o'clock today," Big Jim repeated as he forced his massive shoulders through the revolving door.

"Gotcha," Aitkins replied after the defense lawyer had left.

Other matters, more personal, more tragic in their potentiality, crowded Dan Aitkins' mind. These matters obscured Danny's concern for the welfare of Dean and Nancy Anderson as the litigator watched the red second hand of the Seth Thomas wall clock advance.

CHAPTER 65

"**I** don't know about this case," Dan Aitkins intoned as he poured over the proposed exhibits that the plaintiffs would offer into evidence during the trial against Stevenson's Sci-Swine.

The attorney was armpit deep in paper in the conference room of the Aitkins law firm; sorting the important from the unimportant, tagging documents to be used as evidence. The papers would be three-hole-punched, indexed, and inserted along with indices into large blue binders that would sit on the counsel table, providing ready access to exhibits and outlines during the trial. Depositions of witnesses would be cataloged. Summaries of their testimony would be prepared by the firm's paralegals for quick reference. Combing through such material is a labor intensive, detail oriented task. It's a part of the job that many lawyers disdain and assign to underlings. As a lover of detail, Danny reserved these tasks for himself.

"What's the problem?" Dee Dee asked as she removed staples from a laboratory report.

Outside, the first significant blizzard of the New Year appeared imminent. The prediction for the weekend was that two to three feet of incredibly light powder would drift into Detroit Lakes, clogging the roads and bringing traffic to a stand still. It was late Friday morning, the Friday before trial. The Andersons were coming in for their final pre-trial meeting with their lawyers on Saturday, provided the roads were open. The dedicated efforts of Big Jim Thompson and Danny Aitkins had not resulted in settlement of the case. Stevenson's best offer was $85,000.00, which, when expenses and attorneys fees were deducted, resulted in little more than $30,000.00 going to the plaintiffs. Trial was now a certainty.

"I'd still like to know where the corn used to make the pellets came from," the lawyer mused, rubbing his stinging eyes, the pupils red from overuse. "I mean, we know that the Andersons bought the product from Stevenson's Detroit Lakes operation and that the pellets were manufactured in Grand Forks. Beyond that, we have no idea where the stuff came from."

The female attorney smiled.

"What's so funny?" Dan asked.

"Have you read our witness list?"

Aitkins was puzzled.

"What's that got to do with where the pellets came from?"

Hernesman stood up, patted the fabric of her dress slacks to release trapped static electricity, picked up a set of papers, and leaned over Aitkins' left shoulder.

"You smell good," Danny remarked, a wry grin erupting across his mouth.

"'Aunt Edna's Most Particular Fragrance'," the woman offered.

"Special brand, eh?"

"Ivory Soap. My Aunt Edna used to use it," Dee Dee quipped.

Aitkins laughed.

"Well, whatever it is, it smells nice."

"Thanks. Are you done flirting now?"

"I think so."

"You know it's not going to do any good, don't you?" Hernesman said, smiling kindly.

"I forgot."

"Sure, Daniel. You don't forget anything. Read this," Hernesman urged, placing a document in his hands.

Aitkins studied the material.

"What am I supposed to be looking for? There are over forty names on this list."

Hernesman sat down.

"Look at numbers thirty-three through thirty-six."

Aitkins scanned the names.

"Who the hell are these people? I don't recognize these names."

Dee Dee stood up and walked over to her briefcase. Her hands withdrew a distressed manila envelope from the black leather satchel. She handed an additional document to her partner.

"What's this?"

"Read it," the woman advised.

Daniel studied the battered folder, removed a four-page memorandum, and scrutinized the paperwork.

"Holy shit," he muttered.

"That's exactly what I said when I saw it," Dee Dee agreed.

Aitkins perused the document. His fingers quivered when he placed the wrinkled papers on the table.

"Where'd you get this?" he asked.

"I don't think that's something you really need to know at this point."

"Do you have any idea what this means?" Danny asked as his eyes met those of his partner.

"I'm pretty sure I do."

"Dees, I need to know where you got this."

"Not now. After the case is over."

He stood up and touched the woman's shoulder with the fingers of his right hand.

"Dees, if you're involved in this somehow, I gotta know. I can't be walking into a landmine in front of Harriet."

"Landmine?"

329

"Shit, I don't know where this came from. It's obviously the work product of Malachi Stone. His name is all over it."

"You're not going to use the memorandum. You're just calling the names from the memorandum as witnesses," the woman demurred.

"And how does that overcome the fact that this thing was likely stolen? It looks like the fucking original, Dees. The fucking original document. Stealing another attorney's work product definitely violates the Rules of Professional Responsibility."

The female attorney paced back and forth on the far side of the conference room. An austere essence blazed across Dee Dee's face each time she passed beneath the fluorescent fixture. Her eyes, their murky color ignited by the lights, shone defiantly.

"So who will know?"

"I will."

"And so will I. But beyond the two of us, who will ever know where we came up with the names?"

There was an awkward silence as Danny sought to battle an inclination to agree.

"Look at it this way, Dan," the woman continued. "Suppose we never received the document? Sure, the memo itself is Stone's work product. It's not a statement, not a verbatim transcript, or a writing authored by a witness. It's clearly Stone's understanding of what Bobby Morgan uncovered. Because of that, I'll grant you that we have no business being provided a copy of the memo itself."

"Not a copy, Dees, the fucking original, initialed personally by Malachi Stone."

"The original. Anyway, let me ask you this: Aren't Stevenson's and their lawyers obligated to disclose the names and addresses of all potential witnesses, regardless of how that information was obtained?"

"Yes."

"And didn't they conceal the existence of four viable and relevant witnesses from us?"

Daniel's eyes brightened. There was a glimmer of justification, a scrap of integrity, to what his partner was saying.

"That's true."

"And isn't that a violation of the Rules of Civil Procedure as well as the Rules of Professional Responsibility?"

"But two wrongs don't make a right."

"Cut the kindergarten psychology. We're talking as attorneys here. Litigators. People charged with bringing out the truth," she advocated.

"OK."

"So then how is it that our fortuitous acquisition of these four names, names that were wrongfully withheld from us by the defense, is in any way immoral or unethical?"

Daniel stood up and paced from one end of the table to the other. His right hand stroked the baby-soft skin of his chin; the whiskers having been shorn clean a few hours earlier under the extreme light of his bathroom vanity. The trial lawyer stretched across the table to retrieve the memorandum.

"I'm gonna write these four names and addresses down on a legal pad. If anyone ever asks, that's where you saw them; that's where you obtained them. If anyone ever presses me, I'll come up with some lame story about how I happened upon them when we doing our document inventory in Winnipeg."

Aitkins jotted down the information on a legal pad. He reached into the drawer of a nearby end table and removed a book of matches. Holding the sheets of paper over a metal wastebasket, he ignited a match. The paper caught fire.

"Shouldn't we keep the memo to use on cross exam if the witnesses' stories don't match what they told Bobby Morgan?" Hernesman asked.

"Can't risk it. Even if Thompson is clean on this, and that looks to be the case because his name isn't on the distribution list, I can't pull out Stone's memo and wave it in front of a recanting witness. Enwright would have my balls. The Lawyer's Board would have my license."

Flames climbed the document in rapid succession. Fire lapped at Dan's fingers. The lawyer dropped the fiery mess into the empty garbage can and stepped on the debris with his shoe.

"Alison Buckvold and I'll take a ride out there tomorrow to talk to as many of these four as we can," Aitkins said, referencing the private investigator the firm relied upon. "If they tell us a different tale, we won't call them for trial."

Dee Dee Hernesman resumed her seat.

"There's just one other thing," Aitkins indicated, moving closer to the woman.

"What's that?"

"Do you think that this missing memorandum has anything to do with why Stone and F.W. Barnes were arguing like crazy in the Fort Garry restaurant?"

"A clever supposition, counselor," Hernesman replied, faint gaiety imbedded in her voice.

"Also seems interesting that, since our final witness list just went out, Stone picked the day of the pretrial to vamoose to Canada in search of more cash to resolve this case."

The woman lowered her eyes and refused to engage in further discussion. For the rest of the morning, Dee Dee

Hernesman's attention was purposefully riveted upon the paperwork in front of her.

CHAPTER 66

Rather than telephone ahead, Aitkins took a chance. He postponed his meeting with the Anderson family until Sunday afternoon. He and Dee Dee would drive out to the Anderson Farm after church, bringing with them the portions of the file that were appropriate, and discuss the testimony of Dean, Nancy, and the four Anderson children with the family. Matthew Anderson was due to leave for Marine Corps basic training in San Diego early in February. The trial would be over by then.

The predicted storm passed over the western fringe of Minnesota without fanfare. Instead of several feet of snow, a few inches of fluffy white flakes settled over the existing snow cover. The drive to Eastern North Dakota in the Ranger was uneventful. Danny brought along Alison Buckvold, the independent private investigator retained by the Aitkins firm in high profile cases.

Alison was long legged. Her naturally dark hair was artificially bleached. She was intelligent but hard-edged. Her husband Deke was a member of the Climax Motorcycle Club, a band of reformed desperados who had once terrorized the Dakotas. Now, the CMC was mostly relegated to holding pig roasts and motorcycle touring events. The members were older, their pastimes, more sociable than the bank robberies, drug running, and assaults that plagued their formative years. Daniel really didn't need Alison along for any particular reason. He just liked her company.

Buckvold jumped into the passenger's seat of the pickup early Saturday morning, a Marlboro hanging out of the right corner of her mouth between thick lips made larger still by significant lipstick. Deke, a mountain of a man with waist length hair and tattoos over every spare inch of his arms, ambled out to the truck as Danny waited for the investigator to buckle up.

"What you waiting for?" she asked.

"For you to put your harness on," Dan replied.

"Shit, I don't wear a seat belt," she said through a laugh. "Hell, I don't even wear a helmet when I ride behind my crazy old man on his bike."

"Howdy, Dan," Deke said, his voice gravelly and low. The man approached the passenger window, waving a large paw of a hand as he stopped alongside the Ford.

"Hey, Deke."

"Nice day for a drive," the PI's husband offered.

"Sure is."

"See you sometime this afternoon, hon," the woman said, kissing the stubbled face of her mate, leaving an impression of red behind on the man's skin.

"OK," the less than talkative biker responded.

The little six-cylinder truck pulled away from the Buckvold's disintegrating house on a dead end street located on the south side of Detroit Lakes.

"Where we headed?"

Though the PI had been briefed about who there were going to see, she had no idea of where they were going.

"North Dakota."

"Lovely. The dullest place in North American," the woman moaned. "Where 'bouts?"

"We're gonna stop and see a German Bachelor farmer by the name of Dave Mueller."

"What's the connection to the Andersons?"

"I think he may have grown the corn that ultimately ended up in the pellets the Andersons bought."

"Ah", the woman opined, "chain of custody."

Danny smiled. He liked Alison, though lately, he ended up doing much of the investigative work for his files on his own. It wasn't that he didn't trust her instincts; she was good, damn good. It went back to his perfectionist nature. He felt more secure knowing that he had personally covered all the bases.

Mueller's farm was a long ways from any place else. With four thousand acres of land, the sheer size of the bachelor's spread precluded neighbors. As the truck bounced along the frozen ruts of the rudimentary road into the Mueller place, Aitkins marveled at the decay evident in Mueller's operation.

Old livestock barns had fallen on hard times and were near collapse. The house itself tilted, as if the defeated framing, roof, and white clapboards of the place were ready to slide right off the building's foundation into a heap of rubble. Four gigantic pole buildings, the structures obviously used for storage, the metal sheeting painted a standard oxidized red with white trim, dominated a slight rise behind the house. Rusting tractors and machinery, clearly inoperable and being used for parts, were parked in disarray around the perimeter of the farm's expansive lawn. Waist high shards of wild grass, the stalks frozen and asleep, had taken firm root, defining the open spaces of the place, spaces unclaimed as yet by deceased equipment.

A meager globe constituting a faint suggestion of a sun stood above the prairie. There was no wind, no sound, as Aitkins' truck stopped in front of the decrepit front porch of the home. The black metal frame of a significant satellite dish stood next to the house. The dish was the only structure on the place other than the pole buildings in good repair.

"This guy's rich?" the woman asked skeptically.

"That's what I hear."

"Who told you that?"

"Can't recall," the lawyer answered, taking in the narrow hips and waist of the fifty-something investigator.

"Well, seems to me that your information ain't worth a shit. Take a look at this dump."

"Looks can be deceiving," Aitkins observed.

"That's a line Deke's been trying to get me to swallow for years. But he's still butt-ugly, no matter how you slice it."

Aitkins laughed.

They exited the truck. A large Rottweiler dashed out from beneath the porch and made straight for the woman.

"Slow down there, pup," Alison admonished. The dog, its viciousness called into question by the tone of the woman's voice, stopped dead in its tracks, cocked its ugly head, and studied the humans.

"He won't bite," a voice called out from the porch.

The attorney looked towards the farmhouse. Dan's eyes focused on a man exiting the front door.

"Mr. Mueller?"

"That'd be me."

The stocky grain farmer stepped out into the chill in a short-sleeved white T-shirt, brown corduroys, and ravaged moccasins.

"And you are?"

"Dan Aitkins. This is Alison Buckvold. I'm a lawyer. She's a PI."

Mueller's eyes squinted. The farmer's ruddy cheeks puffed in and out in slow fashion, as if he was getting ready to spit. He stared straight at Aitkins as he spoke.

"I'm not so sure I want to know what this is about."

Alison stepped in, using her femininity as a shield. Though her days as a coquette were long passed, she wasn't above using her gender to place men at ease by playing to their weakness.

"Not to worry, Mr. Mueller. It's Dave, right?"

Mueller nodded.

"Mind if I call you Dave?" she asked.

"Please do," the bachelor said, studying the investigator from head to toe, lingering on all the appropriate places.

Alison smiled.

"Like I said, this isn't about you. No problem for the Mueller place in what Mr. Aitkins and I have to discuss with you. That's a guaranty from Alison Buckvold."

"OK. So why are you here?" the farmer asked.

Aitkins shifted his weight. He'd left his winter jacket in the truck. Cold infiltrated his joints.

"Is there someplace we can get out of this weather and talk?" the attorney inquired.

"Sure. Come on inside. I've got a pot of hot water brewing for tea. Got some instant cocoa if you don't like tea."

The PI and the lawyer followed Mueller into the house. Once inside, the farmer brought them down a long hallway, the plaster of the walls cracked and dirty from decades of neglect. They left their boots at the door. Aitkins felt food crumbs crunch beneath his toes as he followed the farmer's lead in his stocking feet.

They sat down at a 1940's vintage pine table in the kitchen, the tabletop marred with burns and gouges; the matching chairs crudely held together with wire and nails.

"Tea?" Mueller asked, pouring hot water over a tea bag in a waiting cup.

"That's fine," Ms. Buckvold responded.

"The same," Aitkins repeated.

"Either of you use milk?"

"Nope," the guests answered simultaneously.

The grain farmer sat on a defeated wooden chair and scrutinized his visitors.

"So what's this all about?"

Aitkins took a deep breath.

"First, I want you to understand that my client will not make any sort of a claim or file any sort of a lawsuit against you."

Mueller's eyes flashed.

"What the hell is that supposed to mean? You come here, strangers. I give you hospitality and you talk about lawsuits? What is this?"

Alison moved her thin fingers onto the bare skin of the man's wrist.

"Just listen. This has nothing to do with you except as a witness."

Mueller's eyes softened. There was a hint of curiosity about his face.

"A witness? To what?"

"My clients bought some grain from Stevenson's Sci-Swine last spring. The stuff turned out to be corn-based pellets. It seems that the corn used in the pellets they bought may have come from your farm," Aitkins revealed.

"Are you sure?"

"It was verified by a Mrs. Martin..."

"That'd be Marge," the farmer interrupted.

"Yes, Marge. She verified that she delivered three truckloads of corn from your farm to the local elevator."

"I remember that crap. Hotter than a pistol. Moisture content of nineteen percent," Mueller volunteered. "Ed LeFaive at the elevator basically took it for salvage price. He was gonna mix it with some dry stuff and sell it as a fattener for butcher hogs."

336

"That's the information I got as well," Aitkins lied.

"So how do you tie your client's feed from Stevenson's back to me?" Mueller asked.

Alison sipped hot liquid in less than quiet gulps as she listened.

"Apparently, in the spring, LeFaive had more of the inferior corn than he could use locally. He sold five truckloads to Stevenson's. As far as we can tell, he thought the stuff was going to be used for grower-finisher pellets, like he intended," the lawyer added.

"Ed was worried about using that corn for gestating animals," the farmer added.

"Smart man," Buckvold observed. "I had a couple of horses get sick on moldy feed once," she indicated. "Not a pretty sight."

"According to LeFaive, he specifically asked the Stevenson's buyer what the corn was going to be used for. He told the guy that it wasn't fit for gestational rations for any livestock. The information we have suggests that the Stevenson's man agreed and advised it was going into pellets for meat animals," Aitkins concluded.

Mueller began to fidget in his seat.

"I sure hope you're being honest with me about the lawsuit thing. I've been sued twice. Won both of 'em but I don't much like the idea of courtrooms."

Buckvold touched the top of the man's hand again.

"Easy, big fella. Dan's as honest as they come. He's told you that you're not a target. Relax, would ya?"

"She's right. My client's claim is against Stevenson's. All fingers point to them as the culprit."

The farmer rose from his chair and looked Aitkins square in the eye.

"What's my part in all this?"

"Trial starts Monday. Come Tuesday, I want to be able to call you as a witness to tell the jury what happened."

"That it?"

"That's all I need."

"No bullshit?"

"No bullshit."

Mueller rolled his eyes as he considered a response. His thinking done, the farmer leaned his coarse frame over the rickety table, holding the weight of his thick chest away from the platform with stubby arms.

"What happened to your client?"

Aitkins drew a serious breath.

"The pellets destroyed their litters. Caused a massive abortion storm that will, if I don't win this thing, wipe them out."

Mueller walked slowly across the weathered pine slats of the kitchen floor, his moccasins scuffling as he moved.

"They got any kids?"

"Four."

"Christ. I knew there had to be. If there weren't kids, I'd tell you to go flour your ass. I know enough about the law that you can't drag me over the border with a subpoena. I don't have to do this. But knowing there are kids at stake, Goddamn you Mr. Aitkins, I don't see as I have much of a choice."

Danny smiled and rose to shake the grain farmer's thick hand.

"Thanks, Dave. You won't regret this."

"I hope not," was all the man said as he ushered them to the door.

CHAPTER 67

They slid onto stools anchored to the greasy tile floor of a luncheonette in the little farming community of Larimore in time for lunch.

Aitkins took a seat next to an elderly gentleman. The old man's long hair was white with age. The attorney pondered how to break the ice. Alison Buckvold sat next to the lawyer looking over a menu printed on glossy cardboard.

"Coffee?" a young boy in an apron, blue jeans, and a sweatshirt asked as he held a steaming pot of black liquid above the surface of the counter with one hand, two white porcelain cups in the other.

"None for me," the lawyer said.

"Sure," the female PI advised.

The server poured the woman a cup of coffee. Vapor drifted a few inches away from the lip of the vessel before evaporating.

"Nice little town you have here," Aitkins observed, speaking to the man seated next to him.

Ed LeFaive looked at the stranger.

"I guess," the man reflected, turning a page in the *Fargo Forum* newspaper he was reading.

"I hear you run the Cooperative Elevator."

"Ran. Thirty-seven year's worth," the Canadian responded, scanning the high school basketball scores.

"I'd like to talk to you about that," Aitkins interjected.

"What's that?"

"About one of your customers, Dave Mueller. I'm a lawyer. Involved in a case over in Minnesota. My associate, Ms. Buckvold, and I just came from Mueller's place."

LeFaive's eyes studied Aitkins' face.

"What's this got to do with the Co-Op?" the foreman asked with evident distrust.

"Maybe we should sit in a booth to keep this private," Alison interjected.

"Private? Say, what's this all about?"

"Nothing against the elevator, Mr. LeFaive. I'm Danny Aitkins, from Detroit Lakes. I think Ms. Buckvold is right. Care to join us in a booth? The tab's on me."

LeFaive grunted.

"I been paying my own freight for over forty years. I'll talk to you but I'll pay my own tab, thank you."

The group found an empty booth and sat down.

"What's this all about?" the elevator employee asked.

"Our clients, the Andersons, bought a load of pelleted feed for their sows and gilts from Stevenson's Sci-Swine in Detroit Lakes. The feed was full of fusarium."

"What happened?" LeFaive inquired.

"A massive abortion storm," Alison offered between tenuous sips of hot coffee.

The conversation ceased when a waitress approached. Their server was a woman with bad acne and a bright personality. She took their order. The discussion resumed.

"Seems that the pellets were made of corn sold by the Co-Op to Stevenson's," Aitkins revealed.

"When did this supposedly take place?"

"In March."

LeFaive pondered a response.

"You're not after the Co-Op on this?"

"No way. The case against Stevenson's is set for trial on Monday. We're only interested in finding out whether Stevenson's knew the condition of the corn they used to make the pellets."

"How do you know the stuff that your guy got originated at Mueller's?"

"We don't," Aitkins admitted. "We've got some hunches. Mueller verified the stuff he sold you was crap, very wet, and sprouting mold. He also verified that you weren't anxious to buy it but that you thought it would be safe enough if it was mixed and not used for breeding animals."

The little Quebecois stroked his left cheek with his left hand. There was bustle and commotion around them but the elevator manager remained contemplative. Their food arrived.

"I remember buying three trucks of wet corn from Dave Mueller," LeFaive affirmed. "I think he sold some of the same crop to another elevator. But the stuff I bought, it was shit. I told him so. I told him I'd try to cut it or sell it elsewhere but that I would not sell it to anyone using it as feed for breeding animals. I ended up selling five truckloads of wet corn, including the three from Mueller, to Stevenson's Grand Forks plant. Norm Vekich, their buyer, paid me exactly what I had paid Mueller and the other farmers for the shit," the manager explained between bites of scrambled eggs and ham.

"Here's the thing," Aitkins explained, "we think Stevenson's used that stuff in their pellets. We're missing a connector. We don't have a manifest or an invoice from them linking the Mueller corn to the pellets our client bought.

"Sorry, there's no way I'd have access to that information," the Canadian replied.

"Shit," the lawyer said.

"Daniel," Buckvold admonished in mock upset. "Watch your language around the ladies."

340

"But you'd be willing to testify that, in a general sense, you supplied Stevenson's with wet corn earlier in the year, corn that you warned their buyer should not be used for pregnant animals?" Aitkins asked.

"That I can do, as long as it's clear your clients aren't coming after me."

The attorney and the investigator finished their food, stood up, and shook hands with the French-Canadian.

"Thanks for your help, Mr. LeFaive. I'll give you a call but you can expect to take the stand sometime on Tuesday afternoon. I've got Mr. Vekich set to testify that Stevenson's purchased only dry, fusarium-free corn for their plant in Grand Forks. I'll put you on the stand right after Mueller to say how that ain't so."

"One thing, barrister," LeFaive said, using the Canadian term for litigator, his tone soft yet firm.

"Yes?"

"I'll want your client's promise not to sue me in writing before I take the witness stand. Don't much care about the rest of it, seeing as how I retired last year, when Stevenson's bought out Northern Dakota Farmers Cooperative and made me a pensioner."

LeFaive smiled and nodded slightly as he resumed his place in the booth to finish his eggs.

CHAPTER 68

Billy Wilson, the teenager who had worked for the Co-Op on the loading dock the day Mueller's three truckloads of wet corn came in, had disappeared. There were no "Wilson's" in the Larimore area. Billie was a dead end. Even Alison Buckvold's considerable skip-tracing abilities would not be able to find the kid in time for trial. Daniel Aitkins and Alison Buckvold moved on.

Martin Trucking was located in Niagara, North Dakota, sixteen miles west of Larimore on US Highway 2. Danny filled up the gas tank of the Ranger at the Larimore Cooperative beneath a sheltering winter sky. He paid for the fuel and brought the truck up through the gears as he and Alison headed out to meet Marge Martin.

He'd broken protocol and called the trucker in advance, just to make sure she wasn't out on a run. She was a local hauler, not over-the-road, so even if she wasn't in the shop, it was likely she'd be around sometime during the day. But Daniel got lucky. She was at her shop and had time to meet with the attorney.

"Mr. Aitkins, I presume," the female driver said, offering an oil-stained hand in greeting as Danny and Alison alighted from the Ford.

Martin was, as Mueller had described her, a large woman. Her hair was cropped short, giving her a distinctly masculine appearance. She wore no make-up, no jewelry of any kind save for a diamond engagement ring and a gold wedding band.

"Pleased to meet you, Ms. Martin," Aitkins said.

"It's Mrs. But you can call me Marge."

There was an odd enthusiasm in the trucker's voice.

"I'm Alison Buckvold," Aitkins' companion indicated, shaking the hand of the other woman, returning the strength of the grip.

"Hey, that's some handshake, lady," Marge admitted.

"We're here to see you about..." Danny attempted to say.

"I know, I know. Stevenson's, the slimy bastards. Dave Mueller called me right after you left his place. Said you might be out to see me."

"You don't have much use for Stevenson's?" Aitkins asked, puzzled by the trucker's opening salvo against the Canadian grain concern.

"You ain't heard the half of it. They screwed me out of a big contract with the Northern Dakota Farmers Co-Op. I had the contract on the Co-Op's twenty-seven elevators. Did you know that Stevenson's owns its own trucking company? Up until a month ago, I hauled everything in the Dakotas for Northern. Stevenson's bought 'em out and bounced me right out the door. Cost six of my drivers their jobs. I had to idle six of my trucks. But the bank hasn't idled the payments on my rigs. I'm in a world of hurt because of those assholes."

They were headed towards the yard office, a mere shack of a structure tucked against a large metal pole building that served as the outfit's garage. Tractors and trailers, all bearing *Martin Trucking...We're Mean Mother Truckers, Niagara, N.D.*, stood silent under an open sky. There were no trees in the yard. A single-wide mobile home stood alone behind the gravel parking lot.

A teenaged boy, his body shape an exact replica of the trucker's, stood beneath a doorway, inspecting the diesel motor of an International truck, as they passed by.

"Todd, you get that damn thing running by tomorrow night, you hear me?" the woman grumbled.

"No problem, ma. It'll be running by tonight."

"Where's your father?" Marge asked.

"He went into town. Said he needed to buy some cigs," the boy answered as he climbed up the front bumper of the rig and went back to tinkering.

Inside the office of the trucking company, Marge Martin took a seat behind an old desk. The wood of the furniture was stained from petroleum products. Stacks of invoices and receipts covered the writing surface of the desk. The walls were covered with calendars displaying muscular men, attractive men, their torsos lean, bare, and suntanned.

"I like your taste in decorating," Alison Buckvold observed as she sat down in a distressed chair and studied the eye candy.

"Thanks. My hubbie isn't crazy about 'em but a girl's got a right to dream, don't she?"

"Ladies, can we remove our eyes from those disgusting posters and concentrate on why we're here?" Aitkins asked in mock upset.

"You're sure no fun, Mr. Lawyer," Marge squeaked.

"Got that right, Marge. Danny's the least fun person I know," Buckvold chimed in.

"So why are you here, Mr. Aitkins?" the trucker queried.

"Danny. Call me Danny."

"Fine."

"Did Mueller share anything with you?"

"A bit. Said you're OK, that you're not interested in starting a commotion with me, that you've got some lawsuit coming up against Stevenson's over bad feed your client bought from them. Hurt some pigs, was the way Mueller told it."

"That's right. Moldy corn wiped out their entire farrowing."

"That's a shame but I could've predicted it. The stuff I was hauling from Northern to Stevenson's production mill in Grand Forks last spring, stuff that the local elevators wouldn't use, was all

343

crap. Wetter than my hair after a shower," the woman observed, running her thick fingers through the stumpy residue of her follicles like a beauty pageant contestant.

Buckvold laughed. Aitkins missed the point.

"What we need is some connection between the stuff Mueller sold to the Co-Op and the pellets manufactured by Stevenson's and sold to my clients."

Martin studied the attorney with blazing blue eyes.

"When did your folks get their stuff from Stevenson's?"

"First week of April."

"Well, I wouldn't have any documents showing what you want to prove, if that's what you're looking for. All I have are the invoices from the elevators to Stevenson's. What they do with the stuff after I deliver it, I have no record of that."

A wave of disappointment crossed the attorney's face.

"Do your records show the moisture content of the corn you picked up and delivered?"

"Nope."

Martin handed Buckvold a thick stack of bills of lading for the period in question. The investigator scrutinized the details of the battered documents, the pages stained with food, motor oil, and fingerprints.

"Danny, I think this can still work," the investigator said with an air of excitement.

"What do you mean?"

"Marge, how many other trucking company's were making deliveries to Stevenson's Grand Forks mill during the last few weeks of February and the month of March?"

"None. The mill was only operating one shift. There was a temporary layoff. Vekich was buying only enough corn to run one shift, and my trucks, because I had the Northern contract, and because Northern was the only one supplying the mill during the lull, were the only ones bringing in corn for the pellet plant."

"That's it, then," Alison said, nodding significantly.

"What's your point?" Aitkins asked, truly puzzled.

"Ma'am, would you feel comfortable telling the folks on the jury that every last load of corn you delivered to Stevenson's during the time frame in question was wet?"

Marge paused to consider the request.

"Darn tooten. That's the God's honest truth of it. I saw the stuff, smelled it, and felt it with my own little fingers. That corn was wet as cooked spaghetti."

The lawyer finally caught on.

"We don't need to trace the exact load of pellets sold to the Andersons back to Mueller's corn," Aitkins said.

"Now you're getting it, Daniel my man," the investigator added.

Margery smiled and revealed that she understood her role.

"If every last load delivered to the plant sucked, the stuff sold to your client also sucked," the trucker advanced, her manner of speaking making it clear she was itching for a fight.

CHAPTER 69

Monday morning. The lawyer watched winter from a bedroom window. His wife slept soundly as he pulled on a pair of black wool-blend trousers, tucked the tail of a light blue dress shirt into the waistband of the pants, and negotiated a black leather belt through the loops of the slacks. A black and white tie bearing an image of Rhett and Scarlet from *Gone with the Wind* hung around his neck.

Outside, a remorseful sun climbed above the trees. The livestock remained inside the pole building, content to hunker down until the day warmed. Snowdrifts flowed across the fields, softening the landscape's demeanor.

Daniel couldn't eat. He'd spent the better part of the night tossing and turning on the basement couch. There were more questions to be answered, more links in the chain to be connected. But he'd run out of time.

The lawyer arrived at the Becker County Courthouse before seven-thirty. The front door was unlocked. Earl Bethard, Judge Davidson's bailiff, watched Aitkins approach the entrance with a two-wheeled dolly loaded with files and loose-leaf notebooks. The ex-cop opened the door for the lawyer.

"Morning, Mr. Aitkins. Quite a load you got there."

"Yep. Trial day."

Bethard lifted the front end of the conveyance up the stairs.

"I know. I'm gonna bailiff for Judge Enwright. We're using the big courtroom upstairs. Judge Davidson is on vacation for the next three weeks. Lucky stiff's in Jamaica."

I wish that's where I was, Aitkins thought.

The attorney pushed the heavily laden dolly across the smooth floor of the courthouse lobby.

"You need some help with that?" the retired lawman asked.

"I think I've got it."

"I'll go get the coffee started. The lights in the courtroom are already on."

Danny was comforted that no one else was in the courtroom. He stopped in front of the counsel table closest to the jury box, his favored position, and began to organize his trial materials.

Three yellow legal pads. Three black felt markers. Two jumbo markers, one black, one red for writing on the white board for the benefit of the jurors. A solar powered calculator. A stapler, staples, and paper clips. Post-it notes in three sizes and two colors. He arranged all of the supplies so that he had quick access to the materials he'd need during the heat of battle. A copy of the Minnesota Rules, including the Rules of Civil Procedure and Evidence, the pages crumpled, the cover ragged from use, was placed next to the yellow pads. Five three ring binders with blue

346

covers, containing pleadings, discovery materials, exhibits, witness statements, depositions, outlines for the questioning of each witness, outlines of voir dire questions for potential jurors, and his opening statement, were lined up in front of Daniels's chair, forming an impervious wall of documents.

A door opened.

"Hi, Dan."

Dee Dee Hernesman, her hair freshly cut, wearing a smart charcoal colored business suit, stepped into the solitude of Aitkins' preparation.

"Hey, Dees."

The woman stood next to her partner.

"Need anything?"

"A cup of coffee would be nice. Earl claims that he's gonna make fresh stuff," Danny said.

"I could use some too. I'll see what I can find."

The woman wandered out the door in search of the bailiff.

Aitkins felt a sudden urgency to use the restroom. He moved quickly to answer nature's call.

"Good morning, Aitkins," F.W. Barnes said as the elder barrister approached Judge Davidson's courtroom through the courthouse lobby at a measured pace.

"Hello, Frank," the younger lawyer offered as he passed by. If the older man was upset at Daniel's use of his first name, F.W. didn't let on.

"Beautiful day to try a lawsuit, I'd say," Barnes responded, his arms weighed down by two large box-style briefcases.

Aitkins didn't answer his adversary.

Danny removed his suit coat and sat on the toilet. He held an outline of his opening statement in one hand and studied the document. It was all there. The entirety of his case. He'd followed Horace Brewster's admonition. The Andersons bought feed. Their pigs seemed healthy. They were fed the feed. They aborted. A pathway of logic linked the destruction of his client's pigs to Stevenson's. That was the story he would tell through the witnesses. That was the path he would coax seven jurors down.

Thompson had not arrived when Aitkins re-entered the courtroom. What he saw when he stepped across the threshold shocked him.

"What the hell do you think you're doing?" Dan Aitkins asked as he approached the counsel tables.

"Seems someone took my traditional spot, first table, first chair by the jury box," F.W. Barnes replied, never removing his eyes from a file folder he was studying as he sat at what had previously been Aitkins' chosen place in the courtroom.

347

"You can't move my stuff, you pompous arrogant ass," the young lawyer hissed.

"I certainly can. And I did," Barnes replied.

Daniel reached across the old man, flicked his hand in front of Barnes' face, and sent a pile of papers fluttering to the floor.

"What do you think you're doing?" Barnes objected, his voice carefully modulated. "Stop acting like a spoiled child."

Aitkins contemplated striking the man in the face.

"What seems to be the problem, gentlemen?" Judge Enwright asked as she appeared from behind a door leading to Judge Davidson's chambers.

"Barnes is playing a fucking little game," Aitkins advised, attempting to retrieve the curse word as it flew off his tongue.

"Watch your language, Mr. Aitkins. What's the story, Frank?"

"Aitkins improperly placed his materials on the defense table. I simply moved his files and supplies to their appropriate place."

Enwright's face wrinkled in a pained expression.

"That's it? That's what this is all about?"

Danny rotated his neck before speaking. Vertebrae cracked audibly in the desolate air of the courtroom.

"Judge, I apologize for the four letter word. It's just that I was here at seven-thirty and had all my stuff set up. I went to the bathroom and when I came back, Frankie here had taken it upon himself to re-arrange everything."

Enwright stepped up to the bench. She towered over the men.

"We haven't even commenced trial and already the bullshit starts? Mr. Barnes, so far as I know, and I do believe this to be true whether we're in my courtroom or Judge Davidson's, there are no assigned seats for lawyers. It's first come, first served."

The jurist's face glowered as she continue.

"I take it you'd agree that Mr. Aitkins had his stuff here first?"

The older man's eyes filled with scorn. He was dangerously close to saying something offensive to the female jurist. His years of experience took over and reined his emotions in.

"Yes."

"Then move your crap to the other table and put Mr. Aitkins' material back in exactly the same order you found it. What are you two, little kids? Christ, I hope this isn't a taste of how this whole case is going to go," the judge muttered as she walked back through the door to Davidson's private office.

Barnes removed his files and notebooks and placed them on the other table. He made no attempt to return Aitkins' belongings to their place of origin. Rather than incur the wrath of the judge by renewing his complaints, Aitkins retrieved his property and rearranged it in its original space.

Dee Dee Hernesman entered the courtroom bearing two tall Styrofoam cups. F.W. Barnes completed his task and left as the woman arrived. The attorneys nodded but exchanged no pleasantries.

"You look pissed," the female attorney observed as she handed Danny his coffee. "So does Barnes. Not so much as a 'hello' from the old coot."

"Fuckin' Barnes," Danny seethed.

"That's his stuff?" Hernesman asked, nodding slightly towards the second counsel table.

"Yeah. He moved all my shit and started putting his crap here, like he owned the Goddamned courthouse."

"You're kidding."

"Nope."

"What'd you do?"

Aitkins looked up and gave her a tired grin.

"I tossed his shit on the floor."

"You didn't."

"Yep. That was the upside. The downside was that Harriet heard the ruckus and stuck her head in the door. She wasn't too happy with us."

Dee Dee laughed.

"Little boys. When do they grow up?"

"Hey, would you let him pull that shit?"

The woman's eyes closed as she thought.

"No. But I think I would have been a little more subtle in my response."

"Whatever. It's done with. This coffee is good. I'm pretty sure Earl didn't make it," Aitkins said, pointing to a label on the cup.

"It's hazel nut mocha. From 'The Bottomless Cup'".

"That tourist trap? I can't believe you're into the latte' scene."

Hernesman sat on the edge of the table and dangled her feet. She sipped mocha and pursed her lips as hot liquid touched her tongue.

"Generally, I'm not. But I took one look at that tarry mess Bethard created and knew that you'd never make it through the day if you drank that brew. You're already wired to the max."

"And this," Daniel said, pointing to his cup, "is better?"

"Half and half. Only fifty percent of the caffeine."

At that moment, James Thompson, Malachi Stone, F.W. Barnes, Ralph Covington, and Jason Billington walked into the courtroom.

"Hello, Mr. Aitkins," Thompson extolled, reaching across Stone's body to offer his hand.

"Good morning, Jim," Aitkins replied, returning the defense attorney's handshake.

"Nice to see you again, ma'am," the big man observed.

"Same here, Mr. Thompson."

The defense entourage opened their briefcases and deposited papers and books across the surface of the table.

"I think we'll need to have Billington and Covington sit behind us in the first row of spectator seating," Thompson noted quietly. "We're going to be cramped up here as it is."

Aitkins took in the broad shoulders of his adversary. The man was dressed in a thousand dollar custom made double breasted black suit, flawlessly polished black loafers with little tassels, matching argyle stockings, a luminous white dress shirt, and a conservative tie. Thompson sat down a fragile oak chair behind the counsel table. His form occupied most of the available space allotted to the defense team.

"Any movement from your people?" Thompson asked, his eyes never leaving his legal pad as he studied his notes.

Aitkins answered curtly.

"None."

"Eighty-five thousand dollars is a lot of money," the defense lawyer said.

"Not enough."

Big Jim Thompson smiled.

"I expected you'd say that. I guess that's why we have juries."

Daniel nodded. The door to the courtroom opened again. His clients had arrived.

CHAPTER 70

"**Judge**, you can't allow Pavo Tynjala to testify," Aitkins urged as the attorneys sat around a conference table in Judge Davidson's chambers before jury selection. The lawyer's were arguing various pre-trial or "in limine" motions prior to seating the jury panel.

"Your honor, I understand what Mr. Aitkins is saying. He's right that there is a danger that Mr. Tynjala might try to have his case against the Andersons, a case already in suit and in the beginning stages of discovery, heard as part of this proceeding. That is a danger," Thompson admitted. "But the court must balance that potentiality with the reality that one of our key defenses in this case involves the findings of Dr. Bronski and Dr. Kelly Long of the University of Illinois. Our experts are prepared to testify that the Anderson swine herd was infected with haemophilus pleural pneumonia on the day of the abortion storm and that HPP is a known cause of fetal distress and abortion in swine."

"I'll give you that, Mr. Thompson," Judge Enwright agreed. "I understand the defense in that respect. But why is it essential to your theory of the case to have Tynjala take the stand and tell his tale of woe to this jury, when he'll undoubtedly do that in his own case, during his own trial, sometime down the road?" the judge asked.

"I can handle that," F.W. Barnes interjected.

Thompson's face drew. A wave of upset clouded his features. The African-American lawyer restrained himself and allowed his cohort to speak.

"Mr. Tynjala will testify that, despite the protestations of the plaintiffs that their swine are asymptomatic and clear of HPP, when he purchased swine from an auction house, swine that came from the Anderson place, and introduced them into his farrow to finish operation, HPP broke out and essentially bankrupted him," Barnes professed. "That belies the Andersons' testimony that HPP was no longer present at the time of the alleged abortions, or if it was, it was inconsequential. Tynjala bought his pigs two weeks before the alleged incident on the Anderson Farm."

"Your honor. It's clear that what the defense is trying to do is to muddy the waters. If you let Tynjala testify as to his claim, then the jury is really trying two cases. The case of the Andersons vs. Stevenson's and the case of Tynjala vs. the Andersons. To require the plaintiffs to defend against an unrelated lawsuit during this trial isn't fair. It'll also confuse the jury," Danny Aitkins argued.

Harriet Enwright sat behind Clement Davidson's desk. She wore a flowered dress; a faint blue pattern set against a field of yellow. Her manner was serious. Her fingers tapped out an uneasy cadence against the desk as she considered the arguments. She cleared her voice and spoke.

"Mr. Aitkins, I believe the court can limit the testimony of Mr. Tynjala and prevent any unfairness to your clients. The defense is entitled to call him for the limited purpose of buttressing Stevenson's claim that there was active HPP in the Anderson herd at the time of the abortion storm. Whether or not that's the cause of the abortions he sustained is for the jury. But to that limited extent, Tynjala will be allowed to testify."

Aitkins' shoulders slumped.

"Any other motions?"

"Judge, we have our own motion to exclude testimony," F.W. Barnes advised.

"And that would be...?" Judge Enwright asked.

"It seems that Aitkins has pulled somewhat of a fast one on the court."

All eyes veered towards Barnes.

"How so?" the judge inquired.

"There are four names on the witness list that were never disclosed prior to the final witness list being filed."

The judge's eyes slid slightly to one side to take in Danny Aitkins and Dee Dee Hernesman.

"Is that true, Mr. Aitkins?"

The plaintiffs' lawyer swallowed hard.

"That's true, your honor. However, there's an explanation for the late disclosure."

"With all due respect, Judge Enwright, there can't be any reasonable explanation for disclosing material witnesses a week before trial," Barnes interrupted.

James Thompson allowed the white-haired litigator to continue. There was no sign that the black man had any idea what F.W. was talking about.

"Mr. Aitkins?" the judge asked.

"I can handle this," Dee Dee Hernesman advised.

"Please do."

"There are four names that were never divulged before. That's because they are rebuttal witnesses, to be called in rebuttal to testimony we believe will be offered by Mr. Norman Vekich of Stevenson's. Mr. Vekich's testimony, at least as outlined in the deposition that I took of him, is that Stevenson's Grand Forks mill purchased only dry corn during the essential time period. These names are folks who will testify that, insofar as particular corn sold to Stevenson's by the Northern Dakota Farmer's Cooperative in Larimore, North Dakota, that isn't true. And we're not talking about four witnesses. We could only find three of them."

"Which ones?" the court asked with a hint of interest.

"LeFaive, Martin, and Mueller. The other young man, Billy Wilson, isn't available."

"Mr. Barnes?"

F.W. bit the skin of his lower lip. Aitkins studied the older man and watched the defense lawyer consider a response. The information to be provided by the rebuttal witnesses was in the possession of Stevenson's and had been for some time. But it had never been disclosed, as required, to the plaintiffs. Barnes was treading on thin ice if he wanted to push a challenge. The old man's bravado shocked the younger attorney.

"Well, your honor. I'd like to know how it is that Mr. Aitkins and Ms. Hernesman came by this information. It seems to me that it's something that should have been revealed to the defense long ago. It might have precipitated more serious settlement discussions, though it appears that what some lay witnesses perceive to be important may be totally irrelevant."

"Irrelevant? How so?"

"Judge, let's suppose that these three do testify that one load, or two loads, or ten loads of corn bought by Stevenson's was wet. That doesn't prove that the corn used to manufacture the pellets sold to the Andersons came from those loads. Indeed, I am certain that Mr. Vekich will testify that if wet corn was purchased, it was used for other products, products directed to non-breeding livestock where fusarium would not be a significant issue."

"That's an interesting position. What about the relevance, Ms. Hernesman?" the judge asked.

"I think you need to hear Mr. Vekich's testimony and then, at that time, I'd be prepared to make an offer of proof in terms of rebuttal. Before these three take the stand, but after Vekich has completed his testimony, I'd outline their testimony for the court out of the hearing of the jury. I'm certain that the court will be satisfied that the information being offered is relevant," Hernesman concluded.

"Fair enough. Mr. Thompson, your comments?"

Big Jim cast a gaze of reproach towards Malachi Stone and F.W. Barnes. It was clear to Aitkins and Hernesman that the lead defense attorney had no idea what was going on.

"I'm interested in learning how Ms. Hernesman came to possess the names of these folks. So far as I'm aware, it's information that even our own investigator, Mr. Morgan, didn't uncover," Thompson advised.

Silence enveloped the room. Malachi Stone's great thighs began to shake. Barnes maintained an innocent look.

"That's something I can address," Aitkins indicated, drawing his face into a picture of credibility before speaking.

The lawyer knew he was a terrible liar and that, in most instances, he would be found out. There was considerable concentration on his brow as he sought to convey a falsehood.

"I found the names on documents that Dee Dee and I ran across when we were in Winnipeg. I jotted the names on a yellow pad and..."

"And I recently found Dan's notes in the investigative portion of our file and followed up on them," Hernesman added, her eyes glaring with steady defiance at Stone.

"Well, given that, I'll reserve judgment on whether these three witnesses testify or not until after Mr. Vekich has told his story. I'm a little troubled by the fact that these names were floating around in the plaintiffs' file before anyone thought to investigate what the folks had to say. Any change in the defendant's settlement position in light of this potential new testimony, Mr. Thompson?"

Thompson studied the face of Stevenson's Customer Service Manager, Mr. Billington. The big man scrutinized Malachi Stone. There was a palpable sense that Thompson wanted to say something disparaging. The opportunity to do so passed. The lawyer simply shook his head.

"Very well, let's go pick a jury," Judge Enwright said, rising to her feet, indicating that the case was now ready for trial.

CHAPTER 71

He hadn't thought about her during the early morning hours. His mind was thoroughly occupied by the details of trial preparation. When the red haired woman walked through the doors of the courtroom in the Becker County Courthouse, all of the angst, pain, and sordid details of their connection flooded over him. Daniel noted that Melanie's left wrist was out of the cast. Her facial bruising was covered by makeup. In every way, Melanie Barnes appeared to have recovered from the injuries she sustained in the car accident.

"What the hell is wrong with you?" Dee Dee asked, noting that her partner's hands trembled uncontrollably as he sat in a chair behind the counsel table waiting for Judge Enwright to enter the courtroom.

Aitkins shook his head.

"For Chrissakes, Danny. The jury is ready to come in. The Andersons will be coming back from coffee. What in God's name has come over you?"

He offered no response.

Dee Dee scanned the confines of the room. A young male reporter from *The Gazette* was the only spectator. The Anderson children sat quietly in seats immediately behind their lawyers. Nancy and Dean Anderson were working their way cautiously towards two empty chairs at the counsel table. Hernesman focused on the defense team. There was no mistaking Melanie Barnes's profile.

"Oh, now I see what's bugging you. An attack of post-coital guilt, eh? Get over it. We've got a job to do. Our clients are about to sit down next to us and entrust their lives to us. Deal with your personal problems on your own time. Understand?"

Hernesman protected her words but there was harshness in her admonition. Aitkins nodded. Potential jurors filed into the courtroom.

"That's better," Dee Dee whispered.

"All rise," Bethard announced. "District Court for the State of Minnesota, County of Becker is now in session, the Honorable Harriet Enwright presiding."

The judge entered the courtroom and took her seat behind the bench.

"Good morning," the jurist said with a sincere smile. "Please be seated."

The judge took a sip of water before continuing.

"Ladies and gentlemen, you're here as potential jurors in the case of Anderson's vs. Stevenson's Sci-Swine. Before we go any further, I'll have the court clerk, Mr. Olson; swear all of you in as possible members of the jury."

Mark Olson rose. The jurors did the same. Olson raised his right hand, commanding the citizens present to follow his lead. The clerk read the oath and the members of the panel resumed their seats.

"Very well," Judge Enwright said. "Soon the attorney's will question you, during what we call 'voir dire' (which the court pronounced 'vor dear') with an eye towards picking seven of you to serve as jurors. However, before counsel does that, I have some preliminary information and a few opening questions for all of you."

The judge proceeded to advise that the case involved a civil lawsuit regarding a claim for damages brought by the plaintiffs against the defendant. Judge Enwright introduced the attorneys and the parties. She asked the panel if any of the folks knew the attorneys or the participants. No one raised a hand. Eleven names were called. Eleven potential jurors took their seats in the jury box. It was then up to the lawyers to inquire, beginning with Jim Thompson.

During questioning by counsel, either side has the right to contest the seating of a juror who expresses bias, prejudice, or any other automatic basis for disqualification. No jurors were excused from service by Judge Enwright for cause, though several such challenges were raised by the attorneys.

At the conclusion of voir dire, the attorneys studied the list of eleven names. The parties had two strikes each; they were allowed to remove two potential jurors without cause, without giving a reason.

Aitkins was troubled. There were three people that he didn't want on the jury. One was a claims investigator for National Indemnity and Casualty Insurance Company. Dan didn't know the man but by virtue of the adjuster's body language, eye contact, and his likely bias against awarding substantial damages, the lawyer knew the man had to be stricken.

Daniel's second problem was a woman. Mrs. Eunice Johnston indicated that she felt the American Civil Justice System promoted unfounded litigation; that bogus lawsuits, such as the McDonald's coffee cup claim, were rampant, destroying the financial strength of the country. Try as he would to have her admit she could not fairly sit in judgment on the Andersons with such pent up feelings of animas, the woman refused to confess that she couldn't be fair. Had she been more honest, Judge Enwright would have granted Aitkins' motion to strike the female juror for cause. Because the woman wouldn't fess up, Daniel was leaning to removing her.

The final problem juror in Aitkins' mind was Donald Blomquist. Blomquist was a farmer, a shareholder in a local Cooperative elevator, and, worst of all in Daniel's estimation, a Minnesota State trooper. Blomquist was tight-lipped in his interaction with the attorneys and seemed reluctant to state his opinions on most topics. The fact that Blomquist was employed in law enforcement, a profession prone to its own share of civil suits for car chases gone bad and civil rights violations, was further reason to remove the man. But the adjuster and the conservative woman were far more dangerous. Despite his intuition that leaving Blomquist on would likely prove to be his undoing, with full knowledge that the lawman's resolute personality would likely lead to his election as the jury foreperson, Danny had no choice but to accept the man. He was the least dangerous of the three.

"I don't like leaving the Trooper on," Aitkins whispered to Dean Anderson as he struck the insurance adjuster and the woman from the roster. "But these two are worse."

Dean Anderson studied the names.

"I agree. Those two would cook our goose."

Aitkins handed the sheet to James Thompson who noted the plaintiffs' strikes. When the names were whittled down to seven, the list was handed to Judge Enwright. The judge noted the strikes on her copy of the form and handed the original to Mr. Olson.

"The clerk will now read the names of those selected to serve as jurors in this case. When you hear your name, please stand and raise your right hand."

Seven folks, including Donald Blomquist, took a second oath relating to their service as jurors. Judge Enwright dismissed the four folks removed from the panel and the citizens remaining in the audience who had not been selected for service. The seven members of the jury were issued writing tablets and pencils for taking notes. Judge Enwright gave the jurors a series of preliminary instructions, delineating most importantly that the jurors were to be the judges of honesty and credibility and that she was the judge of the law.

"Because it's nearly eleven thirty, we'll take our lunch break at this time," Judge Enwright announced at the end of her instructions. "The jurors are reminded not to speak to anyone about this case. You're not investigators. Don't go out seeking evidence or information about this matter. Your decision in this lawsuit must be based upon the testimony and evidence you hear and see in this courtroom and not from other sources. We'll see you back here at one o'clock, at which time, the attorneys will present their opening statements."

Trooper Blomquist rose. Aitkins looked at the officer. As the lawman passed the counsel table, there was no question in Daniel Aitkins' mind that he'd made a terrible mistake by keeping the aloof Trooper on the jury.

CHAPTER 72

"So that your testimony is clear here today, Mr. Vekich, you're absolutely certain that Stevenson's Grand Forks Mill, where you are the primary grain buyer, was only purchasing dry Number One corn for the period during which the pelleted feed sold to my clients was manufactured?" Dee Dee Hernesman asked.

Vekich, a swarthy little man with long black hair and a goatee, nodded his head.

"That's right. That's what I'm saying."

Dee Dee opened a copy of the witness' deposition and sought to compare his answer at trial with his prior testimony. Before Hernesman could nail the man, Vekich squirmed in his seat ever-so-slightly and added a caveat.

"There's a possibility we purchased some corn that wasn't Number One grade during that time frame. In fact, I'm sure we did. I haven't checked all our records to determine how much. But I know this: none of our pelleted feed contained moldy corn. That's a guaranty from yours truly."

Hernesman leaned back in her chair and closed her eyes. She knew better than to fight with Vekich, to give him the satisfaction of losing her cool. She was tired. The lawyers had given their opening statements before Vekich took the stand. The female litigator had questioned him for less than forty-five minutes. And yet, it had been mentally vexing work.

"Nothing further," Hernesman conceded.

"Your witness, Mr. Thompson."

Big Jim rose regally from his chair. The oak seat groaned as the attorney stood.

"We'll reserve our direct examination of this witness for our case in chief, your honor."

Judge Enwright turned to the jury panel.

"Ladies and gentlemen of the jury. Ms. Hernesman called Mr. Vekich as a witness under our Rules of Procedure. Mr. Thompson has indicated he may ask Mr. Vekich additional questions when the defense puts in its case."

The judge turned her steady gaze on the witness.

"You're excused for now, Mr. Vekich."

The witness departed the stand.

"It's almost three-thirty. Because the attorneys and I have some things to go over, we'll recess testimony until eight-thirty tomorrow morning. I'll see the lawyer's back in chambers. Be assured that we are working on the case long after you folks leave for home. And as before, ladies and gentlemen, don't talk to anyone about this case. Don't read about it in the paper or listen to it on the news. Don't try to be investigators."

A wry smile passed over the jurist's lips.

"Especially you, Trooper Blomquist, even though you may be sorely tempted to put your detective skills to use."

Everyone in the courtroom laughed save Donald Blomquist. The law enforcement officer simply shook his head affirmatively.

"I understand, judge," he replied without a hint of gaiety.

"That was a joke, officer," the judge added.

"I knew that," Blomquist said stiffly as he stepped down from the jury box, his eyes focused straight ahead as if he were on parade.

A puzzled look crossed Judge Enwright's face as she stared at the cop.

Very odd fellow," she thought.

"Let's hear the arguments concerning whether Mrs. Martin should be allowed to testify," Harriet Enwright advised as the attorneys resumed their seats in Davidson's chambers.

Angie Devlin, the judge's court reporter, sat at her stenography machine. Her earrings, large orbs of significant color, hung heavy from her earlobes. There was a look of frustration on the woman's face. She sighed, impatient for the attorneys to begin.

"Your honor, the three witnesses will, if allowed to testify, provide the jury with a sufficient basis to establish that Stevenson's purchased moisture-infected corn during the period in question. That corn was used in the manufacture of the pellets sold to our clients," Hernesman began. "In order, Mr. Mueller will testify that he sold three loads of soggy corn, with a moisture content in excess of nineteen percent, to Northern Dakota Farmer's Cooperative. He'll testify that he and Mr. LeFaive, the supervisor at Northern, checked the grain and found that it was tainted with fusarium as determined by black light inspection. Mueller will verify that he and LeFaive discussed the fact that the corn could not be used as feed for gestating livestock.

Mr. LeFaive will then testify that he sold five loads of 'hot' or wet corn to Stevenson's during the weeks before and after the likely production date of the pellets in question. Vekich already testified that a batch of hog feed would last two weeks at the Mill. We know the delivery date of the shipment from Stevenson's to their Detroit Lakes elevator so we know the approximate date of manufacture. LeFaive will testify that he spoke to Vekich about the dangers of using the wet corn sold to Stevenson's as food for gestating livestock. LeFaive will state that Vekich knew that the corn should not be used as feed for pregnant animals.

Finally, Mrs. Martin will testify that she was the exclusive hauler for Northern and that hers was the only trucking company supplying grain to Stevenson's Grand Forks plant during the time frame at issue. She'll also testify, from her personal observations, that every load she delivered to Stevenson's contained wet corn. She'll verify that the corn she delivered to Stevenson's included product grown by Mueller and shipped via Martin to Northern, stuff that Northern could not use and sold to Stevenson's. She will supply first hand testimony that establishes Stevenson' Grand Forks Mill had only one line, the pelleting line, in operation during the period of time she was making these deliveries."

Hernesman folded her hands and looked directly at James Thompson.

"Mr. Thompson?" the court asked.

"I think I'll let Mr. Barnes respond. He seems to have a better understanding of this topic than I do," the big attorney said, a hint of disdain tainting his words.

"Judge, what the plaintiffs propose to do is try to prove by the indirect what they cannot prove directly. They have no way of tying the corn grown by Mueller and sold to Northern Dakota to the pellets produced by our client and sold to the plaintiffs. They have no invoice from Stevenson's by which the alleged tainted corn can be traced back to its farm of origin. This is a backhanded attempt to circumvent the Rules of Evidence. It is an invitation to speculation, something that the jury cannot be allowed to do. I would urge the court to reject all of the proffered testimony and exclude all three witnesses."

"Ms. Hernesman, Mr. Barnes seems to have hit on something there."

You bet he has, judge, Aitkins thought. *Either he or that sonofabitch Stone pocketed the invoice from the batch in question. They concealed that information just like they concealed the names of these witnesses, the assholes.*

Aitkins, having obtained the names at issue through questionable means, held his tongue.

"Judge, Mr. Barnes is correct," Hernesman agreed. "We don't have the invoice. It's interesting that we were able to find, in Stevenson' Winnipeg records, all of the invoices for the past year except the one we needed." The female attorney paused.

Barnes sought to interrupt.

"Your honor, I resent the implication..."

Hernesman ignored the intrusion and continued.

"Be that as it may, the testimony of Mrs. Martin should definitely be allowed, if for no other reason than impeachment. Vekich claims the majority of the corn he bought during the crucial period was dry as a bone. Fine. Let Mrs. Martin testify to the contrary, as set forth in my offer of proof."

"I'm inclined to agree," the jurist advised, thinking aloud as she deliberated a ruling. "I'm convinced that Mueller and LeFaive are out, that without a direct link between the pellets purchased by the Andersons through some sort of formalized 'chain of custody' if you will, their testimony will do more harm than good. It is extremely prejudicial and smacks of guess work."

"That's an enlightened view, your honor. The defendant applauds your ruling to exclude these witnesses," Stone interjected.

"Hold the accolades, Mr. Stone. Mrs. Martin can take the stand and tell the jury what she knows about purchases of wet corn during the time frame at issue as rebuttal to Mr. Vekich's testimony. He dug himself a hole. Now you'll have to help him climb out of it. Mueller and LeFaive are out; Martin is in, but only for purposes of contradicting Vekich."

"That's an evidentiary error, your honor. It's an appealable issue," Barnes lamented.

"Well, that's my decision. Let's see what the jury does with this case and if you feel the need, Frank, you can always appeal. I'll see you folks tomorrow, bright and early. Eight sharp."

It was clear that the judge was ready to go home. The attorneys left the office with dispatch.

Aitkins and Hernesman stood next to the Anderson family in the lobby of the courthouse. Danny was about to explain the day's events to his client's when a loud argument erupted between Malachi Stone and Jim Thompson. The exchange was distorted by the acoustics of the space. Despite the distortion, Danny Aitkins became convinced of one thing: Whatever happened to the missing invoice, Big Jim apparently shared Aitkins' suspicion that the document's disappearance wasn't the product of mere chance.

CHAPTER 73

The courtroom gallery filled with the curious on the second day of testimony. Dean Anderson began to recognize faces in the modest crowd of spectators, faces of men that had been out at his farm on the day of the auction, men who had arrived on the big yellow bus with Eli Bremer. Marge Martin was testifying, enduring steady questioning by the defense, as the day unfolded.

"Mrs. Martin, you're not the biggest fan of Stevenson's Sci-Swine, right?" James Thompson postulated. The advocate's voice was quiet and respectful, without any indication of animosity or antagonism.

The woman smiled. Her broad body took up most of the jury box. Her hips rubbed against the wooden side panels of the enclosure as she withheld her response.

"You might say that," she agreed.

"And that's because Stevenson's, when they took over the Northern Dakota Cooperative Elevator system, installed their trucking firm, Stevenson's Trucking, as the carrier for all of their elevators, including the Northern facilities that you once served."

"True."

"You had to lay off drivers?"

"Six."

"And support staff."

"One mechanic and a 'go-fer'."

"Gopher?"

"Parts runner. Kid that runs to get parts for the shop."

"Oh. And of course, the loss of Northern idled some of your trucks."

"Six."

Thompson smiled.

"Must have been a pretty severe blow."

"We'll get past it. I've been in business for over twenty years. I've seen worse times, I've seen better."

The big man's eyes fluttered.

"Still, you're no fan of my client."

Marge shifted uneasily in her chair.

"That's true."

Thompson took a theatrical breath.

"And that's why you're testifying here today, isn't it? To sort of settle the score?"

"Nope."

The defense lawyer knew better than to ask an open-ended question, one that would allow the witness to explain her answer.

"You're here because Stevenson's, at least to your way of thinking, somehow mistreated you when the company replaced your trucks with its own."

"Nope."

"And you're here, ready to speculate and conjure up all manner of insupportable accusations against my client simply because you were bested by Stevenson's in a business deal."

"Not true," Martin replied through a light grin.

The defense attorney knew he wasn't getting anywhere with the trucking company owner. Thompson changed the direction of his cross-examination.

"Now you're not saying that you know for certain that every load of corn delivered to Stevenson's during the time frame in question was contaminated with Mycotoxins, are you?"

"Mycotoxins?"

"You're not aware that the plaintiffs' claim in this case is that their swineherd was negatively impacted by Mycotoxins contained in feed allegedly manufactured by my client?"

"I don't know anything about Mycotoxins. And I can't say for certain that the Grand Forks mill didn't get a load or two of corn from somewhere else during that month."

"That's what I thought," Thompson said, his face tightly drawn to prevent a smile of self-satisfaction.

"But that don't really change things," the woman added.

Again, Thompson refused to bite. He ignored the open-ended nature of the woman's comment and pushed on.

"And of course you don't know what the moisture content of the so-called 'wet' corn that you say you delivered to Stevenson's was, as measured in terms of percentage, do you?"

"Nope. I only know it was wetter than the spit on the end of my tongue."

The gallery chuckled in unison.

"I appreciate the demonstrative example. But that isn't responsive to my question and I'd ask that the court instruct the jury to disregard the last portion of Mrs. Martin's testimony. It's a question she can answer 'yes' or 'no'."

Harriet Enwright lifted her ballpoint pen from the page of her courtroom minute book and looked intently into faces of the jurors.

"The last portion of the answer was not responsive and is stricken. You are advised to ignore Mrs. Martin's example and afford it no weight."

Marge Martin rolled her eyes.

"Well I never..." the trucker muttered.

"That'll be enough, Mrs. Martin. Just stick to answering Mr. Thompson's questions and things will be a lot easier," the judge commanded.

"Yes ma'am."

"So, after all is said and done, Mrs. Martin, you are here simply to express an opinion that, to your knowledge, the loads of corn that you delivered to the Grand Forks facility were, as you describe them, 'wet'?"

"Wetter than the spit on the end of my tongue," the trucker testified, asserting the same demonstrative example the court had previously redacted from the record.

"Your honor, she just inserted the very words you cautioned her were inappropriate. I'd ask..."

"Not this time, Mr. Thompson," Judge Enwright said. "You opened up the door by asking the question. In that respect, the answer is responsive and will stand."

Margery Martin turned and winked at the jurors. The entire panel except Donald Blomquist giggled.

"Your honor, she's winking at the jury," F.W. Barnes roared, leaping to his feet, oblivious to the fact that Jim Thompson was conducting the cross-examination.

"Sit down, Mr. Barnes. You're not conducting the inquiry of this witness. Mr. Thompson?"

A sheepish grin crept across the black man's wide face.

"I'm sorry, ma'am. I was reviewing my notes to figure out what my last question was. I didn't see what happened."

"Neither did I," Harriet mumbled, turning the page of her minute book to a fresh sheet of paper. "Don't wink at the jury, Mrs. Martin."

"Understood," the trucker said, closing her eyelids ever so slowly so as to avoid being chastised for a clandestine wink.

"Mr. Thompson?"

"Finally, Mrs. Martin, you can't tell us that every load of corn purchased by Mr. Vekich for use at the Grand Forks plant during the last couple of weeks of February, and the beginning of March, was contaminated with anything, can you? I mean, you conducted no scientific testing of those loads, correct?"

"That's true."

"You are not an expert in fusarium mold or the resultant Mycotoxins produced by that species, are you?"

"I haven't the vaguest idea what you just said," Mrs. Martin murmured, carefully avoiding any untoward glances in the direction of the jurors, "much less what the hell Mycotoxins are or where they come from."

"Mrs. Martin," the judge admonished.

"Sorry judge. I'm a trucker. That's how we talk."

Giggles from the audience.

"Not here, Mrs. Martin. Not in my courtroom."

"Yes ma'am. I'm sorry."

Thompson rested the tip of his marker on his legal pad.

"I believe that's all the questions I have, your honor."

"Mr. Aitkins, re-direct?"

"Briefly."

Danny looked intently at the jurors before beginning.

"So you're a truck driver, not a scientist?"

"Yep."

"How many loads of grain, specifically corn, does your company haul in a year?"

"Whew. There'd be no way I could begin to guess."

"Ball park, Margery. A hundred?"

"Way more than that."

"A thousand?"

"At least."

"How many of them would you be the driver on?"

"About a quarter."

"So two hundred and fifty runs a year?"

"Easily."

"How many years have you personally driven rigs carrying corn to elevators and mills?"

"Twenty."

"Have the number of loads of corn that you're personally responsible for changed over the years?"

"Nope."

"They're about the same-250 loads per year."

"That's an estimate. Some years more, some years less."

"That's in excess of 5,000 truck loads of corn over the course of your career?"

"Seems about right."

"How is it that you recall, out of all those thousands of loads of corn, a few dozen trucks filled with corn delivered to Grand Forks during the months in question?"

There was a break in the exchange as the woman pondered the question.

"That's a good one," she said, her face set thoughtfully. "You might think one load would blend into another. That's normally the case. But these hoppers of corn were something I'll never forget."

Aitkins looked towards the jury box and zeroed his gaze on an elderly woman, Mrs. O'Connell, in the first row, a woman who had nodded her head in apparent agreement with every point Daniel had made up to that juncture in the trial.

"How's that?" Danny repeated.

"Like I said before, when you were asking me, I can honestly say I never smelled shit that bad, even on a hot August afternoon inside a hog barn."

"Mrs. Martin," the judge intoned, her eyes flaring, her hand reaching for Davidson's gavel.

"Sorry judge. It's just that, the smell inside those trucks, once you took off the tarps, well, it was worse than any one-holer on the prairie that I ever did my business in."

More laughter from the jurors. Aitkins noted that Trooper Blomquist was looking out a window, watching a school bus deposit kids at the end of the street. There was no sign that the juror was listening.

"What's so important about the smell?"

"Well, that's the way you can tell if it's too hot, too wet, burning up from the inside. These loads, the ones that I saw coming in, stunk of mildew to high heaven."

Aitkins picked up his notepad and stood in front of the witness.

"Mr. Vekich says that he bought only Number One dry corn and that if any wet corn was purchased by the Mill, it was an isolated load, not the norm, during the period that the pellets sold to my clients were made. What do you think of that?"

Thompson stood up.

"Judge, I object. Mr. Aitkin's is utilizing his own personal recollection of what Mr. Vekich said as a substitute for Mr. Vekich's testimony. That's improper impeachment, relying on facts not in evidence."

"Objection overruled. The jury is instructed to consider Mr. Aitkin's rendition of Mr. Vekich's testimony and evaluate it with reference to your own memories as to what Mr. Vekich said."

Mrs. Martin sat up straight and aimed her stern countenance at the jury.

"If Vekich said that, I'd say that he either has a poor memory or a selective one. It ain't the truth," she advised.

"No further questions."

James Thompson's eyes stared at the scribbling he'd accumulated on his legal pad during Margery Martin's time under oath. As he sat silently contemplating whether there was any ground left to cover, F.W. Barnes leaned over and whispered in the big man's ear with determined animation.

Thompson sat patiently, allowing Barnes to have his say. From the white haired attorney's body language, there was little question that the barrister wanted the lead defense counsel to attack other facets of the woman's version of events.

Instead of walking his impressive nose into the rhetorical right cross he knew the woman had waiting for him, Jim Thompson calmly disclosed.

"The defense has no further questions for this witness."

CHAPTER 74

There was a break in the testimony. The man and woman went for a walk. Dan Aitkins wore a black wool overcoat and black leather gloves, the calfskin of the gauntlets shiny and new, against the hostile January cold. Melanie Barnes was dressed in a tan, nearly yellow, leather coat that covered her to mid-thigh, brown wool mittens, a matching scarf, and a complimentary beret. Her hair hung loose and touched the collar of her coat as she moved. They left the Becker County Courthouse separately.

"How's it going?" the attorney asked, the expression conveying multiple meanings.

"OK. It's an interesting trial."

"Got that right. Jim Thompson tries a nice lawsuit. He's a lot more straight forward about it than your father-in-law is."

"Daniel, F.W.'s essentially a good man. He's been a lifesaver for the kids and me. You've got him pegged all wrong."

The attorney moved at the woman's pace. They walked in the direction of the Detroit Lakes Amtrak station. Tufts of white clouds drifted high above slumbering hills. Residual snow snapped under their feet, the flakes turned to ice by a week of sub-zero temperatures.

"I'm sorry I don't share your love of the man," Dan said. "Frank's the one attorney who's given me grief since I started. He's egomaniacal, bombastic and, judging from how he's handled himself in this case, slightly devious."

Melanie turned and studied her lover's face with a flash of anger.

"You of all people. The pot calling the kettle black."

Her reference to their situation and his reliance upon layers of intrigue to insulate their affair from Julie stung him like the hastening wind off the plains.

"I'll be the first to admit I've got some work to do in the individual integrity department," Daniel conceded. "But when it comes to my profession, I've never stooped to concealing evidence or pocketing relevant documents to secure a victory in court."

The woman stopped and grasped the sleeve of her companion's coat.

"What the hell are you saying?"

The attorney's blue eyes reflected the late morning sun.

"What I'm saying is that your saintly father-in-law, the pillar of Fergus Falls society, isn't above making invoices, and witnesses for that matter, disappear, when those tactics suit his needs."

"That's cheap, Daniel, making accusations about a man whose reputation is above reproach because you've never defeated him in trial."

The comment stung. Aitkins looked into Melanie's eyes, intent upon being offensive. But there was something there; vulnerability, a trace of what they had shared together, that blocked his desire to retaliate.

"You have your opinion, I have mine," he muttered with a shrug. "We better get going. The jury will be coming in."

They turned and headed back towards the Becker County Courthouse.

"When do you intend to tell Julie?" the paralegal asked, her words trailing behind them like the vapor of their breath.

"I told you, after the trial is over."

"You're sure of that? I don't want to be waddling around the grocery store, bump into her, and have to make excuses."

"I'll tell her," the lawyer responded.

"As soon as the verdict is in?"

"As soon as the verdict is in."

The courtroom was flooded with winter light. Jim Thompson stared intently at Henry Guttormson, DVM. Aitkins had finished his direct exam of the Andersons' veterinarian. Dr. Guttormson's testimony left little doubt that the abortion storm was an unusually horrific event. The Vet was succinct and straightforward, recounting how he was summoned, the very night of the abortions, by a panic-stricken Dean Anderson. Guttormson verified that he coordinated the follow-up testing and referral of the matter to Dr. Ivan Thomas at NDSU. But the Vet had not referred the Andersons to the other expert who was waiting to testify along with Thomas, Dr. Horace Brewster. That's the point at which James Thompson chose to begin his attack.

"Now Dr. Guttormson, you're familiar with a gentleman by the name of Horace Brewster?"

"Dr. Brewster? Sure, I know him."

"And he's a veterinarian, just like you?"

"He is indeed a Vet."

"You know that he is scheduled to testify, possibly today, possibly tomorrow, on behalf of the Andersons?"

"I've been told that."

"But you've never spoken with Dr. Brewster about this case?"

"Not until this morning, out in the hallway."

Thompson's mouth drew into a grin.

"Oh, you two talked about the case this morning? What did you talk about?"

Guttormson, a meagerly constructed man boasting sandy blond hair and a square, dimpled chin, smiled uncomfortably.

"He had a few basic questions about the Andersons veterinary history that he wanted to run by me. I answered the questions the best I could."

"Such as?"

"He wanted to know about the HPP outbreak and any involvement I had with the disease when the Andersons had their HPP problem several years ago."

"And what did you tell him?"

"That I came out to the farm when the HPP problem surfaced. That I recommended a vaccination program. That I made one follow-up visit after the Andersons began vaccinating the herd for HPP."

Thompson pushed his elbows back and stretched his upper arms.

"But of course, doctor, we know that the Andersons vaccination program was not the one that you recommended."

"That's true."

"You urged them to have a vaccine made from the serum, the blood of their own animals."

"True."

"But Mr. Anderson, Dean, if you will, chose a cheaper route. He purchased ready-made vaccine from a commercial supplier."

"Again, all correct."

"So he didn't do what you recommended?"

"No he didn't."

The big man tilted his head and studied his notes.

"And of course, the reason he didn't was because your suggestion was more expensive."

"I can't state what reasons were behind Mr. Anderson's decision. He used something that I didn't recommend."

"Something that, in your view as the professional hired by Mr. Anderson to give advice, was less effective?"

"Commercial vaccines aren't ineffective. It wasn't like he did nothing."

"Agreed. But he didn't do what you, the professional, suggested. And you'll agree that the commercial product was a less satisfactory alternative?"

"I'd have to say 'yes'."

"Now then, after Mr. Anderson chose to ignore your instructions, you came out to the farm on one other occasion before the abortions?"

"Correct."

"A follow-up to the HPP situation?"

"Yes."

"And during that visit, you admonished Mr. Anderson for ignoring your advice. You also found that there was still disease in the herd."

"I wouldn't say I 'admonished' Mr. Anderson. I questioned his choice. And it's true that HPP was still present, though asymptomatic, in his animals at the time of my second visit."

"So, as far as your personal observations are concerned, the last time you were on the Anderson Farm prior to the abortion event, you witnessed the presence of HPP in their herd?"

Guttormson frowned.

"That's not exactly how I'd put it."

"Your honor, that's a question that the doctor can answer yes or no. I'd ask he be instructed to do so."

Judge Enwright considered the request.

"Doctor, please answer the question with a 'yes' or a 'no'."

Guttormson looked towards the jurors.

"Yes."

"Thank you. It is true, is it not, that HPP can cause abortions in swine?"

"In relatively isolated situations."

"The answer to my question is 'yes'?"

"Yes."

"In addition, the use of fuel oil and lindane for the treatment of mange, the infection of swine by parasites, is now proscribed? It's not a good management practice, is it?"

"The literature suggests it's not the best practice."

"And in a herd infected with HPP, particularity gestational animals, the affect of fuel oil and lindane on pregnant animals exhibiting signs of pneumonia could be significant?"

"Could be."

"And the results could include, could they not, widespread abortions, feed refusal, failure to thrive, and massive loss of breeding animals?"

"I wouldn't go that far."

"But all of the things I've described have been documented as possible consequences of the use of fuel oil and lindane in already distressed swine."

"True, though not to the extent experienced here."

Thompson stood up to stretch. The mammoth defense lawyer resumed his seat.

"How many dead fetuses did you personally see out on the Anderson Farm?"

"I'm not certain."

"More than ten?"

"Yes."

"More than a hundred?"

"I couldn't say."

"You've testified that your visit to the Andersons on the evening of the abortion incident took approximately four hours?"

"That's what I remember."

You took no samples of the Andersons' well water?"

"No."

"By the way, do you know how many wells they have out there on their farm?"

"No."

"And there are water borne pathogens, germs if you like, that can also cause abortions in swine?"

"There are a couple that come to mind."

"You didn't take any tissue samples from the adult female animals from the farrowing and nursery barns?"

"Not that evening. We did some time later."

"You necropsied two sows from the farrowing barn."

"That's right."

"Necropsy being an autopsy of an animal."

"Yes."

"And when NDSU analyzed the lung tissues from those dead animals, HPP lesions were found in the samples."

"Again, correct."

Thompson slowed his pace to establish that the next series of questions would be significant.

"Did you necropsy any of the fetuses from the abortions?"

"NDSU tried."

"But there was nothing recoverable?"

"They had been trampled by the mothers into a congealed mess. There wasn't a lot one could learn from studying the tissues."

"Just so I understand, NDSU found evidence of HPP, the disease that the Andersons had in their herd long before they bought the feed at issue from my client, by virtue of necropsies of adult swine, but the university found no direct evidence of fusarium mold poisoning in the fetal tissue samples collected by Mr. Anderson at your direction."

"Yes."

Big Jim scanned his notepad. His eyes closed as he traced a thought. The attorney's eyes snapped open as if struck by a sudden inspiration.

"Are you aware sir that at least one local farmer, someone who purchased swine raised by the Andersons in the recent past, has complained that pigs originating with the Andersons contaminated his herd with HPP?"

"I've been told that."

"By whom?"

"By Mr. Aitkins and Ms. Hernesman."

"Have you been provided with the test results from that situation showing that the strain of HPP found in the other swineherd, pigs owned by a Mr. Tynjala from Wheaton, Minnesota, is the same strain of HPP found in the Andersons' pigs?"

"I was told that."

"You know Dr. Charles Bronski, don't you?"

"I know Chuck."

The veterinarian twisted in the witness box. Guttormson's eyes scanned the spectators in the courtroom until he found Bronski.

"In fact, he's sitting right out there," the Vet added, pointing to the expert in the gallery.

"You respect him as a professional?"

"He's very well credentialed."

"You'd agree that he is a world renowned expert in the field of swine nutrition and health?"

"That's one way to put it."

"Is there another way?" Thompson let his words lash out a bit, showing the jury that he was capable of toughness when a witness ad-libbed.

"I guess not. He's a much sought after consultant regarding pigs."

"Foreign governments hire him to visit their countries and make recommendations about pork production?"

Guttormson's eyes narrowed.

"And lawyers hire him to testify."

"Your honor..."

Before Judge Enwright could issue an admonishment, the veterinarian continued.

"Which is something of a specialty unto itself."

"I'd ask that the last portion of the witness' answer be stricken as unresponsive," Thompson requested.

"Dr. Guttormson, please refrain from editorializing," the jurist admonished. "The jury is to disregard the reference to Dr. Bronski being a specialist as to testimony."

Once the judge uttered the words, Thompson knew it had been a mistake to seek the ruling. The jury had learned that the primary defense witness was a hired gun from the mouth of an essentially disinterested local veterinarian, whom many of the members of the jury panel knew, and then heard that information reiterated by the judge. The defense lawyer studied the face of Harriet Enwright, seeking to determine if he should request a sidebar conference. He thought better of it and moved on.

"You'd agree that Dr. Bronski and Dr. Kelly Long of the University of Illinois Animal Poison Control Center both enjoy national, and indeed, international reputations as experts in their fields."

"That's a true statement. I don't know Dr. Long personally but I know her work."

"And you understand that both of these experts disagree with your conclusions in this case."

"I've read their reports and their discovery depositions to that effect."

"You in fact have consulted with Dr. Bronski on any number of swine problems you've encountered in the past, isn't that true?"

"Yes."

"And you've referred cases to the University of Illinois Center, if not to Dr. Long, at least to the facility."

"You know I have. That information was conveyed to you during my deposition," the witness related with a seed of impatience.

Thompson smiled. He had no intention of attempting to take on the community's leading veterinarian directly.

"I believe those are all the questions I have."

"Mr. Aitkins?"

"Just a few brief follow-up questions, your honor."

Guttormson coughed and ran his fingers through his aging blond hair.

"When you were out at the Andersons while the abortions were taking place, you said earlier that you found tell-tale symptoms of Mycotoxin poisoning in the female gestating animals. These were observations you made personally?"

"Yes."

"And they included?"

"Well, we now know, from the work done at NDSU, that the gilts and sows, three hundred or so I believe, in the farrowing house, were exposed to two specific Mycotoxins; zearalenone and DON. Of the two, the first one I mentioned is the one that impacts the gestational cycle. What I found examining the female animals were that their vulva, the outside of their vaginal areas if you will, were red and inflamed. Their mammary glands were also enlarged."

"Could you explain that?"

"Zearalenone acts like a hormone enhancer. It accelerates the gestational process beyond what the adult animals and the fetuses can tolerate. The increase in the size of a sow's mammary glands is one reaction that is readily visible and easily documented. The teats swell to a size one would normally see in swine already nursing their young. Here, of course, the fetuses were nowhere near birth size when they were aborted. That's documented in the plastic baggie of fetal tissue I photographed and you marked as an exhibit. The embryonic mortality of fetuses at the stage shown by the tissue in that exhibit is another tell-tale sign of Mycotoxin involvement."

"These symptoms, so the ladies and gentlemen of the jury are clear, are they in any way consistent with HPP infection?"

"No."

A wry grin crossed Daniel Aitkins' face as he readied himself for the next inquiry.

"Doctor, do you know Mr. Pavo Tynjala?"

"I certainly do."

"How do you know him?"

Thompson felt a sudden urge to rise to his feet and say something.

"Your honor, may we approach?"

"You may."

Five attorneys left their places and congregated in front of Judge Enwright.

"What's the problem, counselor?" the jurist whispered.

"Judge, I was not aware, there was no disclosure made, of any prior relationship between this witness and Mr. Tynjala."

"That true, Mr. Aitkins?" the jurist asked.

"Judge, I didn't even know about the connection myself until after this court made its decision to allow Tynjala to testify about his problems, problems that he's all ready placed before the court in his own lawsuit. I mentioned Tynjala's name to Dr. Guttormson as we were preparing for the doctor's testimony this morning. That's when he told me Tynjala had been a client of his office."

Enwright studied the face of the plaintiffs' lawyer, searching for a sign that she was being misled.

"Mr. Thompson?"

"Well, your honor," F.W. Barnes interceded. "It's clear that Mr. Aitkins is again trying to inject information into this case that was not disclosed during discovery. We should have been told about any connection between Dr. Guttormson and Tynjala, either in Interrogatory Answers or during the Vet's deposition."

Hernesman surreptitiously pinched the skin of Aitkins' left wrist, a gesture urging restraint.

"Judge, seems to me that since I didn't even know that Tynjala was going to be allowed to testify about his allegations until we came here to the courthouse, and since I just learned about the connection, it's not unfair for me to explore that relationship with the doctor," Aitkins urged.

The judge nodded. Her nearly invisible eyebrows rolled.

"He's right, Mr. Barnes. Your own witness, Mr. Tynjala, knew about his connection to Dr. Guttormson. He was in the best position to disclose that information to you. I'm going to allow Dr. Guttormson to testify on this point so long as what he says is relevant."

374

"But your honor..." Barnes whined. "That's tantamount to allowing Mr. Aitkins' to get away with concealing evidence."

Enwright fumed.

"Lower your voice, sir. I won't have this jury infected by unfounded accusations. Step back and keep your mouth shut. Mr. Thompson, please control your cohort or I will be forced to do so."

Thompson turned towards F.W. Barnes. There was no need for the big man to say a word. Barnes held his tongue, though his face revealed scorn for the female judge.

Aitkins whispered something to Dee Dee Hernesman. She nodded her head in agreement.

"At this time, your honor, I have no other questions for Dr. Guttormson. However, we reserve to right to recall him as a rebuttal witness."

"Very well. We'll take our afternoon break at this time and be back at three o'clock," the trial judge said, adding the standard cautions for the benefit of the jury.

Aitkins, Hernesman, and Dean Anderson stood in a corner of the courthouse discussing the day's events.

"I think we just caught our first big break," Danny related as they watched the defense lawyers, the executives from Stevenson's, and Melanie Barnes walk by.

"How so?" Dean Anderson asked.

"Dr. Guttormson knows a thing or two about Mr. Tynjala."

"Like what?"

"Patience, Dean. All in good time. Let's just say that, with my father Emery's intuition, Ms. Hernesman's persistence, and Dr. Guttormson's knowledge, Mr. Tynjala is going to turn out to be a very ineffective witness."

The farmer looked at his lawyers. Unlike the days leading up to trial, specifically Sunday, when they had met at the Anderson Farmhouse to discuss the testimony of the Anderson family, there was no sign of anxiety on Danny Aitkins' face. There was nothing but calm reflected in the attorney's eyes. The farmer turned to watch his wife and his children take turns sipping cold water from a water fountain located in the lobby of the old courthouse.

"How's Nancy feeling?" Dee Dee asked.

"Not so good. She can't sleep," Dean Anderson admitted.

Join the club, Aitkins thought.

"We'll put her on right after the break," Dan advised.

"I thought we were calling Horace next," Dee Dee responded.

"He can wait. He's here for the duration, taking notes, offering suggestions. Let's get Mrs. Anderson on and off so she can sleep tonight."

The expression on the farmer's face didn't vanish.

"I'm not so sure that's going to do it," he said.

"It certainly can't hurt," Dee Dee observed.

Dean Anderson looked longingly at his wife. The farmer appeared poised to continue the conversation. Instead, Dean Anderson kept his thoughts to himself.

CHAPTER 75

Nancy Anderson's time in the witness box on direct examination was uneventful. In little over an hour, Dan Aitkins deftly manipulated the woman through the history of her marriage, the Anderson Farm, and the abortion storm, insofar as she was aware of the details of that event. Big Jim Thompson, his pride slightly wounded by the continued interference of F.W. Barnes, realizing that the testimony of the farmer's wife was relatively inconsequential in terms of the big picture, treated her with kindness and respect, while painting an inference of a disease-ridden, fiscally troubled farming operation.

"Mrs. Anderson, you understand that your pigs were infected at some point with haemophilus pleural pneumonia, HPP?"

"Yes."

"I take it you didn't have much to do with the response to disease on your farm because your husband deals with those sorts of issues."

The woman appeared vulnerable. Her light blond hair was held in place by an enameled clasp depicting a purple butterfly. Her frame appeared withered beneath a pastel skirt and blouse, the background of the fabric faint mauve, the print; purple flowers, a color complimenting the hair clasp.

Nancy's fingernails, normally rough and worn from the hard work of the farm, were smooth and shiny, the result of Millicent's considerable efforts. The woman's blue eyes demurely acknowledged the enormity of the black man asking her questions without staring imprudently at Thompson's face.

"Dean handles the pigs. I handle the vegetable garden and the house," she replied.

"A division of labor?" the attorney asked through a genuine smile.

"That's right."

"But you did go out to the farrowing barn on the night of the alleged abortion storm?"

A sliver of upset invaded the woman's cheeks.

"There's nothing 'alleged' about it. I saw it sir, saw it with my own eyes."

"I apologize for my poor choice of words. That's the way we lawyers are trained to talk. Seems like most times, only other lawyers can understand what we're trying to say. You told Mr. Aitkins you saw some fetuses?"

"Yes."

"How many?"

"I can't give a number. I wasn't out there for very long. Dean came in and got me. He was really upset. I've never seen him like that, at least not about anything related to the farm. I went out, walked the aisle between the farrowing crates with him and saw the mess."

"But you can't tell us how many dead or aborted piglets there were?"

"No. You have to understand something. When the mothers abort, they immediately begin eating the afterbirth. It's instinct. Because you're dealing with dead fetuses only a few inches in size, the sows and gilts don't differentiate. They clean up the whole sloppy, disgusting mess."

"I see."

"And what they don't clean up, they trample. That night, they were in a pretty high state of excitement. It was a mystery to them, I'm sure, as to what was going on."

Thompson cast a look towards the jury. All of the jurors except the cop were riveted on the woman. The defense lawyer knew that it was best to move on.

"You're not aware that Dr. Guttormson prescribed an autogenous vaccine for the HPP strain on your farm, are you?"

"Autogenous?"

"Sorry. A vaccine made from the actual disease strain in your pigs as opposed to buying off the shelf, so to speak?"

"I heard him say that today. But prior to today, no sir, I didn't know that was something he recommended."

"And it's fair to say your husband never consulted you about buying off the shelf as opposed to following the veterinarian's suggestion?"

"He did not."

"Does your husband often make major decisions about your farm without consulting you?"

"Not often."

"But you'll agree that, at least on this one occasion, he did?"

Nancy looked at her husband. Her eyes diverted towards the ceiling.

"I guess so."

"Did you know that your swine herd still had traces of HPP in it the night of the abortion storm?"

"No."

"Did you know that customers of your farming operation, specifically, a Mr. Tynjala, complained about your pigs being sold infected with HPP?"

"I wasn't a party to any such conversations," the woman acknowledged, her voice beginning to crack.

The defense lawyer eased up.

"Can you, as one-half owner of the Anderson Farm, state with reasonable clarity, how it is that you believe the events in question have caused damage to your operation in an amount in excess of $300,000.00 as claimed by Mr. Nelson, the economist you've hired to testify in this matter?"

"I'm not sure. I believe it's based upon two years of lost profits and opportunity costs. Those are words that Mr. Nelson has used, in any event."

"You folks have an accountant who does your taxes?"

"Yes."

"Ms. Lori Peltich, from over in Vergas, I believe?"

"That's right."

"Ms. Peltich isn't going to testify here, correct?"

"So far as I know."

"And Mr. Nelson, he's not your accountant?"

"True."

"He was, so far as you are aware, wholly unfamiliar with the operation of your farm before he was hired by your lawyers to determine your alleged level of damages?"

"I believe that's true. I never met him before this case that I know of."

"So the jury understands, Mrs. Anderson, Mr. Nelson was retained specifically and specially to figure out losses for purposes of testimony in this case."

"As far as I know," the woman admitted, her voice reduced to a whisper.

"And for no other reason?"

"That's the only one I know of."

Thompson looked at the jury.

"But your accountant, the person with the greatest knowledge of the financial aspects of your farm, isn't even going to testify."

"As far as I know, your statement is correct."

"No further questions."

Danny studied the tired features of his client. The woman sat with her hands folded in her lap, her eyes near tears, the responsibility of her words heaped upon her slender femininity to an extent nearly beyond her endurance. There were points the lawyer wanted to clarify, arrows slung by the defense that had hit targets that Danny Aitkins wanted to withdraw, testimonial wounds that needed healing. But the woman's body language told the attorney that his client could endure no further scrutiny.

"No re-direct," he said, nodding appreciatively to the woman as she began to rise from her seat.

"That's as good a breaking point for the day as any," Judge Enwright advanced. "Remember to keep your own counsel, no investigating, avoid any discussions about the case and avoid reading anything or listening to any media accounts of this matter between now and tomorrow. We'll see you all back here at eight-thirty tomorrow for another day of trial."

The sound of gavel striking wood resonated.

Nancy Anderson's body shook. She stood by a freestanding bird's eye maple coat rack located next to the jury box and fumbled with her winter coat. Dean Anderson eased the frayed garment over the woman's arms, planting a small, delicate kiss on Nancy's right cheek as he secured the buttons of her coat.

"You did well, Nancy," Dee Dee Hernesman said. "Not many folks could stand up to Mr. Thompson the way you did."

"She's right, Mrs. Anderson. You were a trooper up there today," Aitkins agreed. "You don't have to worry about being recalled. Your part in this trial is over, kaput."

The woman forced a weary smile.

"Thanks. I just want to go home and take a long, hot bath."

"Maybe a glass of wine?" Dean Anderson added suggestively.

"Glass, hell. After sitting up in front of all these folks, I want the whole damn bottle."

"Mother," Millicent gasped. "I didn't know you knew how to swear."

"There's a lot about your mother that you don't know," Dean Anderson advised. "A whole hell of a lot."

The farmer kissed his wife again, this time, square on the lips.

"Dean," the woman muttered, her husband's name distorted by their embrace.

"Save it for later, dad," Matthew admonished. "At least wait until you're out in the car."

The farmer smiled. His wife shrugged her shoulders, allowing the coat to settle.

"I'll pick up that bottle of wine on the way home," Dean Anderson offered as he ushered his family towards the door.

"A big bottle," Dee Dee suggested. "And one with a cork, not a screw top."

Laughter cut through the residual intensity of the day as the lawyers retrieved their notes, intent on preparing for another day of testimony.

CHAPTER 76

Julie Aitkins found it odd that she hadn't heard from her friend Melanie Barnes. This was true even though, since Michael's passing and Mel's subsequent move to the Twin Cities, their contacts had been reduced to perfunctory chats on the telephone. Despite the geographic distance, they had remained friends. There remained a bond between the women, though their closeness was distinctly moderated by the red head's disclosure of her near-affair with Danny Aitkins. That revelation altered the strength of their connectedness, creating an invisible wall of suspicion that wasn't easily scaled. Still, the women had preserved a level of intimacy.

The writer sat behind her computer in the loft of the pole building. She was editing the concluding chapter of her novel. The working title for the book was *Affairs of Habit*. The novel told the story of a nun: the woman's surrender to temporal desire as a young woman, her struggle, in her mid-thirties, after a decade of celibacy, to defeat the images of her past, and the futility of the nun's attempts to rid her memory of the smell of Father Joseph's aftershave, the touch of his fingers along her spine, the heat of his breath.

The first draft of the book was coming together. Julie was proud of the effort. She'd succeeded in convincing a friend of hers from the Loft Literary Organization in Minneapolis to introduce the writer to an agent from Chicago. Hartley Bennett was the agent's name. He was well respected and took on only one or two new clients a year, adding them to the stable of twenty quality authors he already represented. Hartley had telephoned Julie Aitkins after Alice Tate, the woman from the Loft, praised the book and sent the first three chapters of the manuscript to Hartley. They were going to have lunch, the three of them, at a Thai restaurant located on the West Bank of the University of Minnesota Campus, near where another Minnesota writer first gained the public spotlight. Julie Aitkins wasn't looking to become the next Garrison Keillor, though she was anxious to see her words in print:

I'd be happy if I became a successful regional author, she thought as she scrutinized the concluding paragraph of her novel.

The lunch was set for Saturday. Danny could watch the kids for the weekend. Time away from her husband was essential. She needed space. From Danny, from his moods, from their life together.

"Hopefully not permanent space," Julie reflected, looking out a window. Her eyes fixed upon the farm's three horses. The animals stood motionless in the winter sunlight. Her fingers clutched an expensive pen, the instrument she used for re-writing. There was a carton of identical pens in her desk drawer. She insisted on a particular feel, a particular size of pen, and always black ink, never red or blue, with which to edit.

Sadness afflicted Julie's heart. It ate away at her as she tried to concentrate. Three days remained before her meeting with the agent. She wanted to correct the rough draft she was going to leave with Hartley Bennett. She wanted Bennett to appreciate the full measure of her protagonist's saga, to know the height of the character's passion, the depths of the nun's despair. Julie fought mightily against the intrusion of her personal situation but the features of her husband's face came roaring back into her thoughts as she sat in reflective solitude. Danny: it was always Danny.

Is he sleeping with someone else? she pondered.

Julie felt like she was strong enough to deal with most anything that might come between them, the exception being physical betrayal. Emotional longings, those she understood. Those sorts of feelings were not reserved for the males of the planet. Julie had experienced the influence of outside attention. She was always flattered when such situations arose but quick to dissuade the notion that anything physical could ever develop. Security, trust, a sense of belonging to another. These were the keys to her sensuality and happiness. Daniel, despite all of his faults, the wanderings of his eyes, and, on at least two occasions, his hands, had always seemed to understand that there was a border between them, a boundary of trust, that he dared not breach. Now, she wasn't so certain of her husband's commitment to that line of demarcation.

A sigh escaped the woman's lips. She watched her husband's pickup truck negotiate the driveway. Dusk was fast approaching. She knew he was having a hell of a time with the trial. He was unable to conceal the turmoil from her even as he continued to avoid her in bed.

"Why are you still sleeping in the basement?" Julie had asked that morning.

"It's better this way," he'd responded. She had watched her children's faces as Daniel answered, a note of disrespect deep and hurtful in his voice.

"What do you mean?" she replied, her eyes ready to tear.

He had obviously sensed her distress and backed off from his injurious intent.

"It's just that I'm tossing and turning all night, what with this trial going on and all," he offered, some truth, more falsehood, obvious behind his words.

Julie hadn't pressed the issue further with the children in the room.

"OK," she'd said.

The writer's gaze followed the steady progress of the Ranger as it slowed and parked on snow-covered gravel in front of the house. She watched her husband, his arms weighed down by two large briefcases; try to close the driver's side door of the truck with the toe of his boot. The lawyer lost his footing, nearly falling to the ground before successfully shutting the door. The woman's eyes returned to the work in front of her.

The scene Julie Aitkins struggled with was one where the Sister stood before a convent, a beautiful Victorian mansion, prominently situated on a ridge rising above the City of Milwaukee along the shores of Lake Michigan. A phrase the writer wanted the nun to utter as the prophetic, final expression of wisdom revealed by the book, ran over and over in Julie's head. The phrase was:

Life is meant to be lived one story at a time.

With certainty, the author suspected the line was relevant to the present status of her own marriage.

CHAPTER 77

Clyde Armstrong, the twenty-nine year old less-than-hygienic farmer and ultrasound technician, testified proudly in a new JC Penney suit provided with the compliments of Danny Aitkins. Clyde also boasted a fresh haircut and a significant application of Brute aftershave, both of which improved the farmer's general appearance and fragrance.

Jim Thompson tried a variety of approaches to knock Armstrong off his game. Nothing seemed to faze the farmer. His intellect was too limited for lies; his mental outlook, too matter-of-fact for embellishment. In the final analysis, the witness escaped Thompson's assault with only incidental damage to his testimony. He weathered the defense lawyer's onslaught by pure ignorance.

Ivan Thomas from NDSU was another solid witness for the Andersons. Though Thompson made a few early points by differentiating Thomas' background as a research scientist from the working résumés of Drs. Bronski and Long, experts aligned with the defense camp, by the time the defense lawyer sought to redirect the jurors' attentions away from the rat feeding trial data and mass spectrometer readings relied upon by Dr. Thomas, the contest was over in terms of attempting to inflict damage on the professor.

The performance of Horace Brewster, DVM, the plaintiffs' final liability witness, was set up perfectly by the testimony of Dean Anderson. Though Dean showed several flashes of anger during an arduous cross-examination by James Thompson, the farmer kept his cool. When Thompson insisted that Anderson knew that the feeder pigs purchased by Pavo Tynjala were ill with HPP when the animals left the Anderson Farm, Dean held his tongue and issued a mild denial. When the black man cited hog breeding manuals that called the use of lindane and fuel oil for mange "antiquated", Anderson countered that his methods were, in many respects, considered antiquated by large corporate concerns running factory feed lots. And finally, when Thompson attempted to cast doubt upon the extent of the dead litters and the financial loss encountered by the Anderson family due to the abortion storm, the farmer calmly reiterated, over Thompson's vehement objection, the basic facts of the extent of his family's claimed loss at the hands of the feed manufacturer.

At the time of the incident, the Andersons had three hundred sows and gilts in production, which farrowed, on average, 2.26 times per year. The records of the Anderson herd established that the average litter size on the farm was 9.2 hogs per litter. The farmer recounted that, using a conservative ten-year average of forty dollars per hundredweight for hogs, his estimate of the loss incurred exceeded $400,000.00.

Thompson attacked the farmer's numbers. He engaged in all-out war, zeroing in on the premise that it would take two years to rebuild their destroyed herd. James Thompson pointed out that replacement animals could be bought from certified dealers and put into production, thereby shortening the recovery period. The defense lawyer also suggested that there was no need for Dean Anderson to liquidate his female breeding stock, that the animals could be rebred, reducing the damages claimed to the loss of one farrowing cycle.

"That's all well and good from where you sit, Mr. Thompson. I mean, the experts; my veterinarian, and folks at NDSU, an institution that I respect, told me the safest course would be to replace the animals. No one could promise that the sows and gilts would be able to conceive, carry their litters, or successfully nurse after being poisoned," Anderson responded.

Before the defense lawyer could ask a follow-up question, the burly farmer finished his thought.

"Your client certainly wasn't going to guaranty that, now was it? I mean, seeing as how your investigator was the one who turned all our customers against us. Your client wasn't about to finance the cost of buying fancy certified replacement hogs for our farm."

Though the judge had rebuked Dean Anderson for making the speech and ordered it stricken from the record, Danny Aitkins noted, with surreptitious satisfaction, that several jurors had nodded their heads approvingly during the farmer's diatribe. Thompson was hamstrung. He couldn't point out to the jury that settlement monies, significant monies, had been made available to the Andersons to use for such purchases. He was unable to advise the jury that the offers had been rejected; settlement discussions being a taboo subject in front of a jury.

Horace Brewster was a no-nonsense witness. Brewster down played the HPP incursion, minimized the adverse effects of using fuel oil and lindane as a treatment for mange, and stuck to a singular cogent theme.

"Doctor, after hearing the testimony in this trial, after considering all of the depositions, affidavits, and Answers to Interrogatories filed with the court, and having studied the expert reports prepared by Drs. Covington, Long, and Bronski regarding the Andersons' claim, have you formed any opinions as to whether the Anderson swineherd was damaged by the feed sold by Stevenson's Sci-Swine?"

"Yes."

"Are the opinions you hold stated to a reasonable degree of probability?"

"Yes."

Aitkins smiled.

"Would you kindly tell the ladies and gentlemen of the jury what opinions you hold in this case?"

Thomas took to his feet to object.

"Your honor, I object. The question calls for an answer based upon a hypothetical and facts not in evidence. It also calls for speculation on the part of this witness as he was not present on the Anderson Farm at any point during the alleged abortion incident and did not provide any veterinary services, at any time, to the plaintiffs with regard to the claimed event."

Judge Enwright clenched and unclenched her hands several times.

"Overruled. I believe there's been adequate foundation laid. Go ahead and answer the question, Dr. Brewster."

The veterinarian turned his ruggedly handsome face towards the jury.

"There's no question that the hogs on the Anderson place, primarily the gestating sows and gilts in the farrowing barn, received feed that was tainted with fusarium mold resulting in Mycotoxin poisoning. The physical signs noted by Dr. Guttormson and the Andersons: the reddened vulvas, the enlarged mammary glands, the feed refusal, the spontaneous, catastrophic abortion of nearly all of the litters, together with the underlying reality that the only change in the operation was a change in feed, points directly and undeniably to a problem with the pellets."

Aitkins interrupted the man.

"You raise hogs yourself?"

"Yes."

"On a farrow to finish basis, like the Andersons? You buy only boars from outside your herd?"

"That's right."

"How many sows and gilts do you run?"

"A little over seventy at a time. I'm a small operator. I run more cattle than hogs. You might say that my affinity is for large, smelly cows, not small, smelly pigs." the Vet offered.

Several jurors grinned. Their response was not lost on Jim Thompson.

"You also do some work for the Hutterites?"

"And the Amish as well."

"Explain what that entails."

"Well, I'm a consultant to both religious groups. The Amish, as most folks know, are completely Nineteenth Century. No mechanization. The Hutterites, on the other hand, though socially conservative and tight-knit, use modern farming implements; tractors, harvesters, computers. But for both sects, I come onto their land and offer expertise within the constraints of the groups' religious tenets. It's a little harder working with the Amish, but they're pretty good about spelling out the limitations I have to follow."

Aitkins pondered a question.

"You heard Mr. Thompson's suggestion that the Andersons should have either re-bred the females that suffered the abortions or purchased certified disease-free animals from outside their farm."

"Yes."

"What do you think of those options?"

F.W. Barnes, silent for nearly a day, erupted.

"Your honor, the question calls for a narrative answer."

Harriet Enwright smoothed a coil of hair dangling next to her left ear. Her fingers played with the wayward sprite for a few seconds, attempting to return the strand to its proper place as she considered the old litigator's position. The hair refused to comply with her efforts.

"It may well call for a narrative, Mr. Barnes. Unfortunately, there is no prohibition in the Rules of Evidence against allowing a narrative response when it's warranted. I believe that in this instance, such latitude should be exercised. Your objection is overruled."

"I've never..."

Malachi Stone thrust his thick hand out and grasped the wrist of the silver haired attorney, lurching Barnes off his feet and back into his chair before the old man could finish the untoward comment. The judge remained impassive. Her eyes simply stared at the defense lawyers until she was satisfied that the commotion was concluded.

"Mr. Aitkins, please proceed," the judge advised.

"You remember the question?"

Brewster nodded.

"Yes sir, I do."

"Your answer?"

The Vet directed his response at the jury.

"I think that, in a perfect world, with unlimited money, Mr. Thompson's suggestion, that the Andersons buy all new breeding stock from certified disease-free suppliers is feasible. But this is not a perfect world. When the abortion storm hit, it disrupted the Andersons' cash flow to a point where they did not have sufficient financial resources to exercise that option. Borrowing money, given the uncertain status of their lawsuit, would have been ill-advised, and, as stated by Mr. Anderson, difficult given the overall fiscal picture of their farming operation. So, based upon the facts confronting Mr. and Mrs. Anderson, buying expensive breeding stock wasn't a viable option."

"What about rebreeding their own sows and gilts?"

387

A grimace stormed across the veterinarian's face.

"Not a chance. Guttormson and Thomas gave sound advice. There are ample studies that indicate that the breeding, gestating, and nursing capabilities of swine experiencing the type of widespread, violent abortions present here, are permanently compromised by the toxins. Under no circumstances would any prudent Vet advise a client to rebreed the affected animals."

Thompson attempted several verbal jabs on re-cross but did not move Dr. Brewster from the Vet's simple, down home approach. The feed was tainted. It was fed to the Andersons' pigs. It caused abortions. It was Stevenson's fault. There was no other explanation for what had happened.

Andrew Nelson looked too young to be an agricultural economist. His face appeared to be that of a twenty-something college student rather than a thirty-something professor of economics at Moorhead State University. Though the professor had graduated from Detroit Lakes High School with Daniel and Julie Aitkins, he wasn't a member of their group. He was a brain, a 1960's rock and roll lover who spent most of his time listening to scratched vinyl recordings of The Doors and the Grateful Dead when everyone else was turned on to Queen, Rush, and Bruce Springsteen. Despite his odd persona, he and Danny stayed in touch after high school. They went way back, back to afternoon kindergarten with Miss Bunting; a gray haired old matron who spoiled them both as her class favorites. Danny had used his connection to Andrew Nelson over the years to secure the professor's assistance as an expert in cases.

The economist prepared a variety of charts and graphs for display; enlarged images projected from a notebook computer onto a movie screen in the courtroom. Aitkins kept a tight rein on the witness, making him testify in short, declarative sentences. Tally up the pigs, compute the costs, come up with a bottom line.

In the end, the economist's projections, using rebuilding of the herd from within as a given, using replacement sows and gilts originally destined for slaughter as feeder pigs, were nearly identical to the suppositions of Dean Anderson. Nelson's final number was between $350,000.00 and $400,000.00, depending upon variables.

Big Jim went to work on the underlying economic premises used by Andrew Nelson. The farrowing rates were too high, above the national average. The Andersons' mortgage and utility costs were understated, making the projected profits too fat. The assumed hog prices were speculative, above the current market reflection per hundredweight. The feed costs were too low, again making the predicted profit margin per hog too large. Through it all Andrew Nelson, his boyish good looks aimed at the female members of the jury, retained his cool demeanor.

As a last resort, Thompson delicately attacked the witness as a "hired gun", a professional expert willing to say anything for pay. Nelson simply smiled and revealed that his hourly rate was sixty-five dollars per hour, less than the prevailing rate for a plumber's call in Western Minnesota. He also pointed out that the last trial he was involved in, where Dr. Eunice Underwood, the economist scheduled to appear on behalf of Stevenson's testified, her rate was one hundred and fifty dollars per hour.

Danny Aitkins had only one question on re-direct of the economist.

"Just so the jury understands your final opinion, Mr. Nelson. You're saying that, based upon the actual financial documents and farming records of the Anderson Farm, the damages incurred by my clients as a result of the abortion storm, accepting Dr. Brewster's premise that the herd must be rebuilt from within, exceed $400,000.00?"

"That's correct."

"Your opinion is stated, as indicated previously, to a reasonable degree of economic probability?"

"It is."

Aitkins looked at Dee Dee Hernesman. The lawyer leaned towards his female partner and spoke in a hushed tone.

"Anything I missed?"

"Nope. That's a wrap," she whispered.

"Dean, you agree?"

"I can't see where there's anything left out," the client concurred.

Aitkins drew to the limit of his short stature and addressed the court.

"Your honor, the plaintiffs rest."

Harriet Enwright looked at the clock on the wall. It was nearly four in the afternoon. It was Friday. The week was over. It was time to clear her head, to ready herself for the defense motions she knew were going to be launched at her on Monday morning.

"We'll recess for the weekend," the female jurist disclosed, adding her normal caveats. "I'll see counsel in Judge Davidson's chambers on Monday morning at eight. The jury doesn't need to report until nine-thirty. Have a good weekend," she concluded, rapping Davidson's wooden gavel on the top of the bench.

Aitkins motioned to his clients.

"I'll meet you in the lobby."

The Anderson family put on their jackets, caps, and mittens and left the room. As the door closed behind the plaintiffs, James Thompson held an animated discussion with Malachi Stone, F.W. Barnes, and Jason Billington. Thompson's voice rumbled low and obvious. Billington nodded. The customer service man held a cell phone to his right ear, listening to the lawyers and his supervisor in Winnipeg at the same time. There was a lull in the discussion. Big Jim left the group and made his way to the opposing counsel table.

"Can we talk?" the defense lawyer asked Daniel Aitkins.

"Certainly. What's on your mind, Jim?"

"That was some pretty sordid chicanery your economist pulled today," Thompson said, a meager smirk, an uncharacteristic gesture, settling across his face.

"How so?"

"Those numbers are a work of fiction. Dr. Underwood will tear them apart. That's if the jury doesn't simply find that your clients' caused their own problems."

"Jim, it's Friday night. I want to go home," Aitkins said. "I'm tired. I don't want to argue with you. Save it for Monday."

"Fair enough. I'll get right to it. Stevenson's is willing to add some money to the pot if you're clients will sign a confidentiality agreement and settle this case before trial resumes on Monday."

"How much?"

The big man's eyes caught the light of the overhead florescent bulbs.

"They'll pay $125,000."

"That's a pretty big jump," Dee Dee Hernesman noted.

"You got that right, ma'am. It's also the end of the line. The last dollar is being spent."

Daniel studied his opponent's face. For the first time since he'd met Big Jim Thompson, Aitkins watched a bead of sweat slip down the defense lawyer's cheek.

"I'll talk to the Andersons."

"Before Monday?" Thompson asked, no hint of eagerness in his voice despite the sudden appearance of perspiration.

"Before Monday," Aitkins promised

.

CHAPTER 78

Calm settled over the valley as the man pushed a shovel full of snow across the perfect ice of a stream. It was Saturday morning, just after the crack of dawn. Adam Aitkins sat on a hay bale nestled against an adjacent snow bank tying his goalie skates. The boy's fingers worked from habit. He laced up his Bauer's. It was warm for January. A cold snap had passed through propelled by an Alberta Clipper. There wasn't a cloud in the sky. Diminutive Chickadees danced from tree limb to tree limb.

Amanda, her white figure skates scuffed from use, twirled violently within a cleared space on the creek's smooth surface. Michael, his ankles barely supporting his weight, ice-walked precariously behind his father as the man shoveled. Willow branches hung low, creating interlocking tunnels around the edge of the pond.

"The ice is smooth," Amanda said.

"The best I've ever seen it," Dan responded.

"Just wait until I get out there," Adam chimed in.

Though his oldest child made an attempt at conveying a light heart, Daniel detected anxiousness in the boy's speech.

He's thirteen, the father thought. *He knows things aren't going so well between his mother and me.*

"Watch me, daddy," Michael yelled, the child spinning crazily as his skate blades propelled him in an uncontrolled circle.

"You'll be joining Peggy Fleming in no time," Dan observed.

"Who's that?" Amanda asked.

"I forget just how young you are," the man responded through a smile, "and how old I've become. She's a famous figure skater, an Olympic star from the 1970's."

"Like Michelle Kwan?" Adam postulated, rising to his feet.

"Like her," Danny agreed.

"I wanna play hockey," Amanda said through a small pout.

"Girls don't play hockey," Adam retorted, racing across the ice, planting his skates in a hockey stop, spraying his sister with shavings.

"Not true," the father corrected the son. "There's a girl's program starting in DL."

"So there," Amanda retorted, sticking out her tongue for emphasis.

"In fact," Dan observed as he leaned heavily on the shovel, his Red Wing winter packs planted firmly against the slickness of the ice, "most high schools up north are adding girls' hockey."

"Yuck," the goalie responded, performing cross-over turns with precision. "Who wants a sweaty old girl hockey player for a girlfriend?"

Amanda chased her brother. The two older children flew past Michael, who remained nearly motionless, his ankles touching, his balance, precarious.

Ralph, the family Border Collie, dodged in and out of a distant thicket chasing a snowshoe hare. The dog stopped its pursuit of the rabbit when it lost its prey in the tangled alders.

"Here, Ralph," the youngest Aitkins child called. "Here boy."

The dog leapt onto the ice and promptly collapsed on its belly, all four legs splayed akimbo.

Danny shuffled across ice. He claimed a seat on the hay bale. He'd never learned to skate. The intricacies of the task eluded him. As he watched his children at play, the lawyer felt uncertainty infest his mind. Uncertainty about his family's future. Uncertainty about the red haired woman. Twin threads of doubt wrapped and unwrapped themselves around his thoughts until it felt like his brain was suffocating. His thoughts became directed towards his wife.

Julie was in the Twin Cities, meeting a literary agent from Chicago. There was a chance, a sliver of optimistic hope, that the agent would like her first novel. Julie had not allowed Dan to read the manuscript. She was vehement. He could not see the novel unless and until it was accepted for publication. A few times, when he was up in her studio on errands, he glanced at the work in progress. What he read astounded him. The book wasn't good; it was great, a book that, if someone looked closely enough at its construction, could be labeled genius. He hadn't shared his opinion with his wife. Such an admission of a violation of Julie's privacy would have increased the acrimony between them. There would be a time for him to reveal his thoughts. Someday, sometime.

It was the "someday" that stuck in his craw. There'd be a period where all hell would break loose, where he would be tossed out of their house unceremoniously on his ass. There'd be a time when she would contemplate divorce, maybe hire a lawyer, someone from Fargo or Duluth, someone she could trust, whose judgment wouldn't be affected by Daniel's connections to the local judiciary and the local legal community. Whether she'd go through with it was the ultimate question. He simply couldn't predict what she would do in the final scene of the drama about to be played out between them.

The lawyer grimaced. He couldn't live without his children. He couldn't bear to be a part-time dad. They were, to use a Biblical reference, his treasure, his trove. Julie knew that. She had to understand that.

"Hell, she might use that against me," the attorney sadly reflected.

The lone bright spot in his life was the Anderson lawsuit. Big Jim's assaults on the plaintiffs' case hadn't achieved the measure of success an attorney of Thompson's credentials would expect. Aitkins knew that the defense lawyer remained dangerous. Stevenson's would parade Drs. Long, Bronski, and Covington in front of the jury in hopes of smashing the scientific principles adduced by the plaintiffs' experts. Prof. Eunice Underwood would testify that, even if the Andersons sustained some loss at the hands of the feed manufacturer, the number to be attached to those damages was less than $50,000.00. And finally, when all of the experts had completed their barrage against the plaintiffs' case, Pavo Tynjala would step up to the plate hoping to hit a home run for the defendant.

A tired grin found the attorney's lips as he watched his children ice skate. Of all the witnesses that were yet to be called, the young lawyer had a fervent desire to watch the performance of Pavo Tynjala. Dan wanted to measure the man beneath the equalizing assault of Dee Dee Hernesman's cross-examination. Dee Dee had put together a nice package of surprises for the goldbricking Finlander. That thought, and that thought alone, would have to be enough to sustain Danny Aitkins.

CHAPTER 79

"**The** defendant moves for a directed verdict on all theories of liability," James Thompson advised, standing behind the table occupied by the defense.

It was slightly after eight on Monday morning. Aitkins had discussed Stevenson's proposal to settle the case on a confidential basis for $125,000.00 with his clients in a conference room prior to coming into court.

"They've increased their offer," Daniel had indicated to Dean and Nancy Anderson as the entire Anderson family sat reverently awaiting the attorney's disclosure.

"To what?" Dean had asked.

"One-twenty-five," Aitkins advised as he stood at the end of a table. Dee Dee Hernesman, her cheeks aglow from the brisk walk from her car to the building, sat in a chair next to her partner.

Nancy Anderson's eyes darted. She met her husband's gaze head on.

"That's a lot of money," the woman observed. "How much of that would we see?"

"With our costs and everything, after reducing our fee from a third to a quarter, about sixty thousand," Hernesman replied.

Dean Anderson studied the face of his primary lawyer.

"It's not enough," the farmer stated.

Dan smiled hesitantly.

"It's your call. You want some time to talk it over?"

The farmer's wife cast a pleading look at her husband.

"I'd like that," she said.

"Can you give us a few minutes?" Dean Anderson requested.

Dan and Dee Dee had left the room.

No sounds of discussion had escaped the conference room. After five minutes, the door had opened. Matt Anderson held the knob as the attorneys entered the room.

"Well?" Aitkins asked.

"It's not enough," Dean had reiterated. "They've got to get to $185,000 before we'll think about it."

"With a twenty-five percent fee and the $30,000.00 in costs, that would net you a little over a hundred thousand," Dee Dee revealed.

Nancy folded her hands together on the beaten surface of the table.

"We're not going to let you reduce your fee, Mr. Aitkins," the woman murmured. "We took a family vote. It was unanimous. Your firm has stood by us and done more than could be expected to try and save our farm. You get paid the full one-third. That's all there is to it."

Millicent Anderson had stared at the male attorney.

"You have a family to feed too, Mr. Aitkins. Ms. Hernesman has payments to make. You have bills to pay just like we do. We all want to see that you guys get what's due you."

Daniel had shifted uneasily as he stood at the end of the table.

"Thanks for the confidence. Don't worry about us. We'll do just fine at twenty-five percent, so long as the expenses are covered separately."

"You're not listening, Dan. We won't settle the case, no matter how much the offer, unless you take your full fee. We signed an agreement. The Andersons don't go back on their word," Dean added sternly.

Aitkins had looked at his partner. She shrugged.

"You've made your position clear. You'd take one-eighty-five, right?"

"That's the bottom line. No less," Dean Anderson emphasized, "and no reduction in fees."

"You've made that very clear," Danny had observed.

Aitkins had presented the Andersons' position to James Thompson the moment the defense lawyer and his entourage arrived at the Becker County Courthouse.

"They willing to talk any further?" Thompson responded.

Before Aitkins could reply, the big man added.

"Understand, Stevenson's told me what I passed along last Friday was the last Canadian dime available."

"They'd take two hundred," Danny advised. "American," Aitkins' added with a grin.

"No way, Daniel. I can't go back to them with that."

"Then let's let the jury decide the case."

Thompson's eyes had studied the smaller man.

"That's why we're here, isn't it?" Dan interjected.

Aitkins thought he detected sadness on the big man's face, as if the Twin Citian hoped the matter would simply and finally resolve itself.

"I guess so," Thompson had replied without conviction.

During his argument for a directed verdict, James Thompson pointed out many of the same perceived deficiencies he'd raised when summary judgment was argued. The lawyer's magnificent baritone voice echoed smartly inside the courtroom. When he was finished with his argument, his comrades nodded their heads in congratulatory support.

"Your honor," Aitkins began, his voice small and tinny in comparison to the defense attorney's polished rhetorical instrument, "we have presented, through the direct testimony of our witnesses, sufficient facts from which a reasonable jury could conclude that Stevenson's Sci-Swine sold tainted feed to my clients. Such conduct was not only a breach of warranty under the Uniform Commercial Code; it's also violative of the Adulterated Feed Act, which gives rise, as the court is aware, to negligence per se."

The attorney paused. An odd look occupied Harriet Enwright's face. It was an expression, a posture that Danny Aitkins couldn't place. The jurist cleared her throat.

"With respect to the claims brought under the UCC, the court agrees with Mr. Aitkins. There is more than enough testimony for the jury to conclude, if it so desires, that the grain in question was not fit for the use intended and that, in a general sense, it wasn't as advertised."

The judge took a deep breath. Daniel sensed the other shoe was about to drop.

"However, upon careful reconsideration of the doctrine of negligence per se, when one zeros in on the fact that this was a commercial transaction, between merchants, to which the holding of *Superwood* and its progeny would apply, I am not at all certain that a negligence claim, even one incorporating a statutory violation, can be sustained under the present status of the law. Therefore, with respect to that element of the plaintiffs' claim, I am granting Mr. Thompson's motion. This case, barring something unforeseen happening, will go to the jury on theories of breach of warranty only."

Aitkins turned in disbelief and searched the mottled gray of his partner's eyes. Hernesman's gaze was steady. The surprise decision had not made an impact upon her in any discernible way. A bright, infectious smile crossed the female attorney's lips.

"Remember what Dr. Brewster said? Keep the case simple. Well, now it is. Let's go kick their ass," Dee Dee whispered, her confidence brimming.

Dean Anderson overheard Hernesman's comment and leaned over to address Danny Aitkins in a low voice.

"I like this lady lawyer. Screw Stevenson's. Let's see what the jury will do."

Aitkins was momentarily stunned. The jurors began to enter the courtroom to reclaim their seats.

CHAPTER 80

"**Is** the use of lindane and fuel oil to control mange a recommended methodology, Dr. Bronski?"

The reedy veterinarian from Wadena studied the face of the African American attorney posing the question.

"According to recent literature from the University of Nebraska at Lincoln, lindane is still an acceptable treatment when applied topically to kill adult mange mites."

"Explain, if you would, Doctor, why a farmer such as Mr. Anderson, would want to get rid of mange?"

Bronski smiled and pushed his glasses up the bridge of his angular nose until the instruments were correctly seated.

"Mange causes adult pigs to eat poorly. The mites bore into the skin of the hogs and cause unrepentant itching. The skin gets bruised from constant rubbing and the health of the animals, even those not pregnant, begins to fail. In farrowing and nursing females, the problem gets worse. The constant scratching and failure to eat impacts the mother's health and leads to reproductive or delivery problems. The gilts and sows neglect their young while they try to rid themselves of the mites. All in all, it's a nasty infection. A farmer needs to control the adult bugs so fewer eggs get laid."

Thompson looked up from his notes.

"What about using fuel oil with the lindane?"

"An old remedy no longer considered to be good practice. Fuel oil itself impacts mites but it also impacts swine. Farmers combine oil with lindane to make the more expensive lindane go further. It's not an advisable combination given its toxic effects."

"You have criticism of the Andersons' application of lindane and fuel oil in their operation?"

"Beyond the mere fact that fuel oil shouldn't be used at all as the carrying agent?"

"Yes."

"I do."

"What opinion do you hold in that regard?"

"Here, the Andersons want to point their fingers at the feed as the primary cause of the abortions they claim took place."

"Let's stop there, Dr. Bronski. You say, 'claim' took place?"

"Yes."

"You don't believe there were any abortion problems on the Anderson Farm?"

"I wouldn't go so far as to say 'no' abortions took place. But I do take issue with the use of ultrasound voodoo and speculation by other professionals, such as Dr. Guttormson, who primarily deals with cats and dogs in his veterinary practice, and Dr. Thomas, who is a researcher in a university setting, that some sort of herd-wide abortion storm took place."

"How is that?"

"Well, sir, I've been to eighteen foreign countries and thirty-two states in America, all with regard to hogs and the raising and management of hogs. I have never, in my two-plus decades of veterinary practice, encountered an abortion storm where more than twenty percent of a breeding herd lost its litters."

"You said twenty percent? Was that a feed situation, as alleged here?"

"No, that was a disease incident, the very disease that was found in the Anderson herd when I drew blood."

"HPP?"

"That's the one. Nasty stuff."

"So you don't believe that the Andersons experienced a ninety percent-plus loss of litters?"

"I am confident no such loss took place."

"Getting back to the use of lindane and fuel oil..."

"Yes?"

Thompson smiled. He had stopped taking notes and was merely following the expert's lead. It was clear that Bronski had been in court before.

"You were about to explain another reason that the Andersons' use of lindane and fuel oil to control mange wasn't a good idea."

"Ah yes. Well, from the Andersons' records, it appears that the last use of lindane may have, and I say may because the records I am relying upon include an old calendar from the farrowing barn which isn't the easiest to decipher, may have been within the proscribed time frame, when it is ill-advised to use lindane on pregnant or recently farrowed swine. You're not supposed to use the compound two weeks before or three weeks after farrowing."

"And you think that happened here?"

"It's a distinct possibility, if the calendar showing the application dates is accurate."

"So we have the HPP that you've all ready indicated causes abortions, the use of lindane against recommended guidelines. What other criticisms do you have of the Andersons' operation as it relates to the allegations in this case?"

Bronski scanned a pile of notes resting before him on the witness stand.

"I'd have to say that the high levels of mange in the adult pigs, which I saw personally when I was on the Anderson Farm, reinforces my opinion that Mr. Anderson is not a high quality operator. There's a lot of cutting of corners, doing things the cheap and dangerous way rather than the safe and sometimes expensive way. The drilled well serving the home came back fine. But the shallow well supplying water to the hog barns is contaminated with e-coli; fecal bacteria from animal waste allowed to accumulate in the farmyard, which is another potential cause of health problems, including reproductive lapses and abortions in the gilts and sows."

"You've seen the results of the testing done at NDSU regarding the presence of fusarium and Mycotoxins in the feed sold to the Andersons by Stevenson's?"

"I have."

"You've been provided all of the depositions taken in this case, including those of Drs. Guttormson, Thomas, and Brewster?"

"Yes."

"In fact, you've been here for their testimony?"

"That's correct."

"You've had the chance to review the report of Dr. Kelly Long and you've been provided with her deposition as well?"

"That's right."

"These experts that I've just named, do you know any of them personally?"

"I know Dr. Guttormson and Dr. Brewster. I don't use NDSU's plant pathology or toxicology services so I don't know Dr. Thomas. I know Dr. Long very well. I've done seven or eight research papers with her and her colleagues at Illinois. I've also sent several hundred cases of animal poisoning to her for evaluation."

Big Jim stretched out, nearly popping the seams of his brown tweed suit coat in the process of working through a kink.

"I know Mr. Aitkins will jump on this one so I'll ask it. Do you consider Dr. Long a friend?"

"Yes I do."

"Would you allow that relationship to alter or change your opinions in this case?"

"Absolutely not."

"You'd be able to reach a position counter to Dr. Long's if the facts were there?"

"I would and I have. In several other cases we have been on opposite sides of the aisle, so to speak."

"Taking all of the data and testimony you've been presented in this case, do you have an opinion to a reasonable degree of probability, as to whether the abortions alleged to have occurred on the Anderson Farm were caused by feed sold by the defendant?"

"I have an opinion."

"What is that opinion?"

Danny didn't stir. He knew that any objection he would raise would be overruled. He knew his best hope as not to assault the man's intellect, but to attack his integrity. Aitkins allowed the veterinarian to answer the "home run" question as posed.

"My opinion is that whatever abortions took place were caused by a combination of HPP, the weakened condition of the pigs due to the improvident use of lindane and fuel oil, mange infestation, and the presence of e-coli in the water supply. The feed, containing scant traces of Mycotoxins and no detectable fusarium mold, had nothing to do with whatever took place on the Anderson Farm."

Thompson watched the jury. Appreciation for the man's testimony seemed to alight on the juror's faces; all save for the countenance of the unreadable trooper.

"No further questions."

The court took a brief morning recess.

In the corridor leading to the bathrooms, Danny encountered the red haired woman.

"Hey, Mel," he said, a limp smile sneaking across his lips.

"Hi, Danny," she responded, a trace of interest cracking her leaden expression.

He knew better than to talk about anything of substance with the woman in public view.

"Can we catch a bite to eat over lunch?" the lawyer suggested.

"Why? I thought we'd said everything that needed saying."

"You're probably right. Still, I'd like to talk."

"I'm about all talked out, Danny. I feel like shit. My stomach is starting to bust out. What the hell are we gonna talk about?"

His eyes displayed the pain caused by her rebuke. She modified her reply.

"Nothing more is going to happen, at least not now, not with me in this God awful no-man's-land between you and Julie."

"I know. I just want to talk."

"Meet me at my car at noon. We'll go for a ride. I'll drive," she said.

His eyes cleared.

"I'll be there."

Back in the courtroom, Danny put the exchange behind him and concentrated his cross exam on chinks in the armor of the vaunted defense expert.

"Now, Dr. Bronski, you've been to court before?"

"Yes."

"Many times?"

"Define 'many'," the expert said defensively.

"You've testified over fifty times."

"Yes."

"Over a hundred times."

"I believe so."

"In fact, just looking at cases where you've given depositions, information you provided to Mr. Thompson for an answer to one of my Interrogatories, there are over two hundred cases listed in that answer where you've been a witness."

"If that's what I said, that's what it is."

"You make a considerable living as a professional witness."

"Define 'considerable'," Bronski answered, his words becoming hard.

"Well, looking at your tax return from last year... 'Bronski Consulting', that's your expert consulting firm, the entity that bills for your services to lawyers like Mr. Thompson, correct?"

"Yes."

"Well, last year, your gross receipts for such consultations exceeded $250,000.00," Aitkins' observed.

"Where'd you get that number?"

"You have a copy of your last year's tax return in your file documents?"

"Yes."

"You see the schedule attached to the return headed 'Bronski Consulting', about the fourth schedule in?"

"Oh yes. You're correct, $255,100.00" the expert admitted, his words turning so that it almost sounded as if he was volunteering the information.

Aitkins studied his opponent.

"And if we take a peek at the years before last year, say for the four years previous, we'd see fees ranging from $150,000.00 to $335,000.00 for cases where you were hired as a consultant."

"If you say so."

"You disagree?"

"I'll accept your word on it."

"Now, so the ladies and gentlemen of the jury understand, that amount is not your sole income, is it?"

"No, it's not."

"In fact, just looking at last year again, it's only a small portion your total gross income."

The witness' face reddened.

"Define 'small'."

"Well, your total gross income was well into the seven figures, when you consider the receipts of your veterinarian service, 'Swine Scientific', where you're the sole shareholder of the corporation, along with the profits from 'Scientific Swine Farms, Inc.,' the farrow to finish operation you own one-half of; together with other miscellaneous sources of income. True?"

The expert's eyes flared.

"If that's what my tax return shows, that's what it is."

401

"So my statement, indicating that your fees as a professional witness are only a portion of your total gross income in any given year, is accurate?"

"Your honor, I object to the characterization of this man's income from a legitimate consulting business as being that of a professional witness," Big Jim injected, trying to deflate the onerous label being applied to Dr. Bronski.

"Sustained. Mr. Aitkins, please refrain from editorializing," Judge Enwright advised, her eyes scanning the faces of the jurors.

"My statement, except for the 'professional witness' part, which the judge wants the jury to figure out on its own, was accurate, correct?" Aitkins blurted out, ready to incur the wrath of the trial court, accepting of the costs, knowing his comment was a poisonous seed that would resonate with the jurors even if the Court ordered them to disregard it.

"Judge, he can't do that," Stone erupted, struggling to remove his buttocks from the grip of his seat. "You just told him not too."

Enwright's eyes blazed.

"Counsel, in my chambers," the jurist spat, ignoring the fact that the office she was using was actually Judge Davidson's. "Now."

An awful, on-the-record dressing down of Daniel Aitkins ensued behind closed doors with all of the involved attorneys in attendance. Thompson moved for sanctions, for the imposition of a monetary fine as punishment. The court refused to react punitively, relying instead upon an admonition as sufficient deterrence.

"You do it again, and I'll grant a mistrial. As a contingency lawyer in a small firm, I can't imagine you want that, do you Mr. Aitkins? You want to have to come back, start all over again, incurring the same terrific costs of trial for your experts, not to mention your time? I don't think so," Judge Enwright lectured. "Now get back out there and play it straight. Understand?"

"Yes ma'am," Daniel Aitkins mumbled contritely.

"That was a little too close to the edge, Daniel Emery Aitkins," Dee Dee observed as they resumed their seats in the courtroom. "But it was fucking brilliant," she added, her face breaking into a smirk.

"Thanks. I'll let you take the next shot to the head from the judge," Aitkins replied.

"The jury is to disregard Mr. Aitkins' last commentary. Move on, counsel," Judge Enwright instructed.

"Your earnings from lawsuits, while significant, are only a part of your yearly income?"

"Correct."

"And of course, in this case, you're being paid well for your services."

"I'm not sure how to answer that."

"Let me try it another way. You bill what, two hundred and fifty dollars per hour?"

"For myself. One hundred dollars per hour if one of my associates is involved."

"And something less if a technician from your firm is on board?"

"Seventy-five dollars per hour for tech time."

"You also bill for supplies and lab time. I assume there's profit built into those charges as well."

"Yes."

"So that we can cut to the chase, what's your billing to Mr. Thompson to date on this case?"

"I haven't the foggiest notion."

"Less than $10,000.00?"

"Surely not."

"More than $50,000.00?"

"I wish that were the case," the witness replied with false humor.

None of the jurors smiled.

"If your current bill is somewhere between those numbers, is it closer to the smaller or the larger number?'

"The larger."

"So between $25,000.00 and $50,000.00 to date?"

"Yes."

"You're not appearing here for free, are you?"

"No."

"So isn't it safe to say, for seven days of trial, we could add another $14,000-$16,000.00 to the total, using your hourly rate and the fact you're here about eight hours a day?"

"That's not correct."

"Why not?"

"I charge by the day for trials and depositions, not by the hour."

"So per day, what will you bill for this trial?"

"A thousand dollars a day."

"Whether it's one hour or eight?"

"Of course not. If it's less than four hours, I only charge a half day."

"So if this trial concludes after eight days, as it looks like it might, we could add another $8,000.00 onto your bill," Aitkins suggested.

"That's fair."

"So the minimum charge Mr. Thompson can expect from you, using all of the numbers we've talked about, would be $25,000.00 plus $8,000.00 or $33,000.00."

"Seems about right."

Aitkins looked slyly at the judge.

"And you're OK with that, Dr. Bronski?"

Judge Enwright's brow crinkled. The witness answered before either the Court or defense counsel could intercede.

"Perfectly," Bronski said with a little too much pride.

Aitkins spent little time confronting the doctor about his opinions. The lawyer's attacks in that regard were half-hearted and brief. He knew that Bronski, as a well-seasoned veteran of the courtroom, was not going to suddenly make a mistake or retract his views. Little would be accomplished if Danny asked questions that allowed the expert to reiterate his position. The lawyer was satisfied he'd shown Bronski to be a rich, powerful man; a man who made a pretty good living beating up on folks like Dean and Nancy Anderson. He let the rest of it alone.

Harriet Enwright recessed the trial at quarter to noon and announced she would be late getting started after lunch. She was the featured luncheon speaker at the Battered Woman's Shelter in Osage, a little town located east of Detroit Lakes on the rim of the Smokey Hills.

"Be back at two," she advised the lawyers, the parties and the members of the jury. "And be prepared to go past five if we need to."

Danny ducked lunch with Dee Dee Hernesman by telling her that he had to check back at their office regarding a break-through that Alison Buckvold had uncovered in the ATV rollover case. Hernesman took the Andersons aside and praised Danny's tactics in a voice loud enough for him to hear as he walked away.

Aitkins stepped out into the mild January day. Danny's eyes searched desperately for Melanie Barnes' Lumina, the car she had purchased to replace the Audi destroyed in the accident. The woman's new vehicle was nowhere to be found.

CHAPTER 81

The courtroom was filled with observers, jurors, and participants. Danny searched for her. Melanie Barnes didn't return after lunch. The lawyer forced his attentions back to the battle being waged in the courtroom, silently hoping that the woman would reappear so that they could talk.

The afternoon passed quickly. Dr. Kelly Long, a vibrant, thick-necked professor from Champaign-Urbana, Illinois, the main campus of the University of Illinois, and the head of the National Animal Poison Control Center located on the grounds of the University, buttressed Dr. Bronski and Covington's contentions that the amounts of trace Mycotoxins found by NDSU were not responsible for the abortions experienced by the Andersons' swine.

"You've been provided with the reports of Dr. Ivan Thomas from NDSU?" Aitkins' asked on cross-examination.

"I have."

"Do you know Dr. Thomas?"

"Only by reputation. Our facility has received referrals from NDSU."

"You understand that Dr. Thomas has come to a completely different conclusion regarding the significance of the mass spectrometry findings?"

"He has a different opinion."

"Now, as we learned from your deposition, when Ms. Hernesman from my office questioned you back in August under oath on the Illini campus, you are not a toxicologist by training?"

"I am not."

"You're a veterinarian, like Dr. Thomas, but your specialty, before becoming the director of the Poison Control Center, was as an equine nutritional specialist. A horse expert."

"True."

"You'll agree that you've had no specialized schooling in toxicology, as Dr. Thomas has?"

"I've had training since coming on board as the Center's Director."

"But no advanced degree or anything in that area? Only on-the-job and continuing education stuff."

"That's fair."

Aitkins studied his notes and scanned a summary of the professor's deposition.

"You also understand that Dr. Thomas conducted a feed trial using the suspect pellets?"

"Using rodents," the woman answered with a hint of derision.

"There's something wrong with using rodents for feeding trials?"

405

"I would have used gestating sows. I would have sought to reproduce the abortions in similar animals. I would have set up a control group of pigs as well."

"So, even though you are not a toxicologist by trade and not university educated in the specialty of poisons, you take issue with the tests conducted by Dr. Thomas, someone who is a specialist in that field."

The witness smirked.

"The toxicologists on my staff agree with me in this regard."

"I'd ask that the last answer be stricken as hearsay," Aitkins requested, his voice calm, his direction undeterred.

"Mr. Thompson?" the court inquired.

"She's an expert, the director of the facility, your honor. She has the right to rely upon hearsay in forming her opinions."

"True enough," Danny interjected. "But she can't quote opinions from folks who aren't hear to testify in front of this jury."

"Point taken, Mr. Aitkins," Judge Enwright noted. "The last answer is stricken. The jury is instructed to disregard the hearsay statement."

"What don't you like about the feeding trial?" Aitkins asked, allowing the witness some latitude.

"Rats are not pigs. They have a completely different digestive system. Their reaction to small amounts of Mycotoxin, given their relative size compared to a three hundred-pound plus sow or gilt, will likely be catastrophic. If Dr. Thomas attempted to publish his so-called study in a professional journal, given his lack of protocol, he'd be laughed out of the profession."

Aitkins tightened his lips. He refrained from an overly zealous attack.

"Of course, Dr. Thomas didn't do the testing in this case for purposes of establishing general veterinary principles, did he? He ran the tests as an adjunct to a forensic investigation regarding the Anderson herd."

"That's true."

"You have no information that NDSU was planning on publishing the results obtained by their lab regarding this case?"

"Correct."

Daniel eased up.

"And of course, your center often runs tests or experiments regarding problems in the field which are not intended to be published, correct?"

"Fair enough."

"So your real criticism of NDSU, if we can get back to it, is that their study used rats, not pigs?"

"That and their reliance upon Dr. Ojala's reported research indicating that parts per billion of zearalenone can cause abortions in gestating livestock, including pigs."

"You don't recognize Dr. Ojala as one of the world's preeminent plant pathologists?"

"He is that. But he isn't a veterinarian. He's a plant pathologist. His findings, with respect to virtually undetectable amounts of various Mycotoxins causing significant health problems in livestock, are pretty far out there."

Aitkins pondered a response. Dr. Long swept her bangs, the color of the hair an unnatural blond, out of her eyes. She was a plain, scholarly woman with small hazel eyes and thick plastic-framed glasses. The attorney studied the forty-something expert before launching into a new line of inquiry.

"Your opinion in this case mirrors that of Dr. Bronski?"

"I've heard that."

"You haven't talked to Dr. Bronski about this case?"

"We talked a couple of times by phone."

"Did you ever get together with Bronski in person, and I'm not asking for any meetings where Mr. Thompson or any other lawyer from Stevenson's was present?"

"Understood. Once."

"When and where did that meeting take place?"

There was a long pause as the woman searched the face of James Thompson for assistance. The big man simply pursed his lips and allowed the question to stand.

"Could you repeat the question?" the witness asked, hesitancy building in her voice.

"Rather than do that, let me ask you this. You and Dr. Bronski know each other very well, don't you?"

Malachi Stone became visibly upset and shuffled uneasily in his seat. The corporate lawyer lunged across the table to whisper in Thompson's ear. The lead defense attorney rose to the full elevation of his imposing height.

"Your honor, I'm not certain where counsel is going with this but if it involves the personal life of Dr. Long, I would object to the relevance of such an inquiry," Big Jim said.

"It doesn't," Aitkins promised the Court.

Enwright's mouth reformed from a grimace to a look of noncommittal.

"On that basis, and that basis alone, go ahead and answer the question, Dr. Long."

The professor's eyes grew wide.

"Please explain what you mean by 'know each other very well.'"

"Well, your husband, Russell O'Brien, that is your husband's name, correct?"

"Yes," the witness responded weakly.

"Mr. O'Brien and Dr. Bronski are business associates, correct?"

Thompson's eyes drew together as he looked sternly at the woman. The defense lawyer was obviously unaware of any financial connection between the witness and Dr. Bronski.

"I believe that's true."

Aitkins' mouth opened in a wicked grin.

"Come on, Dr. Long. You're well aware that your husband is the other share holder in 'Scientific Swine Farms', the farrow to finish operation located on Dr. Bronski's spread near Wadena, Minnesota aren't you?"

The witness remained mute.

"And looking at Dr. Bronski's 1999 federal tax returns, it appears that the business, of which your husband is one-half owner, generated a profit, split by the two shareholders, in excess of one point seven million dollars."

Long's face turned from looking pained to a display of anger.

"That's not something I'm privy to. I'm not an owner in that business and I don't have any knowledge of that operation."

"I'll accept that. How do your husband and Dr. Bronski know each other, outside of this business venture, I mean?"

"They went to college together."

"University of Missouri?"

"Yes."

"Big school. How did they connect?"

Thompson stood up.

"Judge, is there really any relevance to how this woman's husband knows one of the other witnesses called by the defense in this case?"

"Good question, counsel. Mr. Aitkins, how far is this little fishing expedition going to go?"

"Just about done, your honor. I'd suggest that the fact that this witness' husband and Dr. Bronski are involved in an ongoing farrow to finish farming operation, which generates nearly two million dollars a year in profit, is indeed relevant in terms of potential interest and bias."

The judge frowned.

"Mr. Thompson, I'll let him go a little further but that's all. Go ahead, Mr. Aitkins."

"Ma'am, do you remember the question?" the attorney asked the professor.

"Yes."

"And your answer?"

"They ran track together. They were long distance runners at the University of Missouri."

"So their connection goes way back?"

"You could say that."

"Of course, you told Mr. Thompson over there about this before you agreed to testify?"

A sheepish look crossed the female professor's chalky face.

"No, I didn't."

"But once you knew Dr. Bronski was involved, both you and Dr. Bronski advised Mr. Thompson of this connection?"

"I can't speak for Dr. Bronski. I know I didn't say anything," the witness said, her anger rising. "Quite frankly, I don't see what it has to do with whether or not your clients' pigs were poisoned by Mycotoxins."

Aitkins smiled.

"I'm not sure what it has to with that either, ma'am. But we'll leave that for the jury to sort out. I have nothing further to ask of this witness, your honor."

"I'd like to decide whether I have any re-direct over the evening hours," James Thompson requested.

It was four-fifteen in the afternoon.

"Any objection from plaintiffs' counsel?" the judge asked.

"None," Daniel responded.

Judge Enwright adjourned the trial for the day.

Outside Judge Davidson's courtroom, a vicious exchange ensued between Big Jim Thompson and Malachi Stone. The Andersons had departed but their lawyers remained behind to eavesdrop on the other camp. Hernesman and Aitkins heard bits and pieces of the argument, most importantly, Thompson's repeated mantra.

"Why the fuck didn't you tell me about this?"

"Nice catch by Alison," Dee Dee whispered, referencing the private investigator, Alison Buckvold. "I never would have suspected that Bronski and that ice maiden were connected."

"Alison had a hunch. She thought that maybe Bronski and the woman professor had some commonality. By pure luck she figured out that O'Brien was married to Long. Discovered that little piece of trivia by going online and reading Long's vitae and her biography on the 'Fighting Illini' website," Aitkins revealed. "O'Brien's school and year of graduation were included in his wife's bio. After that it was a matter of Alison poking around in the materials we got from Bronski in response to our discovery requests. There it was, plain as day. O'Brien and Bronski are partners."

Hernesman draped her hand on Aitkins' shoulder. The woman's skin smelled of Ivory soap and expensive perfume. Her movement wasn't one of intimacy but was accomplished so that Dee Dee could gain her partner's attention.

"It looks like someone forgot to share that little detail with Big Jim," Dee Dee observed, her words breaking into a giggle.

Aitkins chuckled softly. The antics of the defense lawyers momentarily distracted him. Despite the success of the day, he felt heartsick. He wanted to see Melanie Barnes, to talk to her, to find answers for questions that came to him with increasing intensity. She was gone. He knew better than to chase after her.

"Something bothering you?" his partner asked, removing her hand.

"I'll be fine," the lawyer muttered.

Dee Dee's eyes squeezed together. She opened them and stared at Danny.

"I hope so. We're almost done. You gotta hold together through final arguments. Then you can get at whatever the hell is eating you."

Daniel blinked and stared hard at James Thompson as the defense attorney stormed away from Malachi Stone.

"I'd say Big Jim is none too happy about being left out of the loop," Aitkins observed, ignoring the female litigator's expression of concern.

CHAPTER 82

Pavo Tynjala had not bargained for what he got during the Anderson trial. The plaintiffs were in possession of information, culled from the depths of Tynjala's financial records, pieced together by Andrew Nelson, and Dee Dee Hernesman, that became the basis for the eventual unraveling of the house of cards erected by Alan Ignatius, Tynjala's attorney.

"Your herd became violently ill after purchasing feeder pigs from the auction barn?"

James Thompson watched the little farmer, the man's Finnish complexion and yellow tufts of hair in sharp contrast with those of the attorney, as the defense lawyer asked questions. F.W. Barnes had been the primary contact between Alan Ignatius and the Stevenson's defense team. After the surprises of the past week, during which Thompson witnessed the destruction of several significant portions of his defense, the big man was no longer certain of the information he possessed regarding any particular witness.

"That's right."

"You bought thirty-five head that turned out to be Anderson hogs?"

"Feeder-weight females. I bought 'em as replacement gilts."

"You had your herd examined by Dr. Plasac from Wheaton, your regular Vet, after the animals began to get sick?"

"Yep."

"And the blood titers showed HPP, the same strain as found in the Anderson herd?"

"That's what I've been told."

Aitkins didn't object to the hearsay. He allowed Thompson to cultivate a sense of security with the witness, providing Tynjala with a measure of comfort before Dee Dee's cross-examination would rip the Finn's self-esteem to shreds.

Besides, Daniel mused to himself, *they'll just call one of the Vet's to verify that the HPP is the same type. It's not at issue,* he thought.

"The HPP infection, what was the course of the illness?" Thompson asked.

"Well, within a few days, the gilts and sows started coughing. I used the feeders we bought as additional breeding stock because the winter stressed my herd. They weren't breeding. After getting the cough, it got so bad, they wouldn't eat, they was hacking and choking on their own spit. Then it spread to the growers, the finishers, and the nursery. Within a couple of weeks, every hog on the place had HPP."

Thompson scrutinized his witness. He wanted to avoid any gross embellishment.

"Are you sure every hog was infected?"

"Well, Dr. Plasac drew blood from animals in all of our buildings. Every last barn had hogs sick with that damn HPP."

Judge Enwright looked down her nose at the farmer.

"Watch your language, Mr. Tynjala," she warned.

"Sorry, your honor."

"Any question in your mind where the HPP came from?" the defense lawyer inquired, looking in Daniel's direction, certain an objection as to a lack of foundation was imminent.

Aitkins mulled over intervening. The pathogenic history of the HPP on the Tynjala Farm was beyond the expertise of Pavo Tynjala. Again, the attorney let the question stand. Dee Dee cast a perplexed glance at Dan.

"I don't generally buy hogs from outside my place. I'm a farrow to finish operator, just like Anderson. But in this instance, with the summer coming and a shortage of breeding stock on hand, I took a chance," Tynjala admitted.

"A calculated risk?"

"Well, animals from auctions carry certificates from the owners, here, Anderson, that the owners' aren't aware of any infectious diseases or other health conditions in the hogs. I relied upon that. I dealt with Anderson before, knew the man. I figured he wouldn't pull a fast one. I was wrong."

"Your animals never had HPP before you bought those thirty-five feeder pigs?"

"Never."

"You bought no other hogs in the time frame before the HPP outbreak, say in the six months before that?"

"Not that I recall."

Thompson sensed that the witness desperately wanted to blurt out the fact that he'd brought his own lawsuit against the Andersons regarding his loss. Big Jim knew that such a disclosure was precluded by the court's earlier ruling. Stevenson's couldn't risk antagonizing the judge near the end of the case. Thompson folded his hands, looked up from his notes, and declared that he had no further questions.

Dee Dee Hernesman began the cross-examination of the farmer. She maintained a steady pace as she questioned the middle-aged man from Wheaton.

"Mr. Tynjala, am I to understand that you didn't purchase any other stock during the six months prior to the auction trip where you bought thirty-five hogs that originated with the Anderson Farm?"

412

"Like I told the big fella over there, I don't recall making any other purchases."

"Remember when my partner, Emery Aitkins, took your deposition in your lawyer's office down in St. Cloud, what, about two weeks ago?"

"Can't hardly forget that experience," the farmer spit out with a degree of acid.

"You remember being asked a question then, by Mr. Aitkins, a different Mr. Aitkins, as follows, page twenty-seven, line four:

'Question: During the six months prior to the auction purchase, did you buy any other pigs of any kind and bring those animals onto your farm?'"

"I don't rightly recall that question."

Dee Dee flipped on Andrew Nelson's computer. The page of the deposition appeared substantially enlarged on a white movie screen on the wall across from the jury.

"With the court's permission, I'd like to use this laptop to highlight the deposition pages I'll be referencing."

"Go ahead."

A red dot, the beam of a laser pointer, directed the witness' attention to the appropriate place on the projected image.

"See the question, Mr. Tynjala?"

"I see it."

"You'll agree you were asked that question, with Mr. Barnes, co-counsel for the defense, and your own lawyer, Mr. Ignatius, present?"

"I'd have to say I was."

The lawyer smiled and turned to face the hog farmer from her position standing behind the counsel table.

"Do remember how you answered the question back then, two weeks ago?"

Tynjala stared blankly at the deposition excerpt.

"Without refreshing your recollection by reading the text," Hernesman added.

The man's face turned red. It was obvious he was embarrassed by the woman's directness.

"I can't say."

"Take a look. Didn't you answer 'no'?"

Tynjala studied the enlargement.

"That's what it says up there."

"You were under oath."

"I guess so."

The woman's eyes pinched together in annoyance.

"Do I have to put the oath portion of the deposition up there to refresh your memory?"

Pavo glared.

413

"No, you don't. I was under oath."

Aitkins sat back in his chair. He had contemplated taking notes. Instead, he simply watched the performance of his understudy with pride.

"So two weeks ago, you were definite. You told Mr. Emery Aitkins that you did not purchase any pigs from outside your farm other than the thirty-five we've been talking about, correct?"

"Seems to be what I said."

"And today, when asked by Mr. Thompson that very same question, you had a different answer."

"Whatdoyamean?" the farmer questioned, running the words together in alarm.

"Well, you told Mr. Thompson you didn't know if you bought other outside animals, isn't that what you said."

"Boy, your memory is better than mine. I'm not sure."

Dee Dee looked at Angie Devlin.

"You want me to have the Court Reporter find your answer and read for you just to make sure?"

Tynjala drew in a huge breath and exhumed heavily through his mouth. The pressure of the escaping carbon dioxide caused his lips to flap.

"I'll take your word for it."

Hernesman eased up.

"So you'll agree that you have stated, under oath, that you did not purchase any other pigs, during the six months before you bought the thirty-five at the auction, nor did you bring any pigs other than those thirty-five onto your farm in those same six months, true?"

"It seems I did say that."

The lawyer resumed her seat.

"Did you make a mistake?"

"No."

"So that's a true picture of your hog purchases for the period of time in question?"

"I think I might have bought a boar or two?"

Hernesman's smile increased.

"That's reflected in your records."

The farmer nodded in self-satisfaction.

"You also answered written questions for Mr. Aitkins, Sr., correct?"

"Rogatories or somethin'?"

"Right, interrogatories."

Tynjala pursed his lips.

"Well, Mr. Ignatius put the answers together, had 'em all typed up for me."

414

"But again, you read them and then signed them under oath, right?"

The farmer grinned.

"Well, I signed them, that's for certain. I don't recollect reading them, though."

The attorney changed the image on the screen.

"Here's the signature page. It shows you signed the Answers to Interrogatories. It also shows they were under oath."

"I see that."

Dee Dee paused and reflected.

"You in the habit of signing things you've sworn are true without reading them first?"

"Not normally."

"Did you read these Answers before you swore to them?"

"I guess."

The female lawyer switched images on the projector. She shut off the light source to the device while she moved on.

"You also provided us with copies of your financial records, invoices, tax returns, the whole nine yards regarding your farming operation for the past three years, up to the end of last month, December."

"Yep."

"And if we look at your inventory sheets for January, February, March, and April of last year, we'll see that you've reflected purchasing the two boars you told us about, and the thirty-five feeder pigs from the auction, correct?"

The attorney turned on the light and paged through the inventory sheets by using the projector.

"Agreed?'

"That's what it shows."

Aitkins knew that his partner's pulse was beginning to race. She was zeroing in on her prey.

"But of course, that's not the truth, is it Mr. Tynjala?"

Thompson clambered to his feet.

"Your honor, this badgering of the witness has got to stop. I'd ask that the court admonish counsel not to make inferences not supported by the record."

"I was just getting to that, judge."

"With the understanding that you will connect, proceed."

"Remember my question?" Hernesman asked.

"No."

Dee Dee turned to Ms. Devlin.

"Please read the question back."

Angie found the passage and read the question aloud.

"That's not right. It is the truth," Tynjala asserted.

415

Aitkins detected the pounding of his partner's heart through the thin fabric of her blouse.

"You're certain of that, are you Mr. Tynjala? Then can you tell me why your Agrifax sheets, not the ones you keep in your personal records, but the ones you turned over to your FHA loan officer, show that, between January fifteenth and May seventeenth, Tynjala Hog Farms bought over four hundred feeder pigs, sows, and gilts from seven separate sources?"

There was an audible click. A neatly prepared chart appeared on the movie screen, casting an image of deception and untruth for all of the jurors to see. The farmer from Wheaton stared at the numbers and names. It was all there; all the information that he had so carefully removed from his personal file had been uncovered. He was caught, trapped, as visible as a bison in a supermarket.

"Well I'll be damned," was all the Finlander said.

"I have no further questions," the advocate announced between rare breaths.

"On that note, I think we'll take our morning recess, folks," Judge Enwright advised, her eyes struggling not to stare unkindly at the witness.

James Thompson sat expressionless. His eyes were closed. His great hands were clenched and rested uneasily on a notepad. As the rest of the defense team vacated their seats, the black man rotated in his chair to follow the retreat of Pavo Tynjala. Thompson watched Alan Ignatius with palpable scorn as the disgraced attorney uttered words of steady reassurance to the Finlander before leading the despondent farmer out of the building.

CHAPTER 83

An unsteady truce remained in effect. Daniel reappeared in the Aitkins marital bed the evening before the final day of trial. There had been no in-depth dialogue between the husband and the wife. No sudden revelation precipitated the attorney's return to the attic. It simply happened.

Julie sat up in bed, a massive down pillow supporting her upper body. The writer was reading a book, *These Granite Islands,* a debut novel written by Sarah Stonich, a writer from Proctor, Minnesota, a little railroad town that no one west of Brainerd had ever heard of. Julie followed the printed words, entranced by the story, longing to see her own work published.

Danny reclined in bed next to his wife. The room was quiet. Only the steady blow of a furnace fan distributing hot air from the basement utility room intruded upon the artificial silence.

The lawyer was working out the details of his final argument. The case was riding on the precision of his words. A family farm hung in the balance. He knew that Stevenson's had taken some serious licks during the trial. So had the Andersons. The loss of the negligence per se theory, the absence of the simple, concrete premise: "If it's adulterated feed, it's in violation of the law. If it's in violation of the law, it's negligence;" was a loss that could not be easily calculated. In contrast, the concept of breach of implied warranty, all that remained of the plaintiffs' claim, was amorphous, like the dust clouds of a nebula. Dan knew he would have to work hard to construct a bridge between abstract legal theory and the practical application of that theory during his summation.

The lawyer grew tired. A steady wind buffeted the eaves of the house. Periodic gusts of migratory cold found their way across the room.

"I know you said the agent guy... what was his name?" Dan asked, opening a brief dialogue with his wife.

"Hartley Bennett," Julie responded without looking up from her book.

"Ya, Bennett...was interested in your novel. Has he called back?"

The corners of the woman's eyes scrutinized her husband.

"He called today."

The disclosure surprised Danny.

"And you never said a word?" he asked.

"You didn't seem too interested," she replied, her gaze locked on the pages of the book in her hands.

"Jules, you know that's not true," he whispered, injury plain in his expression. "I'm your biggest fan when it comes to your writing."

Danny wanted to reveal that he loved her novel; that he had read excerpts and thought only great things about the story. He remained silent to preserve decorum.

Her eyes met his. A sheet was pulled up to the base of her neck. She wore her hair loose. Strands of yellow flared out behind her head on the pillow. Her hands relaxed, allowing the book to rest in her lap.

"Hartley's sending me a contract," she said quietly. "He's negotiating with a regional publisher, one that prints literary fiction. There'll be an advance. Somewhere between twenty and thirty thousand. The first printing will be hard cover, guaranteed ten thousand copies, distributed nation-wide."

There was no boastfulness in the woman's voice.

"You're kidding, right?"

"Nope. The contract should be here before the weekend," Julie said, removing the hardbound novel from her lap, placing the book on an adjacent end table. "I was going to have my attorney look it over before I signed it," she added, allowing a slight influence of humor to infiltrate the overly courteous setting.

"My wife the famous novelist," the attorney mused softly. He pushed his notes away and negotiated the covers.

"What do you think you're doing?" the woman asked, the impact of her comment softened by its tone.

"Finding out what it's like to make love to a published writer," he joked.

"Mmmm. Let me think about this. You've been a silent, reclusive jerk with too much on your mind and no time for me for more than a month. Does someone like that deserve the attention of the author of the next Book-Of-The-Month-Club selection?"

His hands slid under the cool cotton of her pajama top and found the warmth of her bare skin. Julie Aitkins reached out and turned off a lamp on the nightstand before moving towards a point of significant compromise in the middle of their bed.

As their lips met in a tender, patient kiss, the embrace of two people who believed they understood everything there was to know about each other, the hurt within Daniel Aitkins compressed. His eyes opened to study the lines of his mate's face, the curve of her forehead, the shape of her nose. He loved her. There was no question that was true. His next comment caught both of them off guard.

"Does this mean I have to join your fan club?" he asked as his hands slipped up her stomach.

CHAPTER 84

Horace Brewster, DVM leaned back in the witness chair considering his answer. Pale morning light infiltrated the upper floor of the Becker County Courthouse and enveloped Judge Davidson's bench. The defense lawyers, their faces identically impassive, their eyes concealed from the jurors, remained motionless, as if in suspended animation, as they waited for the witness to respond to Aitkins' rebuttal examination.

"Well, Mr. Aitkins," Dr. Brewster began, "here's what I think about the testimony provided by Mr. Tynjala. The fact is, the accounting problem that your partner pointed out has a significant impact upon Mr. Tynjala's accusations against the Andersons with respect to the outbreak of HPP in his pigs."

"How so?"

"As Dr. Bronski, Dr. Covington, and Dr. Long so aptly testified, HPP is highly contagious. Here, as we now know," the expert said, his eyes diverting to make significant eye contact with the jury, "Mr. Tynjala bought all sorts of pigs from all sorts of sources. Seven other places supplied him with hogs, hogs that, if he was truly a closed herd, farrow to finish operator as he claimed, should never have walked onto his farm."

"Why is that?"

"Like Mr. Anderson said, if you're a closed herd operator, you raise every last pig on your farm from your farm, with the exception of the boars. You bring in certified, healthy boars from reputable suppliers so as to add positive attributes to the bloodlines you're trying to build. In that sense, the Anderson Farm is a true farrow to finish farm. The only hogs that walk onto their property are the breeding males, the boars. And those are quarantined for a minimum of thirty days to protect against any bugs that the animals might harbor. Mr. Tynjala, for whatever reason, and there is no good animal husbandry reason to take the risks he took by willy-nilly buying stock all over the countryside and introducing potential disease carriers into his previously closed herd, violated the principles of a closed herd. And he paid the price."

Aitkins phrased an additional question.

"But how does that impact Tynjala's claim that his animals were infected by pigs from the Anderson place?"

Brewster stretched his small frame.

"There's no way to know where the HPP came from. Unless you blood test every last bargain basement pig, and that's exactly what this Tynjala fellow was buying when he bought stock from hog jockeys and auction houses, there's no way to trace the origin of the disease. It might be from the Andersons; it might also be from any of the other seven sources of hogs. There's no way to make an educated guess, much less prove it."

"The court's gonna instruct the fine folks of the jury that a point doesn't have to be proven to a certainty by either party. All the defense needs to prove is that the HPP probably came from the Andersons."

Brewster stroked his chin with his strong fingers.

"There's no way anyone can say that it's more likely the disease came from the Andersons versus one of the other suppliers. That would be absurd."

Aitkins smiled.

"Anything else you think needs mentioning while we're at it, Dr. Brewster?"

The witness turned towards the jurors again.

"The idea that the Andersons' problems were caused by e-coli, HPP, the use of lindane and fuel oil, or even mange, is ridiculous."

"Why?"

Big Jim Thompson tossed an insincere objection out into the still air of the courtroom.

"Improper rebuttal, your honor. I object to the witness editorializing, using the word 'ridiculous'."

"He's entitled to state his opinion, Judge, in his own words," Aitkins argued.

"Overruled."

"Go ahead and answer," Daniel advised.

"Because short of Mr. and Mrs. Anderson injecting their gilts and sows with lindane and oil, there's no way that any combination of the factors listed by Dr. Bronski is a likely culprit. None of those items can account for the catastrophic levels of abortion experienced on the evening in question."

"That leaves only the pelleted feed supplied by Stevenson's?"

"That's right. It's my opinion that the feed is not just the number one suspect here, it's the guilty party."

"Any other concerns about the evidence presented by the defendant?"

"Surely."

"Such as?"

The veterinarian licked the edges of his lips. He raised a paper cup of room temperature water to his mouth and drank.

"The notion that the Andersons were free to rebreed the affected sows and gilts, thereby cutting their damages to one or two lost farrowings, is also flawed."

"What about that accusation troubles you?"

James Thompson cleared his throat but did not voice an objection. Aitkins chanced a look at the members of the jury. Mrs.

O'Connell, the juror who had been riveted to every question he asked, and every answer his witnesses had given, was writing with fervor. In the back row, in the seat closest to the bank of windows spanning the rear of the jury box, Trooper Blomquist sat loosely in his seat, his eyes riveted upon the steady rotation of a fan secured to the ceiling high above the courtroom floor.

Shit, Aitkins thought. *I've lost him.*

The trial lawyer turned his attention back to the veterinarian.

"There's new research that indicates exposure to fusarium mold, even in small amounts, compromises not only the gestational and nursing capabilities of sows and gilts but also impairs their general ability to resist disease. In a nutshell, the advice that Dr. Guttormson and Dr. Thomas gave to the Andersons was prudent: sell the female animals impacted by the Mycotoxins and begin rebuilding your closed herd from within."

"What about buying certified breeding animals from the outside as suggested by the defense and incorporated into Dr. Eunice Underwood's computations?"

"Like I said on direct exam, that's a great approach in a perfect world. But here, where the cash flow of the Anderson Farm was disrupted by the abortions, the Andersons didn't have the money to put such a plan into practice. But even if they did, to require the Andersons to do that doesn't recognize, nor compensate, for the years of work that they put into developing their own line of hogs. A point that no one has yet mentioned is that the Andersons hogs were the products of years of selective breeding; close monitoring and tinkering. In one disastrous event, all of that effort was destroyed. Using outside females as replacement breeding animals doesn't begin to compensate for this loss of genetic engineering."

"Anything else?"

"As a farrow to finish, closed herd operator myself, my own opinion of the numbers advanced by Mr. Nelson is that they are infinitely reasonable, and, perhaps, a little conservative."

Thompson's nostrils flared as he stood up, disrupting the relative calm of the examination.

"That's unsupported testimony from someone with no foundation to supply financial or economic testimony. There's been no showing that Mr. Brewster is in a position to provide a financial analysis of the plaintiffs' losses."

"The objection is sustained as to a lack of foundation. The jury is to disregard the last answer of the witness."

Aitkins was angry. His ears, clearly visible above his short blond hair, turned crimson.

"Don't I get a chance to make an argument, judge?"

"Not on this one, Mr. Aitkins. Move on."

"With all due respect, your honor..."

"Move on," Judge Enwright stated emphatically.

The lawyer stared at the jurist. Aitkins wanted to do battle with the judge over the ruling. He looked at the jury. Acknowledging the power of the bench, the attorney backed down.

"No further questions."

F.W. Barnes handled the re-cross of Dr. Brewster, attacking the veterinarian's credentials, comparing the plainspoken Vet's lack of international standing to the considerable resumes of Drs. Bronski and Long. In the end, the North Dakotan remained calm. Barnes became frustrated. Brewster's eyes retained a clear, determined gaze as the defense lawyer launched a fruitless assault on the expert's opinion. Exasperated, the litigator ran his fingers nervously through the field of white covering his head, stared hard at the unrepentant witness, and sat down in utter defeat.

"Nothing more from the defense," Thompson inserted at the end of Barnes' failed onslaught.

Behind James Thompson's small eyes, a vision of his daughter, the treasure of his life he'd not seen in nearly two weeks, began to sing. His little girl, her tawny skin aglow beneath the steady pulse of spotlights, was on a stage, her hair piled high on top of her head, her figure mature, seemingly a carbon-copy of her mother. He listened intently as the woman who had once been his daughter began to sing in a sweet, high soprano. He wasn't able to decipher the lyrics of the song, but the tune, the tune was captivating.

"Counsel?" the judge prodded, her eyes staring at the lead defense attorney, the intrusion shattering the man's respite.

"I was asking if you can be here by seven-forty-five tomorrow morning to go over the proposed jury instructions and the special verdict form," Judge Enwright disclosed.

Outwardly, James Thompson smiled. Inwardly, he sought to recall the vision of his daughter that had been disturbed by the jurist's intrusion.

"That's fine, Judge Enwright. We'll be here."

The judge dismissed the jury with the admonition that they would be getting the case for deliberation in the morning, after the jury instructions were read and the attorneys had completed their final arguments.

"You OK, Jim?" Malachi Stone asked as the defense team began to round up their files. "You seem sort of distracted."

The ex-Gopher looked at the shorter man through blazing eyes.

"I'm fine, Malachi. Never been better," the black man responded. "But thanks for asking."

"I thought so," the Iowan added, patting the big man on the back.

"I'll see you folks for breakfast at six-thirty," Thompson advised, packing the last of his trial notes in a briefcase.

"We're not going to work on the argument together?" F.W. Barnes asked in a manner meant to convey a feeling of having been slighted.

Big Jim didn't turn to face the older attorney as he responded.

"Seems like you folks have helped me way more than necessary during the course of this trial," Thompson said, malice apparent in his voice. "I think I'll handle writing the summation on my own, if you don't mind."

CHAPTER 85

The low hum of a photocopier drifted across the conference room. Daniel Aitkins rubbed his eyes and tried to focus his thought. He'd reclaimed his blue binders from the courtroom, the contents of the notebooks significantly diminished after the attorneys had selected documents during the trial, removed them from the folders, and introduced them as evidence. Danny focused on the reams of hand scrawled notes he'd produced during the trial. The law firm's staff, associates, and most of the firm's partners had left the office.

Dee Dee sat across from him. She was reviewing proposed jury instructions; written outlines of the law that both parties would request Judge Enwright read to the jurors before the attorneys argued their cases. There had been a time when jurors heard the lawyers' arguments and then received the rules of law from the Court; the instructions came after the arguments. Over the years, the court system in Becker County, as in many parts of the state, came to recognize that providing the legal parameters, the instructions, to the jurors before final argument made more sense. Jurors were better able to apply instructions given to them by the court to the attorneys' arguments if the jurors were informed about the law before the summations took place.

Harriet Enwright's practice was to provide jurors with written copies of the final jury instructions. The folks on the jury could, if they chose, follow along as she read the instructions to them. They also received copies of the special verdict form, the questions that the jury needed to answer as a deliberative body. Once the lawyers' summations were concluded, the bailiff would retrieve all copies of the jury instructions and the special verdict form. One original set of instructions and verdict, along with all of the documentary and physical evidence, would accompany the jurors into the deliberation room.

In other parts of the country, in other parts of Minnesota, judges were experimenting with further innovations, including allowing jurors to submit written questions to the court during the trial. Harriet Enwright was too cautious a jurist to go that far in fiddling with the jury process.

It would be up to the judge, come the next morning, to decide which of the competing jury instructions submitted by the parties would be read to the jury. Given that the jurist had limited the plaintiffs' theory of recovery to breach of the implied warranty of merchantability under Minnesota Statute 336.2-314 and breach of the implied warranty of fitness for a particular use under 336.2-315, the areas of conflict between the parties in terms of jury instructions would be relatively minor.

"This case has become remarkably simple," Dee Dee noted as she placed her pen on the conference table surface and looked across the ocean of paper separating her from her partner.

Danny's face contorted.

"You're saying that Judge Enwright did us a big favor by tossing out our other theories of recovery?"

Hernesman tilted her head.

"That's exactly what I'm saying."

"I don't know, Dees. I'd much rather be arguing strict liability or negligence per se than warranty."

"I disagree," the female litigator responded. "Think of it this way. Everyone on the jury stares at us with puzzled looks when we parade out multiple theories of recovery. Plus, they've never, except in passing, heard terms like 'tortfeasor', 'negligence', 'causation' and 'strict liability'. But they all know, every last housewife, farmer, or laborer on the jury knows about warranties. It's likely every last one of them has, at some point in time, bumped up against a manufacturer who was less than quick to honor a warranty."

Aitkins studied the face of the woman.

"Ya, but those usually involve express warranties, promises made in writing."

"Doesn't matter. Think about it. If they've been burned in their own circumstance, how likely is it they're gonna be sympathetic to a company that sells food for pregnant pigs loaded with poison?"

"Good point."

"Tackle it from the premise that this is, and always was, a simple case. Don't get too far a field beating up on old Pavo Tynjala or wandering into the wasteland of alternative causes thrown up by the defense. Stick to Horace Brewster's mantra: 'they sold it as hog feed; the Andersons bought it as hog feed; the feed contained poisons that killed the hogs.'"

Daniel broadened his mouth.

"I knew there was a reason I hired you."

"Just stick with me, mister and only good things will come to you," Hernesman quipped, directing her attention back to the proposed jury instructions.

"I'm still worried about Trooper Blomquist."

Dee Dee raised her head.

"I am too. But there's not much we can about that now. Maybe if we're lucky, he'll be the only hold-out and the others will stall until the sixth hour, allowing a six-sevenths verdict."

"He's pretty strong willed. I'm concerned that he'll turn them, one at a time."

425

"I doubt he'll turn Mrs. O'Connell. She was riveted on you during the whole trial," the female attorney observed. "I think she's sweet on you."

A light laugh passed between Aitkins' lips.

"She's a little too experienced for me."

"That's a kind way of putting it. Whatever, she'll be as loyal as a dog to Daniel Emery Aitkins and his cause."

They resumed their respective tasks and worked past ten o'clock.

Danny drove towards the farmhouse in his truck. The dwelling was dark. An exuberant moon stood above the trees, illuminating the yard and pasture in gracious light. His stomach was upset. His hands were nervous with sweat as he released his grip on the steering wheel of the Ranger and exited the vehicle. The case was only a small part of what was eating at him. Larger issues, topics of grave importance to his place in the world, awaited exhumation and examination under calculated scrutiny. The cold metal of the doorknob seared the lawyer's bare hand as he opened the back door of the home.

Strains of folk music, a song by Fargo's Brenda Weiler, floated through the house. He followed the music into the living room. Julie, her hair in disarray, her eyes fluttering unconsciously to changing guitar chords, was slumped in a recliner, her body covered with her grandmother's hand stitched quilt. The only light in the room came from limpid images scrolling across the television set. Some late night host on some late night show that Danny never cared for and never watched babbled on endlessly, the man's words muted deliberately so that Julie could listen to music.

There was grace, there was tenderness, and there was integrity displayed in the worn lines of his wife's face. The attorney bent to kiss the woman's cheek.

"Hi," she said weakly, her eyelids quivering at his touch. "Long night?"

"Dee Dee and I just finished a half hour ago. I've got my closing all done. She's ready to argue the jury instructions."

His wife's eyes opened.

"I took tomorrow off. I want to hear your closing," she whispered.

"I'd like that," he replied.

The springs of the recliner objected as the attorney joined his wife in the chair. They snuggled in front of the muted television, listening to the bittersweet music of the female singer, until they both fell fast asleep.

I was standing at the corner of Ashland and Oxford Street

it was cold enough to turn the rain drizzling down into sleet

I was sitting in a place I could not remember
to feed and be at one with
and my father started speaking softly in my ear
saying 'this is what you want and this is what can save you'

fly me back to where I belong
fly me back to my family
why don't you look down in our faces sometime
and fly us out of here?

I was holding onto a child as if it were my own
I had everything all figured out with everything unknown
and I stared into his eyes, and I stared into my own
saying 'this is what can save, though my body may fail me'

fly me back to where I belong
fly me back to my family
why don't you look down in our faces sometime
and fly us out of here?

I looked up to gaze into the sky instead of at my feet
nothing can describe the feeling
I could hardly speak.

CHAPTER 86

Melanie Barnes tossed and turned. Her children remained in deep slumber. The trial was due to end tomorrow. She had avoided Danny. There was nothing left to talk about, to mull over, to discuss. It wasn't that she didn't long to see him, to feel the faint distress of his breath against her skin as he slept next to her. All the feelings of want, of love, of physical desire, remained intact. She fought them every day, every waking moment, as she fought the urge to call Julie Aitkins and unburden her soul. There was no hiding her condition from close scrutiny. The nausea was passing. Her body was adjusting to the reality of carrying a child far quicker than her mind was.

"Where are we headed?" Melanie asked herself, her hands clenching cotton sheets, her eyes watering without respite. "There is no 'we' " she acknowledged, conversing with herself in low tones, the outline of high, distant clouds brightened by the escaping moon visible through her window. "There never will be a 'we'."

It was something she'd known from the very start. There was never any question that Danny Aitkins would choose to remain with his wife and his family.

"How could I be so stupid?" she asked herself.

There was no relief for the woman as she debated her circumstance for the entirety of the long, bleak night.

The air of her bedroom was thick with moisture at daybreak. Melanie sought to roust her son and her daughter from their beds. Her feet labored to propel her body. She shuffled across the carpeting of her bedroom floor, her steps leaden and heavy despite her diminutive stature. Her scarlet hair hung limp across the base of her neck. The woman's cheeks were stained with salt and appeared lifeless as she made her way to her children.

The courtroom was filled to capacity. Additional members of the Grafton faction of the Patriots were in attendance. The militiamen had learned that the case would be submitted to the jury. Emil Bremer and his cohorts were dressed in casual attire and remained unobtrusive, their anti-government fervor significantly diminished after the debacle involving their compatriot from Indiana. Earl Bethard noted the increasing presence of the Patriots and requested that deputies be assigned to the courthouse. As court opened that morning, two armed lawmen occupied either side of the doorway to the courtroom. Their faces were drawn in mirror-images of confidence. The lawmen satisfied their curiosity with pat searches of selected spectators. Julie Aitkins, dressed casually in a bright magenta sweater and blue jeans, entered the courtroom without scrutiny.

"Judge, I agree that the defense is entitled to a mitigation of damages instruction," Dee Dee Hernesman conceded as the attorneys discussed the jury instructions outside the hearing of the jurors in Judge Davidson's chambers. "JIG (referring to jury instruction) 20.65 makes it clear that in contract cases, and a breach of warranty case is a contract case, the defense is entitled to a mitigation instruction. However, the defense hasn't cited 20.65. Instead, they've drafted their own instruction which doesn't comport to the standard JIG," Hernesman added.

The judge frowned.

"I saw that. Mr. Thompson, any particular reason why you chose to try to craft something when there's a standard JIG available?"

James Thompson looked across the table at his adversaries. He cleared his throat before coming eye to eye with the judge.

"We've cited language from several Minnesota Supreme Court decisions in the footnote to our proposed instruction. We believe that, because this is an agricultural contract, the specific language from agricultural cases should be used, not the more general language of 20.65."

Hernesman winced.

"Judge, the problem with the cases cited by the defense is that they all pre-date the adoption of the new JIGs. Clearly, if the committee drafting the instructions wanted to incorporate some special language for farm-related contracts, it could have. The cases cited by Mr. Thompson also pre-date the adoption of the Uniform Commercial Code in Minnesota. They don't reflect the UCC discussion of mitigation included in the present JIG."

Angie Devlin's fingers poured across the stenography keypad as she followed the arguments.

"I'm going to side with plaintiffs on this one," Judge Enwright advised. "We'll use the standard instruction. Your objection, Mr. Thompson, is noted for the record."

"Very well," the big man acquiesced.

"The defense has asked for 90.25, adjustment of future damages to present cash value," Harriet observed, her eyes scanning the respective paragraphs of the competing instructions. "But the plaintiffs don't have it in their submission."

"We don't think it applies," Dee Dee asserted. "It's set out in the personal injury portion of the JIGs, not in the breach of contract/warranty section. We don't like it's applicable."

"Interesting. Mr. Thompson?"

James' eyes blinked.

"Well, ma'am, that's nonsensical. If the court adopts plaintiffs' view, the jury wouldn't be told that they are to consider any award of future damages based upon what an award today, in terms of today's dollars, would earn if invested. If the instruction isn't given, the jury may well award a number to the plaintiffs that doesn't take into account the present value of money in hand."

"Point made. Looking at the comments, Ms. Hernesman, I see no limitation included which prohibits this instruction from broader application."

"But your honor..."

"I've made my decision, counselor. You can argue that, in addition to taking into account a discount due to the present value of money, the jury can take into account the issue of inflation. In fact. I believe your economist, what was his name...?" Judge Enwright paused.

"Nelson."

"Yes, Mr. Nelson. He testified along those lines, both as to present value and as to inflation. It's an instruction that has to be given."

F.W. Barnes nodded knowingly and smiled a crooked little sliver of a smile.

"Anything else?"

"Nothing from the plaintiffs."

"Defense would renew its motion to dismiss the claim in its entirety," Jim Thompson asserted.

"And for the record, that motion is once again denied. There is sufficient testimony for the jury to conclude that a breach of implied warranty occurred. Whether they do so or not, we're about to find out," the jurist ruled. "We'll take ten minutes, and then begin instructions."

Aitkins studied the state patrolman as the judge read the precise language of the jury instructions and the special verdict form to the jury. Blomquist's hands never left his lap. The man's eyes remained closed while all of the other jurors furiously scribbled notes or read along silently as Judge Enwright explained their roles as the fact finders in the case and detailed the law that they were to apply in answering the questions on the verdict form.

Daniel shook his head imperceptibly as he envisioned the trooper, staid and erect, sitting in the sanctity of the jury room. He'd likely be elected foreperson. The man had the look of leadership written all over his face. Though he was considerably younger than anyone else on the panel, he would end up directing the jury's deliberations. Of that, Danny Aitkins had no doubt. And when it came time to speak, the lawman would do so intelligently, calmly, and without passion. He would sabotage the case. That's what would happen. It was certain, as certain as the rising and setting of the sun.

Big Jim walked up to the podium. He brought no notes with him to the lectern. All of his argument was lodged in his brain, committed to memory, an art; a trick that Daniel had never mastered. The younger lawyer would have to rely upon an outline to get him through his final summation. The black man needed no such crutch.

"It is an unfortunate thing that the Andersons are here in front of you today," the defense lawyer began. "And it would be natural, if you believe that their farm has been affected in a severe and adverse way by the events at issue, for you to have sympathy for them. It would be easy for you to find Stevenson's, a faceless legal entity, a fiction created by commerce, to be responsible for whatever the Andersons say happened simply because the Andersons are your neighbors and Stevenson's is not. To do that, to come to that place, you would have to disregard your oath, your sworn promise as jurors, and you would have to ignore Judge Enwright's instructions in this case."

Thompson paused and closed his eyes as if in prayer.

"Let us talk about what it is that we know, not what we might be able to conjecture, conjure up, or speculate about. Once we review that which is concrete, that which is real, I assure you, absent some violation of your sworn oath and duty, there will be no conclusion left to you but a finding that Stevenson's Sci-Swine had nothing to do with the malady that allegedly befell your neighbors."

The big man proceeded to weave a seamless story consistent with the defendant's theory of the case: that the Andersons were well meaning but careless; inefficient farmers who ignored the admonitions of their own veterinarian. That they allowed HPP to infect their herd and, failing to do what Dr. Guttormson required of them, that their hogs infected the herds of other innocent farmers. That the plaintiffs used archaic and ineffective methods of controlling mange, methods that adversely impacted their own pigs. That the water supply to their barn was contaminated. That if there was anything to the story told by the plaintiffs regarding the abortion storm, the incident was caused by their own failings and had, as testified to by world-renowned experts called by the defense, nothing to do with the feed sold to the Andersons by the defendant.

After thirty minutes of punching holes in the wall of the plaintiffs' breach of warranty case, Big Jim finally came to the issue of recompense.

"Now, understand that, no matter how you decide the questions regarding liability, those questions dealing with the alleged breach of warranty and mitigation of damages, the instructions on the special verdict form require that you answer the damages questions. There are two. One deals with damages from the

431

date of the alleged incident through today's date. The other covers damages into the future."

Thompson swallowed hard. His eyes never left the faces of the jurors. Daniel noted that the defense lawyer had the same inclination as Aitkins' did about the state trooper. Though Big Jim made certain he kept eye contact with every member of the panel, it was plain to Danny that Thompson was focusing his efforts upon Donald Blomquist.

"I do not concede or agree that the Andersons are entitled to any sum of money. But because you must fill in those blanks with something, I will suggest figures for each. As you heard from our economist and our experts, the Andersons, if they sustained any loss at all, should have been able to rebuild their herd within one or two farrowing cycles. They could have borrowed the funds to purchase certified breeding stock and limited, mitigated if you will, their claimed losses to something around $30,000.00. That's the figure you should insert as past damages suffered. And remember, this figure would be the maximum because, as Dr. Bronski noted, there is no way to confirm that every sow and gilt on the Anderson Farm lost its litter during the incident at issue."

The lawyer drew a deep breath and looked hard at the Trooper.

"As far as the future is concerned, had the Andersons followed Dr. Bronski's analysis, they would be back in operation today, with no ill effects beyond a couple of lost farrowings. Thus, the amount to be inserted in the blank for future damages is zero."

Thompson walked up and down the jury box as he brought his argument to its climax.

"You may feel sorry for your neighbors. Don't fall into that trap, ladies and gentlemen of the jury. Don't let a misguided notion of compassion interfere with your sworn duty to arrive, as a collective and deliberative body, at justice. Justice in this case requires that you ignore your ordinary human feelings of sympathy and render a decision in favor of the defendant. You do that, and you'll wake up tomorrow morning feeling that you've followed the law as Judge Enwright instructed."

Aitkins gulped. His hands began to shake. The young lawyer held out little hope that he could embrace the jury as James Thompson had, melding them, kneading them, bringing them with dignity and honor into the camp of his client. The young lawyer scanned the courtroom. His gaze lingered on his wife's profile. A faint smile crossed Julie's lips as their eyes connected.

"Mr. Aitkins?" Judge Enwright prodded.

The attorney stood up, grasped a yellow pad full of notes, and walked hesitantly to the podium. Earl Bethard removed the paper cup that Big Jim had used and replaced it with a new container full of water. Aitkins nodded his thanks to the bailiff, took a small drink from the cup, and began.

"There's a strong public sentiment today that lawyers, though officers of the Court, sworn to uphold the ethics of their profession, cannot be trusted. There may be a temptation amongst you, sitting in judgment in a cause before the court, to discount my clients' position because of all the talk you hear on television regarding lawyers and lawsuits. This is not something new for the American system of justice," Aitkins said softly, his voice losing its tremor as he warmed to his own words.

"Charles McCabe of the San Francisco Chronicle once remarked as follows:

I am one of that vast body of loyal, devoted, red-blooded American cynics who despise lawyers as they despise no other class of fauna...The three times I was most deceived and most poorly served were when I allowed my affairs to go into the hands of officers of the court, sworn to protect my interests...My experience led me to believe, doubtless mistaken, that most lawyers are swine. And not even nice swine."

Smiles formed on the faces of most of the jurors. Trooper Blomquist jotted a short note on the pad of paper resting in his lap. The officer didn't smile.

"I bring this quote to your attention because I need to insure that you understand what this case is not about. It is not about who is the better advocate. It's not about who is the more prepared or who brings the greater number of witnesses into the courtroom or about which lawyer's political or philosophical views, real or perceived, mirror your own. It is about an event, an incident in the life of the Andersons that you are being asked to consider and judge."

Daniel looked at his clients. Dean and Nancy Anderson were seated at counsel table next to Dee Dee Hernesman.

"Mr. Thompson cautions you to discard notions of sympathy and compassion as you consider this matter. I agree. The Andersons have received those things from their friends, family, and neighbors. They do not expect such things from you. They cannot expect such things from you. What they expect, and have every right to demand of you, a jury of their peers, is that you will do the job entrusted to you by our Constitution and described in detail to you by Judge Enwright."

Aitkins took another sip of water.

"All that they ask, and all that can be expected of you, is that you scrutinize the credibility, honesty, and integrity of those folks who took the oath and spoke from the witness stand. If you do that, and do it with no preconceived bias against my clients, against myself or Ms. Hernesman, or based upon any other personal philosophy or belief you may hold, that, ladies and gentlemen, will satisfy Dean and Nancy Anderson."

Aitkins proceeded to outline the simple litany of the plaintiffs' case. He spent little time on Pavo Tynjala's claims or the impact of HPP beyond pointing out that the disease, if present the day of the abortion storm, could not have caused the deaths experienced in the Andersons' herd. The lawyer saved his acrimony and contempt for two witnesses retained by the defense.

"As eloquent as Mr. Thompson may be in explaining that nothing happened out on the Anderson Farm, or, in the alternative, that if something did happen, it had nothing to do with the feed supplied to the Andersons by Mr. Thompson's client, I must spend some time discussing with you the flawed premise behind my opponent's position."

The lawyer paused.

"Recall, if you will, the two folks called by the defense who came before you and testified that the pelleted feed, despite the feeding trials conducted at NDSU and despite the presence of fusarium mold and Mycotoxins, was not the cause of the mass abortions experienced by the Anderson herd. Who were these folks? What were their interests in this case? Were their words genuine and sincere or were they tainted, as the corn in this case was tainted, with poison?"

Malachi Stone fidgeted with documents. F.W. Barnes maintained a stony expression. James Thompson watched the face of his adversary.

"The answer, I believe, but you will have to be the ones to ultimately sort it all out, is that Dr. Bronski's and Dr. Long's testimony cannot be trusted, no matter what their credentials, no matter how significant their impressive resumes may be. For, in the end, once all of the camouflage has been removed, it can only be said that the experts called to testify in this case by the defense said what they said because of a strong economic tie existing between them, a tie I might remind you that neither witness revealed to Mr. Thompson before taking the witness stand. In addition, and, most assuredly in the case of Dr. Bronski, their words flowed in return for the payment of cold hard cash in the form of an expert witness fee.

There's an old adage amongst defense lawyers that the more complex a case can be made, the less likely a jury will find for the plaintiff. So, in this case, you heard about HPP, a non-issue, according to Drs. Guttormson and Brewster. You heard about mange and the use of lindane and fuel oil. A red herring, according to the Andersons' veterinarian. You heard about e-coli in the well water, which was shown to have nothing to do with widespread abortions. To what purpose was all of this irrelevant and immaterial information brought to you? I've told you the premise: Complicating a case makes it unlikely a jury can sort through the chaff to find the wheat. I don't believe it will work in this case. I have faith that you will see through the ruse and find the facts."

Danny stepped out from behind the lectern and approached the jury box. His voice was calm. He'd hit his stride. Though he lacked the elegant oratory style of his more experienced adversary, Dan Aitkins remained true to himself; a simple man from a small town relaying a simple message.

"The Andersons bought feed. The feed caused their herd to abort. Is there any doubt in your mind, after hearing the unassuming testimony of Clyde Armstrong, an honest, hard working farmer who used his own ultrasound equipment to confirm the Andersons' loss; and after hearing from Dr. Guttormson, who came out and witnessed with his own eyes the calamity as it took place, that the event in question destroyed the lifeblood of the Anderson Farm? This is the truth. This is the simple, plain story that we have told, that we have proven by the greater weight of the evidence."

Danny looked into the faces of the jurors.

"I cannot tell you how to decide this case. Mr. Thompson cannot tell you how to decide this case. Judge Enwright cannot tell you how to decide this case. That is for you and you alone. However, I will suggest, that when you consider answering the questions; that, when you consider whether or not Stevenson's breached the warranty of merchantability, you answer Question Number One in that regard on the special verdict form, 'yes'. I also suggest that the greater weight of the evidence mandates that you find their breach was a direct cause of damage to the Andersons, so that you answer Question Number Two 'yes' as well. Similarily, when you consider Questions Three and Four, regarding a breach of warranty for the use intended, you answer both questions 'yes'."

Aitkins studied his hands. His notes remained on the lectern. There was no anxiety in his voice as he continued.

"Where you are asked, at Question Five, whether or not the plaintiffs' mitigated their loss, you should answer 'yes'. There is no question, as you were advised by Mr. Nelson and Dr. Brewster, that the Andersons did everything within their economic power, by selling off the affected female animals and reducing their damage claim by the amount received, to mitigate their loss. "

The lawyer walked over to a white board and removed the top of a black felt marker. He wrote the number "$400,000.00" on the surface of the display.

"I will not try to tell you how to divide the damage amount testified to by Mr. Nelson, and verified by Dean Anderson, in terms of past and future damages. That's for you to decide. Understand that whatever number you come to, whether it is more, or whether it is less than the number I suggest, is solely within the province of you, the jury. You are to decide that issue, like all of the other issues, based upon your collective wisdom and under the law as given to you by Judge Enwright."

Daniel Aitkins felt a surge of anxiety. The advocate's face betrayed concern. He noted that all of the members of the jury panel, including Donald Blomquist, had declined to copy his suggested damage amount on their notepads. As the attorney struggled to regroup and press onward, he walked idly in front of the jurors, turned, and migrated towards the podium in search of a direction. Danny's attention was drawn to the woman seated next to Jason Billington. Melanie Barnes occupied a place on the oak bench immediately behind the defense team. Her hands held a notebook in her lap.

Aitkins appreciated that Melanie had returned to the courtroom. Their eyes met. Until that pivotal moment, he hadn't let the woman's presence distract him. Weakened by the seeming indifference of the jury, he froze. A sense of profound confusion burst through the lawyer's veneer of feigned invincibility. The red haired woman retracted her gaze, causing Daniel Emery Aitkins to fall silent. At that moment, he became fully aware that he was in danger of losing more than just a lawsuit.

CHAPTER 87

"That was really something," Dean Anderson remarked as Danny Aitkins sat down next to his client. "The way you remembered all those facts, put them together. The best of it was the way you left the jury wondering at the end, as if they were supposed to fill in the blanks."

The lawyer cast a sheepish grin towards Dean and Nancy Anderson.

"Thanks," the attorney muttered.

In reality, Daniel lost his place. His eyes, instead of focusing on the jurors, or closing in contemplation until he could regain his form, embraced a woman. Not his wife, loyally sitting in the rear of the room, silently cheering him on, providing him with needed moral support, but another. He kept that reality locked inside as he accepted his client's accolades.

"Nice job," Dee Dee said approvingly. "What happened there at the end?" she whispered.

"Just thought it was as good a place as any to finish up."

"I watched the jurors. They seemed sort of confused."

Danny frowned.

"That wasn't the reaction I was hoping for."

Hernesman sensed that her critique stung her partner. She refrained from further comment.

Earl Bethard was sworn to prevent communications between the jury and the outside world. Any questions the jurors raised would be conveyed to Judge Enwright by the bailiff. The lawyers and spectators watched as the jurors rose from their seats and followed Bethard through a door. It was a quarter-past-twelve. The jurors had not yet had lunch.

"Gentlemen, Ms. Hernesman, anything else to be placed of record at this time?" Harriet asked after the jury was removed.

"Nothing from the plaintiffs," Danny Aitkins advised without rising.

James Thompson stood.

"The defense has nothing additional to place of record," the big man replied.

"I'd ask that you give Mr. Olson, my courtroom clerk, a phone number where you can be reached if there are any questions from the jury," the judge asserted.

"The defense does not plan to be here for the reading of the verdict, your honor. I'll give Mark my cell number. My daughter's in a play tonight back home in the Cities. I'd like to be there to see her," the black attorney indicated.

Judge Enwright rose as she addressed the attorney.

"How's your little girl doing?"

The judge was obviously interested in Ajudica's welfare.

"Very well, your honor. She's had nightmares. We got her into counseling. My wife and I went with. That seemed to help. She's pretty much back to square one. Thanks for asking."

"Give her the court's best."

Thompson smiled. He began to retrieve his files as he answered.

"I'll do that, judge. If the jury has a question, Mr. Barnes has agreed to stand in for me."

Aitkins waited for the exchange to be completed.

"I'll be hanging around the courthouse with the Andersons, at least for a while," he disclosed.

"OK. You fellows tried a mighty fine case," Judge Enwright intimated. "As good a job as I've seen in my short time on the bench. Both parties were well represented."

Malachi Stone nodded his acceptance of the compliment. Jason Billington smiled. F.W. Barnes gathered his file documents without any indication that he'd heard the judge's remark.

"Thanks," Aitkins responded.

"I second that," Thompson added as he closed his briefcase and walked towards opposing counsel.

"Ms. Hernesman, nice to try a case against you. If you're ever looking to relocate, give me a call. Our firm could use a good female litigator," the black man gushed as he shook the woman's hand.

"I'll keep that in mind," Dee Dee said, her hazel eyes dancing.

"And you," Thompson said with a huge grin, reaching to shake Aitkins' hand. "I'd never be able to convince you to come over to the side of righteousness," the black man chided. "You tried a hell of a case, Dan."

The smaller attorney returned the grip.

"You did a fine job as well," Aitkins replied.

"Good luck to you, Mr. And Mrs. Anderson," Big Jim said as he turned to leave.

Aitkins watched the lead defense attorney amble out of the courtroom.

"Did he just wish us good luck or am I dreaming?" Dean Anderson asked, scooping loose papers up in his hands and handing them to Hernesman.

"That he did," Aitkins responded. "That he did."

"Strange, don't you think?" Dee Dee asked.

"Very," Aitkins observed. "He's pretty straight-up. I wonder if he meant it."

"He did," Nancy Anderson said. "He's a Christian man. He means what he says."

The defense entourage made its way through the lobby towards the front door. The deputies kept a close watch on the dispersal of the militia. Eli Bremer and his cohorts didn't hang around. The farmers, shopkeepers, and other men who'd sat through the final arguments offered the Andersons words of encouragement before exiting the building.

Sheriff Isak Iverson was preoccupied. On his arrival at the courthouse, he noted the presence of a Safari van with a broken passenger's side window; a piece of thick cardboard duct taped across the opening where glass should be. The van was parked in front of the building. The van had caught his eye, the broken window, the temporary North Dakota registration slip taped to the rear windshield; the general appearance of the thing seemed vaguely familiar. Iverson had ambled from his squad car into the building, and occupied a seat in the back of courtroom while maintaining a watchful eye on the proceedings. Nothing unusual struck a chord with the lawman. He twisted and untwisted the peppered fibers of his moustache with his fingers. Iverson had splayed out his beanpole body on the hard oak of a bench as he listened to the lawyers' final arguments and scrutinized the spectators.

He focused his attention on a select few. Bremer, he knew. The others, he'd seen around or, at the very least, they looked like they belonged. One very tall, angular soul, didn't fit in. The stranger's eyes were clear and blue. His jaw was set square. His hair was shaved to the scalp. The man's concentration was riveted on the proceedings. There was something about the big white man, a man nearly as tall and athletic as James Thompson, which unnerved the sheriff. The officer determined there was a need to keep an eye on the stranger. Without leaving his seat or becoming obvious, using surreptitious glances, Iverson had conveyed his suspicions to his deputies.

As the jury was ushered into the deliberation room, as the courtroom began to clear, the sheriff kept close tabs on the stranger. The man made no move towards the attorneys or the judge. He simply picked up his coat, a yellow and green ski jacket resting as a crumpled ball on the pew beside him, and filed out with the rest of the crowd. When the stranger passed by Iverson, the man looked directly at the sheriff and touched the inside edge of his right index finger to his eyebrow in an informal salute. Iverson was tall. The man who walked by him was taller, standing significantly over six-five.

Out in the lobby, the stranger disappeared in the men's room. Trying to remain inconspicuous, Iverson posted himself informally across the way and positioned the other officers in significant locations around the interior of the lobby.

Thompson and the others dragged their battle-weary bodies along. Melanie Barnes walked next to her father-in-law, visibly shaken by a chance meeting with Julie Aitkins. The group was poised to descend a stone staircase when the tall white man, his Columbia parka hanging open, exited the courthouse and moved towards the defense entourage. Sheriff Iverson followed the stranger by a few steps.

"Mr. Thompson," the man called out, his hands shoved into the pockets of his jacket, his size eighteen Etonic Cross Trainers slapping hard against stone as he advanced.

Big Jim turned. His puny eyes stared hard at the stranger.

"Yes?"

Before the intruder could say another word, Iverson snaked his narrow body between the men.

"Hold on, sir," the sheriff advised.

"There a problem here?" F.W. Barnes asked, sliding protectively in front of his daughter-in-law.

"I'd like a word with the big fella," Isak Iverson said. "Could you take your hands out of your pockets?" the sheriff added.

"Not a problem," the stranger answered.

The man complied and exposed his bare hands, the fingers long and athletic, along the seams of his trousers.

"I haven't seen you around here before," Iverson commented, his face shaded by a campaign hat.

"I'm from Indiana."

The attorneys stood behind a phalanx formed by the sheriff and one deputy. Another officer stood behind the stranger.

"I thought as much," Iverson said before launching a significant gob of old chew out of his mouth. "You got business here in Detroit Lakes?"

The man smiled.

"Yes sir, I believe I do."

"I don't know as I caught your name."

The wind gusted.

"John Winchip."

Isak Iverson's eyes squinted. His lips moved as if to spit again. Instead, the sheriff simply scratched the right tip of his moustache with an index finger and resumed talking.

"I thought as much. The van looked familiar. I'd guess you're kin to the man who took Mr. Thompson's little girl."

Winchip's face lost color.

"I'm his younger brother."

The man's demeanor was sparse.

Thompson started to turn away.

The sheriff extended his scrawny right arm and halted the African American's progress.

"Hold up there, Jim. Let the man state his piece."

Winchip cleared his throat. His hand dug into the confines of an inside pocket of the jacket and cautiously withdrew a battered envelope. The lawmen appeared nervous during the gesture.

"Here," the Indianan advised, handing the document to the sheriff. "For the little girl."

Iverson transferred the package.

James Thompson opened the envelope.

"There's over two thousand dollars in here."

"Likely get another two when I sell the van. I'll send that to you as well."

"Where'd the money come from?" the sheriff queried.

John Winchip shifted his body, his height towering over everyone except Big Jim.

"First, you have to understand, Mr. Thompson, that my brother had a hard life. He grew up too fast, had to; both our parents weren't worth snot. He took care of me, at least until I was old enough to take care of myself. Then he joined the Army. It was a bad fit. He came back bitter, confused, and a bigot. Got in with the wrong crowd."

Thompson followed the man's revelation, all the while holding the envelope in his significant hands.

"Anyway, I'm all George had. We haven't been close for years. But when I heard, I had to come and get him, bring him back home."

Iverson nodded.

"He's out there in the van?"

"Yes sir, he is. Plain wood casket, ready to be planted back in Terre Haute."

"A noble gesture," Malachi Stone observed.

John Winchip demurred.

"I should have done more to straighten him out. But it's hard when it's your older brother. The dynamics for lecturin' don't fit so smooth."

The sheriff nodded and continued.

"The money?"

"I sold what few things George had. A computer, some furniture. He had a little over a grand in the bank, his life savings, so far as I know. It isn't much but it's everything he had. When she's old enough, you tell her that, Mr. Thompson. Tell her he didn't know what he was doing, that something got to him and turned him from being my big brother into someone else."

Thompson nodded.

"You're on the job, aren't you," Iverson offered, fixing hard on the man's profile, his manner of speech, his attitude.

"Yes sir, I am. Ten years with the Indianapolis Police Department. Last three in homicide."

"It's somethin' you just can't hide," Isak said through a brightening smile.

"That's a fact," Winchip agreed. "I best get going. It's a long drive and George needs to get home."

Iverson stepped aside. Thompson shoved the envelope in his pocket and extended a hand.

"No need for that, Mr. Thompson. It's not much and I didn't do it for your thanks," Winchip noted, stopping in front of the lawyer.

Big Jim's face studied the tall white detective.

"But you did it. Didn't have to. But you did," Thompson replied, extending his fingers.

Their hands grasped. Thompson drew the white man close. After an instant, Winchip withdrew.

"I'll be leaving now," the detective said as he began to descend the steps. "You take care of that little girl, Mr. Thompson," he added, never turning to look back.

"You can count on that," Big Jim replied.

They watched the tall policeman open the driver's door of the van. Rusty fragments of sheet metal dropped to the snow-covered pavement as the driver's door slammed shut. Blue exhaust, clear evidence that Winchip would be lucky to get $2,000.00 for the vehicle back in Terre Haute, gasped from the exhaust pipe. The Safari pulled away from the curb. The law officers and the defense team departed.

Inside the courthouse, Dean Anderson studied the face of his wife. The woman looked exhausted. Her skin was pallid. Suddenly, her legs buckled and Nancy Anderson collapsed.

"Oh my God," Dean screamed.

The Anderson children had been milling around the back of the courtroom talking to Julie Aitkins. They rushed towards their mother in unison.

"What's wrong?" Matthew asked, fear infecting his speech as he arrived at his mother's side.

"I'm not sure," Dean answered, holding Nancy's head in his hands, keeping her neck away from the floor.

Dee Dee dialed 911 on her cellular phone.

"We need an ambulance in Judge Davidson's courtroom," she commanded. "A woman just collapsed."

Julie Aitkins joined them.

"What's happening, Danny?" she asked, her breath quick and excited.

"Mrs. Anderson passed out. Ambulance is on its way."

"Is she breathing?" Julie queried.

Dean nodded his head.

"Her pulse is racing like crazy," the farmer advised. "She's been having heart spells, some sort of electrical problem. She's supposed to go down to Mayo for a new kind of pacemaker next month."

"Will she be OK?" Millicent asked, her voice quaking as she bent to one knee and held her mother's right hand.

"I think so. As long as those damn paramedics get here soon," Dean commented, his words seeming calm but for the inflection of his voice.

An ambulance team arrived. A man and a woman carried the equipment of their trade, including a defibrillator, into the courtroom. One of the deputies who had just left the courtroom entered behind the paramedics.

"Folks, stand aside. Sir, you the husband?" the male paramedic asked, the name "S. Stuart" stitched above the left pocket of his navy blue uniform shirt.

Dean nodded.

"She passed out?" the female EMT asked, her moniker, "L. Kellet", appearing in a similar location.

Dean nodded again.

"Any health history we should know about?" Stuart asked.

"She's had some heart irregularities. She's having a pacemaker/micro-defibrillator implanted next month at Mayo," Dean Anderson advised.

The woman checked the patient's heart rate and pulse.

"We need to shock her heart back into rhythm," Kellet said. "Everyone please stand back."

Stuart uncoiled the paddles, cut open Nancy's dress from the neck to her waist, found bare skin above the unconscious woman's brassiere, and applied the business end of the defibrillator to her chest. Electricity flowed. The monitor picked up a steady heartbeat.

"That's it," Stuart murmured.

"We'll need to get her to Detroit Lakes Lutheran," Kellet advised as she pulled the stretcher close to the patient.

"I'll meet you there," Dean Anderson said. "Millie and Matt, you stay here with Mr. Aitkins and Ms. Hernesman to wait for the verdict. You younger boys come with me."

"Dad, I want to go with," Millie intoned.

"I need you and Matt here in case something happens. I'll call you on Ms. Hernesman's phone if anything changes. Mom will be fine."

Millicent Anderson quietly acquiesced.

"You're sure you don't want us to go with?" Danny Aitkins asked.

"She's gonna be fine, right Ms. Kellet?"

"I think so. We'll know more once we're at the hospital. She's stable, with a strong heartbeat and pulse. I don't think there'll be any surprises."

"Stay and take the verdict," the farmer commanded. "I'll call you as soon as I know more."

"OK," Dan replied.

Three fire fighters and the other deputy who had been on duty during the final arguments burst through the doors in time to help wheel the stretcher away. Dean Anderson and his two young sons followed the gurney out of the courtroom.

"She's too young for something like this," Julie observed.

"She's only a few years older than we are," Dee Dee agreed.

Millicent looked at the attorneys with frightened eyes. Matt Anderson noted his sister's fear and placed his strong arms around her.

"She'll be fine, Mill. She'll be fine," Matthew urged in a comforting tone.

"He's right," Julie Aitkins added. "Your mom is in good hands. The excitement of the trial must have triggered something. They'll get it straightened out."

The group stood in utter quiet.

"Let's go down the street and get something to eat," Danny said after an appropriate interlude. "The jury won't be coming back for a while. They'll be taking lunch if they're not done after the first hour. It'll be after three by the time they get back from eating."

"I'd rather take a ride over to the hospital to be with my mom," Millicent gasped through declining tears.

"Ditto for me," Matt added.

"I don't see the harm. Be back here by three, though," Daniel mandated.

"We will."

The oldest Anderson children exited the Becker County Courthouse.

"I'll grab a table at Betty's," Dee Dee advised, hoisting a large briefcase with each hand.

"We'll be right there," Dan responded, packing additional trial materials in another valise.

The courtroom door opened and closed.

Julie sat in a pew behind her husband as he worked. Her fingers fidgeted with the drawstring of her winter coat, a deep brown parka that came to the middle of her thighs, as she contemplated events.

"That was scary."

Daniel looked up from the table.

"You got that right."

"Your final argument was great," she said through a staggered grin.

"Thanks."

"I got the sense that you left the jury hanging deliberately."

He smiled. She was the one person he could be totally honest with.

"I'm glad it looked that way. I got flummoxed when I wrote the damage number on the board and no one on the jury copied it down. I felt like I'd lost the case right there."

"Maybe they all agree with you."

"I doubt it."

"I think you're being too hard on yourself," the woman said as she left her seat and gave her husband a peck on the cheek.

Danny Aitkins relished the feel of his wife's warm mouth against his skin. His face flushed. He stood up, pulled his overcoat from the back of his chair, and slid the sleeves of the garment over his arms.

"Dee Dee's waiting for us," he observed as Julie hugged him tightly.

"You were great. Your argument conveyed a sense of integrity, a true belief in your clients' cause. The jury will see that," she added as they walked through the doors and out into the lobby.

They followed a sidewalk, the concrete surface of the walkway swept clean of snow. As they crossed the street, Julie Aitkins changed the topic of their conversation.

"I talked to Melanie," she said.

Aitkins fought a pained expression, fought to keep his secret buried, as he addressed his wife.

"Oh?"

"She seemed depressed. Have you noticed that, I mean, working on the case against her and all?"

"Not really," he lied.

There was a subtle change in his wife's demeanor. She had always been able to detect a lie coming out of his mouth.

"You sure? You don't seem certain."

"I haven't really noticed anything in particular. We haven't spent that much time working together on the case."

"I thought she was up in Winnipeg, in the warehouse when you and Dees were looking for stuff."

He tried to maintain his composure.

"She was. But Dee Dee spent more time working with her than I did. I worked more with Stone. I really didn't see any depression. Mel seemed her old self."

They stepped across the curb on the other side of the street. Julie's boot caught the concrete lip of the gutter. The lawyer prevented his wife from falling.

"Thanks," Julie said.

They walked a few more paces.

"Have you noticed anything else about her?" Julie Aitkins asked.

"Like what?" the lawyer responded.

Dan's face grimaced. The gesture was visible. Julie was distracted by a flock of pigeons flying high above the cityscape and didn't see the expression.

"Like the fact that she's regained most of the weight she'd lost," the lawyer's wife observed.

"I hadn't noticed," he lied.

"You expect me to believe that? You can't keep your eyes off a woman's ass, any woman's ass, much less one as attractive as Melanie's," his wife observed.

"I really hadn't," Daniel lied again, opening the door to the restaurant as they spoke.

"Whatever. The really strange thing is that, if I had to guess, I'd almost think Mel was pregnant. Weird, huh?"

Danny Aitkins avoided looking at his wife as they crossed the threshold into Betty's Café. The lawyer found it hard to grip the doorknob with his sweat-covered hand. He was content to allow his wife's supposition to evaporate as the warm air of the eatery, an atmosphere imbedded with the odor of freshly baked pumpkin pie, greeted them.

CHAPTER 88

"**They're** keeping Nance until tomorrow morning just to make sure everything's all right,' Dean Anderson advised.

The hog farmer sat with his attorneys on a bench in the courthouse lobby outside of Judge Davidson's courtroom. Julie Aitkins left after lunch to insure she was home when Adam, Amanda, and Michael got off their respective school buses. The Anderson children were still at the hospital visiting their mother. Nancy Anderson's condition had stabilized. She'd regained consciousness during the five-minute ambulance ride to Detroit Lakes Lutheran and was coherent by the time she met the doctor in the emergency room. Her pulse and other vital signs had returned to normal. Blood work was drawn and an EKG was ordered as a precaution. Once the physician knew her history, he felt reasonably confident, based upon the EKG, that the farmer's wife had experienced an electrical interruption to her heart's normal contractions. She had not experienced a heart attack.

"That's great news, Dean," Danny Aitkins offered as the men sat next to each other on the bench.

Dee Dee Hernesman studied the Seth Thomas clock on the wall. It was nearly six-thirty. The jury had been out six hours. The jurors ordered food but insisted on having a working lunch. There had been no questions requiring the court's attention. Judge Enwright and her staff remained at work behind the doors leading to Judge Davidson's inner sanctum.

The exterior doors to the courthouse opened. Matt, Millicent, Joey, and Chad Anderson walked forlornly into the chamber.

"Hey, kids," Dean greeted, rising from his feet to hug his daughter.

"Hey, dad," the kids' responded in unison.

"What's up?" Matt asked Daniel Aitkins.

"They're still out."

"Is that good?"

"It might mean they're considering damages or it might mean that there's a hold out. They just passed six hours so I'm not certain what to make of it," the attorney offered.

Judge Enwright exited the courtroom and walked over to the group. Her eyes were clear and bright, her face freshly scrubbed, as she stopped in front of the plaintiff.

"How's your wife, Mr. Anderson? I heard from Mr. Bethard that she had to be taken to the hospital. I hope it isn't anything serious."

A frown interrupted the jurist's forehead. A look of genuine concern settled upon her face.

"She's got a little heart problem, something we knew about. She's doing fine. The kids just came from seeing her," Dean Anderson answered.

The judge smiled.

"These cases take a lot out of everyone. I hope things go well for you and your children," the judge said as she turned away and walked down the hall.

"Nice lady," Dean mumbled.

"Smart lady too," Dee Dee Hernesman added. "She's a good judge."

Darkness settled over Detroit Lakes. The lights of the lobby, their aura subdued against the largeness of the room, brought friendly warmth to the space. All of the offices in the building save Judge Davidson's chambers and the administrator's office were closed. Most of the personnel had left. Only Judge Enwright, the judge's staff, and Earl Bethard remained on duty.

Time progressed slowly as the Andersons waited for the jury to decide the fate of their farm. Judge Enwright exited the administrator's office, turning out the lights as she closed the door.

"Earl called. The jury's back," the judge reported as she passed by.

"We'll be right in," Danny acknowledged.

Dean Anderson studied his own large, well-worked hands before rising from the bench.

"Come 'on kids."

The Anderson children left their respective places and followed their father and their attorneys into the courtroom.

After a short wait, Judge Enwright, her law clerk, her courtroom clerk, and Angie Devlin took their seats. The bailiff did not require the Andersons or their lawyers to rise as the judge entered the room. Daniel studied the face of Earl Bethard, searching for a hint as to what the jury's decision was going to be. The former deputy maintained his game face as he brought the seven jurors back into the room.

"Damn it," Aitkins muttered to himself. "Blomquist's the foreman," the lawyer observed. He watched as the state trooper, maintaining his ever-vigilant posture and indecipherable face, walked across the carpeting with the special verdict form clenched tightly in his left hand.

"Has the jury reached a verdict?" Judge Enwright asked.

Danny's heart began to pound. Adrenaline rushed through his body. There was so much raw emotion coursing through his veins that Aitkins felt for a moment that he too would end up passed out on the floor. His mouth became dry, parched as the Nevada desert. His body began to shake: not insignificant tremors but bold twitches of agitation.

448

"Something wrong, Dan?" Dee Dee whispered, observing her partner's legs trembling beneath the table.

"I don't like the fact that Blomquist is the foreman."

Hernesman smiled a knowing smile. She was as calm as a Minnesota lake before a thunderstorm. There was a depth of knowing about the woman. She was no longer the pupil. In many ways, she was now the teacher. Danny looked at his partner and silently acknowledged that he couldn't handle the pressure of not knowing like she could. He couldn't handle the physical assault on his body that the emotional turmoil of trial created.

I can't do this anymore, he thought to himself, watching Dee Dee's eyes pry beneath his machismo.

"I'm telling you, it's after six hours. It'll be fine," the woman whispered.

"Please pass the verdict to the bailiff," the judge directed.

Blomquist complied. Bethard dragged his injured body across the floor, retrieved the form, and handed it to the courtroom clerk. The clerk, Mark Olson, passed the papers to the judge.

Harriet Enwright reviewed the verdict form. Aitkins struggled to determine the result of the case by divining the expression on the jurist's face. He was unable to glean anything from the woman's reaction.

"The clerk will now read the verdict."

Mark Olson received the form from the judge.

"Dean and Nancy Anderson versus Stevenson's Sci-Swine, a foreign corporation. We the jury, find as follows..."

Aitkins' listened. His personal situation, the complexities of his life that would follow, were not at issue and did not press for his attention. The lawyer was concerned only for his clients; decent, honest, hard working folks who had been wronged by a faceless, soulless, conglomerate. It was their farm on the line. It was their future. It was their life. As he waited, his eyes scanned the handsome faces of the farmer and his children. This was for them. This was their time. He began to pray.

"Question One: Did defendant breach the implied warranty for fitness for a particular use by the sale of feed to plaintiffs? Answer...'yes'"

Blood rushed into the attorney's brain. His face turned beat red.

"Question Two: If you answered Question Number One 'yes' then and only then, answer this question: Did the breach of implied warranty for fitness for a particular purpose cause plaintiffs to sustain damages? Answer: 'yes'."

Aitkins looked at Hernesman.

"Question Three: Did defendant breach the implied warranty of merchantability by the sale of feed to plaintiffs? Answer: 'yes'."

The second 'cause' question was answered in the plaintiffs' favor as well. The jury also found that the plaintiffs had mitigated their losses.

Daniel leaned over and whispered in Dean Anderson's ear.

"Excuse my French, but I can't fucking believe this is happening," the lawyer said through the broadest smile Dean Anderson had ever seen.

The farmer chuckled.

"Question Six: What sum of money will adequately compensate plaintiffs for any and all losses incurred up until the time of trial?"

"This is it," Anderson whispered. "This is the whole shooting match."

"Answer: $200,000.00"

"Oh my God," Millicent Anderson blurted out.

Judge Enwright looked crossly at the girl.

"Sorry your honor," the young woman apologized. The jurors, with the notable exception of Donald Blomquist, smiled.

"Holy shit," Danny murmured in agreement, careful not to speak loud enough for the judge to hear.

"And how," Hernesman chimed in, her eyes riveted on the jury foreman.

The clerk took a sip of water. Ice clinked against glass as Mark Olson drank heavily.

"I think he's with us, Dan," Dee Dee whispered.

"What?"

"I think that sonofabitch played you like a cheap pinball machine."

"Who?"

"The trooper."

"No way."

"I'll bet you a hundred bucks that he signed the form with the majority."

"You're on, Dees. Ain't no way that sorry-assed cop gave away the store."

"Question Seven: What sum of money will adequately compensate plaintiffs for any and all future losses to be incurred from the day of trial forward? Answer: $200,000.00."

"I can't believe it," Dean Anderson yelped, slapping Dan Aitkins on the back. "I can't believe it." Before the jurist could intervene, the farmer quickly added:

"Sorry about that, your honor."

Judge Enwright nodded.

"It's a six-sevenths verdict. I'll poll the six who signed the form as to whether this is their true and correct verdict," Mark Olson advised.

Aitkins thought he saw Harriet Enwright wink at him as the clerk began the poll. The first five jurors who signed the form all confirmed their intentions. Only Mrs. O'Connell and Trooper Donald Blomquist remained to be questioned.

Hernesman smiled. She tried to suppress the urge to break into a laugh but found she was powerless to control herself. A slight chuckle escaped. The judge ignored her. Daniel looked sternly at his partner but said nothing.

"Donald Blomquist, foreperson, do you affirm and swear that this is a true and correct rendition of your verdict in this case?"

Blomquist looked directly at the clerk and simply said:

"I do."

"Shit," Aitkins mumbled.

"You can pay up later," Hernesman advised through an all-knowing smirk.

Danny took to his feet when the jurors descended. His attention was drawn to the face of Mrs. O'Connell. He extended his hand to thank her for her service.

"Even though you weren't for us, Mrs. O'Connell, I want to thank you for your attention to this case," he said.

There was no response from the old woman as she ignored his gesture.

"Strange," Aitkins thought to himself as she walked mutely away.

Trooper Blomquist strode towards the lawyer, Daniel detected the impression of a modest smile on the man's face.

"Thanks for your service," Aitkins said as he extended his hand to the lawman. "My client is most appreciative."

Blomquist leaned hard into Danny and shook the attorney's hand forcefully.

"I hope we gave them enough money, Mr. Aitkins," the trooper whispered. "We would have given more if you had asked for it."

Before the litigator could reply, the officer walked past Aitkins, intent upon retrieving his belongings from the deliberation room. Daniel was numb. He mechanically thanked the remaining jurors.

"Wonderful result, Mr. Aitkins," Judge Enwright observed from behind the bench. "That's the biggest verdict in the past five years in Becker County."

Turning to Dean Anderson, the judge said her farewells.

"You had two great lawyers working for you, Mr. Anderson. But more than that, your family came across as honest and sincere. I think that won the case, not to downplay the efforts expended by Ms. Hernesman and Mr. Aitkins on your behalf. Take care of your family, Mr. Anderson. Take care of your wife."

"Thanks judge, I will," the farmer promised, watching the jurist depart.

Daniel took a deep breath.

"I can't believe it."

"What?" Hernesman asked.

"Mrs. O'Connell, when I thanked her, it was like I wasn't even here."

The bailiff approached them.

"I hate to tell you this, Mr. Aitkins," Earl Bethard said, stopping to convey his congratulations. "But her mind was set against your case the moment she was picked."

"Earl, how would you know that?"

"Her doodles."

"Doodles?"

"The drawings she made when she was pretending to listen."

"I thought she was taking notes."

"Pay attention, counselor," Dee Dee admonished. "You might learn something."

Bethard continued.

"She stopped listening right after opening statements and started drawing little pictures. I thought she was taking notes until she left her notebook in the jury washroom. I picked it up. I should have saved it to show you."

"Show me what?" Aitkins asked.

"Well, one of the pictures had a bunch of dead pigs on their backs, feet stuck up in the air. That was one that I remember. She did that one right close to the beginning of the trial."

"So?"

"Underneath the dead pigs, she wrote 'killed by farmer stupidity' or somethin' like that."

Aitkins' face turned red again.

"You've got to be kidding me."

"I probably shouldn't be telling you this, but since things turned out OK for your clients, I thought you'd wanna know."

The old deputy continued his final inspection of the courtroom.

"See what I mean?" Dee Dee asserted.

"I owe you a hundred bucks. I can't believe it. How did you figure it out?"

Hernesman smiled.

"Women know these things about other women."

The remark stung Daniel unintentionally.

How much does Julie know? the trial lawyer asked himself as he borrowed Hernesman's cellular phone to call his wife.

CHAPTER 89

The day dawned. It was the end time. The moment had arrived for the lawyer to reveal his indiscretions The Anderson matter had been dealt with. Danny Aitkins had achieved the most satisfying victory of his legal career. And yet, because of his impending disclosure, his appreciation for the verdict carried a distant quality.

In the days following the trial, Danny, Julie, Dee Dee, Tom Murphy, and Emery, attended a victory celebration at the Anderson Farm. Brandy and keg beer flowed freely, an interesting circumstance given the rigid doctrines of the farmer's conservative Missouri Synod Lutheran faith. Nancy Anderson quickly regained her strength. By the time of the celebration, she was only a few weeks away from undergoing surgery at the Mayo Clinic.

Up in Winnipeg, the decision was made by Stevenson's to negotiate payment of the jury award together with costs and expenses. The reason behind the capitulation was simple: Stevenson's was within a whiskers breath of finalizing their long-planned corporate acquisition. Rather than risk publicity during sensitive negotiations, James Thompson was directed to secure a confidentiality agreement and pay the verdict. Unwilling to engage in a protracted appellate battle, Dean and Nancy Anderson agreed to keep the terms of the settlement a secret. The documents and the settlement check were already en route to Aitkins' office.

Within days of the jury decision, Emery Aitkins effectively cut off Alan Ignatius at the knees. Pavo Tynjala's disclosures during the Anderson trial were used against the farmer from Wheaton. His admissions became sharp needles of truth that caused his lawsuit to dissipate like air from a punctured balloon.

Daniel arranged to take Julie to lunch at Bordson's Bed and Breakfast in Pelican Rapids. His plan was to slowly exhume his immoderation while his wife consumed an inordinate amount of wine. He would not drink. He could not drink. That was past. He would eat his meal, acting the part of the triumphant litigator celebrating the vanquishing of a foe, all the while knowing the terrible, awful truth of what he was about to unveil. He made certain that they would be alone, in an upstairs parlor of the Inn, when the time came to unburden his soul.

Wind whipped across the winter landscape. Amanda Jane stood next to her father bundled in suede riding coat, the tan leather brushed smooth, the collar and seams displaying clean lamb's wool. The child's hands were bare. Insulated ski gloves were tucked into the depths of her pockets as the girl rigged Pumpkin's tack.

Daniel smiled and tugged on the belly strap of a saddle resting on the back of his daughter's mare. Hope remained patient as the lawyer tightened the leather.

"I'd like to ride Hope one more time to make sure she's sound," the father said to his daughter.

"But dad, she's so calm. I don't think there's anything to worry about," Amanda protested.

"I thought you'd say that," Daniel said through a smile as he looped leather reins over the saddle horn. Both animals remained tethered to the steel bars of stall doors by nylon leads secured to halters. "All the same, I'd like to take her out one last time. Then she's all yours, kiddo."

Snow fell gently across the landscape as they emerged from the pole building leading their mounts. Danny, his head covered with his Australian bush hat, his hands bare to winter, shuffled through the soft white powder. His daughter followed, gently urging her father's horse along.

The attorney stopped and cast a wistful glance back at their home. Against the gray sky, the clouds having disappeared in the squall that had settled over the Smokey Hills, the lights of the farmhouse shone like misplaced stars. Wood smoke, the sweet scent of maple, curled upward from the antique brick chimney of the home. The idyllic setting was distinctly at odds with the agony Daniel was about to unleash upon his wife and family. Once the significance of his secret was revealed, once the awkward reality of Melanie's circumstance was published, things would end. How many things, how many details of his life would be demolished was impossible to predict. But the lawyer knew that the destruction would be swift and brutal when visited upon those he loved most.

"Let's ride," he whispered, containing his emotions, placing his left foot in a stirrup, lifting himself into his daughter's new saddle as he spoke. The dull toes of his old cowboy boots, Tony Lama's that had seen better days, their brown leather faded and cracked, found the limits of the irons as he settled into the seat of the roping saddle.

"Is something wrong dad?" Amanda asked, her eyes searching her father's face.

'No, darlin'. Just a snowflake stuck in my eye," he fibbed.

"What trail we gonna take?" she asked as the horses began to walk down the driveway.

"How about the Hill Lake Trail? It's so pretty climbing up to the top and winding back down towards the lake through those old ironwood trees."

"I like that one too," the girl responded, clicking her tongue against her teeth, using the heels of her black riding boots to urge Pumpkin on.

"Hill Lake Trail it is," the attorney announced.

Flakes twirled slowly in the breeze; their great size catching the air as they descended, forcing them to shift on their decline. Amanda stuck her tongue out, playfully inhaling insignificant water as the snow melted in her mouth. They entered the depths of mature forest. The ironwoods were welcoming and protective. The riders kept their thoughts to themselves. All around them, the woods presented a repose that was deep, peaceful, and ancient.

Daniel thought about how he would break the truth to Julie. Would he excuse himself, rise up from the table, and amble into the bathroom of the Bed and Breakfast to assemble his words, to plan his plea for forgiveness? Or would he simply watch her until he was confident that she had finished her meal, likely a salad, and drank as much wine as she wanted, before ruining her afternoon, and with it, perhaps, her life? He didn't know how one should disclose unfaithfulness that resulted in the conception of a child. There were no rules, no books of etiquette, so far as he was aware, that covered such an event. He envisioned Julie's eyes as he related the information. With prescience as clear as a television screen, he watched a tremendous shudder of upset steal across his wife's body, shaking her faith in humanity to the very foundations of her heart. No matter how it came out, it would devastate her and likely mean the end.

Pumpkin snorted. Danny turned in the saddle to view his daughter.

"This is nice," Amanda said through a smile.

"No, this is perfect," he responded.

The pewter sky seemed to climb forever. Trees surrounded them and stood fast against the wind. The horses labored up a steep slope until the riders and their mounts achieved the top of a knob. Below them, rolling hills slid off to the north. The black ice of Hill Lake, its surface polished smooth and clean of snow by constant prairie winds, formed a mysterious mirror of frozen water that reflected the steely hue of the obscured sky. Someone had cleared trees from the knoll and placed a wooden table at the summit. They were not carrying lunch. They did not dismount.

"Some day we'll have to eat up here," Danny told his daughter, "when we have more time."

"That'd be nice," Amanda replied, her eyes taking in the beauty of the valley.

Straggling snow continued to fall, though the greater weight of the flurry was behind them. The horses stood quietly above the desolation of the winter scenery, nervously lifting their hooves from time to time in anticipation of departure.

"Maybe mom will come along on Happy," the girl added, making reference to her mother's well-ridden, twenty-year-old Arab gelding.

The irony of the horse's name stung. Danny could not bear the thought of his daughter blaming him for the changes that were about to come into her life. He knew that the culpability for what was about to happen rested solely and squarely on his shoulders. Still, the weight of Amanda, Michael, and Adam's likely recriminations seemed too cruel a punishment to face. But there was no option. He had promised Melanie that he'd make an avowal to Julie. Today was the day. There was no escaping his duty.

Father and daughter began a slow, winding descent. The sounds of snowmobiles crossing unblemished ice resonated mechanically through the air. The noise was of little significance to the litigator.

Danny often encountered snowmobilers while horseback riding during the winter. There was nothing to fear from neighbors who preferred motorized transport to horses. There was plenty of room in the Smokey Hills for both forms of activity. The engine exhaust disturbed the tranquility of the morning. Hope's ears perked up. Danny felt a subtle quickening of the animal's heart rate. Out of the corner of his eye, he saw the yellow globe of a snowmobile headlight. An Arctic Cat dodged timber. Then he saw another. And another. Three sleds were advancing towards them at a rapid clip.

"Better ease off the trial to let the machines pass," he advised Amanda.

"OK," the girl responded, reining her mount towards the edge of the path.

Hope fought Daniel's command to move off the trail. The animal's eyes widened.

"Something's eaten your horse," the attorney advised. "I don't think she likes snowmobiles."

The lead machine roared up the slope followed in close succession by its companions. Hope pranced anxiously.

"Slow down, damn it," Danny hollered. The attorney's hat slid off his head, came to the end of its lanyard, and dangled against the back of his neck.

The driver of the first machine did not hear Aitkins' plea over the throaty rumble of his snowmobile.

"Slow down, Goddamn it," Danny shouted as the mare thrashed its forelegs towards the perceived threat.

"Daddy," the girl cried out as Hope cavorted along the edge of the woods.

There was fear in Amanda's voice as she witnessed the out-of-control antics of her horse. Then it happened. He was on her, straight up in the saddle, riding out the worst of it when the animal

456

bucked, lifting Danny free of leather, then pitched, throwing the man's torso over her neck. The attorney struggled to defy gravity. He clawed at the steel of the stirrups with the wounded toes of his boots.

Daniel's efforts were meaningless. He was engulfed by a cloud of snow tossed into the air by the frantic bolting of the horse. The whiteout obscured his vision. He was thrown from his mount. The back of Daniel's head slammed against the hard surface of the frozen ground, rendering him unconscious, as sharp hooves assaulted the limp extremities of the lawyer's helpless body.

CHAPTER 90

There was a stream. The water was cool and pristine, the kind of water that nurtures trout. A man stood waist deep in the current, working a Fenwick graphite rod with smooth precision. A dry fly danced over the surface of the river in mock flight until it settled near a cedar root, the texture of the wood gnarled and foreign, the canopy of the great tree significant and presenting a voluminous shadow. His waders were damaged. Cold water seeped in through precarious patches glued to neoprene with adhesive. The intruding water pooled around his stocking feet. The clouds were distant and rippled like the ribs of an athlete. Blue sky hung beneath the folds of the high atmosphere. Canada Geese, large and black in perspective against the ivory and aquamarine, searched for newly cut fields to gorge upon as they flew over the river.

The man drifted the dry fly, a late summer look-alike, through a swirling pool behind the obstructing cedar. He thought there would be a fish there; a smooth skinned, ancient German Brown, grown fat and smart through patience. The art of deception was all the fisherman had at his disposal. Deceit, trickery, and mimicry were his stock in trade. There was a small disturbance beneath the surface of the stream. The big fish was wary. It would not be so foolish as to lunge at the first offering.

He eased the fly out of the water and dried it with soft breath. A girl watched him from the bank. The high grass of the meadow had been trampled by her feet. The woolen blanket she sat on followed the contours of the earth. Her almond eyes, their power undiminished despite her condition, studied the man's effort in silent appreciation.

The fly settled on the water. A sudden flash of color, of green and silver, turned beneath the water's surface and struck the barb. He let the line go slack until he was certain the fish had taken the bait. His fingers nimbly retracted the loose line until there was no excess hanging below the reel. He set the hook and felt the point of the device bury itself into the thick skeletal structure of the trout's mouth.

The man stumbled through the water, catching the toes of his boots on rocks and logs below the surface as he sought to keep up with his prey. The Brown thrashed powerfully, seeking the protection of an overhanging bank, seeking to break the monofilament leader on a rock ledge. It was all the fisherman could do to hold the rod tip up and to keep the fish away from danger.

"You've got him," the Indian girl cried out. "You've really got him."

"Her," the man responded. "From the size of the fight, I'd guess it's a female getting ready to spawn."

He stumbled. Water crested the edges of his waders and soaked his stockings. The fish gave no notice of tiring. The man steadied himself in the middle of a small ripple and began to retrieve the line, pulling hard against the strength of the trout.

The water was shallow. The fisherman scanned the river bottom. A tail splashed. The fish turned, attempting to break the union between man and animal. The line held fast.

Now the trout was in a foot of water. Its resplendent worm-like markings and colors became visible as the exhausted creature coasted near the toe of the man's boot.

"It's a beauty," the fisherman said, beaming broadly at the little girl. "It's got to go three pounds."

"I wanna see it before you let it go," the child responded, her dark hair dancing as she stood in expectation, slender blades of grass rising around her like a protective wall.

He urged the fish into the webbing of a landing net, the handle; smoothly oiled hickory; the mesh crisp and strong. The trout thrashed excitedly as the angler lifted it out of the water.

"Wow," the man's youthful companion exclaimed as he advanced towards the shoreline with his catch. "That's the biggest fish I've ever seen caught here."

The man smiled and untangled the trout from the net. Holding the fish gingerly in one hand as he knelt on a gravel bar, the angler removed the hook from the animal's jaw.

"She's getting ready to lay her eggs," the fisherman observed, studying the tiny bursts of color interrupting the ordinary steel and emerald flank of the German Brown. " She's fat with them."

"Let her go," the girl urged softly.

"That's just what I intend to do," the man replied, placing the fish in objection to the cool flow of the river. He released his grip. In an instant, the trout was gone.

"Do you want to see Audrey now?" the youth asked, her native skin dark against the red and yellows of her slacks and blouse. She was barefoot, her oxidized feet the color of the earth. There was a look of doubt in the man's eyes.

"I'm not sure I'm ready."

"I thought it's what you wanted," the girl replied.

"So did I. Now, I'm not so certain," the angler disclosed, his voice tired and sad.

"You're the one who prayed for this."

He stood at the base of the stream bank and looked pleadingly into the face of the Indian child.

"Maybe I didn't know what it would mean."

The girl extended her hand to the man and assisted him up the bank. His boots slipped as he sought the top of the incline.

"I didn't have a choice, you know," the child said harshly. "I didn't pray for it to happen to me."

"I know that."

"Maybe I don't want to be here either," she pouted. "Though, it has its moments," she revealed, her demeanor brightening.

The man searched the woodlands for familiar landmarks.

"What river is this?"

The girl smiled.

"Any one you want it to be."

"The Brule, over in Wisconsin?"

"If that's what will make you happy."

"Is that how it is here: you simply will a thing and it is?"

"There are exceptions."

He looked into the eyes of his companion for answers.

"Such as?"

"You have to learn those on your own. They're not so different from the rules you're used to."

She stuck a piece of timothy between her teeth and stared hard at the man.

"I can see you're troubled by this."

"That's an understatement," he replied.

"Once it's done, it can't be undone," the girl advised.

"Someone else said that to me once."

The child smiled.

"Ms. Barnes."

His eyes widened.

"How did you...?"

"No one has secrets here. Everything is an open book."

He removed his baseball cap and scratched his head. Despite the warmth of the day, there were no bugs. He was not sweating. The whole circumstance of his fishing the unnamed river and talking to the girl was unnerving.

Visions of his children collided with the present. Infinite melancholy injected itself into his veins as he studied the perfect trees, the perfect sky, the perfect world.

"Am I required to stay here?"

A sigh escaped the child.

"Normally, yes. Once you ask for something and your request is honored, that's usually the end of it."

His eyes took on an aspect of fright.

"No exceptions?"

The little girl looked steadily into the heavens and remained perfectly still. There was a sudden, minute touch of a breeze, something that had been totally lacking before that moment.

"You're certain you want to do this?" she asked, returning her focus on the man's face. Her head tilted upward so that she could study his eyes as they spoke. "Things won't be the same, I hope you know that."

"What do you mean?"

She shook her head.

"That's for you to discover. But if you want to go back, He says it's all right with Him."

"Who is 'He'?"

"Sorry."

His face grew impatient.

"You're not going to tell me, are you?"

"You don't need to be told what you already know."

He placed the rod and the landing net at a base of an aspen.

"I'm ready," he said, closing his eyes.

The girl laughed.

"What's so funny?" he said, staring hard as she convulsed, as she held her hands to her mouth to suppress giggling.

"You expect that I'll wave a wand or something?"

He failed to see the humor in her remark.

"What's so Goddamn funny?" he asked.

"Watch your language. Your return trip can be canceled, you know," she cautioned. "You leave the same way you came."

"I don't remember how I got here."

She extended an index finger and pointed to a trail winding its way through shimmering trees.

"You walked."

"That's it?"

"That's it," she replied, turning to leave.

"Where are you going?" he asked, a trace of sadness coloring his inquiry.

"Where I belong," the child said, wiping a tear from her eye. A few steps down another path, she turned and spoke in a voice infected with longing.

"Tell my mom I'm waiting for her, will you? Tell her I love her."

He tried to answer. The words were stuck and unable to escape. The fisherman simply nodded and began his long journey back.

CHAPTER 91

Demerol dripped from an IV bag and flowed slowly into his veins. There was no pain, no discomfort despite the fact that the entirety of the left side of his pelvis had been crushed under the flailing hooves of the mare. Splinters of bone had damaged Daniel's bladder; had pierced his liver and spleen, and had come dangerously close to severing his aorta.

The snowmobiler's stopped in response to the screams of the terrified girl as she watched her horse trample the unconscious form of her father, his limp body dragged by one foot caught in a stirrup, the man tossed violently by each unreasoning buck of the mare until strangers were able to grasp the leather reins and control the upset animal.

Amanda leaped off Pumpkin at the sight of her father's body coming to rest, his hatless head nestled in the snow, his left leg twisted behind him, a cowboy boot maintaining attachment to the stirrup as the horse becalmed. Once the horses were secured, the girl knelt in the snow next to her father. Tears rolled from the little girl's eyes as she waited apprehensively for emergency personnel from the Height of the Land Volunteer Fire Department to arrive.

Two of the snowmobiler's stayed with Danny Aitkins, carefully covering his mangled body, his left leg unnaturally pinned beneath the weight of his torso, no blood flowing from any wound, the damage done by Hope completely concealed by clothing and skin.

The third rider, his snow machine roaring at peak RPM's, dashed down the slope to his truck. Waiting for evacuation, the stricken man's face turned to chalk. His body surged through a series of unnatural shivers. Waves of shock cascaded over the victim, a consequence of internal injury.

They brought him down the hillside behind a snow machine and flew him by helicopter from the parking lot adjacent to Hill Lake to Fargo. Daniel's ride down the hillside, first in a bouncing toboggan pulled by an Arctic Cat, and then by chopper to the hospital, was uneventful. There was no pain, no recognition from the attorney of his surroundings or his circumstances as he was evacuated. Sheriff Iverson arrived, took custody of the little girl, and arranged with a neighboring farmer to board the horses. Amanda Jane accompanied the old lawman to her home where painful revelations were made to Julie Aitkins.

"They're taking him to St. Lucia's in Fargo. Should be there within half an hour," Isak Iverson revealed standing on the solidly frozen surface of the gravel drive in front of the Aitkins' farmhouse, his weight shifting awkwardly from foot to foot as he spoke to the woman.

"How did this happen?" Julie asked, her face ashen in grief.

"Seems your daughter's horse spooked from the noise of the snow machines," the sheriff offered. "Lucky he wasn't killed outright by the way the animal went off."

The woman convulsed.

"How is he?" she asked weakly.

"Critical. Best the paramedics and the RN on the chopper could determine, he's stable but he has one hell of a fight on his hands," the lawman advised.

"I'd better get driving," the woman said, looking forlornly at her child. The girl's face was buried in her mother's stomach. Amanda's tears soaked Julie's blouse as the two of them stood exposed to the weather.

"I'll give you a lift," the sheriff offered.

Julie's mouth opened.

"That's not necessary."

"Yes, it is," Iverson replied, a gentle tone to his voice. "You got someone to watch the kids?"

"Dee Dee Hernesman is on her way," the woman indicated. "Only Amanda's home. The boys are staying with friends." Just as Julie's words ended, Hernesman's Volkswagen sped into view. "Here's Dee Dee now."

The vehicle wheeled into the parking area and stopped abruptly, scattering rocks.

"Hey," Dee Dee observed, sliding quickly from behind the wheel. "You get going. I'll take care of 'Manda," the lawyer said in a concerned tone.

"We better hit the road Mrs. Aitkins. That chopper has a good start on us as it is."

Julie Aitkins eased her daughter away from her body.

"You stay here with Ms. Hernesman," the mother advised.

"I wanna go with," Amanda protested, her voice cracking.

"Your dad's gonna be fine," Dee Dee promised, taking Amanda by the hand and drawing the girl to her hip. "Best let your mom and Sheriff Iverson be on their way. They'll call as soon as they can, right mom?"

"That's right," Julie promised, entering the warmth of the squad car. "As soon as I know anything, I'll call."

A large lump formed in the girl's throat as she watched the sheriff back up the vehicle, shift the squad car's transmission into drive, and ease away from the house.

Julie discovered that her husband was in surgery. It was feared that splinters of pelvic bone were in danger of dissecting Daniel's aorta, rendering him paralyzed, or worse. There was also a significant possibility that shards of bone had already penetrated Danny's intestines, exposing the interior cavity of his body to waste, setting up a scenario for sepsis.

As it turned out, none of these things happened. Surgeons worked on the man; reconnecting his urethra where disrupted; rebuilding the left side of his pelvis with donor bone from the right thigh, securing it with surgical wire; suturing internal wounds, closing off arteries and veins that had been nicked by migrating pieces of bone. Daniel knew nothing of these efforts to save his life. He was somewhere else; somewhere the love of his wife and children couldn't reach.

"Danny?" Julie asked, her words tired, her eyes heavy and near sleep, during his fifth night in the hospital. "Are you awake?"

He was breathing on his own. All of the tubes, save a catheter and a single IV delivering antibiotics and pain medication, had been removed. His eyes had remained closed from the moment he flew off the horse until he recognized his wife's intonations.

There was a look of supreme puzzlement on Danny's face when he came to.

"Julie?"

"Yes."

"I'm thirsty."

She held a glass of ice water in one hand and placed a plastic straw in the corner of his mouth. He sipped lightly. The effort was taxing. Most of the liquid dribbled down his chin. She wiped the moisture from his face with a tissue.

"How do you feel?"

"Where the hell am I?"

"In Fargo, in the hospital."

"What the hell..."

"You had an accident.'Manda's horse threw you on Hill Lake Trail."

His eyes narrowed. Her face hovered over him. He could see each pore of her skin. And yet, she seemed so far away, so distant, through the light gauze of the narcotics.

"Really?"

"Really."

His lips formed a smile.

"I thought I was trout fishing."

Her eyes darted and considered the entirety of his face.

"You mentioned something about that while you were out."

Daniel studied his wife's lips, her dark eyes, her endearing features.

"I was looking for Audrey."

"Uh huh."

"The Pelletier girl was trying to help me."

A frown formed on his wife's face.

"She was telling me I could stay where she was. But I didn't. Something drove me away, made me come back."

Julie's eyes clouded.

"I'm glad," she replied, squeezing his limp hand in hers.

"How are the kids?"

"They've been here every day, waiting for you to come 'round. They're at school. Your dad's bringing them back after their classes get out."

He shook his head. He was tired. His eyes drifted towards sleep. Before he dozed, recognition of the unspoken crept into his mind.

"You've had a lot of well-wishers," she advised, pointing to three shelves full of flower arrangements and plants, the gay foliage accented by several dozen get well cards and a cluster of helium balloons.

"Really?"

"Everyone from your office has been here. Dee Dee's been here every damn day."

He smiled.

"I'm beginning to think there might be something going on between you," Julie added.

"That would be news to her, I'd guess," he replied, his eyes now fully shut, the drugs taking over.

"Melanie's been here nearly as often," Julie whispered, knowing her husband was fading.

His eyes fluttered. He possessed enough residual control to avert opening them.

"She's been a big help. She's taken care of the kids a few times when your dad and my parents haven't been able to."

The lawyer nodded.

Julie Aitkins watched her husband's face. There was more weakness, more frailty in his profile than she had ever seen. His breathing became heavy. His hand went limp in hers. She understood that now was not the time to reveal the totality of what she knew.

CHAPTER 92

The horses were sent off the place, boarded at the Hubbard County Fairgrounds in Park Rapids. Transferring the animals was hardest on Amanda. The girl resisted sending the horses away. With Daniel in the long and painful process of recovery Julie had no choice. There was no one around the house with the time or energy to care for livestock. The steer and hogs were slaughtered early. The writer contemplated selling the horses at the Park Rapids Livestock Auction. Once that possibility was made known to Amanda, the girl fell into a deep and significant pout.

Dan was incapable of work. Disability insurance checks paid their bills. Julie took three weeks off from her teaching position during the most critical time of Daniel's readjustment. She helped him learn to go to the toilet without a catheter and prompted him to begin slow, painful excursions around the main floor of the house with a walker.

The living room became Danny's bedroom. A rented hospital bed replaced the couch in front of the fireplace. Dan's buddies accomplished all of the heavy lifting under Julie's watchful eye. These same friends took turns driving the attorney to medical appointments and rehabilitation sessions in Detroit Lakes. With the aid of painkillers, Danny attended Adam's playoff hockey game at the Becker County Fairgrounds Ice Arena. His enthusiasm subdued by medication, the lawyer proudly watched his son win the game, handing Bemidji's Bantam A team their first loss of the year, a shutout victory for the Lakers. He didn't attend the next game. It was Adam's turn to sit. It was just as well. Fergus Falls won the contest in overtime, ending the season.

Daniel Emery Aitkins had no memory of the accident. Dee Dee urged him to bring a claim against the snowmobiler's for disturbing the horses, for not using sufficient caution. Alternatively, she suggested commencing a lawsuit against the auction house for not disclosing the negative attributes of the mare. He rejected Dee Dee's suggestions. Danny Aitkins wasn't interested in becoming a party to litigation.

He came to another personal decision. Whatever happened between himself and Julie, once the truth was out in the open, searing their love in its unholy flame, Daniel promised himself that his career as a litigator was over. He didn't share this epiphany with Dee Dee Hernesman. He would, once he sorted out all of the details pertaining to his marriage. That was, to his way of thinking, something that needed to be done in short order. Melanie's plight was obvious. It was common knowledge that Michael Barnes' widow was pregnant. There were no rumors; at least that he knew of, speculating on the identity of the father. That was likely to change as Melanie's due date drew closer.

"How you feeling?" Julie asked as she approached her husband. He was standing precariously on late winter ground, his weight held off the recuperating leg by aluminum crutches shoved under his armpits.

The lawyer smiled. His eyes followed the advance of his life partner, the mother of his children, the one person he'd entrusted with nearly every secret of his life. He considered the moment.

"Hey," was his only response.

He focused his eyes on the farm's vacant pasture. He leaned precariously against the top rail of the cedar fence, steadying himself with his hands, and rested the crutches against the wooden rail next to him.

"I get nervous when you're out here walking around on your own," Julie remarked, her arms crossed beneath her chest, her torso covered by a wool pullover displaying black wolves against a red background.

"I'm fine. Another week and these crutches are history," Dan replied, never looking at the woman.

"Think that's wise? The doctors want you on them at least two more weeks."

"I'm ready. The hip feels good. I'm off painkillers. The swimming sessions are rebuilding the muscle. I don't even feel the wires anymore."

She stared hard at his face. The line of his jaw was clean and straight. The age that appeared on him during his hospital stay was gone.

"Whatever you think is best," she agreed. "Just don't push yourself too hard."

His tone lightened.

"What's up with the book?"

"Hartley sent me a contract last week."

"Oh?" he responded.

Her eyes diverted.

"I had Murph go over it," she replied, referencing Tom Murphy, Daniel's partner.

"And?" the lawyer asked.

"He said to go for it. I signed it."

There was a glimmer of hurt in the man's face.

"Some reason you didn't want me to look at the contract?" he inquired.

She shoved her hands into the back pockets of her warm ups. A cool late winter breeze rustled mischievous strands of her hair.

"I didn't want to trouble you, is all," she advised, her lips tight around the words.

He nodded. A significant passage of time followed.

"Are you going to tell me what they paid as an advance?" he asked, small inflections of upset clear beneath the question.

Her hand came to rest on his right shoulder. She looked directly at him as she responded.

"I don't think that's such a good idea. When you're feeling better, we'll go over all that."

Her reply puzzled him. There was no reason he could fathom why his wife would want to conceal her good fortune from him. They had always shared everything, every bit of positive or negative news that they encountered during their relationship.

"I don't understand," he said.

"Let's just leave it there for now," she replied, removing her hand and heading back towards the house.

Danny stood at the fence. The sun departed, leaving long shadows and the mantle of an uncommitted sky standing above the hobby farm. The lawyer watched his wife depart, her strides controlled and patient, as he considered the end of another day.

CHAPTER 93

Melanie Barnes dreamed. When she slept, the faces of the men she had loved during her life visited her. Her imagination wasn't crowded. Despite the fact that she was a striking woman, someone other women envied as being able to attract suitors with a subtle glance or by virtue of a well-orchestrated smile, only a handful of men visited Melanie in her dreams. She had been married to one. She wanted, more than anything else, to marry another.

It had been easier than she thought to explain the pregnancy to her two children. They were spared the details as to who the father was, though each child inquired privately as to that missing piece of information. Despite the curiosity of her children, she didn't share Daniel's role in causing her condition with Megan or Josh. That would happen later, once the attorney sat down and discussed the situation with his wife. Melanie had purposefully maintained a low profile, avoiding extended telephone calls or overly personal visits during his recovery, in hopes of keeping Julie's inquisitiveness at bay. Too much contact with the stricken lawyer would have caused scrutiny. She remained a steady friend, one who pledged her assistance to the Aitkins family through appropriate visits and telephone contacts. Though she longed to bring their secret out into the open, she maintained a suffering silence.

When Julie Aitkins showed up on Saturday morning, a week after Daniel came home from the hospital, knocking softly on the back door of Melanie's modest home, the writer's appearance came as a total surprise.

"I should have called," Julie stated plainly, standing beneath an open sky, her hair sheared short, her eyes fixed tightly on the face of the red head.

"Julie. I wasn't expecting you," Melanie whispered as she answered the door. "What brings you to Fergus so early on a Saturday?"

The writer forced an answer.

"We need to talk."

The paralegal looked intently at the woman.

"I'll get my coat."

"That's fine. We can go for a walk. That'd be best," Julie Aitkins agreed, nodding her head slightly, her gaze staring at the stomach of her friend, yielding to an inclination to give the woman's pregnancy the full weight of her attention.

The paralegal retrieved a long winter coat from a closet, slipped on her running shoes, and stepped out into the morning air.

"There any place to get coffee close by?" Julie asked.

469

"Caroline's, just down the street. They serve breakfast too," Melanie added as the women began to walk. Meager snow remained alongside the sidewalk. The crowns of the snowbanks had been scoured by the wind.

"Coffee will be fine. I don't feel much like eating," Julie replied.

There was a definite bite to the woman's words.

"The kids are still sleeping," Melanie added for no obvious reason, filling in an opening in their conversation out of nervousness.

"That's good," Julie replied flatly.

They approached the café. Melanie stopped and placed a bare hand on the poplin fabric of her companion's ski jacket.

"Is this something we can do in public?" the red head whispered tremulously.

Julie's dark brown eyes studied the slices of emerald floating in Melanie's irises.

"I think so."

The paralegal nodded, released the woman, and opened the door to the restaurant.

A sign advised the women to seat themselves. There were ten or so other folks in the place engaged in conversations or in reading the morning paper. The women found a booth and sat down on opposite sides of the table. A young man, no more than twenty, approached them with ceramic cups and a glass pot.

"Coffee?"

"Please," Melanie said, avoiding eye contact with Julie Aitkins.

"Take anything in it?" the boy asked.

"Just black."

Julie stared blankly.

"I'll have the same," she murmured.

The young man filled two cups. Steam rose from the lip of the pot as black liquid chugged into the mugs.

"The Number Two is on special, Three-twenty-five, with your choice of meat and toast," the waiter offered, holding the pot in one hand, wiping excess moisture from the palm of his hand on his white apron. "I'll be back in minute or so."

"Thanks," the red head said weakly.

A ceiling fan turned slowly. A faint squeak accompanied the lazy rotation of the blades. There was no frost on the plate glass window overlooking the street at the far end of the room. Muted discussion hummed around the women as they sipped coffee in strained silence.

"You know why I'm here," Julie Aitkins said.

470

Thickness enveloped Melanie Barnes' tongue. Her response was nearly inaudible.

"I think I have a pretty good idea."

The writer held her cup between her hands and inhaled.

"I thought we were friends."

A lump blocked the other woman's throat.

"We are," Mel replied meekly.

"I don't see how that's possible."

The red head shut her eyes to escape Julie's incriminating gaze.

"Do you?" the wife of the lawyer added, sarcasm embedded in the question.

"I guess that's your call," the pregnant woman replied. "I really don't know what to say."

Julie tilted her head and studied the face of her companion.

"You're probably right about that. An 'I'm sorry' just doesn't seem to fit the situation, now does it? I guess if I were you, I'd be more than a little unsure of just how to deal with getting impregnated by somebody else's husband, of how to explain that to someone I considered a friend, if I were you, I mean," the teacher said with acrimony.

Melanie clenched her eyes. Her face trembled. There was no holding back the torrent.

Julie Aitkins waited for the crying spell to pass. The waiter reappeared. Julie waved him off with a terse flip of her hand. The writer took a hefty draw of coffee and studied pedestrians passing by the big window. Unadulterated sunlight cast a golden glow across the diner. Time inched along like a heavily loaded freight train as the red haired woman sought to regain her composure.

"That's not really going to help much, now, is it?" Julie interposed. "Crying won't solve what's come between us, what's hanging above us like a sharpened sword."

Sunlight caught the green of the stricken woman's eyes.

"How can you be so cold?"

"Me?" Aitkins' responded incredulously. "I'm not the one that fucked my friend's husband in some hotel room in Winnipeg and then compounded my deceit by becoming pregnant," she added with measured scorn.

Silence imposed itself between the women. Melanie touched the corners of her eyes with the edge of a tissue while staring at a cheap oil painting, the product of a local artist, hanging against grease-stained wallpaper.

"I deserve that," Melanie Barnes whispered pathetically.

"Yes you do."

The paralegal took a swig of coffee, swallowed, cleared her throat, and spoke.

"What am I supposed to do?"

"Before we talk about that, I'm curious about one thing, Mel."

"Yes?"

"Why in God's name are you still pregnant?"

Exhaled breath exploded from the other woman.

"I couldn't."

"You mean, you wouldn't."

"No, I couldn't."

Julie's hands tightened around her cup.

"You've never been all that religious."

The woman shook her head affirmatively.

"That's true," Melanie admitted.

"Then why?"

A paralyzing fear descended over the pregnant woman as she contemplated telling an untruth.

No more lies, she told herself as she stared into the eyes of her friend. *No more lies.*

"I love him."

"Christ," Julie muttered, disgust and loathing clear and present in her voice.

"It's not like that."

"Like what? You dumb bitch; I'm married to the man. You and I are friends. Doesn't that mean anything to you?"

The tears returned.

"Cut the act, sister."

"This isn't an act, Julie. I can't help myself. I love him."

Something in the pregnant woman's voice impacted the writer and compelled her to soften. A long period of silence interceded before Julie Aitkins leaned over the tabletop and placed a hand on Melanie Barnes' bare wrist.

"I don't mean that it's all on you, Mel. Danny's as much to blame, maybe more. I'd love to pinch his little balls in a vice grip about now. That's how much I hate the bastard for doing this to me, to our kids."

The waiter nervously watched the women from behind the cash register. Julie motioned for the man to attend to them.

"I'll have the special, easy over, with bacon, and wheat toast," Julie said.

Melanie Barnes stared in disbelief.

"How can you eat?"

"Easy," the teacher confided. "I've been dealing with this thing for over a month. Order something."

The paralegal studied the menu.

"I'll have a bowl of oatmeal, a glass of orange juice and an English muffin. Make it whole wheat," she mumbled. The waiter retreated.

"When did you figure it out?" the paralegal asked.

"I'd been getting weird vibes from you and Danny ever since Winnipeg. You don't know people for two decades and not understand their moods, their daily patterns of being."

The red head refilled her cup. She attempted to pour coffee for Julie. The writer signaled for her to stop.

"I don't need any more caffeine."

Melanie returned the carafe to its place on the table.

"When did you figure out that the baby was Danny's?"

"I suspected that it was when I saw you at the end of the Anderson trial. I grew more suspicious when you kept showing up in the hospital to visit Daniel. But I didn't know for sure until I saw your face today, until I knocked on your door. You should have seen the look you gave me."

Another period of respite followed. Their food came. The women ate their meals in relative silence.

"I don't hate you, Melanie," the teacher volunteered, wiping egg yolk from her lips with a napkin.

The other woman chewed her food in methodical fashion.

"I should. But I don't. And I don't hate Danny, though I can't say I'll ever forgive either of you, especially when you consider I'll be reminded about this over the course of my entire lifetime by the child you've made. "

"I appreciate that."

The wife of the lawyer took a significant breath.

"Here's what I think. I think that no matter what I did in life, no matter how loving, how loyal, how hard I tried to be beautiful, to be sexy, to fill whatever needs Daniel has, it was never going to be enough."

Julie Aitkins sipped water before continuing.

"Truth is, Danny Aitkins is still mourning his mother. He's been looking for her in every woman he's met since she died. There's nothing I can do, regardless of how hard I work at it, to fill the dark, deep hole that her passing left. Couple that with the demise of his sister, Audrey. Well, it's just my opinion, but I don't see how any woman can compensate for all of that loss."

Melanie spooned soggy cereal into her mouth.

"You and Danny are both tied to ghosts," Julie advised. "Dan to his mother and sister, you to your dead husband. Maybe that's part of the reason you ended up falling together, despite all of the common sense reasons why you should have steered clear of it. Like I say, I understand it, to a degree. I don't hate either of you. Just don't ask me to be happy about it or try to sweep it under the rug as some inconsequential event. Even without the baby, what the two of you did is implausible, unforgivable. I'd like to say forgivable, but unforgettable, but my faith isn't that strong."

The writer drew a breath.

"Of course, it could be that the two of you just lusted after each other, that you've been wanting to fuck each other silly since high school. What the hell do I know about it anyway?" the woman asked rhetorically, her eyes briefly batting at fragile tears.

"That wasn't it at all," Melanie added, her hand touching her companion's palm. "It wasn't something cheap or tawdry."

Julie Aitkins looked sternly at her friend.

"Is that supposed to make me feel better?"

"No. I don't think anything Daniel or I choose to say will make you feel better."

The bill came. They finished their coffee and sat perplexed, poised over an expression of release that escaped them both.

"I should get back," the writer observed. "Danny took the kids to visit his dad. It's the first time he's been out driving by himself since the accident."

Melanie smiled weakly.

"How's he doing?"

"He's got a ways to go. His hip is sore. He'll likely always walk with a limp. Everything else seems back to square one. No more catheter; no more pain pills. "

As they stood to put their coats on, Melanie took an extended period of time to catch her breath.

"Anything wrong?" Julie asked.

"I'll be fine. It'll pass."

"How are you doing, with the baby and all?" Julie inquired in a maternal tone of voice, the context odd given the respective positions of the women.

"It's going OK," the paralegal responded as she drew her coat around her expanded stomach. "It sure was a lot easier when I was younger."

The lawyer's wife thought about uttering a recriminating remark but refrained. They paid their respective bills and walked out the door, breathing the fresh air of winter as they labored up the hill towards Melanie's bungalow.

"What are you going to do?" Melanie asked.

"About...?"

"Daniel."

"I expect he'll have to find some place else to call home," the woman explained matter-of-factly.

"Divorce?" the pregnant woman asked, carefully couching her question, avoiding any hint that she might profit if the couple's marriage came to an end.

Julie Aitkins looked away.

"That's the part I'm not sure of. He's out of the house, that much I'm clear on," she said, her voice frail and lonely. "Promise me you won't say a word to him until I take care of it. Promise me," she implored.

"I won't say anything. I've kept my distance, lately, anyways."

The wife of the trial lawyer nodded.

"I've noticed that," Julie admitted. "Something else you need to know."

The women didn't look at each other as they climbed the short rise from downtown Fergus Falls.

"What's that?"

"Danny's quitting the practice."

Melanie, her pace already impeded by the child she was carrying, slowed further.

"What?"

"He says he's had enough. The Anderson case is the last one he'll ever try."

They stood in front of Melanie's house. The Barnes children peeked at the women through a gap in the living room curtains. Julie Aitkins waved to the children.

"I can't believe it. I thought he loved being a lawyer," Melanie observed.

Another thing you didn't know about my husband, Julie Aitkins thought, studying the pregnant woman with less than charitable eyes.

"Couldn't be further from the truth. He hates the law. He's hated it since he was sworn in thirteen years ago. I'm convinced stress is what caused most of his physical problems, though he's never admitted as much to me."

"I guess I never saw that in him. The few times I watched him in court, he was brilliant. I thought he loved being a trial attorney."

Julie opened the driver's door to her car, a Lexus SUV.

"Nice," Melanie observed. "Is it new?"

The writer smiled.

"It is. Bought it with my advance. My book's in line to be published before summer. I signed a three-book deal with the publisher. My agent thought we'd be using a small regional press. Turns out, we ended up with three national publishers bidding for the rights."

"That's great," Melanie said without hesitancy, though the anxiety in her voice was palpable.

"Something else that needs to be said?" the writer asked, turning towards the pregnant woman.

"Julie, I am so damn sorry that this happened," Melanie Barnes wailed, releasing a flood of tears as she embraced her friend.

The Barnes children watched the women hug through the clean glass of the picture window.

"So am I," Julie said, "so am I," the teacher repeated, as she reluctantly embraced the red head's thickening body.

CHAPTER 94

They walked the downtown streets of Detroit Lakes. The sun warmed their faces. A hint of wind kept them from perspiring. The man walked with an impaired gait, his left leg ambulating slightly slower than his right, as they negotiated the sidewalk. The woman's pace was restrained to match her companion's.

"You sure this is what you want to do?" the female attorney asked her partner.

"It's what I have to do, Dees. I can't take trial work any more. I'm not much good at real estate or business law. Seems to me it's time to make a change," Dan Aitkins confided.

"I never saw you as the academic type," she replied, her gray eyes maintaining focus on the streetscape in front of them. "I have a hard time putting the label 'professor' in front of your name."

Aitkins grinned.

"You're not the only one."

"How you gonna pay your bills on a law professor's salary? The University of North Dakota doesn't pay all that much, from what I hear."

Danny coughed. Their path took them towards a residential neighborhood adjoining the commercial district of the town. Early migratory robins flitted through the air, their feathers colorful against the sun.

"Julie's book deal pretty much set us up."

"You're shameless, you know that. Letting the woman of the house bring home the bacon," the female attorney quipped.

"It's about time. She's been dragging her feet, earning that paltry teacher's salary for too damn long. 'Bout time she carried her weight," Dan joked.

They followed a street demarcating the business district from the residential area.

"You told Emery yet?" Hernesman asked.

"Yep. He was more supportive than I could've hoped for. I think having you in the firm as a partner smoothed the transition. You're one hell of a litigator, you know that Hernesman?"

"Thanks. I never thought your old man was all that enamored with my work."

Aitkins grinned.

"He wasn't. But it's hard to argue with results. He's come around. Don't you worry about old Emery. He'll be there for you, without question."

She returned the smile, showing small, off-white teeth, her murky eyes seemingly distracted.

"You've got something more to tell me, don't you Daniel? Something beyond changing careers and beginning a daily commute to Grand Forks."

His throat became tight.

"I guess."

"Is it about the red haired woman?"

"Yep."

Hernesman sighed.

"Shit, you're in love with her?"

"You already knew that."

She stopped in mid-stride and faced him.

"What is it then?"

The breeze caught the loose edges of Dee Dee's ebony hair; the strands flecked with slight dashes of white. Her plainly honest face considered the man as she waited for a response. The lawyer drew a large breath, holding it for emphasis before exhaling.

"Mel's pregnant."

"Tell me something I don't know. She's as round as a beach ball. Got to be at least five months along."

"Six."

"How in the hell would you know that?"

They resumed their walk.

"Because I'm the father."

"That supposed to be some kind of a joke?"

"I wish it were."

The woman's eyes closed. When they opened, their aspect was angry.

"Are you serious? How in God's name did you let this happen?"

He shook his head slowly, as if a large object was attached to his skull.

"It just did."

Dee Dee clasped her lower jaw with her right hand and stroked the skin in methodical fashion.

"What the fuck is wrong with you, Danny?"

"I wish I knew," the man quietly responded.

The female lawyer stopped walking.

"Does Julie know?"

"Not yet."

"Well, you better tell her pretty damn soon. You think she won't put two and two together on her own? I had an inclination that the baby might be yours. Never said anything because I wasn't a hundred percent sure. But the timing sure seemed convenient."

Aitkins avoided the woman's stare.

"It was Winnipeg, wasn't it?"

"I think so."

"You know so. What, you screwed her without taking any precautions?"

"She was on the pill."

The woman's mouth turned into a curious grin.

"What?" Daniel asked.

"She planned this," Dee Dee postulated.

"Are you out of your fucking mind? Planned to get pregnant, with two kids at home, and a dead husband?"

"Maybe not consciously. You don't forget to take a birth control pill when you're thirty-seven years old. Maybe at eighteen. Not at thirty-seven. I'm not saying she did it deliberately or with malice. But some part of her, some inner portion of her being, allowed her to conveniently forget to do what needed to be done."

"Bullshit."

Danny turned harshly and began to walk towards their office.

"You think so? She loves you, Dan, the way a mature woman loves a man. I've seen that look in her eyes whenever you're around her."

Aitkins spun on his heals, his left foot hesitant from the injury, and spat ugly words at his partner.

"What the hell would you know about it?"

If the remark hit its target, Dee Dee didn't let it slow her down.

"Oh, that's it, turn this into an 'insult the dyke' discussion. I'm not biting, Aitkins. I know plenty. Even if I have a different view on romance, I'm a woman, remember? I understand how women think, how they work. That's all I'm saying."

The male attorney resumed his pace.

"I apologize," he murmured as Dee Dee caught up with him and matched his stride.

"Apology accepted."

Aitkins' voice cracked.

"I guess I really screwed up, huh?"

Hernesman coated her response with sympathy.

"That would be a mild understatement."

Their building came into view.

"When are you going to tell Julie?"

Aitkins remained silent.

"Danny..."

"I know, I know. Tonight, after work. The kids will be off doing stuff. It'll be easier that way."

The female lawyer pulled hard on the metal handle of the entry door.

"How in God's name did you ever get yourself into this mess? Wait, don't tell me. I know. You let your little head do all your thinking."

"Funny, Hernesman. Real funny," Danny Aitkins muttered as the attorneys entered their office building.

The drive home was bleak. Scattered thoughts of alternative scenarios and plans for life infiltrated the lawyer's mind as the Ford bounded towards the farm. None of the ideas he came up with seemed satisfactory. There was no way to reclaim his marital integrity and remain in love with Melanie Barnes. Choices were going to have to be made; choices he was ill prepared to make.

"It should be easy," he said to himself as the tires of the truck rolled harshly over the pockmarked pavement. "I've always loved Julie. Still do. She's my partner, my soul mate. We've made a life together. Despite all its warts and imperfections, it's something good and sacred and honorable," he repeated to himself, as if the mantra would lessen the looming confrontation.

His thinking began to wander. Visions of moments spent with the red haired woman began to assert themselves, to acquire power over him in ways that he did not want them to.

"Damn it," he mumbled. "Damn it to fucking hell," he shouted as his fists pounded against the hard plastic of the steering wheel.

The lights of the farmhouse were on despite the fact that nightfall was still an hour or more away. A steady glow occupied the western limits of the sky, detailing the last glimmer of sunlight. Orange, magenta, and purple streamers extended upwards from the horizon, the color of the atmosphere slowly darkening to royal blue as natural light faded. He parked the Ranger and sat quietly in the driver's seat, steadying his nerves.

He noted a large array of items, personal belongings, stacked neatly along the sidewalk leading to the kitchen door. There were several suitcases, an assortment of wooden peach crates, and cardboard boxes filled in orderly fashion with a gathering of property. Items of clothing were suspended in the chilling air from hangers arranged across a temporary clothesline strung beneath the eaves of the back porch between two nails; nails that had not been in place when he left for work that morning.

What the fuck is going on? the attorney thought, stepping out of the warm cab of the truck.

The porch light came on. His wife opened a screen door and emerged onto the painted wooden platform of the covered porch. She was in her stocking feet. Julie's arms embraced her own body as she watched him approach.

"What the hell is this?" Danny asked in a tight voice.

480

"I think you know," Julie advised.

"No, I don't know. What is all my stuff doing out here?"

His wife's eyes, their deep brown distorted by water and salt, looked defiant.

"Don't bullshit me, Daniel Aitkins. You know very well what's going on here."

He stopped in front of his belongings. He tilted his head towards the sky. His eyes looked past the house, past the pasture, past the farm that they had shared for over a decade. He kept the truth inside, bottled up, trying to fathom how she could possibly know.

"I don't understand," he repeated.

"When do the lies stop, Danny? When do your deceptions give way to honesty? I know. That should be pretty fucking obvious to someone as bright as you," she expressed with rancor. "I know."

He brought his gaze down from heaven and stared at the pretty face of his wife. His eyes followed the feminine contours of her body, the wisps of dirty blond hair framing her face, the stark terror in her eyes obvious and painful despite her bravado.

"You're kicking me out?"

She sniggered, an expression of nervous tension, not mirth.

"Now you're catching on."

His face turned ashen.

"You want a divorce?"

She averted her eyes, shielding her uncertainty.

"I don't know."

"Where the hell am I supposed to go?"

She bit the side of her cheek before responding.

"You figure it out. You claim to be so Goddamned smart."

His immediate impulse was to cast out something foolish, such as a threat to take up living with Melanie. He refrained from committing that error, recognizing that his wife, pushed into a corner, would likely give her blessing for him to do so.

Danny picked up a heavy valise, the canvas sides of the bag bulging with clothes, and shuffled towards his pickup. He deposited the luggage in the metal box of the Ranger and returned for another load. The woman remained still, her face intentionally pulled tight to conceal her distress.

"Can't we talk about this?" he asked as he bent to pick up a canvas duffel bag filled with sporting equipment.

"I've got nothing to say to you," she whispered, her voice shaking, her temper magnificently restrained.

He started to reply. His words drifted away before they were spoken. Her inflection left open a possibility; a slender ray of hope that she might be willing to talk it through after some time had passed. Danny grasped onto that slim suggestion like a drowning man gripping a life buoy in a seething sea.

He climbed the stairs to the porch, his boots treading heavily against treated lumber as he moved. She retreated, placing plenty of distance between them. Julie Aitkins watched in controlled despair as her husband snatched shirt after shirt free of the temporary clothesline and carried the garments back to his truck. She remained motionless as he deposited the items in the cargo area of the Ranger's Club Cab and continued her watchful silence as he recovered the remaining items hanging across the porch.

"Aren't you going to say anything?" he asked, carelessly tossing the last of his clothing into the cab of the pick up.

"There's nothing left to say."

His eyes watered, the first weeping he'd experienced since arriving home.

"Julie, I am so sorry."

"Someone else told me that."

"Melanie?"

The woman shook her head affirmatively.

"You talked to Melanie?'

Another affirming gesture.

"She told you?"

The woman swallowed hard and shifted her weight, causing the hem of her gingham skirt to sway in the air.

"No."

"You already knew, didn't you?"

There was no acknowledgement from the lawyer's wife.

"How long have you known?"

She shook her head from side to side.

"It's not important, not any more," she insisted.

He looked helplessly into the eyes of the woman he loved, the woman he had married, the mother of his three children.

"Do the kids know?"

Her eyes grew large.

"I'm going to tell them tonight."

"Shouldn't I be here?"

Sobs claimed the woman's body, disrupting her stoicism.

"I don't think that's a good idea," she managed to murmur between spasms.

"You sure?"

She mouthed a "yes", shielding her eyes from her husband.

He climbed into his truck.

"Julie, I don't want to lose you," he said with tenderness through the open driver's door of the Ranger.

"It's too late for that," she replied, seeking the means to regain her composure.

"I'll call you," he offered.

The writer maintained silence and looked past the man. Standing on the porch, the woman fixed her eyes on the Smokey Hills. She considered the distant heights, their flanks covered by a mantle of new foliage. Freshly unfurled leaves of oaks and maples stood in marked contrast to the newly tilled soil of surrounding croplands.

Fighting the urge to scream out her upset, Julie watched Daniel slip into the driver's seat of the Ford, engage the shoulder harness, start the truck, and pull away from the farmhouse, unsure of the journey that she and her husband were about to begin.

AFTERWARDS

A handwritten copy of a poem was left on the dashboard of his truck by the woman he loved. He didn't remember all of the text. He memorized significant lines of the verse and carried them in his head as he mulled over the twists and turns of his life. The man often felt as if his future were a smooth stone tossed into a shallow pond, the stone having settled in the pond's mud only to remain slightly visible beneath the water's surface. He tried to recall the words to the poem, a piece written by Li-Young Lee, as he walked hand in hand with a toddler, contemplating unspoken memories of others that he'd loved. The words unraveled slowly in his mind:

> *Between two unknowns, I live my life.*
> *Between my mother's hopes, older than I am*
> *by coming before me, and my child's wishes, older than I am*
> *by outliving me. And what's it like?*
> *Is it a door, and good-bye on either side?*
> *A window, and eternity on either side?*
> *Yes, and a little singing between two great rests.*

Above them, the sky stretched on beyond the reach of a man's vision. Sunlight struck their respective heads; his, blond and turning slowly to platinum; hers, flaming red, a vibrant, constant reminder of her mother.

Waves pulsed against the beach of the tourist village, purifying the sand with each surge of the lake. They had come here, to this place, this escape, each summer after the girl had been born.

"Ruthie, see the ducks?" the man said, pointing a finger at a raft of mallards drifting in placid water.

"Ducks," the child repeated. "Ducks fly," she added.

"That's right," the father said. "They fly."

He walked the line of greenish water, his toes curling and uncurling in the sand, as he watched the girl challenge the incoming thrust of the surf. He glimpsed beautiful hints of green and gold captured within his daughter's eyes; fragments of mystery, of hope, of love.

There was always too little time. His moments with her were fleeting, constructed from the details of legal process and subject to arrangements made between the man and the woman. Though the finer points of their agreement were never the subject of controversy or argument, artificial concepts governed his fatherhood and restricted his connection with the little girl in ways that were unnatural.

She bounded through ankle deep water; her pale skin turning pink despite the sun block he'd carefully applied to her

484

exposed limbs. Her yellow bathing suit, the rump covered in moist sand as she ran, protected the majority of her torso from radiation. Brown freckles paraded across her upper back, standing obvious against her skin, against a complexion nearly identical to her mother's. The only resemblance between the little girl and her father was her nose; the bridge set up high, the end tapering to elegance, defining the center of her pretty face; and also her smile. When Ruth smiled, her cheeks expanded to twice their normal size. She, like her father, held nothing back when afflicted by joy.

Gulls wheeled above the dancing child, circling Winnipeg Beach beneath an azure atmosphere. At intervals throughout the park, tourists sat on beach towels or in lawn chairs imbedded in the sand, watching their own children while reading snippets of best selling novels propped against their reddening thighs.

The man, his left leg noticeably lagging behind him as he walked, his pace visibly cautious across the shifting surface of the beach, stopped near a young couple. He stood patiently next to a male sunbather; the young man bronzed from days of exposure, and the man's female companion, the woman similarly colored, her yellow hair shiny and clean from swimming in the lake.

"You're reading *Affairs of Habit?*" the father of the little girl asked; his words eloquent and quiet, his pattern of speech modified by academia.

The young woman, her body thick and well-formed, her shape admirably confined in a one-piece bathing suit, smiled, and looked up from the book she was reading. She maintained her place in the novel with a thumb as she studied the stranger.

"You've read it?"

"Not yet. It's on my list of books to read," the man disclosed, his eyes studying the angular chin of the woman, his smile genuine; his ears relishing her Canadian accent.

"I'm enjoying it. I'd recommend it highly," the woman advised, viewing him over the silver rims of expensive sunglasses.

The woman's muscular companion began to gauge the professor with a slightly jealous eye. The older man diverted his gaze and watched his daughter romp through crashing waves. Ruth had joined other children, three small boys, at play, near the water's edge.

"Lovely child," the woman offered. "Yours?"

"Yes."

"We're expecting our first," she advised, her stomach still flat and trim.

"Congratulations. She's my fourth."

The young lady smiled. Her companion frowned. The stranger knew it was time to move on. He turned to walk away.

"Like I said, I'd recommend the book highly," the woman repeated.

The man pivoted slowly.

"My wife would appreciate that," he said.

"How's that?" the woman asked.

"My wife, she wrote the book you're reading. She's the author."

The woman's smile broadened.

"Tell her how much I'm enjoying it. I'm looking forward to her next one."

"I'll let her know," the man said, turning away.

"And tell her how beautiful her little girl is," the young lady added.

The comment occasioned hesitation. The man's left foot caught a ridge of compacted beach. He stumbled. Regaining his balance, the man waded into shallow water, caught his little girl and lifted her free of Lake Winnipeg's warm grasp. The father kissed his daughter on her forehead before carrying the child across the sand and over freshly mown grass towards a familiar lakeside cottage where three older children waited.

ABOUT THE AUTHOR

Mark Munger is a life long resident of Northeastern Minnesota. He and his wife Rene' and their four sons live on the banks of the wild and scenic Cloquet River north of Duluth. When not writing fiction, Mark writes a regular column for *The Hermantown Star* newspaper and is a District Court Judge.

The Author and his son Christian, at Indian Lake, ready to begin a fifty mile canoe trip down the Cloquet River.

OTHER WORKS BY THE AUTHOR

The Legacy (ISBN 0972005080, Cloquet River Press)
Set against the backdrop of WWII Yugoslavia and present-day Minnesota, this debut novel combines elements of military history, romance, thriller, and mystery. Rated 3 and 1/2 daggers out of 4 by *The Mystery Review Quarterly*.
Trade Paperback-$20.00 USA, $25.00 CAN

River Stories (ISBN 0972005013; Cloquet River Press)
A collection of essays describing life in Northern Minnesota with a strong emphasis on the out-of-doors, the rearing of children, and the environment. A mixture of humor and thought-provoking prose gleaned from the author's columns in *The Hermantown Star*.
Trade Paperback-$20.00 USA, $25.00 CAN

Ordinary Lives (ISBN 9780979217517 (Second Edition) Cloquet River Press)
Creative fiction from one of Northern Minnesota's newest writers, these stories touch upon all elements of the human condition and leave the reader asking for more.
Trade Paperback-$20.00 USA, $25.00 CAN

Pigs, a Trial Lawyer's Story (ISBN 097200503x; Cloquet River Press)
A story of a young trial attorney, a giant corporation, marital infidelity, moral conflict, and choices made, ***Pigs*** takes place against the backdrop of Western Minnesota's beautiful Smokey Hills. This tale is being compared by reviewers to Grisham's best.
Trade Paperback - $20.00 USA, $25.00 CAN

Doc the Bunny and Other Short Tales (ISBN 0972005072, Cloquet River Press)
A sequel to ***River Stories*** packed with over three dozen humorous, touching, and thought-provoking essays about life lived large in NE Minnesota. Munger demonstrates once again why he is fast becoming recognized as a regional writer of finely crafted fiction and creative non-fiction.
Trade Paperback-$15.00 USA, $20.00 CAN

Esther's Race (ISBN 9780972005098, Cloquet River Press)
A story of an African American registered nurse who confronts race, religion, and tragedy in her quest for love, this novel is set against the stark and vivid beauty of Wisconsin's Apostle Islands, the pastoral landscape of Central Iowa, and the steel and